BALEFIRE

BALEFIRE

Cate Tiernan

BOOK ONE:
A CHALICE OF WIND

BOOK TWO:
A CIRCLE OF ASHES

BOOK THREE:
A FEATHER OF STONE

BOOK FOUR:
A NECKLACE OF WATER

razorbill

An Imprint of Penguin Group (USA) Inc.

Balefire Omnibus

RAZORBILL

Published by the Penguin Group
Penguin Young Readers Group
345 Hudson Street, New York, New York 10014, U.S.A.
Penguin Group (USA) Inc., 375 Hudson Street, New York, New York 10014, U.S.A.
Penguin Group (Canada), 90 Eglinton Avenue East, Suite 700, Toronto, Ontario, Canada
M4P 2Y3 (a division of Pearson Penguin Canada Inc.)
Penguin Books Ltd, 80 Strand, London WC2R 0RL, England
Penguin Ireland, 25 St Stephen's Green, Dublin 2, Ireland (a division of Penguin Books Ltd)
Penguin Group (Australia), 250 Camberwell Road, Camberwell, Victoria 3124, Australia
(a division of Pearson Australia Group Pty Ltd)
Penguin Books India Pvt Ltd, 11 Community Centre, Panchsheel Park,
New Delhi – 110 017, India
Penguin Group (NZ), 67 Apollo Drive, Mairangi Bay, Auckland 1311, New Zealand
(a division of Pearson New Zealand Ltd)
Penguin Books (South Africa) (Pty) Ltd, 24 Sturdee Avenue, Rosebank, Johannesburg
2196, South Africa

Penguin Books Ltd, Registered Offices: 80 Strand, London WC2R 0RL, England

10 9 8 7 6 5 4 3 2 1

ISBN: 978-1-59514-411-9

Library of Congress Cataloging-in-Publication Data is available

Printed in the United States of America

BALEFIRE

Cate Tiernan

BOOK ONE:
A CHALICE OF WIND

BALEFIRE

BOOK ONE:
A CHALICE OF WIND

✦ Prologue

WHEN THE SHADES WERE DOWN, YOU HAD TO actually open the train compartment door to see who's inside. The last four minutes had taught us this, as my friends Alison, Lynne, and I raced through the train cars, looking for our trip supervisor.

"Not this one!" Alison said, checking out one compartment.

I looked through a window and saw a bunch of tweed-suited German businessmen. "Not here," I reported.

"Do you think it was something she ate?" Alison asked. "I mean, poor Anne. Yuck."

"Whatever it was, I'm not going back in there," Lynne said, popping open another door. "Oops! Entschuldigung!" Bowing, she closed the door on the couple making out inside. We burst into laughter.

Poor Anne. We were only on day three of our junior-year trip to Europe—having done Belgium in a whirlwind, we were speeding through Germany and would end up in France in another four days. But if Anne was really sick, she would be flown home. Maybe it was just something she ate. Our supervisor Ms. Polems could decide.

"Thais, get that one!" Lynne called, pointing, as she looked through a compartment window.

I cupped my hands around my eyes like a scuba mask and pressed them against the glass. Just as quickly I pulled away, as four junior-class pinhead jocks started catcalling and whistling.

"Oh, I'm so sure," I muttered in repulsion. "Like I'm going to be, 'Come on, guys!'"

"Oops! Entschuld—entschuh—" Alison began in another doorway.

"Entschuldigung!" Lynne sang, pulling Alison back into the corridor.

I grinned at them. Despite poor Anne, so far we were having a blast on this trip.

I seized the handle of the next compartment and yanked. Four tourists were inside—no Ms. Polems. Where the hell had she squirreled herself away? "Oh, sorry," I said, pulling back. Two of the men stared at me, and I groaned inwardly. I'd already dealt with some over-friendly natives, and I didn't need more now.

"Clio?" one of the men said in a smooth, educated voice.

Yeah, right. Nice try. "Nope, sorry," I said briskly and slid the door shut. "Not here," I told Alison.

Three doors up ahead, Lynne swung out into the corridor. "Found her!" she called, and I relaxed against the swaying train window, miles of stunning mountainy German landscape flashing by. Ms. Polems and Lynne hurried by me, and I slowly followed them, hoping Pats and Jess had tried to clean up our compartment a little.

· · ·

Jules gazed silently at the compartment door that had just clicked loudly into place. That face . . .

He turned and looked at his companion, a friend he had known for more years than he cared to count. Daedalus looked as shocked as Jules felt.

"Surely that was Clio," Daedalus said, speaking softly so their seatmates wouldn't hear. He ran an elegant, long-fingered hand through hair graying at the temples, though still thick despite his age. "Wasn't Clio her name? Or was it . . . Clémence?"

"Clémence was the mother," Jules murmured. "The one who died. When was the last time you saw the child?"

Daedalus held his chin, thinking. Both men looked up as a small knot of students, led by an official-looking older woman, bobbed down the rocking corridor. He saw her again—that face—and then she was gone. "Maybe four years ago?" he guessed. "She was thirteen, and Petra was initiating her. I saw her only from a distance."

"But of course, they're unmistakable, that line," Jules said in an undertone. "They always have been."

"Yes." Daedalus frowned: Confronted with an impossibility, his brain spun with thoughts. How to make sense of this? "She had to be the child, and yet she wasn't," he said at last. "She really wasn't—there was nothing about her—"

Cate Tiernan

"Nothing in her eyes," Jules broke in, agreeing.

"Unmistakably the child, and yet not the child," Daedalus catalogued facts on his fingers. "Clearly not an older child, nor a younger."

"No," Jules said grimly.

The same conclusion occurred to them at the same instant. Daedalus's mouth actually dropped open, and Jules put his hand over his heart. "Oh my God," he whispered. "Twins. Two of them! *Two* of them! *Two!*"

He hadn't see Daedalus smile like that in—he didn't know how long.

❧ Chapter One

Clio

THIS WAS SO EFFING *FRUSTRATING.* IF I CLENCHED my jaws any tighter, my face would snap.

My grandmother sat across from me, serenity emanating from her like perfume, a scent she dabbed behind her ears in the morning that carried her smoothly through her day.

Well, I had *forgotten* to dab on my freaking *serenity* this morning, and now I was holding this piece of copper in my left fist, my fingernails making angry half-moons in my palm. Another minute of this and I would throw the copper across the room, sweep the candle over with my hand, and just *go*, like, shopping or something.

But I wanted this so bad.

So bad I could taste it. And now, looking into my grandmother's eyes, calm and blue over the candle's flame, I felt like she was reading every thought that flit through my brain. And that she was amused.

I closed my eyes and took a deep breath, all the way down to my belly ring. Then I released it slowly, slowly, willing it to take tension, doubt, ignorance, and impatience with it. *Please.*

Cuivre, orientez ma force. Copper, direct my power, I thought. Actually, not even thought—lighter than that. Expressing that idea so lightly that it wasn't even a thought or words. Just pure feeling, as slight as a ribbon of smoke, weaving into the power of *Bonne Magie.*

Montrez-moi, I breathed. *Show me. Breathe in, breathe out.*

You have to walk before you can run. You have to crawl before you can walk.

Montrez-moi.

Quartz crystals and rough chunks of emerald surrounded my grandmother and me in twelve points. A white candle burned on the ground between us. My ass had gone numb, like, yesterday. *Breathe.*

Montrez-moi.

It wasn't working, it wasn't working. *Je n'ai pas de force, rien du tout.* I opened my eyes, ready to scream.

And saw a huge cypress tree before me.

No grandmother. An enormous cypress tree almost blocked out the sky and the heavy gray clouds. I looked down: I still held the copper, hot now from my hand. I was in the woods somewhere—I didn't recognize where. *Une cyprière.* A woodsy swamp—cypress knees pushing up through still, brown-green water. But I was standing on land, something solid, moss-covered.

The clouds grew darker, roiling with an internal storm. Leaves whipped past me, landed on the water, brushed my face. I heard thunder, a deep rumbling that fluttered in my chest and filled my ears. Fat raindrops spattered the ground, ran down my cheeks like tears. Then an enormous *crack!* shook me where I stood, and a simultaneous stroke of lightning blinded me. Almost instantly, I heard a shuddering, splintering sound, like a wooden boat grinding against rocks. I blinked, trying to look through brilliant red and orange afterimages in my eyes. Right in front of me, the huge cypress tree was split in two, its halves bending precariously outward, already cracking, pulled down by their weight.

At the base, between two thick roots that were slowly being tugged from the earth, I saw a sudden upsurging of—what? I squinted. Was it water? Oil? It was dark like oil, thick—but the next lightning flash revealed the opaque dark red of blood. The rivulet of blood also split into two and ran across the ground, seeping slowly into the sodden moss, the red startling against the greenish gray. I looked down and saw the blood swelling, running faster, gushing heavily from between the tree roots. My feet! My feet were being splashed with blood, my shins flecked with it. I lost it then, covered my mouth, and screamed into my tight palm, trying to move but finding myself more firmly rooted than the tree itself—

"Clio! Clio!"

A cool hand took my chin in a no-nonsense grip. My head wobbled. I blinked rapidly, trying to clear rain out of my eyes. My grandmother was holding my chin in one hand and had her other under my elbow.

"Stand up, child," Nan instructed calmly. The candle between us had been knocked over, its wax running on the wooden floor. My knees felt wobbly, and I was gulping air, looking around wildly, orienting myself.

"Nan," I gasped, swallowing air like a fish. "Nan, oh, *Déesse*, that sucked."

"Tell me what you saw," she said, leading me out of the workroom and into our somewhat shabby kitchen.

I didn't want to talk about it, as if the words would recall the vision, putting me back into it. My grandmother's blue eyes stayed on mine, even as she automatically began fixing tea. "I saw a tree," I said reluctantly. "A cypress. I was in a swamp kind of place. There was a storm, and then—the tree got hit by lightning. It got split in two. And then—blood gushed out of its roots."

"Blood?" Her gaze was sharp.

I nodded, feeling shivery and kind of sick. "Blood, a river of blood. And it split into two and started running over my feet, and then I yelled. Yuck." I trembled and couldn't help looking at my bare feet. Not bloody. Tan feet, purple-painted toenails. Fine.

"A tree split by lightning," my grandmother mused, pouring hot water into a pot. The steamy, wet smell of herbs filled the room, and my shivering eased. "And then a river of blood from its roots. And the river split in two."

"Yeah," I said, holding my mug in my cold hands, inhaling the steam. "That pretty much sums it up. Man." I shook my head and sipped. "What," I said, noticing that my grandmother was watching me.

"It's interesting," she said in that way that meant there were a thousand other words inside her that weren't coming out. "Interesting vision. Looks like copper's good for you. We'll work on it again tomorrow."

"Not if I see you first," I muttered into my mug.

✦ Chapter Two

Thais

THIS ISN'T HAPPENING.

I could tell myself that a thousand times, and a thousand times the cold reality of my life would ruthlessly sink in again.

Next to me, Mrs. Thompkins gave my hand a pat. We were sitting side by side in hard wooden chairs in the third-district civil court of Welsford, Connecticut. Two weeks ago, I had been happily scarfing down a *patisserie Anglaise* in a little bakery in Tours. Today I was waiting to hear a judge discuss the terms of my father's will.

Because my father was dead.

Two weeks ago, I'd had a dad, a home, a life. Then someone had had a stroke behind the wheel of a Buick Regal, and the out-of-control car had jumped a curb on Main Street and killed my dad. Things like that don't happen to people, not really. They happen in movies, sometimes books. Not to real people, not to real dads. Not to me.

And yet here I was, listening to a judge read a will I'd never even known existed. Mrs. Thompkins, who'd been our neighbor my whole life, dabbed at my cheeks with a lavender-scented hankie, and I realized I'd been crying.

"The minor child, Thais Allard, has been granted in custody to a family friend." The judge pushed her bifocals farther up the bridge of her nose and looked at me kindly. I glanced at Mrs. Thompkins next to me, thinking how strange it would be to go home to her house, right next door to my old life, to sleep in her guest room for the next four months, until I turned eighteen. And then what?

If I had a boyfriend, I could move in with him. So I guess breaking up with Chad Woolcott right before I went to Europe had been premature. I sighed, but the sigh turned into a sob, and I choked it back.

The judge began talking about probate and executors, and my mind got fuzzy.

I loved Bridget Thompkins—she'd been the grandmother I'd never had. When her husband had died three years ago, it was like losing a grandfather. Could I stay in my own house and just have her be my guardian, next door?

"And is the person named Axel Govin in the courtroom?" Judge Dailey asked, looking over her glasses.

"Ax*elle* Gau-*vanh*," a voice behind me said, giving the name a crisp French pronunciation.

"Axelle Gauvin," the judge repeated patiently.

Mrs. Thompkins and I frowned at each other.

"Ms. Gauvin, Michel Allard's will clearly states that he

wished you to become the guardian of his only minor child, Thais Allard. Is this your understanding?"

I blinked rapidly. Whaaat?

"Yes, it is, your honor," said the voice behind me, and I whirled around. Axelle Gauvin, whom I'd never heard of in my life, looked like the head dominatrix of an expensive bordello. She had shining black hair cut in a perfect, swingy bell right above her shoulders. Black bangs framed black eyes heavily made up. Bright blood-red lips either pouted naturally or had been injected with collagen. The rest of her was a blur of shining black leather and silver buckles. In summer. Welsford, Connecticut, had never seen anything like this.

"Who is that?" Mrs. Thompkins whispered in shock.

I shook my head helplessly, trying to swallow with an impossibly dry throat.

"Michel and I hadn't seen each other recently," the woman said in a sultry, smoker's voice, "but we'd always promised each other I'd take care of little Thais if anything happened to him. I just never thought it would." Her voice broke, and I turned around to see her dabbing at eyes as dark as a well.

She'd said my name correctly—even the judge had pronounced it Thay-iss, but Axelle had known it was Tye-ees. Had she known my dad? How? My whole life, it had been me and my dad. I'd known he'd dated, but I'd always met the women. None of them had been Axelle Gauvin.

"Your honor, I—" Mrs. Thompkins began, upset.

"I'm sorry," the judge said gently. "You're still the executor for all of Mr. Allard's personal possessions, but the will clearly states that Ms. Axelle Gauvin is to assume custody of the minor. Of course, you could challenge the will in court . . . but it would be an expensive and lengthy process." The judge took off her glasses, and the icy knowledge that this was real, that I really might end up with this hard-looking stranger in back of me, began to filter into my panicked mind. "Thais will be eighteen in only four months, and at that time she'll be legally free to decide where she wants to live, and with whom. Although I would hope that Ms. Gauvin is sensible to the fact that Thais is about to start her senior year of high school, and that it would be least disruptive if she could simply stay in Welsford to do so."

"I know," said the woman, sounding regretful. "But sadly, my home is in New Orleans, and my business precludes my being able to relocate here for the next year. Thais will be coming to New Orleans with me."

• • •

I stood in my room, looking at everything I couldn't possibly fit into a suitcase. Actually, I had three suitcases and a large trunk that had belonged to Mr. Thompkins in World War II. My desk wasn't about to fit in any of them.

I sagged down on my bed, feeling my somewhat threadbare quilt under my fingers. I felt numb. I was embracing numbness. If I ever let myself not feel numb, a huge, howling pain would tear up from my gut and burst out into the world in a shrieking, unstoppable, hysterical hurricane of anguish.

I was going to New Orleans, Louisiana, with a leather-happy stranger. I hated to even speculate on how she knew my dad. If they'd had any kind of romantic relationship, it would take away the dad I knew and replace him with some brain-damaged unknown. She'd said they'd been friends. Such good friends that he'd given her his only child and yet had never mentioned her name to me once.

A tap on my door. I looked up blankly as Mrs. Thompkins came in, her gentle, plump face drawn and sad. She carried a sandwich and a glass of lemonade on a tray, which she set on my desk. She stood by me, brushing her fingers over my hair while I tried not to feel anything.

"Do you need any help, dear?" she whispered.

I shook my head no and tried to manage a brave smile, which failed miserably. Inside me a hollow wail of pain threatened to break through. It hit me over and over again, and yet I still couldn't quite take it in. My dad was dead. Gone forever. It was literally unbelievable.

"You and I know everything we want to say," Mrs. Thompkins went on in a soft voice. "Saying it just seems too hard right now. But I'll tell you this: It's just for four months. If it works out and you want to stay down there"—she made it sound like hell—"then that's fine, and I'll wish you well. But if you want to come back after four months, I'll be here with open arms. Do you understand?"

I nodded and did smile then, and she smiled back at me and left.

I couldn't eat. I didn't know what to pack. What had happened to my life? I was about to leave everything and everyone I had ever known. I'd been looking forward to going away to college next year—had imagined leaving this place, this room. But I wasn't ready now, a year early. I wasn't ready for any of this.

⚜ Chapter Three

Connected by Fate

I reach out through the darkness
To touch the ones I need
I send my spirit with a message
It finds their spirits where they reside
We are connected by time
We are connected by fate
We are connected by life
We are connected by death
Go

IN THIS STILL ROOM, THE CANDLE FLAME barely wavered. How lucky, truly, for them to find such a suitable place. Daedalus liked this little room, with its attic ceiling sloping sharply downward toward the walls. He sat comfortably on the wooden floor, nailed into place more than two hundred years before. Breathing slowly, he watched the candle flame shine unwaveringly, upside down in the faintly amethyst-colored glass, as if the ball itself were a large eye peering out into the world.

"Sophie," Daedalus breathed, imagining her, the way she'd looked when he'd seen her last. What, ten years ago? More. *Sophie. Feel my connection, hear my message.* Daedalus closed his eyes, scarcely breathing, sending thoughts across continents, across time itself.

• • •

Reherche: L'histoire de France. Sophie tapped the words out on her keyboard, enjoying the instant gratification, the enormous well of knowledge at her fingertips. With every passing age, things became more wondrous. Yes, there were downsides to progress. There were many, many things she missed. But each new day revealed a new wonder also.

"Veux-tu du saumon?" Manon asked, the phone pressed against her ear. "Pour dîner," she clarified when Sophie looked at her.

Sophie nodded. She didn't care what she ate. She couldn't understand Manon's various hungers: food, drink, cigarettes, people. Sophie thirsted for knowledge, for learning. One day, somehow, if she could fill her brain with enough truth and understanding, then perhaps she could begin to understand herself, her life, the lives that were irrevocably entwined with hers. Maybe.

A thin tendril of cigarette smoke floated over to her. Manon was still walking around, phone pressed against her ear, ordering food from the concierge.

The results of Sophie's search filled her laptop screen, and she leaned forward. At that moment, with no warning, the words wavered, as if underwater. Sophie frowned, glancing at the floor to make sure the surge protector was active. This computer was practically brand-new. What—

Sophie, my love. Come to New Orleans. It's important. Daedalus.

The words resolved themselves on Sophie's screen as she watched them, taking them in. Manon hung up the phone and came to see what Sophie was staring at.

"We haven't heard from him in a while," Manon said unnecessarily.

Sophie said nothing.

"Are we going to go?" Manon asked.

Again Sophie didn't reply. Her large brown eyes searched the room, the air, seeming to stare across thousands of miles, straight at Daedalus.

• • •

"And now Ouida," Daedalus murmured, clearing his mind of all thought, all feeling. He existed but was unaware of his own being. He was one with the wood, the air, the glass, the flame. . . .

• • •

Okay, assuming this sample wasn't contaminated, she could isolate about thirty cells, put them through trypsin-giemsa staining, and have a nice set of chromosomes to examine. Ouida Jeffers carefully maneuvered the dish containing the genetic material out of the centrifuge. She heard the lab door swing open and shut but didn't look up until the sample was securely on a shelf and the fridge door closed. Not after what had happened last Tuesday. A month's worth of work literally down the drain. God.

"Excuse me, Doctor."

Ouida looked over to see her assistant holding out a pink telephone message.

"This came for you."

"Okay, thanks, Scott." Ouida took the message. Maybe it was about that intern she'd interviewed.

Come to New Orleans, Ouida, it said. The hairs on the back of her neck stood up. Breathing quickly, she glanced around the lab, her lab, so familiar, representing everything she'd worked so hard for. *We need you,* said the message. *At last. Daedalus.*

Swallowing, Ouida sank down on a lab stool and reread the message. *Relax, calm down. You don't have to go.* She looked through the window, honeycombed with wire for security. Outside the sky was clear and blue. New Orleans. New Orleans would be very hot right now.

• • •

As soon as he saw Claire, Daedalus grimaced. Clearly she hadn't made huge leaps forward since the last time they'd met. He saw her sprawled gracelessly in a cheap wooden chair. Two uneven rows of upside-down shot glasses gleamed stickily on the Formica table where she rested her elbows.

Claire.

The crowd chanted around her. A beefy, middle-aged man, some sort of Asian, Daedalus couldn't tell which, seemed to rally himself. He tossed back another jolt of whatever white-lightning alcohol they were drinking. Beyond feeling the stinging burn on the back of his throat, he wiped his mouth on his worker's sleeve. Dark, half-closed eyes strained to focus on his opponent.

Claire's attention was caught momentarily by the insistent ringing of the bar's wall phone.

Answer it, Claire. Ask not for whom the phone rings; it rings for thee. . . .

The ringing was blinked away as if it were an annoying insect. Claire smiled, and the crowd cheered at this show of bravado. Someone thunked down another heavy shot glass; an unmarked bottle tilted and splashed more rotgut, filling the glass and dousing the table around it.

The crowd started clapping in unison, shouting something. Her name? Some Asian word that meant "crazy white lady"? Daedalus couldn't tell. She wasn't going to answer the phone—no one was. She wouldn't hear his message. He would have to try to catch her when she was more sober. Good luck. It would take her days, at least, to dry out from today's little episode.

Her eyes glowing greenly, as if lit from within, Claire's unsteady hand reached out for the glass. It wobbled; clear liquid running over her fingers. She didn't notice. She held the shot glass to her lips and tossed back her head. Then, triumphantly, she slammed it down on the table. The crowd roared its approval; money openly changed hands. Across from her, the Asian man bluffed by reaching out his hand for another glass, but then slowly leaned sideways, sliding gently against the table. He was lying on the floor, eyes shut, shirt wet, before anyone had realized he was out.

Daedalus groaned. All right, later for her.

• • •

At least Marcel wasn't likely to be pickling himself from the inside out, Daedalus thought, closing his eyes and focusing on the man who'd been a mystery for as long as Daedalus had known him. *Marcel.* He pictured the youthful face, the smooth, fair skin, the blue eyes, the pale auburn hair.

The candlelight's reflection didn't move while Daedalus gazed at it. *Marcel.*

Daedalus could practically feel the chill wafting off the stone walls in his vision. He mused that he could be seeing Marcel today, a hundred years ago, three hundred years ago, and it would all look the same: the rough stone monastery walls, the dim light, the orderly rows of desks. Three hundred years ago, every desk would have been occupied. But today few Irish families committed younger sons to God so they'd have one less mouth to feed. As a result, only two other occupants kept Marcel silent company in the large hall.

Marcel was hunched over a large book—an original, hand-illuminated manuscript. The gold leaf had faded hardly at all since the time it was ever-so-carefully pressed in place by a penitent servant of the Holy Mother Church.

Daedalus sent his message, smiling at his own creativity, proud of his strength. Marcel could deny what he was;

Daedalus never would. Ouida could ignore her powers, the same powers that Daedalus reveled in daily. Sophie could fill her time with learning and other intellectual pursuits. Daedalus spent his time harvesting strength.

Which was why he was greater than they; why he was the sender, and they the receivers.

In the monastery Marcel's thin shoulders hunched over his manuscript. The beauty of the art in the margins was filling his soul with a too-pleasurable torment—was it a sin to feel such human joy upon seeing the work of men before him? Or had their hands been divinely guided, their illuminations divinely inspired? In which case Marcel was only paying homage to their God by his admiration.

His lips barely moved as he read the Latin words. But—he frowned. He blinked and rubbed a rough sleeve over his eyes. The letters were moving . . . *oh no.*

Panicked, Marcel looked up. No one was paying attention. He shielded the book with his body, keeping it out of sight. He would never escape. Never, never. Never was such a long time. Now he accepted that the fine-edged black letters had rearranged themselves. He read the newly formed words. *Important. Urgent. Come to New Orleans at once. Daedalus.*

Marcel brushed his rough sleeve across the cold sweat dampening his brow. Then he sat, struggling to feel nothing, as he waited for the words to disappear, to become again a prayer in Latin, lauding God. He had to wait a long time.

· · ·

The last storm had stirred the waters so that fishing or crabbing was pointless. Better to wait till the water cleared, a week, maybe two. Besides clouding the waters with silt, the storm had littered the sandy beaches with all manner of driftwood, dead fish, an empty turtleshell, uglier human detritus: a bicycle tire, someone's bra. There was a story about *that*, Richard bet.

He wanted a smoke, but last time he'd lit up, four different people had given him hell. Whether it was because he looked so young—despite the pierced nose, pierced eyebrow, and visible tattoos—or they were just worried about this part of the world being polluted, he didn't know.

Might as well give up for now. Go back home, sleep, whatever.

An unexpected tug on his line caught Richard by surprise, and he almost dropped his pole. But his fingers tightened automatically, and he quickly turned his reel. He hoped it wasn't a catfish. They were a bitch to get off the line, and ones this big weren't good eating. The flash of sun on silver told him it was something else.

The reel whirred while he pulled. Long, slender body, shiny silver with spots. Spanish mackerel. Under the length limit—it would have to go back. Richard pulled the line closer, running his fingers down the wet line to unhook the fish.

Its mouth opened. "Richard," the fish croaked. *Ree-shard*.

Richard blinked and then started to grin. He glanced around—unlikely that anyone else could hear his talking fish. He laughed. What a funny idea! A talking fish! This was hysterical.

"Richard," the fish said again. "Come back to New Orleans. It'll be worth your while, I promise. Daedalus."

Richard waited a moment, but the fish had exhausted its message apparently. Quickly he slipped his fingers down the hook, flipped the fish off it. The mackerel dropped the eight feet to the cloudy olive-drab water, its flanks flashing.

Hmm, New Orleans. It hadn't been that long since he'd been back. But long enough. He grinned. A road trip. Just what he needed to cheer himself up.

• • •

Daedalus laughed softly to himself, watching Richard gather his gear. It would be good to see him again. Probably.

A sound downstairs drew Daedalus's attention. Moving deliberately, not quickly, he doused his candle and put his glass globe in the cupboard, draping a square of black silk over it. He smudged the circle of salt on the floor, erasing its lines with his foot, then smoothed his hair back.

He felt drained, hungry, thirsty. He'd done a lot in one day—perhaps too much. But there was no time to waste. They didn't have a lot of time. There was much, much to be done.

✦ Chapter Four

Clio

"YEAH, SO SHE WAS PISSED," RACEY REPORTED, flipping her streaked hair back. She leaned against the wall in the tiny curtained dressing cubicle and took a sip of iced coffee.

"Yeah?" I asked absently, unhooking my bra so I could try on a tie-dyed halter top. "What'd she say?"

"She said the next time I missed a circle, my ass would be grass." Racey cocked her head to one side, which made her short, asymmetrical haircut look almost even.

I gave a quick grin—Racey's mom was a riot. More like an older sister than a mom. My grandmother was cool in her own way, but you couldn't get away from the fact that she was a grandmother. True, she was aging well—in fact, her looks hadn't changed much for as long as I could remember. Those were the genes I wanted to inherit—those, and Nan's *force de magie*. "And she'd be the lawnmower?" I guessed.

"Yep. Turn around so I can see the back," Racey instructed. "Cool. Hot. Both."

"I'm going to look." I pushed open the Indian-bedspread curtain and stepped out to look at the full-length mirror mounted on one wall. I loved Botanika—they always had cool stuff. It was my home away from home. Food, coffee, tea, witch supplies like candles, oils, crystals, etc. Books, music, incense. A small selection of retro clothes, tie-dyed and batik and funky. Plus, it felt so normal here. I'd told Racey about my horrible vision, but only a bit, and I hadn't really told her how freaked I'd been. Even now, days later, I felt a bit weird, like something was about to happen. It was stupid.

Outside, the mirror was cheap and warped, so that I had to stand on my tiptoes to get a good view of the halter. I looked at myself, thinking, *I so lucked out.* Conceited? Well, yeah. But also realistic. Why should I pretend that I didn't enjoy my natural assets? I tugged the shirt up so my silver belly ring showed. Cool.

"Was your grandmother mad?" Racey asked, stirring her coffee with the straw.

"Oh, yeah." I grimaced. "She was burned. I had to vacuum the whole house."

"Poor Cinderella." Racey grinned. "Good thing you have a small house." The contrast of her dark brown hair streaked with white gave her a faintly camouflaged look, like a zebra or a tiger. Her big brown eyes were rimmed in teal today. She'd been my best friend and partner in crime since kindergarten. It helped that her parents and my grandmother belonged to the same coven. The coven we had blown off the night of the new moon, so we could go bar-hopping in the Quarter.

"But it was worth it," I said firmly, checking out my rear view. "I love Amadeo's—full of college guys and tourists. Didn't you have fun?" I smiled, remembering how I hadn't needed to buy myself a single drink—and not because I was working on those guys with spells. It had been just good old-fashioned female charms.

"Yeah, I did, but my magick wasn't worth crap the next day. The alcohol."

"There *is* that," I admitted, deciding to buy the halter. Someday, I'd have to find a way around that annoying truth. Still looking at myself, I pushed my black hair over my shoulders, then saw how it looked against my skin in back. Excellent. *Thanks, Mom.* Nan had one picture of my mom, and I looked like her: black hair, green eyes, and the weirdest thing of all—we both had a strawberry birthmark in the exact same place. I was still trying to decide if I wanted to get it lasered off. It was on my left cheekbone and looked like, well, frankly, what it looked like depended on how much you'd had to drink. Sometimes a small thistle flower, sometimes an animal footprint (Racey said a very tiny three-toed sloth), sometimes a fleur-de-lis. And my mom, who had died when I was born, had had the same thing. Bizarre, n'est-ce pas?

I was heading back into the cubicle when I felt, literally felt, someone's gaze on me. I looked through the few clothing racks, out to the main part of the store. And saw him.

My breath stopped in my throat and I froze where I stood.

Déesse. This was the definition of *poleaxed*, this stunned feeling, where time was standing still, and all that crap.

"What?" said Racey, almost bumping into me. She followed my line of vision. "Whoa. Jeez, Louise."

The Hottest Guy in the World was staring right at me. I've known my share of hot guys, but this one was in a whole different league. His sable-colored hair was too long, as if he couldn't be bothered to get it cut properly. Dark eyebrows angled sharply over dark eyes. He was young but with strong bones, strong features, like a man, not a boy. In that instant, I knew we would be together. And I also somehow knew that he wouldn't be easy to wrap around my little finger, like other guys. His open, interested look was a challenge. One that I was going to accept.

I raised my eyebrows slightly, then went slowly into the cubicle, giving him a good look at my back, all bare skin because of the halter. Racey followed me in a second later, and I made an awed, oh-my-God face at her. She shrugged non-committally.

"You don't think he's too old?" she whispered.

I shook my head and laughed, surprised and a little freaked to notice that my fingers were trembling. Racey helped me undo the back ties, and I scrambled back into my bra and tank top. I felt like I'd just run a thousand-meter race, hot and cold and trembly all over.

I was dressed for comfort in an overdyed man's tank top and a ratty pair of jean shorts that were cut off right below my underwear. While it would have been nice to be wearing something more sophisticated, I knew that most guys would think I looked damn fine.

"That guy is fantastic," I said in an excited understatement.

Racey shrugged again. "We don't know him," she pointed out. "He could be anyone."

I looked at her. Racey had never been like this—usually she was as go-get-'em as I was. Did she want him for herself? I didn't think so. She didn't look jealous. Just . . . concerned.

I had to get up my nerve to saunter out of the changing cubicle, the halter in my hand. Which was very unlike me. A guy—any guy—hadn't made me nervous since I was about four years old. I was sure I knew all the ins and outs of the whole male/female thing, but for some reason Mr. Fabulous was suddenly making me wonder if I knew anything at all.

He was still there, not even pretending to be cool or casual. His gaze locked on me like a dark laser, and I felt an actual, bonafide shiver go down my spine. Oh my God, this was going to be fun. And scary. Anything that was truly fun always had an element of scary to it.

He didn't smile, or wave, or try to look approachable. Instead, keeping his eyes on me, he nudged a chair out a bit with his foot. *Très* suave.

I was dimly aware of Racey fading into the background like a good best friend. Out of the corner of my eye, I saw her settle into a seat at the bar. Then I was at his table, and he pushed a chair out the rest of the way for me. I sat down, dropped the halter on the table, and reached over for his drink. Our eyes stayed locked as I took a sip—he was drinking iced espresso, which seemed impossibly cool. He was perfection. The ultimate. And I was going to show him that we were a matched set.

"I haven't seen you here before," I said, thrilled to hear my voice sound a tiny bit husky, a tiny bit lower than usual. This close I could see his eyes were actually an incredibly dark blue, like the sky at midnight. It made him look that much more intense.

"I'm new in town," he said, and *he had a French accent*. God help me.

"How are you liking the local scenery?" I asked and drank more of his coffee.

He looked at me, and I felt like he was picturing me lying down somewhere, with him, and he was thinking about what we would do when we got there. My heartbeat sped up.

So scary. And so exciting.

"I'm liking it," he said, understanding my meaning. He took back his glass and drank from it. "I'm André."

I smiled. "Clio."

"Clio," he repeated, and my name with a French accent sounded incredible. I mean, I spoke some French, like my grandmother did. Our religion was all based in French from hundreds of years ago. But I didn't have an accent, I mean, except an American one. "Tell me, Clio," he said, leaning toward me over the small table. "Are you what you seem? Would you be dangerous for me to . . . know?"

"Yes. And no," I said steadily, lying through my teeth. I had no idea what I seemed to be, and no way would I tell him that I was dangerous only because I didn't intend to ever let him get away. "What about you?" I asked, feeling like I was walking some fine edge. "Are you dangerous for me to know?"

He smiled then, and I felt my heart shudder to a stop inside my chest. At that moment, I would have given him my hand and let him take me across the world, giving up my home, my grandmother, my friends. "Yes, Clio," he said softly, still smiling. "I'm dangerous for you to know."

I looked back at him, feeling utterly, utterly lost. "Good," I managed, my throat dry.

An instant of surprise crossed his beautiful, sculpted face, and then he actually laughed. He took my hand with both of his. Little sparks of electricity made me tingle all over, and then he turned my palm up. He looked at it and slowly traced a finger down the lines, as if reading my fortune. Then he took out a pen and wrote a phone number on my skin.

"Unfortunately, I'm already late," he said in a voice that was so intimate, so personal, it was as if we were the only two people in Botanika. He stood up—he was tall—and put some money on the table for a tip. "But that's my number, and I'm telling you: If you don't call me, I'll come find you."

"We'll see, won't we?" I said coolly, though inside I was doing an ecstatic victory dance. Something in his eyes flared, making me take a shallow breath, and then it was gone, leaving me to wonder if I had imagined it.

"Yes," he said, sounding deceptively mild. "We will." Turning, he walked with long, easy strides to the door and pushed it open. I watched him pass the plate glass window and had to struggle with myself not to jump up, run after him, and tackle him right there.

Racey slid into the seat opposite mine. "Well?" she said. "What was he like? Did he seem okay?"

I let out a deep breath I hadn't realized I'd been holding. "More than okay." I uncurled my fingers, showing Racey his number written on my palm.

Racey looked at me, unusually solemn.

"What?" I asked her. "I've never seen you like this."

"Yeah," she said and looked away. "I don't know what it is. Usually, you know, we see a guy, and bam, we know what the deal is, how to handle him—no surprises, you know? They're all kind of the same. But this one—I don't know," she said again. "I mean, I just got a funny feeling from him."

"You and me both," I said sincerely, looking at his phone number in my palm.

"It was like I instantly knew he was . . . really different," Racey persisted.

I looked at her, interested. She was one of the strongest witches our age in the coven, and besides that, she was my best friend. I totally trusted her.

"Different bad?" I asked. "I didn't see that. He knocked me off my feet, but it all felt good." Besides the scary stuff, I meant.

Racey shrugged, as if shaking off bad feelings. She smiled at me, looking more normal. "I don't know what I'm doing," she said. "Don't listen to me. He *is* really hot. And I didn't even talk to him." Then she looked at me again. "Just—be careful."

"Yeah, of course," I said, having no idea what that meant. We got up, and I paid for my new halter, which I planned to wear the next time I saw André.

Because I was going to call him. I was going to see him again. And I was going to make him mine.

✦ Chapter Five

Thais

OKAY, ONE GOOD THING—BEIGNETS—WEIGHED against the katrillion bad things. Mostly, not having Dad, who had been there every day of my life, let me win at Monopoly, taught me to drive. He'd held me when I cried, and my eyes filled up now just thinking about it. He'd been quietly funny, gentle, maybe a little bit remote, but I'd always known he'd loved me. And I hoped he'd known how much I loved him.

I swallowed hard and moved on to all the other horrible things: Axelle, the rest of New Orleans, my entire life, Axelle's creepy friends, being an orphan, my life, the heat, the bugs, the ridiculous humidity that felt like a damp fist punching your head when you stepped outside, my life, missing my dad, missing Welsford, missing Mrs. Thompkins, Axelle, not having a car, being seventeen and starting a new school for senior year, oh yeah, my *life*, the noise, the crowds, the clogging throngs of tourists everywhere, drunk and sunbaked by two in the afternoon because New Orleans is the devil's playground, Axelle, oh, and did I mention going crazy missing my dad?

But the beignets and coffee were unbelievable. Nothing like light, airy, puffs of dough deep-fried in lard and coated with powdered sugar to pick a girl up. And the coffee—oh, God. I'd always hated coffee—didn't even like the smell when Dad made it. But the coffee here was boiled with milk, and it was fabulous. I now came to Café du Monde every day for my caffeine 'n' cholesterol fix. Another couple weeks and I would be permanently hyped up and weigh two hundred pounds. The sad thing was, that wouldn't even make my life any worse. I was already at rock bottom. And now I was crying again, dripping tears onto the powdered sugar, as I did almost every time I came here. I pulled more napkins out of the dispenser and wiped my eyes.

I had no idea how this had happened to me. A month ago I was totally normal in every way, living a totally normal life with my totally normal dad. Now, barely four weeks later, I was living with a strange woman (I mean literally strange, as in *bizarre*, not just *unknown*) who had zero idea of what guardianship was all about. She'd told me that she and my dad had had a deep and meaningful friendship, but had sometimes lost touch with each other through the years. I was way, way thankful that apparently they'd never actually dated.

Still, Dad must have been out of his gourd to think for even one second that my living with Axelle would be anything close to a good idea. I'd lost track of how many times a day I prayed for this to be a nightmare so I could wake up.

I got up and walked across the street, through Jackson

Square. Axelle lived in the French Quarter, the oldest part of New Orleans. I had to admit, it was pretty. The buildings looked European, not Southern or colonial, and there was an old-fashioned grace and timelessness to the place that even I in my misery could appreciate. On the other hand, it was incredibly dirty almost everywhere, and some streets were touristy in a horrible, seedy kind of way. Like all the strip joints on Bourbon Street. Yep, just blocks of strip joints and bars, all being peered into by anyone passing by, even if the person passing by was a *child*.

But there were other streets, not touristy, quiet and serene in a timeless way. Even Welsford was founded only in about 1860. New Orleans had had some sort of settlement here for about 150 years before that. Through hours and hours of walking aimlessly, I had realized that there was a whole separate Quarter that most people never see: the private gardens, hidden courtyards, pockets of lush green almost pulsing with life.

And yet, even in the midst of ageless beauty, there was an undercurrent of—what? Danger? Not as strong as danger. Not as strong as dread. But like, when I walked under a balcony, I expected a safe to fall on my head. If the same person walked behind me for more than a block, I got nervous. There was a lot of crime here, but my nervousness wasn't even that based in reality. It was more like I expected the sun never to shine again in my life. Or like I had driven into a train tunnel, and there was no end in sight, and a train was coming at me. It was weird but probably normal after everything I had been through.

I turned left and cut down a narrow, one-block-long little street. I waded through a busload of tourists on a walking tour and turned another corner. Two blocks down this street was where I was sentenced to live, at least for the next four months.

Axelle's apartment had once been part of an incredible private home. There was a side gate made of wrought iron, which I unlocked. It led to a narrow, covered driveway, wide enough for carriages, not cars. My feet made faint echoing noises on the cool flagstones, worn from hundreds of years of use. The front door was in the back of the house. Four buildings bordered a private courtyard, which had a weensy swimming pool and lushly overgrown plant beds around the walls.

Sighing, feeling like an anvil was on my chest, I turned my key in the lock. With any luck Axelle wouldn't be here—she'd already be out for the evening, and I wouldn't have to go with her. Last night she'd brought me to three different bars, despite my reminding her that not only was I not twenty-one, but I wasn't even eighteen yet. At all three places, the bouncer or doorman had looked at me, opened his mouth as if to card me, which I was hoping for, because then I could go home and go to bed—but then they'd just shut their mouths and let me pass. I guessed Axelle knew them, and they'd let her do whatever.

I pushed open the door to be met by a blessed whoosh of air conditioning and found I was out of luck. Axelle lounged on her black leather sofa, her clothes making slight sibilant noises when she shifted. She was smoking and talking on the phone and barely looked up at me when I came in.

To add to my fun, her creepy friends Jules and Daedalus were there too. I'd met them practically the moment we got off the plane in New Orleans. Neither of them was her boyfriend, but they were around a lot. Jules was good-looking in a Denzel Washington kind of way, and seemed about Axelle's age, early thirties. Daedalus was old enough to be her father, like in his mid-fifties. He reminded me of a used-car salesman, always smiling, but the smile never reaching his eyes.

"Ah! Thais," said Daedalus, looking up from a thick book. Jules also looked up and smiled, then continued examining a map on the small round dining table at one end of the huge main room. At the other end was a fireplace and sitting area. The tiny kitchen was open to the big room, separated by a black granite counter. Axelle's bedroom and huge, pathologically crowded and messy closet were down a short hallway. My tiny bedroom, which was essentially a former lean-to tacked onto the main house as an outdoor kitchen, opened off the back of the current kitchen.

"Hi," I said, heading for privacy.

"Wait, Thais," Jules said. He had a beautiful, deep voice, like James Earl Jones's, but dipped in honey. "I'd like you to meet our friend, Richard Landry." He gestured toward the main room, and someone I hadn't noticed stepped through the haze of Axelle's cigarette smoke.

"Hey," he said.

I blinked. At first glance he was my age, but in the next second I realized he was actually younger—maybe fourteen? He was a bit taller than me, and had warm brown hair, streaked from the sun, and brown eyes. I couldn't help standing still for a moment to take him in: He was the only fourteen-year-old I'd ever seen with a silver stud through his eyebrow, a silver ring through one nostril, and tattoos. He was wearing a black T-shirt with the sleeves torn off and long black jeans, despite the heat.

I realized I was staring and tried to recover. "Hi, Richard," I said, pronouncing it the way Jules had: Ree-shard. He just nodded, looking at me in a weirdly adult way, as if appraising. Yes, he won the weirdest-kid-I'd-ever-met award. And why on earth was he hanging out with these people? Maybe his parents were friends of theirs?

Axelle hung up the phone and got to her feet. Today, in deference to the ninety-eight-degree weather, she was wearing a black satiny catsuit. "Oh, good, you met Richard," she said. "Well, you all ready?"

Jules, Daedalus, and Richard nodded, and Richard put down his glass.

"We won't be long," said Axelle, unlocking a door that I hadn't even seen the first four days I was here. It was built into the deep molding of the main room, a hidden door. I'd almost jumped out of my skin one day when I'd thought I was alone and then suddenly Daedalus appeared out of the wall. Now that I knew it was there, I could easily see its outline and the round brass lock. It led to stairs, I knew that much, but I wasn't allowed in—it was always locked when Axelle wasn't home.

I watched silently as the three guys followed Axelle.

I was convinced they did drugs up there. And now they were dragging a kid into their web. True, a strange, hardcore kid, but still. The door clicked shut with a heavy finality, and I prowled restlessly around the main room, wondering if I should do something. Okay, for the three weird adults, that was one thing. They might be complete dope fiends, but they'd never hit me or come on to me or anything. But now they were corrupting a kid—if there was anything left in Richard to corrupt. That was definitely wrong.

Unsure what to do with my concern, I wandered around, picking up used glasses and loading them into the dishwasher. Axelle was the world's biggest slob, and I'd started tidying up out of self-defense, just so I'd have clean plates to eat off of, etc.

"Mreow?" Minou, Axelle's cat, jumped up on the kitchen counter. I scratched him absently behind the ears and then refilled his food bowl. Like the hidden door, Minou had shown up several days after I got here, but Axelle knew him and actually had cat food, so I figured he was hers. Guess what color he was?

I gathered a stack of newspapers, and the weird domesticness of the situation suddenly hit me. I blinked back tears, remembering how I'd done the same kind of stuff at home with Dad and how I'd grumbled about it and made him remind me five times and stuff. Now, what I wouldn't give to be at home with Dad nagging me! I would be the perfect daughter if I could only have another chance. I gulped, thinking maybe it was time to go cry on my bed for a while.

"Excuse me."

I whirled, sniffing and brushing my hand across my eyes. I hadn't heard Richard come up behind me. I closed the dishwasher door. "What," I said, feeling unnerved.

"Axelle sent me down for matches," he explained in a husky, unkidlike voice, stepping past me into the narrow kitchen. He was slender but wiry, with defined muscles. He was wearing black motorcycle boots.

"Don't you—" I began, and he glanced up at me. I could see that even though he was a little kid, he would probably be really good-looking when he grew up. If he lost the face jewelry. "Don't you think you're a little young for that?" I waved my hand toward the hidden stairway. Richard looked at me, expressionless. "I mean—do your folks know where you are? Don't you worry about getting in trouble or having it lead to bigger stuff that could actually really be dangerous?"

Richard picked up the box of matches. "I'm an orphan, honey," he said with a funny little smile. "And it's not what you think, upstairs. You'll find out."

Uh-oh. That didn't sound good. "I mean, it's not too late to quit," I said, feeling more and more unsure.

He did smile then, showing a hint of the man he would become in a couple years. "It's way too late to quit," he said and gave a little laugh, like there was a private joke somewhere. He left me and went back through the door, and feeling completely weirded out, I glanced absently at the stack of newspapers.

Time to register for school, those attending Orleans Parish public schools, I read. I had to move Minou's tail to finish the headline. School started on August 27, barely three weeks away. It listed a website where you could register online.

"Oh, Thais," said Axelle, coming into the kitchen. She rummaged in the cupboards and pulled out a box of salt. "Listen, don't go anywhere—we'll be done in a while, and then we're going out to dinner."

I nodded. We always went out to dinner. "Um, I have to register for school."

Axelle looked at me blankly.

I tapped the paper. "It says it's time to register if you're going to public school. Which I assume I am."

She seemed to recover and said, "Well, you know, you don't have to go if you don't want to. You've probably gone enough, right?"

Now I stared at her, her beautiful face that never seemed to show lack of sleep or hangovers or anything else, the black eyes that had no pupils. "I haven't graduated high school," I said slowly, as if I were explaining something to a child. "I have one more year."

"Well, what's one year?" she asked, shrugging. "I bet you know everything you need to know. Why don't you just hang out, relax?"

My mouth dropped open. "If I don't graduate high school, I won't be able to go to college."

"You mean you'd sign up for four more years?" She looked appalled.

"How am I going to get a *job*?" *Or do I not need one, here on Planet Unreality?*

Now she looked downright shocked. "*Job?*"

Okay. I was getting nowhere. I could see that. *Thanks, Dad,* I thought, tasting bitterness in the back of my throat. *You sure can pick 'em.* I took a deep breath and let it out. "Don't worry about it," I said calmly. "I'll take care of it. I'm going to school, and I'll register myself. I'll let you know what happens."

Axelle looked as if she were trying to think up a good argument, but couldn't come up with anything. "Well, if that's what you want to do," she said reluctantly.

"Yes," I said firmly. "Don't worry about it."

"Okay." She sighed heavily, as if she couldn't believe Michel Allard's child could be so incredibly unreasonable. I picked up the newspaper and headed back into my room, where I carefully shut the door. Then I lay down on my bed, put a pillow over my face, and howled.

Chapter Six

So Much Has Changed

"C'EST IMPOSSIBLE," DAEDALUS MUTTERED IN disgust. He banged his fist down on the hood of the car. "C'est impossible!"

"Hey!" said Axelle, throwing her cigarette to the ground. "La voiture, c'est à moi!" She leaned over and carefully examined the hood of her pink Cadillac, checking for dents.

This was unbelievable. Daedalus folded his arms across his chest and joined Richard and Jules, who were leaning against the side of Axelle's car, staring across the street. Axelle lit another cigarette. Richard held out his hand, his bracelet made of alligator teeth glistening in the dull light. Axelle shook a cigarette into it, and he lit it off hers.

Jules made a face. "Must you smoke even here?"

"Yes," Axelle said evenly, blowing smoke out the side of her mouth. "Are you going to lecture me about the health disadvantages?"

Richard chuckled, and Jules looked away.

"It's unpleasant, is all," he said.

"Then stand *downwind*," said Axelle.

"Stop it, you two," said Daedalus. "Of course we're all upset and disappointed. But we can't start arguing among ourselves. Now, more than ever, we have to stand together."

"Has Sophie come yet?" Axelle asked.

"I think she and Manon are coming tomorrow," said Daedalus, running a hand through his thick gray hair. He let out a breath and looked across the street, still unbelieving. "This *is* the place?" he asked for the fifth time.

"It's the place," Jules said dispiritedly. "It has to be."

The four of them stood in a line against the car. Across the street, where they had expected to find thick woods and swamps as far as the eye could see, there was instead a huge Super Walmart. And a huge parking lot. And other stores in a line next to it.

"When's the last time anyone was here?" Daedalus asked.

They thought, shrugged.

"Long time," Axelle said at last. "Obviously."

"Hang on." Richard leaned into the open window of the car and pulled out their old map. He took the recent map from Daedalus and spread them both out on the hood of the car. "Okay, here's New Orleans," he said, pointing to the city within the crescent bend of the river. "And this is about where we are." He traced a slender finger down a blue highway line, south-southwest of New Orleans.

"They're two completely different maps," said Axelle.

Daedalus saw what she meant. "What's the date on that first map?"

"Uh, 1843," Richard said, finding the date in one corner.

"And this is a current map," Daedalus clarified. "Clearly, the older map is wildly inaccurate—it's not a satellite-data topographical map. The same features don't even appear on both. Look, the Lac Mechant, the Lac Penchant. This one is called Grand Barataria, and now it's called, uh, Lake Salvador, I think." He squinted at the two maps, then glanced up and saw that this afternoon's quick, heavy thunderstorm was on its way.

"Crap," Axelle said.

"But this is the map we always used," Jules said.

"But it's been a long time," Richard pointed out. "Even the actual courses of the rivers have changed. The coastline has changed a lot. With every hurricane that's hit Louisiana, some aspect of the landscape *changed.*"

"Now what?" Jules asked, frustration in his voice. "This is a major point."

"Yes, Jules, we *know,*" Daedalus said, hearing himself sound testy. He tried to dampen his irritation. They needed to pull together, to work as one. It was important now as never before. He reached out and put a hand on Jules's shoulder. "I'm sorry, old friend. I'm upset. But this is only a temporary setback, I'm sure. We'll do more research. We'll look at maps from different years and compare them. It will show us how the land markers have changed. From that we can extrapolate where we need to be looking. It will take time, but we can do it."

"We only have a little time," Jules said.

Again Daedalus squelched his temper. "We have time enough," he said, trying to sound both certain and reassuring. "We'll get started tonight." He looked over at Richard, who'd been quiet. That handsome child's face, those old, old eyes. Richard met his gaze and nodded, flicked his cigarette to the ground. Daedalus saw Jules's pursed lips: littering. Daedalus got into the car just as the first big raindrops hit the windshield. They had to pull this off. This was their only chance. Who knew if they would ever have another?

✦ Chapter Seven

Clio

HALF AN HOUR LATE. THAT SEEMED ABOUT right. If he was still here, he was serious and had staying power; if he was gone, then good riddance.

(Actually, if he was gone, I would track him down like a dog.)

We were supposed to meet at Amadeo's at nine. It was nine thirty, and the place was starting to fill up. I looked at the bouncer when I went in, and he automatically started to card me.

You don't want to do that, I thought, sending him a quick distraction spell. Just then, something at the back of the bar caught his eye, and he turned, striding through the crowd like a bull through a field of wheat.

I slipped inside and smiled as I saw some regulars. I could feel admiring looks from people and hoped André appreciated the skintight white jeans and tie-dyed halter. I flipped my hair back, looking unconcerned, and slowly examined the patrons.

I felt him before I saw him. All of a sudden, my skin

tingled, as if someone had shocked me. The next moment, a warm hand was on my bare back, and when I turned, I was practically in his arms.

"You're late," he said, looking into my eyes until I felt breathless.

"I'm here now."

"Yes. What do you want to drink?" Expertly he weaved us through the crowd until we could stand at the bar to order. Nothing too crass or too childish. "A margarita," I said. "No salt."

Five minutes later we had made our way into Amadeo's back room, where a small stage filled one end. Sometimes on weekends they had live bands. But it was a weeknight, and instead people were clustered around tiny tables and clumped onto the easy chairs and small couches scattered around the room. It was very dark, and the walls were covered with flocked red wallpaper, so kitschy it was in again.

André led me to a battered purple love seat that was already occupied by a couple of college guys. He didn't say anything, just stood there, but somehow they suddenly got the urge to get refills on their drafts.

I sank down first, taking André's hand and pulling him down next me. He smiled slightly and didn't resist. Then he was on the love seat and, with no hesitation, kept coming at me until our mouths were touching, our eyes wide open. I held my right hand still over the back of the love seat so I wouldn't spill my drink, but the rest of me leaned against André, wanting to sink into him, eat him up, melt our bodies together.

Minutes later one of us pulled back—I don't know who. I took a sip of my drink, feeling stunned and hot and nervous and very, very turned on. I glanced uncertainly at him, and he looked like everything I was feeling.

"What do you have?" I asked, nodding toward his drink. I sounded breathless.

"Seven Up," he said, fishing the maraschino cherry out with long, graceful fingers. He held it out to me, and I went for it, loving the burst of candied over-sweetness in my mouth. When I could talk I said, "Oh, sure, get the girl drunk, while you stay totally in control." Which, to tell you the truth, did not seem like a good situation for me to be in. I mean, I was practically blind with lust for André, but I still had one or possibly two wits about me.

André gave me a crooked smile, and I silenced an involuntary whimper. "Number one," he said softly in his accented voice, "I don't think you would need to be drunk, and number two, I'm not drinking, but somehow I feel I've lost control anyway."

Okay, I was in love. And this is how sappy it was: I was totally, completely, 100 percent happy and content to be sitting on that lumpy love seat in that crowded bar, drinking my drink and just staring into his dark blue eyes. I wanted nothing, needed nothing, had to go nowhere. I could sit there and feast my eyes on him till the end of time.

I looked at him thoughtfully, running one finger around the

edge of my glass. "No, I wouldn't have to be drunk," I agreed shakily. I leaned back against the side of the love seat and stretched my legs across his lap. My bare feet felt the warmth of his hard thigh through his black jeans, and I pressed them down experimentally. He had muscles.

"Tell me about yourself," I said, pushing my hair back. I played with the straw in my glass and smiled. "Where have you been all my life?"

He smiled too, getting the corny reference. Despite everything, I remembered how Racey had felt about him, and I owed it to her—and to myself—to find out a little bit about him before, say, we got married.

"André what?" I prompted when he didn't answer. "Are you still in school? Where do you live?"

"André Martin," he said, giving his last name the French pronunciation: Mar-taihn. I blinked. "I'm taking a year off, out of university, to work for my uncle's law firm here. As a paralegal. I have my own apartment in the Quarter." His warm hands slid under my jeans and massaged my calves. It made my brain feel like mush, or maybe that was because I had drained my large margarita. "Not far from here," he volunteered, smiling wickedly. I put the glass down on the little table next to the love seat.

"André Martin?" I said, making sure.

"Yes."

I felt like I'd been looking at his face my whole life. "That's so weird," I said.

"No, many people in France get experience working with their relatives," André said, massaging my feet, each little green-polished toe.

"No, your name," I said, feeling distinctly fuzzy-headed. "That's my name too. Clio Martin. Isn't that weird?"

He looked amused, then considered it. "Martin is not so unusual a name," he pointed out. "And here, many names have a French pronunciation."

Which was true, of course. Last year we'd had a biology teacher from up north whose name had been Mr. Herbert. Hur-burt. By the end of the first month, he was so tired of correcting everyone when they pronounced it Ay-bear that he gave up and just went by Ay-bear. There were tons of names like that.

"Yeah, I guess you're right," I said. "It just seemed funny—having the same last name." I dropped my head back over the arm of the love seat—it was suddenly very heavy. Involuntarily I moaned at the strength of André's fingers rubbing my legs.

He laughed, then swung my legs over the side again, which pulled me up next to him. He put his arms around me and kissed me again.

Things after that were a little blurry. I know he asked me to go home with him, and miracle of miracles, I said no. I couldn't make it *too* easy for him. I know we kissed and made out and held each other so tightly that at one point my top had his shirt's button impressions on it, which struck us both as really funny.

I know I wanted another margarita and instead got a 7UP,

which made me fall even more in love with him. I could trust him.

And I know that by the time we finally said good-bye, he walked me to my car and made sure I was straight enough to drive, which I truly was—especially since I did a silent dissipation spell as soon as I was behind the wheel. Tonight's alcohol would dampen my abilities tomorrow, but right now the magick sang through my veins. Losing every bit of the margarita's effect was sad, but I also knew if I drove impaired and killed myself, my grandmother would pull me back from the dead so she could kill me all over again.

I rolled down my window, the engine of my battered little Camry humming.

"I had a good time tonight," I said. Major understatement.

He brushed his fingers along my cheek, rubbing his thumb over my birthmark. "So did I," he said seriously, then leaned in the window and kissed me long and hard. "It's okay if I call you?" I had given him my cell-phone number.

"Yes," I said, surpassing the first understatement.

"Drive carefully." His look made me feel like we were already joined, one, forever.

I nodded, put the car in gear, and pulled out. He was in my rearview mirror until I turned the corner.

• • •

Seed of life, I nourish you
I give you room to grow
I give you friends to grow with

The sun and rain are all for you
Your leaves unfurl, your budding show
To all I am your gardensmith.

I knew better than to roll my eyes or act impatient. Nan always said little spells when she planted things, and of course her garden, the whole yard, was the most perfectly balanced, beautiful garden for blocks. And yet there was a part of me that was thinking, *It's just okra.*

She patted the earth down firmly around the okra seed, a little smile on her face. She looked perfectly calm, at ease. I was *dying.* It was a thousand degrees outside, and my T-shirt was already damp with sweat. I felt totally gross. At least no one but Nan would see me like this.

Nan looked up at me in that way that felt like she was seeing right through my eyes into the back of my skull. "Not your cup of tea, is it?" she asked with humor.

I showed her my dirty, broken fingernails and the blister beginning on my thumb. She laughed outright.

"Thank you for your sympathy," I muttered, and she laughed again.

"How are you going to be a witch without a garden?" she asked.

"I'll hire someone," I said.

"Will you hire someone to study for you?" she asked more seriously. "Or maybe you should hire someone to do your drinking for you."

I looked up in alarm. "I haven't been drinking."

She gave me an oh-come-on face. "Clio—your magick is very strong." She brushed my damp hair off my cheek. "It was strong in your mother also. But she died before she could come into her full power." Her eyes had a faraway, sad look in them. "I want to see *you* come into your full power. Unfortunately, the only way to get there is actually to study, to learn, to practice. The only way to practice meaningfully is to not have dulled your senses. You can be a strong witch, or you can be a weak witch. It's up to you."

I hated these kinds of talks. They were embarrassing, they made me feel terrible, and most of all, they were always true.

"It's summertime," I said, hating how whiny and childish I sounded. "I want to have fun."

"All right, have fun," she said. "But you'll be eighteen in November. And I'm telling you now, you're nowhere near ready for your rite of ascension."

Now she had my full and undivided attention. "What? Really? I didn't know it was that bad."

She nodded, looking sad and wise and somehow older than she usually looked. "It's that bad, honey. If you work your butt off, you might be able to pass it. Or you can wait a year, when you turn nineteen."

"Oh, I'm so sure," I sputtered, thinking of all the other kids who'd made their rites of ascension when they were eighteen. No one had *ever* failed and had to wait till they were nineteen. I would never live it down. I would embarrass my grandmother, whom everyone considered one of the best teachers. I would look like a total loser when really I should be impressing the hell out of everyone. Damn it! All I wanted to do was see André. I didn't want to study, didn't want to practice, didn't want to stop ingesting fun things, like margaritas.

"It's just that sometimes studying seems a little, well, boring," I said delicately. "I always feel like I want lightning and sparks and *big* magick, you know?" I held my arms out to the sides to demonstrate "Big Magick."

Nan looked at me sharply. "Big magick is dangerous magick," she said. "Even if it's for good. Remember, what has a front, has a back, and the bigger the front, the bigger the back."

I nodded, thinking, *Whatever the hell that means.* "Okay, I'll try to study more."

Nan stood and brushed her hands off on her old-fashioned apron. "Like I said, it's up to—" she stopped, her words trailing away. She stood very still, her hands frozen, while she looked all around us. Up at the sky where the usual afternoon storm clouds were gathering, down the street, across the street, at our house and side yard.

"What's the matter?" I stood up also.

Nan looked at me as if surprised to see me—I mean, really looked at me, like she was actually trying to tell who I was. It was creepy, and I wondered for a second if she'd had a stroke or something.

"What's the matter?" I said. "Nan, are you okay? Let's go

into the house—I'll get you some cold lemonade, okay?"

She blinked then and glanced around us once more. "No, I'm all right, honey. It's just—a storm is coming."

"It always comes in the afternoon in the summer," I said, still gently tugging her toward the front steps. "Every day around three, a storm. But they always blow over fast."

"No," she said. "No." Her voice sounded stronger, more like her. "Not a rainstorm. I mean a bigger storm, one that will . . ." Her words trailed off again, and she looked at the ground, lost in thought.

"A hurricane?" I asked, trying to understand. She was totally creeping me out.

She didn't answer.

✦ Chapter Eight

Thais

I LOOKED AROUND AND SIGHED. GREAT. ONE of these dreams. Just what I need.

I'd always had incredibly realistic, Technicolor, all-sensories-on dreams my whole life. I'd tried telling Dad about them, but though he was sympathetic, he didn't really get what I was talking about. It wasn't every single night, of course. But maybe 65 percent of the time. In my dreams I felt cold and hot, could smell things, taste things, feel the texture of something in my mouth.

Once, after a shop downtown had been held up, I'd dreamed I'd been in that shop and had gotten shot. I'd felt the burning heat of the bullet as it bored through my chest, felt the impact from the blow knock me off my feet. Tasted the warm blood that rose up in my mouth. Felt myself staring at the shop ceiling, old-fashioned tin, while I slowly lost consciousness, bleeding to death. But it had been just a dream.

The really annoying thing was, even though I almost always knew I was dreaming, I was powerless to stop these dreams.

Only a few times I had called, "Cut!" and managed to get myself out of some situation. Mostly I just had to suck it up.

Which explained why I was standing in the middle of this swamp/jungle place, thinking, *Damn it.*

This would teach me to buy touristy postcards to send to my friends back home. At the time I'd thought they were funny—pictures of a Louisiana swamp, or a huge plantation house, or the front of a strip joint on Bourbon Street—all with a tiny picture of myself pasted on them. But apparently the images had sunk into my subconscious too well.

Hence the swamp. *Okay, I need to release any feelings about this place,* I thought, *and just see what happens, what the dream needs to show me.* I looked around. My bare feet were ankle-deep in reddish-green-brownish water, surprisingly warm. Beneath my feet the bottom was superslick clay, fine silt that squished up between my toes. The air was thick and heavy and wet, and my skin was covered with sweat that couldn't evaporate. Hardly any sunlight penetrated to the ground, and I tried to convince myself it was a fascinating example of a rainforest-like habitat.

Then I saw the ghosts. Translucent, gray, Disney World ghosts, floating from one tree to the next, as if playing ghost hide-and-seek. I saw a woman in old-fashioned clothes, a gray-haired man in his Sunday best. There was a hollow-eyed child, wearing rags, eating rice from a bowl with her fingers. And a slave, wrists wrapped in chains, the skin scraped raw and bleeding. I began to feel cold, and all the tiny little hairs all over my body stood on end. There was no sound—no splash of water, no call of bird, no rustle of leaves. Dead silence.

"Okay, I've seen enough," I told myself firmly. "Time to wake up."

The mist around me got thicker, more opaque, swirling in a smoky paisley pattern around the trees, the cypress knees, the Spanish moss. Maybe ten yards away, a log rolled—no, it was an alligator, covered with thick, dark green skin. I saw its small yellow eyes for a moment, right before it silently slid into the water, headed my way.

Crap.

Something touched my bare ankle, and I yelped, jumping a foot in the air. Heart pounding, I looked down. An enormous snake was twining around my bare leg. It was huge, as thick around as my waist, impossibly strong, dark, and wet. Its triangular head framed two cold reptilian eyes. The constant flick of its tongue across my skin made me feel like I was covered with crawling insects. Adrenaline raced coldly through my veins, tightening my throat, speeding up my heart. I tried to run, but it held me fast. Uselessly I pushed at it with all my strength, trying to uncoil it from around me. I punched its head and barely made it bob. It coiled around me till I was weighted down by snake, surrounded by snake, my breath being squeezed from my lungs. I gasped for breath, trying to scream, digging my fingernails into the heavy, coiled muscles around my neck, and suddenly I knew that I was going to die here in this swamp, without understanding why.

"Daddy!" With my very last shred of strength, a scream burst from my throat. Then it was choked off—the snake was around my neck. I couldn't feel my arms anymore. I was light-headed and couldn't see. . . .

Then all around me the world grew bright, like a flood light had been turned on. I gasped and blinked wildly, unable to see, the snake still around my neck—

"Hold still, dammit," said a voice, and strong hands worked at my neck. I sucked in a deep breath as the snake's grip loosened and I could breathe again. I gulped in cool, air-conditioned air, feeling the cold sweat run down my temple, down my back.

"Wha, wha—"

"I heard you yell," Axelle said, and with difficulty I brought her into focus.

Slowly I struggled upright, my hand to my throat. I was still gasping, still choked by panic. I looked around. I was in my little room at Axelle's in New Orleans. She looked uncharacteristically disheveled—hair rumpled from sleep, grumpy, her body barely contained inside a red lace slip.

"What happened?" I croaked, my voice as hoarse as if I'd been coughing all night. Looking down, I saw that my top sheet had gotten twisted into a thick rope, and this had been wound around my neck. "I was having a nightmare," I said, still trying to orient myself. "A snake . . ." I pushed the sheet away, kicking it away from me, wiping my hand across my damp forehead. "God."

"I heard you yell," Axelle said again.

"How did you get in? My door was locked."

She shrugged. "It's my apartment. Nothing is locked to me."

Great. "Well, thank you," I said awkwardly. "I thought I was dying—it was . . . really realistic." I swallowed again, my hand brushing my throat, which ached.

Axelle frowned and nudged my fingers away, tilting my chin. She looked at my neck, at the sheet, and back at my neck. At the expression on her face, I got up and shakily made my way to the little mirror over the white bamboo dresser. My neck was bruised, scraped, as if I truly had been strangled.

My eyes widened. Axelle frowned. She went to my one window and ran her hands around the edge of it. The shutters were pulled and bolted from inside, and the window had been locked.

"It was just a dream," I said faintly. Unless of course Axelle had been trying to kill me. But I didn't sense danger from her—she'd just woken me up. It sounded stupid—it was hard to explain. But sometimes I had a sense about people—like in seventh grade, when I had instantly hated Coach Deakin, even though everyone else had loved him and thought he was so great. I'd hated him immediately, for no reason. And then six months later he was arrested for sexually harassing four students.

I went to the bathroom and splashed water on my face, then drank some, feeling the ache in my throat as it went down.

"I don't see how you could do that to yourself," Axelle

murmured as I shook out the covers, untwisting the sheet and spreading everything flat. "You dreamed it was a snake?"

I nodded, folding my covers way down out of the way at the bottom of the bed. I didn't want them anywhere near my head. "In a swamp."

Axelle looked at me thoughtfully, and for the first time since I'd known her, I saw shrewd intelligence in her black eyes. "Well, leave your door open tonight," she said, pushing it wide. "In case you—need anything."

"Okay."

Murmuring to herself, Axelle traced her fingers lightly around my door frame, almost as if she were writing a secret message with her fingers.

"What are you doing?"

She shrugged. "Just making sure the door is all right."

O-kaaaay.

"Call me if you—get scared, or anything," Axelle said before she turned to go.

I nodded. And the weird part was: I actually found that *comforting*.

Then she was gone, her red slip swishing lightly through the kitchen.

I sat up in bed, propped against the headboard, and didn't go back to sleep until the sun came through my shutters.

✦ Chapter Nine

Time Is Running Out

JULES SPREAD HIS LATEST ACQUISITION OVER the work table in Axelle's attic room.

"What year is that?" Daedalus asked.

Jules checked. "Nineteen-ten."

This is painstaking, often frustrating work, Jules thought. But perhaps they were making slow progress.

"Look," Jules said, tracing a finger down the Atchafalaya River. "It's different here and here."

Daedalus nodded. "It must have jumped its banks between the time this map was drawn and the one from . . . 1903."

"Let's get a computer up here, so we can double-check hurricane dates, floods, things like that," Jules said.

Daedalus gave him that patient-father look he hated. "We can't have a computer up here," he said, just as Jules remembered that electrical appliances wreaked havoc with magickal fields.

"Oh, yeah," he said, irritated that he hadn't thought of that. "It's just a pain to run up and down those stairs every time we need to check something. And that girl is on it a lot."

Daedalus glanced at him, keeping his finger on a map. "Is Axelle monitoring her?"

Jules shrugged. "I don't know."

He heard Daedalus sigh, as though once again, he himself had to do everything, had to make sure everything was being done right, done his way. Jules clenched his jaw. He was getting fed up with Daedalus's attitude. Daedalus wasn't the mayor, after all. They were all equal in the Treize, right? Isn't that what they had agreed? So why was Daedalus issuing orders—find this, get that, go look up such and such? And Jules knew he wasn't the only one whose nerves Daedalus was stepping on.

Richard came in, holding a bottle of beer. Jules tried not to glance at his watch, but couldn't help it. And of course Richard saw him.

"Hey, it's five o'clock *somewhere*," he said, popping the top. He took a deep drink, then breathed a contented sigh. "Now *that's* a beer," he said, shaking his hair back. "Thank God for microbreweries. Have you tried this Turbodog?"

"I don't drink," Jules said stiffly, moving to the bookcase and selecting a thick volume with a cracked leather binding.

"It *does* dull your magick, Riche," Daedalus said mildly, still poring over the maps.

"I'll cross that bridge when we come to it," Richard said, seating himself on a stool by the work table. One knee poked through the huge rip in his jeans. "We don't seem to be close to needing my magick, such as it is."

"It won't be long," Jules said. "We're working on the maps. We're getting the rite into shape, practically everyone is here—we each have a role to perform, and we're doing it." Unconsciously he looked at Daedalus, and the other man met his eyes. Some roles were more challenging than others.

"Practically," Richard said, seizing on the word. "We're missing Claire, Marcel, Ouida, and who else?"

"Ouida's on her way," said Daedalus. "As are Manon and Sophie, I believe. We're still working on Claire and Marcel."

Richard gave a short laugh. "Good luck. So we'll have the map, the rite, the water, the wood—and a full Treize, yes?"

Daedalus straightened and smiled at him. "That's right. This is the closest we've ever come. Nothing will go wrong—we won't let it."

Richard nodded and took another swig from his bottle. Jules didn't look up from the book, pretending to scan the old-fashioned French words. He didn't share Daedalus's optimism. There were too many variables—too many things that could go wrong. And time was running out.

✦ Chapter Ten

MY LIFE HAD SETTLED INTO A ROUTINE AT Casa Loco: I had somehow become the general houseboy, maid, gofer, and all-around Girl Friday. Not that Axelle was forcing me into these roles at gunpoint. Some things I did for my own comfort and survival, some out of boredom, and then there were a few things that Axelle asked me to do and I had no good reason not to.

Now that I lived here, there was usually actual food around, the ant problem in the kitchen had been licked, and I could cross the main room in the dark without killing myself. I tried not to think about home or what I would be doing there, but every once in a while, I was overwhelmed by longing for my dad and my old life. He used to take me canoeing on the weekends. Or skiing, in the winter. Once he'd broken his ankle, skiing, and he'd let me decorate his cast, all of it, by myself.

When I got older, my best friend Caralyn and I would both get summer jobs at whatever shop in town that was hiring. I'd worked at Friendly's Hardware, Marybeth's Ice

Cream Shoppe, Joe & Joe's Coffee Emporium, you name it. And after work we'd meet at the pool and go swimming, or hit the movies, or go to the closest mall, twenty miles away.

When I'd mentioned getting a summer job to Axelle, she's looked at me blankly, as she so often did, and then had pulled two hundred dollars out of her wallet and handed it to me. I had no idea why I shouldn't get a job, but whatever.

After a couple days of lying on my bed, wallowing in despair, I'd realized that I needed to do something, anything, to stay busy and keep my mind off My Tragic Life. Hence my springing into action and becoming a domestic goddess.

Today I'd braved the heat and the wet, thick air to go out to get the mail—pathetically, getting the mail was the highlight of my day. Axelle got tons of catalogs, and I got a kick out of looking through them. Some of them sold freaky stuff for, like, pagans and "witches" and stuff. I didn't know how anyone could take this stuff seriously, but she obviously did. I remembered how she'd run her fingers around my doorframe, after my nightmare. Had she been trying to do magick? How? What for?

Anyway. I loved her clothes catalogs, for the little bit of leather queen in all of us.

Sometimes I got letters from my friends or Mrs. Thompkins, back home. Mostly we e-mailed, but they also sent me funny articles and pictures—which almost always made me cry.

I hadn't gotten anything from my dad's lawyer about my father's estate, and Mrs. Thompkins said they were still sorting through everything. It sounded like a total headache. I wanted it to be all settled—I could put the house furniture into storage, and when I escaped from this loony bin, I could set up my own apartment or house back home. I was counting the days.

Thais Allard, one envelope said. It was from the Orleans Parish Public School System. I ripped it open to find I was to attend Ecole Bernardin, which was the nearest public school. It started in six days. My homeroom teacher would be Ms. Aubert.

So, okay. I'd wanted to go to school, but somehow accepting the fact that I would attend school *here* felt like a ton of harsh reality all at once. An oh-so-familiar wave of despair washed over me as I headed up the narrow carriageway to the back of the building.

I went in, got blasted by the air conditioning, and dumped Axelle's mail in a pile on the kitchen counter. A weird burning smell made me sneeze, and I followed it through the kitchen and into my bedroom, where Axelle was—get this—burning a little green branch and chanting.

"What the heck are you doing?" I asked, waving my arms to clear out the smoke.

"Burning sage," Axelle said briefly and kept going, waving the smoldering green leaves in every corner of my room.

Burning sage? "You know, they make actual air fresheners," I said, dumping my stuff on my bed. "Or we could just open the window."

"This isn't for that," Axelle said. Her lips moved silently, and I finally got it: The burning sage was some "magick" thing she was doing. Like she was doing a "spell" in my room for some reason. So. This was my life: I lived with an unknown stranger who was right now performing a *voodoo* spell in my own *bedroom*. Because she actually believed all that crap. I mean, Jesus. Not to take the Lord's name in vain.

Axelle ignored me, murmuring some sort of chant under her breath as she moved about the room. In her other hand, she held a crystal, the kind you can buy at a science shop, and she ran this around the window frame while she chanted.

I freaked. I couldn't help it. At that moment my life seemed so completely *insane*. Without saying a word, I turned around, ran out of that apartment, down the carriageway, and through the gate. Then I was on the narrow street, with slow-moving cars, tourists, street performers. It was all too much, and I pressed my hand against my mouth, trying not to cry. I hated this place! I wanted to be somewhere normal! I wanted to be home! While Welsford wasn't exactly a mime-free zone, still, I wouldn't encounter them on the street right outside my *house*.

My eyes blurred, and I stumbled on the curb. I had nowhere to go, no refuge. Then the word *refuge* made me think of a church, and that made me remember a place I had seen a couple of days before: a small hidden garden behind a tall brick wall. It was attached to St. Peter's, a Catholic church between Axelle's apartment and the small corner grocery store where I shopped.

I headed there now, walking fast down the brick-paved

sidewalk. When I reached it, I pressed my face to the small iron grille inset into one wall, about five feet up. I walked the length of the brick wall and pushed some ivy aside to find a small wooden door, made for tiny Creole people two centuries ago.

With no hesitation, I wrenched on the latch and shook the door hard until it popped open. Then I slipped under the ivy and entered a serene, private world.

The garden was small, maybe sixty feet square, and bordered by the church in back of it, an alley on one side, a parish office on the other, and the street in front. But although all that separated me from the world was a seven-foot brick fence, this place was unnaturally quiet, set apart, not of the secular world somehow.

I glanced around. A few windows overlooked the garden, but it felt safe and private. Beneath a crape myrtle tree, its bark hanging off in silken shards, stood an ancient marble bench, and I sank down onto it, burying my face in my arms. I didn't make a sound, but hot tears squeezed out of my eyes and dripped into the crooks of my elbows. I expected someone to come tap me on the shoulder at any minute, telling me the garden was private and I had to leave, but no one did. I lay hunched over that cool marble bench for a long time, my mind screaming variations of "Someone, for God's sake, please help me."

Finally, after my arms felt numb and one thigh had gone to sleep, I slowly straightened up. I felt waterlogged and puffy and sniffled, wiping my nose on my shirtsleeve.

"Try this."

I jumped, startled, almost losing my balance over the back of the bench. To make my total humiliation complete, there was a guy about my age there, holding out a crisp white handkerchief.

"How long have you been there?" I demanded, all too aware of what I must have looked like: flush-faced, swollen eyes, Rudolph's nose.

"Long enough to know you could use a handkerchief," he said wryly, shaking it gently in front of me.

Okay. It was either that or blow my nose on my sleeve. Ungraciously I took the handkerchief and wiped my nose and dabbed at my eyes. Then what? Did one return a used hankie? Gross. The guy solved my dilemma by taking it from my hand and standing up. He walked to a small fountain that I hadn't even been aware of: a blue-caped Nordic Virgin Mary, with thin streams of water running from her out-stretched hands.

The guy wet the hankie and came back, wringing it out. I sighed and took it again, and since this situation was already too far gone for me to possibly salvage it, I wiped the cool, damp cloth over my face, feeling tons better.

"Thank you," I said, unable to look at him.

"You're welcome." Uninvited, he sat down next to me. I was in no mood to make friends, so I just pretended he wasn't there. Now that I was calmer, I looked at the fountain, the different flowers growing in the somewhat untidy beds. Narrow walkways of well-worn brick made a knot of paths around the fountain. Small birds chirped in the thick growth of shrubs that hid the brick walls from inside.

The air was still here, marginally cooler than on the street. A vine grew thickly on several walls, its shiny dark-green leaves surrounding heavily scented creamy flowers.

"Confederate jasmine," the guy said, as though he knew where I'd been looking. He kneeled quickly and plucked a crisp white flower off a smaller shrub. I saw that he had dark brown hair, almost black, and was tall, maybe almost six feet?

"Gardenia." He handed it to me, and I took it, inhaling its fragrance. It was almost unbearably sweet, too much scent for one flower. But it was heavenly, and I tucked it behind my ear, which made the guy laugh lightly.

I managed to smile.

"I guess I'm trespassing," I said.

"I guess we both are," he agreed. "But I love to come here in the evenings, to escape the crowds and the heat."

"Do you work at the church?" I asked.

"No. But my apartment is right up there." He pointed to the third story of the building next door. "I didn't mean to spy on you. But I thought you might be sick."

"No," I said glumly, thinking, *sick of New Orleans.*

"I understand," he said gently. "Sometimes it's all too much." He had a precise, crisp way of speaking, as if he'd gone to school in England. I looked at him, into his eyes, and wondered if he *could* possibly understand.

No. Of course not. I got up and rewet the handkerchief in

the fountain. I knelt by its base, wrung out the thin cloth, and wiped my face again, and the back of my neck.

"I'll have to start carrying one of these," I said, pressing the wet cloth against my forehead.

"You're not used to the heat," he said.

"No. I'm from Connecticut," I said. "I've only been here a couple of weeks. I'm used to my air actually feeling like air."

He laughed, putting his head back. I realized that he was actually really good-looking, his throat smooth and tan, and I wondered if his chest was that color. I felt my face heat at that thought and looked down, embarrassed. When I looked up again he was watching me intently.

"They say the heat makes people crazy," he said, his voice very quiet in the private garden. "That's why there are so many crimes of passion here—the unending heat works on you, frays your nerves. Next thing you know, your best friend has a knife to your throat."

Well, I was a *little* creeped out, but mostly his voice worked slowly through my veins like a drug, soothing me, calming me, taking away my raw pain.

"What did you do?" I asked seriously, and a glint of surprise lit his eyes for a moment.

He laughed again, and there was no mistaking it—I saw admiration in his eyes. Attraction. "I was speaking metaphorically. Fortunately, so far I haven't stolen my best friend's girl."

For just an instant, I pictured myself, going out with some unnamed best friend, and then meeting this guy, feeling this electric attraction, and knowing that soon he would steal me away. I shivered.

"What's your name?" he asked, his words falling as softly as leaves.

"Thais," I said. Tye-ees.

He stood and offered me his hand. I looked up at him, his even features, the dark eyebrows slanting over incredible eyes. I took his hand. Unbelievably, he pressed my open palm against his lips, leaving a whisper of a kiss. "My pleasure, Thais," he said, awakening every nerve ending I had. "My name is Luc."

Luc, I repeated silently.

"Come here again soon," he said, looking at me as if to memorize my features. "I'll watch for you."

"I don't know when it will be," I hedged.

"It will be soon," he said confidently, and I knew that he was right.

Chapter Eleven

I Have Sinned

"FORGIVE ME, FATHER, FOR I HAVE SINNED." Marcel whispered the familiar words, already anticipating the comfort of absolution. In this dark cubicle he was completely himself, and it was all right. Everything was all right. "It's been one week since my last confession."

"Have you any sins to confess, my son?"

Ah. It was Brother Eric. He was always understanding.

"Yes, Father," Marcel murmured. "I have—felt anger. Great anger."

"Feeling anger in itself is not a sin, Marcel," murmured Brother Eric. "It is only when you enjoy the feeling of anger, or act upon it."

"I fear—were I to confront this anger, it could lead to . . . violence." There, it was out.

"Violence?"

Marcel took a deep breath. "I have been contacted by former . . . associates. People I knew a long time ago. I've tried to leave these people behind, Father. I've tried to escape them.

I've come *here*. These people do not acknowledge the Lord our God. They play with—fate. They have unholy power." Marcel felt his throat close. He shut his eyes, remembering that power, how it had flowed from his hands, how beautiful the world seemed when he held it.

"Explain about the violence, son," said Brother Eric.

"If I see them, or one in particular—I'm afraid I will do him harm." A cold sweat broke out on Marcel's forehead. Yes, God was listening—but He might not be the only one. What a risk he was taking . . . he looked around himself, contained in this dark cubicle.

"Do him harm out of anger?"

"Yes," said Marcel. "For trying to make me renounce what is good."

There was silence while Brother Eric thought.

"Does he so threaten you, lad, that in order to protect yourself, you'd destroy him?"

"Yes," Marcel whispered.

"You don't see another path, Marcel?"

"I can never see him again," Marcel offered. "I can refuse to go to him, to help him."

"He's asked for your help?"

"Not yet. But I think he might. He's asked to see me."

"Perhaps he's changed his ways?" suggested Brother Eric.

"No," Marcel said with certainty.

"Perhaps he wants to ask your advice."

"No."

"Then what does he want from you?"

"My . . . power." The words were so faint as to barely penetrate the wooden pierce-work screen.

"No one can take your power from you, Marcel."

Instantly Marcel saw that this was pointless, that Brother Eric could never understand, that there was no salvation for him here. He almost wept. He needed a strong hand to hold his, to say, "We will not let you go." But that was not the Church's way. With the Church it was all about free will. How to explain that sometimes his will was not truly his own?

Liar. His conscience was a small, cold voice, mocking him inside his head. *Your will is your own. You like the power, Marcel. You like wielding it. You love feeling life, energy, pure force flowing from you, from your hands. You like what you can do with it. You like what you can do to others.*

"No! No, I don't! You're lying," Marcel cried, covering his face with his hands.

"Marcel?"

It doesn't have to be bad, Marcel, said his conscience. *Remember, "Nothing is good or bad, but thinking makes it so." You can use your power for good. You can convince the others. They want to be good anyway. It's only Daedalus—Daedalus and Jules and Axelle. Maybe Manon. Maybe Richard. But the others, they're for good. They follow the* Bonne Magie. *You can too. Your power could elevate them to goodness.*

"No, no," Marcel sobbed as the velvet curtain opened and Brother Eric touched his shoulder. "I can't go back. I can't."

"Marcel, we must all face our demons," Brother Eric said softly. "Now come, rest. You've been working too hard. I'll have Brother Simon bring you some soup. Come, let me help you."

Marcel let himself be led out of the chapel, its stones standing watch over God's disciples since 1348. But Marcel knew they could no longer protect him. It was only a matter of time. Every step he took was a step closer to his own personal hell, and whatever awaited him in New Orleans.

✦ Chapter Twelve

Clio

"YOU'RE LATE." I GAVE ANDRE THE FULL FORCE of my "peeved" look, which had always made lesser guys quake. André just grinned and swooped in to quickly kiss my neck, which pretty much shorted out all rational thought.

"So we're even then," he said, with such an unrepentant, wicked expression on his face that I laughed and couldn't hold it against him. Instead I pushed against his chest, barely moving him, and then walked ahead, trying to get my fluttering nerves under control. My palms tingled where I'd touched him.

"You're lucky I waited," I tossed over my shoulder. I'd worn my hair in two braids today, to get it off my neck.

After a few paces André caught up to me, matching his steps with mine. It was dusk, the sun just beginning to set over the bend of the Mississippi River. It was a magickal time. I mean, literally magickal, when the force of the sun was yielding to the force of the moon. Some rites used this time on purpose, to harness the effects of both. Of course, I didn't mention this to André. Why give away all my secrets?

"This is a pretty park," he said.

I looked around. The small golf course had been molded with weensy, artificial hills. Huge live oaks towered over us, spreading shade beneath their branches. It was so familiar to me that I barely noticed anymore. "I like how green New Orleans is," I said. "My grandmother and I went to Arizona a couple years ago, and it was awful. I mean, actually, it was pretty, in a really dry, dusty way. But I felt just parched somehow. I like being surrounded by green."

I pressed my lips together. *Déesse*, I sounded like a freaking idiot. Or a travel guide. What was wrong with me? Why did he throw me off balance? I took a deep breath, momentarily closed my eyes. *Center. Center yourself.*

"Come this way," I said, holding out my hand.

André took it, his skin warm against mine. "Where are you leading me?"

Everything he said seemed to have two meanings. He could make anything sound sexy or forbidden.

I smiled back at him, pulling him along. Years ago Racey and I had found a place we called our clubhouse. Really, it was just a dip in the ground between the massive roots of three live oaks. If you lay flat, no one could see you until they were right on top of you. We used to lie there for hours, talking, practicing little baby spells, giggling to ourselves when we heard passing golfers swear and throw down their clubs.

Now, standing at the entrance, I suddenly remembered my horrible vision—the one where blood had bubbled up from between a tree's roots. But that had been a cypress tree. I swallowed hard and forced myself to step over the large roots. It had just been a dumb vision—you could see all kinds of freaky stuff when you let your magick rip. I wasn't going to think about it.

Now I sat down, tucking my skirt under me. It was lavender and tiered, almost reaching my ankles, long and loose and flowing. Guys loved stuff like that. On top I wore a little white cotton camisole that buttoned up the back and had embroidered lavender butterflies.

I kicked off my sandals and patted the ground next to me.

"You should feel honored. You're the first non-blood sister to see this place," I said teasingly, tapping his knee with a long piece of centipede grass.

He looked at me quickly. "Blood sister?"

I nodded solemnly. "My best friend Racey and I are blood sisters—we did a rite when we were ten. I think I still have the scar." I looked at my thumb, but the tiny cut where I had shared my blood with Racey's had long become invisible.

"She was with you at Botanika," André said, leaning back on his elbows. He was wearing a blue oxford shirt that looked incredibly soft and worn. The sleeves were rolled halfway up to his elbows. Like his shirt, his khaki cargo shorts were well broken in, the fabric velvety.

"Yes." I looked up to find him smiling knowingly at me. Without even really thinking about it, the words sprang into my mind: *I am the woman you desire, my will is strong, my passion's fire. I will give myself to you, once you prove that you are true.*

It wasn't a proper spell, not really. There was no real intent in my mind, I had no tools, and I wasn't even trying to achieve any specific thing. It was more—opening his mind to the idea. Allowing him to see me as his true love. Sort of moving things along, in a way.

He blinked once, quickly, and looked at me, almost as if he'd heard my thought, which was impossible. But that's how finely we were already attuned to each other, that he could somehow sense something, some strong emotion flowing from me.

"How are you liking the local scenery?" he asked, echoing my words to him the first time we had met.

I swallowed, feeling shivery and excited. "I'm liking it," I said, and my voice sounded a little rough, a little unsure. Perfect.

"Come here," he said, his face intent, his slight French accent making his *h* almost silent.

Moments later it was just like at Amadeo's. We fit together perfectly, and for the first time in my life, I actually felt overwhelmed. Before, no matter who I was with, part of my brain was always doing an imaginary manicure, or going over a lesson with Nan, or thinking about clothes I wanted to buy. This time all my senses were focused on André, the way he felt, tasted, the scent of his skin, the heat in his hands as he held me. *This is the one,* I thought. *I'm only seventeen, and I've found my one perfect love.* It was amazing and also a tiny bit scary. All my emotions made perfect sense to me, but part of me was still marveling at how strongly I felt about him, so quickly. But I couldn't stop it—I was caught on this swift ride of emotion, and there was no way to slow it down. I didn't even want to.

I couldn't help smiling with happiness against his lips, and he pulled back to look at me.

"What's funny?" he asked, looking at me.

"Not funny," I said, pressing my hips against him. "Happy."

"Happy?"

I laughed at his confused expression. "Yes, *happy.*" I raised my eyebrows. "Or are you not happy to be here with me?"

"No." He smiled. "I'm happy." He traced my eyebrow with one finger, letting it trail down my cheek. "Happy to be here with you." He leaned back so that he was lying next to me and looked up at the sky. Never in my life had any boy ever stopped kissing me *himself,* I mean, without me knocking him off me so I could take a breath. So it wasn't all physical with André— he wanted to be with me for more than just that. He was so much *deeper* than anyone else I'd ever known, and my heart swelled. I looked at his beautiful profile, like a classical statue, and felt like the luckiest person in the world.

"Tell me about yourself," he said, still gazing at the thicket of oak leaves overhead. The growing darkness made it even more private. "Who do you live with?"

I laughed. "What kind of a question is that? You don't think I live with my parents?"

He looked at me curiously. "Oh. And do you?" Maybe he'd been hoping I had a roommate, my own place, and I suddenly felt stupid, childish.

"Actually, no," I said. "I live with my grandmother. I always have."

"It's very sad to lose your parents so young," he said, turning on his side to face me. He took my hand and held it in his own against his chest. I could feel his heart beating. I wondered why he'd assumed that I had actually *lost* my parents—they could have been divorced, or in prison, or maybe just one of them was dead.

I shook my head. I'd *told* him I'd always lived with my grandmother—of course it sounded like I'd never had any parents.

"What about you?" I asked. "Where's your family from?"

"My parents died a long time ago too," he said. "But some of my extended family still lives in France—a little town called Saint-Malo."

"I would love to go to France," I said dreamily. *Hint, hint.* "My family was originally from there, a couple hundred years ago. I'd love to go visit."

"You've never been there?"

"No." I looked into his dark eyes. "I bet it's so beautiful there. Bet it has good food."

André smiled easily and tapped my lip with one gentle finger. "Yes. Very good food. Who knows? Maybe one day we'll see France together."

Yes! "I'd like that," I said and put my hand on his neck, beneath the collar of his shirt. I drew his head toward me and kissed him again. "I can see us doing lots of things together," I whispered.

He kissed me back, pressing my shoulders into the soft ground. His dark head blotted out the day's final bit of light, and I closed my eyes. André kissed my eyelids, my forehead, my cheeks, my birthmark, my chin, and I lay quietly, smiling, soaking it all up. I was filled with happiness and felt the rush of love and light and power swell inside me. I so wished I could make real magick, a proper spell, right there—I knew I'd be more powerful than ever before. I would try to hold on to this feeling when I went home. Nan would be impressed. The power of love.

Someday I would be able to show André who and what I was. If he loved me as deeply as I loved him, then magick would be just another experience for us to share, another aspect of my life I would open to him.

His hand moved slowly from my waist, over my camisole, and my muscles went taut as it brushed lightly over my breast. I shuddered, eyes closed, holding him tightly, feeling his knee press between mine.

"Come home with me." The words were barely whispered against my temple.

Everything in me said *yes.* I pictured us alone and private. I saw his skin against mine, us joining completely, how magickal it would be. All it would take is for me to stand up, take his hand, and go to his apartment. Then we could be together.

I didn't want to open my eyes. If I kept my eyes shut, I could still imagine us together, see how it would be.

"Clio?"

I sighed. I opened my eyes. It was dark out. Cicadas were thrumming rhythmically around us, an insistent chorus.

"Clio. Come." André stroked wisps of my hair back against my temple. I felt my heartbeat echo everywhere he touched.

"I can't."

His dark eyebrows rose, and the phrase *handsome as the devil* popped into my mind. "What?" He looked taken aback, and I felt angry at reality, resentful, and . . . bound to obey Nan.

I licked my lips. "I'm sorry, André. Tonight, I can't. Another time? Any other time, practically. But—"

"I've pushed you." He looked regretful.

"No! It isn't that at all," I said. "I've pushed you as much as you've pushed me." I swallowed hard, my blood still running strong and hot with longing. "It's so stupid. But tomorrow is the first day of school. Believe it or not. And even though everything in me wants to just be with you—still, my grandmother would absolutely kill me if I came home really late on the night before school started."

I felt my face flush even more if possible. I, Clio Martin, felt so incredibly uncool for perhaps the first time in my life. Ninety-eight percent of me said to blow Nan off, to go with André, to seize life, etc. But the other two percent held powerful sway: I loved Nan, and I hated disappointing her or making her angry.

André was expressionless, propped up on one elbow, looking down at me. For a few moments, I felt so acutely horrible that I was absolutely ready to jump up and grab André's hand and say I was just kidding.

I sat up fast. "Actually, I—" I began, just as André said, "I understand."

"What?" I stared at him, his face with its strong bones.

"I understand," he repeated. He smiled ruefully. "Of course you need to get home. I wasn't thinking—I'm sorry. I was listening to my heart, and not my head."

I blinked, astonished to feel the beginnings of tears in my eyes. Could André be more perfect? He was everything wild and dangerous and sexy that I could ever hope for, and he was *also* caring, unselfish, and considerate.

I took his strong tan hand and kissed it. He smiled and looked boyishly pleased.

"Come," he said. "I'll take you home."

I hesitated. Something in me didn't want Nan to meet him just yet. She always asked questions about the guys I dated, and I wanted to know André a little better before I went through the inquisition. Besides, she'd have plenty of time to get used to him as her future grandson-in-law.

I shook my head. "I can walk from here. It's perfectly safe." Since I could zap a freezing spell on any jerk who messed with me.

He frowned. "No, Clio, please—let me see you home."

I shook my head and stood up, brushing the leaves off my clothes. "I get out of school at three," I told him. "Can I see you tomorrow?"

He laughed and pulled me to him. "You can see me any-time you want."

✤ Chapter Thirteen

Thais

I LAY IN BED, WONDERING WHAT I SHOULD DO first: cry or throw up. It seemed pointless to "wake up," since I'd been staring at my ceiling, sleepless, pretty much all night. Today was my first day of school in a new place. The first day of school in my whole life that my dad wouldn't be there to take me, holding my hand when I was little, waving good-bye when I got older. I felt intensely alone, waking up in this strange apartment, everything so foreign around me.

My eyelids felt like sandpaper. I rolled over in bed, hugging my pillow. Ever since my nightmare, I'd hated falling asleep. Axelle insisted I keep the door to my room open, and on the one hand, I actually appreciated her being able to hear me if I cried out. On the other hand, I sorely missed my privacy and the implied safety of a locked door. Especially when Jules and Daedalus stayed over, which they did every once in a while.

I sleepwalked to the bathroom and got under the shower. In New Orleans the cold water was actually never cold like in Connecticut. Back home, the "C" on the faucet meant business. Here, the "C" meant "tepid"—I never even bothered with hot water.

And another thing: Back home, the first day of school always meant new school clothes, autumny clothes. School starts; Autumn's on the way. The forecast for today was a high of 96, 100 percent humidity. I wore a short skirt and a sleeveless top, both gray with pink athletic stripes. I guessed I would soon find out what was considered cool to wear here.

I spritzed my hair and bunched it up to make the layers stand out. I started crying. I put drops in my eyes and tried to put on mascara. I started crying again. I quit with the makeup and headed out to the kitchen. So now only throwing up was left.

In the main room, I found Axelle, Jules, and Daedalus sitting around the table, wearing the same clothes from last night. The ashtray was full of cigarettes. Empty soda cans and bottles of water circled the table. They had clearly been up all night, and I was amazed they hadn't been louder.

"Hey," I said unenthusiastically, and they looked up.

"You're up early," Axelle said, glancing at the antique clock on the mantel.

"School," I said, trying to eat a plain piece of bread.

Axelle let out a breath, giving Jules and Daedalus a meaningful look. I was so zany and unpredictable, wanting to go to school.

"You were *serious* about that," she muttered. Then, "What time will you be home?"

"School gets out at three," I said, chewing, struggling to swallow. "I guess around three thirty? I don't know how long the streetcar will take."

"Give her a cell phone," Daedalus told Axelle, and I stopped chewing in surprise.

She looked at him, her black eyes thoughtful. Then she stood, fished around in her huge black leather purse, and pulled out a cell phone. For a moment she stood looking at it, tracing her fingers over it as if, like, memorizing it, saying good-bye. To a cell phone. Jeez.

Finally she brought it over to me. I couldn't believe it.

"Let us know if you're going to be late," she said.

O-kaaaay. And you'll have cookies hot from the oven ready for me, right?

I had bought myself a backpack and stocked it with a few first-day supplies. I zipped the phone into a little pocket.

"Thais, come here," Jules said, and I walked over. Now what?

The three of them were hunched over all kinds of old maps and new maps and books and what looked like geographical surveys.

"Have you ever seen anything like this before?" Axelle asked. Though she'd been up all night, she didn't look beat. Her skin was clear, her eyes bright—even her makeup looked okay.

"Maps? Yeah—I've seen *maps* before." I had no idea what she meant.

"No, more—maps like this," she said, pulling one out. It looked like an ole-timey reproduction on fake parchment, the edges tattered. I expected to see a big black *X* somewhere, where the treasure was buried.

I shook my head. "Like a pirate map? Not any real ones."

Jules snorted with laughter, and Axelle looked irritated.

"Not a pirate map," she said. "Old maps. *Real* old maps. Like, did your father have anything like this, among his things? Did you ever see anything else like this when you were little?"

Well, that ranked right up there as being one of the weirder questions I'd ever been asked. "No." I shook my head again and started moving toward the door. "Dad didn't have anything like that. See you later."

I slipped out the door into the lush, damp courtyard. It was early—I'd allowed plenty of time to get to school by public transportation—but already incredibly, jungle-style hot. Before I'd even reached the side gate, I felt damp and limp. Great. I swallowed the last of my bread, feeling it stick in my throat. Somehow, this morning, I missed my dad even more than the day before.

❧ Chapter Fourteen

Clio

"YOU READY?" I GLANCED OVER AT RACEY, WHO held up one finger and sucked down the last of her coffee.

"I guess so." She leaned down and grabbed her retro plaid backpack, then leaned back against the car seat and closed her eyes. "I'm not ready," she moaned.

I leaned back and closed my eyes too. I'd already shut off the Camry's engine, so it was going to get hot in here in about two seconds, but we needed to take a moment. "I know," I said. "Where did the summer go?"

"We got to the beach, what, once?" Racey complained.

I thought back to the long, hot summer days and the long, hot summer nights. "Still, we had some fun," I pointed out. "And I met André."

"Yeah." Racey opened her eyes and looked out the window. Some of our posse was already gathered around the "Friendship Tree," which had a cement bench in front of it. She looked down at her nails, which were painted black with little white lightning bolts on them.

"Your nails match your hair," I said as I made the realization.

She grinned at me. "I know I've got kind of a skunk thing going, but I like it." She took a deep breath and let it out, then unlocked her door. "Okay, I'm ready. Let's go rock this joint."

Laughing, I got out and unsuccessfully tugged my tank top down so it would meet my board shorts. Surely the school couldn't enforce their quaint "dress code" ideas today, not in this heat.

"Yo!" called Eugenie LaFaye, holding up a hand in greeting.

Racey and I were the only witches in our group, but it wasn't a secret. There have always been witches in New Orleans, so it wasn't a big deal. Witches, Catholics, voodoo, Santeria, Jews . . . there was a lot of latitude about acceptable religions. Our friends thought it was kind of more of a hobby, rather than a whole system of power. I didn't correct them.

"So you got home all right last week?" Della asked with a smirk. The last time I'd seen her, I'd been trying to remember where the hell I'd left my car in a mall parking lot. That day felt like ages and ages ago—it was hard to believe I'd known André less than a week. He'd changed my life so much—it was like his appearance had separated my history into two parts: before him and after him.

"Oh, sure," I said airily. "How many blue 1998 Toyota Camrys could there possibly be in a mall parking lot? Like, two thousand?"

"Yeah, and she found hers after only 1, 378," Racey said, and they all laughed.

"So we got lucky," I said brightly.

"We've been checking out the talent," said Nicole, nodding at a bunch of guys over by the basketball hoops. Racey's little brother Trey was among them.

I looked over, but without a lot of interest. Ordinarily, of course, my antenna would be quivering—gauging the guys, obsessing over what I was wearing, seeing who was checking me out, enjoying being able to stun guys with a look, a word. Now even the most studly senior guys looked like second graders. Realizing I was already feeling clammy at eight forty-five in the morning, I twisted my hair into a knot, fished a chopstick out of my backpack, and stuck it through. "Voilà," I said. "Chic yet simple."

"Goofy, yet messy," Eugenie said in the same tone.

"Ladies," said a voice, and I turned to see Kris Edwards stroll up.

"Yo, girl," I said, giving her a hug. "And how were the Swiss alps?" Kris's family was stinking rich, and she'd spent the summer in Europe.

"Swissy," she said, hugging Racey next. "Alpy."

"And the Swiss lads?" Nicole asked. "Your IMs left much to the imagination."

"For which we're thankful," I said, and Kris laughed.

"The Swiss talent was very . . . talented," she said, smirking, and Della slapped her a high five. "And you?" she asked me. "Racey IMed that you'd met someone tall, dark, and dangerous."

"Dangerous?" I looked at Racey, who shrugged, looking a

little embarrassed. "Well, he's tall, dark, and *fabulous,* but he's not dangerous. His name is André," I said, trying unsuccessfully not to look too smug.

"Ooh, *André,*" said Nicole, just as the first morning bell rang.

"He's French," I said. "With a real French accent. He could read the phone book, and I'd be drooling." We started moving toward the side doors, following the stream of other students. As usual, the freshman looked like they should be in sixth grade. I was sure we'd never looked that young.

"I love French accents," Della said enviously.

"He *is* incredibly good-looking," Racey said loyally, and I smiled at her.

"Okay, let's see who we've got for homerooms," Kris said, and we headed for the senior lists on the walls.

I looked, but my mind wasn't on it. I kept thinking about lying with André beneath the tree and how sure I was that we were meant to be together. It was a completely different feeling than I'd ever had, and it changed everything—school, friends, my whole world. I felt older somehow. Two weeks ago I'd been another seventeen-year-old about to start senior year. Now senior year was just a stepping stone to the rest of my life, and the person I wanted to spend it with. It was weird: I felt somehow calmer and surer than I'd ever felt, but also more excited and full of anticipation than I'd ever felt. Two weeks ago I'd been just like all my friends. Now I had this huge relationship, and they didn't. And it made me different from them, forever.

✦ Chapter Fifteen

Thais

THE STREETCAR STOPPED RIGHT ACROSS THE street from Ecole Bernardin. I'd been practically hanging out the open window, totally nervous that I would somehow miss it. I felt more alone than I ever had in my whole life, even when a bunch of other kids got off the streetcar with me, obviously going to the same school.

I know it's always hard being the new kid—I mean, I'd *read* about it. But I'd never *been* the new kid before. And from the looks I was getting, this school didn't seem to get too many new kids. Some people glanced at me and gave me casual waves or smiles, but others stared at me like I was an alien—edging me closer to freaking nervous breakdowndom.

The school building looked like it had been built back in the '60s and was garishly painted blue and orange. Inside, one of the first doors I saw said "Girls," and I ducked in there fast. Inside, three sinks sat below three mirrors, and I looked at myself to see if I had toothpaste on my face, or had grown horns, or something.

I was still trying to figure it out when a girl emerged from a cubicle and stood next to me to wash her hands. She glanced casually at me in the mirror and said, "Oh, hey." Then she stopped and actually did a double take.

"*What?*" I asked, my nerves about to snap. "What's wrong with me?"

"Uh . . ." the girl looked totally taken aback. "Uh, who *are* you? Are you new here?"

"Yes," I said, crossing my arms over my chest. "Do you guys never get new people? Everyone's looking at me like I have two heads. What *is* it?" I swallowed hard, praying that I wouldn't start crying.

The girl shook her head. "Nothing's wrong with you," she said, trying to be nice. "But it's just that you—you really look like someone who already goes to school here."

I stared at her, thinking of the few casual "Heys" I'd gotten. "*What?* I look *so* similar to someone that people are *staring* at me when I go by? You've got to be kidding."

"No," the girl said, giving me an apologetic smile. "You really do look like her. It's kind of weird, actually."

I didn't know what to say. Once again I had entered some crazy New Orleans *X-Files* where the rules of reality didn't apply.

"I'm sorry," the girl said and held out her hand. "I'm Sylvie. Do you want me to show you where the office is?"

I shook her hand, feeling a pathetic amount of relief that I'd met someone kind. "I'm Thais," I said. "That would be great."

Just walking beside Sylvie helped so much, to the point where I could quit freaking out and actually pay attention to the reactions I was getting. It wasn't from everyone—mostly older kids. I saw what Sylvie meant: Some kids said hello, as if they already knew me. Others looked like they were going to say hi, then frowned and looked confused. But I bet when I saw this other person, we wouldn't really look that much alike. Maybe just our coloring or something.

"Okay, here it is," said Sylvie, showing me to an open door by a wide counter. Clearly the school office. "Homerooms are by last name. What's yours?"

"Allard," I said, and she smiled and nodded.

"I'm Allen—Sylvie Allen! So we'll be in the same one. I'll see you soon, okay?"

"Thanks," I said gratefully.

Sylvie nodded and headed down the hall, and I waited at the counter. A middle-aged woman with curly gray hair came over to me.

"Yes, Clio," she said briefly, taking out a form from under the counter. "What can I do for you?"

There was no one standing there but me. "Um, I'm not Clio," I said.

The woman stopped and looked at me full on. Embarrassed, I stood there, feeling like a zoo exhibit. A bell rang, and the halls filled with even more kids. The bell stopped, and still she hadn't said anything to me.

"You're not Clio," she said finally.

"No. Someone told me I look like someone who already goes to school here." *But can you get over it?* "Here are my transcripts from my last school." I pushed them across the counter. "I just moved here this summer. From Connecticut."

Slowly she took my transcripts and the registration letter I'd gotten in the mail. Her name tag said Ms. DiLiberti. "Thais Allard," she said, pronouncing it correctly.

"Yes."

"Yes, well, welcome, Thais," she said, seeming to recover enough to give me a professional smile. "I see you were a very good student back in Connecticut. I'm sure you'll do well here."

"Thank you."

"Your homeroom teacher will be Ms. Delaney, room 206. You'll just take the first set of stairs over there, to your left."

"Thanks."

"And here's some other information." Now she was all business. "Here's a copy of our school handbook—you might find that helpful. Here's our school contract—please read it, sign it, and get it back to me by the end of the day. And if you could fill in this emergency contact form."

"Yes, okay." This stuff I could deal with. What a relief. Then something almost imperceptible made my shoulders tense. I looked up just in time to see Ms. DiLiberti straighten, looking over my shoulder.

"Wait," she said to me. "Clio!"

I looked around—at last, they'd see us both together and

we could stop all this double-take crap. A group of girls was walking toward us, laughing among themselves. The light was behind them, so they were just dark silhouettes.

"Clio! Clio Martin!" Ms. DiLiberti called.

I turned to face the counter, suddenly aware of a shaky feeling in the pit of my stomach. It was barely nine o'clock, and I was exhausted and emotionally wrung out. *Just meet Clio and get it over with.* But still I felt nervous and anxious all over again.

"See y'all," said a voice. It sounded like my voice—except the word *y'all* would never pass my lips. A fist of something like dread grabbed my stomach. I didn't know why I felt this way, but I was barely able to keep it together. "Yes, Ms. DiLiberti? It wasn't me," said the voice. "I just got here."

Ms. DiLiberti smiled wryly. "Amazingly, I haven't called you over to discuss your latest transgression," she said. "After all, it's only nine o'clock on the first day. I'll give you a little more time. But there's someone I want you to meet. Thais?"

Slowly I turned, finally face-to-face with the mysterious— Me.

I blinked, and for one second I almost put up a hand to see if someone had slipped a mirror in front of me. My eyes widened, and identical green eyes widened simultaneously. My mouth opened a tiny bit, and a mouth shaped like mine but with slightly darker lip gloss also opened. I stepped back automatically and quickly scanned this other me, this Clio.

Our hair was different—hers was longer, I guessed, since

it was in a messy knot on the back of her head. Mine was feathered in layers above my shoulders. She was wearing a white tank top and pink-and-red surfer shorts that laced up the front. She had a silver belly ring. We had the same long legs, the same arms. She had a slightly darker tan. We were the same height and looked like we were the same weight, or almost. And here was the really, really unbelievable part:

We had the exact same strawberry birthmark, shaped like a crushed flower. Only hers was on her left cheekbone, and mine was on the right. We were freaking *identical*, two copies of the same person, peeled apart at some point to make mirror images of each other.

Even though my brain was screaming in confusion, one coherent thought surfaced: There was only one possible explanation.

Clio was my twin sister.

✦ Chapter Sixteen

Clio

"OH. MY. FREAKING. GOD." I WAS VAGUELY AWARE the voice was mine, but everything else had faded away. The only thing in my universe just then was this girl, who had obviously been cloned from my DNA. Obvious—but impossible.

Racey quickly looked at me, then at the other me, and she literally gasped. "Holy Mother," she breathed.

The other me looked like someone had just put a binding spell on her—frozen in place, eyes open wide, muscles stiff. Then I noticed one difference between us:

"Your face is green," I said, just as her eyelids fluttered and she started to collapse.

Racey and I caught her, and Ms. DiLiberti hustled out from behind the counter and led us into the assistant principal's office. Someone got a wet paper towel. I fanned the new girl's face with a copy of the student handbook.

Almost immediately, she opened her eyes and sat up, though she was still kind of whitish-green around the edges.

I hadn't taken my eyes off her. *So that's what I would look like with layered hair,* I thought, realizing I felt stunned and not enjoying the experience. My heart was beating hard, and a million thoughts pushed insistently at my brain. I didn't want to let them in.

"Who *are* you?" I asked. "Where are you from? Why are you here?"

She drank some water that Ms. DiLiberti brought her and pushed her hair off her face. "I'm Thais Allard," she said, sounding almost exactly like me, but more Yankeeish. "I'm from Connecticut. This past summer my dad died, and my new guardian lives here, so I moved here."

Her dad died. *Who was he?* I wanted to shout. Had he been my dad too? Had we been separated at birth, and Thais adopted by strangers? Or maybe I—was Nan my nan? She had to be. But she'd never, ever mentioned that I might have a sister. And this girl, even if she were from the planet Xoron, had to be my sister. We were just too freakishly identical, down to our matching *birthmarks.* We had the exact same *birthmark.* The birthmark that I'd alternately loved and hated, the one André had traced, had kissed just yesterday—was on her face.

"Who was your dad?" I said. "Who's your new guardian?"

Thais wavered and looked like she was about to turn on the faucets. Outside the office, we heard other students coming and going.

"I'm going to be late for homeroom," she said faintly, and I thought, *Sacrée mère, she's a weenie.*

"Your teachers will understand," Ms. DiLiberti said firmly.

"My dad was Michel Allard," the girl said. I'd never heard of him. "My new guardian is some weird friend of his." She shrugged, frowning.

It was all too much to take in. I felt a little weak-kneed myself, but unlike the Fainter, I sagged gracefully into a chair.

The girl—Thais—seemed to be coming back to life. "Do you have parents?" she asked. I saw the sudden eagerness on her face, and it was only then that I realized that Nan *had* to be her grandmother too. I would have to *share* Nan.

I'm a successful only child. I mean, I'm successful at *being* an only child. I bit my lip and said, "I live with my grandmother. My parents are dead." *Our* parents were dead. "When's your birthday?" I asked brusquely.

"November twenty-third." Now her eyes were examining me, her strength coming back. *Déesse,* was she even a *witch*? Well, of course, she had to be—but did she grow up being a witch? How could she not?

I frowned. "I'm November twenty-second. " I looked up at Racey to find her staring at me, like, *What the hell is going on?* Such a good question. One that I intended to ask Nan, as soon as possible. I thought Nan was probably not home now. She was a midwife, a nurse-practitioner at a local clinic. She had irregular hours, but she'd been getting ready to leave when I was walking out the door this morning.

"Where were you born?" Thais asked me.

"Here, New Orleans," I said. "Weren't you?"

Thais frowned. "No—I was born in Boston."

Racey raised her eyebrows. "That must have been a neat trick."

The first-period bell rang. I couldn't remember a time when I'd felt less like going to class, which in my case is saying something. All I wanted to do was go home and confront Nan, ask her why a stranger had shown up at *my* school in *my* town, with *my* face. I'd just have to wait till she got back tonight.

"Well, this is certainly a mystery," said Ms. DiLiberti, standing up. "You two obviously have some figuring out to do. But right now I'm going to write you passes for your teachers, and you're going to get to your first-period classes."

I consulted my class schedule. "I have American history."

Thais looked at hers. She still seemed shaken and pale, which made her birthmark stand out like red ink on her cheek. "I have senior English."

"Well, you girls get going," said Ms. DiLiberti briskly, handing us pink slips. "You too, Racey. And I can't wait to hear how this all plays out."

"Me neither," I muttered, gathering my stuff.

"Me neither," said Thais, sounding like an instant replay of me.

"Me neither," said Racey, and Thais looked at her, seeming to notice her for the first time. "I'm Racey Copeland," she told Thais.

"I don't know who I am," Thais said in a small voice, and suddenly I kind of felt sorry for her. And for me. For both of us.

"We're going to find out," I said.

• • •

Nan didn't come home until almost six o'clock. When she works late, I'm in charge of dinner, which we call Emergency Dinners, because cooking is yet another domestic art I'm not strong at.

Tonight's emergency dinner was a frozen pizza and a salad. I ripped up a head of lettuce and got a tomato from the garden in back. Ta da.

From the moment I'd walked in the door, I'd been wound as tight as a window shade. My shoulders literally ached. This afternoon I'd planned to see André—I'd finally been going to go to his apartment, and who knew what would happen? But now all I could think about was the fact that my double was walking around New Orleans, looking like me, sounding like me, and yet not being me. I mean, it wasn't her fault, obviously, but I felt like a Versace bag that had suddenly seen a vinyl imitation being sold on a street corner.

So I just paced around the house, my jaw aching from being clenched, missing André and wanting to run to him and have him make me forget all about this, and instead counting the minutes until my grandmother got home.

Finally I felt her pushing open the front gate. I didn't go meet her, but waited while she turned her key in the lock and came in. She looked tired, but when she saw my face, she straightened up, very alert.

"What is it?" she said. "What's happened?"

And that was when Clio Martin, stoic queen, non-cryer

in public, non-cryer in general, burst into tears and fell on her shoulder.

Nan was so startled it took her a moment to put her arms around me.

I pulled back and looked at her. "I'm a *twin!*" I cried. "I have an identical twin!"

To say I'd managed to take Nan by surprise was a gross understatement. I had absolutely floored her, and believe me, Nan did not floor easily. She'd always seemed like she'd seen everything, that nothing could rock her or make her upset. Even in second grade, when I'd slipped on a watermelon seed and split my head open on our neighbor's cement porch, Nan had simply filled a dishtowel with ice, told me to hold it in place, and had driven me to the hospital. Our neighbor had been about to have a nervous breakdown.

But this, *this* had really managed to stun her. Her face turned white, her eyes were dark and huge in her face, and she actually staggered back. "What?" she said weakly.

Okay, now—most people, if they went home and told their grandmother they were a twin, the grandmother would laugh and say, "Oh, you are *not.*"

So this was not good.

Nan wobbled backward, and I stuck a chair under her just in time. She grabbed my hands and held them, and said, "Clio, what are you talking about?"

I sat down in another chair, still sobbing. "There's another me at school! This morning they called me to the office, and there was *me*, standing there, but with a haircut! Nan, I mean, we're *identical!* We're exactly alike, except she's a Yankee, and she even has my exact same *birthmark*! I mean, what the hell is *going on?*" My last words ended in a totally unCliolike shriek.

Nan looked like she'd seen a ghost, only I bet if she saw a real ghost, it wouldn't faze her. She swallowed, still speechless.

Something was so, so wrong with this picture. I felt like the two of us were sitting there, waiting for a hurricane to hit our house, to yank it right off its foundation, to sweep us up with it. I quit crying and just gaped at her, thinking, *Oh, my God, oh, my God, oh, my God.* She knew.

"Nan—" I said, and then stopped.

She seemed to come back to herself then, shaking her head and focusing on me. A tiny bit of color leached back into her face, but she still looked pretty whacked. "Clio," she said in this old, old voice. "She had your same birthmark?"

I nodded and touched my cheekbone. "Hers is on the other side. It's exactly like mine. Nan—*tell me.*"

"What's her name?" Nan's voice was thin and strained, barely more than a whisper.

"Thais Allard," I said. "She said her dad had just died, and now she lives here with a friend of her dad's. She used to live in Connecticut. She says she was born in Boston, but the day after me."

Nan put her fingers to her lips. I saw her soundlessly form the name *Thais*. "Michel is dead?" she asked sadly, as if from faraway.

"*You knew him?* Was that—he wasn't *my* real dad, was he? Wasn't he just someone who adopted *Thais?*" I felt like my sanity was about to rip in half. "Nan, explain this to me. NOW."

At last, her eyes sparked with recognition. She looked at me with her familiar, sharp gaze, and I could recognize her again.

"Yes," she said, her voice firmer. "Yes, of course, *chérie.* I'll explain. I'll explain everything. But first—first there are some things I must do, very quickly."

While I sat with my jaw hanging open like a largemouth bass, she sprang to her feet with her usual energy. She hurried into our workroom, and I heard the cupboard open. I sat there, unable to move, to process anything except a series of cataclysmic thoughts: *I had a sister, a twin sister. I'd had a father, maybe, until this past summer. I'd have to share Nan. Nan had been lying to me my whole life.*

Over and over, those thoughts burned a pattern into my brain.

Numbly I watched Nan come out, dressed in a black silk robe, the one she wore for serious work, or when it was her turn to lead our coven's monthly circle. She held her wand, a slim length of cypress no thicker than my pinkie. She didn't look at me, but quickly centered herself and started chanting in old French, only a few words of which I recognized. Her first coven, Balefire, had always worked in a kind of language all their own, she'd told me—a mixture of old French, Latin, and one of the African dialects brought here during the dark days of slavery.

She went outside, and I felt her circling our house, our yard. She came onto the porch and stood before our front door. She came back inside and moved through each room, tracing each window with a crystal, singing softly in a language that had been passed down by our family for hundreds of years.

Every now and then I caught a word, but even before then, it had sunk in, what she was doing.

She was weaving layer after layer of spells, all around our house, our yard, around us, around our lives.

Spells of protection and to ward off evil.

✦ Chapter Seventeen

Life at the Golden Blossom

SUNLIGHT IS A PAINFUL THING, CLAIRE THOUGHT, trying to drag a sheet over her eyes. But thin pinpricks of morning seared her retinas, and she knew it was pointless to hold it off any longer.

She must get up.

Carefully she pried one eyelid open. The hazy view of her broken wooden window screen showed her it was maybe only two in the afternoon. Not too bad.

The bed was sunken weirdly—she was rolling toward the middle. A survey revealed a human form sleeping next to her, his straight black hair tossed across a pillow. No one she recognized. Well, that happened.

She sighed. A bath. A bath would revive her, and no one did baths better than the Golden Blossom Hotel. She would ring for a maid. Bravely she hauled herself into an unenthusiastic slump and rested for a moment, exhausted and dizzy.

"Please, ma'am?"

Claire willed her head to turn and somehow managed to

switch her gaze a bit to the left. A small Thai maid, no more than fifteen, knelt on the black wooden floor. She held up a small silver tray covered with a stack of neatly folded telephone messages. Her head was bowed—she was reluctant to disturb ma'am. Especially this ma'am, who often threw things and broke things when she was unwillingly disturbed.

"Please, ma'am? Messages for you. Man call many times. He say very urgent."

She held the small tray above her head, as if it was a sacrificial offering.

With supreme effort, Claire swung her feet over the side of the bed. She glanced at herself in the mirror. Ouch. Reaching out for the messages, she felt a sudden surge of nausea that made her freeze momentarily. She muttered some words under her breath and waited a moment for the feeling to pass. The little maid, tiny in her old-fashioned pink uniform, bowed her head lower, as if to avoid a blow.

Claire took the messages. She muttered thanks in Thai.

The little maid bowed deeply, then stood and started to shuffle backward out of the room.

"Make a bath for me!" Claire remembered to call, then winced as the words reverberated inside her pain-racked skull, making it feel like all the little blood vessels in her brain were leaking. "Please make a bath," Claire whispered again, adding the word "bath" in Thai. The maid bustled into the bathroom.

Claire glanced at the first message. From Daedalus. She

tossed it on the floor and looked at the second. Daedalus. Onto the floor. Third one read, "Get your ass to New Orleans, damn you." She laughed and tossed it after its companions. The rest were just more of the same, just old Daedalus playing mayor, wanting an audience so he could pontificate about nothing, blah, blah, blah.

Claire reached over and found a bottle by the bed with a few inches of a pale yellow liquor in it. She took a swig, winced, and drew her sleeve across her mouth. Time to start the day.

Chapter Eighteen

Thais

I DIDN'T REMEMBER GETTING BACK TO AXELLE'S. The whole surreal day swam through my consciousness like bits of a movie I'd seen long ago. For six periods I'd dealt with stares and whispers, dealt with seeing Clio again and again as we passed each other in the hall, both of us jerking in renewed surprise, as if zapped with a cattle prod. Thank God for Sylvie. In her I sensed a true friend—she treated me normally, helped me get my bearings, told me where classes were, how to meet her at lunch. Without her, I would have just lain down somewhere and let the world wash over me, not sure if I could ever get up again.

Clio was going to talk to her grandmother. So *I* had a grandmother too, for the first time in seventeen years. Doubt was pointless. It had been overwhelmingly obvious that Clio and I had once been a single cell, split in two. Now that I knew I had an identical twin, I somehow felt twice as lost, twice as incomplete as before. Would that feeling go away if we became close? I had family now, real blood family, where before I hadn't. I still felt so alone.

Dad hadn't known. I felt that instinctively. Never in any way had he ever revealed that he knew I'd been a twin. Which was a whole other mystery in itself.

I'd managed to get on the streetcar going downtown and got off at Canal Street, the end of the line. Like a trained dog, I found my way to Axelle's apartment. For just a minute, I rested my forehead against the sun-warmed iron of the gate. *Please, please, let Axelle not be home. Or Daedalus, or Jules. Please.*

I passed the small swimming pool in the courtyard and hesitated before I unlocked the door. How had Axelle gotten me? Who was she, really? Had she even known my dad? Because just as surely as I knew Clio was my sister, I also instinctively felt that I had been brought to New Orleans on purpose, and part of that purpose must have been Clio. I paused for a moment, my key in my hand. Oh my God. Had Axelle caused my dad's death somehow? The timing was so—I took a deep breath and thought it through.

I didn't see how she could have done it. Remembering it was a fresh pain: My dad had been killed when an old woman had fallen asleep at the wheel of her car. It had jumped the curb and crashed through the drugstore window. My dad had been in the way. But the woman was from our town—old Mrs. Beadle. I'd known her by sight. There was no way Axelle could have bribed her—it had been terrible for Mrs. Beadle as well. She'd broken her nose and her collarbone and gotten glass in one eye. Her driving license had been taken away forever. Despite everything, even Mrs. Thompkins had felt sorry for her. No. Axelle and her gang of merry weirdos couldn't have had anything to do with it.

I opened the door and was met by a blast of air conditioning as usual. The air inside was stale with cigarettes but blessedly quiet and empty. That instant I knew no one was home, as if I could have felt the jangling energy their presence would make.

I dumped my backpack in my room and sat down on my bed, feeling numb. What was happening with my life? Even if Axelle hadn't caused my dad's death, still, it wasn't a coincidence that I had been brought halfway across America to a city where I'd never been before, only to run into my *identical twin*—the twin I never knew existed. And yet, given how unconcerned Axelle had been about my going to school, I didn't see how meeting Clio today had been planned. If Axelle knew Clio was here, she hadn't planned on us meeting—at least not yet.

Restlessly I got up. I had no idea when she'd be back. Listening for her outside in the carriageway, I started roaming the apartment, deliberately snooping for the first time. My eyes fell on the door that led to the secret attic room. If anything was hidden in this apartment, it was in that room. I listened again for Axelle. I heard nothing, felt nothing. There was a small brass knob right below the small brass lock. Could she have left it unlocked, this once? I knew she carried the key with her.

I turned the doorknob and pulled.

Nothing happened. It was locked. Of course.

A wave of frustration made me grit my teeth. I needed answers! I closed my eyes, trying to calm the thousand questions swirling in my brain. I took some deep breaths. A lock, a lock . . . I was about to cry, as I hadn't all day, not since this morning when I'd gotten up. I pictured the lock in my mind. All I needed was a stupid key! I could see how the small key would slide into the lock, how its indentations would line up with the little row of pins in the cylinder. . . .

I needed to think, to decide what to do. I leaned against the cool wall, my eyes closed, hand still on the knob. I reached my finger up and traced the keyhole. One stupid key. I would just put the key in, turn it, the pins would fall into place . . . I could *see* it. I sighed heavily. Maybe I should go take a long tepid shower.

Then, under my finger, I imagined I felt the smallest of vibrations.

I opened my eyes. I listened. Silence. Stillness. I turned the doorknob and pulled gently.

The door opened.

I was in! Without hesitation I ran up the worn wooden steps. The plaster walls were decaying slightly, like everything else in New Orleans. Here and there bare brick was exposed.

I held my breath as I reached the door at the top of the stairs. God only knew what was behind here, and all of a sudden, horror-movie images filled my mind.

"Don't be ridiculous," I muttered, and turned the doorknob.

The door led to one dimly lit room, the only illumination

coming from shuttered half-moon windows at either end. The ceiling was low, maybe eight feet in the center, and sloped down on both sides to maybe four feet. The air was completely still and the exact temperature of my skin. I could smell wood, incense, fire, and too many other intermingled scents for me to name. At one end was a scarred work table, which was covered with the same kinds of maps and plans and books I'd seen downstairs. At first glance, I saw no suitcase full of heroin, no huge opium pipes, as I'd feared. So it was just about the voodoo, then.

Low bookshelves lined the wall on one side, and curious, I knelt to read their spines. Some of the titles were in French, but others were *Candle-Burning Rituals for the Full Moon*, *Witch—a History*, *Astral Magick*, *Principles of Spellcraft*, *Magick, White and Black*.

I sat back on my heels. Oh, jeez. Magick. Witchcraft. Not a surprise, but a depressing confirmation. I looked around. The bare wooden floor had layers of dripped wax from candles. There were pale, smeared lines of circles within circles, all different sizes, around the candle wax. Other shelves held candles of all colors. An astrology chart was pinned to one crumbling wall. There were rows of glass jars, labeled in some other language—maybe French? Latin?

How incredibly asinine. It was like finding out they were Moonies. I couldn't believe anyone would spend so much time and energy and money on all this stuff. What idiots.

So the three of them did their "rites" up here. And that kid Richard too. God.

But . . . after my nightmare, Axelle had done spells in my room, like they would help protect me or something. Which meant she thought someone was trying to hurt me. As if my nightmare had been witchcraft by someone else.

I suddenly felt dizzy, my head pounding. I had to get out of here this *second*. I ran to the door, raced down the steps, and pulled the door shut behind me. I heard a slight *snick*—it was locked again. Adrenaline raced through me, making my heart hammer, my breath come fast. I didn't even think of where to go but flew out of the apartment and out the side gate.

On the street I stopped short. It was still daylight, the sun intermittently covered with dark gray clouds. Tourists were walking by, as if nothing were unusual, as if my life hadn't changed hugely, not once, but too many times to count in the last three months, and today most of all. I slowed to a walk and crossed the narrow cobbled street. What to do, where to go— my thoughts weren't even that coherent. I just kept taking one step at a time, one foot in front of the other, feeling my skin film with cold sweat.

Then I found myself in front of the private garden, the garden where I'd met Luc only—what—two days before?

Quickly I moved the ivy aside and pushed open the small wooden door. As soon as I was inside and the door shut behind me, I felt the cold dread start to leave me. Inside this quiet garden, I felt calmer, saner. Safe.

Once again I sank onto the marble bench, feeling its welcome coolness against my skin. I didn't want to search the windows of the surrounding buildings, but hoped that Luc could see I was here. In a life filled with strangers, he and Sylvie were the only people I felt at ease with.

In the meantime I sat, letting my heartbeat slow, my breathing become regular. I couldn't think, couldn't begin to piece this puzzle together. I could only sit and listen to the muted sounds around me: the trickling fountain, the few small birds hopping among the jasmine, the very distant sounds of horses and carriages, tugboats on the river, streetcars rattling on their tracks.

I had a sister, a twin sister. I had a grandmother. Each time, I realized it all over again. Things with Clio had been strange. Maybe she didn't want a sister. Maybe she didn't want to share her grandmother—my grandmother. But surely my grandmother would want me? I closed my eyes and said a prayer that this was all real, that I had a real family now, that my grandmother would love me and take me to live with her, like in a fairy tale. *Please don't let me be alone anymore,* I prayed.

As before, I didn't hear the gate open, but when I looked up, Luc was walking toward me. A tight knot inside my chest eased, and all my tension started to evaporate. He was taller than I'd realized, wearing worn jeans and a white button-down shirt rolled back at the sleeves. A gentle smile lit his face, and I marveled at how good-looking he was. And then I became aware of how grubby and dusty and hot I was, and my morning shower seemed a lifetime ago. Great.

"We meet again." He sat next to me on the bench, leaning

forward to rest his arms on his knees. "You look upset. Again. Is your life so crazy right now?"

I gave a short laugh, wishing I had brushed my hair sometime in the last eight hours. "Yes."

He gave a sympathetic sigh, and it struck me how incredibly comforting he was to be with. He couldn't be more than a year or two older than me, but he seemed light-years away from most guys I'd known. I put my head to one side, thinking about it.

"What?" He smiled at me.

"I was just thinking . . . you have a—deep stillness to you," I said. His eyes lost their dreamy expression, became more alert. "As if all of this"—I waved my hand to encompass the whole world—"washes over you without affecting you very much. You seem like a—" I paused, considering. "Like a tree in the middle of a river, kind of. Like you're a tree, and the river washes around you and past you, but the tree never moves." I laughed self-consciously at my description.

Luc didn't speak for a minute, just looked at me. "Is that how I seem to you?" he asked softly.

"Yes," I said, not caring if I sounded stupid. "Everything in my life has changed. It keeps changing every day. But when I sit here with you, it's like the world has stopped." I shrugged. "Like time has stopped. It's . . . peaceful. It makes me feel better. I can't explain it."

Luc leaned back against the vine-covered brick wall. I heard the sleepy hum of bees as they went from flower to flower among the confederate jasmine. I remembered how Luc had told me the names of some of the plants and, leaning forward, I picked another perfect, creamy gardenia blossom. I inhaled its fragrance, its heady sweetness, and then I tucked it through a buttonhole on his shirt pocket.

"One for you," I said, smiling.

Luc was very still, and now he looked at me with a slight, puzzled smile.

"What do you want from me, Thais?" he asked.

"What do I *want* from you?" I didn't understand.

"In relationships, people want things from each other," he explained, his voice patient. "Girls might want protection, or someone to pay for things . . . someone to show off to their friends. Guys might want arm candy or someone to take care of them, or just someone to sleep with. People are afraid to be alone, and so they cling to each other like flotsam after a shipwreck. So, what is it that you *want* from me? And also, what is it that you're *offering* me?" His crisply accented voice was very quiet, for my ears only in this still, private garden.

My mouth was hanging open. "Well, that was just about the most depressing, old-fashioned, sexist-pig view of relationships I've heard in a long time," I said. I felt hurt, as if he were implying that I wanted to use him somehow. "What rock have you been living under? How did you get so cynical, this young?"

Luc cocked his head to one side, studying me. His dark hair, his beautiful eyes made me even madder because my strong attraction to his gorgeous outside was being spoiled by his dumb inside.

"And since when do we have a relationship?" I said, feeling anger rise in my veins. "We've run into each other *twice!*" My jaw set as I thought rapidly, already feeling the loss of something I hadn't even realized I wanted. "I am offering you *nothing*," I went on, practically spitting at him. "I'd rather stay alone the rest of my life than hook up with a guy who's only wondering what I *want* from him. And why would you even be worried? You *clearly* have nothing to offer *me*,"

I pushed off from the bench and strode to the garden gate, furious at him for ruining everything when I'd felt so peaceful and calm. I'd reached out to yank the gate open when suddenly Luc grabbed my arm and swung me around. Emotion crossed his face: uncertainty, hope, and something I recognized at the last second as strong, intense wanting.

"You'd be surprised at what I can offer you," he said roughly, and then he was kissing me like Chad Woolcott had never kissed me in eight months of going out. Like no one had ever kissed me, ever. My head bent back over his arm, and I felt the heat of his body through my clothes. It never occurred to me to resist, and I knew then that I'd wanted him all along. I felt the hardness of his arms holding me, pressing me to him. My eyes drifted shut, my mouth opened to his, and my arms wrapped around his neck as if I had no control over my own body. And maybe I didn't.

It felt like we kissed for ages, standing there, and finally we pulled away, as reluctantly as if pulling away meant death. Luc looked as shocked as I felt. I put my fingers to my lips—they felt bruised. Luc was breathing hard. He ran a hand through his dark hair and looked away.

All I could think was—*My world has just tilted.* It was just a kiss, standing up, even, and yet in that kiss it felt like everything in my life fell quietly into place and made sense.

Which it didn't, of course. My life was still a huge, thorny freaking mess. But during that kiss I had been able to forget about it, forget about everything.

"I'm sorry," he muttered, looking completely unlike his usual cool, suave self.

"Don't be sorry," I whispered, trying to pull myself together. I glanced at the sky, almost dark, and then I felt the first heavy raindrop explode against my arm. My skin felt so hot I expected to see a little puff of steam. "I have to go." I didn't want to go. I wanted to stay there forever.

He looked at me then, intensely, as if trying to see my soul. "We have a relationship," he said, and I got a weird feeling that he hadn't meant to say that, that it had come out anyway. "Even if I'm . . . old-fashioned and sexist and cynical." He gave a short laugh.

"I'll be back," I said. And looking into his eyes, I saw my reflected knowledge that with one kiss everything had spun out of control.

⚜ Chapter Nineteen

Clio

"HOLY MOTHER," RACEY BREATHED, LOOKING at me. "I can't get over it."

I took the bag of Raisinets from her and got a small handful. "Me neither."

"So Petra knew about your mystery twin," she said.

I nodded. "She had to. She was stunned, but not surprised, if you know what I mean."

Racey nodded, leaning against my wall, stuffing my bed pillow behind her back. It was getting late; soon she'd have to go. School night, etc. Like I could deal with school now. I could barely stand school when my life was somewhat normal—now, it would be an unending agony.

"Well, oh my God," Racey said, trying to sound normal. She tucked her white-streaked hair behind one ear. "You have a sister. You told me you wanted a sister, once."

"No. I said I wanted *you* to be my sister," I reminded her. "I don't want another *me* as a sister."

"That *would* be a nightmare," Racey agreed, and I kicked

at her with my bare foot. She laughed and said, "So what's Petra's explanation, then?"

"Don't know," I said shortly. "Haven't heard it." I leaned against my headboard and pulled a pillow into my lap. "She said she'd explain it, but she started doing all these protection spells, and then later she said that she wanted to see Thais and me together."

"Do you think Thais'll come live here?"

I groaned. "I don't know. She's living with some friend of her dad's. But if Nan is an actual living relative . . . I mean, there's no room here! We'd have to share a room!" I kicked a pillow on the floor.

"Okay—it's a freak show," Racey agreed. "Got it. Let's talk about something else. How's the mysterious André?" She raised her eyebrows suggestively.

"How would I know?" I snarled. "I haven't seen him today, because, oh, *yeah*, I found out that I had an identical twin sister that my grandmother has been lying to me about for seventeen years!"

Racey pursed her lips. "All *righty*, then. Who'd you get for chem lab?"

Unwillingly, trying to hold on to my outrage, I laughed. Only Racey could make me laugh at a time like this. "Foster."

"Me too! We can swap notes. Now, quick segue: So you still like André?"

"More than like. I mean, he's . . . he's just everything I could want." I shook my head. "He's perfect for me. I can't imagine ever wanting to be with anyone else."

Racey's eyes widened in alarm. She'd never heard me talk this way. I'd never heard me talk this way either. Or even think this way. I'd been with tons of guys, and André was the first one who'd even gotten close to touching my heart. And he was more than close. This was all new territory for me. It was exciting. Kind of dangerous.

"Huh," she said, obviously thinking this through.

"Anyway: you and Jonah," I said. "What gives?" Racey and Jonah Weinberg had had a summer fling, and now he was in her English class. Outside, I heard heavy rain start to hit the windowpanes—it had been pouring off and on all evening.

"I may have underestimated him," Racey allowed.

I grinned. "He did look pretty good today, didn't he?"

"Yeah." She was about to elaborate when her cell phone rang. She answered it and said, "Hey, Mom. Uh-huh. Yeah. Yeah, okay. Got it." She clicked the phone off. "It's a school night," she said brightly. "I better get my ass home so I can get a good night's sleep!"

I laughed, feeling better since she'd come over. "Okay. But thanks, Race. You're my lifeline." I hugged her.

"Clio—it'll be okay." She pulled back and looked into my eyes. "No matter what happens, it'll be okay, and I'll be here for you." We didn't usually get all sappy with each other, so I was touched.

"Thanks. And after all, *you* have sisters, right?" She had two sisters, both older, and Trey, just a year younger than us.

"Yeah." She frowned. "They suck." Then she pasted on

a falsely enthusiastic face. "But I'm sure *your* sister will be *great!*"

I snorted and kicked her in the butt on the way out. *Thank you, Déesse, for friends.* It was the most heartfelt prayer I'd said all day.

✦ Chapter Twenty

STREETCARS ARE NOT AIR-CONDITIONED, LIKE buses or subways. Instead they have windows that go up and down. Except for the window *I* was sitting next to, which was broken or something and wouldn't budge. I was already clammy and sticky, and it was barely eight thirty in the morning.

Axelle hadn't come home until almost ten o'clock last night. After I'd left Luc, I'd gone back and taken a long shower. When Axelle walked in, I was calmly eating a microwaved chicken pot pie and going through my school papers at the table. So much for her wanting me to come straight home from school.

We hadn't talked much. I was dying to shriek questions at her: Who was she, why was I here? But something held me back. Meeting Clio had made this whole scenario even stranger and more upsetting, and Axelle was a big part of it. Though she didn't actually seem dangerous, I was much more on my guard. Did she know about Clio? If she knew about Clio, but hadn't mentioned her to me, then she didn't want me to know about her, for some reason. So if I told Axelle that Clio went to my school, would she ever let me go back? Or would this whole situation unravel horribly? So I just tried to act normal, Axelle was distracted and uninterested, and I slipped off to bed as soon as I could.

This morning she'd still been sleeping when I left the house.

Now I sat on the swaying, clacking streetcar, leaning forward to catch the warm breeze from the open window by the seat in front of me. Once again I was nervous, on edge, as if Axelle would run up and pull me off the trolley. Or maybe a huge live oak would topple across the tracks and mash us. Or someone would try to snatch my backpack. Just something, some unnamed dread was weighing on me, winding me tight.

Maybe I should switch to decaf.

I was sitting toward the back. Every seat was taken by people going to work, kids in Catholic-school uniforms, kids going to Ecole Bernardin and other schools. Riding a streetcar to school seemed so quaint and old-fashioned, compared to, say, a subway.

When we passed Sacré Coeur, a Catholic girls' school, a lot of seats emptied. Still nervous, jumpy, I suddenly decided to move up front so I could see when Ecole Bernardin appeared. I stood up, grabbed my backpack, and was three feet down the aisle when I heard someone gasp. Time stretched out as I slowly turned.

Outside the back windows, a big, bright red pickup truck had jumped the curb and was flying toward the streetcar. I hardly had time to blink as the truck plowed into one of the streetlights that lines St. Charles Avenue. The streetlight snapped off a foot above the ground, and the top of it speared through the streetcar window, smashing the glass and reaching halfway across the aisle.

Right where I'd been sitting.

Streetcars can't stop on a dime, so we dragged the streetlight about twenty feet as the brakes screeched and shot sparks. I had grabbed a seat handle, and now I sank, weak-kneed, into the closest seat. If I hadn't moved, that broken, jagged streetlight would have speared me like a fish.

The driver strode toward the back of the streetcar and looked at the damage. He was huge, and he was mad.

"Anybody hurt?" he boomed, and we all looked at each other.

Despite the broken glass, no one had even a scratch. People had gotten almost knocked off their seats, but no one had fallen. It was amazing. I felt shaky, realizing what a close call I'd had.

"Okay, everybody move to the front of the car," the driver said authoritatively. "Watch out for the glass." He opened the back door of the streetcar and went onto the neutral ground, the median, where a dazed teenager wearing a baseball cap was unfolding himself from the pickup.

The streetcar driver started yelling at the teenager, who looked scared and upset. I heard him moan, "My dad is gonna kill me."

"He's gonna haveta get in line!" the streetcar driver said angrily. "Look what you did to my trolley, fool!"

Then the police came. After they had checked everything out, that streetcar went out of service. I didn't want to wait for another one and walked the last ten blocks to school. The aftereffects of my near escape made me feel hyped-up and anxious. Limp from humidity and damp with sweat, I got to school just after the first bell had rung. The halls were emptying fast, and I hurried in, wanting to see Clio, to see what her grandmother had said—and also just to see her, to make sure I hadn't hallucinated the whole thing.

A couple of people said hi—the whole twin story had probably made its rounds. I smiled shakily and said hi, grateful for any friendly face.

"Thais! Hi," said Sylvie, walking up. "Did you find your one-inch, three-ring binder with the clear panel outside for your name?" It had been on one of our supply lists.

I nodded and smiled faintly. "Yeah. But I just almost experienced death by light pole." I told her what had happened, trying to sound not as scared as I felt.

"Oh, no!" she said sympathetically. "What a sucky way to start the day. But I'm glad you're all right."

Sylvie liked me as me, not just as one of the bizarre separated twins. A thought of Luc popped into my mind—I also wanted him to like me as me. Granted, he didn't know that I had a twin. The image of his burning kiss seared my mind for just a moment, and I felt heat flush my cheeks.

"Yeah, it's already hot," Sylvie said as the second, tardy bell rang. "We better get to homeroom."

But as I turned, I saw Clio disappear into a room down the hall. For a second she met my eyes, and I tapped Sylvie's arm.

"You go ahead—I'm going to get a drink of water."

She nodded, and I took off down the hall, looking through glass doors. One room was unlit and empty, and I almost passed it. But then I saw a dark silhouette. I opened the door and peered in.

"Clio?"

She was leaning against a desk, her long hair down around her shoulders. "Hey." She looked me up and down, as if to remind herself of how identical we were. She gestured to her right. "This is my—uh, Nan. My grandmother. Nan, this is Thais."

An older woman stepped out of the shadows. I searched her face, but I'd definitely never seen her before. She didn't look like me or Clio or our mother.

"Thais," she said softly, stepping closer to me. She glanced from me to Clio and back. "My name is Petra Martin. You've—both—grown up beautifully. I'm so happy to finally see you again." Clio's grandmother. So my grandmother too. This was my grandmother. My mother's mother.

I'd never even known about her, and Clio had had her for seventeen years.

I swallowed nervously, hoping she would want me too, that I had found my family. Quickly Petra hugged me. Her hair smelled like lavender.

She pulled back and smiled at me. "You've got to come

with me now," she said, starting to walk to the outside door on the other side of the room.

Petra opened the outside door and started to walk briskly across the school yard, to go off property. I hurried after her, and Clio followed me.

"Are we skipping out of school?" I had never done that in my life.

Petra gave me a quick glance, her eyes clear and blue and piercing. "Yes."

"Oh. Well." I nodded. "Okay." There's a first time for everything.

She led us to a Volvo station wagon, and five minutes later we pulled up in front of a small house, set back from the sidewalk and surrounded by one of the cast-iron fences I saw all over the place. The front garden was lush, so thickly planted that it practically concealed the house from the street. The house was small and painted a dark rust color, with natural wood trim. Two tall French windows opened onto the small porch, and the front door had stained glass around the main frosted pane. It was adorable.

After my dad had died, I'd felt more alone than I had thought possible. I'd practically wanted to die myself. Since I'd seen Clio yesterday, I'd been hoping and praying that somehow this would work out, and the horrible, unbelievable turn my life had taken in the last couple months would be over. I wanted normalcy, a grandmother, a home, a sister. Real, normal people who would never take Dad's place but be a close second.

The front door opened directly into a sparsely furnished living room. I looked around with interest, as if examining my new home. I wished.

The furniture was simple and old-fashioned. The walls were painted a dusty rose. I felt comfortable here—it was so much homier than Axelle's black-leather art deco stuff. Like Axelle's main room, the ceilings were ridiculously tall, maybe twelve feet? Fourteen? Two wooden bookcases were centered on the far wall, and I read their titles, hoping they would give me clues as to what kind of person Petra was.

"*Crystal Working.*"

My breath caught in my throat as I hoped desperately that Petra was all into beading.

"*Wiccan Sabbats. Herbal Magick. Metal and Stone Work in Spells.*"

I couldn't keep the dismay off my face. All the hopes that had been born yesterday—my dreams for a real family, my sad need for a home and normalcy—withered inside me.

"You do voodoo," I muttered, blinking back tears. Then it hit me: Petra and Clio did this magick stuff—just like Axelle and the others. What were the chances of that? Just how common was it, in New Orleans? I swallowed, feeling suddenly cold. Petra and Clio were my only family. Couldn't I trust them? Could I give them up, not have anything to do with them? I took a breath. I would hear Petra out. Then decide. Everything in me wanted Petra and Clio to belong to me, and me to them. I would wait and see. If they were connected to Axelle somehow . . .

"Not voodoo," said Petra with a little smile. "*Bonne Magie.* The Craft. Similar to Wicca, with the same roots. Now, come into the kitchen. We'll have tea."

The kitchen was painted a pretty green, and the two windows both had shelves of healthy houseplants in front of them. A large white cat was asleep on top of some newspapers on the kitchen table. I felt crushed, devastated. I'd been so stupid to get my hopes up.

"Get the cat off the table," Petra said, going to the cupboard and taking out three glasses.

Clio picked up the cat and handed him to me. "This is Q-tip."

I held him awkwardly. Q-tip sleepily opened his blue eyes and looked at me. Then he closed his eyes and went heavily limp in my arms. For a moment I was surprised at how he'd accepted me, but then I realized I didn't look like a stranger.

"Q-tip is a big boy," I murmured, looking around for a place to put him down. I didn't see one and finally just sat in a chair and arranged him on my lap. Petra put a tall glass of tea in front of me, and then the three of us were sitting there, together. In a witch's house.

"He's deaf," Clio said as an icebreaker. "A lot of white, blue-eyed cats are."

"How do you call him?" I asked, trying to be polite.

Petra smiled, and suddenly her somewhat forbidding, stern-looking face relaxed, and an affectionate warmth stunned me. I was still blinking in surprise when she said, "We stomp on the floor, hard enough to send vibrations through the house. Then he comes running. He comes even if he's outside, if he's close enough."

I looked down at the huge cat, impressed. He purred.

"Unfortunately, until just a few years ago, when Clio was mad she'd stamp her feet and slam doors," Petra went on wryly. Clio made a semi-embarrassed face from across the table. "Finally she had to learn to get her temper under control, if only for the cat's sake."

"He kept running up, wanting treats," Clio admitted, and I smiled.

"Why do you do magick?" I blurted. "It seems so—"

"It's our family's religion, dear," Petra said, as if explaining why we were Lutherans. "What do you have against it?"

I realized I was on thin ice. Despite everything, I wanted to make a good impression. Despite the magick, despite my worries about Axelle, I couldn't help wanting Petra to love me, to want me. I shrugged and drank my tea.

"I don't think I've ever stamped my foot or slammed a door," I said, returning to the earlier conversation. "Dad and I didn't fight much."

Petra's face softened when I mentioned my dad. "I'm very sorry you lost Michel, dear," she said gently. "I only met him once, but I thought he seemed very nice."

"If you met him, why didn't we both go with him?" I asked, and saw the same curiosity on Clio's face.

Petra sighed and took a deep drink of her tea. I was halfway through mine—it was unusual, not sweet, though I tasted traces of mint and honey. With surprise I realized that I felt unexpectedly comfortable, even relaxed.

"I'm going to tell you both what happened," Petra said, folding her fingers around her glass. "Yes, obviously, you're twins. Identical twins. And I was the one who separated you."

Chapter Twenty-One

Clio

THIS OUGHTA BE GOOD, I THOUGHT. ACROSS THE table, Thais had her gaze locked on Nan, and I wondered if the tea had kicked in yet. Nan hadn't said anything to me, but I could taste the catnip and just a trace of valerian and knew she'd brewed something to calm us all down, make this easier. I had seen how completely freaked Thais looked when she saw our books.

"I knew your mother, Clémence, was pregnant, of course, but she wasn't married. And I didn't know who the father was until the night she came to me in labor." Nan took a deep breath. "I'm a midwife, and Clémence wanted me to deliver her baby at home, not in a hospital," she explained to Thais.

"Why?" Thais asked.

"Because—she trusted me more than a hospital," Nan said slowly, as if reliving that time. "Because I'm a witch. As was Clémence."

I hid my smile behind my sip of tea. Thais sat back in her chair, looking, if possible, more horrified. I got up and put some cookies on the table. Numbly she reached out for one and took a distracted bite. I saw Q-tip's ear twitch as she dropped crumbs on him.

"Witch how, exactly?" she asked, and I looked at her thoughtfully. She was bummed, but not shocked. That was interesting.

"I mean, our family's religion is called *Bonne Magie,*" Petra said. "Good Magick in English. White Magick if you will. It's been our family's religion for hundreds of years—since about the sixth century. Our ancestors brought it to Canada, then down into America, to Louisiana, hundreds of years ago. But there's more to it than that."

Thais sipped her drink and absently stroked Q-tip's fur. I could hear his purring from where I sat. I wanted Nan to get to the part where she deprived me of my father. And deprived Thais of her grandmother, I admitted. If I thought of it that way, I couldn't help feeling I'd been the lucky one.

"Many people practice the Craft in different forms," Nan went on. "Wicca is a big example, and the closest religion to what we have. *Bonne Magie* descended from the earliest forms of Wicca—the Celts brought it to Brittany when they came as refugees to escape the Anglo-Saxons."

I took a deep, impatient breath. *Cut to the* chase, I thought.

"Anyway," said Nan, "we and our ancestors have achieved something more. We've tapped into the deep magick contained within Nature herself. We have power."

Thais looked at her blankly. I'd grown up knowing all this,

so it was like watching someone fold laundry. But to Thais it was all new, and I wondered what she was thinking.

"Uh-*huh*," she said, sounding as if she were humoring a nutcase. Again I had to hide a smile. "Power."

Petra heard Thais's tone. "Yes, my dear, 'power.' Power and energy are contained within every natural thing on this planet, there to be tapped into, used, if you know how. Our religion is about knowing how, and even more important, knowing *why*."

Thais licked her lips and glanced sideways, as if plotting an escape route.

"Look," I said, pushing my glass away. I took the salt cellar and dumped a small pile onto the table. I looked at it, then closed my eyes. I slowed my breathing and centered myself, then started singing softly under my breath. The basic form was in Old French, and it rhymed. I substituted a few words to make it apply to this situation.

Salt of the earth
Power of life
I shape you
I make you mine
We become one.

I pictured the tiny, individual salt grains. I let my energy flow out and around them, so it was like I had no boundaries in my body anymore. I was part of everything, and because I was part of everything, I could affect everything.

A minute later I opened my eyes. Thais looked like someone had just smacked her upside the head. She stared at the table, then up at me. She scooted her chair back, leaned over Q-tip, and looked beneath the table for hidden wires or magnets.

"It's just salt," I told her. "It's not, like, metal shavings. Not a lot can affect it. Except magick."

She looked at the table again, where a round happy face made of salt smiled at her.

"Of course," Petra said dryly, "magick also has larger, more important purposes. But that was just one small demonstration of what we call power. I don't think Michel knew your mother was a witch. He himself was not. And I tell you all this to set the stage, to help explain why I acted as I did."

"Our family can trace its line back more than five centuries," Nan said. "And since the very beginning, it's had an issue with twins."

"What?" I'd never heard that before. "*An issue?*"

"Yes," Nan said. "In our line, twins are special, because they can join their magick to become very powerful—much more powerful than any other two people using their magick together. Identical twins who know what they're doing can really have a great deal of power indeed." Nan met my eyes, then Thais's. "Even a dangerous amount of power."

This was the most interesting thing I'd heard in ages. I looked at Thais speculatively, wondering how long it would take to get her up to speed, magick-wise.

"So people in our line fear twins," Nan went on, and I frowned. "More than once, a set of identical twins has used their combined power not for good but for dark purposes.

They caused destruction, disaster, and death. The most recent time was about two hundred years ago."

"Were they crazy to use it for evil?" I asked. Seeing Thais's face, I explained, "Any magick you put out into the world comes back to you threefold. So anyone with half a brain is careful to use their force only for good. Anyone who uses magick for a dark purpose is risking having hellfire come down on them."

"Yes," Nan agreed. "And hellfire did come down on them, their families, their communities, with disastrous consequences. This happened at least three times in our history. So even today, in the twenty-first century, our people are wary of twins. More than wary—afraid. And fear makes people dangerous. When your mother gave birth that night, almost eighteen years ago, to twins, identical girls, I instantly knew that you would face prejudice, fear, persecution, and even danger from people afraid of you."

"But—I mean, how many of you are there? Why couldn't we have just moved someplace else and grown up normally? How many people would even know about us, and would care enough to actually try to hurt us?" Thais shook her head. "I still don't get it."

"Of people who practice *Bonne Magie*, of course it's hard to know an exact number," said Nan. "I believe there are roughly twenty thousand or so. Maybe six thousand in America, more in France and other parts of Europe. Maybe eight thousand in Canada."

"That still doesn't seem like that many," Thais argued. "There're over three hundred million people in America."

Cate Tiernan

"Comparatively, it's not," Nan agreed. "But you don't need huge numbers for a group of people to wield a great deal of influence and for their powers to stretch over far distances. Our particular famille, with less than a thousand hereditary witches, all grew up with the cultural fear of our kind having twins."

"So you split us up," I said. "Voilà, no more twins."

"Did my dad know?" Thais asked.

Nan seemed uncomfortable. She shook her head, looking sad, remembering. "Your mother knew, of course. That's another reason she came to me. She was afraid for you, even before you were born. She kept you a secret from everyone, even me, even your father, until the night she had you. That night, she begged me to keep you safe. Clio, you were born just before midnight, and Thais, you were born just after midnight. That's why you have different birthdates. And then, with her dying breath, Clémence made me promise to do everything within my power to keep you safe."

Thais's eyes were brimming with tears. Seeing that made my own eyes fill.

Nan went on. "When I found out that Michel didn't know there was more than one baby, I didn't know what to do. Then— something went wrong during the delivery. Even if Clémence had been in a hospital, nothing could have saved her. It all happened so fast. But she had a minute, and she knew she was dying, and she begged me to save her daughters."

Nan cleared her throat and took a sip of tea. Thais's tears

were running down her cheeks, falling onto Q-tip's fur. I wiped my own eyes and swallowed the lump in my throat.

"I had no time to think." Nan took a strand of hair and tucked it back into her long braid. "Michel was waiting in the next room. Clémence had just died, and I would have to call the police, the hospital." I couldn't even imagine what that night had been like for her.

"And I had these two infants, wrapped in blankets," Nan said. "So I hid one, and I called Michel in and placed the other in his arms. In that one instant, he gained a daughter and lost his lover. I never mentioned the other baby or the twin curse. I told him where to take the baby for her to be checked out. I told him where they would take Clémence and about the arrangements he would need to make. He was shocked and heartbroken, and never have I felt sorrier for any human being as I did that night for Michel, holding his daughter, mourning his lost love."

Now I was crying too, for the young parents I had never known, for how painful it must have been for Nan, for myself, losing a mother, father, and sister all in one night. And for Thaïs, because she had lost her mother, grandmother, and sister in one stroke too.

"That was in Boston," said Nan. "Within a week, I had closed my midwifery practice and moved with Clio to New Orleans." She put her hand on mine. "I had a birth certificate made for you, and then you were mine. And though it absolutely broke my heart in two, I didn't leave my forwarding address with Michel, and I threw his information away. I didn't want to take any chances that one of the members of our famille would discover you and perhaps make their own plans for ensuring that you never have a chance to wreak your powers of destruction."

"But then why am I here?" Thais cried, her voice broken with tears. "What's happened?"

"Obviously someone has found out," said Nan, an edge of steel underlying her calm voice. "Which leads me to ask: How did your father die, and who do you live with now?"

Thais blinked, trying to gather her thoughts. "Uh, Dad died in an accident," she said, taking a tissue from the box on the table. "He got hit by a car that jumped the curb." For a moment she frowned, thinking, as if something was just occurring to her, but then her face cleared and she went on. "Then in court I thought I was going to go live with Mrs. Thompkins, who was our best friend, like a grandmother to me. But Dad's will gave me to an old friend of his, who I'd never even heard of."

"*Who?*" Nan said, her fingers tightening around her glass.

"Her name is Axelle Gauvin," Thais said, and Nan's glass tipped, spilling tea. I saw Thais's eyes narrow slightly as I jumped up to get a dishtowel. Tea and ice had spilled on Q-tip, and he leaped down in disgust and trotted into the other room.

"So I take it you've heard of Axelle Gauvin?" I said dryly as I mopped up spilled tea.

"Yes," Nan said grimly. "She's from our line, our original line. Her ancestors and mine were in the same famille."

"She's a relative?" Thais asked intently.

"Not by blood," Nan said. "It's more like a clan. Many people came here from Canada, of course. Many of them are now called Cajuns. But our particular group, a group that practiced *Bonne Magie,* had fifteen families. Clearly, Axelle knows about you and Clio. Just as clearly, she's brought you here for a reason."

Thais looked stricken. "That's what I've been worried about. How did she know when my dad died? How did she get to have me? And then both of you do magick—" Thais's chin trembled. "Oh, God," she said faintly, sounding near tears. "Did she kill my dad?"

"Axelle is a lot of things, but a murderer? I have to say I don't think she could do it," said Nan firmly. "You've been safe with her this far. No one's tried to harm you, have they?"

Thais frowned, thinking. "Not really, no." She shook her head. "Do you know Jules and Daedalus too?"

Nan nodded.

"They're over at Axelle's a lot," said Thais. "They're a little creepy, but no one's ever tried to hurt me. In her own way, Axelle seems kind of concerned about me. She gave me a cell phone. Oh, and one night I had a bad dream. Axelle did spells in my room after that."

For several minutes we sat there, each of us lost in thought. This was a lot of stuff to take in. Now I understood why Nan had freaked about Thais, and why she'd put all the protection spells on the house and yard. I wondered if I had to go back to school today, and if there was any way I could sneak over to see André instead.

"I think for now, it's safe for you to stay at Axelle's," Nan decided. "I'll talk to her, and then we should consider your living here."

Thais's face lit up just as I felt mine shut down. There was no room here for Thais. I mean, she was okay, and she was my sister, but this was all happening too fast.

"But for right now, stay at Axelle's. Keep your eyes and ears open, be extra careful, extra cautious," said Nan. "And I also think it would be safer if you started learning some magick. It would help you protect yourself."

"Uh . . ." Thais looked less than thrilled at this idea.

"Now I'm going to take you both back to school," said Nan. "I'll write notes so you won't have any trouble. Clio, you come straight home after school, and Thais, you go straight to Axelle's, understand?"

I somehow avoided making a face. I would run home after school, drop off my books, change, and go see André.

Then Nan hugged me and Thais in turn. "Despite everything, I am very glad to have you two reunited again. I'm so happy to see both of you at once, to know both of you. We're a family, and once we get all this sorted out, it will all seem much better."

✦ Chapter Twenty-Two

Thais

"WHAT," I WHISPERED.

Sylvie gave an embarrassed smile and propped her work-book up so the study-hall monitor wouldn't see us talking. "Sorry. I don't mean to stare. It's just—I've known Clio for three years, and now I know you, and you guys are so differ-ent. I mean, I was never good friends with Clio or anything. But still, you *look* so much alike, but you're really nothing alike."

"We dress differently," I said. Being back at school after my *X-Files* morning was weird, but school felt safer and more familiar than the rest of my life.

"It's more than that," Sylvie said. "You're just really *nice*."

I winced. "Ouch."

She grinned. "Not goody-goody nice. But not a user, you know? I'm not saying Clio's mean, exactly. She's never been mean to me. But she's always been one of the really popular girls. Girls want to be her, and guys want to date her. And she knows it. And she gets into it." Sylvie stopped, as if she'd just realized she was talking about my sister and didn't want to hurt my feelings.

I thought about my life back in Welsford. I had been one of the popular girls, and guys asked me out. I knew people had thought I was pretty. In a way, I hadn't known how pretty I was until I had seen Clio. I saw her and how people reacted to her, and I realized they would react to me that way too. Is that what Luc saw? I thought again of his kiss, for the nine millionth time that day. Even at Petra's, hearing about my family's unbelievable past, I had thought of him again and again. What would happen the next time I saw him? Was I ready for it?

"What are you thinking about?" Sylvie asked behind her hand.

"Oh—just back home, you know," I said, putting Luc out of my mind before I blushed. "It was so different than it is here. My school was really small, and we'd all started together in kindergarten, and no one was all that much better or worse than anyone else. So being pretty or popular didn't really get you anywhere." Ecole Bernardin was about ten times bigger than my last school had been, and even on my second day, I could see clear tiers of social strata. Clio and her friends were at the top.

I wondered where I would end up.

• • •

Axelle was waiting for me at the door of the apartment, pacing and smoking. I came in, and our eyes met, a world of knowledge passing between us.

"Petra called me," she said unnecessarily.

I walked past her and dumped my backpack in my room, then came out into the kitchen and poured myself a glass of seltzer. Finally, practically trembling, I faced her. Despite what Petra had said, I had to ask Axelle myself.

"Did you kill my father?" My voice was like ice. I'd never heard it sound like that.

"No." Axelle frowned. "I didn't even know him."

"Then how did I end up with you?" I yelled, taking us both by surprise.

Axelle looked defensive. "We . . . kept in touch with your father because of Clémence," she said. "When he died . . . unexpectedly, we thought it would be best if you came here, where you have people in your famille. I admit I pulled a few strings after your father died. It was important that I get you here. And really, don't you agree it's in your best interest? Aren't you glad you met your sister? And your . . . grandmother?"

"Of course," I said with gritted teeth. "But you did all this behind my back. And if I hadn't run into Clio at school, I still wouldn't know about my sister and grandmother. When were you planning to tell me?"

Axelle took a moment. I could practically see the mental gears turning. "The less you know, the safer it is for you," she said. "Of course I would have told you—when the time was right. You just found out a little sooner, is all. Eventually, everything will be clear."

"So you're a witch too?"

161

"Of course," said Axelle. "Just as you are."

I ignored that. "You're part of the same famille as Petra?" I tried to pronounce the French word as I'd heard Petra say it.

Axelle looked at me consideringly, her black eyes thoughtful. "Yes. The same as you."

"What about Jules and Daedalus?"

"Yes."

"Even that kid Richard, the Goth guy? He's a witch?"

"Yes."

"Petra knows all of you?"

Axelle nodded.

"And you've always known Clio?"

"No. I saw her once from a distance. But none of us knows her, and she doesn't actually know any of us."

"So what's going to happen now?" I crossed my arms over my chest and stared at her.

Axelle's face seemed to close, as if I could actually see emotions shutting down. "Nothing. Business as usual. No huge fireworks or anything. Listen, I'm going upstairs for a while. Later we'll order in Chinese." She turned on her spiked heel and went into the main room. I heard the door open and then the click of her sandals on the wooden steps. She didn't know I'd been up there. I had my secrets too.

An image of Luc flitted through my thoughts, and I got up to go to the garden. But just as I opened the front door, a thunderstorm blew in from out of nowhere. I'd gotten used to this happening almost every day, sometimes twice a day.

One minute it was sunny; the next it would be literally black outside, with rain falling so hard and thick that you literally couldn't see through it. Not even Connecticut nor'easters came close to a regular New Orleans summer storm.

Inside the apartment it was dark and cool. Outside it was pouring, with lightning and thunder. I sighed. We'd probably lose power soon. Since I'd lived here, we'd lost power maybe five times already. Just for a few minutes or an hour, but it was still disconcerting to have everything suddenly shut down.

An instantaneous *boom!* of thunder and a blinding flash of lightning that made the courtyard glow made up my mind for me. I closed the door. Back in my room, I lay on my bed, listening to the buckets of rain drumming on the low roof over me. It was oddly soothing, comforting, and despite thunder that reverberated inside my chest and lightning that made the world go white, I actually fell asleep.

✤ Chapter Twenty-Three

We Have a Full Treize

OUIDA JEFFERS PARKED HER SMALL RENTAL car in a pay lot and walked the last two blocks to Daedalus's rented apartment. The heavy rain had stopped, and now thin curtains of steam rose from the cobbled streets. She didn't know how he could stand the French Quarter. It was always loud, always crowded, and there was no place to park. Years ago it had been lovely, much less touristy, more charming and authentic. But that had been a long time ago.

Ouida double-checked the apartment number and rang the bell.

"Yes?" A voice called from the upstairs balcony, and Ouida backed up into the street so he could see her. "Ouida!" said Jules, pleasure lighting his face. "I'll buzz you up!"

Ouida pushed the door when it buzzed and walked up the beautiful, floating staircase that curved around the courtyard to the second story. *Jules looks strained,* she thought. He often did. He put so much pressure on himself.

As Ouida reached the landing, a tall wooden door opened,

and Jules came out to hug her.

"Long time, old friend," he said, and she nodded into his shoulder. "I'm glad you're here."

"What's going on?" Ouida said in a low voice, but Jules didn't answer, just led her into the front parlor. Ouida looked around. Daedalus had always had impeccable taste. This apartment's balconies overlooked Chartres Street, with huge Boston ferns shielding the view a bit. Inside, graceful Empire furniture created an elegant, old-fashioned ambience. The whole effect was light, airy, and whispered old money.

"Ouida." Daedalus came forward, holding out his hands. They kissed formally on both cheeks and looked at each other. *We always do this*, Ouida thought. *When we see other members of the Treize, we examine them like medical curiosities.*

"How nice to see you, my dear," Daedalus said. "Come in, make yourself comfortable."

Ouida sank onto a delicate love seat. It had been hectic and difficult to arrange to come here. Fortunately her research project could be put on hold, at least for a while. The chromosome samples weren't going anywhere. Daedalus had never summoned her like this, and she was curious.

"What's going on, Daedalus?" she asked as he handed her a tall, cold drink.

"You won't believe it," he said with a smile, sitting down opposite her. Jules sat down also. He didn't look nearly as cheerful as Daedalus did.

Ouida waited. Daedalus had always been a showman. Now

he leaned forward, his blue eyes bright, energetic. "We can do the rite. We have a full Treize, once more."

"Wh—" Ouida began, but her voice failed her. She looked quickly from Daedalus to Jules, and Jules nodded in confirmation. The breath had left her lungs, and now she tried to get enough air to speak. "What do you mean? Surely Melita—"

Daedalus waved his hand impatiently. "God, no. I have no idea where Melita is. As far as anyone can tell, she was swallowed up by the earth right after she left. But now, at last, we have a full thirteen. Thirteen witches of the famille to perform the rite."

"How? Who?" Ouida asked. Emotions she hadn't felt in years flooded her brain. Memories, yearnings, things that happened so long ago it was as if they'd happened to a completely different person.

"Twins," said Daedalus with great satisfaction. "From Cerise's line. Identical, female twins."

"Twins? Where are they?" Ouida asked, so taken aback that her head was swimming.

"Here, in New Orleans," said Jules. "It turns out Petra's had one for the last seventeen years. And then this summer, Daedalus and I found the other. Quite by chance."

Ouida frowned, thinking. "I saw Clio, when she was a little girl. But she wasn't a twin."

"Turns out she was," Jules said. "Petra had divided them and hidden one."

"To prevent this from happening." Ouida understood immediately.

"Yes," Daedalus admitted. "But it isn't only Petra's decision. It affects all of us. It's something we've always wanted."

"Ouida."

Ouida turned to see the voice's owner. Her eyes met Richard's intensely, and for a moment everything was quiet. Then she rose and went to him. Ouida was barely five feet two, and her head fit neatly into Richard's shoulder. They hugged for a long time, until Richard drew back and smiled at her. "How was your flight?"

"It sucked," she said, smiling back. He knew she hated flying. She looked at his pierced eyebrow—that was new. He could get away with something like that, where it would look ridiculous on Jules or Daedalus. "You look very—young," she said, and he laughed.

"Love you, babe," he said and went to pour himself a drink.

"So, these twins theoretically complete the thirteen," Ouida said, sitting back down. "But what about the actual rest of the Treize?"

"Petra is here, of course," said Daedalus, his eyes on Richard as he went to sit next to Ouida. "We haven't hashed out all the details—and I for one feel that she owes us a serious accounting of why she took matters into her own hands. Not telling us? Hiding a twin? She's done us all a great disservice. At best. But she's still one of us in the end, and I assume she won't let us down. Sophie and Manon are arriving tomorrow, I believe. Everyone is coming."

Ouida looked at Daedalus knowingly. He was assuming a lot, and not only about Petra. "Everyone?" she questioned.

Daedalus shrugged. "We might have a few hitches. But everyone will be here soon."

Richard put his head back and tossed a pecan in the air, catching it expertly in his mouth. "Yeah. A few hitches. That's one way to put it."

"Claire?" Ouida asked, and Daedalus's face gave her the answer. "And . . . Marcel?"

Daedalus made an impatient gesture. "They will come."

Richard met Ouida's eye. Clearly he was skeptical that Daedalus could get the last two members here. Ouida suddenly felt very tired. She leaned back against the heavy silk upholstery. "It isn't just the Treize," she said. "There are so many other factors."

"All of which we've been working on," Daedalus said smoothly. "Everything is well under control. It could even happen by *Récolte*. But more likely by *Monvoile*."

Ouida found this all so hard to believe. After all this time, was this even what they wanted? Clearly Daedalus did. And Jules. But Richard? She looked at his young face. He looked back at her, and she found it hard to read his expression.

Abruptly she got up and put her glass on the table. "Well, this was certainly unexpected," she said. "It's a lot to think about. Right now I'm going to my B & B to sleep for a day."

Daedalus's eyes followed her. "Certainly, my dear. Rest. I know this is a lot to take in. Jules and I have had several months to absorb its implications. I know we'll be able to count on you when the time comes."

Ouida looked at him and didn't reply. She picked up her purse and walked to the door. "I'll be in touch." She let herself out, feeling three pairs of speculative eyes on her back.

✦ Chapter Twenty-Four

Salvation Being Snatched Away

SLEEP ELUDED HIM. MARCEL TURNED restlessly on his pallet, its straw rustling with every movement. In truth, he dreaded sleep. In his sleep he was prey to dreams. Awake, he was prey to Daedalus. Today he had served as an acolyte at mass. As he'd lit the tall altar candle, young Sean, sent up from the village to assist here and there, had turned to him and said, "Come to New Orleans." Startled, Marcel had almost dropped his tall taper. He'd seen the blankness in Sean's eyes and realized the boy had no memory of having spoken.

So waking hours were unbearably tense. And sleep—the dreams that twisted through his mind, making him wake sobbing, tears running down his face—

Death would be such a sweet release.

If only, if only . . .

The small cell he'd occupied for the last five years had become such a refuge for him. He'd almost become hopeful, as his days blended one into another, the seasons flowing through his hands like rain. He worked hard, studied hard, prayed with the fervor of the converted. And now, after everything, it was being taken away from him. His hope, his peace, his possible salvation, all being snatched away by Daedalus. And for what?

Marcel turned again, his face to the stone wall. From a foot away he felt the chill wafting off the stones, and he closed his eyes. His single candle had guttered and gone out hours ago. Soon it would be time for matins, and he would have passed the brief night with no sleep. Through the one small high window, he had seen the sliver of moon arc across the sky and disappear from view.

Then it was there with no warning: Marcel was once again standing in a circle before the huge cypress tree. Melita was beginning the incantation. He could see everyone's faces: Daedalus, watchful, intrigued; Jules frightened, unable to move; Ouida curious; Manon excited, like the child she was. Himself curious, eager, yet with a dark weight on his chest: fear.

The storm, the crack of lightning. The white glow on everyone's faces, sending their features into sharp relief, like a frieze. He saw Cerise, her face young and open, her belly heavy and round. The child not due for almost two months. Then the blast of power, striking them all like a fist. His mind clasping the energy like a snake, writhing within him. The exaltation . . . the unbelievable power, the fierce, proud hunger they all felt, tasting that power. The gurgling spring, bubbling up from the ground, dark, like blood. Then the lightning flashed, and they saw it *was* blood. Cerise was holding her belly, her face twisting in pain. The blood around her ankles, Petra springing to her side, Richard's face so young and white . . .

Marcel hadn't moved, had watched everything in a stupor, still drunk with the power that flowed through him.

Cerise had died as everyone crowded around her. Everyone except him and Melita. Melita had also been reveling in the power, had glanced across at him with a supremely victorious expression. The power lit her in glory, and she felt only an exquisite joy so sharp it bordered on pain. He saw that, saw Melita's face, as her younger sister died in childbirth on the ground.

Petra had held up the bloody, wriggling infant, small and weak, but mewling, alive.

"Whose child is this?" she had called, her voice barely audible over the pouring rain that was already washing Cerise's body clean. "Whose child is this?"

No one had answered. Cerise had died without revealing the name of her child's father.

But Marcel had known.

Now, in his cell, he was jarred by the deep, pealing sound of the bells announcing matins, calling the faithful to morning prayer. It was still dark outside. Automatically, Marcel rose and walked to the chipped metal basin that stood on a rough table. He splashed icy water on his face. The water mingled with his tears and left his face flushed and tingling.

Moving as if drawn by an invisible thread, Marcel plodded silently down the dark stone hall. Time to pray for his soul, once again. To beg for mercy from the all-merciful Father.

It would do no good.

Chapter Twenty-Five

Clio

"I CAN'T BELIEVE PETRA LET YOU OUT," RACEY said under her breath. Of all my friends, Racey was the only one I'd told about the whole curse-of-the-twins thing. Everyone else just thought that Nan had somehow, tragically, lost track of Thais and her dad until now. Now we were going to be one big happy, and so on.

Ahead of us, Eugenie and Della were laughing, their high-heeled slides tapping against the sidewalk. We'd left Racey's mom's car down on Rue Burgundy—parking close to Amadeo's was impossible. It was only a few blocks, anyway.

"I'm in a group," I pointed out, giving Racey the same rationale I'd given Nan. "And I have to be back by eleven."

Racey grimaced, and I nodded glumly. "I told her I *needed* to go out and have a good time, not worry about anything," I said. "This whole thing has totally freaked me out. I can't think about it right now. But I have to be really careful, stay with you guys, yada yada yada."

Racey nodded sympathetically. "Did you get hold of André?"

I nodded. "I left a message—hope he gets it. I'm dying to see him." To put it mildly. It felt like a year since we had lain together under the oak tree in the park. That had been the last time I'd felt normal or at ease, and I was desperate to feel that way again, desperate to see the one person who made me forget about everything else that was happening.

"So Della's hot for Collier Collier," Eugenie called back over her shoulder, and Della whopped her on the shoulder.

My eyebrows rose. "The *sophomore?*"

Della looked embarrassed as Racey and I caught up with them. "He's a really hot sophomore," she defended herself. As if to change the subject, she gestured at a shortcut, a small alley that would let us skip two tourist-clogged blocks. We turned down it.

I thought about Collier Collier. "Yeah, in a young, con-tributing-to-the-delinquency-of-a-minor kind of way," I said. "He's what, fifteen? And you're going to be eighteen, when? Next week?" This alley was narrow and unlit, but I could already see the light and noise of Royal Street ahead of us.

"He's *almost* sixteen, and I won't be eighteen till next *April,*" Della said. "There's not that huge a difference. And I mean, God. He's gorgeous."

Actually, he *was* gorgeous, which was the only reason I knew the name of a sophomore.

"I noticed him last year," Della admitted. "Remember? He was almost pretty. But over the summer, he grew, like, five inches—"

"Let's hope in the right place," Eugenie murmured, and I laughed out loud.

Della whopped her again on the arm. "And he's just really, really hot."

"Plus, he's a lowly sophomore, you're a hot senior babe, and he's going to follow you around like a puppy," Racey said dryly.

"He *has* been very agreeable," Della said innocently.

"And pathetically grateful?" I asked.

"Don't know yet," Della said with a wicked smile. "But I assume so."

I was laughing again, but it suddenly choked off. Alarm flashed through me, but from what? I looked at Racey quickly, and she frowned. Then her eyes widened and she looked around—

"Gimme your wallets!" He stepped out of the shadows so fast that Eugenie squeaked and tottered on her heels. The guy had a knife and looked rough, unshaven, with torn clothes and a wild expression in his eyes. I cast my senses out—he wasn't a witch, which is why I didn't pick up on him till it was too late.

I held up my hands. "Okay, okay," I said tensely. My heart was hammering in my chest, and I felt jittery with fear.

"Shut up! Gimme your wallet, bitch!" he snarled again, looking at me, and my throat closed even as my brain kicked into high gear.

We all fumbled for our purses. Eugenie was visibly shaking and accidentally tipped hers out, so everything spilled to the ground.

"Damn it!" she hissed, sounding near tears.

"It's okay," I said again, trying to sound calm. "Just pick your stuff up, Eu. Look, I'm taking out my wallet. . . ."

Everything happened so fast after that. For no reason, the guy suddenly freaked out and tried to backhand me across the face. I managed to jump back in time, and I saw Racey make a quick motion. The guy blinked, confused for a second, and I snapped my hand out and shot a bolt of *fourjet* at him.

He reeled as if he'd been punched in the shoulder, but then his crazed, bloodshot eyes fastened on me again, and he lunged at me with his knife. The blade whipped close enough for me to feel its *swish*, but I leaped to one side and sent another bolt of *fourjet* at his knees, which promptly buckled.

Looking surprised, he dropped to his knees, and then Della snarled in rage and swung her purse at his head as hard as she could. Della carries *everything* in her purse—I'd picked it up once and said, "What do you have in here? Bricks?"

It cracked against the mugger's head just as I whispered a *sortilège d'attacher*—a binding spell—feeling grateful that Nan had made me practice them until I wept with fatigue. The mugger went over sideways, looking stunned. I flicked my wrist and knocked his knife away, then shot it over and down a drain I saw out of the corner of my eye. Racey stood over him, silently adding her spells to mine to hold him in place.

He started howling, swearing, and calling us names as he struggled futilely against the invisible bonds. Racey made a tiny gesture and then even his voice went mute. His eyes bugged out of his head in fear, and the four of us started backing away.

"What did you do, Della?" Eugenie cried.

"Maybe he's epileptic," Della said, sounding scared.

At that moment, I saw a tall, dark figure enter the alley and start running toward us.

"Guys, run!" I cried, grabbing Eugenie's arm. "He has a partner!" We turned and raced for the other end of the alley, which would take us out into the crowded light of Royal Street. We were almost out when I heard my name being called.

"Clio! Clio, wait!"

I screeched to a halt. "It's André!" I whirled and peered down the dark alley.

André ran right past the mugger, barely glancing down at him. We waited at the end of the alley, in clear view of everyone passing on the street. André caught up to us and grabbed my arms. "Are you okay? I was half a block behind you. Didn't you hear me calling you?"

"No," I said, looking past him. The mugger was still lying on the ground. I could feel his helpless rage from here. "That guy tried to mug us!"

André swore under his breath, looking angry. Della and Eugenie hadn't met him yet, and despite the shaky aftermath of almost being mugged, they were looking at him, impressed.

"I tried to catch up to you," André said. "That alley was *not* a good idea."

I saw a beat policeman strolling down the street, and I ran toward him. "Um, a guy fell down in that alley back there,"

I said, pointing. "Maybe he's having an epileptic fit." The cop hurried toward the alley, reaching for his walkie-talkie. I debated telling him that the guy had tried to mug us, but the cop was going to have a hard time dealing with the binding spell as it was. I didn't want to give an official statement or have to explain anything.

"That cop is going to go check on him," I told everyone.

"Should we file a report?" Della asked. "If I do, and my parents find out—"

"Me too," said Eugenie. "Good-bye, Quarter."

"Let's get out of here," I said. "The cop will take care of it. I just want to sit down."

We had walked quickly down half a block before I remembered to introduce Della and Eugenie to André. He gave them a smile, and I could see his magic working. Not real magick, of course—just his own personal attraction.

We turned into Amadeo's, where it was blessedly dark after the overlit street. The bouncer let André in, but wanted to card us. I sent him a *we're of age, don't worry about it* thought, and he waved us through, looking bored.

"Friend of yours?" André said, nodding at the bouncer. He knew I was still in high school.

I shrugged. "Something like that. Hey, what about you? You're what, nineteen?"

André grinned, looking dark and mysterious. "Fake ID."

We got drinks and went to the back room. A live band was going to start soon, since it was Friday, but we found a small empty couch and pulled some chairs over to it. Again, I felt that Racey was watching André, as if trying to figure him out. Then she seemed to shake off the feeling and put a smile on her face. I saw her make eye contact with a guy sitting at another table, and soon they had a flirtation going. Within minutes Della and Eugenie had drifted off to check out guys, leaving André and me alone.

"Are you all right?" he asked, getting closer and putting his arm around my shoulder. "I practically felt my heart stop when I saw you duck down that dark alley. I've only been here two months, but even I know that you never go down a dark alley in New Orleans."

A delayed reaction to the mugging suddenly came over me, and I shivered and sat as close to him as possible. "I know," I said. "We weren't thinking—we were teasing Della about something, and she just pointed to the alley and we went down it without paying attention. And I've taken that shortcut a million times—just not at night."

André pressed a kiss into my hair. "How did you get away from him? I saw him drop, and then you started running."

What would I say? Racey and I were witches, and we zapped him with spells? I didn't think so. "Della hit him with her purse," I said, smiling at the memory. "He went down like an ox. She carries, like, lead weights in her purse."

André laughed. "He's sorry he messed with you, no doubt."

I nodded, starting to feel smug about how we had dealt

with that scumbag. "He'll think twice before he picks on lone girls again."

I looked into André's eyes, and my smile faded. I could get lost in his eyes so quickly, so totally. I reached out and touched his lips softly. "I'm glad you got my message to meet us here," I said. "I missed you yesterday."

"What happened? I was hoping to see you."

I hesitated. *Oh, my whole world changed, that's all.* Suddenly, explaining everything to André—Thais, my past—it was all too much. I needed to figure out a way to tell him without mentioning all the witch stuff. Someday he could know everything. Someday soon. But not tonight. "School, and then Nan needed me at home."

"Everything okay?" he asked, smoothing my hair away from my face. His finger traced down my cheek, then my neck, past my collarbone. It dipped slightly under my lacey black camisole, and I shivered again, but not with fear.

I shrugged. "Just family stuff." *Huge, bizarre family stuff.* I spread my hands on his hard, warm shoulders and smiled flirtatiously at him. "When can we be alone?"

Sharp interest lit his eyes, and he gave me a predatory look that made butterfly wings feather lightly inside my chest. I was usually the predator with guys. Sometimes I let them pretend to be the one who pounced, but really, it was always me. Which is how I liked it.

Now, with André, I realized how exciting it was for him to come after me. He leaned in to kiss me and I smiled. I held his dark head in my hands, pulling him to me.

He pressed me back against the couch, and I wished that I was powerful enough to cross my arms and blink twice and send us somewhere else. I wanted to take his shirt off to see the hard chest pressed against me. I wanted to watch his face when he saw me naked. Our kisses were so hard and deep, and my body was melting, wanting to join with him, wanting to be as close as possible. The club faded away around me as I held him to me as tightly as I could. Dimly I heard the first opening notes of a band warming up, but mostly all I was aware of was André's heart, thudding fast against mine. Blood rushed through my veins, and every cell in my body felt more alive, more sensitive, more attuned to his body than I'd ever felt with anyone before.

I pulled my head back, feeling drugged, to see his half-closed eyes glittering over me. "What?" he muttered.

"Let's go to your apartment," I said, my voice husky. I swallowed and tried to catch my breath as my words sank into his brain. He nodded and started to sit up, pulling me with him.

"Clio!"

I blinked, still dazed, and looked over to see Racey kneeling next to the couch. She had a drink in her hand and the stem of a maraschino cherry sticking out of her mouth.

"It's quarter to eleven," she said urgently, tapping her watch.

It took a moment for her meaning to penetrate my lust-crazed consciousness. "What? Not already," I said, as if denying the knowledge would make the situation go away.

She gave me a patient look, not even glancing at André. I would have to figure out why she didn't like him. She'd never been like this before. Well, okay, she'd hated Jason Fisher, but he'd been an ass.

"It's quarter to eleven," she said slowly and distinctly, trying not to say the words *you have a curfew* in front of this hot guy. A loyal friend.

First, what would Nan do to me if I were late? Like, if I blew off getting home anywhere close to eleven? I considered it, sitting all the way up and sipping my mojito. Ordinarily, I didn't have much of a curfew. But whenever I'd ignored her occasional request to have me home at a certain hour, she hadn't been happy. Glum memories of me doing tons of housework made me frown.

And now, when she was already strung tight about the curse-of-the-twins thing? It would not be good.

"I have to go," I said abruptly and swigged the rest of my drink.

"No," André said coaxingly. His warm hand stroked my bare arm, leaving excited little ripples in its wake. "Stay. I'll drive you home later."

"I'm going to get Della and Eugenie," Racey said, standing up. "I'll be back in a moment." *To get you* was left unsaid.

I traced the vee of warm tan skin at the collar of his shirt. "I really have to go. My grandmother needs me home early tonight. I promised her."

"Call her," André said, his fingers moving on me persuasively, sending shivers down my spine. "Explain. Tell her I'll see you home safely soon. Just not now."

I sighed, and Racey returned to stand by me, all but tapping her foot.

"Are they ready?" I asked, stalling.

"They're catching a ride with Susan Saltbier," Racey said. That *she* was willing to leave early with me because she had driven was not lost on me.

I thought it all through, as André's hand curled around my waist between the bottom of my camisole and the top of my short camouflage cargo skirt.

"Maybe André could drive me home," I said slowly, as Bad Clio on my shoulder nodded eagerly.

"Maybe your grandmother could put your *head* on a *stake* in the front yard," Racey said, crossing her arms over her chest.

I bit my lip. She was right, of course. I would be *lucky* to get the stake treatment. *Do it now, before you weaken,* I told myself firmly, while Good Clio sighed with relief. Using every bit of my willpower, I left André's heat and the promise of intense pleasure and stood up.

"Really?" André said, and my knees threatened to buckle.

I nodded mutely. Leaving now went against every desire I had. Racey pulled her car keys out of her purse and let them jingle.

André stood, and I loved how tall he was, at least six inches taller than me. "I'll walk you to your car," he said, running his hand through his hair and looking bummed, but gallant.

"Oh, that's okay," Racey began, but André cut her off.

"No. You were almost mugged earlier. I'll walk you to your car." He and Racey locked eyes for a moment. Then Racey nodded with ill grace and turned on her heel.

I smiled at André and put my arm around him as we moved through the noise of the bar.

"My hero," I said and went on tiptoe to kiss him. He smiled and kissed me back, and I savored every second we had before we reached Racey's mom's car.

"Call me," he said as I got into the car. I nodded and kissed the hand that was leaning against the car door.

He smiled and made a tiny kissing motion with his lips, then turned and headed down the street, alone into the night.

I sighed. "You were right, Racey. You're my salvation. I thank you, and I grovel before your superior sense of duty."

"Damn right," Racey said and started the car.

✤ Chapter Twenty-Six

A Messy Business

"DID YOU REALLY THINK YOU COULD GET AWAY with it?" Daedalus's voice was cutting.

"Oh, Daedalus," Petra said. "Get over yourself." She ignored his look of outrage and went to the small bar. She found a bottle of spring water, then went to look out the tall French window at the people passing on the street below.

The air was heavy today, heavy and wet. She'd left Clio at home, working on her "principles of metal in magick" lesson. Clio had been only ten minutes late last night, but she was keeping a secret. Petra was sure of it. But Racey had dropped her off—so they had probably stayed together during the evening. Petra tried to control her tension. She had spoiled Clio, and now she was reaping the results. Petra was sick of secrets. Almost her entire life had been a series of secrets. After all this time, she had no idea how to live without them.

"Petra!"

Petra looked up to see Ouida coming toward her, hands outstretched. The younger woman looked a bit drawn, Petra thought. A bit tense. Well, this was a messy business.

They hugged, and Petra wondered how long it had been since they'd seen each other. Not that long, surely. Petra pulled back to look at her, smoothing her hand over the soft coffee-colored cheek. "Last time I saw you, you had cornrows and beads," Petra said, smiling.

Ouida patted her short-cropped afro. "This is easier. Wait till you see Richard."

Petra's glance was sharp. "How is he?"

Ouida nodded thoughtfully. "He's good," she said, but Petra felt her uncertainty.

The doorbell below rang, and Jules buzzed someone in. Moments later Sophie and Manon came through the door, Sophie as lovely as always, with her fair skin and large brown eyes. And Manon still had her girlish prettiness, her pale blonde curls, her dark eyes, the slender body poised on the edge of puberty.

"My dears." Petra hugged them each in turn. "Still in school?" she teased Sophie. Sophie blushed and nodded.

"Art history, this time," said Manon. "But we're going to the Riviera for *Soliver*—she's promised."

"You look beautiful, my dear," Petra told Manon tenderly. Manon and Richard would always have the hardest time, and Petra understood how intensely they wished it were different.

Manon smiled and shrugged. She moved to the small sofa and sat down, propping delicate feet on the Directoire table in front of her. Petra saw Daedalus wince.

"Well, isn't this quite the little reunion?" Richard's dry voice cut through the air. Petra turned to see him.

Ouida said cheerfully, "He's Goth now."

Petra embraced Richard, holding his tight body, feeling his tension. He held himself stiffly for a moment, then seemed to relax against his will, putting his arms around her in a brief, hard hug. When she looked into his brown eyes, she saw pain, as usual.

"You kept it from us," he said under his breath so only she could hear.

She nodded sadly. "I had to, love. I—"

"Yeah." Richard released himself and went to pour himself several fingers of whiskey over ice. *So he's drinking again.* Petra wondered how long that had been going on.

Petra looked around the room. "Where's Claire? Marcel?" Who else was missing? "And our favorite rake?" she asked dryly.

Axelle grinned, running her finger around the top of her wineglass. "He's out," she said. "Raking through the locals, no doubt."

"We can start without him," said Daedalus. "He knows all this, anyway. And Claire and Marcel are on their way. Petra— we know about the twins, obviously. We know that you kept it from all of us for seventeen years. What do you have to say for yourself?"

It was a measure of Daedalus's arrogance that he was most offended by her not telling *him*—Petra was sure that if he alone had known, he would have been content to keep the secret from the others if it suited his purpose.

"I did as I thought best," Petra said calmly. "I honored Clémence's last wish; I honored the wishes of the twins' father. And truly, all this never occurred to me—" She waved her hand, summing up Daedalus's whole scheme. "Cerise's descendants have always been my responsibility—none of you have offered to take on the burden. Why would I trouble you with these orphans, when you couldn't be bothered before?" She shrugged, sounding eminently reasonable.

"But surely you must have recognized the significance of twins!" Daedalus said coldly. "How many years ago did we start thinking about the possibility of a ritual? A ritual that all of us have wanted, at one time or another."

"Not all of us, Daedalus," said Petra. "And frankly, after I had watched Clémence bleed to death, as I had watched Cerise's other descendants bleed to death, instantly plugging her children into your grand plan never occurred to me." Petra let her voice take on an edge of steel. Daedalus was trying to extend his influence—she would draw the line of where it would stop. "I found myself with two newborn, motherless infants. Their father had no idea of Clémence's background or who I was. He was heartbroken at her death, barely able to function. He felt he could deal with only one child, if that, and begged me to take care of the other. We kept in touch for years, but gradually our letters became less and less frequent. And then he moved and left no forwarding address. I've had no idea of Thais's whereabouts for years."

Petra was aware that the others were watching this exchange back and forth like a tennis match. Some would agree with Daedalus, some with her, but above all else, each witch there was truly loyal only to him- or herself.

"All that is in the past, and the twins weren't significant much before this, anyway," Ouida said. "The question is, what's happening now?"

Daedalus moved to stand before the marble fireplace, striking a pose that Petra saw as rehearsed and theatrical. Really, did he think anyone would buy this persona? Didn't he realize that the years had stripped away all their innocence forever? None of them would ever regain a fresh perspective, ever trust anything at face value, ever truly let down their guard again. Not even Sophie or Jules, who had always been the most trusting of them all.

"What's happening now is that we're working hard to put the rite together," Daedalus said pompously. "Jules, Richard, and I. And now that you're all here, we can move more quickly, with your help."

Petra put disbelief and just a touch of scorn into her voice. "The rite? *Déesse*, Daedalus, is that still the focus of your being? Have you not branched out by now?"

Daedalus schooled his face into calm, but Petra had seen the brief flash of rage in his eyes. She wondered if anyone else had. "Of course, Petra," he said. "You're not the only one who has pursued interests and achieved goals in this life. But, yes, beneath all my business dealings, the companies I've founded, my pursuit of all of life's experiences, there has always been a strong interest in—recapturing the past, shall we say. Some of you may have let that desire go. Some of you may not agree with how urgently I feel it's necessary. But in my view, yes, the rite is imperative. I have never released that hope, never lost sight of that goal."

He's managed to make everyone else sound faithless and short-sighted, Petra acknowledged wryly. *Point for him.*

"To what end, Daedalus?" she asked, one eyebrow raised.

"To whatever end we agree on," he came back. "That's the beauty. With this one rite, we could each achieve whatever personal goals we have. But more important, we could reclaim a treasure that was lost to us long ago, one invaluable to our ancestors. It has kept this famille alive. This treasure would give us, the Treize, incalculable power—and it's rightly ours. Surely you're not truly prepared to let it go forever? Does it mean so little to you, Petra? After everything?"

Petra glanced around the room. His words had made people thoughtful, perhaps given new life to dreams that she thought had been left behind.

"This is all within reach again," he went on. "Now that we know Cerise's line has produced twins. They will make twelve and thirteen: a complete Treize. Not that they are the only consideration." He gestured to Jules and Richard. "Jules and I have been trying to pinpoint the exact location of the Source. The land itself has shifted. Richard is working on the rite.

Perhaps Sophie or Manon could help him with that. Axelle has the four cups." Axelle nodded. "Ouida has the vial of water." Daedalus deliberately met Petra's eyes. "And you have the twins. It's all coming together."

"So I assume the twins are safe, then?" Petra said sternly. "No harm will come to them from any of you?"

"Of course not," Ouida said, shocked, but Ouida hadn't been the one Petra was talking to.

"The girls are quite safe," Daedalus said with a frown. "We do, after all, need them."

Petra nodded, not meeting anyone's eyes. Inside her a feeling was rising that she recognized as panic. Ruthlessly she shut it down. *Not time yet to panic,* she told herself. After all, Claire was so unreliable, and she never could stand Daedalus. And then Marcel—Marcel would be a tough nut to crack. No. There was no reason to panic. Not yet. And before the time to panic came, she would have come up with a plan to save the twins, to keep them from being used in this way, in a rite that would surely kill one of them.

Chapter Twenty-Seven

Thais

"I WAS AFRAID YOU WOULDN'T COME BACK," Luc said, not looking at me.

We were headed to the levee of the river—broad steps led to a sort of boardwalk. When I'd gone to the garden earlier, he'd been waiting for me, leaning back against the vine-covered wall, his eyes closed. When I'd gotten close to him, his breathing looked so deep and regular that I'd wondered if he was asleep. But then his eyes had slowly opened, had met mine. He hadn't smiled, but I'd felt an alertness come over his body as I approached.

I'd sat down next to him, not touching him, not saying anything.

At last he'd stood, held out one hand, and said, "Come."

I'd had no idea where he was leading me, and I didn't care. Now we were getting close to the river. I could smell the water and hear the tugboats moving barges downstream.

We walked up the steps and all the way down the board-walk, avoiding tourists taking pictures of each other in front of the mighty Mississippi. Luc led me to where the levee was just shorn grass and crushed oyster shells. Still we walked on, until we were far away from anyone else. The French Quarter was at our backs, the river spread before us, almost a mile across. We sat cross-legged on the grass, not touching, not talking, and watched the afternoon pass by.

It was dusk before he spoke. "I was afraid you wouldn't come back." He pulled a long piece of grass out of the ground and started stripping it methodically.

"You knew I'd come back."

He turned to me then, his eyes the exact color of the darkening sky. Reaching out, he took my hand, twining our fingers together. "You're the most restful person I've ever known," he said quietly. "You have a . . . serenity, an ability to just be, without wanting anything, without needing anything. It's . . . remarkable. I actually feel almost peaceful when I'm with you." He gave a short laugh. "If you knew me better, you'd understand how amazing that is."

I felt the same way about him. "Luc," I said. A question had been on my mind since the evening he'd kissed me in the garden, stunning me to the bottom of my soul. Nothing that had happened since then detracted from how deeply he'd touched me. "What is it that *you* want from me, and what is it that you're offering me?"

His eyes seemed to grow darker, or maybe it just looked that way. A thick cloud cover had been moving over us, like God pulling a bedspread into place.

"I'm not mocking you," I said. "I really want to know."

"I know." His fingers stroked my hand while he thought. "If you'd asked me that several days ago, I would have had one answer. Now, I don't know."

I smiled, curious. "What would you have answered?"

He gave me a mischievous look that was devastating on his handsome face. "I would have said, I wanted to get into your pants, and I was offering you a chance to get into mine."

I snatched my hand back. "Luc!"

He laughed, and I wanted to kiss him, hard. I blinked with surprise at that thought—not my usual kind of thing. But I felt fierce about him, as if I wanted to mark him as mine. I blushed, and Luc misunderstood.

"Have I shocked you?" he teased. "Surely you've lost count of how many guys have said that to you?"

I answered him seriously. "No, not really. I mean, people always knew that I'd say no, so they kind of quit asking."

He went still, his eyes searching my face. I realized what information I had just given up, and I groaned to myself, mortified. *Oh, God, Thais, just tell him every embarrassing thing you can think of.*

"Thais." He sounded deeply shocked, and there was something else in his voice that I couldn't identify. I was smothering with embarrassment. I wanted to self-combust right there, just burst into flames and disappear into a puff of smoke.

I covered my face with my hands. "I don't want to talk about it!"

"You can't be saying—"

"I don't want to talk about it!" Without looking, I kicked him. My flip-flops had fallen off, and now he grabbed my bare foot and held it.

"Thais," Luc said, a velvet determination in his voice. He waited, as patient as time. He would sit there until I answered him.

"Thais. You're saying you've never said yes? To anyone?" He leaned closer, his voice as soothing as honey, his breath barely brushing my skin.

I gritted my teeth, pressing my covered face against my drawn-up knees, trying to make myself as small as possible— so small that I might disappear. *Good luck.*

Luc put one hand against my shoulder and one against my knee and pushed, as if I were a bear trap he was unspringing. He was much stronger than I was, and not for the first time, I regretted not having abs of steel.

Then I was on my back on the grass, and an oddly cool, rain-scented breeze blew against my heated skin. Luc pinned my legs down with one of his so I couldn't curl up again, and I could feel him pressed against my whole length.

"Why do you want to know?" I choked out, pointlessly stalling for time—there was no way to recover from this.

"Oh, I'm very interested, Thais," he said against my ear. "I'm very, very interested."

I wanted to die. I wanted him to kiss me. I wanted . . .

Again Luc waited—he had all night, wasn't going anywhere.

I had no idea what time it was or when Axelle would be back. She'd left shortly after lunch and hadn't exactly clued me in on her plans. I felt a raindrop hit my forehead. Time was running out.

"Well, if you must know," I said in a muffled, ill-tempered voice. "Then no, I haven't said yes. There, are you happy?"

I could feel him smile. He pressed his lips against my hands where they covered my face, kissing each finger.

"Not yet," he said teasingly, and I groaned and took my hands away to glare at him.

But his face, when he looked down at me, turned serious. "Why are you ashamed? It's a beautiful thing to save yourself. To not squander your beauty, your gifts, on pimple-faced, stupid boys who won't value you."

He sounded positively medieval, and I looked at him, puzzled.

"I didn't mean to embarrass you," he said, smoothing my hair away. The one drop I'd felt had presaged a fine, warm rain as gentle as a breeze—hardly more than a mist. It formed tiny, tiny diamonds on Luc's hair and gave his skin a beautiful sheen in the darkness. "I'm just surprised. It's hard to believe that someone as beautiful as you has escaped the pressure of giving yourself away."

"I got pressured," I said wryly, remembering a night when Chad's predecessor, Travis Gammel, had actually kicked me out of his car and made me walk home at *night* because I wouldn't sleep with him. Bastard. I was still mad about it.

"What stopped you?" Luc asked softly. "And don't tell me you never wanted to. I can feel passion flowing under your skin. You're made of desire."

Luc had a way of saying flowery things that sounded completely natural and sincere. Out of anyone else's mouth they would have sounded stupid or artificial. And he was right. I had wanted to. Sometimes so much that I had felt almost crazy. But never enough to actually go ahead and do it. Now I shrugged. "Never met the right guy," I said.

One dark eyebrow rose, giving me a perfect opportunity to say, "Until you." But I didn't—couldn't. After a moment, Luc leaned over and brushed light kisses along my jawbone, making my eyes drift shut and my bones go limp.

"I guess you've said yes to millions of girls," I said and then swallowed as an unexpected shaft of poisonous jealousy pierced me so sharply I almost gasped. The thought of him with anyone else made me feel like crying. For a long moment he looked into my eyes, and then he sat up, leaving me cold.

I realized our clothes were soaking wet from the light rain and felt many tiny drops come together to roll as one down my neck. Luc's shirt was translucent, sticking to his skin. I felt humiliated, gauche, like some stupid high school girl. Which I was, of course.

He turned back to me, a look of gentle regret on his face.

"Not millions," he said, sounding almost sad. "But—a lot. And until now, I never wished it were different. But you, Thais—" He leaned back down on one elbow next to me. "For the first time, I wish that I could have no memory of anyone but you."

I burst into tears, in that suave woman-of-the-world way I have. In that moment I knew I loved him, and even more frightening, I felt he loved me. Then he was kissing me, kissing the tears in my eyes, my rain-washed face, my mouth. I smoothed my hands over his wet shirt, feeling the heat of his skin through the cloth. Our legs were tangled together, and for the first time in my life, no alarms went off in my head, no warnings told me to get myself out of there. In my mind, there was a peaceful silence, an acceptance. The warm, gentle rain drifted down on us, making me feel invisible, private, elemental.

A line from an old song floated into my consciousness, and if I had been a real witch, I would have let it float over to Luc, all raw emotion and timeless melody. It went: *I'm all for you, body and soul.*

Chapter Twenty-Eight

Clio

I YAWNED AND STRETCHED, SMILING AS I relived some of last night's dreams. I had dreamed about André, how he looked as he came down to kiss me. I could practically feel him in my arms, feel his weight and his strength. He was perfection. It had killed me to have to leave him Friday night. Maybe today I could get away, and we could take up where we had left off.

But first, breakfast. I could smell coffee—excellent. I rolled out of bed and headed out onto the landing. Nan's bedroom was separated from mine by a short hall that led to the one upstairs bathroom. Our house is called a camelback shotgun: You could stand in the front door and shoot a gun, and the bullet could go out the back door without hitting anything in the four rooms in between. And it was a camelback because we had only two rooms upstairs to the four rooms below. The only-two-bedrooms factor was one of the main reasons I hated the idea of Thais coming to live here.

I had others.

Glancing into Nan's bedroom, I saw her standing at the foot of her bed. She was completely dressed, which was unusual: Sunday was our traditional laze-around, get-a-slow-start day. I wandered in, then stopped in surprise.

Nan was packing a suitcase that lay open on her bed. Q-tip was trying to climb into it—prime napping territory—and Nan lifted him out.

"Good morning, dear," she said briskly, barely glancing at me.

"What are you doing?"

"Packing. There's coffee made, downstairs, but you're on your own for breakfast."

"Why are you packing? Are we going somewhere?" A nervous flutter started in the pit of my stomach. Nan had been acting oddly since right before we'd found out about Thais.

"Not you—just me," she said, folding an Indian cotton top. She lifted Q-tip out of the suitcase again and packed it.

"What's going *on*?"

Nan's calm blue-gray eyes regarded me. "I need to go away for a while. I'm not sure how long. While I'm gone, you need to be extra careful, completely on guard. Don't trust anything or anyone. If anyone gives you a message they say came from me, don't believe them. If I need to contact you, I'll do it directly."

My mouth dropped open. "Where are you going? What's happening?"

"I need to take care of some things," she said. I saw that she had gathered some spell-craft supplies—crystals, small candles, some essential oils, her copper bracelets. These she now put into a purple velvet bag and pulled the drawstring.

"Tomorrow is Monday," she said. "I expect you to go to school this week, complete the metal-study course we began, and to go to your tutoring session with Melysa Hawkcraft next Wednesday afternoon."

"You won't be back by *Wednesday*?"

"I'm not sure," she said. "I hope so, but I'm not sure. However, if I'm not back by next Thursday, I've left a letter for you in the cupboard in the workroom." She gave me a wry, knowing smile. "Don't bother trying to open it before next Thursday. It's spelled—you won't be able to. But come next Thursday, if I'm not back, you'll read it and follow the instructions inside. Understand?"

"Yeah, I guess," I said uncertainly. I hadn't told Nan about getting a knife pulled on me the other night—I didn't want her to say I couldn't go out at night with my friends or something. But now the fear of that night rushed back with all of Nan's cryptic warnings and instructions. I didn't want her to go like this.

Except. I would have the house to myself.

André could come over. Scared is one thing I wouldn't be feeling if he were here.

Nan came over and put her hands on my shoulders. Looking deeply into my eyes, she said, "You'll be okay, Clio. You're seventeen, and the house is spelled with layers of protection.

Just watch yourself, refresh the spells every night before you go to bed, and everything will be fine." She put her head to one side, considering. "Do you want me to ask Racey's parents if you can stay over there for a few days?"

"Let me try staying on my own," I said. "If I get too freaked out, I'll go to Racey's."

"Okay." Nan hefted Q-tip out one last time and closed her suitcase. I followed her downstairs, still in my nightgown, feeling a rising excitement. I would have the whole house to myself! The situation was clouded by worry about what Nan was going to "take care of," but still.

At the front door, Nan put down her suitcase, and we hugged. I had a sudden unreasonable fear that this would be the last time I saw her, or hugged her; that from this moment on I was on my own. Sappy tears sprang to my eyes, and I blinked them back. Everything was fine—Nan said so. I would be fine, she would come back. I would have a fun little free holiday. Then she would return, and our lives would go on as they were before.

I was sure of it.

· · ·

"Well, *that's* bizarre," Racey said, frowning. She'd met me at Botanika after lunch. The morning, after Nan had left, had stretched out surprisingly long and quiet. I'd called Racey and left a message for André. He never answered his phone, it seemed. "And she didn't tell you where she was going, or for what?"

"Nope. She was going out of town, not just off to a job or

something." In Nan's work as a midwife, she had been gone overnight before, but just in the city. "It was weird, a bit alarming, and yet—not without possibilities." I gave Racey a meaningful look.

Her eyebrows rose. "Like what?" she asked, her tone hopeful.

"A *party*, for starters," I said. "Muchas fiestas. All manner of merriment." I waved my hand expansively. "Blender drinks. Fun magick, depending on who we invite. Unbridled teenage mayhem."

Racey's face lit up as various possibilities bloomed in her mind. "Sweet! How many people do you want to invite?"

"Enough to make it fun. Not so many that the neighbors will call the cops."

"Okay. Let's make a list," said Racey, pulling a pen out of her purse. I grinned. Racey was always very big on lists.

"The usual suspects, I assume," she said, busily writing. "And guys. I'll ask Della and Kris and Eugenie for ideas."

"Good. And let's make margaritas," I said. "And oh! Get this! I'll do a dampening spell around the house, so people outside can't hear the noise from inside! Then we can have loud music!"

"Brilliant," Racey said admiringly, writing it down. "And food?"

Just then my macramé purse started wriggling on the table. Racey glanced up. "Your purse is ringing," she said briefly while I dug for my phone.

Its small screen said *unlisted number*. I clicked the answer button.

"Hello?"

"Hey, babe." André's voice made my skin tingle. "I got your message. What's up? Do you think you can see me today?"

"Oh, *yeah*," I said with feeling. Smiling hugely, I leaned back in my chair and tried to ignore how Racey's face had assumed a look of careful neutrality. "I can see a *lot* of you. In fact, I'm giving a party tonight—just you, me, and forty of my closest friends. Can you come?"

"At your house?" André sounded surprised—I'd never invited him over before.

"Yep." I gave him the address and directions on how to get there. Uptown isn't built on a grid—the streets follow the curve of the river. "Like, at nine? And maybe you can stay and help, after everyone else has gone." I was practically quivering with anticipation.

"Help with what?" André sounded wary.

I shrugged. "Anything that needs doing. After all, with my grandmother out of town, I'll be on my own. I'll need all the help I can get."

I could almost feel his interest quickening, over the phone. "Your grandmother's out of town?" he asked. "Since when?"

"Since this morning. I didn't even know about it till I saw her packing. She'll be gone several days, at least." For right now, I put away all my unease about when she was coming back. I would deal with it when the time came.

André was silent for a minute. "So you're saying that your grandmother is out of town, leaving you alone in the house."

"Uh-huh." I took a sip of my drink, careful not to make slurping noises into the phone.

"And you, being the good granddaughter who gets home on time because you promised, are immediately seizing this opportunity to raise hell."

I considered. "Pretty much, yeah."

"And tell me if I'm getting your meaning correctly, little Clio," said André's dark, delicious voice, "but are you suggesting that I stay with you after everyone has left to, um, help you with . . . something?"

I could hardly breathe. The minute the front door closed after the last person, I was going to rip his clothes off. "That's right," I managed to get out.

"Well, well, well," he said, his tone making my heart beat faster. "That sounds like a very good idea. I would love to stay later and help you—with anything you want."

With great self-control I avoided whimpering. "Terrific," I said, trying to sound together. "Anytime after nine."

"Can I bring anything? Besides myself?"

"Um, let's see." I thought quickly, glancing at Racey's list. "Can you bring some tequila? For the margaritas?"

"It will be my pleasure."

My eyes shut slowly and I swallowed. "Okay," I said, barely able to speak. "See you then." I clicked off my phone and took some deep breaths, as if recovering from running.

Racey was watching me shrewdly from across the table. "Don't tell me," she said. "Let me guess. He is, by some *miracle*, going to take you up on your offer."

I regarded my best friend. "How come you don't like him?" There, it was out in the open.

Racey looked taken aback. "I never said I didn't like him. It's just—you're moving awful fast. You don't really know him."

"That's never stopped us before," I pointed out. Since we were fifteen, Racey and I had been wrapping the lesser sex around our pinkies. This was the first time she had encouraged me to put on the brakes. "What is it?"

Racey shifted her weight in her seat, looking uncomfortable. "I don't know," she admitted. "He's different somehow than all the others."

"*Yeah,*" I said. "Absolutely."

Racey still looked hesitant. "I don't know what it is. He just makes me feel—cautious."

I looked at her speculatively. Did Racey have the hots for André? I didn't think so. I'd be able to pick up on it if she did. Well, they just didn't click for some reason. I wasn't going to worry about it.

"Okay," I said, switching into party mode. "Show me your list. We gotta hit the store."

✦ Chapter Twenty-Nine

Thais

"DAMN IT! *DAMN IT!* WHERE THE *HELL* ARE they?" *Crash.*

As a way to wake up, this was worse than an alarm clock, but better than having a bucket of cold water dumped on my head. Next to me, Minou yawned and looked offended. I blinked groggily at my clock. Ten a.m. Another restless night had led me to sleep in.

But what was Axelle doing up so suspiciously early?

"They were right *here!*" she shrieked from the living room.

I pulled on some gym shorts and cautiously made my way out to the main room. Axelle had torn the place apart—sofa cushions on the floor, a table overturned, the basket of kindling by the fireplace knocked over. Newspapers, magazines, and clothes were strewn everywhere.

In short, the place was even more a wreck than usual, and guess who was the only person who would care enough to clean it up?

Still shouting, Axelle picked up my French-English

dictionary and heaved it across the room. It smacked the opposite wall with force, which showed me that the door to the secret room was wide open, as if the search had started up there and spilled over into the secular area of the apartment.

"Hey!" I cried, hurrying over to get the book. "That's mine!"

Axelle looked up at me, wild-eyed. I'd never seen her so wiggy—usually she lived at a slinky, feline saunter, summoning energy only to decide what shoes went with which purse. But now she looked as if she'd been up for hours, and even her characteristic silky, shiny black bob was totally mussed.

"What's wrong?" I asked. "What are you looking for?"

"My cups!" she shrieked, grabbing handfuls of her hair, as if to keep a tenuous grip on her sanity. "Family heirlooms!"

I looked around, trying to remember if I'd seen anything like that. "Were they silver, or crystal, or what?"

"They were *wood!*" Axelle cried, distraught. "Carved cypress! They're invaluable! I mean, for personal reasons! This is a *disaster!*"

"Wooden cups?" I felt a sense of dread come over me. "How many?" I already knew.

"Four!" Axelle cried, looking near tears. "Four wooden cups!" Then she seemed to catch something in my voice and looked up, her black eyes locking on me like a laser. "Why? Have you seen them? Four wooden cups?"

"Uh—" I froze like a frightened rabbit.

Axelle's eyes narrowed, and then she rushed past me, into

my room. I saw my pillow fly out into the hall, heard her sweep all my stuff off my desk. Minou raced out of my room and disappeared. I gritted my teeth, and then Axelle tore into my small bathroom.

Her howl was a mixture of relief, rage, and triumph.

Head bowed, dreading the inevitable, I shuffled toward the bathroom. Axelle was holding her carved wooden cups—the cups that had seemed so old and battered I was sure no one would miss them from the living-room armoire. Her face was a mixture of strong emotions as she stared at the one that held cotton swabs, the one that held cotton balls. . . .

When she spoke, her voice was low and trembling. "These four cups are the most valuable things you'll ever see in your whole life. If you had ruined them—"

There was nothing I could say. I hadn't known. If they were so valuable, why weren't they upstairs in the locked room? I mean, they weren't much to look at—just four old wooden cups.

With great effort, Axelle seemed to get herself under control. "From now on, ask if you borrow anything of mine."

This was much more reasonable than she usually was, and I nodded, embarrassed. She swept out of the bathroom, having dumped the cups' contents onto the floor, and then I heard her head upstairs.

I sank down onto the closed toilet lid, my head in my hands. What a way to start a Sunday. I needed to get out of here. After all the emotion last night with Luc, I felt self-conscious about going to the garden to find him, like I needed to give us both a little time and space. I was also still burning to see Clio and Petra, get some more questions answered, spend time with them. I got up and headed for the phone.

❧ Chapter Thirty

Clio

"BUT WHERE DOES THE MAGICK COME FROM?"

I tried to summon up patience—never my strong point. When Racey and I had gotten home, there'd been a message from Thais, wanting to come over. Well, we were having a party, the more the merrier, and after all, she was my sister.

We'd gotten in a pizza for dinner, and she'd started asking about magick.

To hide my resigned sigh, I got up and went to the fridge. "Want a beer?"

Thais paused in mid-bite. "But—we're only seventeen," she said, her mouth full.

I looked at her blankly. "And? . . ."

"Oh. No thanks," she mumbled, and I could swear a faint pink tinge flushed her cheeks.

Racey and I exchanged a look over Thais's head. I sat back down, and Racey and I popped the tops on our bottles. This was like a science experiment: The whole nature versus nurture thing. Thais had grown up with our dad, who, even though I so wished I could have met him, seemed to have raised her to be a straight-arrow weenie. Then there was me. Even though Nan was strict about some things, she was pretty cool about others, and I had grown up blessedly free of most hang-ups and willing to experience life to the fullest.

"But where does the magick come from?" Thais asked again.

"Everything," Racey said. Q-tip jumped up on the table, and she gave him a piece of her pizza cheese.

"Like Nan said, there's a bit of power, or energy, or magick, in everything in the natural world," I said. "In rocks, trees, water, the earth itself. The art and craft of magick is all about learning to tap into that power."

"For what?" Thais asked. "Can I have some iced tea?"

"In the fridge," I told her. "For *what?* Because you *can.* Using magick ties you into the earth, into nature, more powerfully than anything else. It's incredible."

"It's also useful," Racey pointed out. "Magick can help us make decisions, figure things out. Or for healing, fixing things. Or people."

"Hmm." Thais poured herself some iced tea, looking thoughtful.

"Look, I'll show you," I said, taking my plate to the sink.

"I think I'll run out and get some last-minute stuff," said Racey, getting up. "And I'll swing by my house and get some more CDs."

"Good idea," I said.

Thais looked hesitant—she'd been spooked the last time, when I'd rearranged the salt, which I had thought was so funny. But magick was one of those things that was better to experience than to hear about.

"Come on," I said briskly, looking at the clock. "We have a little bit of time before we have to get ready for the party."

Our workroom was bare except for the wooden altar and bookcases. A small cupboard stood beneath the window. I took out a piece of chalk and our four pewter rite cups. They'd been made for Nan by a friend of hers and had zodiac symbols around the edges.

First I drew most of a circle on the wooden floor, but left it open. Then I got the four cups ready. "These four cups will represent the four elements," I explained.

"Four cups," said Thais in an "ohhhh" kind of way.

"What?" I asked.

"Axelle has four cups too," she said briefly, and I nodded.

"Well, she's a witch. Now, this one in the north position is for water, or *l'eau*. In the south, this cup holds a candle." I lit it. "Which stands for fire, or *le feu*. This incense, with its trail of smoke, represents air, or as we say in French, *l'air*." I grinned and looked over at Thais. She still looked wary, as if deciding whether she should bolt now before the naughty magick got her.

I kept on. This stuff was all so familiar and basic: *Bonne Magie's* ABCs. "And lastly, this cup holds literal dirt to represent *la terre,* but it could also be sand, pebbles, stuff like that. Now, step into the circle."

Thais stepped in, and I drew the circle closed. Q-tip wandered into the room and sat right outside the circle. He never crossed a circle line.

"Okay, now it's closed, and you can't break it until we open it again. I'm going to lead you through a basic visualization exercise," I explained. Nan had first started doing this with me when I was three years old. "Don't worry, you're not going to freak out and start tripping. Here, sit down across from me."

I set a white candle between us and gave Thais a box of matches. "Conjure fire. Just strike the match as normal, but say—" I did a quick translation in my head, rather than start trying to teach Thais old French. "—Fire, fire, hot and light, help me have the second sight." I was pleased with myself for making it rhyme.

Thais murmured the words and struck the match as if she thought it would explode. It went out before the candle caught. She did it again and lit the candle, and then I took her hands in mine.

"Now, we both just look at the candle and sort of let our minds go," I said. "And magick will show us what we need to see."

"Is this like self-hypnosis?" Thais asked.

"Well, with self-hypnosis you're putting yourself into kind of a magickal state," I said. "You're releasing outside influences and concentrating on your inner knowledge, your subconscious. It's your subconscious that's attuned to magick."

"Oh."

"Just let your boundaries dissolve," I told Thais in a soft, slow voice. "Become one with the fire, with me, with your surroundings. Open your mind to anything and everything. Trust *la magie* to show you what you need to know. Focus on your breathing, slowing it down, making it shallow and smooth, so you can hardly feel it."

It was interesting—when you're little and learning this, you often practice in front of a mirror. I'd spent countless hours in front of a mirror with a candle, working on being able to sink quickly and easily into the trance state that makes magick possible. Looking at Thais, holding her hands, it was eerily like those days, only this time Thais was the mirror.

I felt myself sinking and drew Thais along with me. This was working well, despite the slight distance I felt because I'd drunk half a beer. I really had to remember the negative effect alcohol had on magick. It was a bummer.

Then, with no warning, Thais and I were standing in a *cyprière*—a swamp. It happened suddenly and abruptly, which is not usually how a vision works. And this was utterly complete—there was no sign of my workroom. I started to get a bad feeling.

Thais looked at me, startled, and I tried not to let her see my concern. "This is a swamp," I whispered, figuring they didn't have too many back in Connecticut. It was dark all around us, nighttime, and I felt a heavy, oppressive weight in the air.

Thais nodded, not looking thrilled. "I've been in a swamp," she said.

Then we saw a group of witches through the trees. Thais gripped my hand, and I realized we hadn't let go of each other.

With dismay I recognized the huge cypress tree and the dark water bubbling up between its roots from my vision with Nan. *Déesse.* No way did I want to go through this again, and no way did I want this to be Thais's first experience with visions.

I literally backed away from the tree, starting to murmur words that would take us out of here. Nothing happened. I said the words again, sure I was remembering correctly, but still nothing happened.

"Who are they? What are they doing?" Thais whispered.

I didn't know. "I'm trying to get us out of here," I said in a low voice, as if speaking loudly would draw attention to us. The witches, all wearing long robes of different colors, some with hoods, started moving *dalmonde*, clockwise, in a circle before the tree. We heard a faint humming sound, their chanting, but I couldn't make out any words.

Thais's face was white and scared.

Before, Nan had pulled me out of my bad vision. But no one was waiting for us back at the workroom.

Boom! A burst of light and a huge shockwave of sound almost lifted us off our feet. Thais and I gripped each other's arms, our hair practically on end from electricity. I saw the circle of witches glowing as the energy entered them, saw their backs arch with either ecstasy or pain, their hands outstretched.

One of the witches was laughing—I think it was a woman.

We saw another witch grab her stomach and fall to the ground. Two other witches bent over her, and even through the storm, the pouring rain that drenched us, we could hear her wails.

"Get us out of here!" Thais cried.

"I'm trying!" I told her and repeated the words that *should* have pulled us right back to reality.

Time seemed to speed up. We could see everything more clearly, though we weren't too close. The witch on the ground gave birth—another witch helped the baby out, and the rain started washing it clean. It was tiny and hardly moving. Then the baby's mother sank back on the black, wet ground, her face pale and bloodless, her eyes open. Even from here we could tell she had died. The rest of the coven seemed horrified and shocked, except for the witch who was still in the throes of enjoying her surge of power.

Just like in my vision, blood was seeping into the same ground as the spring burbling up through the tree roots. I had no idea what any of this meant.

"What's that?" Thais asked, trembling, and I heard a slow bell ringing, sort of a drone.

"I don't know," I said.

A woman picked the baby up and held it. The baby cried with a high, thin, kitteny sound, and I heard the bell peal again. I frowned at Thais, and she shook her head—she had no idea what it was either.

"It's the doorbell!" I cried, just as the hood of the witch fell back. A flash of lightning lit her face, the baby, the whole circle, and the ground red with blood. In the next instant, Thais and I were blinking at each other across the lit candle in the middle of the floor. Our hands were white-knuckled, numb from clutching each other so tightly.

The doorbell rang again. Feeling shaky, I blew out the candle and stood up, quickly dismantling the circle. Thais went to open the door, moving slowly.

"Yo! Party!" Racey yelled, holding bottles above her head. A crowd of people swarmed in after her, someone put a CD into the stereo, and instantly the house was filled with noise and light and people. Q-tip raced out the front door between their legs and escaped into the night. Smart cat. I glanced at my watch—it was past nine. I was horrified, shaken, and wanted only to go sit down somewhere and process what we'd just seen. Thais looked ill and uncomfortable. But we didn't have much choice right now.

Just as Thais was closing the door, it pushed open again, and more people came in. She gave them brief, uncomfortable smiles as they all began to say hi, realized it was her, and then headed on, looking for me.

"Hi! Hi!" I said, trying to sound enthusiastic, feeling like I'd rather be anywhere but here. Fortunately, Racey was in the kitchen, already making blender drinks. Collier Collier came in with a twenty-pound bag of ice on his shoulder. I saw Della head for him, and I smiled and winked at her, feeling odd and numb. With an unhappy glance at me, Thais headed for the dining room, where Eugenie and Kris were starting to rip open bags of chips.

She didn't need to say anything. We both knew what we had seen in that last second before the doorbell had pulled us home. The older witch's hood had fallen off as she held up the newborn baby. It had been Nan. And the lightning had shown us the dead mother's face: She'd had a birthmark, just like ours, a red splotch on one cheekbone.

The baby had had one too.

"Fabulous idea!" Kris said, her long blonde hair swinging as she whirled past me. "Where's your trash?"

"Kitchen," I said automatically, trying to put myself into the here and now. "But we better set one up in the dining room too."

I took a deep breath and ran a hand through my hair. I had no idea what I looked like but decided I could not look very festive. I ran upstairs, tore through my closet, and pulled on a bra-strap tank and a short black skirt. In the bathroom, my eyes looked huge and haunted, but I whipped through my makeup routine. Two minutes later I ran downstairs barefoot just as the doorbell rang again.

"I'll get it!" Miranda Hughes said, grabbing the door.

André stood in the doorway—tall, dark, and mouth-watering—and surveyed the noisy crowd inside. I smiled, full of relief and happiness that he was here: His presence would erase the trauma of the vision. He caught sight of me, and his dark eyes widened in appreciation. He held up a paper bag: the tequila.

"André!" I called, pushing through the crowd to get to him. "Everybody, this is André! André, this is everybody!"

Laughing, he swept me up into his arms, kissing me on the mouth. I sighed with pleasure and relaxed against him, so, so happy he was here, feeling safe and cared for and not alone.

"Hey, babe," he said into my ear, and a fluttery sense of delight ran down my spine.

"Hey, yourself," I said as he put me on my feet again.

Still smiling, he glanced around the room, and then suddenly, his face paled and he froze.

"What is it?" I asked. I whirled to see what he was looking at. To my surprise, Thais was standing in the dining room doorway, wearing the same thunderstruck, horrified expression that André had.

"Luc," she breathed, looking like death.

Chapter Thirty-One

Thais

"LUC?" CLIO SAID TO ME. "NO. THIS IS ANDRE, MY boyfriend. André, this is my sister, Thais."

Luc didn't say anything, just stared at me. His face looked grim and white, and tension made his body as tight as a bowstring.

I felt like I'd been hit by a car. I tried to swallow. Luc still had his arm around Clio's waist. I'd seen him kissing her, seen him pick her up and whirl her off her feet. Instantly Luc dropped his hand and stood apart from Clio, not touching her, and I saw a look of alarm come over her face.

"Luc," I said again numbly, my voice sounding broken, brittle as glass. By now people around us had started to realize that something weird and much more interesting than the party was happening, and heads were turning.

Just last night, we'd lain in the wet grass on the levee, and he'd held me while I cried and told me he wished he could have no memory of making love with anyone but me. Now I'd just seen him kiss my sister, kiss her deeply on the mouth, their hands on each other as if they knew each other very, very well.

At that moment I knew I was going to be sick. I turned and raced upstairs. I found a small bathroom and slammed the door shut in back of me. I made it to the toilet just in time, just as all the pain and horror and disbelief made my stomach turn inside out.

I don't know how long I was up there, but I had washed my face and was sitting on the floor against the tub when I realized someone was knocking on the door. If it was either Clio or Luc, I would stab them through the heart, I swore to God.

"Go away," I croaked, fresh tears starting to sting my eyes. *Stop it, idiot!* I lashed out at myself.

Still, the door opened, and Della, one of Clio's friends, came in. She wore a sympathetic look and held a can of Sprite. "Drink this," she said. "It'll help settle your stomach."

Given how much alcohol I suspected Clio and her friends put away, I figured she knew what she was talking about. I took it and sipped. It was deliciously cold, fresh, and it tasted incredible. "Thanks," I muttered, feeling more wretched than I had since my father had died.

Della leaned back against the tub next to me. "Well," she said brightly, "this is one party people won't forget any time soon."

A quick, surprised laugh escaped my throat, and I envied her so much, to be able to look at this situation in that way. "Nope," I agreed, bleak again. "What's going on downstairs?"

"World War III," Della said matter-of-factly. "Needless to say, people are slinking out the door as fast as they can, and the ones who want to stay and see the fireworks are getting herded out by Racey and Eugenie. So it appears your guy was two-timing you both."

A fresh pain stabbed me, and I almost choked on the Sprite. "It appears that way," I managed to say.

"Clio is furious—throwing things at him and trying to kick his ass out of here—but he's out front, saying he won't leave until he talks to you."

"Why?" I was flabbergasted. "I don't want to hear anything he says."

Della shrugged. "Don't blame you. Still, he says he's not leaving till he talks to you."

My jaw set as a welcome wave of fury lit inside me. "Fine," I snapped, getting to my feet. "I'll go talk to him."

As I stomped downstairs, I refused to dwell on how utterly humiliated I felt and instead seized the anger that was consuming me inside. In the dining room, Kris and Eugenie glanced up as they snapped plastic lids onto dip bowls. They took one look at my face and quickly feigned disinterest in the horrible soap opera that was playing out in front of them.

Clio was standing in her open front door, her body arched and taut as she yelled at Luc. I saw his outline in the small front yard, right before the gate. His hands were held wide, and I couldn't imagine what he could possibly be saying to defend himself.

Clio whirled when she felt my angry footsteps vibrating the floorboards. We stared at each other, taking in the other's furious expression, and for an instant a bolt of pain shot into my heart as I pictured her and Luc together.

"Get rid of him!" Clio snarled. "Before I start whipping steak knives at him."

I nodded grimly and strode past her to the open door. Clio crossed her arms and stood behind me. I didn't know if it was to lend support or to make sure he and I didn't somehow end up together.

"What do you want?" I demanded when I was close enough. My voice was thrumming with fury—I could hardly speak. Even to myself I sounded like a cornered, spitting cat, growling deep in its throat before it struck.

"Thais." Luc took a deep breath and ran a hand through his dark hair. He was frowning, his jaw set, his eyes dark with emotion.

"Clio told you to go," I bit out. "So go." I forbade myself to not look vulnerable, hurt, or heartbroken. All of which I was, of course.

Luc glanced at Clio, then stepped forward, his eyes on my face. "Thais," he said again in a low voice. "I never meant to hurt you or Clio. I never meant for this to happen."

"How could it *not!*" I exclaimed. "What were you *thinking,* you bastard?"

"Neither of you mentioned having a sister," he said. "I actually didn't know if you knew each other."

"*So what?*" I exploded. "*You* knew we were sisters! Not only sisters, but *twins*! *You* knew what you were doing! And you were lying through your teeth and using us. You even gave us different names! I don't even know your name! How long did you expect to get away with it?" I shook my head in disbelief. "I know the lies you were telling *me*," I said in a lower voice. "I don't even want to think about what you were doing with Clio."

"Maybe he was hoping for a threeway," Clio said behind me, and I winced.

"Of course I wasn't!" Luc said angrily, then he forcibly got himself under control. He looked away from me, and it made my soul hurt to see the profile I'd traced under my fingers, my lips. I felt beyond heartbroken and didn't know how I would stand the pain.

"I'm sorry, Thais," he said. "I'm very sorry that I hurt you and hurt Clio. I never meant to. Everything happened so fast—I didn't expect us all to take everything so . . . seriously."

I stared at him.

"But we did—and I took you both very seriously, in my way," he went on, his voice dark and strained. "Thais—my name *is* Luc. Luc-André Martin. I *do* live where I told you. I *have* been in New Orleans only a few months." He lowered his voice so only I could hear, his dark blue eyes focused intently on mine. "Everything I told you about how I felt about you is true. Everything I said when we were together was absolutely sincere and from my heart."

"*What?*" Clio burst out, storming past me. "So you were being sincere with *her*? What was I? *Nothing*? A *diversion*? You fricking bastard!"

"No, Clio—of course I care about you. You're beautiful, fun, and exciting. You make me forget—"

"Now you can forget about both of *us!*" I cried. "Get out of here!"

Luc looked first at Clio, then at me, and raised one hand as if to ask me for something. In his eyes I saw both regret and anger, and I hardened my heart against him.

"Thais—"

If he didn't get out of here this second, I was going to turn into a shrieking, frothing, out-of-control banshee. "You're a lying, faithless bastard," I said, speaking slowly and clearly to keep myself from breaking down. "And I'll hate you for the rest of my life." I turned on my heel and went back inside the house. Clio snapped something else at him, kind of sing-songy. Then she came in and slammed the door shut so hard that one of its stained-glass panes cracked.

She and I were both wild-eyed, breathing hard, shaking.

"I put the guard spells back on the gate," she muttered. "Took 'em off for the party."

Racey, Eugenie, Della, and Kris peeped out from the work-room. Racey took one look at us and immediately assumed a brisk, no-nonsense control.

"Into the kitchen," she said, motioning with her hand. "Come on."

I followed Clio into the kitchen and almost fell into a chair.

"I need a shot of something," Clio said faintly. "For medicinal purposes."

"No—no alcohol," said Racey firmly. "Here. Racey's private recipe. Guaranteed to help soothe frayed nerves." She poured two cups of a steaming herbal tea and set them in front of us.

Mindlessly I took my cup and drank, not caring that it was too hot. I saw Clio pass her hand over her cup, as if to feel the steam, and then she drank without wincing.

Within two minutes I felt as if someone was smoothing aloe on all the burning pain inside me, over my heart that felt wrapped in barbed wire, around my mind that felt as if acid had been dumped on it. The tea was putting out fire after fire, and I found I could almost think clearly.

"I feel better," I said, looking up at Racey. "Thanks. I'll have to get that recipe."

She smiled at me. "You'll be able to come up with one yourself soon."

I put my head in my hands. She meant if I learned magick. Which reminded me of the awful vision Clio and I'd had, right before Luc had ripped our hearts out.

This was pretty much one of the top-three worst nights of my entire life.

"I think we're going to go," said Della. "Unless you need us to stay."

Clio shook her head and drank more tea. "No," she said, her voice thin. "Thanks, guys. And thanks for cleaning up and everything."

"I'll call you tomorrow," Eugenie said. Clio gave a wan smile and nodded.

"Want me to stay?" Racey asked after the other three had left.

Clio glanced up at me and bit her lip. "That's okay," she said softly. "I guess we can take it from here. But thank you." She stood up and hugged Racey.

"Yeah, thanks for the tea and for being here," I added inadequately. Racey patted my shoulder, picked up her purse, and left.

And Clio and I were left alone.

Chapter Thirty-Two

Clio

IF I LOOKED AS BAD AS THAIS DID, I WAS seriously going downhill. Her face was pinched and bloodless, and her shiny black hair lay limply on her shoulders.

"I think I'll go too," Thais said, starting to get up. "I just want to go to bed."

"How are you going to get home?"

"Streetcar," she said, putting her teacup in the sink.

"Not this late." I shook my head. "I'll drive you home."

She looked like she wanted to refuse, but she was too sensible to. "I wish I'd never come to New Orleans!" she burst out.

That makes two of us. My skin was crawling: André had actually meant what he had said to Thais, and I had been just the good-time girl. He might even love her. *Her.*

He hadn't left until *she'd* come down and talked to him. Even out on the porch, it was *her* understanding he'd wanted, not mine. He'd kept talking to *her*, explaining to *her*. Oh, yeah, I'd been beautiful and exciting and fun. Yay for me. But he'd *cared* about *her*. I felt like I was going to shatter into sharp, bitter shards, like colored glass.

I drank my tea, trying to think about anything else. Unwanted, the image of the crying newborn popped into my mind. Why had we seen that? Why had it all been so real? Because we were doing it together?

"Who do you think that baby was, earlier?" I asked, and Thais blinked at the shift in gears.

"Uh, I don't know," she said. "I was thinking, maybe our mom? Dad told me that Mom had this same birthmark." She touched her cheekbone lightly. "He thought it was so strange that I had it too—birthmarks aren't usually inherited."

"So you think it was real, what we were seeing?"

Thais looked up, surprised. "You mean, maybe it wasn't? How do those things usually work? Do you usually see real things or just possibilities, or even stuff that never happened and couldn't happen?"

I thought. "All of the above," I decided. "But that one felt so real, more real than they usually do. Sometimes it's like watching TV, kind of, where you're still aware of your surroundings. That one was so complete. I wish Nan were here to talk about it."

"Where is she, anyway? Isn't she coming back tonight?"

Amazingly enough, it was barely ten o'clock. It felt like three in the morning.

I shook my head. "She had to go out of town for a little while. She should be back in a day or two." I hoped. Memories of how I'd planned to spend my free days—and nights—made my teeth clench.

"You're lucky," said Thais. "I wish Axelle would go out of town. For a long time." Suddenly she looked over at me. "Did you love him?" she asked in a broken voice, her face miserable.

I let out a slow breath. "No," I lied. "I was just using him. He was hot, you know? And I wanted a fling. But I'm still *really* pissed," I added.

She nodded. It was so obvious that she'd really loved him too. She sighed, and I could practically see her heart bleeding inside her. I wondered if we were linked somehow—I'd heard of twins who could finish each other's sentences and did the same things at the same time, even if they were in different cities.

"Can I go home now?" she said. "Are you sure I shouldn't take the trolley?"

"Not this late. It's not safe. Hang on and I'll get my purse. And I'm going to change." I hated this skirt, hated this top, never wanted to see them again. I headed upstairs and heard the front door open.

"I'm going to wait on the porch," Thais called. "Get some air."

"Okay," I called back. In my room I put on gym shorts and an old T-shirt and pulled my long hair back into a ponytail.

Pathetic, desperate thoughts swirled around me like dust devils. *Maybe André was still outside. Maybe they would both be gone when I got out there. Or maybe after I dropped Thais off, I would see André on the street, and he would be so miserable and tell me he had been trying not to hurt Thais's feelings. But it was me he loved* . . .

I raced out through the house and found Thais by herself on the front porch, looking up at the stars.

"It was cloudy earlier," she said, sounding as if she'd been crying. "Now it's clear."

"Yeah." There was a bitterness at the back of my throat that I couldn't swallow away. My blue Camry was parked on the street; hardly anyone has a garage in New Orleans, and not many people even had driveways.

Thais went out through our front gate while I locked the door behind me. I felt drained, totally spent and exhausted, and just wanted to get rid of Thais so I could go collapse in bed and cry without anyone seeing.

I started down the front steps, and just as I reached the front gate I heard a dull buzzing, humming sound that was growing louder with every second. I looked up at the overhead telephone and electricity wires—was something going funky? Was it music from somewhere?

"Clio!"

I snapped my head down to look at Thais, then gasped. A huge dark cloud was moving toward her fast. "Thais!" I yelled. "Get back inside the gate!"

But it was too late—the dark cloud enveloped her, and she screamed. In horror I realized it was a cloud of *wasps*, a huge, droning mass of angry wasps, and they were attacking her. In the next second I realized that this was unnatural, that wasps didn't do this. Which meant they'd been sent on purpose, to harm Thais or me or both. Rushing out the gate, I started a dispelling spell, drawing the powerful protective sign of *ailche* in the air, followed by *bay*, the sign for wind.

"Clio!" Thais shrieked, the sound muffled.

"I'm coming!" I yelled, and then I dove into the middle of the cloud and grabbed her. If I could pull her back inside the gate, the protection spells should help. Suddenly it felt like a thousand hot needles plunged into my skin, and I cried out. Thais was crying, waving her arms, lurching around, and I started pulling her back toward the gate.

I was frantic—my eyes were swelling shut, one stung me inside my ear—my entire being was a mass of burning pain. I shouted a banishing spell, and it seemed the droning let up for just a second. But then the wasps were around us again, so thickly that I couldn't even see the gate or the house. The two of us stumbled off the curb into the street—we'd gone in the wrong direction!

"Thais!" I shouted. "Give me your energy!"

"Wha—I can't!" she cried, sounding hysterical.

"Just send me your energy, your strength—any way you know!" I yelled. "Think!"

I had her by both shoulders. My hands were so swollen and numb that it felt like my skin was splitting. Everything in me wanted to scream my head off and run a hundred miles, but I forced myself to stand still and concentrate, trying to ignore the pain, ignore the burning, salty tears running down my swollen, stinging face.

"*Ailche*, protect us!" I said, crying, my tongue thick. "*Bay*, dispel this swarm! *Déesse*, aidez-nous!" I concentrated on Thais, pushing past her outer, terrified body and into her core, where her unawakened energy lay. It was familiar to me, similar to mine, and I sought out the power she didn't know she had. I joined my power to hers and repeated my banishing spell:

Force of darkness, leave us be
Your power's gone, your secret found—
My twin has given strength to me
Three times this curse on you rebound!

· · ·

My eyes were almost completely swollen shut, but my ears heard the droning lessen, and I thought I felt fewer new stinger jabs. I risked opening my eyes and saw that the swarm had in fact started to disperse, untidy clumps of wasps staggering through the air as if unsure of how they got there or what they were doing. Our feet were covered with wasp bodies.

A minute later they were all gone, and Thais and I were standing in the street. Amazingly, no neighbors had come out to see what the shouting was about, but they might have been spelled to stay indoors.

"Come on," I said, barely understandable. My tongue filled my mouth, and I knew we needed help fast—we'd both been stung hundreds of times.

Thais was shaking, sobbing, her eyes shut, her grossly bloated arms still covering her head. I took her shoulder and started towing her back to the house. In my mind, I sent one of my teachers, Melysa, an urgent help message. I couldn't talk on the phone at this point, and I didn't know how much time we had.

Before now, I'd always had Nan to help me if I was in trouble or hurt. I'd depended on her to fix everything. With her gone, I had to be the strong one, the one who saved us.

"I hate this place!" Thais sobbed thickly. "Sheets attack you here, trucks drive through streetcars, and now killer wasps! This place is a death trap!"

"Shh, shh," I said automatically, gently pulling Thais through our garden gate. I immediately felt safer. We stumbled up the porch steps, and I had a hell of a time stuffing my hand into my pocket to fish out the house key.

I was barely able to turn the key, and then I felt Melysa coming, running down the street. She lived only three blocks away—she was one of Nan's best friends, one of the top witches in our coven, and had been tutoring me in healing spells for the past year.

She burst through the gate, her full, wavy gray hair flying.

"Clio!" she exclaimed, looking at us.

I made a mumbled "uunnhhh" sound.

"Inside, inside," Melysa said, careful not to touch us.

I was starting to feel dizzy, lightheaded, and oddly cold. I couldn't think straight, couldn't explain Thais to Melysa, or even tell her what happened. My world was narrowing, growing chilly and black around the edges, and then I felt myself falling, falling in slow motion.

✦ Chapter Thirty-Three

Thais

A HEAVY WEIGHT WAS ON MY CHEST, MAKING it hard to breathe. Alarmed, I opened my eyes.

A broad white furry face was looking back at me. Q-tip.

"Jeez, kitty—you've got to take dieting seriously," I murmured, easing him off my chest. Ah. I could breathe again.

So I was at Clio's. This must have been Nan's room. I got out of bed and moved slowly to the door, feeling like I'd been hit all over with a baseball bat. Out on the landing I suddenly remembered the whole horrible night before. It had started with finding out that I had meant nothing to Luc and ended with wasps almost killing me. I glanced at my arms—I had faint pink spots all over me, hundreds of them, but they were hardly noticeable.

I looked into Clio's room. It was empty.

Downstairs I padded barefoot into the kitchen. Clio sat at the small table, her hands wrapped around a mug. When she looked up at me, her green eyes were clear and weirdly calm.

"Coffee?" she asked.

"God, yes," I said and poured myself a cup.

"Tell me again, what you said last night, about being attacked, and streetcars and stuff," she said.

"Oh my God, Axelle!" I remembered, my hand over my mouth. She was going to be furious! I'd stayed out all night—

"Melysa called her," Clio told me. "She knows where you are. It's cool. And I called us in sick this morning, to school."

School was the last thing on my mind. "Was Melysa the woman with gray hair?" I asked, barely able to remember what she looked like, only that she had been calm and kind and had taken all my pain away. *She is no doubt a witch,* I thought with resignation.

"Yeah," Clio answered. "She's one of my teachers. She's a healer, and she lives close by. So that was lucky. She left early this morning."

I sank down into a chair, shivering at the memory of the wasps. "That was very bad," I said, and Clio nodded.

"Yes. Now tell me again what you said last night. What's happened to make you think New Orleans is a death trap?" Clio pressed, calm and unstoppable. She seemed unlike herself this morning, older somehow, less offhand. Well, near death can do that to a girl.

"I had a bad dream," I said, still hating to think of it. "An incredibly realistic dream where I was in a swamp. A huge snake came and wrapped itself around me, choking me. I felt like I was dying, couldn't breathe. Somehow, I yelled, and then Axelle came in—though my door was locked—and she woke me up. My sheet was twisted into a thick rope, and it was wrapped around my neck tight enough to choke me. I had bruises for days, as if I'd been strangled." I shivered. Clio was listening intently, following every word.

"And then, on the second day of school, I was on the street-car, going to school. A teenager driving a pickup truck jumped the curb and hit a light post. It snapped off and crashed through a closed window on the streetcar—right where I'd been sitting until, like, a second before. If I hadn't moved, it could have killed me. And now the wasps. I mean, God."

Clio nodded, thoughtful.

"Why?" I said.

"A few nights ago, a mugger pulled a knife on me," she said. "He didn't even really try to rob us, me, Della, Eu, and Racey. What he really wanted to do was knife me. Me in par-ticular. And then the wasps last night. And your dream and the streetcar. I mean, suddenly it seems so clear, right? Someone's trying to kill us. Someone from Nan's old famille found out about us and has been trying to kill us because we're twins."

My stomach dropped. "You're right," I said, shocked. "That has to be it. But who? If Axelle wanted to kill me, she could have done it a long time ago. She's the one who saved me from my dream. Same with Jules and Daedalus—Axelle isn't always there. They could have gotten to me far more easily before now."

"And it's not Nan," Clio said wryly.

"Who else is there?" I asked, trying to think.

Clio shrugged. "It could be anyone from their famille.

Which could be . . . let's see—there were fifteen original families three hundred years ago. Now we have all their descendents. It could be more than a thousand people."

"Great," I said, wanting to race back to Welsford on the next plane. But they'd found me there—I wouldn't be any safer now.

"Nan isn't here to ask," Clio said. "Of course, now I wish I'd told Nan about being mugged."

"Well, I can think of one place to start," I said. "Axelle."

• • •

We found Axelle standing in the kitchen, eating cold leftover Chinese food out of its carton.

"Are you all right, then?" she asked, examining me.

"Yes," I said. "But it wasn't pretty. This is Clio."

Clio looked around the apartment—it had quite a different ambience than the comfortable, homey existence she had with Nan.

Axelle studied Clio. "Interesting," she said, and I realized that Clio and Axelle were somewhat alike in their personalities. They were both kind of showy and used to getting their own ways. Axelle was a more exaggerated version.

"We want some answers," Clio said coolly. She pulled up a chrome-and-leather barstool and sat down. Axelle looked at us both, a little smile playing around her lips.

"Such as?"

"What other members of Petra's famille are here in New Orleans?" I asked.

Axelle's glance turned speculative. "Why do you want to know?"

"Look," Clio said tightly. "We're twins. Nan has explained that we're probably setting off mass hysteria in members of her original *famille*. But there's more to it than that. We're in danger. We want to know what's going on. And you're going to tell us."

Axelle smiled wider, as if she approved of Clio's take-no-prisoners attitude. *Great,* I thought. *She can come live here with the leather queen, and I can go live with Nan.*

"Well." Axelle seemed to come to a decision. "Maybe you're right," she said. "Maybe it's time for you to be let in on the whole enchilada."

Why did this not sound like a better idea?

Axelle went into the main room and picked up the phone. "Let me make a few calls."

• • •

Half an hour later the door opened and Daedalus came in. He examined Clio, and she met his gaze calmly. Jules was with him, of course, and Richard came a few minutes after that. Axelle smugly made the introductions, as if she was enjoying presenting the Other Twin to everyone.

I saw Clio blink when she met Richard, taking in his piercings, tattoos, and oddly adult demeanor.

"Yo, babe," Richard said to me, moving into the kitchen.

There was a knock on the door, and Axelle opened it.

"Thais, Clio, this is Sophie and Manon."

Sophie was a pretty woman in her early twenties, and, oh my God, Manon was another *kid*, even younger than Richard, maybe twelve? But like Richard, she seemed older and creepily knowing, like a grown-up.

"Hello," I said, as Sophie and Manon checked us out. I saw Manon wink at Richard, and he grinned at her. Those weird kids knew so much more than I did, were much more comfortable in this world than I was. Was Manon an orphan, like Richard? Or did her parents just not care?

Richard was pouring himself an *alcoholic* drink. Mouth open in shock, I waited for someone to stop him, but though several people saw it, they didn't seem to think anything of it. Clio looked at him curiously, then held out her hand in a pinching gesture, her fingers two inches apart. Richard nodded and got down another glass. I shook my head.

"I guess I'm not in Kansas anymore," I whispered bitterly to Minou, who had jumped up on the counter.

The door opened again, and a black woman came in. Maybe four inches shorter than me, she was fine-boned, elegant, and graceful.

"This is Ouida," Axelle said, and gestured at us. Unlike everyone else, who had just stared at us like we were an exhibit, Ouida caught on to the fact that we were actually people. She crossed the room, holding out her hands.

"I'm so happy to meet you," she said in an attractive, cultivated voice and hugged Clio first. When she hugged me, I felt warm and happy. "I'm Ouida Jeffers, and I'm a good friend of . . . Petra's. Now let me see. . . ." She looked at us both, then nodded at Clio. "You're Clio, and you're Thais," she said to me. I nodded, smiling at her. She seemed blessedly normal and unweird. "I know this is all strange and confusing—maybe a little scary? I wish Petra was here today to help. But she'll be back soon."

"Where did she go?" Clio asked quickly.

Ouida patted her arm. "It will all be clear soon," she promised. "Today might be upsetting for you—but afterward, maybe we can all go out and get something to eat somewhere? I'm anxious to know you both better."

"I'd like that," I said, feeling more comfortable than I had in days.

The doorbell rang again, and Axelle yelled, "Come in!" The apartment had taken on a party atmosphere, with people getting themselves things to drink, milling around, talking. Yep, just a bunch of modern witches hanging out, schmoozing. . . . I wondered if Ouida would be interested in escaping sometime soon.

The door opened, and—

My heart pounded one last time and thudded to a halt. I saw Clio turn, then her body froze and the hand holding her glass clenched.

"Luc," Richard said casually, tossing a pecan into his mouth.

Daedalus and Jules nodded at him. Luc nodded back at them. Axelle waved at him as she talked to Sophie. Luc ran one hand through his dark hair and nodded back. He looked tense, upset.

Clio turned very slowly in her seat and met my eyes. I'm sure we wore the same sick, horrified expression: The situation that had already been as wretched and heartbreaking as it possibly could be had just gotten worse.

Luc was one of *them*.

✦ Chapter Thirty-Four

Clio

OKAY, CALL ME IMPULSIVE. IT TOOK ONLY A few seconds to process André's presence, meet Thais's eyes, and then take aim and hum my heavy glass hard at André's head. Being a *witch*, he felt it coming at the last second and managed to deflect it, just barely. It whisked by his head, splashing his shirt, and he stared at me, grimly shocked.

Instantly his eyes shifted, looking for Thais. He saw her standing behind the kitchen counter, and the new wash of pain in his eyes made my insides twist.

Of course, all conversation stopped, and the other seven witches now stared at the stupid, humiliating drama spread before them. André was a witch, and brilliant me had been so lust-crazed and in love that I had totally missed it. I'd been so swamped by my raging emotions that I'd thought the strong vibes I got from him were all sexual attraction.

My stomach dropped at my next thought. *Could it be André? Could it have been André who was trying to kill us? He'd lied about so many other things. . . .*

I sucked in a silent breath and spun on my barstool, my back to André. I met Thais's eyes, letting my feelings show, and I saw the dawning comprehension in hers. A new stunned look came over her face, and then she looked at me like, *Do you really think so?* I shrugged, then stared stonily out the small kitchen window behind Thais. I didn't know anything anymore.

"Good God, Luc, already?" Axelle's tone was both amused and irritated.

"Luc, I told you this—" the old guy, Daedalus, began, but André cut him off.

"Shut up." He sounded furious.

Thais's eyes were downcast, looking only at Axelle's black cat as she stroked it.

Richard gave a somewhat bitter-sounding laugh. "The more things change, the more they stay the same, eh, Luc?"

"Shut up!" André snapped again, and Richard made a "whatever" gesture.

I felt a soft hand on my back and tensed, ready to smack whoever it was. "I'm sorry, Clio," Ouida whispered, then sighed heavily. "I should have come back a week ago."

"It doesn't matter," I said stiffly. I turned around again and faced Axelle, who was still carrying on a silent, exasperated conversation of gestures with André.

"So are we all here?" I said, making my voice as cold as possible. "Why don't you get this show on the road? Is anyone going to tell us what the hell is going on?"

I heard Richard chuckle behind me and resisted the strong temptation to turn around and deck him.

"Yes," Axelle said. "I think it's time to initiate our newest members."

I frowned. Not exactly what I'd had in mind. "I want some answers first. Who are you?"

The older guy stepped forward. His practiced smile reminded me of a circus ringmaster. How appropriate. "We are members of the Treize," he said. His open hands encompassed everyone in the room. "As are you and your sister."

Huh. "Okay, *treize* means *thirteen* in French, so I'm guessing you're a coven. But how does my grandmother fit into all this? We already belong to a coven."

"Petra belonged to this one first," said Jules. "We don't get together very often."

"To put it mildly," said Richard under his breath.

"How are Thais and I members of this so-called coven too?" I asked.

"This coven is made up of members from the fifteen original families who founded our ancestors' settlement hundreds of years ago," Daedalus went on. "Not every family is represented, of course. But the twelve of us, plus one of your ancestors, a woman named Cerise, made up our coven. Cerise died . . . long ago, and another member disappeared and is presumed dead. So we've been only eleven for a long time. But then one of Cerise's descendents, your mother, Clémence, had twins. So you and Thais unexpectedly make a full thirteen possible again."

Eyes narrowed, I looked around at all the witches in the room, carefully avoiding André. Even seeing him hurt unbearably. There was something weird here—I mean, something even weirder than all the obvious weirdness.

Thais spoke up. "Even with us, there are still only ten people here."

"Your—Petra is out of town," said Jules. "And two other members haven't arrived yet."

"But they will," Daedalus said firmly.

"Wait a second." I held up my hand. "All of you were members of the Treize?"

Axelle nodded, shrugging, and Daedalus said, "Yes."

"And now you found out that we're twins and that we're almost ready for our rite of ascension." I was, anyway. "So we'd be useful in a coven."

"Yes, my dear," Daedalus said, practically rubbing his hands together.

"Okay. Explain *them*," I said bluntly, pointing at Richard and Manon, who clearly weren't anywhere close to seventeen, especially Manon.

Awkward silence.

"She's smarter than the average bear," Richard said dryly, and I spun on my barstool.

"Shut *up*, you weird kid!" I hissed, and he raised his eyebrows and looked back at Axelle.

"You're right, of course," Ouida said, glancing at the others in the room. "And being a witch yourself, you understand that there are often mysteries and things that aren't how they appear on the surface."

"Why don't we have a circle?" Jules suggested. "It would be a good place to start."

Being smarter than the average bear, I knew that having a magick circle with a bunch of strangers, one of whom I thought might be trying to kill Thais and me, was not a good idea. I started to say so, and then I caught Ouida's face.

She looked accepting, as if she knew what I was thinking, and it was okay. She would support whatever Thais and I would decide. Assuming we had a choice about this. I turned around, and Thais and I met eyes. Her shoulders gave a tiny shrug, as if to say, *Maybe we should.*

I nodded. Maybe one or more persons here were dangerous to us. But not all of them. Not Ouida. Probably not Axelle, Daedalus, or Jules, according to Thais.

Thais came and stood next to me. Together we faced Daedalus. "Okay," I said.

Thais had told me about Axelle's secret room upstairs. We went up. It looked like any other witch's workroom. I stayed close to Ouida, hating being in the same room with André. Worse, I hated his being in the same room as Thais. All my senses were on alert, watching to make sure they didn't somehow end up together, and not just because I thought he might be trying to hurt us. I knew this was sick and paranoid of me, but I couldn't help it.

Daedalus drew a large circle on the floor. Axelle got four

old wooden cups and set them in the points of the compass, with their respective elements. Feeling someone's eyes on me, I glanced up to find André watching me. As soon as I saw him, he looked away. He still seemed tight and angry, and his face was pale and unshaven, as if he hadn't slept well last night.

Good, I thought. *I hope he never sleeps well again.* I started to think about spells to accomplish this, conveniently forgetting the threefold rule, and then Axelle said, "Everyone join hands."

Ouida was on one side of me. On my other side was Sophie, who seemed nice and shy and had a stronger French accent than most of them. Next to her was Richard, then André, then Jules, Thais, Manon, Daedalus, and Axelle on Ouida's other side.

Daedalus started chanting, and we began to walk slowly *dalmonde*. I actually didn't recognize what Daedalus was saying—it sounded like it might be Old French, but I could make out only a few words: *vent* and *pierre, cercle, plume*. Wind and stone, circle, feather. They didn't make sense. The others joined in, but Thais and I met eyes and shrugged. My sister looked curious and cautious but kept in step and carefully walked right inside the large circle.

We began walking faster, as their voices seemed to separate like ribbons to intertwine and lace through and under and around each other. This happened in my regular coven too, and I always loved this part, the weaving together of the whole. Wisps of magick started to swirl around us, like fine threads of cotton candy. I waited for the familiar rush of magick to fill me, but I felt dull around the edges, not fully present.

Against my will, I glanced across the circle and saw André watching Thais. She wasn't looking back. Quick rage filled my chest, and I realized that my anger was getting in my way.

It was almost impossible to release it. I wanted to rake my fingernails down his face—almost as much as I wanted to grab him and kiss him hard, make him forget my sister. Gritting my teeth, I closed my eyes and took several deep breaths, putting both of them out of my mind. I tried to release all emotion, all feelings, to open myself to receive magick.

We quickened our pace, and I kept my eyes closed, concentrating on being here and being blank, a blank canvas for magick to color. I caught more words: *calice, d'eau, cendres.* Chalice, water, ashes. No idea what they meant. But at last, it worked: A familiar excitement and anticipation came over me, and magick began to swell within my chest. I breathed it in like light, letting myself feel the joy, the completeness of being surrounded by magick. It dwarfed everything else, and from this exalted height, my anguish over André's betrayal seemed far away.

I opened my eyes and looked at Thais, wondering what she was thinking and feeling. Her eyes were open wide, as if in astonishment, her face transformed from wary to welcoming. I smiled at her, and she smiled back breathlessly. She felt the exhilaration of magick too, and it was her first time. I was glad we were together now, despite all the mixed feelings I had about her, about us, about our future.

I felt the lovely rush of power and life, felt myself meld with the other forces in this circle, that heady sense of connection, the joining of spirits. Our circle moved swiftly, round like the earth, like the sun, eternal like the tides of the oceans. The chant reached a crescendo, and I found myself joining in: "Un calice du vent, un cercle de cendres, une plume de pierre, un collier d'eau." Again and again we sang the words, and though I thought I got their translation, they still didn't make sense to me. I offered up a prayer to *Déesse: Please help my sister and me become what we are supposed to become. Please help us keep safe.*

Then as if one, the circle suddenly stopped. We threw our hands in the air, releasing our energy, sending out our power, which is the only way to receive the power back into you. I felt stronger within myself, felt I could work miraculous spells, and then Ouida and I were smiling and hugging.

The ten of us were flushed, panting, glorying in the aftereffects of magick. Thais was hugging Sophie. Hating myself, my eyes sought André. His face was dark, he was breathing hard, his emotions jangled and discordant. He looked as he had when we were twined together, kissing, when I had been offering him everything, and he had almost taken it. I sent out a quick general thanks that we hadn't actually gotten farther than that.

Then Thais was in front of me, blocking my view. I saw faint tear tracks on her pink cheeks as she put her arms around me. I hugged her back, feeling less alone, less wretched. I had a sister. I think it truly only hit me right then: I had a *sister*, forever. We shared the same blood, the same bone. We were one person, split into two. We would never be alone again. It seemed huge and amazing in a way that it hadn't, until then, and my eyes filled with tears.

"What did you think?" I whispered.

Her face, so eerily like my own, was solemn. "It was—scary," she said finally, trying to gather her thoughts. "And . . . so beautiful. I wish—" She broke off, biting her lip. "I wish I had never known of anything so beautiful, so powerful." Her face was almost sad.

"What do you mean? I don't understand."

"Before, I didn't know what I was missing," she said softly. "Now I do. And now I know—I have to have it. I'll do anything to feel it again."

I nodded. What has a front, has a back. And the bigger the front, the bigger the back. The joy and beauty of magick were married to the awful responsibility of wielding it. The pleasure of calling on magick was tempered by the need to do so.

"Did you get any of the words?" she asked me.

I nodded. "Some, but they didn't make sense. Part of it was, 'A chalice of wind, a circle of ashes, a feather of stone, a necklace of water.' All connected like that."

Thais looked thoughtful, repeating the words to herself. "You don't know what it meant?"

"No—never heard it before. We can ask Ouida," I said.

"Now I think it's time." Ouida's clear voice cut through the lingering effects of the magick. "Time to know the truth. The whole truth."

✦ Chapter Thirty-Five

Thais

MAYBE I'D HAD ENOUGH TRUTH FOR ONE DAY.
I felt drained. My skin was still alive and glowing from what
I'd just discovered. I didn't know how it had happened, where
it had come from, or even what "magick" really was. I only
knew that I'd felt it, and for a few minutes, I'd been part of
everything. I hadn't been alone, everything had made sense,
and my pain had lessened. If that was magick, sign me up.

"Can we go back downstairs?" Manon asked in her little-
girl voice. "It's hot up here."

The whole truth. I thought about finding Clio, realizing
she and Petra were witches, finding out Luc was really André,
finding out he was a witch. I really didn't think I could take any
more. Could I escape somehow? But Ouida seemed to have a
plan, and Clio looked determined.

Downstairs, every time I glanced at Clio, she was watching Luc. Her face was angry, but I recognized another emotion
as well: desire. She'd said she'd just been using him, that she
didn't love him. It wasn't true. She'd wondered if he was the

one behind the attacks. I didn't know—when I tried to follow that line of thought, my brain just shut down.

"Sit here, Thais," said Ouida, gesturing to the sofa. I was stuck. Clio sat at the other end of the sofa, and Richard sat between us. I couldn't wait to hear *his* story.

Axelle, Ouida, Daedalus, and Jules all looked at each other, as if silently figuring out who should start. My curiosity was mixed with dread about what might be coming. After today everything that had happened in my life before New Orleans would be gone forever, as if it had happened to someone else. I felt Luc's eyes on me, and Clio's eyes on him. I ignored him as best I could, but heat rose in my cheeks just from being in the same room.

"Well, really, our story started quite a long time ago," Ouida said slowly. "Our families came from France, through Canada, and settled in southern Louisiana, not far from New Orleans. That was in the late 1600s. There were fifteen families, fifty-eight people total. They lived in peace and made their lives and homes in their new chosen land. They practiced *Bonne Magie* and stayed true to the old ways.

"This continued for almost a hundred years," Ouida went on. "As with any group of people, there were leaders and followers—people who were stronger and people who were weaker. Within the fifteen families, and the new families that had been created by intermarrying, there were several different covens."

"Eight, I think," said Jules, frowning in thought.

"Now, I have to tell you a bit about *Magie Noir*," Ouida said, taking a deep breath.

"Dark magick?" Clio said in surprise.

"Yes," Ouida went on more firmly. "In our community, young people, teenagers, often experimented with *Magie Noir*, before they made their rite of ascension. The corollary today would be experimenting with drugs, or drinking, or sex."

"Or all three," Richard murmured, and my skin crawled. Bizarrely, there was something very likeable about Richard, but he was also just so young to be so dark. It was creepy.

"In those days, it was usually *Magie Noir*," Ouida said. "They were punished if caught, but in general the feeling was that they would play with it, get it out of their systems, and then be ready to settle down into the community, as they should. And for the most part, that's what happened."

"Until Melita," Daedalus said, his voice heavy with memory, as if it had all happened just last year.

"Yes," Ouida said. "Until Melita. Melita was a very powerful witch, with the kind of power that comes along once every hundred years. She learned fast, soaking up information, rites, history like a sponge. Before she was sixteen, she made her rite of ascension, thus giving her even more power."

I had been watching Ouida, but when I looked around the room, I was surprised by people's expressions. Almost everyone here wore a mantle of gloom. These witches who only ten minutes before had been singing with clear joy now looked as if they were immersed in sadness and pain. I risked glancing at

Luc, and he looked even worse than before. He met my eyes, a still, speculative look on his face. I shifted and looked away from him, my heart pounding.

"The community ignored what was happening and closed their eyes to the fact that Melita wasn't just passing through her *Magie Noir* phase—she was reveling in it, pursuing it, and working hard to increase her power all the time through dark and dangerous methods."

Jules lowered his head and rubbed his eyes with one hand, as if suddenly tired beyond words. Daedalus for once had no used-car salesman's smile but looked drawn and stiff.

"One night Melita was in the woods, performing her dark rites. It's still unclear whether she caused this to happen, or whether it was just there and she found it—but she came upon a small, bubbling spring, *une Source*. The water was red-tinted and very cold, and she drank from it."

"She said she made it, conjured it," said Richard, and Daedalus whirled on him.

"I don't believe it. It was sheer happenstance that led her to it."

"However it happened," Ouida continued, "from that day on, Melita was never ill. When the whole community had the flu, and more than twenty people died, Melita never got sick. Any small injury healed unnaturally quickly. She was strong and healthy in a way that few people were in those days, before antibiotics and vaccinations. But more important, her magick increased maybe a hundredfold.

"Several years passed. There had always been people whose magick seemed stronger or more true, but now Melita overshadowed the best of them. It was obvious that she had special powers. The boys in the village fell in love with her, but she didn't care for them—only for power. She began to dominate the whole community, both through her force of will and by her magick. The *Magie Noir* had taken hold of her, and unlike other people, it didn't let her go."

"She studied the ancient texts," Jules said quietly. "And researched herbology and astrology. Within seven years, she was the strongest witch anyone had ever seen. At the end of those seven years, Melita had devised a plan to forever consolidate her power by a ritual at the Source, this time with twelve carefully chosen fellow witches. These witches would represent a cross-section of abilities, affinities, ages, sexes, and so on, as her research had indicated was necessary."

"There was an older man," said Daedalus, his voice dull. He was looking at the floor and didn't raise his eyes. "An elder in the community—the mayor, if you will."

"There was a powerful, headstrong woman," said Axelle, sounding sad and unAxellelike.

"There was a virginal young woman," said Sophie, not looking at anyone.

"There was an older woman, a wise healer," Ouida said. "And there was a female slave."

"And another slave," said Jules. "Arrogant and ambitious."

"There was a girl," Manon said slowly. "Who had not yet

reached puberty."

"There was a heartless rake," said Luc wearily.

It was then that all the hairs on the back of my neck stood up, and my blood turned cold. My breaths became faster and shallower, and I watched this play unfold with horror.

"There was a boy." Richard's voice was bitter and full of pain. "Halfway to becoming a man."

"There was an innocent young man," said Ouida, "who was emotional and easily led."

"There was the village outcast, a woman of loose morals," said Daedalus with distaste.

"And there was Melita's younger sister, Cerise," said Axelle. "She was unmarried, but pregnant. No one knew who the father was."

"The baby was due in two months," said Sophie, sounding near tears.

My eyes wide, I sought out Clio's face. Silent knowledge passed between us: our vision. They were describing our vision. Holy crap.

"Through various means—bribes, threats, coercion—she rounded up these twelve witches and performed the ritual with them," Ouida said. "During the ritual, they all drank from the spring, thereby increasing all their magickal powers—beyond where Melita's had been."

"During the rite, Melita called on all the dark forces she knew," Sophie said softly. "Forces the others didn't know existed. And her magick was so strong, and the combined forces of the thirteen were so strong, that it called down the wrath of heaven."

My eyebrows must have gone up, because Ouida explained, "It called down a tremendous surge of power that entered Melita and poured into the souls of the twelve with her."

"Dark power," Jules said.

"It stunned everyone," said Manon, her voice wispy and light. "It felt . . . like the beginning and the end of everything, of life itself."

"Which it was in a way." Luc sounded very tired.

"No one knows why, but Cerise went into early labor," Ouida continued. "The rest of the twelve were practically glowing in the dark with power and magick and energy, but it didn't have the same effect on Cerise. She went into labor and died in childbirth."

I almost said, "But the child lived," thinking of the pale, mewling baby washed clean by the rain.

"Maybe Melita knew it would happen," Richard said. "Maybe not. But Cerise, her sister, died that night."

"The eleven others who were left were horrified and scared of what had happened," Sophie said.

"Melita was too dangerous." Axelle examined her blood-red fingernails. "It wasn't safe to have her around. So the eleven remaining witches lay in wait for her. They were going to kill her."

I couldn't believe I was hearing this, that this was a real story, real history. And I couldn't believe the terrible conclusions my mind was leading me to. I glanced at Clio, who seemed as spellbound as I was.

"But it didn't work," Daedalus put in. "Melita was too strong even for the eleven together. Instead of dying, she escaped and disappeared. No one ever saw her again."

"Before she left, she went back to the Source and the great cypress tree, where she'd performed the rite." Ouida took a deep breath, looking at her hands, folded in her lap. "She destroyed the tree, and the Source disappeared."

"Fast-forward fifteen years," said Manon. "By then it was obvious that the rite had had unexpected, lingering effects. None of the eleven was ever ill. Their magick was strong and clear and very, very powerful."

"Cerise's daughter, born that night, grew normally," Ouida said. "Oddly enough, she had the exact same birthmark that Cerise had had—a bright fleur-de-lis on her cheekbone. Somehow the magick that night had entered her as well, and her powers were unnaturally strong. Her name was Hélène. In time she married and became with child. She died in childbirth, as her mother had. Her daughter Félice was marked with the fleur-de-lis."

My own birthmark felt like it was burning against my skin.

"Félice grew to adulthood, married, and died in childbirth," Daedalus said flatly. "It was like Cerise's line was cursed because she had died the night of the ritual."

"And it continued that way," Ouida said. "Cerise's line

never died out completely. Each successive generation produced one child. Your mother, Clémence, was the twelfth generation of Cerise's line. You, my dears, are the thirteenth. In your line, the power is very strong. You two have the potential to be extremely powerful witches."

"Especially if we put our powers together," said Clio coolly.

Ouida frowned. "Well, I don't know about that. I guess, in theory. I haven't really heard of other identical twins being able to do that. Have you?" she asked Daedalus.

I worked hard to keep the shock off my face and not to look at Clio.

Daedalus looked thoughtful. "I can recall only two other sets of identical twins among our famille," he said. "In the first pair, a twin died in childhood before his rite of ascension. I don't remember anything remarkable about the other set."

"You must remember," Jules pointed out, "that only the eleven that took part in Melita's dark rite became, well, superpowerful. The rest of the community practiced *Bonne Magie* and were strong witches, but not supernaturally so. And of the eleven, you two are the first and only set of twins in any line."

I tried to look calm and interested. This was completely opposite what Petra had told us. They were lying. They wanted us to feel safe, as twins. They didn't realize that we'd already figured out someone was trying to harm us.

"What happened to the other eleven lines?" I asked.

"That brings us to the next important part of our story," said Daedalus. He stood before the fireplace, hands clasped behind his back. "You see—and this is the remarkable part—in addition to having incredibly strong magickal powers after that rite, in addition to never becoming ill, and having injuries heal quickly, there was another unmistakable legacy granted to those who had drunk from the Source that night."

"They never . . . aged." Richard's voice was characteristically bitter.

My hands started to tremble, and I clasped them together tightly. *No, no, oh, no . . .*

"What do you mean?" Clio asked tightly.

Richard looked at her. "They never aged. Have you not figured this out yet, Clio? As smart as you are?" he asked mockingly.

I felt cold through and through, and the knuckles on my fingers were white.

Ouida smiled sadly. "A woman named Claire is the village outcast. Marcel is the innocent young man."

"Do you mean Petra isn't really our grandmother?" I asked.

Ouida shook her head. "No, not your grandmother. She's your ancestor, though. You see, Petra was Melita and Cerise's mother. That night she saw one daughter die and her other revealed as a power-mad monster. She's been helping the descendents of Cerise's line ever since. Though Clio was the first child she actually raised herself."

I looked over at Luc. "Don't tell me," I said, sounding as cool and smooth as a stone. "You're the heartless rake."

He made a gesture with his hand and looked away, looking tired and almost ill. Which I guessed was impossible—the ill part.

"Let me get this straight," said Clio. "You are the original eleven. You're saying you are *immortal?*"

Eight heads nodded with various levels of enthusiasm.

"I mean, so far, at least," Richard said.

How could this possibly be true?

"Okay, fine," said Clio briskly. "You guys are immortal, my grandmother isn't my grandmother, I understand why my mom died. But why did you want to find me and Thais? Get us together?"

"Because you would complete the Treize," said Daedalus. "As we said earlier."

"And that's important why?" Clio asked, her eyebrows raised.

"So we can re-create the rite, of course," said Jules. "Then you can be immortal too."

Uh . . . okay. I found my voice. "Why do you care if we're immortal?"

"He would get something out of it," Luc said, his voice as dry as bone. "Everyone would. Doing the rite would conjure up a huge amount of power—power that could be twisted and shaped to do anything anyone wanted it to. For example, we could increase even the power we already have. If we reopen the Source, we can save people we . . . love. Save their lives."

Jules and Sophie shifted uneasily in their seats. Daedalus

seemed coldly angry, a muscle in his jaw twitching as he watched Luc. Luc looked directly at me, and I found myself unable to tear my gaze away. "And some of us," he went on quietly, "are tired of immortality. And we would like to die."

✦ Epilogue

THE AIRPLANE INTERCOM CRACKLED. "LADIES and gentlemen, we're experiencing a bit of turbulence. At this time, please put your trays and seats in their upright and locked positions. Please make sure your seat belt is securely fastened. The captain has put on the 'remain seated' light, so do not move about the cabin until the light is turned off. Thank you."

Petra turned off her small overhead light and sat with her hands in her lap. Flashes of lightning illuminated the dark night outside, and horizontal lashes of rain streaked across her window. The plane suddenly dropped ten feet, and a woman gave a short cry of alarm. A baby started crying.

It began to feel like a roller-coaster ride with sudden jarring jumps and drops and general shuddering in between. Across the aisle a woman started praying out loud.

Petra closed her eyes, cleared her mind of everything, and began to murmur a general calming spell under her breath. Into the airplane cabin she sent soothing tendrils of calm and serenity, easing fears, cooling raw nerves, blunting the sharp edges of fear and panic. She didn't bother with a protection spell for the plane. She knew it would be all right.

Ten minutes later the atmosphere inside the cabin had achieved a lulling sense of divine reassurance. The man next to Petra gave her a small smile when another bolt of lightning cracked outside.

"Nature's fireworks," he said.

"Yes," Petra agreed. In fact, Petra was deeply afraid. Not for herself—that was pointless. Nor for the plane and its occupants, whom she knew to be safe. No, Petra was afraid of what might be happening below, thirty-three thousand feet down, in New Orleans. Despite leaving Ouida in charge, Petra felt her base of power in danger of eroding.

The sooner she got back to New Orleans, the better. She had accomplished her mission: Thais would come to live with her, and Petra could keep an eye on both twins. Then she would try to formulate more of a plan, quickly. One that would take the twins away, keep them out of the Treize's long reach. Right now, only one thing stood between the twins and certain danger, possibly even death. That one thing was Petra.

She hoped she was up for the task.

BALEFIRE

Cate Tiernan

BOOK TWO:
A CIRCLE OF ASHES

BALEFIRE

BOOK TWO:
A CIRCLE OF ASHES

✦ Chapter One

Clio

"HERE." I PUSHED THE COOKIES OVER TO THAIS. "Crumble them on top. It's good."

Thais took a couple cookies and dutifully crumbled them over her ice cream. Then she took a bite and nodded. "S' good."

We kept up the everything's normal ice-cream eating for another two minutes, and then at the exact same time, we put down our spoons and stared at each other.

"Immortal," said Thais.

"Yeah. If we believe them." I had a sudden thought. Quickly I ran upstairs to my room and pulled out an old photo album. I brought it downstairs and opened it on the kitchen table between us. Together Thais and I looked at pictures from when I was way little, a baby, and on up till when I was about three. I was an extremely pretty baby.

Nan—Petra—looked exactly the same as she did today. She hadn't aged a bit in seventeen years. And I, with my razor-sharp skills of observation, had never noticed it. She'd always just been Nan. I was trying to process the knowledge that she was so much more than she'd ever told me.

"So," I said, closing the book with a sigh. "They were probably telling the truth. Or mostly."

Thais nodded. "I'm totally freaking."

I gave a short laugh. "That's one word for it." I sighed again. I was having a rough summer, and so far I had no signs that anything was going to get easier.

"Just all of it," said Thais. "Twins." She pointed at me, then at herself, summing up the whole, huge, identical-twins-separated-at-birth thing with one gesture. "Luc." She closed her eyes and breathed out heavily, summing up the whole, huge, two-timing-lying-bastard-witch-boyfriend thing. "Witches." She shook her head slowly about the whole, huge, finding-out-you're-a-witch-and-so-is-your-family thing.

"And now the possibility of being immortal," I said. "Oh, and almost being killed a bunch of times."

"It's been a crazed couple of months," Thais said, and that reminded me that on top of everything else, she'd lost her father—our father—just this summer. Even though I'd never known him, I still felt pangs of loss, so I could barely imagine what she had to be going through.

"Been a roller-coaster ride," I agreed.

"So what now?" Thais asked. "It's all too much. I don't know where to start."

I thought for a minute. Usually I left the dealing with stuff to my not-grandmother Petra. Nan. I mean, I'd always thought she was my grandmother. She'd said she was. She'd raised me after my mother had died giving birth to me and my surprise sister. But as it turned out, she was an *ancestor*, a great-grandmother so many times back that I couldn't even put in enough *greats*. And she'd kept my sister and my dad a secret from me. I could have known them both all this time. Now he was dead and my chance was gone. I still couldn't believe Nan had done it, no matter what her reasons were. And I had missed growing up with a sister.

Now Nan was who knew where, and I didn't know when or if she was coming back. If she wasn't back by midnight on Wednesday, I was supposed to open a spelled cabinet in the workroom and find instructions there. In the meantime, I had to handle everything.

"Okay, so the Treize," I said, sitting down and taking another swipe at my ice cream. "They want us to complete their coven so they can do the big schmancy spell that will blow everyone's minds with power."

"*Is* there a spell like that?" Thais asked. "Where everyone would get power and then be able to use it for whatever they want?"

"I don't know. I guess they think there is. I don't know how it would work or what it would do to them or us."

"Besides make us immortal," said Thais.

"Well, yeah, besides that. So they say. I've never heard of anything like that."

"Luc said he wanted to die," Thais said, not looking at me. "That he was tired of immortality and wanted to die."

Luc. Would I ever not flinch when I heard his name? Luc-

André. I'd known him as André. Thais had known him as Luc. Each of us had gone out with him, kissed him, fallen in love with him. He had betrayed us twice: first with each other and then by being one of the Treize. Even now, with my rage still burning, some part inside me ached for him, longed for him, wished he could be mine. Mine and not Thais's.

But he loved *her*.

I swallowed hard. "Yeah. I'm willing to give him a hand with that."

Thais gave me a wry look, then her face sobered. "Do you think he means it?"

I looked back at her. "Do you care?"

She turned away and didn't answer.

I took a deep breath and pushed my bowl away. "Would you want immortality?"

"I don't know."

"We have to figure this stuff out. Like, now we've met all of them. Who in the Treize is trying to kill us?"

"If it *is* someone from the Treize. We don't know that for sure," Thais pointed out.

"Well, no," I agreed. "But they're the obvious place to start. I mean, the attacks had magick behind them." Someone had been trying to hurt both Thais and me ever since she moved to New Orleans. At first it had seemed like "accidents," but then when whoever it was finally came after us both together with an angry mass of wasps, we realized there had to be a connection with all the other near misses.

"Yeah, you're right. Okay, then. Someone from the Treize. Not Petra," said Thais.

"No. Not Axelle or Daedalus or Jules," I added, naming three witches we'd just met. "They've had plenty of clear shots at you." Thais had been living at Axelle's since her—our—dad had died.

"And not Ouida. I hope." Thais looked troubled. "I really liked her. But I just couldn't face dinner with her—after all that."

"No. And Sophie and Manon just got to town," I said. "So we can rule them out."

"And the ones who aren't here, what, Marcel? And—Claire? Not them."

I nodded, then got up and grabbed a sheet of paper and a pen. I made a list of everyone we had put in the not-guilty category. "Who's left?"

Thais thought. "You and me. Richard," she said, pronouncing his name Ree-shard. "Luc."

"Richard was around Axelle's a lot too, wasn't he? So probably not him. And we're not doing it," I said. I looked at the paper. Only Luc left, which was impossible. Unbelievable. Probably. "Wait—what if Axelle, Jules, Richard, or Daedalus didn't try to kill you at Axelle's because it would be too obvious? That doesn't necessarily put them in the clear."

"But Axelle is the one who saved me with my dream," Thais objected. "She stopped me from choking myself."

I looked at her. "That's what she told you. Any chance she

was doing the opposite? Tightening the twisted sheet around your neck, but then you woke up and stopped her?"

Thais frowned. "I don't know." She sighed and looked at the clock. It was almost two a.m. "So that still gives us Richard and Luc and those three. And Richard isn't just a really weird fifteen-year-old with tattoos and a pierced eyebrow. He's a grown-up. A really old grown-up in a kid's body."

I forced myself to say it. "What about Luc? He lied to us about so many things. Maybe he was trying to lull us into loving him so we wouldn't think he would try to kill us."

"I don't know," Thais said after a long pause. "I can't wrap my mind around it. Logically, it's possible. But I can't get myself there."

"Yeah. I know." I let my breath out, feeling incredibly tired. Well, finding out your entire life has been a web of lies can do that to a girl. "But still—we shouldn't be blind about this. He outright lied about so many things. Made us believe—I mean, he was way convincing, right? Who knows what he's capable of?" I said it, though something inside me just couldn't believe it. Then something else occurred to me.

"We're not out of danger," I said. "Especially with Nan still MIA. But I just thought of something—there's a spell."

I expected Thais to get her sour-milk expression at the mention of a spell, and I wasn't disappointed. She was still finding it hard to get cozy with all the witch stuff, despite how much she'd loved the feel of magick at the Treize's circle.

"It's a spell where two people sort of share their power,"

I said, trying to remember where I'd seen it. "Like, people in love use it to strengthen their bond, make them closer. Or a parent might do it with a child to help with learning magick or make the child stronger. It makes it easier to join your powers together afterward. If we did it . . . both of us would be stronger—against anything that might come at us."

Thais nodded thoughtfully. "Is it dangerous?"

I frowned. "I don't think so. Let me get the book." I knew what she meant—Thais and I had done magick, shared a vision, and it had gotten weirdly huge and powerful, out of control. I didn't know why. Our grandmo—Petra—had told us that in our magickal *famille,* people were afraid of twins because their magick put together was frighteningly strong. I wasn't sure if that was true.

In the little house I shared with Nan, we had a living room, workroom, dining room, small bathroom, and kitchen on the first floor. Upstairs were two small bedrooms and another bathroom. Our workroom had bookcases full of magickal texts. The first time Thais had come into this house, she'd been horrified when she saw our books, our supplies for magick. I snickered now, thinking about it.

"Would it be indexed in the back?" Thais asked. "Can I help look?"

"Do you speak old French?"

"I don't even speak new French," she said. "Not much, anyway."

"Okay. Then just sit tight. I should be able to find . . ."

A few minutes later I had found it in an old *grimoire* that belonged to Nan. It was in Old French, which I wasn't completely fluent in but could hack my way through. The spell was called *"Joindre tous les deux,"* or "Join both."

Quickly I got our supplies together.

"Why do I feel like I'm in the Addams family?" Thais asked, watching me. "Aren't you leaving out the eye of newt, wing of bat?"

I looked at her. "You liked it at Axelle's house, the magick."

She lowered her eyes and quit smiling. "Yeah."

"Okay, get in," I said. Thais came to stand next to me as I drew a chalk circle around us on the workroom floor.

"You're really good at drawing circles," Thais said, sounding nervous.

"Lots of practice. Circle-drawing 101." I did it again with salt, then I got Nan's four pewter cups to represent the four elements and put them at the points of the compass. One held water, one held incense to represent air, one held dirt from our backyard to represent, well, earth, and one held a candle for fire.

"Fire is our element," I reminded Thais. "Every witch has an affinity with one element, and she focuses on that element in her magick. It makes it smoother, more effective."

I lit another candle and put it on the floor between us. We sat cross-legged, facing each other. I found the right page again and began to read.

"Can you do it in English?" Thais asked.

I thought. "Well, it might be more effective in French—it all rhymes and everything. Sometimes the very words themselves hold magickal power."

"But I won't understand it," said Thais, and I thought I heard fear in her voice.

"And you think I'll turn you into a frog?"

Thais just looked unhappy.

"Okay, um, I think I can just translate this as I go," I muttered, reading down. "Maybe it doesn't really have to be in French. Let's see. First let's center ourselves and get in touch with our magick. Then I'll read this little section. There are four sections, and at each section, you'll combine two things together. I'll explain as we go. Okay?"

Thais nodded, looking uncertain.

I closed my eyes and reached out to barely touch the tips of my fingers to Thais's knees. After a moment she did the same to me. "Slow your breathing," I said very softly. "Slow your mind. Let everything relax. Let go of fear and fatigue. Inside you is a joyous door that leads to magick. When you relax completely, the door doesn't open—it dissolves, letting you become one with magick. Magick is everywhere around you, in everything, living and inert. That's the strength and power we tap. Now breathe very, very slowly."

From just the little connection I already had with Thais, I was in tune with her aura, and I could feel her gradually relax and become centered. It took several minutes, but as Nan said, quality magick takes time.

Slowly I opened my eyes and referred back to the book. My translation was clumsy, and it was hard to make it into a nice, smooth chant.

"I join with you, my sister, so that we will be one."

I had Thais repeat that, then I went on.

"We are of the same blood. Now let us be of the same heart and the same mind. I join with you and offer you my power and strength."

Thais repeated it.

"Water is our witness." I motioned to Thais, and she poured two silver cups of water into one larger cup.

"Air is our witness." Thais took two long incense sticks and held their tips together so that their thin spirals of smoke twined together like vines.

"Earth is our witness." Thais took white sand and black sand and rubbed them together in her palms, like salt and pepper. When they were evenly mixed, she dribbled them out of her hand into the rune shape I showed her, *goeffe*, which looks like an *X*. It stood for gift, partnership, generosity.

"Fire is our witness," I said. Thais picked up two smaller candles and lit them simultaneously from the candle between us. Then she set them into a small silver candleholder that had two joined stems.

"We join our strength and power," we said together, and I nodded at two small willow twigs. With red string, Thais tied them securely together in the middle.

"Life is our witness."

I took a piece of chalk and drew the rune *quenne* on the floor. "This is for fire, our element," I said. "It's our passion, our creativity."

I gave Thais the piece of chalk and showed her the rune in the book that I wanted her to draw. She did. "*Lage* is for knowledge, creativity, psychic power," I said. "We call on the power of these runes to make our spell complete."

Then Thais and I put our hands on each other's shoulders and closed our eyes.

"Nous voulons nous joindre toutes les deux," I said. We said it together and then said it a third time. And that was when we got blown across the room.

✤ Chapter Two

Thais

I HIT THE WALL HEADFIRST AND CRIED OUT. After several moments of being stunned, I slowly sat up, trying not to groan. Clio lay in a heap on the other side of the room, and I got up and ran to her. She was already blinking and trying to sit up.

"What the hell was that?" she said.

I knelt and put my arm around her. "Are you okay? You didn't say that would happen!"

Her eyes were wide, and she rubbed her head where it had hit a bookcase. "Because I didn't know!" she said. "We got blown right out of that circle! I've never heard of anything like that happening. Holy crap."

"Then what went wrong?" I asked.

"I have no fricking idea." Clio stood up and brushed off her butt. She rubbed her head again. "Ow. That has never, ever happened to me." She looked at me, and I felt the usual little spark of surprise that we looked so much alike. Her hair was longer, and our birthmarks were on opposite cheeks, but there was no doubt we were identical. "Maybe it was the twin-power thing," she said, sounding kind of awed.

"God. Well, no wonder everyone's freaked about it." I realized I was shaking and looked over at the circle. The candles and incense had been snuffed out, and the salt circle wasn't even there anymore. "So are we joined now?"

We looked at each other, and I sent out a systems check to see if I felt different.

"I'm not sure," said Clio. "I don't know if the spell had time to work or what."

But as I stood there, I realized that I was picking up stuff from Clio—I could *feel* her next to me, but not physically. It was like I felt a form, a shape, next to me. Not like a ghost. Not even human looking. But it was Clio, definitely Clio. I felt her puzzlement and excitement. I felt fear in myself, but not from her.

"Hey. Is that you?" I asked.

Looking amazed, Clio laughed and nodded. "I feel you too. It's like—Flubber. Like a Flubber Thais, only I can't see it. This is way cool."

"It's strange," I said. "I wonder if it works when we're farther apart."

"I guess we'll find out," she said, grinning.

• • •

At dawn I went back to Axelle's. I still didn't know how Axelle Gauvin had wrangled custody of me after Dad had died. A spell? Strings pulled? I hoped that Petra would come back soon and that I'd be able to live with her and Clio when she did.

In the meantime, all my stuff was in Axelle's apartment in the French Quarter.

At dawn in September, it was about eighty-five degrees. I walked down narrow, almost quiet streets, thinking how pretty the Quarter was with not many people in it. Later today it would be crowded and noisy and smell like beer and sunscreen.

I was still awed by the spell with Clio. I mean, I had gotten thrown eight feet across a room. By magick. It was hard to believe. Except I had a knot on my head to prove it. Clio said she would try to figure out what had gone wrong, but if she'd never even heard of anything like that happening . . .

I used my key and went through the wrought-iron side gate that led to Axelle's apartment. The narrow carriageway was cool and damp, and I could barely hear my shoes on the ancient flagstones, worn by centuries of use. The small courtyard was a mini-Eden, with birds fluttering around the subtropical plants that lined the tiny swimming pool.

And here was Axelle's front door. Despite feeling shaken by last night's spell, a new strength had solidified in me, and I felt complete and sure of myself. I opened the door and went in. As usual, the scent of cigarette smoke made my nostrils twitch. It was cool and dark inside, and as I shut the door, Minou, Axelle's cat, ran past my legs into the apartment.

"Thais."

My eyes were adjusting to the dim light, and I saw Axelle

lying on her black leather couch. Putting aside the newspaper she was reading, she stood and came over to me.

"You're up early. Catching up on current events?" I said evenly, moving into the kitchen.

"Up all night. Reading the comics." Her dark shiny page-boy swung right at her chin, every hair in place. She might have been awake for the previous twenty-four hours, but you'd never be able to tell. "So you stayed out all night. Another wasp attack?"

"More like shock and horror over my family's history." Not looking at her, I poured myself some orange juice and put two slices of bread into the toaster.

"Shock? Okay, I'll give you that. You had a lot dumped on you yesterday. But horror?" Her red lips formed a smile. She poured herself a glass of juice, then got a bottle of vodka from the top of the fridge. She splashed some into her orange juice and took an appreciative sip. It was barely seven a.m.

"Thais," she said, with a warm, almost seductive note in her voice. "You've been handed the opportunity of a lifetime. The chance to become immortal—it's what fantasies are made of."

"Or nightmares," I said. "You guys, the ones I've met so far—the Treize—you're not exactly the poster kids for health and happiness."

Axelle stretched, her lithe, catlike body arching. "You might be surprised at how much pleasure one can experience with an endless lifetime to pursue it."

"News flash," I said. "Pleasure isn't the same thing as

happiness." I felt bitter and angry that my life was entwined with the Treize at all. It wasn't that I hated Axelle—I didn't. But I didn't trust her, and we had nothing in common.

"Ooh," said Axelle, finishing her orange juice and vodka. "Such wisdom from one so *young*. But Thais, tell me you aren't happy to know you have a family, a background, a history. You know who you are and where you're from. Isn't that better than being a little boat adrift at sea?"

I didn't answer as I ate my toast. She had me. My whole life, it had been just me and my dad. When he'd died, I'd had no one—just a family friend, a neighbor who cared about me. But no family. It was true—I'd felt lost. Then Axelle had brought me to New Orleans, and Clio and I had found each other. Discovering that I had a sister and a grandmother was like winning the lottery. I belonged to someone. I wasn't alone.

Then I'd found out they were witches. I'd never taken witchcraft or Wicca or any of that stuff seriously—I'd thought it was all a joke. The disappointment that they were involved in it had been sharp and immediate. Now I was more used to the idea. I had accepted that it ran in *my* blood too. But it hadn't been what I wanted. And after last night's explosive spell, my doubts seemed justified.

I'd found my family, and they were witches.

I'd found my soul mate, my true love, and he had betrayed me.

And all of this was woven into the unbelievable, movie-plot background that Petra, Axelle, Luc, and a bunch of other people were in fact still experiencing a spell that had been set into motion in 1763, more than 240 years ago. They were immortal.

Now they wanted to make Clio and me immortal too. And we had to decide.

I felt Axelle's eyes on me and hoped my feelings weren't transparent. Immortality. Luc was immortal—he would never age. If we had stayed together, I would get old and die someday, and he wouldn't, ever. But if I was immortal . . .

It wouldn't even matter because we wouldn't be together, because he was a lying, cheating bastard.

I heard footsteps on the wooden stairs that led to Axelle's attic workroom. *Great.* Now I had to deal with Daedalus or Jules, who practically lived here.

"Is she back yet?"

The voice came to me in the kitchen and sent chills down my spine.

"Can't you call Petra?" Luc went on, crossing the dimly lit room.

Axelle waited till he was in sight, then wordlessly pointed to me, a small cat's smile on her face.

Luc stopped short when he saw me.

I glanced at him for a second, just long enough to stop my heart and sear his image into my brain. Luc. Unlike Axelle, he did look like he'd been up all night. He was in the same clothes as yesterday. His face was darkened by a day's worth of beard. His eyes, the color of the sky at twilight, were upset, shadowed.

Good.

"Thais." He took a step closer, and I saw him run a hand through his disheveled, too-long dark hair. I turned and put my plate in the sink, unable to swallow.

"I was worried," he said, and it sounded like getting those words out cost him. I was all too aware of Axelle's black, interested eyes following this exchange like a tennis match.

I tried to wipe any expression from my face and turned back to him.

"And this matters because . . . ?" I said coolly.

He frowned. "Are you okay, then?"

"I'm fine. I mean, my heart hasn't been ripped out and stomped on *today*." I was surprising myself—it was like I could channel my inner bitch all of a sudden. I'd never spoken so coldly to anyone in my life.

Luc flushed, which of course increased his gorgeousness level to about a forty-seven on a scale from one to ten. "That isn't fair," he said in a low voice, and I saw his hands clench at his sides.

"Unfair? *You're* talking to *me* about unfair?" I felt my cheeks heat with anger. "Are you *nuts?* Who the hell do you think you are?"

Suddenly I felt like I was going to lose it in a huge, humiliating way. I spun and stalked to my room, which was a little addition past the kitchen. I slammed the door behind me, but it hit Luc's shoulder with a thud, and he shoved it open so hard it crashed against the wall, rattling the pictures.

I'd never seen him look so angry, not even on that horrible night when Clio and I had found out he'd been two-timing us—with each other. I still felt sick when I thought of it.

"I think I'm *yours*," he said furiously. I backed away from him until I reached my bed, but I wasn't scared. I was furious too, my anger and pain rising in me like a tidal wave.

"I think I was made for you and you for me," he went on, his jaw clenched and his body rigid with tension. "I think I found you just when I wanted to die. I think I found someone to live for. At last."

I was in hell. This was what hell was.

"But I screwed up," he said. "I made a huge mistake because I was stupid and scared—" He stopped suddenly, as if startled that word had left his lips. "I screwed up," he said more calmly. "I'm sorrier than I can say. I regret it more than anything." He looked into my eyes, and he was so familiar to me, so much who I loved, that I wanted to scream. "Out of 250 years' worth of regrets, this is the biggest one."

I couldn't breathe. My heart was pounding so hard it was a physical pain in my chest. Here's the really humiliating part: *I wanted to buy it,* to say, *I forgive you.* I wanted to reach out and grab him and hold his head in my hands so I could kiss him hard, *hard.* I wanted to pull him down onto my bed with me and feel him pressed all against me, like I had before, on the levee by the river. I wanted it so much I could taste it, feel it.

"Thais," he said, moving closer, his voice much softer. "Hit me if you want. Throw things at me. Yell and scream and curse my name until your voice is gone. But come back to me. I'll spend the rest of my life trying to make it up to you." He paused. "Which is saying something." The rest of his life would be quite a long time. Unless he used the Treize's spell to die.

Still I couldn't speak. My eyes felt wide and huge, staring at him with a longing so deep it felt like thirst.

He reached out one hand and slowly, slowly stroked one finger up my bare arm. His hands, his knowing hands, had been all over my body, and the memory of it choked me.

My brain was shorting out. My world was telescoping inward till it contained only Luc and me. I swallowed hard.

"No," I said in a barely audible whisper. I pulled my arm away from his touch and drew in a shuddering breath. "No."

He took a step back, searching my face. I saw new pain in his eyes, as if I could see hope actually dying, and I looked away.

"I could make you love me," he said, his voice low and tense again.

Cold reason dumped into my brain. I met his eyes again.

"You think? Like with a *spell*?"

His jaw tightened. Then he looked down, and I saw both shame and despair on his face. "Thais, I—" He started to raise a hand, then dropped it. He looked at me for a long time, then finally turned and left my room. As soon as he was through the door, I shut it behind him and locked it.

Then I sat on my bed, shaking, and waited for the tears to come.

⚜ Chapter Three

St. Louis Cemetery No. 1

THE TOMBSTONES WERE SPECKLED WITH lichen and moss, the result of hundreds of years of heat and humidity. Ouida thought it looked beautiful, and she focused her camera at a barely readable inscription. With the grainy black-and-white film she was using, this image would be striking, melancholy, like the cemetery itself. She checked the light meter and decided to underexpose the film so that the inscription would show up darker. Angling her camera on its tripod, she carefully clicked the shutter, then stood back, pleased. That would come out well.

Cemeteries fascinated her. Maybe it was like looking through the window of an exclusive club to which she'd never belong. A quiet laugh escaped her, and she covered her mouth, not wanting to be overheard.

Once her tripod was stowed, Ouida looked around, feeling a light gray sense of—not dread, it wasn't that bad—but maybe just sadness? There was another reason she was in St. Louis Cemetery No. 1 besides just a photo op.

Head down, she started walking to the far southeast corner, one of the first areas to be filled in, back in the 1790s. God, that had been a long time ago. Yet the memories of it were still sharply engraved in her mind, not softened or weathered by time.

A few minutes' walking brought her to a place she visited every time she was in New Orleans. There was a small bench opposite the family crypt, and she sat on it, putting down her camera equipment bag. The sun was hot, reflecting off the white marble everywhere, the cement-sealed tombs. People had learned long ago to clear a graveyard of trees unless they wanted thick roots to start popping coffins out of the ground ten years down the road.

Ouida thought of all the winters she'd spent freezing up in Massachusetts. She was a Southerner, all right. The cold had gone right through her bones to her marrow. Here the heat seemed to melt through her skin, softening her inside, relaxing layers of tension. She was more at home here, more herself. But the burden of memories was so much easier to bear in Massachusetts. She knew she'd return.

After several minutes Ouida frowned. Someone was coming. Someone she knew. She let her mind expand into the space around her, let slim tendrils of awareness pick up information in a growing circle.

Daedalus.

A minute later he appeared, looking incongruous in a black polo shirt and tan linen pants.

"Ouida," he said. "I thought I felt you over here." He regarded her, then looked around. Seeing the name on the tomb opposite her, he smiled thinly. "La Famille Martin," he read. "Armand. Grégoire. Antonine. Still rehashing the past, eh, Ouida?"

It was not something she was going to discuss with him. "What are you doing here?"

He shrugged and, uninvited, sat next to her on the bench. "Collecting useful things." He gestured to the canvas shopping bag he held. "There are always broken graves in a cemetery this old. Sometimes one can find the occasional bone for one's supply cabinet. Also, Spanish moss, other mosses, any number of useful things."

Ouida looked at him with distaste, and he laughed. "What, you get your bones from a mail-order catalog? Please."

"I don't seem to do many spells that call for human bones, Daedalus."

"Don't give me that superior attitude, Ouida," he said, not angrily. "We've always known that our interests are different." He waved a hand around the cemetery. "Plus, you know, I always check for Melita."

Ouida was truly surprised. "Check for her? As if she might be buried somewhere? You're kidding. How could she possibly be dead?"

Daedalus shrugged. "Most likely she isn't. But I've come to believe there's a slim chance the rite may have affected her differently somehow—maybe because of all the magick she'd done before or for some other reason. After all, it killed Cerise. So maybe it did something different to Melita. There's always hope, however far-fetched. The important thing would be to find her, dead or alive, before she found any of us."

Ouida scoffed. "She's had two hundred and fifty years to find us if she wanted. None of us has been in hiding."

"Yes, but now we're trying to do the rite," Daedalus reminded her.

"Or at least you are," Ouida returned.

Daedalus frowned. "We all are. Everyone is."

Ouida didn't say anything. Gathering bones? Looking for Melita? What was Daedalus actually doing here? Did he know something about Melita that he hadn't told anyone? Had he found her—could he even be in league with her or somehow have usurped her power?

Ouida shook her head, aware that Daedalus was watching her. She'd blocked her thoughts and knew he couldn't be eavesdropping. She had her secrets, just as Daedalus did. She sighed. The Treize was about as safe and trustworthy as an adder's nest.

Chapter Four

Red with Her Blood

ROCKS. IF THERE WAS ONE THING LOUISIANA had over Ireland, it was that there were no cursed rocks in the ground. Plowing was easy there. The dirt was rich and black, bursting with life and nourished by the Delta basin.

Here the soil was thin and pale gray, and you couldn't spit without hitting rock after rock after rock. Marcel had been working this same plot of ground for, what, seven years now? Yet each spring and each autumn, he managed to plow up yet another ton of rocks, as if the earth herself were slowly pushing them to the surface all throughout the year.

And maybe she was.

Marcel paused and wiped his wet brow with the coarse brown wool of his monk's robe, then bent his back over the man-powered plow again. Earth. Giver of life. Mindlessly he watched as the thick steel blade cut through the thin turf and peeled it up in two curling layers. He heard the chink of the blade hitting a rock, of course, because he'd gone about four inches, and he knelt to wrest it up and add it to the growing pile by the side of the field. It would be made into a wall, like the rest.

The ground was cold as his fingers scrabbled around the large stone. It was September; soon it would be winter here and bitter, with icy winds borne off the western sea. Marcel's fingers grabbed the rock, and suddenly he felt something slice his finger.

Wincing, he pulled up his hand and found an ancient shard of glass embedded in his skin. *Good job.* Carefully he pulled the shard out and was surprised by the sudden rush of blood from the relatively small cut. In seconds the blood had run across his hand and begun dripping onto the ground. He'd better get to the infirmary, have Brother Niall do something.

He glanced down, and with no warning, Marcel was hurled back through time, to another place, another life.

It had been dark, pouring rain, but with every flash of lightning, Marcel had seen how the wet ground beneath Cerise was red with her blood. He closed his eyes, blinking hard, not wanting to remember.

He'd fallen in love with her. He'd been seventeen. She'd been fourteen but already a woman, doing a woman's work. She'd laughed and spurned him, saying that she was too young to settle down, that she was content to stay at home with her mother and sister.

He'd courted her for years, leaving flowers on her doorstep, freshly killed rabbits outside her kitchen. She had been easy to love, her face bright and open, that golden hair like sunlight spun into silk. Her eyes had been as green as Irish hills in springtime, and she'd had a small red mark on her cheek, like a crushed flower.

It had been just Cerise, her mother, and her sister at home. Petra's husband, Armand, had run off to New Orleans years before. Marcel could barely remember him. He'd been tall with black hair. But Marcel couldn't picture his face.

The Martins had needed a man about the house; that much was clear. Marcel had taken it upon himself to chop wood for them, to bring their cow in from the woods. Melita, the older sister, had been as dark as their father and dark in other ways as well. Almost every man in the village had watched her, wanted her. But not Marcel. Cerise's sunlight was infinitely preferable to Melita's darkness.

For years Marcel dedicated himself to Cerise and her family, hoping that she would relent, take him as her husband, that she would be his. After everything he had done, how could she do anything else? But she'd made him no promises and laughed lightly whenever he'd brought it up.

She hadn't been unkind or cruel. But it was like trying to catch a fairy made of light and air—impossible to pin down. Of course, he'd been going about it all wrong. He'd come to realize that.

Now, kneeling on the cold Irish ground, Marcel swallowed hard and shut his eyes against the relentless memories—once started, they were unstoppable. He'd been walking through the woods to check his traps and heard Cerise's laughter. From a distance he had spied her, running among the trees, the dappled sunlight occasionally catching her bright hair. Marcel had smiled to see Cerise, a girl of seventeen, still playing tag.

Even when he'd seen who was chasing her, he'd still thought it was a game. Richard Landry was barely fifteen, though he'd become tall in the last year. Still a boy, compared to Marcel's twenty years. Marcel had started walking toward them, already knowing what he would say, how he'd tease them for playing like children.

But then he'd seen Richard catch Cerise, heard her startled gasp of laughter. He'd seen Richard hold Cerise's wrists above her head and press her against the broad trunk of a sycamore. When had the boy gotten taller than she? Marcel was still, like a deer, watching them between the thick trees. He waited for Cerise to push Richard away, perhaps angrily, to chastise him for taking liberties. Not even Marcel had held her so close.

But Richard had dared more. He'd leaned against her, lowered his head to kiss her. For a few moments Cerise ducked away, still laughing breathlessly, but then she had stilled, and Richard's mouth had taken hers. He'd let go of her hands and she'd held his shoulders, her eyes wide at first with astonishment, then drifting closed with pleasure.

Marcel had gaped, speechless. He himself had never kissed Cerise! He'd tried several times, but she'd evaded him, and he hadn't pushed her. Now he saw his approach had been too mild-mannered.

Richard's wasn't, by any means. He'd wedged his knee

between her legs, through her long cotton skirts. They'd been touching from chin to ankle, Richard's hands braced on the tree behind her.

Marcel didn't know how long he'd stood there, feeling lightning struck. After an endless while, Richard and Cerise had separated, staring at each other. Richard had been breathing hard, his face dark with intent. He moved toward her again, but this time Cerise pushed him away. She'd picked up her skirts and run through the woods, back to the village.

After that, Marcel had begun to pursue Cerise with more purpose and less patience. Again and again she'd said no to him, giving him one excuse after another. She'd continued to laugh at him and evade him. Until that one time, down by the river.

He could still smell the water, feel the heaviness of the air. The heat had made them light-headed. Cerise's eyes had looked up into his. And he had tasted heaven.

Then Marcel was in another memory. He was running through the dark woods, woods he knew like his own home. Spanish moss brushed against his face as he tracked Melita. That night he'd seen her work her evil magick, seen her split the huge oak in two, destroying the Source that bubbled from beneath its roots. The tree had fallen and burned.

And Marcel had followed her. Cerise was dead, and it was Melita's fault. Melita had wanted only power at any price, even the cost of her sister's life. She'd worked her rite, maybe even knowing it would kill Cerise—or at least not caring when it had. Marcel had seen Melita's face that night at the circle, her beautiful face, laughing, drunk with magick, flushed with ecstasy—while her younger sister died giving birth to her bastard daughter.

Cerise should have married him. He'd begged her to. He feared he knew the reason she wouldn't.

Now she was dead, her sunlight entombed forever. Marcel would never see or kiss or hold her again. As long as he lived, he would never love another. So Marcel had followed Melita that night, through the darkness. And he'd caught up with her.

✦ Chapter Five

Clio

EARLY ON FRIDAY, I WENT TO AXELLE'S TO GET Thais. I'd been thinking, and I wanted us to do another spell—hopefully one that wouldn't go nuclear on us. In one of Nan's books, I'd found a spell that could reveal other spells. Maybe it would help us figure out who was behind the attacks on us.

Parking in the French Quarter was a fantasy, so I'd called Thais and asked her to wait outside for me. When I drove down Axelle's block at, like, two miles per hour behind a tourist-laden horse carriage, I saw her standing by the curb.

"Hey," she said, sliding into my little blue Camry. "No school. Yay."

"We love teacher workdays," I said.

"Yes, we do," said Thais. "Three-day weekend. So did you do it? Last night?"

For a second I didn't know what she was talking about, but then I remembered that last night had been when I was supposed to open the cupboard where Nan had left emergency instructions.

"Yeah," I said. "I couldn't open it. She told me exactly what to do, and I think I did it right, but no dice."

Thais turned to me, her eyes worried. I made a bunch of left turns until we were headed uptown again.

"So what now?" she asked. "You don't know where she is or how to get in touch with her."

Thais sounded slightly disapproving: that reckless Nan, leaving me on my own.

"I'll give her one more day," I said. "Then I'm going to ask Ouida for help."

"Okay, good idea," Thais agreed. "Where are we going?"

"To Racey's. I didn't feel that safe at home," I admitted. I drove across the eight lanes of Canal Street and started heading up St. Charles Avenue. A streetcar rattled past us, and I waited till its noise had passed to ask, "How are things at Axelle's?"

Thais rubbed her forehead. "Tense. Daedalus and Jules were over last night. And Richard popped in to say hello. He still weirds me out."

"Were they trying to get you to do the rite? Did you feel safe there?"

"Yes, and not really. I mean, I know all these people, but not that well. I just feel so nervous all the time around everyone, like any minute some crazy thing is going to jump out and start attacking me. Plus Richard totally creeps me out just because. I mean, he looks younger than us, but then I remember he's like 260 years old. He's a grown-up."

It was definitely weird—kind of mind-blowing that any of the Treize was immortal, but especially the ones who looked so young still, like Richard and the girl, Manon.

And, of course, there was the other member of their little group who'd been frozen forever at his age, looking so fricking gorgeous. . . .

"Anyone else drop by?" I asked casually, my eyes on the road.

"No," said Thais. "I was hoping Ouida would, but I guess she's busy. Axelle said most of them are trying to rent apartments in case they're here for a while."

"Makes sense. Did you tell anyone about the kablooey magick?"

"No. Were you able to figure out what went wrong?"

"Nope. I went over everything I could think of. All I can come up with is it's the combination of you and me."

"And now you want to do it again?" Thais sounded less than enthusiastic.

"A different spell. And in a different place and with Racey. That should fix it."

A few minutes later I turned off St. Charles toward the lake and turned again on Willow Street. Racey's family had a medium-size house built over a full basement. Basements sat on top of the ground here—you couldn't dig cellars for the same reason you couldn't bury people underground. The water table was too high.

As usual there were three or four cats hanging around outside the house, and Chelsea, one of Racey's dogs, made a show of alertness at the top of the stairs, fierce guard dog on duty, before letting her head sink onto her paws again and closing her eyes.

I knocked hard on the screen door because their doorbell had been broken as long as I could remember. Ceci, one of Racey's older sisters, opened the door. She was holding a bagel in one hand—it was pretty early.

"Yo," she said, then saw Thais standing next to me. She blinked, looked from me to Thais and back again. Then she grinned and shook some of her dark, purple-streaked hair off her shoulders. "Racey told me about the Doublemint action," she said. "Whew. When you go identical, you really go identical." She let us into the house, then turned her head and yelled, "Hey, guys! Come check this out!"

I glanced at Thais, who seemed a little timid and bemused. *Not so identical.* I thought.

Bill and Hillary, Racey's other two dogs, trotted into the room. They sniffed me: same Clio, and then with interest sniffed Thais, the different Clio.

"Hey, puppy," Thais said, holding her hand out to them. "What kind of dogs are these?"

"Catahoula hounds," I said, leading the way to the kitchen. Racey's house was at least twice as big as mine, with six rooms downstairs and four bedrooms on the second floor. We went through the foyer and the dining room, then into the big kitchen/family room. Azura, Racey's mom, was at her sewing machine, surrounded by a big puddle of purple fabric.

"Hi, Clio," she said, looking up with a smile, then she saw Thais. She took the pins out of her mouth and stood up to come over to us. I felt Thais's self-consciousness.

"Azura, this is my sister Thais," I said. "This is Racey's mom, Azura Copeland."

"Welcome, my dear," said Racey's mom, and gave Thais a hug.

Thais was smiling when they separated, and then I heard footsteps running down the stairs. "Mom! Make Trey get out of the bathroom!" Racey said, stomping into the kitchen. Trey was Racey's brother, a year younger than us. He went to our school, and he and Racey were always yelling at each other about something. "Hey, guys. I'm almost ready." She turned back to Azura. "I mean, we have two other bathrooms. Does he have to hog the one that has my makeup in it?"

"I doubt you need makeup on for what you're going to do," Racey's mom said dryly. "Go do your thing, and I'll get Trey out of the bathroom."

Racey scowled. "Whatever." Nodding at us, she said, "Come on. We might as well go."

She opened the back door and headed down the wooden steps that led to their backyard.

"Our workroom is back here," Racey tossed over her shoulder, for Thais's benefit. "It used to be a garden shed, I guess."

Racey's backyard, like so many yards in New Orleans, was

basically an overgrown jungle. There was a thicket of banana trees along one side fence and another clump of enormous ginger plants overhanging the shed. Some of Azura's favorite bamboo was threatening to take over the yard, and I wondered if Thais would recognize the happy, healthy grove of marijuana plants in the back of the tiny vegetable garden. Racey's dad grew them for people with cancer who were going through chemo.

Racey's dad was an artist, and he'd painted a huge sun on the door of the shed. Inside, two small windows and a cracked skylight illuminated the walls and floor, all of which were covered with symbols, runes, and magickal words.

Of course, I'd seen all this a million times, but I wondered what Thais was making of it. She stopped on the threshold and looked around. I guessed they didn't have anything like this in Welsford, Connecticut, where she'd grown up. Racey went to their cabinet and started getting out supplies. I opened Nan's book and started flipping through the pages to find the right spell.

"What's this?" Thais said, tracing her fingers over a symbol.

I looked up. "Uh, *sain et sauf*," I said. "Like, *safe and sound*. Safety. For protection."

"Like those runes from the other night?"

"No—those were runes. *Sain et sauf* is a magickal symbol but not from any runic alphabet."

"There's more than one rune alphabet?"

"Several," said Racey, setting out her family's four cups. Theirs were made of green marble.

"But our branch of the, uh"—I translated in my head—

"natural religion has symbols of its own that are centuries old and very powerful."

"Is the natural religion the *Bonne Magie* you were telling me about?"

"Yeah," I said absently, trailing my finger down the page. "You have any tiger's eye?" I asked Racey.

"I'll look. What else? Copper?"

"No. Gold. And give me four stones of protection, whatever you've got."

"Okay, let's see," Racey murmured, rooting around in the cabinet. "I've got, well, here's another tiger's eye. I've got some agate and malachite. Jet. Citrine?"

I mentally reviewed their properties. "That should be good. Skip the second tiger's eye. Don't want to be unbalanced." I turned back to Thais while Racey started drawing a circle on the floor. "*Magie Naturelle* is like the big, general, French-based form of Wicca, in a way. Like there's Wicca, and then there are different types of Wicca."

Thais frowned. "There are?"

Oh, *Déesse*, she had so much to learn. I was glad I wasn't in her shoes. "Yeah, like Pictish, Scottish, and so on. A bunch. For us, the natural religion is the umbrella religion. Our own famille's branch of it we call *Bonne Magie*."

"I've heard Petra call it *Notre Chose*," added Racey. "Our thing."

"Like the Mafia?" Thais asked faintly. "*Cosa Nostra?*"

Maybe we were giving her too much info for right now.

"Yeah," I said. "Exactly like that. Except we're French witches drawing on the eternal mystical energy in everything around us to work good, and they're Italian and they kill people. Other than that, just like."

Thais looked a little embarrassed.

I drew her into the circle, and Racey closed it behind us. We sat cross-legged on the floor, facing each other.

"Okay, so what are we doing now?" Racey asked.

I realized I hadn't gotten her caught up on the soap opera in, like, days. I let out a deep breath, wondering where to start.

"Someone's trying to hurt Clio and me," said Thais. "To kill us."

Racey looked from Thais to me. "Huh?"

"Things have gotten weird," I said in a massive understatement.

"You mean, weirder than having a surprise identical twin and then God's gift dating both of you at once?" Racey said bluntly.

"Yes. Weirder than that," I said, suddenly feeling tired. "Nan hasn't come back yet. And as it turns out, God's gift actually belongs to a coven that Nan used to belong to. He's a witch."

"Wow." Racey whistled. "Good riddance."

"Yes," I said, my throat feeling tight. "On top of all this, the fun just keeps coming. Both Thais and I have had, like, near-death experiences." I filled Racey in on Thais's nightmare with the snake, the almost stabbing that Racey had witnessed, the streetcar accident, the wasps.

"So we want to do a spell to show us who's behind all this," I went on. "I mean, I'm not thrilled staying in that house alone, Thais is still living with Axelle, and Nan's not back yet."

"You should both come stay here," Racey said, frowning. "Jeez. Why didn't you come here last night?"

"I stayed up late, trying to work Nan's cupboard spell, and then it was too late," I said.

Racey smacked my knee. "Frickin' idiot. It's never too late, you know that. Tell me you're coming here tonight."

"I might," I said. "If nothing's better by then. In the meantime, let's see if this thing works."

The three of us formed a triangle, sitting inside the circle. I picked up the four stones of protection. "One stone for us, one stone for the problem, one stone for the past, and one stone for the future," I said, putting them in a square around us.

"Do you have an element?" Thais asked Racey.

"Yeah, of course," Racey said, surprised. She tugged on the chain of her necklace and showed Thais the large moonstone pendant she wore. "Earth. I use a crystal to represent it. Also, you know, it's pretty and sets off my tan."

I lit the candle in the center for Thais and me.

Then we all held hands, and I read the spell, translating for Thais's benefit. It was much prettier in French, and I always like it when things rhyme. But oh, well.

We walk in sunlight
Shadows follow us.
We are facing fire

We are standing beneath stone
We are underwater
A storm is coming toward us.
With these words reveal the signature
Give the shadow a face, a name.
Show us who kindles fire against us
Who holds a stone over us
Who pulls us underwater
Who conjures a storm to destroy us.

Then I focused on the candle and started to sing my own personal power song, which sort of had words and sort of didn't. Its sounds had their basis in ancient words, but though the power was still there, the words themselves had leached away, leaving pure sound, pure magick.

After a minute, Racey started twining her song in and around mine, under and over and through. We looked up at each other and smiled. We'd done this too many times to count, yet each time it was fresh and new and exciting.

I didn't expect Thais to say anything—there was no way for her to know her personal song yet. It was something that developed over a period of years as you studied magick. But then a third voice joined in. I looked at Thais in surprise and saw that she was singing softly, watching the candle. I didn't recognize the form of her song, but it sounded real, not like gibberish. Racey and I exchanged glances, and then we all looked at the candle and sang.

Two voices singing are balanced, one against the other,

and they can make a pure and beautiful magick. But somehow Thais's voice centered us, the way a three-legged stool is more stable than a two-legged ladder. And while Thais's speaking voice was incredibly similar to mine, our singing voices were different. Hers was more ethereal somehow. To my ears, mine sounded sharper and stronger, and hers was smoother and more flowy.

This was pretty much the most ambitious spell I'd ever tried without a teacher, and I had no idea what to expect. Our three voices raised and fell and joined and separated, and Thais's voice became stronger and more sure. I felt the magick rising in and around us, felt our combined energy swell. It was really beautiful, and happiness rose in me.

And that was when we got blown across the room.

✦ Chapter Six

What's Going On?

PETRA SAW RICHARD EVEN BEFORE SHE PARKED
the car. He was leaning against the iron gate, looking up at her
house. Were his lips moving? She couldn't tell. With a deep,
exhausted sigh she got out of her car, then pulled her suitcase
out of the back. If he felt her coming, he didn't show it.

"Hello, Riche," she said, and he turned to look at her.

"Honey, you're home," he said. "At last. You've missed some
excitement."

Her gaze sharpened as she opened the gate, muttering a
nulling spell so Richard could follow her in. That is, if Clio
had kept up the layers of protection. "What kind of excitement?" she asked, starting up the steps.

Richard took the suitcase out of her hand and carried it up
for her. He was wiry but surprisingly strong, Petra knew.

Inside the house Petra cast her senses but didn't feel Clio.
She turned to face Richard. "What kind of excitement?" she
asked again. "Where's Clio?"

He shrugged. "If she's not here, I don't know. Nothing's

happened to her that I've heard of. I mean, except the Treize."

"What about the Treize?" Petra said, feeling her nerves quicken.

"How about some tea?" Richard said. "Iced, if you have it. And for God's sake, turn on the air."

Petra stepped closer to him and looked up into his brown eyes, the color of coffee with a tiny bit of milk. "Tell me what I want to know and cut the crap," she said quietly.

He laughed. "Or you'll, what, turn me into a frog?" He shook his head. "As far as I know, both girls are fine. But while you were gone, they confronted Axelle, and she called a meeting. Everyone showed, except for monk boy and slut girl, and they basically told the twins everything."

Petra felt a weight settle on her chest. She turned from Richard and walked back to the kitchen, where she opened the window and the back door and turned on the ceiling fan. The kitchen was messy, with unwashed dishes and glasses on the counters, the trash bag overfull, a rotten banana playing host to a happy horde of fruit flies. Yet Petra could detect the faint signature of Clio's presence, feel her vibrations lingering in the air. She had been here recently, like this morning. She was a slob, but alive.

Richard sat in one of the kitchen chairs, and Q-tip ran into the room. Petra saw that his dish had food in it and his water bowl was full. She stooped to pet him, trying to gather her thoughts.

Damn it. Her errand had taken longer than she'd thought,

but she'd still hoped that the Treize hadn't moved on the twins yet. She'd wanted to be the one who told them. Well, too late now. She stood and poured iced tea for herself and Richard, then sat down opposite him.

"Okay," she said. "Tell me what's going on."

He drank his tea, then shrugged. "Just what I told you. The Treize—"

"You included?"

"Hell, yeah. You think I'd miss that freak show? Yeah, so the Treize gathered, and they dumped our sordid past in the twins' pretty laps. Then we had a circle."

Petra tried to hide the dismayed look in her eyes, with no success.

"A circle?"

Richard nodded and drank more tea. Q-tip jumped up on his lap, and Richard petted him. "Yeah. It was very exciting. Your Thais—elle a mordu admirablement au magie. Like a duck to water."

Petra felt Richard's eyes on her. She loved Richard—she'd always loved him. It had pained her when he'd so obviously wanted Cerise. Cerise had rebuffed him, laughed, and called him a little boy. Petra had seen Richard's hurt and been sorry for it. And Marcel had looked daggers at him.

Then Cerise had died. Marcel had broken down, had been so publicly full of grief. But Richard had kept it all inside. He'd overlain his boyish demeanor with a grown-up's cynicism and coldness.

Now, looking at him, his handsome adolescent face that would never achieve its full beauty in adulthood, she felt pangs of sorrow again for the first time in years. Having the twins know about her past, having the Treize gathering again, it was all bringing up so many memories—memories that she'd hoped would stay buried.

"I'm sorry—" she began, then stopped, startled by the admission.

Richard raised one sardonic eyebrow at her.

Petra swallowed. "I'm sorry Cerise turned you down," she said. "You would have been a good match in a few years. I preferred you to Marcel. But he had done so much—"

She'd never before addressed him so directly about Cerise. Everything they'd both felt had been kept to themselves all this time. Why rub salt in the wound? And now, looking at the ice that crackled in Richard's eyes, she wished she'd kept silent.

Q-tip jumped down and ran out the back door, as if the room's tension was too much for him. Petra leaned her head on her hand, looking down at the wooden grain of the kitchen table.

After a long pause, Richard shifted in his chair. "The Treize told Thais and Clio about the Source, the rite, Melita. They'll have a lot of questions for you, I imagine." His voice sounded distant, impersonal. "Also, it appears that Luc's own personal brand of magick is still going strong."

"What?"

Richard shrugged. "It came out that both girls are incredibly pissed at him, and the tension between the three of them would stop a train."

"Damn it," said Petra. "That fast? Both of them? I'll have to have a talk with Luc, then." Her lips thinned as she thought about how that conversation would go. She let out her breath, wishing she could lie down and sleep for a year. "I'd hoped for more time," she said. "It's all starting much too soon, too fast. Everything I've been dreading for so long."

"So you dread it then, do you?" Richard asked.

Petra looked up quickly. Richard had been hanging out with Daedalus and Jules, presumably to help them, for whatever reason. It was very possible he was here today to get an idea of exactly where Petra stood.

She spoke carefully. "Richard—I've been protecting the twins for seventeen years. Whatever Daedalus thinks might happen with the rite, whatever the rest of us could do with it or would want it for—we're still not sure. No one can be positive about its effects. Whether doing it is inevitable or not, yes, there are times when I absolutely dread finding out."

He nodded calmly, looking at her, then finished his tea and stood up. "I hear you. I think it's half-baked myself. But it's fun to watch the old boy run around."

Petra followed him to the front door. He opened it and stepped through, then turned to look back at her.

"Cerise didn't turn me down," he said quietly. Then he was down the front steps and gone before Petra could find her voice.

Chapter Seven

Thais

I LAY ON THE FLOOR NEXT TO THE CABINET. The left side of my face felt like it had been hit with a baseball bat. Trying not to groan, I eased myself to a sitting position. It had happened *again*. I felt horrible—shaky and scared, like I'd been zapped by lightning or stuck my finger in a light socket. Gingerly I touched my cheek, and pain shot into my skull. I'd hit myself even harder this time since the garden shed/workroom was smaller than Clio's workroom. Less room for me to get thrown.

"Are you guys okay?" I asked, looking over at them.

Racey was lying on her back in the corner, muttering swears.

"Holy mother!" Clio said. "What is happening to us?"

Just then the shed door was flung open, and Mrs. Copeland was there, her eyes wide.

"What happened?" she cried, hurrying to Racey. "What are y'all doing out here?"

Racey's sister Ceci rushed in next. After a quick glance

around, she said, "Race, what did I tell you about conjuring demons?"

"Very funny," Clio muttered, rubbing her shoulder.

"What were you doing?" Mrs. Copeland said again, her arm around Racey. Her long black braid swung over one shoulder. She looked barely older than her daughters.

Racey shook her head, wincing. "Just a normal spell."

"A révéler la griffe," Clio explained.

Mrs. Copeland frowned. "To see other spells? And what happened?"

"I don't know," Clio said slowly, looking at me. Instinctively I felt that she didn't want me to mention the twin-magick thing. "I was following the form, right from Nan's book. We were singing, just normal stuff, stuff we've done before, and then kablooey."

I felt Mrs. Copeland looking at me.

"Are you trained in magick?" she asked gently.

My face burned. Was this all my fault because I didn't know what I was doing? She left Racey and came over to turn my face carefully to the light. "You need ice on this," she said, looking concerned. "All of you need arnica. Ceci, go put the kettle on. I'll make some tea."

Standing up, she looked around the room, at the circle that had all but disappeared. "What was this?" she asked, pointing to a small black pile of gray dust.

"Uh, jet," Clio said. "I'll get you a new one. Sorry."

"It doesn't matter, sweetie. But you guys, do not repeat that spell unless Petra can be with you, okay?"

"Don't worry," I muttered. Right then I never wanted to do magick again.

• • •

We were all so upset that after Mrs. Copeland patched us up, we were forced to go to Botanika and have cheesecake and iced mocha frappés.

"It's either this or go buy shoes," Clio said, stirring her drink glumly.

Racey nodded. "I have to say, that totally sucked. But at least I don't have a shiner."

I made a face. Though Racey's mom had given me stuff to help with the pain and swelling, I still had a black eye. She'd given me arnica to take home and said it would help clear it up really fast, but still, I had a sort of bar-fight look going on that I hated.

"This has to be my fault," I said, stirring my drink. "This never happened to either of you before I came along. I think— maybe my magick is just off somehow. Or it just doesn't work right."

"That's a possibility," Racey said thoughtfully. "Tell me, are you a spawn of Satan? That would explain it."

I looked at her in horror, and Racey said, "Ouch!" when Clio kicked her under the table.

"Don't tease her," Clio said, then turned to me. "Our religion doesn't even believe in Satan or the devil or anything like that. There's nothing wrong with you. I don't know what's going on, but I'm sure there's an explanation. If only Nan—"

I nodded. If only Petra would come home.

The brass bells tied to Botanika's door jingled, and I saw my friend Sylvie Allen come in. She was the first person who'd been nice to me when I had started school here, and we were in the same homeroom and several classes together. She was with her boyfriend, Claude, and another guy.

"Hey!" I said, waving, happy to see her. She was so normal. Not a witch. Not immortal. It was a relief.

"Thais!" Sylvie came over, concern on her face. "Are you okay? What happened?"

"Oh," I said, remembering my black eye. "I ran into a door."

Sylvie just looked at me, then at Clio and Racey.

"She really did run into a door," Clio said.

"Hm," said Sylvie. "Well, anyway—are you guys doing something? Do you want to come sit with us?"

Suddenly I desperately wanted to go sit with them and pretend to be a normal high schooler. Stop worrying that every person I saw on the street was a potential threat, every step I took just bringing me toward a new danger. I glanced at Clio and Racey. Clio gave me a little nod.

"It's cool," she said. "I'll call you if I go to Ouida's, okay? But Racey and I can hang."

"Okay, great," I said, picking up my drink and cheesecake.

"Later," said Clio.

I grabbed a new table by the window while Sylvie, Claude, and the other guy went and ordered. A minute later they came back with their coffees.

"Oh, Thais, this is Kevin," Sylvie said. "Kevin LaTour. He goes to L'Ecole too."

I smiled and nodded. "Yeah, I think I've seen you there."

"I *know* I've seen *you* there," said Kevin, smiling back. I blinked, realizing what he meant at the same time I realized he was pretty cute. He had a great, warm smile—bright against his dark skin. His eyes were a clear, olive green, and his black hair was twisted into little spikes all over his head.

"I loved having today off," said Sylvie. "School would be so much better if we always had three-day weekends."

"Hear, hear," said Claude, emptying a sugar packet into his coffee.

Just then Racey and Clio stopped by our table. "We're taking off," said Clio. "I'll call you later, okay?"

"Okay. And tell your mom thanks," I said to Racey. She nodded, and they left.

"Racey's mom patched up my eye," I explained. "It happened at her house."

"Does it still hurt?" Sylvie asked.

"Not too much. Just looks stupid."

"Not too stupid," said Kevin. "How are you liking school here? You're from up north, right?"

"Connecticut," I said. "Um, I like school here okay. You know, it's school."

Sylvie nodded. "At least we only have eight more months. Yay."

"Then we get to do it all over again for four more years,"

Kevin said.

I made a face and laughed, and he laughed too. He was actually really, really cute. Of course, *cute* didn't even begin to sum up Luc's attraction, but still. The fact that I could even distinguish that about Kevin seemed healthy somehow. Good for me.

"Hey, we were thinking of hitting a matinee and then maybe going to Camellia Grill for a hamburger," Sylvie said. "You want to come with?"

I thought for just a second. Axelle almost never told me where she was going or when she'd be back, and I almost never told her anymore. The idea of being a free agent—just taking off and doing something like this without having to let anyone know—seemed great.

"Matinee'll be air-conditioned," Kevin coaxed.

"You talked me into it," I said, and he grinned. At that moment I felt so happy to be sitting there, so un-witchlike, like I used to be.

Of course, I was kidding myself.

✦ Chapter Eight

Eternité

"THIS APARTMENT IS OKAY, ISN'T IT?" SOPHIE asked Manon. She stood at the sink, washing the lunch dishes. Manon was at the kitchen table, reading the newspaper.

"It's fine," said Manon. "I like being on the second floor."

It was lucky how quickly we found a nice place to live, Sophie thought. The apartment wasn't big, just four rooms, but the two of them didn't need much space. And the building was charming, an old Victorian home that had been cut up and rented out. It was only a block from the streetcar line. Maybe if they stayed here awhile, they would rent a car.

Manon came up behind Sophie and put her arms around her waist. Sophie turned her head and smiled at her, still up to her elbows in suds. They didn't have a dishwasher, but she was used to that.

"Do you think Petra's twins will want to do the rite?" Manon asked her. "Want immortality?"

Sophie thought. "I don't know. Daedalus can't be making a good impression—he has 'power hungry' written all over him.

And I don't know the girls at all. I just don't know. It wouldn't be an easy choice."

Manon was silent for awhile, resting her head against Sophie's back.

"If you could choose this time, would you want it?" Manon asked. "Last time we didn't get to choose. It got shoved down our throats. But do you think you'd have wanted it, *l'eternité*, if you'd had a choice?"

"Hmm. I guess so," said Sophie, thinking. "There's been so much I enjoy doing. I like modern life. I'm so glad I've gotten to experience a life that isn't so hard and short, like it was when we were born."

"Also, it took you about a hundred years to fall in love with me," said Manon, and Sophie laughed, a little embarrassed.

"True," she said. "I was a slow learner."

"I wouldn't choose it," said Manon, letting go of Sophie and walking over to a window. "I wouldn't choose immortality."

Sophie was surprised. Manon had never said anything like that before.

"In fact," Manon said, looking out the window, "I've been doing a lot of thinking. If we can do the rite and change things, the way Daedalus says, I think I would choose to die this time. At last." She turned to look back at Sophie, but Sophie was frozen in place, shock turning her to stone.

Sophie had never, ever considered that Manon might want to *die*. The idea, after all this time, was unthinkable. They'd always been together, even before they were lovers.

They'd always planned to be together in the future. Now, out of nowhere, she wanted to die? Sophie had no words. Without Manon—she would die also. There was no way she would want to continue in this life without Manon to come home to, to share everything with. They made each other laugh, comforted each other, held hands in scary movies. Took care of each other when they were sick. They were two halves, joined together. One half alone would never survive.

Carefully Sophie rinsed the plates and put them in the dish drainer. She couldn't remember the last time she'd felt so panicked, so desperate. Her heart was pounding, and cold sweat had broken out on her forehead. She couldn't even form the words yet to ask Manon why, why she'd want to leave her, to die. She couldn't even look at her.

But there was no way she would allow that to happen, no way she would let Manon die.

✦ Chapter Nine

Clio

I ENDED UP BUYING A PAIR OF NEW SHOES, anyway. Racey and I hit our favorite shoe store on Magazine Street, and they had an adorable pair of Doc Martens on sale that would be great for what passed as winter here.

"Now what?" said Racey. "We've done the medicinal snack and the medicinal shoes. I for one am feeling a little better, though I never want to do magick with Thais again."

"Do you really think it's her?" I said. "But why would she have this effect? She doesn't have hardly any power yet. And it's not just because she isn't trained—I mean, I can do spells with some untrained little kid, and I wouldn't get blown across a fricking room."

"Well, I know it's not *me*," said Racey dryly.

For the hundred-and-oneth time, I wished Nan was back, despite how upset I was with her, and that reminded me: I took out my phone and called Ouida's cell phone number. It rang, but in the end I only got her voice mail. I left a message, asking her to call me.

"Okay, so I'm going to take you up on your sleepover offer," I told Racey. "I just don't want to be in that house alone another night. Let me go home and get some stuff, and I'll come back later, okay?"

"Cool," said Racey, getting out of the car. "Later, then."

"Later."

I drove home, worry really starting to weigh me down. Just a few weeks ago, I'd been totally on top of my life. I'd met André, who was my soul mate and the guy I wanted to spend the rest of my life with, Nan was just my Nan, and everything was normal.

Now nothing was. I had an identical twin—gorgeous Thais who all the guys stared at—I wasn't unique anymore. Nan wasn't really my grandmother, and she was part of some science-fiction setup with a bunch of other witches who made *Survivor* look like a tea party. Nan, my Nan, had lied to me my whole life. Everything I had thought was true about me and her had been a lie. It made me feel like I didn't know her, like I'd been living with a stranger. Yet—she was still my Nan, the only grown-up who always took care of me, and I couldn't help feeling like she was still the only person I could trust to keep me safe, especially with someone out there trying to hurt Thais and me. I shivered, automatically glancing in my rearview mirror at the thought. I knew just what Thais meant about feeling constantly on edge, like someone could be lurking anywhere, ready to come at me. It was beyond freaky to know someone wanted you dead and have no idea who that person was.

I looked back at the road as I drove up to the house, feeling relief wash over me when I spotted Nan's old Volvo parked three cars down. Finally she was back!

Now I would get answers to my questions, hear her explanations. I leaped out of my car and raced through the gate and up the steps. Then Nan was opening the door for me. I hesitated for just a second—I was really angry at her—but old habits and my worry won out, and I threw myself into her arms.

"Nan!" I said. "Nan! I thought you were never coming back!"

She held me tightly, one hand stroking my hair, murmuring, "Shhh, shhh," the way she used to when I was little and I'd skinned my knee. And then, taking us both by surprise, I burst into tears. "Don't go away again," I sobbed, effectively leaving my calm, cool Clio image in the dust.

"I won't, my dear," Nan said. "Come inside now and tell me everything."

We went to the kitchen, and I noticed she'd been home long enough to clean up. I watched her as she poured us cold drinks.

"You lied to me," I said, and saw her wince. "I trusted you. You've been lying to me my whole life. You kept my father from me. I'll never have a chance to know him."

"I'm so sorry, Clio," she said. "I was—afraid. I wanted to keep you safe, at almost any cost. I'm not sure if I did the right thing or not. But you have to believe that I never intended to hurt you."

"That wasn't even all, though," I went on. "Even after all of that came out, and you barely explained it, then you go away and I hear about this whole Treize thing. It's—unbelievable. And I heard about it from a bunch of strangers. They were telling the truth, right?"

"Pretty much," Nan said quietly.

I let out a breath. Some part of me hadn't fully accepted it as real until that moment, hearing her confirm it. "You're not even my grandmother. We're related so far back I can't even figure it out!"

"Thirteen generations," Nan said, her long, slim fingers curled around her glass. "But we are related—I still am your nearest relative, besides Thais. And I wanted to tell you so many times, but I truly didn't know how. I just didn't want the Treize to touch your life."

"Too late," I said.

"I know. And I know they're putting their grand plan into action. You and I and Thais have to determine where we stand on that and on other things."

"Yeah, like whether we want to live *forever*," I said, and consternation crossed her face. I told her about Axelle and how we knew about the rite and met everyone and had a circle.

"So you met Luc, did you?" Nan asked, as if picking up on something.

I shrugged. I'd never told Nan the details of my plunges into the dating pool, and now I felt even less close to her, trusted her less.

"Clio—did Luc hurt you? And Thais?"

There was no way I would admit how bad it had been, to anyone. It was too embarrassing and made me feel like my heart, pumping and bleeding, was hung on the outside of my chest.

I shrugged again and met Nan's eyes. "Not really." I sighed. "But what a jerk. He dated both Thais and me. Luckily, we found out almost right away. We both screamed at him, and then when we saw that he was also part of the Treize, we froze him out."

Nan looked at me, weighing my words. I wondered if she'd heard anything different from someone else and decided it didn't matter. That was my story, and I was sticking to it.

"So it wasn't any worse than that?"

"No. I mean, we're still majorly pissed. But we're dealing."

"Uh-huh."

I had to change the subject. "So where were you all this time? Why didn't you call?"

"I was in Connecticut, fixing Michel Allard's will."

I frowned. "Thais's dad?" I paused, feeling something weird in my stomach. "*My* dad?" I added, the words sounding funny. "Why? What do you mean, fix?"

"Somehow, right after Michel died, either Axelle or Daedalus changed Michel's will so Axelle would get custody of Thais."

"Oh, yeah."

"Yes. So this time I went up and changed his will myself."

My head was spinning. "And they don't have phones in Connecticut? I didn't realize how backward they were."

Nan looked at me wryly. "I was extremely busy the whole time, and I didn't want to be in touch until everything was worked out. I knew you'd have so many questions. . . . The phone didn't seem the right way to do this."

"You changed the will back to how it was? Is Thais going back to Connecticut to be with that neighbor?"

"No. I changed his will so I would have custody," Nan said, her eyes very clear and calm, looking into mine. "I'm Thais's legal guardian now, and she's going to come live with us."

It took a moment for that to sink in. Another huge change in my life. I did feel a quick rush of gladness that she wasn't going back north, yet—

"Do I have to share my room?"

Nan smiled at me, so familiar, and despite my anger, I was relieved she was back. "No," she said with an amused look. "I've thought about it, and I'm going to move myself to the little alcove room under the stairs. Thais will have my room. I don't need much space anyway. It will be fine."

Right now, the tiny little room under the stairs was our junk room.

"Well, if you think so. I'll help you clear it out," I said.

"Thank you."

And then here's the Clio part: It occurred to me that with Thais living here, I'd be much more involved with her life, know what she was doing. Like, if she was seeing Luc, for example. I felt ashamed as soon as I thought that, but I knew it was true.

"Oh my God—there's stuff I haven't even told you," I said, my heart beating faster. "Someone's trying to kill Thais and me, and there's something wrong with Thais's magick."

Nan's eyes opened wide, and I went on to tell her all about our attacks, and the wasps, and how Melysa, one of my teachers, had saved us. I ran down our current theories and who we'd eliminated. Nan looked increasingly concerned as I went on, and her lips pressed together the way they did when she was mad at me.

Finally she nodded slowly, looking thoughtful. "Okay. I'm back, and I'll get to the bottom of that. Now, what do you mean, there's something wrong with Thais's magick?"

So I told her about the spells we'd tried, and how they'd gone wonky, and then we'd done the joining spell, which had blown us across the room. Nan had nodded approvingly at the mention of the spell, but when I mentioned the hand-grenade effect, she looked astonished.

"What?" she said, as if she hadn't heard right.

"We got blown right out of the circle, across the work-room," I said again. I told her how I'd set the spell up, putting in every detail I could think of. "I felt like a rag doll. Then, just this morning, I thought we could try to do a *révéler la griffe* to see if we could find out who was trying to hurt us."

Nan nodded; it was perfectly reasonable.

"We did it at Racey's because I felt weird here. And I set it up carefully, four stones of protection, blah blah blah, and I was doing my song, and Racey joined in like a million times before, and then Thais joined in, singing, and she sounded good, you know? Like she knew what she was doing. Or at least like what was coming out of her mouth was real."

I realized I hadn't asked Thais how she'd known what to sing. I'd ask her later.

"Then what happened?"

"We got blown across the room. All of us. We felt like crap, and Thais hit her face on the cabinet. She has a black eye."

Nan looked at me as if I'd announced I was joining the Peace Corps.

"I can't believe it," she said. "Racey got thrown too?"

I nodded. "And Azura felt it, a big boom of magick, inside their house, and she came running. She said not to mess with it again unless you were with us."

Nan shook her head. "You physically got moved through a closed circle."

"We got thrown across the room," I repeated.

"Thais has a black eye? Where is she now?"

I shrugged. "She ran into some friends from school and was going to hang with them. Azura patched her up pretty good. It should be mostly gone by tomorrow. I mean, do you have any idea what could cause something like that?"

Nan didn't answer.

✦ Chapter Ten

The Marked Girl Brings You Death

THE SNAKE—A NONPOISONOUS BOA CON-
strictor—coiled around the fortune-teller's neck. Claire
watched it, amused. It might actually spook someone who
didn't know squat about snakes.

The tiny Thai woman, her face the color and texture of a
dried tobacco leaf, peered down at Claire's palm very solemnly.
Claire shot a glance at her friend, who'd convinced her to come
see Madame Chu, one of the most respected fortune-tellers in
Phuket. Her friend gave her a be-patient glance and bent her
head to light a cigarette.

This market was like any number of markets Claire had
seen, in any number of countries. Inexact rows of canvas stalls,
beat-up coolers holding fish, squid, shrimp. People hawk-
ing gold jewelry next to a stand selling fried batter. Roasted
animals hung from poles overhead, filling the air with their
scent and steam.

"What, granny, she has no fortune?" Claire's friend joked
at the ongoing silence.

Madame Chu looked up at Claire. "No, she has too much." Her sharp black eyes, almost closed by folds of skin, examined Claire as if she'd just discovered an exotic new creature.

"Too much fortune?" Claire's friend laughed, the stall's single lantern casting shadows on her red cheongsam. "Lucky you."

"No," said Madame Chu. "Not lucky. Too much."

Claire laughed also, feeling the old woman's cool, dry hands holding her own.

Madame Chu bent low over Claire's hand. "Your fortune goes on and on," she said, speaking slowly. "Your time of death has come and gone. A dark one filled you with lightning, and now you live a walking death."

Claire quit laughing. "What?"

"Granny," said Claire's friend, frowning. "You are the best fortune-teller, I told her. Don't make me into a liar. Tell her the truth, and stop your nonsense."

Claire swallowed hard and wished she had a drink. Right after this, they would go to Samasan's bar. Absolutely. She'd paid up her tab and should be welcome again. Samasan never held a grudge.

Madame Chu's black beetle eyes regarded Claire over their hands.

"What else do you see?" Claire said offhandedly, as if she didn't care.

"I see a girl, marked—" The old woman touched her cheekbone. "Like a red lily flower."

Claire sat very still, her heart starting to beat faster. "She's dead," she said lightly. All of them died, sooner or later. Daughter after daughter after daughter.

"No." Madame Chu's eyes burned like coals. "She will kill you at last. The marked girl brings you death."

"Come on, Claire." Her friend sighed. "She's having an off night. We'll come back some other time, okay?"

Claire pulled her hand back and stood up, looking hard at Madame Chu. "Yeah," she said, throwing some money down. "It's all nonsense."

Madame Chu shook her head sadly, as if Claire were already dead.

✤ Chapter Eleven

Thais

BECAUSE OF A FUNERAL, A LOT OF THE STREETS in the Quarter were blocked. After several frustrating minutes of circling blocks, I asked Sylvie to drop me off, and I would walk the rest of the way.

"You sure?" Sylvie asked.

"Yeah—you'll never get through. And I'm only four short blocks away from here."

"Okay, then. I'll see you at school Monday."

"Yeah, okay." I opened my car door and started to get out. "Thanks a lot for bringing me along today. I had a great time."

"I'm so glad we ran into you," said Sylvie, and Claude nodded.

"I'll look for you at school," said Kevin, and the look he gave me was more than a superficial just-met-you glance.

"Um, okay," I said and got out.

I waved good-bye and walked up the street, through the traffic barriers and in and out of the crowds of mourners. I had no idea who had died, but it was someone who rated a full-blown jazz-band parade, complete with umbrella walkers. I felt like an extra in a movie.

It was dark—after the movie we'd gone to Camellia Grill, which I had loved. I'd had pecan waffles. Now it was almost eight o'clock, and I reviewed whether or not I had homework due Monday. The idea that I still had to think about homework, after everything I'd been through in the past few days, seemed crazy. But education waits for no one.

Kevin LaTour. He'd been really nice. Plus he was on the honor roll and was funny too. He seemed so much younger than Luc. Well, yeah, I guess he *was*—but even if Luc were only nineteen or so, the way he looked, Kevin still seemed much younger, still a kid.

But a nice kid.

And Sylvie was great, and she was so cute with her boyfriend. I was so glad that I knew them, a tiny island of normal sanity in my stormy life.

Even after I was out of the funeral, the streets were busy and well-lit. In less than five minutes I was letting myself through the side gate at Axelle's. I hoped Luc wouldn't be there again. I didn't know how many more horrible, heartbreaking, dramatic scenes I could stand. None, actually.

Right before I put my key into the door lock, I heard raised voices from inside. I stood very still and listened, listened with all of me, not just my ears. I closed my eyes and pretended the words inside were little arrows, slipping right through the door. . . .

"How dare you!" That was Daedalus.

"You should have checked with her." Axelle. "You know she's happy here. I can't believe you would go behind my back like this!"

"It's unsupportable!" Daedalus sounded pompous, as usual. "It's a betrayal!"

"Oh, Daedalus, put a sock in it," said another voice. Petra! It was Petra!

I unlocked the door and rushed in. "Petra! You're back!"

Then she was hugging me, and I was hugging her back, my eyes closed, thinking of how incredibly glad I was, considering that really, I didn't know her all that well. But I belonged to her, because my sister did.

Finally we separated, and she held me at arm's length and looked at me closely, examining my black eye.

"When did you get back?" I asked. "Does Clio know?"

"Yes, she does," said Petra, smiling. "I got back late this morning and saw Clio this afternoon. And now I'm seeing you."

"What happened to your eye?" Axelle said, coming closer.

"I . . . walked into a door," I said. I'd tell Petra the truth later.

Axelle's eyes narrowed, as if she knew I was lying. I didn't care.

"Oh, I'm glad you're back," I told Petra, and she smiled again.

"If I'd known I was going to get these enthusiastic welcomes,

I would have gone away sooner," she said. "But I'm very glad to be back and to see you. And I have some news for you."

"Petra," Daedalus said warningly, but she ignored him.

"Are you hungry, Thais?" Axelle broke in. "Do you want something to drink?"

"What?" She'd never worried about that before.

"Listen," said Petra, putting her hands on my shoulders. "I've got some news. I was in Connecticut. I had your father's will changed so that I would have custody of you."

It took a moment for it to sink in. "Me? You have custody of me? How can you change a will?" Her blue-gray eyes looked into mine. "Oh. Magick." What a creepy thought.

"I'd like you to come home with me tonight," said Petra.

This was incredible—everything I'd hoped for.

"Thais—surely you don't want to leave," said Axelle.

I stared at her. Was she kidding? "I want to go live with Petra and Clio. Clio's my sister. And at least I'm related to Petra."

"Don't you want to stay? It hasn't been so bad, has it?" Axelle said coaxingly.

She actually wanted me to stay. I didn't think it was because she'd become fond of me. She had another reason, one I didn't know. And Daedalus was standing there looking furious. Clearly he wanted me here.

Well, that settled it. "Give me ten minutes to pack," I told Petra.

"Thais!" said Axelle.

"Look, you're right, it hasn't been that bad," I said to Axelle.

Despite everything, I didn't want to be mean to her. "But—you know, it just feels more homey at Petra's. I want to be with my family." Plus I didn't want to be in the Quarter anymore, with Luc living maybe six blocks away. I dreaded running into him and would never go into my special secret garden again. "I'm sorry, Axelle. But I just want a regular kind of home." *And to live with someone I don't think could maybe be trying to kill me*, I added inwardly. Somehow I didn't really feel like it could be Axelle, but then again, I didn't know her very well. I didn't know any of them, really, but at least Clio and Petra were related to me!

Axelle glanced around at the chrome and black leather, the full ashtrays, the empty wine bottles on the counters. She looked like she wanted to protest that this was a regular home but knew she didn't have a leg to stand on. "I wish you would stay, Thais." She gave me a smile, and Axelle is not a smiley kind of person. Even her cat would have known it was fake.

"I'm sorry," I said again and went to my room.

It really did take only ten minutes to throw my stuff together. I had some cardboard boxes from my old house that I hadn't even unpacked, and my clothes fit into several suitcases. To my surprise, Richard came in while I was packing.

He leaned against the door frame, and his wide leather bracelet clicked against the wood. "Need some help?"

"Um—could you carry some of this out to Petra's car?"

"Yep." He picked up two heavy boxes as if they weighed nothing and left.

Twenty minutes later the car was loaded, and Petra was driving us uptown to my new home.

"I'm so glad you're back," I said again. "So much has happened. Did Clio tell you everything?"

"I think so," said Petra, smiling at me. "But you tell me again. She said something strange happens when you make magick."

"You could say that," I said, gingerly touching my eye. I told her everything I could remember about the spells we had done and what had happened. She asked questions, and I answered them as best I could. "Do you know what's going on?" I asked.

Petra let out a sigh. "No, I actually don't. Perhaps it's the twin-power thing, though I hadn't expected your strength to be so reactive yet. But I'll look into it, sweetie. Now that I'm back, I'm going to try to get things more under control."

It was a comforting thought, and I felt even more comforted when we pulled up in front of their—our—house. I was going to live here. I felt like I was finally coming home.

"Am I going to be in Clio's room?" I asked as we started carrying my stuff up to the porch. "Or—on the couch?"

"No." Petra put down her load and went back to the car. I followed her. "Clio and I cleared out my room this afternoon. I've moved into the alcove room, under the stairs, and you'll have my room. You can repaint it if you want."

"What?" I was dumbstruck. "You gave up your room?" I was so touched by that and by her even going to Connecticut to get custody of me. Tears welled up in my eyes and I sniffled.

Clio, I thought. Then the front door opened and Clio came out. I looked up at her, hoping she was okay with my moving in.

She smiled at me, not hugely effusive, but sincerely. "What a trip, huh?" she said, picking up one of my suitcases. "Oof. Glad to see you brought all your own personal bricks."

I laughed and Petra smiled, and it was right then that I felt like I really had a family.

•   •   •

That night I lay in my new bed, staring up at my new ceiling. My room at Axelle's had been long and narrow and kind of dark, with only one small window that was shaded by plants outside. This room wasn't big, smaller than my old room had been in Connecticut, but it was full of light in the daytime, with windows on two walls. It was painted light turquoise, which I thought I would keep, at least for a while. There was a painted border all around the room, about a foot from the ten-foot ceiling. It was painted in gold and was made up of a set of symbols, painted over and over again. Petra had explained that they were symbols of health and happiness, of peace and tranquility and magickal power. She'd told me their names, but I only remembered a few.

Now, as I lay with the moonlight shining bright through the Indian-print curtains, I closed my eyes and tried to feel if there was any magick around me. The last couple of times we had tried doing spells, it had been awful and scary. But *I* was magickal, from a family of witches. Magick ran in my blood. I had just started to tap into it—I couldn't avoid it or pretend it wasn't there. It was like one of those party-favor flowers that blooms underwater, slowly unfolding and sending out colorful streams. It felt—different. I felt different. I felt my life until now had been fine, even good, but that I'd been living under a layer of Saran Wrap, kind of. Now the wrap was peeling slowly off, showing me brighter colors, stronger flavors, fresher breezes. It was scary and weird but also kind of exciting.

And here's the really strange thing that I only realized just then: Despite my mixed feelings about magick, despite being kind of afraid of it, I felt centered in myself. Before it was my dad who made me feel centered. The last couple weeks, it had been knowing I had a real sister and Petra, who cared for me. But now I realized that somehow I felt connected and grounded all by myself, and I thought it was probably because of the magick. Like there was a magickal thread that kept me rooted to the earth, tapped into its ancient, unending life and power. I felt strong in myself in a way I hadn't before. Even though part of me wanted to keep away from magick, keep safe, a much larger part of me was being drawn to it, to its beauty and strength and goodness. I wanted to know more.

✤ Chapter Twelve

Clio

SO THAIS MOVED INTO NAN'S ROOM, AND NAN moved into the tiny alcove room downstairs, where you could hardly stand up straight. I felt much less freaked and worried now that Nan was back, but in a way, having her right there was a constant reminder that she had betrayed me by not telling me the truth my whole life. It was hard. I loved her and depended on her, yet I was also kind of seething with resentment and anger.

I still thought of her as Nan, my grandmother, even though now I knew she wasn't. But I'd called her Nan for seventeen years, and it would be too weird to call her anything else. Still, something inside me felt like I couldn't trust her completely, the way I always had.

But with everything else going on, I knew I needed her more than ever now, even if I couldn't look at her the same way.

I also needed to get my mind off all this intense crap.

"Hey, I realized something," I said to Thais Saturday morning. "My wardrobe just doubled. We're the exact same size. Now

I've got twice as many clothes." Always looking on the bright side, that's me. Actually, not really, but this *was* an upside.

Or not.

"Who's been buying your clothes?" I said, examining her closet critically.

"Me," she said, sounding defensive.

"Uh-huh." I stepped back and closed her closet door. "We must get you clothes that I'll actually want to borrow."

Thais gave me a sour look. Of course, she went to school on Monday wearing a layered tank top from the Clio Collection, so clearly she knew what I was talking about.

At school I waited while Thais gave her new address to the office.

She turned back with a smile. "It's official."

We pushed our fists together, then split up to go to our different homerooms. Her last name began with an *A*, mine with an *M*. I wondered if one of us should change.

• • •

So, yeah, we were twins, and now we even lived together, but at lunch we still sat with our separate gangs. Racey, Della, Eugenie, Kris, and I sat outside on the sidewalk under the overhang, out of the sun. Thais sat with Sylvie and her boyfriend and a couple other people over on the grass in the school's side yard. I noticed the same guy from Botanika sit next to Thais. Kevin something?

"Yo," said Trey, coming up to us. He dropped to one knee next to Racey.

Racey popped a few chips in her mouth. "Yo back."

"So. Collier Collier," said Della meaningfully. She tugged her miniskirt down an inch and leaned back against the building.

"Got any money?" Trey asked Racey.

"For lunch?" she asked him, and he shrugged.

"Go on," I said to Della. "Spill."

Racey rummaged in her purse. "All I have is a ten."

Trey plucked it from her fingers. "Tank-u. Later."

Racey sighed and watched her little brother disappear. "That kid hits me up for more money . . ."

"Race, Della's telling us what happened with Collier Collier," I said pointedly.

"Ooh," said Racey, sitting up. "Do tell. How's cradle robbing going?"

Della made a face at her, and Racey held up her hands. "What? He's younger than Trey!"

"That's 'cause Trey is only eleven months younger than you!" Della said. "You're like Irish twins!"

Racey rolled her eyes. "Go on. I'm all ears."

"He's really sweet," Della said kind of lamely since she had all of our attention.

"*Sweet?*" I said.

"Yeah. He's just—really sweet. He doesn't take anything for granted," said Della. "Anything I do, he's all 'thank you' and everything."

"I bet." Kris smirked.

"No, I mean little things, like if I drive or ask him if he

wants something to drink. He just doesn't take me for granted. It's really—different. Nice."

We all looked at her in silence.

Della sighed. "And okay, he's really hot too."

"Now we're talking," Eugenie said. "Are you teaching him everything?"

"He *knows* everything," Della said wryly. "If this is instinct, I'm all for it. That boy was made to please. He's—fabulous. Like he's made for me."

I knew how that felt. *Don't think about it.*

"Huh," Racey said, looking at Della speculatively. "Sounds serious."

"Oh, well, I don't know." Della picked up her soft drink can and drank from it. She seemed embarrassed, as if she hadn't meant to say so much.

I exchanged a look with Racey. Della was usually the love-'em-and-leave-'em girl, like me. Or at least, how I used to be. I'd never heard her say anyone was sweet before or talk about someone's actual personality. I looked around the school grounds and saw Collier Collier sitting with a bunch of sophomore guys. His eyes were on Della, and the puppy-love look on his face made my eyebrows rise.

How nice that some people had guys who were interested in them and only them.

• • •

"So, you know, if you want to borrow this car sometime, it's cool," I told Thais as I pulled up in front of our house.

"Oh, okay. Thanks," she said. "I don't even have a Louisiana driver's license. Guess I should get one."

I got out of the Camry and headed through the front gate. "Yeah. Then you won't have to use turn signals anymore."

Thais laughed, following me up the steps, and for just a second I flashed on how different our lives would have been if we'd grown up together. We would have come home from school together just like this every day. And we would have hung out and fought over stuff and known each other really well. And either she wouldn't have known our dad or I wouldn't have had Nan.

I was putting my key in the lock when Thais said, "I wish you could have known Dad."

Just like that, out of the blue. One of those twin things, I guessed. I bit my lip. "Me too," I said softly.

Inside, Nan was waiting for us with Melysa in the kitchen. I hadn't seen Melysa since she'd saved our lives last week, and now I saw that she was checking us out for aftereffects.

"Ready to do some metal work?" Melysa asked me.

"Yeah—just let me grab something to eat," I said. "And that reminds me—I guess Thais won't be doing her rite of ascension, will she?"

Nan shook her head. "Not this year."

"Well, maybe by the time she's thirty," I said brightly, and Thais groaned.

Nan and Melysa laughed.

"What exactly is the rite of ascension, anyway?" Thais

asked. "I've heard you mention it."

"It's a rite where a witch is tested on how much he or she knows on any number of given subjects," Nan explained. "About spell-craft skills, historical knowledge, decision-making abilities, and even just raw magickal ability."

"It's an incredibly important rite," Melysa clarified. "Passing it, undergoing the process, greatly enhances your own personal power. Quite a few people don't pass it on the first try."

"So it's like the SATs," Thais said glumly. "But for witches. The WSATs."

"Yes, something like that," Melysa said, smiling. "I'm sure your time will come. But Clio's time is coming in only two months, so we better get to work."

"I'd like to learn more," said Thais hesitantly. "But it's been so weird lately. . . ."

"Actually, Thais, if it's okay, I'd like you to hold off working any spells for just a little while," said Nan. "You and I can start to go over some basic knowledge, though, about plants and properties of other elements. But I think you two shouldn't work any magick together until we figure out what's going on. Okay?"

"Okay," said Thais, and I thought she maybe even looked a little relieved.

I shrugged. "Okay."

• • •

That afternoon Melysa and I worked until it got dark—there were a couple of spells that are particularly effective right at dusk. She put me through my paces, and I did really well, except for one little glitch where I accidentally wrote the wrong rune and had to start over.

But other than that, I did great—nothing went wrong.

Nothing got too big or weird.

I didn't get blown across the room.

So what did that say about Thais?

Chapter Thirteen

The Whole Balance of Power

"HAND ME THAT MAGNIFYING GLASS, WILL YOU, Jules?" Daedalus held out his hand without looking up.

Jules got the small round lens from the shelf and handed it to Daedalus, leaning over a map on the worktable in Axelle's attic workroom. Downstairs he could hear Luc's raised voice, as if he and Axelle were arguing. Jules sighed. When he and Daedalus had first come up with this plan, it had sounded so feasible somehow.

"I'd forgotten how unwieldy the Treize is," he said.

"Hmm?" Daedalus glanced up. "Did you say something?"

Jules gestured to the door at the top of the stairs. "Sounds like Luc and Axelle are locking horns again. Somehow I'd forgotten how strong everyone's personalities are. Though I don't remember Luc being so—volatile."

"He never was," Daedalus said absently. Keeping one finger on the ancient map he was studying, he carefully wrote some notes in a small book. He stood up, capped his pen, and looked at Jules. "Luc's always gotten along with everyone—I mean, after Ouida got over their whole thing. We all knew Luc's foibles, but they never got in the way, never interfered with any of us. It's unusual, his being so—emotional."

"Sophie," said Jules, and Daedalus waved one hand dismissively.

"That's old news. It can't have anything to do with how he is now."

"So is it the girls, then?" Jules asked, frowning. "I don't see how it could be. His dalliances never—"

"Never reach his heart?" Daedalus laughed. "You're assuming he has a heart, Jules. You know Luc. He has a porcelain surface—nothing gets in, and nothing gets out. Yes, we'd discussed his plan, his mission, in regard to the twins. And it seems like he failed, which is certainly unique. But I can't believe whatever happened with Thais and Clio has affected him. There must be something else going on." Daedalus looked thoughtful. "Perhaps it would be prudent to find out what that is."

"Maybe he's against doing the rite?"

"No," said Daedalus, leaning over the map again. "Of course not. No, everyone is behind what we're doing."

"Not everyone," Jules said, frowning. "Remember—"

"No, everyone." Daedalus stood up straight again and fixed Jules with a glare. "No one could seriously oppose what I'm doing—you know that. Anyway, even if they did at first, they'll come around." He bent down to his work again. "Besides," he added, almost in an undertone, "even if they did, it wouldn't matter. None of them is at all powerful enough to really impede me. Well, maybe Petra."

Jules was stung. Maybe Petra? Only she? Pressing his lips together, Jules walked over to the gable window and looked out. From here he could see the river and hear the blare of tugboats' horns as they guided the huge tankers upstream. A haze hung over the water, and the last of the day's sunlight shone weakly through it.

Only Petra. Daedalus considered only Petra worthy of concern. So Jules's own power, own acquiescence, was taken for granted or not taken into account at all. And he noticed that this whole scheme, which he and Daedalus had developed together during the summer, now was Daedalus's plan, his idea. Who was Jules? An underling? An *assistant?*

Jules set his jaw, then schooled his face into calmness and turned back. His power. That's exactly what could change if they did this rite with the full Treize. The whole balance of power would change—in an instant.

✦ Chapter Fourteen

Another Level of Desolation

"BAY," RICHARD MURMURED, PAINTING IT ON his wall. The silver paint looked good against the deep blue, and he stood back to admire its effect. "Wind."

Even though this apartment was only rented and even though he would no doubt not be here long, still, Richard had decided to go ahead and make his surroundings more comfy. His bedroom wasn't big, and his bed was a single mattress on the floor. A low altar in one corner was covered with red candle wax. But the rich blue walls felt good, and now he was painting silver symbols and runes in a border encircling the room.

"Collet," he said, dipping his brush into the paint. He drew two small circles connected by a U shape. Necklace. A drop of silver paint dripped off his brush onto his bare chest. Absently he smeared it with a finger, then put down the brush and lit a cigarette. He was standing in the middle of the room, planning his design, when he heard the apartment door slam.

Richard grinned wryly. What a surprise—Luc was still in a bad mood. He heard cabinets open in the kitchen, liquid being poured into a glass. Footsteps came down the hall, and then Luc was in the doorway, taking a sip of his drink.

"If that's the last of my scotch, I'm going to kick your ass," Richard said without heat.

"Left you some for breakfast tomorrow," Luc said, looking at Richard's handiwork. "You're going to have to repaint all this before you leave."

Richard shrugged, blew out some smoke, and tapped ash onto the floor.

Luc's eyes narrowed as he caught some of the symbols. "You doing something here, Riche, or is this just for looks?"

Richard glanced at him. "Looks."

Luc moved closer to the wall and tapped the symbol for feather. "Plume? Collet? Tache? If I didn't know better, I'd say you were working up to something."

Richard regarded him evenly. "Good thing you know better."

Luc drank, looking bleak. *Ah, the twins,* Richard thought. The lovely twins, with hair black as night, eyes green as the sea. Cerise's eyes. Armand's hair. Funny how their looks had been preserved so perfectly after all this time. Each daughter, daughter after daughter after daughter, had married. Some had been men in the *famille*; some had been outsiders. But for all that inpouring of genetic material, here the twins were, almost identical replicas of Cerise. As if they had sprung from her directly, without their blood being watered down over and over. His mouth set in a grim line, and he went to pull on a T-shirt, carefully switching his cigarette from hand to hand.

"So you know Petra's back," he said.

Luc looked up. "Really? When? Where was she?"

"Got back yesterday. Apparently she was up north, refixing Michel Allard's will."

"In what way?" Luc asked.

Richard took a drag on his cigarette, acting casual, drawing out Luc's torment. "She got custody of Thais. Plucked her out of Axelle's like a chicken out of a fox den. But you probably know this." He watched Luc out of the corner of one eye, saw him run a hand through hair already ragged, his face achieve yet another level of desolation.

"Thais isn't at Axelle's anymore?" Luc asked, trying to sound calm and failing. Richard frowned. Luc actually seemed to have it bad, which was disturbing. *Okay, fine, fool around with them, not a problem. But something more? It could be . . . dangerous.*

Richard and Luc had always gotten along, as long as neither hampered the other from getting what he wanted. So far they'd never wanted the same thing.

"Nope," Richard said, putting out his cigarette. He screwed the paint cap back onto the jar and set it aside. "She moved uptown with Petra last night. I helped load the car." He looked at Luc thoughtfully. "If they told Petra about you screwing them both, she's going to have your blood."

Luc flushed. "I didn't screw either one of them."

"Sorry. I meant *screw over.*"

"Bite me." Luc's hand was clenching his glass so hard, Richard thought it might break.

Richard smiled. "And you would call it? . . ."

"A mistake." Luc turned away, heading down the hall to the kitchen. Richard followed him, saw him dump the last of the bottle into his glass and slam it down.

"So much for breakfast tomorrow," Richard said. He leaned against the counter. "I've never seen you like this. And your uncharacteristic lack of finesse in this situation has raised eyebrows. What's going on?" He laughed. "Oh, *Déesse*, don't tell me you actually care."

Luc's face hardened. "Like you should talk," he said, quietly biting. "The way you used to moon over Cerise. The whole village knew. They thought it was funny. Too bad she wasn't interested in a little kid."

Richard felt anger heat his blood and tried to quench it down. His throat hurt, and he swallowed hard, wishing like hell Luc hadn't just drunk the last liquor in the house.

"What makes you think she wasn't interested?" he said mildly. "Anyway, let's just say my technique has improved in the last two hundred years. As has my success rate. Since the twins have given you the brush-off, would you mind if I had a go? How about Clio?"

"Good luck," Luc said bitterly, staring at his empty glass. "She's a handful."

Richard kept his eyes on Luc. "Or maybe Thais?"

Luc looked up, and Richard was surprised, though he

didn't show it. He'd seen Luc in every situation there was, from crazed drunken revelry to the bitter ashes of regret, but he'd never seen this, this cold, weirdly calm look of murderous rage.

"Try it and I'll rip your heart out," Luc said.

✤ Chapter Fifteen

Maybe Another Two Hundred Years

"THEY TOLD YOU THIS?" OUIDA ASKED, AND Petra nodded.

Morning sunlight shone in through the plants hanging in front of the window. It cast green-tinged dappled light over the table, the worn linoleum of the floor. Petra opened the back door to let more breeze in.

"Récolte soon, and as hot as July," she murmured.

"This is New Orleans," Ouida said dryly. "Monvoile will come and go, and it'll be as hot as July. But maybe you're not used to it yet. Maybe another two hundred years."

"Should be cooler by Soliver," Sophie said. "Maybe."

A noise by the screen door made Petra look, and Q-tip smacked the screen with one paw.

"Oh. Present for Mommy," Ouida said, looking through the screen.

"Ick," said Sophie. "Is that a mouse?"

"What's left of one," Petra said with a sigh. She opened the door and let Q-tip in, then held out her hand. "Tranquille," she murmured, sketching a quick sign in the air, and the cat froze in mid-step on the kitchen floor.

"Why does that work if he's deaf?" Ouida asked.

"I don't know," said Petra, kneeling by him. "But I'm glad it does. Okay, Q-tip, drop the mouse. Laisse tomber."

Q-tip's mouth opened, and the mouse corpse fell onto the floor.

"It's a lovely mouse, Q-tip," Petra said, getting a plastic baggie. "Thank you so much." She patted his head, and though he stayed in place, she felt him start to purr. "You are such a good hunter. A fierce and mighty hunter. I'll put this mouse somewhere safe."

Q-tip, released from his holding spell, sat down, and started washing his paw.

Petra put the mouse baggie up on the counter to get rid of later.

"Okay, where were we?" she said, sitting down again.

"Where you were telling us that someone's trying to harm Thais and Clio," said Sophie.

"Yes," said Petra. "And I believe them." She described the different attacks the twins had told her about. "But they said it hasn't happened lately—not since the circle with the Treize, in fact. Did either of you feel anything that night? Anything off or dangerous?"

"You mean besides Daedalus?" Ouida asked.

"The girls were angry at Luc," Sophie said stiffly. "Really angry. And more strong emotion, going between all three of them."

Petra nodded. "Yes. I have to talk to him. Each of them says things with Luc were superficial—that they're angry but dealing. Did you get more than that?"

"Oh, yes," Sophie said, frowning. "I feel sure—there was much bigger stuff between them, big, strong emotions." She shook her head, her lips tight.

Petra thought. Why hadn't the girls told her this? Embarrassed? She looked at Sophie. "Has he told you anything about what happened between them?"

"We don't really talk," Sophie said, twisting a ring around one finger.

"Sophie," said Ouida gently. "It's been too long, chérie."

Sophie looked at Ouida, her eyes wide. "How can you say that? *You*—"

Ouida reached out to put her hand on Sophie's. "It was a very long time ago. He was young and foolish and selfish. I've made my peace with him. He's a different person now, and so am I."

Sophie didn't look up. "We just don't get along."

Across the table, Petra met Ouida's eyes. *Drop it,* she told her silently. *You'll get nowhere.*

"Okay, so we have someone trying to harm or possibly even kill the twins," said Petra. "We have the Luc thing, which I'll get to the bottom of. We have Daedalus and his rite. Where do you two stand on that?"

"I don't want to do it," Sophie said, surprising Petra. She still didn't meet Petra's eyes, which meant she was hiding something.

"I'm not sure," Ouida said slowly. "My first reaction was no way. But as I think about it, I wonder if it could be used to sort of, well, heal things. Heal *us*."

Petra nodded. "I know what you mean. Personally, I don't trust Daedalus. I'm not sure how I feel about the rite. I can see both sides. Thais and Clio haven't told me what they would decide, and I still need to figure out how hurting them would benefit anyone, or benefit or hurt the rite."

"It would hurt *you*," said Ouida. "And we need both of them to do the rite, to be thirteen."

"So it could be someone who wants to specifically hurt Petra but in an emotional way, not a physical way. Or it could be someone who doesn't want the rite to happen," said Sophie. "I mean, besides me. *I'm* not trying to hurt the twins."

Petra nodded again. "I know. I just can't figure it out. The girls did a révéler la griffe but got nowhere. I'm going to have to work on it. In the meantime, I've been thinking about the rite, and it seems like it would be prudent to get, well, insurance, in a way. Something on our side so Daedalus can't pull the rug out from under us. Here's what I was thinking." She outlined her plan, and both Ouida and Sophie nodded thoughtfully.

"I agree," said Ouida. "That's a good idea. I'll help you."

"Me too," said Sophie. "It can't hurt, and it would be good if we get it."

"Okay, then." Petra sat back in her chair. "We'll go tomorrow. Then—there is one more thing," she said slowly, wondering if she should even bring it up. She felt Ouida and

Sophie watching her and decided to take a chance. "The thing is—Thais is starting to learn a bit of magick. She's worked a little with Clio and also with me. And—almost every time, her magick goes big and unpredictable."

Ouida frowned. "What? In what way?"

"It's hard to say," Petra continued. "In a way I haven't seen before. It happens fast. And—they've told me—twice, in the middle of a spell, they've actually gotten blown across a room. Through a circle and physically across the room."

Her two friends stared at her.

"Nooo," Ouida said doubtfully, and Petra nodded.

"I talked to Azura Copeland—the mother of one of Clio's friends. She was in her house when the girls were out in their workroom, in the backyard. And from inside the house, she felt a big clap of magick, like lightning, and when she ran out there, the three of them were lying on the floor in separate corners, stunned."

"But just ordinary magick?" Sophie asked, looking concerned. "Nothing dark, nothing . . . dangerous?"

Petra shook her head. "No. I even did a révéler la griffe on Clio. Nothing dark came up at all. They were working relatively small, totally ordinary spells. And then, when Clio was working much harder and bigger spells with Melysa, everything was fine."

"What are you saying?" asked Ouida. "You think it's something about Thais?"

Petra hated what was coming next, but she really needed their input. "What if . . . what if—Thais is a dark twin?"

Petra saw Ouida blink, saw Sophie's eyes widen.

"Oh, God," Ouida said, a look of dismay on her face.

"That doesn't happen very often," Sophie said. "I mean, I've never known anyone—"

"I know it's rare. And I'm hoping it's impossible," said Petra grimly. "But how they're describing Thais's magick—what else could it be?"

"I've met her," said Ouida. "I didn't pick up on anything dark from her at all."

"Me neither," said Sophie.

Petra shrugged, feeling hopeless. "She might not know it. Not yet. For seventeen years nothing magickal has touched her. Now she's starting to tap into her powers for the first time. Maybe a crack has appeared in her. Maybe it's getting worse."

Ouida shook her head. "I just don't know. They both felt balanced to me, in the short time I was around them. They both had elements of light and dark, mostly light."

"I know," said Petra. "I feel that too. And I don't really know how a dark twin works. I've heard that it's when the one egg splits, and instead of it separating into two even halves, with both positive and negative forces, one twin gets all the light and one gets all the dark."

"Which would be bad," said Sophie.

"Not irretrievable," said Petra. "Not one hundred percent inevitable, but often bad and always a struggle."

Ouida looked up at her. "You just moved her into your house."

"I know. And I'm praying I'm wrong. Most likely I am," said Petra. "But can you help me keep an eye on her, get close to her, try to pick up on anything?"

Ouida nodded, looking upset.

"All right," said Sophie. "I'll try."

"Thanks. And whatever happens, do not tell anyone else about this. No one. Understood?"

Sophie and Ouida nodded, then the three of them sat, lost in thought. The only sound was the rhythmic click of the ceiling fan going around.

Chapter Sixteen

CLIO DROVE US TO AND FROM SCHOOL EACH day. This afternoon I looked out the car window, still learning how New Orleans looked and smelled and felt. Huge live-oak trees lined St. Charles Avenue, which was where the main streetcar line ran. The tree branches almost met over the center of the median, making an incredibly green, lush tunnel to drive through.

Dad. I still missed him so much. Despite everything that had happened, there were a hundred instances in every day when I turned to say something to him, wanted to ask him something, wondered when he would be home for dinner.

He hadn't looked much like me. His hair had been dark, but mine was darker. He'd had brown eyes. But he'd felt so totally mine, my blood father, the one constant in my life since I was born. Realizing all over again that Clio had never known him was sad. I decided I would make her a little scrapbook with pictures of him in it, and I would write about him in the pages so she would know him.

• • •

"Well, can you choose just one thing to work with?" I asked Clio.

It was almost dinnertime, and we were sitting at the kitchen table. Petra—Nan—hadn't come home yet.

"Yeah," she said. "A lot of people have a favorite assortment of materials to work with, like if they have a special affinity for herbs, or crystals, or metals. And you can do powerful spells with just those. But Nan always said that the best spells, the strongest ones, are balanced with elements of each. Though there are also some spells that specifically don't need crystals or herbs or candles or whatever."

"And you know everything about all this?" I felt dismayed by how ignorant I was, how much I had to learn.

Clio grinned. "Not everything. Talking to you helps me realize how much I actually do know. But I've been studying this since I was really little. You'll catch up."

This was so depressing. "It's like every plant in the world has some use." I groaned. "How can I learn them all? I mean, *trig* is too much for me."

"Me too," Clio said. "But with magickal things, it's like any other subject—you learn it a little bit at a time. And, yes, many, many plants in the world can be put to some kind of magickal use or have certain attributes. Pretty much everything does. Every grain of sand, every drop of rain, blah blah blah. Magick is in everything, yours for the taking. And then of course, certain human-made objects can also be very powerful."

"Uh-huh," I said glumly. "Like, give me a plant example."

Clio looked around, thinking. "Okay, something easy and common. Holly."

"Like we have outside? Christmas holly?"

"Actually, we call it Soliver holly," Clio told me. "Soliver is our winter holiday. In Wicca it's called Yule. Yule log, et cetera. At roughly the same time, the Christians have Christmas. Jews have Hanukkah."

"I'm a Christian, sort of," I said. "We don't have Christmas?" This was not good news.

Clio looked at me like I was an idiot. "We have Soliver," she said patiently. "It's a lot of fun. It'll be okay. Very festive. Do you want to know about holly or not?"

I sighed. "Tell me."

"Okay, holly." Clio looked at the ceiling, thinking. "The broad Latin name is *ilex*. You learn the Latin name because it'll be the same in most languages. It's the scientific name and helps you be precise. Then you have its true name, which for the kind of holly we have outside, but not for other types, is *bestgriel*. You use its true name in some kinds of magick. It's considered a masculine plant, not because it actually has a gender, though it does, but because its properties align along the masculine scale. The element associated with holly is fire, our element. Which would make it a bit more effective or appropriate for us than for someone whose element is something else. Mars is the planet associated with it, so certain spells can take Mars's orbit or properties into account. And mostly, holly is used for protection, all sorts of protection. And good luck. At Soliver we decorate the house with it, and it helps us have good luck in the coming year."

Until now, my main knowledge about holly had been "prickers." "And you know this kind of info about a lot of plants?"

"I better. It's going to be a big part of my rite of ascension."

I breathed out. "So maybe when I'm thirty."

"Maybe." Clio looked smug, but not in a mean way. I decided to change the subject.

"You know who's good-looking? Kevin LaTour."

"Sylvie's friend?" Clio considered it. "Yeah. He is. You hung out with him the other day, right?"

"And Sylvie and Claude. Kevin seems nice too."

"I've never talked to him." She looked at me speculatively. "Are you—interested in him?"

There it was again. The unspoken gulf between us. Luc. I hadn't told her a lot of how I felt about him, and she had her secrets too, I was sure. They'd probably even slept together, but I didn't let myself think about it because it made me feel sick.

Anyway, Luc was behind me. I was moving on, facing the future. A future without him.

"*Interested* is a strong word," I said cautiously. "I've just noticed that he's nice and also really good-looking."

"Yeah. Well, more power to you if you like Kevin."

I looked into her eyes, identical to mine, as if I might see what she was thinking behind them. Was she hoping I would forget about Luc? Did she still want him? I looked away.

I shrugged. "We'll see."

We worked silently for a few minutes, each with our own thoughts.

"Do you think there's something wrong with me?" I hadn't meant to ask the question, but it just popped out.

"In a general sense or just your clothes?"

I made a face at her, and she smirked. "I mean my magick. Is it just because I have no idea what I'm doing? Do spells go that wrong very often?"

"No. Hardly at all that I've heard of," said Clio, more seriously. "I mean, maybe they won't work or they'll work but in a skewed way. But getting knocked out of a circle? Doesn't happen."

"So it's just me, then. Something about me." That idea upset me, even though I still hadn't totally embraced *Bonne Magie* as a way of life.

"Hm," said Clio, looking at me.

"What?"

"I just remembered a spell I heard of once," Clio said thoughtfully. "It was, like, to see someone's aura. I mean, during a circle, you can usually see everyone's auras, and some people can see them on other people all the time, just walking around. But I remember reading about a spell that reveals a person's inner state, like an x-ray of your soul. Sort of. I remember thinking it was pointless because people usually know their inner state and express it if it's good—if it's bad, they wouldn't do the spell in the first place and let anyone see."

"Uh-huh," I said. "You mean you want to do that with me? Nan said we shouldn't—"

"Nan said we shouldn't try any twin-magick magick," said Clio, standing up and heading to the workroom. "But this would be more diagnostic. Besides, we'll do it outside so we won't get thrown into a wall. Your eye's finally better—don't want to do *that* again."

• • •

Out in the backyard, Clio cleared a little space on the brick walkway that wound through the foliage, much like Racey's backyard. There were six-foot wooden fences on both sides and a brick one in the back.

It had taken Clio almost half an hour to find the spell and assemble what we needed. Now she set up a brass bowl the size of a cantaloupe and kindled a small fire in it. I was worried that Petra would come home and be mad about this, but she hadn't returned yet. Clio told me that it wasn't unusual for Petra to miss a meal if she was at a birthing.

Clio drew a circle around us with salt, then took a chunk of broken red-clay brick and drew different symbols on the walkways around us. "This is épine," she said, drawing a vertical line with a little triangle on one side. "It's to help us achieve our goal. This is ouine." She drew what looked like a pointy letter *p*. "It's for success and happiness. Porte is for revealing hidden things."

I recognized that one from the spell we had done at Racey's house.

"Ote is all about one's ancestral birthright," Clio explained, drawing the symbol on the ground. "It's about what you've inherited, and it can mean personal or material things. Okay, I think we're about ready."

"No candles? No incense? What about those four little cups?"

"We don't always use those," Clio said, sitting down across from me. "This one is aimed differently."

"Okay."

As with the other spells we'd ever done, we sat facing each other, holding hands on either side of the little fire bowl. The sun was setting. It was hot and humid.

I was afraid to do this. I didn't know what would happen, and I dreaded feeling that blast of magick in my chest, like before. Even the smaller spells we'd done had spiraled out of control and been scary. I was tentatively getting used to feeling the spark of magick in me and even kind of liking it. But actually doing something with it was so much scarier. What was I doing?

"It'll be okay," Clio said confidently, as if she could read my mind. "But this time, don't say anything, or sing, or do anything, okay? I'll do it."

"Okay." I tried to calm my breathing and relax, but it was hard. It seemed to take forever before I felt myself unwind. I closed my eyes. I tried to open myself to the world, like Clio had said, but I didn't even know what that felt like.

And then I did. I felt the "magickal" essence rising in me,

as if a peony was blooming, unfolding inside my chest. I felt happy, peaceful—calm and excited at the same time. I was part of everything, and everything was part of me. Clio and I were connected, and I'd never felt so whole or complete. Was this because we'd done the joining spell?

I vaguely heard Clio chanting, singing a spell in a soft voice. My hands and knees were a little warm from the tiny fire kindled in the brass pot. Clio's fingers tightened on mine, and just like that, we were off.

Suddenly I felt like I was trapped on a roller coaster that was speeding recklessly around a track that I couldn't see ahead of me. My eyes popped open and all I saw was Clio's face, *my* face, looking scared. Was she seeing my soul, my aura? Could she tell what was wrong with me?

Then we were seeing images, flashed in front of us, like before, when we'd had the swamp vision. This was very similar—only this time, I knew who most of the people were. We saw Petra, looking younger than she did now, arguing with a black-haired man. He turned and stormed away from her, and we saw that he had our birthmark on one cheek. We saw Richard, not tattooed and pierced and gothicky, but looking happier, more innocent, and dressed like he was in a colonial movie. He was chasing a girl through a meadow, and she fell, laughing. Richard fell next to her, and then they were rolling through the tall grass, kissing wildly, her hair flying bright against the birthmark on her cheek. With a gasp I recognized her. This happy, laughing girl, so full of life, was the same girl from our other vision—the one who had died in childbirth at the witches' circle. I could see her face still and gray in the rain, the ground beneath her running scarlet. It was only then that I realized she looked almost exactly like Clio. Like me.

The scene shifted abruptly, making me almost motion sick. None of this seemed to be about the spell Clio had cast. I didn't know why we were seeing any of this. We saw another woman, dark-haired, running through a moonless swamp. Her face was beautiful and cruel, her eyes black. She looked behind her, and then we saw her lying facedown in the shallow water, her bare feet stained with mud. There was a dark figure over her, a man holding something in one hand. A tool? A scythe or ax? Had he killed her?

Then once again we saw a huge multi-forked bolt of lightning split a huge tree. The witches in the circle were almost knocked off their feet, and the tree was on fire, burning brightly. I could hear the hissing as the rain hit the fire, sending up tiny jets of smoke.

The tree's fire was so hot I felt it on my face, uncomfortably warm and too bright to watch. I tried to pull back, but Clio was gripping my hands tightly. I blinked and saw her face red with heat, flames dancing all around her. Her eyes were wide and still, unfocused, and somehow that made me more afraid than anything.

"Clio!" I yelled, shaking my hands, locked in hers. "Clio!" I pulled back as hard as I could, knocking us both to one side, and all of a sudden we were lying on the ground in Clio's backyard. I'd broken the spell. It was nighttime, the sky above me dark and speckled with stars and . . . sparks, flying upward? I jumped to my feet.

"Oh, God, Clio!" I yelled, looking past her. I grabbed her shoulder and shook her—she hadn't sat up yet. Now she blinked slowly, looking at me like I was a stranger.

"Clio! Get up! The house is on fire!" I shouted, shaking her hard enough to rattle her bones. With the next breath she seemed to awaken, sitting up quickly and looking around her. She gasped and put her hand over her mouth, as horrified as I was.

This time we hadn't gotten thrown across a room.

We'd started a fire that had leaped away from us, and our house—my new home—was ablaze.

✦ Chapter Seventeen

Clio

FIRST THAIS WAS SHAKING ME, HER FACE pale but brightly lit. She was yelling something, but I couldn't hear it. She shook my shoulders hard, and then I made out the word *fire!*

That woke me up, and I was back in the now. I jumped to my feet and stared, horrified—the whole back half of our house was engulfed in flames.

"Oh, holy sh—where's a phone?" I cried, my brain feeling scrambled. I had to think, get two thoughts together—

Just then, one of the back windows burst from the heat. We were ten feet away but felt crystalline shards of window hissing against us.

"Thais! Go next door! Call 911!" I shouted. I was amazed the fire trucks weren't already here—the fire was huge and must have been burning for at least twenty minutes. It was night, I had no idea what time.

"I can't!" Thais cried, pointing. "The fire!" I looked and saw that she was right—like many New Orleans houses, ours was on a tiny plot of land. The fences separating us from our neigh-bors were only about six feet from each side of the house. The flames were already billowing out on the sides—you couldn't get past them. The wooden fences had just caught on fire too.

I spun, thinking. Six-foot wooden fences, six-foot brick fences. I'd never climbed over them, and it looked like it would be a bitch to try. Thais was watching me anxiously: her fearless leader.

"Under the house," I said.

"What?"

I was already moving forward. "We have to go under the house," I explained quickly, dropping to my knees. Our house was built up on brick pilings, maybe three feet up, in case the river flooded. Most houses were. So there was a crawl space beneath it.

"The fire is mostly higher," I said, crawling toward the house. "Under the house isn't on fire yet. We have to get through out to the street, and then we can call 911."

"What if it collapses?" Thais almost shrieked.

"Move fast," I said through gritted teeth. This close to the house, the fire was so hot it felt like it was scalding my skin. I hunkered down lower and bellied under the house, having to crawl over a water pipe and a natural-gas pipe that went to our stove. *Oh, crap,* I thought. *If the fire gets to the gas pipe—*

"Come on!" I yelled back to Thais, and saw that she was biting her lip and creeping low to the ground right behind me. Quickly I muttered an all-purpose protection spell. Oddly, my studies hadn't included a specific spell for keeping a burning house from falling on you.

I hadn't been under here since I was eight, when I had been hiding and found a rat skeleton. And I wished I hadn't thought of that just now.

Above me, I heard the hungry crackling and roaring of the fire as it happily, eagerly consumed our walls. More glass broke, and I winced, though it couldn't reach us under here. I was crawling as fast as I could through the fine, cool dust under the house, inhaling it up my nose, smelling smoke everywhere. Every couple of feet we had to crawl around pipes or wiring. I felt Thais following me, and then I saw the light of the front yard just ahead.

"We're almost there," I shouted, and scrabbled right out next to the front steps, through the holly bush. I knelt and waited for Thais, and she crawled out a second later, her pale skin showing whitely through her grime.

"Okay, you go next door and call 911," I said. "I'm going to call Nan and Melysa and anyone else who can help!"

Thais nodded and turned to run—then we both heard an anguished howling coming from inside the house.

"Q-tip!" Thais gasped.

"Holy Mother—he's inside the house!" I said. "Wait!"

But Thais had already run down the narrow alley between the house and fence. The fire was still mostly toward the back third of the house but windows were breaking, and I was fearing an explosion at any second.

"Thais!" I yelled again, but she was running along, looking up at the side windows. At the third window in, the one in the workroom, she stopped. I saw the dim whiteness of Q-tip's fur pressed against the screen in the open window. Before I could think of what to do, Thais jumped up and punched a hole right through the window screen. Q-tip shot out and raced down the alley toward the street. He streaked through our front fence.

"He'll be okay," I said, grabbing Thais's arm. "Let's go!"

As we were running through the front gate, I heard the droning of sirens, coming nearer. Thank the goddess, someone had called the fire department.

The huge red fire engine stopped in front of our house. I noticed that neighbors were starting to come out of their houses to see what was happening. Thais and I were on the front sidewalk, and I realized I was shaking. I put my arm around Thais, and she put hers around me.

"Out of the way, miss!" shouted a firefighter as he started pulling loops of flat canvas hose off the truck.

Then it was like watching a movie. Thais and I had to move out of the way as several firefighters surged past us, the hose on their shoulders.

"Is anyone inside?" one yelled to me, and I shook my head. "No!" I was so thankful Q-tip was safe. He was probably under the house across the street. Then I had a paralyzing thought.

"Nan's books!" I gasped. "Her tools!"

"Oh, no!" Thais said, her face dismayed. "She's going to kill us! Maybe we can—" She looked up at the front porch.

"The fire probably hasn't reached the workroom inside," I said slowly. "Maybe if I run in and you catch them as I toss them out the window . . ."

"Girls! Please!" said a firefighter, making us jump. "Get across the street! Now!"

Thais and I looked at each other, then reluctantly moved across the street. I could throw a glamour so that they wouldn't notice me going up the front steps. I could—no. It was stupid. Nan would kill me for taking the chance. And if I happened to blow myself up doing it, I would be grounded forever.

Then I heard the hissing spray of fire hoses and saw great clouds of billowing smoke rising as they began to extinguish the flames. Nan's beautiful garden in front had been trampled, her tomato stakes knocked over, her herbs crushed by the heavy water hoses.

"How did this happen?" I asked, my throat closing. Tears burned my eyes, which were full of smoke and ash.

"I don't know," said Thais, her voice trembling. "But I guess—I guess it was me," she said so softly I could hardly hear her.

I looked at her. "Oh, no," I said. "It was just—I'm sure it was—" But the truth was, I couldn't reassure her. I actually couldn't be sure it *wasn't* Thais. Nothing like this had ever happened to me before she came.

I don't know how long we stayed there, watching our fire slowly be vanquished. There were two fire trucks and three hoses hooked up to the fire hydrant down the block. The street was full of our neighbors, who kept coming over to see if we were okay or needed anything or when Nan would be home. Someone brought us glasses of iced tea, which felt incredibly good on our scorched throats.

Finally the fire was out. The firefighters began coiling their hoses. Thais and I stared numbly at our house. Just from the front, it looked okay, except for the ruined garden. But in back—the whole back half of the house was scorched, and at least four windows were broken. We had no idea what the inside would be like.

We were still standing there when Nan ran up to us. She'd had to leave her Volvo down the block because of the trucks.

"Oh my God!" she cried. "What happened? Are you all right?"

I nodded, feeling close to tears again. I hated crying, but maybe it would help make Nan more sympathetic? I tried a practice sniffle.

"There was, uh, a fire," Thais said hesitantly.

"Ma'am? Is this your house?" The fire chief stood there, looking hot and sweaty.

"Yes. What happened?" Nan asked anxiously, stepping over to him.

"Well, the back of your house got torched," the fire chief said bluntly.

"How?" Nan exclaimed, then quickly turned to me. "Did someone try to—?"

She was asking if this had been another attack on us. The temptation to shout, "Yes!" and have someone else take the blame was almost overpowering. And Nan had lied to *me*.

"No," said Thais, before I could finish thinking it through. "At least, we don't think so." She met my eyes quickly, then went on. "I mean, it could have been. It's hard to know. But there's a chance . . . we started it." Her voice trailed off in a whisper.

Nan just stared at her, trying to take it in. Then she turned to the fire chief.

"Can you tell how it was started?" she asked.

"We almost always can," he answered, taking off his hat and rubbing his sleeve across his forehead. "And our specialist is still checking it out. But I've had twenty-five years of experience, and I've never seen anything like this."

"Like what?" Nan asked faintly.

"It looks like someone threw a . . . sheet of fire directly at the back of your house," he said, frowning, as if knowing his words didn't make a lot of sense. "I mean, fires always start in one place, then spread. Or if an accelerant is used, there's a traceable pattern. The back of your house looks like someone sprayed it with gasoline, then threw a match at it."

Nan put her hand over her mouth and drew me close. Then she put her other arm around Thais.

"But the thing is, so far there's no trace of accelerant," he went on. "There's nothing to suggest that it was deliberately set. Except for the fact that its pattern simply can't be natural."

He shook his hat against the side of his waders and called to his men to finish up loading.

"You should contact your insurance company, ma'am," he said. "And when I get the final report from our specialist, I'll send you a copy. Or the police will want to conduct a further investigation." He made a sympathetic face, then strode toward one fire truck, barking orders.

"We were doing a spell," I confessed in a tiny voice. "In the backyard. I was trying to see Thais's aura, to see if I could tell why her magick always goes weird. But we saw that same tree get hit by lightning and catch on fire, and the next thing we knew, the whole back of the house had gone up." I really did feel like crying now. "I'm so sorry, Nan. We didn't mean to do it. I don't know why it happened."

She nodded, looking tired, and tucked a stray strand of hair back into her loose bun. She looked up quickly. "Q-tip!"

"We got him out," Thais said.

"Thais got him out," I clarified. "She punched a hole in the screen to rescue him."

Nan took Thais's hand and looked at the scratches the metal screen had caused. Then, putting her arms around us both again, she started toward the house.

"I'm so thankful neither of you was hurt," she said.

✦ Eighteen

They've Seen What Happened

"BUT THEY WEREN'T HURT?" OUIDA ASKED, looking back at Petra in her rearview mirror.

"No," Petra said. "They went to school today, but their hands and faces look sunburned."

"And you don't know how it happened?" Sophie asked.

"They were doing a spell," said Petra. She closed her eyes and leaned against her seat back, glad that Ouida was driving. She felt as if she had aged more in the last seventeen years with Clio than she had in the two hundred years before that. "A spell to see what might be causing Thais's magick to explode."

"I'm sorry," said Ouida. "How's your house?"

"Water damaged, from the fire trucks," said Petra, wishing she could block the picture of her charred house from her mind. "The whole back of the house went up. It'll need to be scraped and sanded and painted, and maybe a quarter of the weatherboards replaced. The windows are cracked and need new glass. Inside, the house smells like a smoke pit. Thais and Clio stayed up late, trying to mop up the water in the kitchen, but it's going to take weeks to get the house back to normal."

She opened her eyes and saw Ouida looking at her in the mirror.

"Do you think this lends credence to your dark-twin theory?" she asked.

"I don't know," said Petra, feeling worn out. First that difficult birth all day and then coming home to find her house on fire. Clio had been upset about not being able to save Petra's books and tools, as if she would care about those things. And they hadn't been touched, anyway. Her first, panicked thought had been that someone else had set the fire, trying to harm the girls. But it didn't seem like that was the case.

"Why don't you try to get some rest?" Ouida suggested. "I'll wake you up when we get to Chacahoula."

"Maybe I should." Petra looked out the car window, thinking. "You know, the girls have shared visions of that night, the Treize, by the tree, with Melita. They've described the action as if they were there."

Sophie turned around in her seat, horrified. "Pas vraiment! But how could they?"

"I don't know," Petra answered. "But they've *seen* what happened. More than once. Really seen it—the rain, the power surge, the lightning. Cerise." Even after all this time, it was a fresh pain, the memory of her daughter. Since then, Petra had tried to help as many other women give birth as she could. "And last night, they saw someone facedown in a swamp and a dark figure standing over her, holding something, some kind of weapon. Thais described her as dark-haired, black-eyed, and beautiful."

"Not Axelle," said Ouida.

"No. Axelle's best friend."

"Melita?" Sophie asked. "They saw her dead?"

"I don't know if she was dead," Petra said slowly. "Clio just said she was facedown and someone was standing over her. And it was clearly a scene of danger. Maybe she *was* killed that night—or maybe just threatened or injured? I don't see how she could have died. . . ."

"Daedalus thinks there's a chance the rite affected Melita differently somehow," Ouida said. "He thinks there's a small chance that she wasn't made immortal. But that seems so improbable."

"Impossible," Sophie said, frowning.

"But she did disappear that night without a trace," said Petra. "Without taking any of her things—not that she had much."

"Who was standing over her?" Ouida asked.

"I don't know, and neither do the twins. They think it was a man, but the figure was very dark, completely in shadow. They couldn't describe him at all."

"Petra," said Ouida seriously. "Don't tell anyone else about the girls' visions."

They met eyes in the mirror, warm brown looking into blue-gray.

"I know," said Petra. If anyone else knew the twins were

having these kinds of visions, and if these visions had revealed or would reveal the answers to centuries-old mysteries, then the twins would definitely be in danger, perhaps from someone else and for a different reason than they were now. If that even made sense. Petra sighed, rubbing her hand over her eyes. She could hardly think, could hardly sort out what made sense. Had the girls set the house on fire? Or had someone seen them performing a spell and taken advantage of that to set the fire himself? Or herself?

Why did the girls seem to have more than two hundred years' worth of memories locked inside them? Could they remember all twelve generations of ancestors, back to Cerise? Why?

And was Thais a dark twin? Petra had questioned Clio separately last night, after she made some aloe ointment for their burns. It had been very late. Clio had explained the point of the spell, and Petra had asked her what she'd seen. Clio had described the same thing that Thais had, yet Petra was certain that Clio had seen something else, something that had disturbed her, that she wouldn't talk about.

It was a problem. Her life was becoming layered with problems.

• • •

"Petra," Sophie said gently. "We're here."

Groggily Petra opened her eyes. Through the open car window, she saw tall live-oak trees blocking out the sky. Gray wisps of Spanish moss trailed down like tattered silk. In an instant, Petra was taken back to another time when she would look overhead and see nothing but trees and sky and moss. No buildings, no planes, no wires.

She'd liked their little village. She'd grown up there. Even its name, Ville du Bois, Village of the Woods, reflected how simple and innocent their lives were there. Not easy—never easy—but still, rhythmic and uncomplicated. Predictable, but in a good way. Crops, farm animals, knowing the plants, the birds in the woods, the fish in the streams. The cycles of *Bonne Magie* tied in so beautifully, so naturally. It took more effort to feel connected to the earth, to nature, nowadays.

She'd grown to be a woman there. She'd married Armand, whom she'd known all her life. They'd had children. First Melita. Jacques had died when he was two. Philippe had lived ten months. After that she'd decided to have no more children. But accidents happen, even to witches performing anti-fertile spells. That had been Cerise, born when Petra was almost forty. Cerise had been a joy, never a sick day in her life, and Petra had taken another chance. But Amanda had lived barely long enough to be named and blessed.

Then Armand had tired of village life. He'd gone on a trip to New Orleans to buy tools and lead to make bullets. He'd come home only once—to ask Petra to take the children and move with him to the city. She'd been afraid. She hadn't wanted anything to happen to her daughters.

Very ironic.

She knew that Armand had died of malaria when he was

forty-five. She'd seen his headstone in the cemetery in New Orleans. Where she now lived. After having lost her last two surviving children to disastrous circumstances.

"Petra?"

Petra blinked and looked up into Sophie's face, as smooth and unlined as when she'd been twenty. Sophie looked concerned, and Petra sat up and opened the car door.

"Sorry," she said, climbing out of the car. "Woolgathering."

She looked around. They were parked on a narrow shell road that was used so rarely that grass had sprung up in the cracks. "Where are we?"

Ouida waved to the map spread on the trunk of the car.

"Here," said Sophie, pointing to a spot. "Bit southeast of Chacahoula. We left the main roads about forty minutes ago."

"Get a bit of a rest?" Ouida asked.

"Yes." Petra squared her shoulders. "I can face this now."

• • •

"I miss Boston," Ouida grumbled, wiping the sweat off her brow.

Petra smiled at her, then pushed her own damp hair off her forehead. September was bad enough in the city, but in the middle of the woods, right on the edge of the swamp, it was suffocating.

"You can't just breathe," Ouida said. "You have to actually *swallow* the air. That's how thick it is."

"I miss Paris," said Sophie.

"You and Manon will be able to go back there soon enough," Petra reassured her.

"Yes . . ." said Sophie.

Ouida checked her compass. She looked overhead, looked again at the detailed topographical map she'd gotten from the extension service. "Well, as close as I can figure, we're about here."

Petra looked around, but nothing was familiar. The trees here had been mostly cleared out, probably a hundred years ago. New growth had sprung up, nature reclaiming its own.

"Okay," she said, pulling some supplies out of her dress pocket. "We might as well give it a go."

"It's creepy being here," Sophie said. She glanced over her shoulder as if waiting for someone to spring out of the woods. The light here was filtered and dim, and the only sounds were from insects and birds.

The three women quickly made a circle on the ground, then stood inside it, holding hands. Petra felt a heaviness weighing on her that was more than the heat and the humidity. Damn Daedalus! When he'd brought Thais to New Orleans, he'd opened up a viper's nest. Now snake after snake was slithering out, weaving paths of danger all around both Clio and Thais. The twins had almost been killed several times. Thank the goddess Melysa had been home the night of the wasp attack. Now Petra's own house was a wet, blackened reminder that something was seriously out of balance in her life.

"Petra?" Sophie's voice was gentle.

"Sorry." Petra closed her eyes and breathed out slowly, trying to release every bit of tension, fear, and dread. Finally, finally, Petra felt herself slip into that place between waking and dream, where her boundaries blurred and merged with everything around her. She felt Ouida's breathing, heard Sophie's heart beating, felt their energies, older now and shaped forever by their lives, but still beautiful. She began her song of power and magick, softly at first, resting lightly on the air. Soon she was joined by Sophie, then Ouida, the three of them weaving their chants together as if they were fine threads being spun into a strong, silken rope.

Within her, Petra felt her power rise, felt her magick strengthening. A slight trembling shook the earth below their feet, and Petra's eyes opened. Their voices didn't waver, but they looked at each other. The whole Louisiana Delta was made of layers upon layers of clay and river silt. There were never earthquakes here.

Petra gasped slightly, feeling like a huge hand was pulling the power right out of her chest. She felt Ouida and Sophie squeeze her hands harder, and she closed her eyes again and tried to stay centered.

Their voices rose in a strong, feminine crescendo, and at last the song was over. They broke apart from each other, staggering back. The trembling stopped.

The world looked different. It felt different.

The air was tinged with the scent of rain, and purple clouds swelled overhead. A thin cool wisp of breeze brushed Petra's face as she looked around in the much dimmer light.

"Storm coming in," said Ouida, sounding breathless.

"Yes," said Petra, feeling resignation settle on her.

"Look," Sophie whispered, and Petra and Ouida turned to her. Sophie's face was white, her eyes dark and troubled. One hand was outstretched, pointing, and Petra squinted to see.

"There," Sophie said, her voice shaking.

Then Petra saw it. Ouida's mapmaking had proven true. The three women looked at each other, a mix of emotions on their faces.

"It's still here," Ouida said disbelievingly. "I never thought that would work."

Petra's lips were pressed together hard as she, Ouida, and Sophie walked over to a small clearing right past the first line of trees. There, on the ground, was a blackened ring of scorched earth, a circle of ashes. Where Cerise had died that night.

"We've found the Source," Sophie said sadly.

✦ Nineteen

"IT WASN'T YOUR FAULT," CLIO SAID AGAIN. "WELL, I mean, probably. I mean, you totally didn't mean for anything like that to happen."

I made a wry face at her, tied the top on a bag of apples, and put them in the cart. School had been miserable today. Clio and I both obviously smelled like smoke—everything in our house did, including our entire wardrobes, and we hadn't had time to wash any clothes. My face and hands still stung slightly despite Petra's soothing ointment. Now we were at the grocery store. Petra had left the house early this morning, saying she had a case, and asked us to stop and get some things.

"You want some nectarines?" Clio asked.

"Yeah. A bunch. I love 'em." Sighing, I picked out three baking potatoes and put them in a bag. I felt wiped out, stressed and upset and tired. Of course it had been almost impossible to sleep last night. Also, since my bedroom was the top back one, all my windows were broken and the window frames scorched on the inside. My curtains had burned away, and the whole room had been drenched with water. I'd slept on the floor in Clio's room.

My throat felt tight. I brushed some hair out of my eyes. I had finally found a home, a home full of love and acceptance, and *wham!* I'd almost burned it down. My own room, which Petra had given up for me—

I swallowed and tried to remember if we had anything green in the fridge at—home.

"You can't blame yourself," Clio said, seeing my face. "We're just not sure." She lowered her voice as we pushed the cart forward. "I mean, how do we know it wasn't like Nan said, that maybe someone saw us doing the spell and seized the opportunity to set the house on fire? You know that's possible."

I nodded and let out a deep breath. "Yeah, that's true." But inside, I couldn't help feeling it had been me, something about my magick.

"Are we out of mayonnaise?" Clio asked, pronouncing it "my-nez."

"Close to it," I said.

"Do we need bread?"

I nodded. "It got—toasted." Clio and I looked at each other, and at the same moment, we burst out laughing.

"Oh God, that was awful," she said, laughing.

"I know. But it's true," I said, still giggling. "The plastic was burned off and the bread inside was all—toasted." I felt much better after we had laughed, but I still had heavy thoughts on my mind. "Clio—there must be something wrong with me.

Maybe I'm . . . like, bad or something. Like Melita. Maybe I'm not supposed to make magick."

"No, Thais, don't be silly. They said that Melita was evil. You're not evil. You're not even a little bad. I don't know what's wrong with your magick, but I know it's not *you*. We'll fix it. Nan will fix it. Just be patient."

"I mean, I think I like magick," I said, putting a big can of coffee in the cart. I was used to coffee with chicory now. "Sometimes I think it feels really good. Not like a drug or something unnatural. Not like I'm ecstatic. But just that I feel really calm and connected and strong."

Clio smiled at me. "That's what magick is."

"But then it goes weird, and it's big and scary and I hate it." I shook my head. "I don't know what to do. Maybe I should forget about it." But even as I said that, I realized that I didn't want to now. Maybe a week ago I could have given magick up, never tasted it again. But now something in me was pulling me forward, eager to explore it. The whole thing worried me and made me feel anxious. I hoped that Petra would be back by the time we got home, but then I remembered what that home would look like, smell like, and a weight of depression settled on me.

"Do Petra's cases always take all day?" I asked.

Clio shook her head. "Nope. Sometimes they're really fast. One time she left at noon and was back by three. But they usually take longer."

"Okay. You have the card?"

Clio pulled out her bank card, and we pushed the cart into the checkout line.

Two normal teenagers picking up stuff for dinner. Two ancestral witches, tied to a line of immortals, with combined explosive magick, who someone kept trying to kill, picking up stuff for dinner.

My life had gotten so complicated.

Chapter Twenty

Clio

MY FINGERNAILS WOULD NEVER BE CLEAN OR unbroken again.

Yesterday Nan, Thaïs, and I had glumly cataloged what work needed to be done on the house. Fortunately, insurance would cover a lot of it, but not all. Some of it we would have to hire someone for. And Thaïs and I had to do as much of it as possible. Which we were doing after school and in any spare time.

The outside of the house in back had to be scraped and sanded and repainted. Some of the charred boards had to be completely replaced. The linoleum in the kitchen had to be pulled up because water had gotten under it and would rot the wooden floor beneath it. We had to cut it into pieces, muscle it out of the house, roll it up and tie it, and put it out on the curb for the trash guys to pick up. It was so horrible. We'd done that yesterday after we got back from the store.

Almost every cupboard had to be emptied, everything inside it washed and dried, then put back. The cupboards and even the walls had to be scrubbed to get off the soot and grime and water stains. About half of Nan's plants that hung in the windows had died. We had to clean the rest of them. We'd only been at work three days, and I felt like I'd be doing this for the rest of my life.

"I guess I'll be repainting my room after all," said Thais. She was sitting on the floor, scrubbing the kitchen table legs, which were also covered in oily soot. "And getting new curtains."

"Yep. Did you switch that load of clothes into the dryer and start a new load?"

"Yep. Poor Petra, having to go this late."

I glanced at the clock—it was almost nine. Nan had left an hour ago on a case. I climbed up another step on the ladder so I could clean the ceiling fan. "Midwives don't really keep predictable hours."

The doorbell rang. At this hour? I froze, looking at Thais, my heart rate speeding up. Then I realized that someone trying to murder us probably wouldn't *ring the doorbell*. Relaxing, I tried to feel who was there. "It's Jules—and Richard, I think. Did you know they were coming over?"

Thais shook her head. "You think it's okay?"

I thought as I climbed down from the ladder. "I guess so." But I still felt uneasy. Just then the phone rang, and Thais answered it. She held up one finger for me to wait, and the doorbell rang again.

"Oh, okay," she said, her face clearing. "Actually, they just got here." She motioned at me to go answer the door. "When do you think you'll be home? Okay. No, we're fine. Bye."

She ran to catch up with me just as I was reaching the door.

"That was Petra," Thais said in a whisper. "She asked Richard and Jules to come replace the glass in the windows. I guess they know how."

"How *conveeenient*," I said, and opened the door.

Jules nodded at us and gave a restrained smile. "Hello. Hear you have some windows need reglazing." His voice was deep, all the edges smoothed out by his southern accent.

"Yep," I said, gesturing them inside.

Richard held up a package of windowpanes wrapped in brown paper. "You have a hissy fit?" he asked, throwing his cigarette down on the porch and grinding it out with his boot. "Throw a shoe through a window?"

He was so incredibly irritating. I wished I could say something scathing, but he was here to help, which we needed. He looked me up and down, which was so bizarre coming from someone who looked several years younger than me, and I was suddenly conscious of how grimy and filthy I was.

I forced myself to meet his eyes calmly. "We set the house on fire. Busted the back windows."

His look of quickly masked surprise was intensely gratifying.

"It's late," Thais said, leading them through the house. "Would this be easier to do in the daytime?"

"Yes," said Jules. "But we might as well do it now before it rains again. Sorry we couldn't come earlier—Petra only called us today."

"That's okay," I said. "We appreciate your helping." I glanced quickly at Richard to find him watching me, one eyebrow raised. I set my teeth and moved the butcher-block thing out of the way so they could get to the back window. Jules took my ladder and went outside, and Richard stayed inside. They set to work removing all the jagged hunks of glass still in the frames, and I got some newspapers to wrap them in.

"Thanks, babe," Richard said absently, not even looking at me.

I glared at his back, then looked down at Thais, who was trying not to snicker. I joined her under the table and started washing another table leg.

After the table, Thais began washing plants in the sink, and I started on one of the bottom cupboards. Most of the top ones had been done, thank God. I opened it and pulled everything out, mostly baking pans, which I could run through the dishwasher. I got a new bowl of hot soapy water, leaned way in, and started washing down the sooty walls.

The smoke had even gotten inside the fricking cabinets, I thought angrily, scrubbing away. I wrung out my rag and ducked back in. Inside *closed cabinets*. Smoke could get into everything. All of our clothes had to be washed—we were almost done with that. All the curtains in the whole house needed to be washed, the upholstered furniture taken outside and beaten and vacuumed and aired. The smell of smoke and ash was everywhere, permeated everything. I was sick of it. And it had been all my fault—mine and Thais's. That was the worst part. I couldn't even resent anyone else.

I was swearing to myself, rubbing furiously away, when someone touched my bare foot. I shrieked and banged my head against the top of the cupboard. "*Damn* it!" I pulled my head out of the cabinet to see Richard squatting on his heels in front of me, trying not to grin. A lit cigarette dangled from one hand. I looked at him, unable to keep the anger off my face.

"Put that out," I said curtly, sliding out to sit on the floor. "Nan doesn't let anyone smoke in the house."

"I understand," Richard said, taking a puff and blowing it toward the stained ceiling. "You don't want the house to smell all smoky." His brown eyes, the color of dark coffee, looked like they were challenging me. "Next you'll be telling me it's bad for my health."

My eyes narrowed at him. I didn't care if he was helping— he irritated the piss out of me. "*Your* health isn't the problem," I said, sounding snippy even to myself. "But Thais and I still have just the two, no-lifetime-warranty sets of lungs. So give us a break."

After a moment Richard smiled as if to say, "Point to you." He stood up and put his cigarette out in the sink. I felt uncomfortable and didn't know why. Richard didn't feel dangerous— but he set me on edge, kept me off balance in an incredibly annoying way. I felt too aware of my dirty tank top and short cutoffs that barely covered my underwear.

"Where's Thais?" I asked.

He motioned toward the back door with his head. "Outside, picking up glass. We're all done." His hair was too long and cut all raggedy, as if he'd done it himself. The natural color was the same warm brown as his eyes, but it was streaky with different shades of blond. His eyebrow ring was gone, but he had a small silver wire through one side of his nose and three earrings in one ear and two in the other. One of them was way on the top of his ear. He was wearing a black T-shirt with the sleeves torn off, showing the tribal tattoos on his upper arms. The cloth was so old and worn it had a comet tail of holes spread across his stomach. I could see smooth tan skin through the holes, and then I realized what I was doing and looked up quickly.

Damn, damn, *damn*. He was watching me examining him, and he had that half-amused smile on his face.

"Like what you see?" he said, almost sounding teasing.

"Oh, *right*," I said sarcastically, standing up and brushing off my shorts, completely without result. In the next instant he stepped toward me, and I looked up in surprise. He was only a couple inches taller than me, inches shorter than Luc. I was so taken aback I froze, and he deliberately put one hand on my waist and pulled me to him. Then he lowered his head, watching my eyes, and kissed me. His lips were warm on mine, firm and gentle, and I had the utterly insane, unbelievable thought of *yes*.

In the next second I pushed him back, hard, and put my

hand to my mouth, horrified. Just then the back screen door opened, and Thais came in, looking filthy and exhausted. Jules was behind her, carrying his box of tools, as cool and unruffled as when he'd arrived.

"That window's fixed," he said, nodding toward the one on the back wall. "This one has cracked panes, but nothing that can't wait till tomorrow. I've stapled plastic over the windows upstairs in case it rains. Tomorrow I'll get an earlier start and finish them all up." He looked over at Richard, who was standing unsmiling by the sink. "You ready, Riche?"

Richard nodded and flicked me a glance, then walked out of the kitchen. I let Thais show them out and make all the grateful noises—I was too freaked to deal. Oh my God, Richard had kissed me. I mean, I'd been ducking unwanted kisses since I was twelve—I knew how to avoid them. How had he gotten to me? Was I just so surprised I—

I waited till I heard the front door close, then headed into the hallway where the stairs were. "You look wiped," I told Thais. "Go ahead and take a shower first."

She nodded tiredly and headed upstairs.

I sat down on the bottom step, my chin in my hand. I couldn't *stand* Richard. André—Luc—was the only person I wanted to kiss, the only kiss I wanted to remember. Now Richard had changed that. I knew how he'd felt when he'd held me to him, knew how he kissed.

Damn him.

✦ Chapter Twenty-One

Undermine All Their Plans

A COOL SHOWER. THAT WAS WHAT SHE NEEDED. A cool shower, some Tylenol, some food, and she would feel fine.

Axelle glanced at her watch as she opened her front door. Not much past ten. Thais would be home, maybe already in bed. Inside the apartment, she dropped her purse on the table. Minou trotted up and rubbed against her legs.

"What's the matter?" Axelle murmured. "Thais didn't fee—"

Axelle sighed. Right, no more Thais. She went to put food in Minou's bowl, which she had to find first. Then she opened a bottle of water and rummaged for the Tylenol in a cupboard. She took four of them and washed them down with Pellegrino.

The refrigerator revealed no food. Which would have been fine and normal if Axelle hadn't gotten used to Thais keeping the fridge full of yogurt and interesting cheese and sliced ham and even eggs.

Axelle found half a box of Frosted Mini-Wheats in a cupboard and took them to the living room. She flopped down on the couch, opened the box, and crunched some up dry. With each one her chewing became angrier. This was pathetic! She was pathetic! She'd gotten along all this time with no Thais, no one, and it had been *fine*. Was she going to fall apart now that Petra had stolen Thais away? Not bloody likely. Axelle stood up and threw down the box. She would take a shower, change, and go out for real food. Tons of restaurants stayed open all night. Or she could order in.

She lit a cigarette and blew the smoke across the room. The fact was, she kind of missed Thais. Not that Thais had been a barrel of laughs. Just the opposite. She'd covered the dining table with boring schoolbooks and made pained expressions when Axelle left clothes on the floor. Clio, the other one, would have been much more fun. She would have liked going to bars, while Thais whined about being underage. She would have been fun to shop with, where Thais seemed content with her boring schoolgirl clothes.

But Thais had been something new and interesting in Axelle's life—the first time Axelle had had even a superficial resemblance of responsibility for someone else. Maybe she hadn't done such a great job—she wasn't some TV mom. But still, had it been so bad that Thais should run off to Petra's the first chance she got?

Damn Petra, anyway. She thought she had the right, that she knew best, that she could just undermine Axelle and

Daedalus and all their plans. *Fine. Take Thais.* It didn't change anything. Everything was still going forward as planned.

Axelle found herself in the hall in back of the kitchen, standing in the doorway of Thais's room. She had saved Thais's life! Had she remembered that when she'd been racing out to Petra's car? No.

Axelle had thought about that night a lot but still wasn't sure who'd been behind the magickal attack on Thais. She knew it wasn't Daedalus or Jules—they both wanted, need-ed the twins to do the rite. They were all hell-bent on do-ing the rite, like it was some big magick party where everyone would get a prize. Maybe they didn't remember what it had been like, felt like that night. How could they have forgot-ten? It had felt terrible, like death. Some of the secret magick Axelle had worked with Melita so long ago had been scary, left nasty hangovers. But nothing had ever felt as bad as that night.

And Cerise had died, leaving behind baby Hélène, a pretty thing. Everyone had expected Petra to raise her, but she'd been adopted by Louise and Charles Dedouard.

Axelle picked up one of her wooden cups. After Thais left, Axelle had put them on the little desk in Thais's room. She smiled wryly, remembering when she'd found them in Thais's bathroom, one holding swabs, one holding cotton balls. . . .

The wood was cool and smooth. Axelle rubbed it on her black silk shirt, making the wood shine. The grain of the wood was thin and straight—the tree had been hundreds of years old. Jules had carved these for her out of the charred stump of the Source tree. Maybe he'd felt sorry for her, with Melita being gone. They'd been like sisters. Much more like sisters than Melita and Cerise. Cerise had been a bubble-headed idiot who'd gotten herself knocked up when everyone knew how to prevent it. And why hadn't the father prevented it, if he was a witch? Men could do it too.

Unless the father hadn't been a witch. Or had wanted the baby for some reason.

Axelle put the cup down next to its mates. Jules used to make nice things. That was one of the first things anyone noticed about him, that he could make pretty things out of wood. That and the shackles on his wrists and ankles.

No one in their *famille* had ever owned another human being. It was bizarre, unthinkable. Why would the slave owners do that to themselves? They were probably *still* working out the bad karma.

Marcel had found Jules, Axelle remembered. Almost dead, in the swamp. A runaway. Marcel had brought him to the village and given him to Petra, who was a healer even then. It had taken a month of magick and nursing to bring Jules back to this side of life. The blacksmith had broken the shackles. He'd actually melted them down and made them into an iron knife, and he'd given it to Jules. Axelle couldn't remember his name.

Then Jules was just one of them, one of their *famille*. He made himself a little house, he learned their religion, he got work as a carpenter. But it was the little things, the pretty things he carved that Axelle had always liked best. Jules had changed a great deal over the years.

Sighing with the weight of memories, Axelle went back to the kitchen and started opening cupboards. Richard seemed to have cleaned out all her liquor. Ah! She found a bottle of dry vermouth with maybe a quarter left and poured herself some over ice.

No, owning slaves had never been acceptable in their religion, their clan.

Which was why Luc had caused such a brouhaha when he'd come back from New Orleans, owning Ouida.

Luc's family, the Martins, had been well-off. Petra would have been well-off too if Armand hadn't taken all their money when he moved to New Orleans. Armand's brother, Luc's father, had sent Luc off to Loyola, in New Orleans, to get a college education. Luc had lasted two years before being sent down for behavior unseemly in a gentleman. Big surprise there. He'd had angry fathers coming after him with shotguns when he was fourteen. Luc's father had been incensed. Then Luc had shown up, cocky as hell, owning a female slave.

Axelle laughed softly, remembering how the entire village had been in an uproar. What a scandal. Luc was lucky no one had beaten him to death. He and his father, Grégoire, had had a huge row, right out in the village commons, and Grégoire had publicly divested him of ownership. Ouida was free to stay or go as she pleased.

Ouida had stunned everybody by choosing to stay—with

Luc. Just for a couple of months until she figured out what to do. She could have headed north, where not many people owned slaves, or gone to Europe. Luc's father would have given her the money. But Ouida made friends in the community. Petra and Sophie started teaching her the ways of *Bonne Magie*. Like Jules, Ouida had quickly made a place for herself.

Then she'd decided to see something else of the world and had left. But she had returned, and that time she'd stayed and become one of them.

It had been around then that Sophie had cut Luc out. Axelle had heard rumors but still wasn't sure of the real reason—Sophie had never said why, and neither had Luc. The *famille* had many secrets, and that was just one more of them. Axelle leaned against the kitchen counter and drained her glass. She felt better. Now for a cold shower, and she'd be ready for anything.

It was a shame about Sophie and Luc, Axelle thought as she walked toward her bedroom. They'd been such a handsome pair.

Axelle paused halfway through the main room. She frowned, standing very still. There was an electricity in the air, a heightened sense of—what? Very slowly and quietly Axelle walked the perimeter of the room, trying to feel where it was coming from. Outside, on the street? From the courtyard in back? Had someone spelled her apartment? All her senses sharpened. Then she passed the hidden door that led to her attic workroom. It was open about a quarter of an inch—the latch hadn't quite caught.

Quickly she draped a shadow spell over herself to make it hard for anyone to pick up on her presence. Leaning closer to the door, she slid one long red fingernail into the crack and pulled. The door opened a fraction, enough for her to hear voices.

It was Jules and Daedalus—but she hadn't felt them when she'd come in. They had a key and came and went as they liked, but why hadn't she instantly known they were there?

"Luc?" She heard Jules ask.

"No," Daedalus said impatiently. "He's strong but completely unreliable."

"Not Petra, obviously."

"Obviously."

"Richard?"

"Yes, maybe Richard," Daedalus said, sounding thoughtful. "Possibly Richard."

"There's Axelle," said Jules.

"Please, no," Daedalus said. "Axelle is fine in many respects, but not for this. We need someone more focused, with more true power. Axelle has let herself grow weak."

Axelle's perfect eyebrows arched. Oh, really? Her magick had gotten weak, had it?

"She has other priorities is all," said Jules.

"Which are not our priorities," said Daedalus firmly. "No, Axelle is out. I wonder if Manon . . ." His voice trailed off, and Axelle could no longer make out their murmuring.

Quietly Axelle backed away from the door, picked up her

purse, and let herself out of the apartment. She closed the door soundlessly and went to stand in the dark, covered carriageway that ran alongside the apartment. Leaning against the smooth, cool stucco, she thought.

Well, it was true. She had let her magick grow weak. She'd never been a scholar, a student—instead of learning everything there was to know, she tended to learn only the aspects that would let her perform certain spells. And what was wrong with that?

Besides, she'd thought that she, Daedalus, and Jules were a triangle, an even-sided balance of power behind this whole rite. But they were planning something, the two of them, something they hadn't shared with her. Perhaps she wasn't as tight with Jules and Daedalus as she'd thought. Perhaps she needed to look out for herself more, protect herself more. Yes, Daedalus was very strong, but so was Petra, so was Richard, and so was Luc, when he focused on it.

More than one allegiance could be made.

Daedalus had been so convincing about how this rite would answer everyone's needs, even if they differed, but suddenly Axelle wasn't so sure of that. Daedalus's needs would be answered—he would make certain of that. And anyone whose desires aligned with his would be well served also.

But not everyone wanted the same thing. What Axelle needed to do was really figure out what she herself wanted out of this. Then she would work with whoever could help her get it.

Now, with a plan in place, she headed back to the apartment. This time she let the front door slam shut and made a lot of noise walking around the big room. She rattled some glasses in the kitchen, then lit another cigarette and waited.

Within a minute Jules and Daedalus came down from the workroom.

"Ah! Axelle," Daedalus said with a smile. "We've been waiting for you—there are some questions I have about the old Ville, and I knew if anyone could remember, it would be you."

"We just got here," said Jules. "Maybe five minutes ago. Now that you're here, we can get started."

"Okay. Just let me get something to drink," said Axelle. She poured some vermouth in a clean glass and looked at them. "Ready."

✦ Chahpter Twenty-Two

Mine Alone

IN HIS DREAM, HE STILL HAD A LIFETIME OF potential. He was still looking forward to being a man, taller and broader, stronger. One day, not too far off, he would leave his father's house and have a house of his own. One day, when his father struck him, Richard would be big enough and strong enough to strike *him* down instead.

And he would be a man, a man that Cerise could have if that sap Marcel hadn't managed to blackmail her into wifery by then. Another two years, Richard thought. He would be seventeen. Plenty old enough. In the meantime, he had to hold Cerise's interest. Which he seemed to be doing pretty well.

After months of chasing, during which she'd laughed at him and called him a child, he thought he finally had her attention. She'd never been unkind, but she was older than he, and she had Marcel wooing her in his stolid, persistent way. Last month Richard had finally caught Cerise, caught her and held her against a tree, and kissed her till they were both breathless. They'd kissed twice more since then, longer and wilder each time. She wasn't laughing at him now. Now when she looked at him, he saw his own hunger reflected in her eyes.

Then last week Richard had seen Marcel's patience finally break. After a circle he'd walked her home, while Richard followed in the darkness at a distance. After Cerise's mother and sister had gone in, Marcel had grabbed Cerise and kissed her. She'd squirmed gently out of his arms and held one hand against his cheek. "Dear Marcel," she'd said, and Richard had caught the words as if they were leaves borne to him by the wind. His hand had closed around the hilt of his hunting knife, but then Cerise had gone inside and Marcel had gone home.

She was old enough to marry Marcel, and Marcel was old enough to take her as wife. Legally, Richard could marry at fifteen—he was of age, but he had no profession yet, no way of keeping a wife or providing for a family. It burned him.

But he and Cerise had lain in the meadow together, clinging together, kissing as if their lives depended on it. They couldn't stop themselves, they were wild with wanting, the air hot and damp on their skin. Richard surely had her attention now.

Then the dream changed and Richard was once again standing outside the general store, which was really just one front room of the Chevets' house. Marcel and Cerise were arguing. "You have to marry me," Marcel had said, his pale skin flushed and his fair, reddish hair burning in the sun. "You carry my child."

Richard's heart had squeezed as if in a vise, his breath knocked out of him.

"I'll not marry anyone," Cerise had hissed, while Madame Chevet had watched with fascination. "The child is mine alone!"

She'd grabbed her skirt and swept away, the market basket hanging heavy from her arm. Marcel had stood watching after her, grim determination on his face.

Several minutes had passed before Richard could breathe again, leaning against the building wall, out of sight. He felt like he was coming down with blood fever.

One truth was seared into his brain: Cerise had not admitted the child was Marcel's, but she hadn't denied it, either.

• • •

With a gasp Richard woke up, jackknifing into a sitting position. He was disoriented, looking around wildly. His heart was pounding, and he was covered in a thin film of sweat that had nothing to do with the temperature.

Okay. He was in his room at Luc's. The bed felt clammy and he got up, sitting on the mattress edge as he fumbled for his cigarettes. He lit one with shaking hands and swallowed the hot smoke down. With his other hand he wiped the sweat off his forehead.

Sometimes he still hated Marcel so much his soul was black with it and it was hard to breathe.

Cerise. How could she still haunt his dreams after two centuries? God knew there had been hundreds of women since then. But Cerise had been the first. *Déesse*, how he'd loved her. He pictured her in his mind, then frowned—Cerise didn't have black hair. *Oh no.* Richard sucked in a breath so sharply it hurt. Cold sweat broke out on his skin and his hand trembled. Cerise with black hair was Clio. Or Thais.

He shook his head to clear the image out of his mind. He'd kissed Clio. He hadn't meant to, never planned to. The other day he'd just been rattling Luc's cage, teasing him about the twins just to mess with him. Last night Clio had been snide and unwelcoming—he could tell she didn't like him. He'd gotten a kick out of seeing her work like a dog. Even hot and sweaty and covered with dirt and grime, she was a beauty. They both were. Clio had been wearing that thin tank top and those itty-bitty shorts, and suddenly he'd wanted her. Which had been deeply disturbing and totally unwelcome.

But the way women dressed these days—Cerise had always been covered from neck to ankle. All the village women had. The naked female form had been a wondrous revelation that had almost made his head explode.

And here was Clio, on display. Those long, tan legs, slim, strong arms. Black hair pulled back into a messy ponytail. Green eyes snapping fire at him. He'd wanted her, wondered how those legs would feel wrapped around his waist, how tightly her arms could pull him to her. He still hadn't meant to kiss her, but then he had, and if she hadn't pushed him away, he wouldn't have stopped.

But she had. Which was good. He wished he'd never done it. He knew he'd never do it again. Never.

✦ Chapter Twenty-Three

Thais

"DO YOU WANT TO GET SOME COFFEE?" KEVIN asked. "Or something? Before you go home?"

I smiled at him, which made my face sting just a tiny bit. It was almost all healed. "That would be great." Just for a little while, I would play hooky from the massive house-cleaning job at home. Clio had said it was okay, and I was seizing the opportunity. These days I was so stiff and sore from all the cleanup work we were doing I could hardly move. I deserved a little break.

"Great." He started his car and pulled away from the curb outside of school. I watched him for a second, driving his little red Miata. "How about Botanika?"

"Uh, no," I said. No place where I might run into Luc. I had chanced it when I was with Clio and Racey but couldn't meet him like this, on my own. "How about that other one, on Magazine, off of Jefferson? What's its name?"

"Café de la Rue," said Kevin easily, turning off St. Charles Avenue toward the river. I had learned that no one used north, south, east, or west here when they gave directions. It was either toward or away from the river or toward or away from the lake. Since the river curled around the city like a shell, you had to know where you were first in relation to those two things before any directions made sense. In my mind I thought of the lake as being north and the river as being east. But if you went east and crossed the river, then you were on the West Bank. I didn't get it, but I already knew that New Orleans had lots and lots of eccentricities that people accepted as normal and everyday and didn't question. It was kind of charming in a way, but it also made you feel crazy sometimes.

Café de la Rue was very different from Botanika. The people seemed to be mostly college students, and it had a slightly more formal, Old World feel, whereas Botanika was all about being funky and mystical and on the fringe.

We ordered our drinks and sat down at a little wooden table by the big sidewalk windows. There was a wide ledge there with potted plants and one of those little tabletop fountains that run on electricity. Its subdued trickling sound was soothing. All around us, people were working on laptops, alone or in pairs, some with headphones on. I drank my iced coffee, looking around, and I realized two things: One, I had drunk more coffee in the last three months than I had in the seventeen years before then, and two, New Orleans has some of the best peoplewatching in the world.

"The whole long-lost-twin thing with Clio is so weird," said Kevin, dumping sugar into his iced tea.

He had no idea. "Yeah, it really is. But it's great because I have a family again. Without my dad, I was just lost."

"That must have been really hard on you," Kevin said sympathetically. "My mom died when I was seven, and my dad got married again within a year. I still think it was because he didn't have any idea of what to do with my sister and me."

"I'm sorry," I said. "Do you get along with your stepmother?"

Kevin nodded. "Actually, I do. I mean, I remember it as being horrible at first, but she's been really good to my sister and me. Now she really seems like a mom."

"That's good," I said. "My dad never got married again, so it was always just me and him. Then he was gone. But now I have Clio and Petra, and things are starting to feel almost normal again."

"I'm glad." Kevin gave me a smile that went right from his eyes to my heart. He was just so sweet. Unfortunately, it was impossible not to compare him to Luc, and every time Luc seemed like the movie and Kevin like the TV show. Which was so awful and unfair of me. But Luc wasn't going to happen, and Kevin definitely could. I was determined to like him. And so far, it wasn't hard.

I don't know how long we sat there—Kevin was telling me stories about some of the teachers at school, and I was cracking up. He told me about getting cut off the football team after he broke his wrist, and he gave me the lowdown on some of the kids at school who I'd wondered about.

"Yeah, so she was on the debate team, and she was so

stuck-up," he told me. "She just looked down on everyone, you know? And I worked my ass off—no one was more prepared. I mean, I had notes taped inside my shirt, I practiced on my whole family, I just got everything down cold, because I wanted to crush her."

"What happened?" I loved stories like this, especially because the girl he was talking about was in my French class and I couldn't stand her.

Kevin grinned, and I couldn't help laughing. "She never had a chance. Every single thing she came up with, I was totally ready. I just demolished her. If it had been anyone else, I would have felt really mean. But that girl so had it coming. I tore apart her arguments and hung her out to dry. She was near tears by the end."

"Oh, I wish I could have seen it," I said. "I would have loved it. What was your topic, anyway?"

Kevin smiled wider. "Women on pro football teams," he said. "I was for."

I started laughing again and put my hand on his arm. Then suddenly I felt, literally felt, someone staring holes into the back of my head. Slowly I turned around.

Luc stood there with Richard. He looked better than when I had seen him at Axelle's—he had shaved and was wearing clean clothes—but his face was still drawn, almost haggard, and his eyes were filled with pain. And, uh, a bloodthirsty hatred.

And here I was, my hand on Kevin's arm, laughing up at him, our knees touching.

I was so, so thankful that it was here and now that I was running into Luc and not, say, when I was sobbing on Clio's shoulder or alone in a grocery store with a big zit or something.

Except, of course, that he was looking at me and Kevin like he was about to pull out an ax and come for us.

Kevin turned to see what I was looking at, and his eyes widened as he caught Luc's glare. "You know him?"

I shook my head. "Just a little," I said, thinking sadly how true that was. "He goes to the same church as—my grandmother."

Kevin looked back at me. "Well, he seems to have it bad for you." There was a question behind his words, but I couldn't go into it. I shrugged and shook my head.

Richard was grinning at me, jerk, and I gave him a careless smile and wave. He'd come over twice to help with the windows, after all. Luc I ignored. I turned back to my coffee and took a long, slow sip, trying to get myself together. My heart was pounding, and my cheeks felt hot. I felt Kevin still looking at me, but I took another couple moments to get a grip.

I swallowed hard, feeling like a wave had just rushed me off my feet at the beach. Oh, God, I still wanted him so much. Loved him so much. I just *loved* him, wanted to be with him, to have him hold me. Wanted him to be mine, like he said he was, and for me to be his. My whole body was flooded with memories of Luc, how he felt, how he tasted. . . .

Of course, Clio had those same memories.

I swallowed again and looked up at Kevin with a bright smile. "This has been really great," I said. "Do you think— would you want to go to a movie sometime?"

Kevin looked happy and I felt better. "Yeah, I'd like that a lot. Maybe this weekend? Should I call you?"

I wrote down Petra's number for him, and he put it in his pocket. I still felt awkward, still felt Luc's presence, and absently I reached over to trail my fingers in the little fountain on the window ledge. Then, out of nowhere, a rhyme popped into my head.

Let me choose a path of light
When my world is dark as night
When my heart is so forlorn
And love feels like a rose's thorn.
I am sunlight, I am shade
For love's sweet kiss my heart was made.
But down that path my heartache lies
Hidden in my lover's eyes.

It was a spell, I knew, but I had no idea where it came from or why. Or what it would do. It didn't exactly seem to have a point. *A spell.* Quickly I looked around, expecting the mirror over the counter to shatter or people's computers to start shooting sparks. But all was quiet.

"Uh," said Kevin.

I looked up at him to see him blinking dully at the table, then he started to slump sideways out of his chair.

"Kevin!" I got up quickly and grabbed his shoulders, easing him back into his chair. He felt slender and hard, like a statue, and he shook his head to clear it. "Are you okay?" I asked, trying to keep my voice down.

"Yeah," Kevin said, more strongly, and he blinked several times and sat up straighter. He rubbed his forehead with one hand and shook his head in bewilderment. "I don't know what happened," he said apologetically. "I just suddenly felt . . . weird. Sorry."

"No problem," I said. "I'm just sorry you feel bad. Do you think something's wrong? Are you getting sick?"

"I'm fine now," said Kevin, and he looked it. "I don't know what it was, but it's over." He smiled at me, and I rubbed his shoulder.

"Why don't we just go?" I said, getting my purse. "I need to get home, anyway—I told Clio I'd help her start dinner." It felt so great to know that someone was expecting me home, that I had someone I needed to check in with. Someone cared about me.

"Okay." Kevin stood up, and he looked fine, no hint of dizziness or anything. As we were leaving the coffee shop, I couldn't resist glancing back quickly, just once, at Luc and Richard.

They were both watching me, and they both had odd expressions on their faces. Richard was looking at me with surprise and wariness, but Luc just seemed completely still and focused on me, as if he was an explorer and I was a new species and if he made any sound, I would run off.

Which I was going to do anyway.

I turned around and followed Kevin out of the café. Only I could pack so much emotion and anguish into getting an iced coffee.

Chapter Twenty-Four

You Yourself Want More Power

DAEDALUS LOOKED AT AXELLE, LYING ON THE couch, reading a magazine, and tried to keep the displeasure off his face.

He failed miserably.

She felt him watching her and looked up. "What?" she said, sounding irritated.

Well, he was irritated too. "There's work to be done. Why are you lying there reading that mindless drivel?"

"This is my house," she said flatly. "I do what I please."

"There are more useful things you could be doing," Daedalus said. "We're working toward a common cause. Your part used to be housing Thais until we were ready for her. What is your part now?"

Her eyes narrowed at him. "I bet you're dying to tell me."

"There are all sorts of things you could be doing for me!" Daedalus said. "I asked you to go to the little voodoo shop on Rampart Street, but you refused." He swung to look at Jules, standing in the kitchen. "And, yes, you went, but you acted as if you were doing me a big favor. Do I have to remind you that we're all working together? I can't do everything myself."

"Yet you want to make all the decisions yourself," Axelle said coolly.

Daedalus was dumbfounded. Was she forgetting that he was the leader? He had always been the leader. But he had always shared everything, given people important roles to play. "Did we or did we not agree that we were a team? That the three of us would get this thing done? I am trying to get this thing done." He looked down at Axelle. "What are you planning to contribute?"

Axelle looked at him, her eyes black and cold. "I'm not a servant girl, Daedalus. I'm not an *apprentice*. I agreed to be part of a team. I didn't agree to be your gofer, running about fetching you cold drinks while you pull all the strings from your throne."

Quick anger rose in Daedalus, and with effort he damped it down. "You know," he said, almost to himself. "I'd forgotten it could be like this. But it's all coming back to me—the years I spent in Europe, traveling, learning. I met people, people who could contribute as much as I could. Useful people who understood the give-and-take of a working relationship."

"I wish you'd stayed there," Axelle muttered. She swung her legs off the sofa, leaned forward, and lit a cigarette.

"Now I find myself saddled with witches who have made no forward progress in a hundred years," he said bitingly. "It's unbearably frustrating. Don't you see? I'm doing this for all of us, not just me. I'm trying to satisfy *your* agenda. Not just mine."

Axelle stood up, facing him. "But it's your agenda that really matters, isn't it, Daedalus? You say that this is for everyone, but we don't really know that, do we? Face it—you're putting this together, this whole thing in motion because you yourself want more power. That's what you want. If it works out for the rest of us, fine and dandy. If not, well, at least you got your power."

Daedalus was almost speechless. "How can you say that!" Axelle turned away from him and stalked toward the kitchen. He followed her. Jules was watching them both as he carved off slivers of Brie and layered them neatly on crackers.

"How can you say that!" Daedalus repeated angrily. "I've involved you from the beginning! I didn't have to bring you in on this, arrange to have you get Thais. I could have asked anyone else! I chose you because you're a valuable person to have on the team. I knew I could depend on you, trust you. Now Thais is under Petra's influence, and instead of throwing yourself into the thousand and one other things that need doing, you're sitting on your pretty ass, smoking cigarettes and reading magazines!" His voice ended in a roar, and Axelle turned, her beautiful, porcelain face flushed.

"I *am* valuable to you, Daedalus," she said in a tightly controlled voice. "But I don't think you understand how much. I'm willing to do my share if I'm an equal member of the team. I am not willing to be your errand girl, running to the store to get dried snakeskin or skullcap at your bidding. Get your own damned ingredients. For that matter, get your own food, your own alcohol, and your own car." She stepped closer to Daedalus, her chin raised to him. "Because right now, you're feeling a lot like a parasite."

Daedalus thought he would choke with rage. "A p-parasite!" he sputtered disbelievingly. "That's bloody ironic, coming from you! You, who's never lifted—"

"Hold it!" Jules had stepped forward, physically placing himself between Daedalus and Axelle. "Both of you! Stop it! You're tired and frustrated. You don't want to do this." Daedalus looked at him, so angry he could hardly speak. "Look," Jules went on, "the three of us are in this together. We need each other. You know how difficult it would be to pull this off if we three can't form the base for the others to lean on." He stepped back, looking from one to the other. "Let's take a break for the rest of the day. Tomorrow we'll meet back here, and we can calmly talk everything out, get everything on the table. Récolte is on Sunday—we're having a circle then. If the three of us can't present a united front then, this whole plan is doomed. Understand?"

Daedalus took a step back, forcing his hands to unclench. Jules might have something there. Best to let everyone calm down. No doubt they would be more reasonable tomorrow. He nodded stiffly and headed to the door, letting himself out.

Outside, the air seemed heavier and stiller than usual. The scent of the river, two blocks away, was pervasive. Perhaps there would be a breeze up on the riverfront. He would walk up there and see, sit on a bench, watch the tugboats go by. That always soothed him.

Daedalus turned right, waiting for a horse and carriage to pass before he crossed the street. He hoped Axelle would have come to her senses by tomorrow. If not, the whole thing would become unbearably unwieldy and difficult. And where were Marcel and Claire? They were ignoring his repeated summons. The two lone holdouts. His lips pressed together grimly. So far he had been playing nice with them, with Axelle and Jules, with everyone. But if things didn't fall into line soon, he would have to be more—persuasive. As for Marcel and Claire, it was definitely time for them to be called home by more forceful means.

Chapter Twenty-Five

Crying Was Pointless

MANON LOOKED OVER AT SOPHIE. SHE'D BEEN sitting in front of her computer all morning, but for the last hour, she hadn't moved, hadn't typed anything. Her body was there, but her mind was somewhere else entirely.

Manon lifted her hair off her neck and stretched. Usually she could trust Sophie to tell her everything on her mind, share everything with her. She loved that about Sophie, how her face was so open, her emotions so transparent. But lately Sophie's face had been closed. She'd been distant. Ever since Manon had made her terrible admission.

Getting up, Manon came and hugged Sophie from behind. She leaned over so her head rested on Sophie's shoulder and put her arms around Sophie's waist. Sophie smiled and turned her head to Manon's. Manon curled one hand around Sophie's head and kissed her gently. She looked deeply into Sophie's artless brown eyes.

"What secret are you keeping from me?" she whispered.

"Nothing." Sophie shook her head.

"This is me," Manon persisted gently. "You can tell me anything."

"I don't want you to die," Sophie blurted, then looked away. "I don't want you to leave me."

Manon sighed and rested her head against Sophie's. At least Sophie was finally ready to talk about this. "I'm sorry if that hurts you," she said. "I don't want to leave you—I love you so much."

Sophie was still looking at her with wounded eyes. No one did wounded eyes better than Sophie.

"Sophie, you just don't understand what it's like, being me."

"I do understand," Sophie said, standing up. "I know it's frustrating—"

"It's so much worse than frustrating," Manon cut in. She gestured to herself, her slender, boyish body. "Look at me. I got frozen when I was thirteen years old. I don't even look like a *teenager*. And worse, I got frozen over two hundred years ago, when average heights were shorter. I'm four feet, six inches tall. I'll never look like a woman—it's almost impossible for me to feel like one."

"Manon, there are many grown women who are your height," Sophie said. "It's not as if you're a freak."

"Please," Manon scoffed. "We're all freaks. But Richard and I have it hardest. You know we do. I can't *stand* looking like a child. Women's rights—such as they are—have come a long way in the last hundred years, but I don't even have those.

I can't buy property or wine or get into R-rated movies without you. I can't drive a damn car. I can hardly do anything without you—I'm so dependent on you. It makes me crazy."

"Is that what—"

"Yet, thank the goddess I have you," Manon interrupted, pacing around the room. "Where would I be if I didn't have you? Can you even imagine? And what if you were a man? What if I loved you and you were a man? You would have been arrested a long time ago. There would have been no way for us to be together. People would think you're a pedophile. It's horrible. It turns our whole relationship into something twisted, something sick. Anyone who looked at us, you, a grown woman, me, looking this age, and knew we were lovers—it would be this horrible, unnatural crime in their eyes. I can't stand it! Not anymore."

"There are people who'd think it's sick and unnatural for us to be lovers even if they knew we were both way, way over twenty-one," Sophie pointed out.

Manon shook her head. "I'm doing it again," she said. "How many times have we had this exact same conversation? I rant about the same stuff, you say the same, placating things. But don't you see? We'll be having this talk—I'll be having this problem for the rest of my life. God, Sophie, it's just too long. Unbearably long." She held her cold can of soda against her forehead, trying not to cry. Crying was pointless. She'd been crying over this for more than two centuries, and it hadn't gotten her anywhere. There was only one thing that would help.

Sophie came closer and put her hands on Manon's shoulders. "I know you're in pain. I see it, I see what you live with and go through. But you know I depend on you just as much as you depend on me. You know I would be just as lost without you. Can't I—don't I—aren't you happy enough with me to make it worthwhile to stay? I try to make you happy, I want you to be so happy with me that none of this will matter."

Manon heard tears in Sophie's voice. "You know I'm happy with you," she said quietly. "There's no one else who could make me happier. But how can I be part of a happy couple when my life is such a nightmare? I feel that way more and more, all the time. What can I bring to you, to us, if I feel that way? In another decade, it will have made me stark raving *nuts*. And you'll be trapped with me, this embittered, crazy, desperately unhappy child/woman. How could you bear it? How could I bear doing that to you?"

Sophie was openly crying now. "Don't say that," she said. "How can you say that? I would love you no matter what! You look like a woman to *me*. You look like the only woman I'll ever want. But you want to leave me, to leave me alone forever!"

Manon put her arms around Sophie, feeling her sobs. She rested her head on Sophie's shoulder and held her tight, rocking her gently, stroking her long brown hair. "Forever is a long time to be alone," she said softly. "But it's a longer time to feel hopeless and wretched."

⚜ Chapter Twenty-Six

Clio

"NO."

Thais turned to look at me. "What?"

"No," I said again, crossing my arms. "You may not go out on a fricking date wearing *that*. I mean, Holy Mother, what's wrong with you?"

Thais looked at herself again in the full-length mirror. "Why can't I wear this?"

"Because you look like a Girl Scout selling cookies." I shook my head in disgust. Identical, schmidentical. Clearly *I* had inherited every bit of fashion sense between us.

"What should I wear, then?" Thais sounded irritated, but I was already heading for my closet. Tonight she was going out on a real date with Kevin LaTour, and I'd be damned if I wasn't going to do everything in my power to make sure those two lovebirds hit it off. Given how much we looked alike, it was a nightmare for me to see myself dressed in a plain white T-shirt and a knee-length denim skirt. For a *date*.

Fortunately, my closet was chock-full of clothes that would

make Thais look like the hottie I am. Thais followed me into my room and sat on the bed. I glanced at her as I considered various options. We'd been doing laundry all week, sometimes washing things two and three times to get out the smell of smoke. "We're going for hot and available, but not slutty," I said, holding up a peasant blouse made of thin, crinkled cotton. I held it to my face and breathed in. Only the scent of detergent.

"Oh, good," Thais said dryly.

I looked at her. "Are you nervous?"

"I don't know. Not really, I guess. Kevin's really nice."

She didn't sound hyper with enthusiasm, and my chest tightened. The more she liked Kevin, the less Luc would mean to her. It wasn't that I wanted him for myself, that bastard, but something mean inside me just wanted Thais not to care about him anymore, as if that would somehow make him more mine. It was ugly, but it was there.

I tossed the peasant blouse over to the bed. "Put that on."

"How is this better than what I'm wearing?" Thais asked, pulling off her shirt.

"For one thing, it's just prettier, with all the embroidery. It looks girlie, unlike your dockworker T-shirt. For another thing, all that elastic around the top makes guys feel like they can just tug it down."

Thais froze. "Ew!"

I shrugged. "You don't have to let 'em. But it puts the idea in their minds."

"And I would want that *why?*"

I sighed and shook my head, then found a black miniskirt that looked great with that top. "Just put this on and listen to the master."

Thais held it up. It came to mid-thigh. "And how do I sit down in this?"

"Let it ride up." Honestly, the girl was hopeless.

"How do I pick up something I drop?"

"Like this." I bent my knees, dropped into a crouch, then stood up. "Or let him get it."

She gave me a dirty look but put on the miniskirt. I switched out her plain silver hoops for some dangly earrings that almost brushed her shoulders.

"Your hair is fine, but we have fabulous eyes," I said, examining her face. "You should do more with them. And your skin is still a little pink, so we need to tone it down."

Ten minutes later, when Kevin rang the bell, Thais was ready. She looked fabulous, much more like me.

Nan and I hovered in the background as Thais opened the front door. I saw Kevin standing there, and Thais was right—he really was good-looking.

"*Whoa,*" I heard Kevin say, and then, "uh, I mean, you look—really great."

Thais laughed, then waved good-bye to us and shut the door behind her.

"Did you want to meet him?" I asked Nan.

"I can meet him later," Nan said, heading into the workroom. "He seemed like a nice guy."

"And he's not a witch," I said, following her. "After Luc, anyone else is simple." As soon as I said it, I winced and thought, *Crap*. I'd worked hard to not mention Luc's name— not to Racey, Nan, or Thais. I'd downplayed how I'd felt about Luc, how heartbroken and sick I was about it. I didn't want anyone to know. It was bad enough that *I* knew.

But of course Nan, as sharp as a shard of glass, caught it and turned to me.

"What do you need to tell me about Luc?" she asked gently.

"Nothing." Nor did I need to tell her that Richard had kissed me the other night. A fact I was still trying to suppress in my own memory. And I got to see *both* of them tomorrow night at the Récolte celebration. Goody.

I went to the cupboard and got out our four cups. We'd planned to work on scrying magick tonight, since Thais would be out of the house and pathetic Clio didn't have a date with a normal, appropriate person who wasn't 250 years old.

Nan started to draw a circle on the floor with a thin line of sand flowing through her fingers. Chalk circles are good, all-purpose circles; circles drawn with salt have protective, purifying powers. Circles can be made out of almost anything— shells, rocks, gems, leaves, silk fibers—you name it. Today's circle of sand had powerful protective qualities because of what sand is made of: quartz, lime (in the form of ground-up calcified shells), feldspar, mica, magnetite. They all had protective powers.

I set up the four cups and lit the incense and the candle

and then another pillar candle, a blue one, in the middle of the circle. Nan and I sat down, facing each other. It wasn't like it was before, before I knew she'd lied to me, kept my father from me. Just a month ago I had trusted her completely, put myself in her hands without question. Now I knew that I couldn't. I wondered if it would interfere with our magick, our connection.

I looked up to see her watching me, as if she knew what I was thinking. With a small, sad smile, she took my hands, then closed her eyes.

Eventually Nan started singing, and I joined in with my own song when I felt ready. We each watched the candle flame between us, and soon I had become part of it. I saw the almost-clear base of fire, faintly tinged with blue, that seemed to hover at the bottom of the wick. Then the orange parabola that rose above it, burning steadily. Above that, the peak of white and yellow, swaying, undulating, burning like life itself. The essence of fire became bigger than the candle flame, as though this small mote had broken off a raging inferno and somehow landed here. I could feel its appetite, its eagerness to consume. It seemed so pure, so above considerations of good or bad. It just *was* itself, with neither pride nor remorse.

I wanted to be fire.

Then, as I gazed dreamily at it, my vision opened up to see a campfire on the ground. An iron pot was boiling above it, supported on a trestle. I looked around and saw a village. A narrow road, covered with crushed oyster shells wound through an uneven line of wooden houses. It looked like a movie set, and I walked down the road, curious. A pig ran past, squealing, followed by two small boys with sticks. Loose chickens pecked in the dirt by the side of the road. I smelled wood smoke.

One smaller house stood a little ways off the road. It was painted yellow and had flowers and herbs growing in the yard. It felt like a place I knew, and I walked toward it. The front door was open, and a cat ran out of it, followed by a woman with light brown hair, almost blonde. It was Nan, a much younger Nan, holding a toddler on her hip. Her lips were pressed tightly together, and she seemed distracted.

Then a man came out of the house, holding a valise made of carpet. It was the same man we'd seen arguing with Nan in our vision. He was tall and handsome with black hair. He had my birthmark on one cheek, but his skin was tanned so darkly you could hardly see it. He said something to Nan, and she waved her hand angrily, not looking at him. He let out a breath, shook his head, and walked away from them. A horse was tethered nearby, and he got on it, then rode off into the distance, out of sight.

The scene changed abruptly, and Nan was much older, as old as she looked now. She was in a small room, standing by a narrow bed. Her forehead was damp with sweat, and she looked tired. A girl I recognized as Sophie stepped forward and handed her a basin of steaming water and a towel. A young woman was on the bed, not the girl from the rainy night who died, but someone different. She had brown hair, brown eyes, and our birthmark but still somehow looked like a young Nan.

She was in labor, and Nan was helping. The baby was born, and Nan lifted it and tied the cord with string. Sophie smiled happily and took the baby in a white cloth. Then Nan looked alarmed and leaned over the girl in the bed, grabbing her hand. The girl's face was pleased and relaxed, her eyes staring blankly at the ceiling. She was dead. I felt Nan's grief, her anger, a huge sense of despair. In another scene I saw Nan fill out the death certificate. The girl's name had been Béatriz Rousseau. The year was 1818.

The baby had had a birthmark too. That birthmark had been handed down in our family for generations, as though we were marked for death even before we had lived.

I didn't want to see anymore and felt myself closing off. I was half aware of sitting on the workroom floor, and then I felt Nan's warm hands slowly pulling themselves out of mine. She drew away and left me, clearly meaning for me to continue practicing my skills.

I didn't know what to scry for. I didn't want to see any more of the past, see how generations before me had died, one after another, like dominos, in childbirth. Like my mother. I had the sudden realization that I myself would die like that if I had a child. I would die. I'd never thought about children, didn't even know if I wanted any. If Luc and I had stayed together somehow, would I want to have his child? A gulf of longing and emptiness rose inside me, thinking of it.

I shook my head. This wasn't scrying. I wasn't concentrating. I could think about all this later.

Luc. God, Luc. Would I ever not miss him? Not want him?

Then he was right in front of me; I was scrying him in the flame. I hadn't meant to—my longing had opened this door. But now that I was here, I didn't close it. I hadn't seen him in days, and my eyes feasted on him, as if I could consume him just by looking.

Luc was in a dark, swampy, woodsy place. He was kneeling on the ground, surrounded by crystals and hunks of salt rock. Before him was a broad, shallow bowl of water. He was working magick.

He blinked and looked up, right into my eyes.

I drew in a startled breath and winked out my vision, dousing the candle. I swallowed and opened my circle quickly, my heart pounding. I was ashamed of spying on him, yet everything in me was singing with joy at seeing him again, just for a moment.

I put away our tools and swept up the circle. I heard Nan in the kitchen and hoped she wasn't doing any of the cleanup, which would only make me feel worse. Though of course I would be happy to do less.

I had seen Luc, and he'd been working magick. For what? I would have given anything to know what he'd been doing. What if the two of us made magick together, joining our hearts and minds, losing ourselves in a magickal place where power and life were all around us? It would be heaven, as close as I would ever get to heaven since our religion didn't have a heaven or a hell.

Luc loved Thais. He'd used me and lied to me and made me love him. I hated him for it—yet pathetically, I admitted only to myself that I still loved him despite everything. And I would be seeing him tomorrow night.

✦ Chapter Twenty-Seven

Thais

"SO *PONCHARTRAIN* IS A NATIVE AMERICAN word, right?" I asked Kevin. We were walking along the levee at the lakefront, hoping to catch any kind of breeze. We'd gone to a movie, which I could already hardly remember, but it had been mildly funny and not too bad.

"Yeah," Kevin said, taking my hand. "Look up ahead. There's a neat fountain I want to show you."

As we headed down the sidewalk, I began to catch on to the fact that the lakefront was a major parking and make-out spot. There were also tons of people just standing around their cars, talking, drinking beer. Other cars drove past and called to them or razzed them. It was a whole scene, and we hadn't had anything like it in Welsford.

I was liking Kevin more the better I knew him. It wasn't an overwhelming, joyous, desperate thing, like it had been with Luc, but it was pleasant and nice. Which was a welcome change.

"Oh my gosh," I said as we came closer to the fountain.

"It's called the Mardi Gras fountain," Kevin said. "It was

made back in 1962, and just last year it didn't work and was all broken. But they've restored it. It's cool."

It was an enormous fountain surrounded by a black wrought-iron fence. Around the concrete base was a ring of tiled plaques, and we walked closer to see them.

"Each one is for a different Mardi Gras krewe," Kevin explained. "Some of them don't exist anymore, and the new ones aren't shown. But a lot of them are still around."

We walked slowly around the fountain, reading the plaques. The names of the krewes were weird and funny: Momus, Comus, Zulu, Osiris, Rex. The fountain itself shot maybe twenty feet into the air, with rings of jets that played at different times and heights to make it seem patternless. Plus lights set into the bottom changed the color of the water itself from purple and green and gold, to just one shade, to red and blue and all sorts of combinations.

It was bizarre, overdone, and gaudy yet beautiful and strong. Very New Orleans.

"This is awesome," I said sincerely. "I love this. Thanks for showing it to me."

Kevin smiled down at me. "It's cool, isn't it? My folks used to take me here when I was little."

"And now you bring girls here," I teased him.

"Uh, a few." He grinned.

"Are they supposed to be doing that?" I pointed to some people who had climbed over the fence and were actually playing and splashing in the fountain.

Kevin shrugged. "No. But people always do. Sometimes people soap it too. There are fountains all over the city, and people always play in them. It's too hot to not take advantage of a chance to cool off."

"You're right about that." Here it was, practically October, ten o'clock at night, and it was probably still in the high eighties. I reached back and lifted my hair off my neck to let the breeze get to it. Leaning over, Kevin blew softly on my neck to cool me off.

It was really intimate and really sweet. I looked into his green eyes, a more olive shade than mine, and wondered if he was going to kiss me. But he drew back and gestured to the fountain.

"Wanna join them?"

"Yeah!" We climbed easily over the low fence, and I kicked off my sandals, the only part of my outfit that Clio had approved of. Kevin took off his Tevas, then led me over the shallow rim of the fountain.

Immediately the smaller jets shot up, raining down on us. People around us were playing and laughing, pretending to really splash each other. When we got wet, I gave a little shriek, but Kevin was laughing, and he took my hand and pulled me away from a group that was getting too raucous.

The water was almost cool, and it swirled around my legs. "This feels great," I said, wading, looking at my bare feet lit up by the fountain lights.

"And your skirt's so short you don't have to worry about it getting wet," Kevin said.

Quickly I looked at him and saw a gentle, teasing expression on his face. He made me feel so comfortable, as if I could totally trust him. "You noticed it, did you?" I said.

"Oh, *yeah.*"

I laughed, and then my foot hit something and I almost lost my balance. Kevin grabbed me, and I saw that I'd run into a little faucet handle set into the fountain floor.

"Thanks," I said, then realized he hadn't let me go. He looked at me, not smiling, and I thought, *Here we go,* and caught my breath. Slowly Kevin lowered his head, giving me time to escape, but I didn't and met his lips with mine, actually kissing someone else besides Luc, which I thought I'd never do again for the rest of my life.

Kevin was a good kisser. He was much more sure of himself than Chad Woolcott had been, and there was none of the deep, heavy urgency that Luc's kisses had ignited. Instead it was sweet and exploring, not tentative. I kissed him back, and pathetically, I was glad that Luc wouldn't see this. Then I was so mad that I'd even had that thought, and I went up on my toes and wrapped my arms around Kevin's neck. It didn't seem to matter that we were out in public, that tons of people could see us.

At that moment it was as if someone flicked a switch and turned off the moonlight. Despite the overhead lights around the fountain and the water lights themselves, the area still somehow seemed draped in sudden darkness. A chilly breeze made goose bumps rise on my arms, and I pulled back from

Kevin and looked at the sky. Huge, dark thunderclouds were rolling in off the lake, blocking the moon and stars.

Suddenly everything was washed out, so brightly lit with lightning that all color was leached out of my sight, as if an enormous camera flash had gone off.

"Move!" Kevin said, starting to pull me to get out of the fountain. Everyone else was scrambling to get out, and then a huge *boom!* of thunder seemed to shake the earth itself. I was hurrying through the knee-deep water, but about a foot from the edge I had a shocking premonition of death, danger, dying. Without a moment to think, I yanked my hand out of Kevin's and threw my arms into the air. Closing my eyes, I cried out the strongest protection spell Petra had taught me, hoping I had memorized the syllables correctly. Then I said, "Goddess, hear me! I call on earth, water, fire, and air! Protect us!"

In the next millisecond, an enormous bolt of lightning snaked down from the sky, making my hair fly up with electricity. I smelled something burning, and then the lightning hit the water we were standing in. My whole body tingled, and the fountain's lights all around us burst, with glass and sparks flying everywhere. But Kevin and I were protected, as if we were in a bubble that slowed time down and absorbed the enormous voltage of the lightning bolt. I whirled in slow motion and saw Kevin, looking stunned, reaching for me. Oh goddess, my magick had worked! For once, it had worked properly! Ecstatic joy flooded me, and I raised my face to the sky and laughed. In the next fraction of a second, I saw Luc's face, right in front of me, his eyes wide and startled, alarm making him still. But my magick had worked and now flowed out of me seamlessly, and I was part of the world again.

Then Kevin started to fall, the moment seemed to pop, and suddenly I was back in the now, hearing scared cries, the fountain's silence, the distant honking of cars. I lunged forward, almost slipping, and caught Kevin. He was heavy, and the best I could do was sink down against the fountain ledge, propping him against me. Had my spell protected only me? I was suddenly terrified. We'd been standing in water that lightning struck—we should have been killed. But was Kevin more hurt than I was?

"Kevin! Kevin!" I said, holding him in my arms. A man ran over and helped me get him out of the fountain. Kevin shook his head and blinked, looking up at me.

"My God!" said the man. "Never seen anything like it! You two should be dead!"

"Are you okay?" I asked Kevin worriedly, keeping my arms around him.

"Yeah," he said slowly. "What happened?"

"We got hit by lightning, sort of," I said with a nervous laugh.

"Y'all better get out of here before you get hit again," said the man as heavy rain began to fall. "Storm looks bad."

"Can you walk? Are you okay?" I asked again.

Kevin nodded and got to his feet. He rubbed his forehead with one hand, looking confused. "I'm okay," he said. "I just don't remember what happened." He seemed more himself, and he took my hand. "Let's get to the car—we're getting soaked."

Together we ran back to where he had parked the little Miata. Inside I felt cold, either from the temperature drop or a delayed reaction. I had made magick. I had saved us. It was exhilarating. And scary. And I had seen Luc, right when my spell had occurred. Why? What did that mean? Had he—been part of it somehow?

"You're shaking," said Kevin.

"I am? Oh. Yeah, I am."

He reached into the minuscule backseat and pulled out a soft cotton throw. It was big enough to wrap around both of us, even over the stick shift, and I immediately felt better.

"Are you okay?" I asked for the third time. "Should we go to a doctor?"

"My dad's a doctor," he said, "but actually, I feel okay. A little shook up, maybe, but fine. So lightning hit the actual water?"

I nodded. "It broke all the lights. It was pretty scary. I felt like I'd stuck my finger in a light socket."

He shook his head, trying to figure it out. "It should have killed us—a fountain that small, a direct hit. I don't know why it didn't."

I shrugged, wide-eyed, realizing suddenly that Kevin hadn't heard my spell. "Just lucky, I guess."

"Yeah," he said, not sounding convinced. The rain was

pouring down now, with more lightning and huge, rolling booms of thunder, but I felt cozy and safe inside the small dark car. Kevin seemed normal again at last, and he started the engine and took me home.

At Petra's, I asked if he wanted to come in and dry off, but he shook his head.

"Think I'll just go home. But—do you want to go out with me again? If I promise not to put you in death-defying situations?" He actually sounded uncertain, and I laughed.

In answer I reached up and put my arms around him, and smiling, he kissed me. He felt warm and smooth and very comforting, and we kissed for a long time, standing there on the porch. Then I felt Clio coming toward the front door, and I broke away.

"I better go in," I said. The rain had stopped while we were kissing, and now the world was dripping wetly.

"Okay. I'll call you." He let me go reluctantly, and I watched him get back into his car and drive away.

I couldn't get one thought out of my brain: I had made magick. And it had worked.

✦ Chapter Twenty-Eight

Endless, Pain-Edged Days

LUC WIPED THE COLD SWEAT FROM HIS BROW. He sat back on his heels, breathing hard, as if he'd been running. *Get a grip.* The intense darkness surrounded him, and he blew out the candles he'd been using to make the darkness more complete. All around him he could hear night sounds—animals foraging or stalking, insects humming, the rustling of owls as they flew through the trees.

God. Thais. The endless, pain-edged days were making him literally sick—he'd lost weight, couldn't sleep, could hardly eat. He'd been drinking most of his meals ever since she'd ripped him out of her life.

He felt like he'd been flayed alive, and Thais was the balm that would heal everything, make him whole again. He missed her solemn face, her quick laugh, the way she touched him. She'd been shy and a little scared, yet she'd never held back from him. She'd given everything he'd asked for, given it freely and with all her strength.

He'd seen her tonight, scrying. She'd been wrapped around

that kid, kissing, their mouths open, drinking from each other. It twisted in Luc's gut like an *athem*. It had been unbearable.

His heart was going to explode. Angrily he smashed the bowl of water aside, then picked it up and brought it down hard on the salt chunks he'd been using. The heavy stone bowl smashed them into powder, and feeling rage wash over him, Luc raised the bowl again and slammed it down, twice, three times. The third time the bowl itself broke, and Luc stared at the shards in disbelief.

This was his main tool, the bowl his mother had used and her mother before that. It was incredibly old and had a carved border of *plumes* around the top. His grandfather's element had been air, his grandmother's water, and the bowl had symbolized their joined powers. He'd always used it in his magick, used it to scry, to hold water or fire. Now he'd broken it, and it could never be repaired. One of the biggest shards had an almost complete *plume,* a feather, on it. He picked it up and stroked the cool stone against his cheek.

Remorse doused his rage. Dropping his head into his hands, he tried to slow his breathing, cool his blood. The bowl was broken forever, like his relationship with the one person he'd actually loved over the last two hundred years.

Sighing, Luc stripped off his shirt and walked over to the narrow river running twenty feet away. The cold water was clear and red-tinged. He dunked his shirt into it and wrung it out, then squeezed it over his face and shoulders. It felt incredible. Standing up, he pushed off his jeans and then, naked, walked out into the river. It was shallow, barely up to his waist, and cool against his hot skin. He dunked under, getting his hair wet and pushing it out of his eyes. He leaned back, looking at the sky. Tall trees on either side of the river left only a narrow channel of dark sky above him. Sinking down till the water was up to his shoulders, Luc watched the stars and thought.

He wanted Thais. Neither twin wanted him. Or . . . was that really true? It always came back to the plan. The plan called for his being with one of them. It didn't matter which one. And it had to happen soon if it was going to work at all.

✦ Chapter Twenty-Nine

Thais

"WHAT'S UP?" CLIO SAID, LOOKING AROUND THE front door at me. Then she really saw me. "Whoa. Guess you got caught in the rain. You look like you got dragged through a hedge backward."

I made a face and followed her into the house. "Thanks." I felt cold and damp and chilled all the way through.

"Thais?" said Petra, running into the room, her brow furrowed with worry. "Are you all right? A while ago I felt—I don't know. I just felt you somehow." She looked me up and down, and her frown deepened. "You're all wet."

"Yeah. It's been kind of a full night. Let me put on something dry, okay?"

"I'll make something hot to drink," said Petra, watching me as I climbed the stairs. "But you're sure you're okay?"

I nodded. "Yeah, pretty okay. Considering I got hit by lightning."

• • •

"Tell me again." Petra looked at me seriously across the

kitchen table.

I took another sip of hot chocolate, surprised it wasn't some herbal magickal anti-damp-and-wet concoction.

"We went to the Mardi Gras fountain by the lake," I said again. I'd already told them once, but I guess Petra was hankering for any juicy details I'd missed. "A bunch of people were playing in it, so we got in too. And then, completely out of nowhere, it was storm city. There was lightning, and everyone was yelling to get out of the fountain. Do we have any cookies?"

Clio tilted her head toward the pantry, and I went and got the package of cookies.

"So everyone was scrambling to get out of the fountain," I went on, trying not to spit crumbs. "We were rushing to the side, but then I suddenly felt that we were about to get hit by lightning. So I just shouted out that protection spell you taught me, not even sure I was remembering it correctly. And I called on earth, water, fire, and air to protect us. And it was like we were in a little bubble, and the lightning hit the water and made my hair stand on end, practically. Then the bubble popped, it was all over, and Kevin fainted."

Petra didn't say anything, thinking it through. She looked very solemn, her long fingers wrapped around her mug. I ate another cookie.

"It's lucky he only fainted," said Clio. "You guys both should have been killed."

"That's what some guy said at the fountain," I said. "But I

mean, I think my magick actually worked somehow. It felt—smooth. Usually it feels like something extra, like a cloak that I'm shrugging off or pushing off, you know? But this felt so . . . light and easy, but really strong and smooth. It's hard to describe. It felt right, like . . . like I was a flower and the magick was a scent. Part of me, but going out into the world. But I made it." I realized how stupid that sounded and shook my head, embarrassed. And still Petra was looking at me. "Isn't this good? Isn't this what it's supposed to be? I didn't blow anything up."

"It's good," said Petra.

"I know what you mean," Clio said, surprising me, and Petra nodded.

"That's what it's supposed to feel like," she said. "It hasn't felt like that before?"

"No, not really," I said. Then I remembered something. "Oh, one other time. I was at the coffee shop with Kevin, and all of a sudden a little rhyme came into my mind. I said it, and it felt like that, smooth and easy and part of me, but going out."

Petra frowned. "What were you doing in the coffee shop?"

"Um, just getting coffee?"

She smiled briefly and shook her head. "No, I meant, what exactly were you doing at the exact moment the rhyme came to you?"

"You were with Kevin that time too," said Clio. "Like he helps your magick somehow. Interesting."

"Was there a tea light on the table? Were you playing with it?" Petra asked.

I thought. "No. Oh, but you know, there was a little electric fountain in the window, a little tabletop one. I remember I was playing with it, dipping my fingers in it."

"Hmm." Petra sat back, looking both satisfied and thoughtful at the same time.

"What?" I asked.

"I think I understand something now, something I didn't see before," said Petra. "I'm surprised, but of course now it makes perfect sense."

"What?" I said again.

"Yeah, *what?*" said Clio.

"Your element," said Petra. "We've assumed that it was fire because Clio's is, and actually mine is too. But it seems clear now—that protection spell worked so well, and felt so right, because you were surrounded by your true element—water."

Clio and I just sat there, speechless for a moment. Finally I found my voice.

"Water! But why would water be my element?"

"It's the opposite of fire," said Petra. "You two are *mirrors* of each other, not clones."

"That explains your fashion sense," Clio said brightly, and I kicked her. "Ow!"

"Huh. Water." I was having trouble taking it in. I hadn't been doing magick long, but what I'd done had been focused around fire. "But what does this mean?"

"It's probably why the magick you've been trying to make has backfired," said Petra. "And why it's felt hard and unnatural."

"I thought it was just because making magick *is* hard and unnatural," I said.

Petra smiled bigger. "Is that still what you think?"

I thought back to when I'd cried out the protection spell, how exhilarated I'd felt, how simple everything had seemed. In that one moment, it was as if the whole world had fallen into place, and everything had made sense, if only for a second. My magick had worked perfectly, flowing seamlessly out from me into the world. Tears came to my eyes as I remembered that beautiful, ecstatic feeling.

"No." I smiled. Now I knew. My element was water. If I worked with my true element, magick felt like nothing else in the world, like perfection. And it was within my grasp.

Petra reached across the table and took my hand in hers, lightly patting it. "Water," she murmured, looking at me. "I never would have thought. . . ."

Chapter Thirty

Clio

"WE'RE DOING WHAT NOW?" THAIS ASKED. "Today is what?"

"Récolte," I said. I straightened from where I was dribbling seed on the ground in a pattern. The backyard still looked like a demilitarized zone, with scorched plants, cracked flowerpots, and leftover building material from where some of the weatherboards had been replaced. We were due to go to our circle pretty soon—because it had to be outside, it was being held over in Covington, across the lake. It would take about forty minutes to get there.

"The autumn equinox," Nan said. "In our religion there are eight jours sacrés. Eight holy days, remember, I told you about them? The four main ones and four minor ones?"

Thais looked embarrassed. "I don't remember them too well."

"Well, Récolte is one of the minor ones," Nan said. "It's the second of three traditional harvest festivals, and it takes place on the autumn equinox every year."

"Today the length of the night and the day are exactly the same," I explained. "All the days after this will be shorter, and the nights longer, until spring. It's sort of about getting the harvest in, getting ready for winter."

"So what's with the seeds?" Thais asked.

"I'm making the rune *seige* with seeds," I said, kneeling down to finish it. "The rune for the sun. Today the sun is going underground for winter, and we'll see him again in the spring."

"Uh-huh." Thais sounded unconvinced.

"You'll understand more at the circle," Nan said, brushing off her hands. She glanced at her watch. "Actually, we better get moving. We need to be there before dusk."

• • •

Covington was directly across the lake, so we took the causeway, the longest bridge in the world, to get there.

"Why do we have to do the circle outside?" Thais looked out her window. We were at the middle part of the causeway, where you couldn't see land on either side—only water all around. Little whitecaps kicked up here and there, and gulls circled overhead, occasionally dipping down to snatch a fish.

"Because it's about celebrating nature," Nan said, keeping her eyes on the road. "It's about thanking the earth for the bounty we've harvested and honoring her as a life giver. After the circle, we'll have a feast, with lots of fresh-baked breads, wine, and seed cakes."

"You usually do this with your other coven?" Thais asked.

Nan nodded. "Yes. But they understand that I need to do some things with the Treize right now. I need to find out more about what they're gathering for and find out how they all feel about it."

"You know what they've gathered for," I said from the backseat. "They want to do the rite that'll find their fountain of youth again and get them even more power."

"Yes." Nan met my eyes in the rearview mirror. "But I think there are other layers to what's going on. I want you two to be extra careful and keep your eyes open. Don't wander off, okay?"

"Okay," I said, and Thais nodded, looking less than thrilled.

I was concerned myself. Tonight I would see Luc in person for the first time since the night I'd kicked him out of the house. So much had happened since then. I smoothed my thin linen *bouvre* over my knees. Thais had started off wearing a blue T-shirt and a jeans skirt, but Nan had asked her to borrow a *bouvre* from me. "A what?" she'd asked, and Nan had explained that usually at circles and always on holidays, witches wore the long, loose gown. Nan's was almost always a sky blue silk, but she had a gold one for the harvest festivals. I'd lent Thais a flowy, thin cotton one in a russet that looked pretty with our coloring. It had a gathered neck and loose sleeves that wouldn't be too hot. I hadn't been able to get her out of her Tevas.

I, on the other hand, was stretching the definition of *bouvre*. Yes, it was long and a little loose and flowy, but it was also a halter top and made out of scarlet linen. Racey always said it looked like it came from Tarts "R" Us, but I loved it and knew I looked incredibly hot in it. And I needed to look incredibly hot tonight. I wanted Luc to see exactly what he had lost. Maybe he thought he loved Thais, but he'd felt something for me. Maybe not love, maybe only desire, but something, and I wanted to rub it in.

"It will be interesting, seeing if you feel this circle any differently now that you know your true element," Nan went on to Thais.

"Yeah. I want to try to work some magick again, like with Clio," she said.

"That's fine, but I'd like you to make sure I'm around when you do," said Nan.

"Why?" Thais looked surprised, but just then Nan reached the end of the causeway. She took the first left, following a small road that wound around the lake.

She never did answer.

• • •

Five minutes later Nan turned and drove through an open wooden gate marked *Private Property*.

"This belongs to one of my friends," she explained, heading down a winding, overgrown road. "I like being on familiar territory. We've had circles here before."

I'd never been here, so I wasn't sure what circles she was talking about. I knew she and about five other women met sometimes to deepen their study of magick—maybe that had been it.

There was no visible house, but we saw several other cars under a row of live oaks, and Nan pulled up next to one. "Can you two get our things from the trunk? I'd like to find Ouida," she said, turning off the engine.

"Sure," said Thais, and Nan got out, leaving us in the car.

"How do you feel?" I asked.

Thais turned around to look at me. "Nervous. I don't want to see him."

I liked how we were so often in tune with what the other was thinking. One of our twin things. Racey and I were like that, but Thais and I didn't even really know each other that well yet.

"I know," I said. "But I also want to show him that I'm perfectly fine and not all torn up, you know? I want to look totally normal, like I don't care. Like it didn't affect me."

Thais nodded. "It's going to be hard."

"Yeah." I was also going to face Richard. Every time I remembered that I'd let him kiss me, I felt weird all over again.

"Plus, you know, the whole someone's-trying-to-kill-us thing," said Thais, leaning her head against her window. "Probably someone here."

I sighed. "Well, we can't stay in the car all night. The circle has to start right before dusk. They'll come get us in a minute."

Thais sighed too, sounding exactly like me. "Okay. Let's go."

• • •

Right through the trees was a large natural clearing. Wild grass grew halfway to my knees. At one end, tables had been set up, and several members of the Treize were there, putting out platters and glasses.

"I'm not eating or drinking anything until I see someone else try it first," Thais muttered as we brought Nan's bread over.

I smiled grimly and nodded. Nan was standing next to Ouida. I saw Sophie and the little-girl-looking witch, Manon, standing by themselves talking, not far away. Sophie was always so solemn—it made her seem much older than she looked.

Oh, right. God, the whole immortal thing was still really hard to deal with.

"Here's the quinoa salad," said Thais, placing it on the table.

"Thanks," said Nan.

"And bread." I put it on a wooden cutting board that had already been set out.

"How have you two been?" Ouida asked sympathetically.

"Okay," I said. "Better, now that Nan's back."

"I bet. Has anything else dangerous happened?"

"You mean, besides us setting the house on fire?" I said dryly. "No. Oh, except Thais got hit by lightning."

"I wanted to tell you about that," Nan said as Ouida's eyes widened. She started to tell the story about Thais's true element.

"Did you bring the wine?" I asked Thais, looking at the table.

"No—there's already some here."

"Nan brought some too. You know, I think it's in the

backseat." I hoped Thais would offer to get it, but she didn't, so I headed back to the car myself. It was within full view of where we were, fortunately.

I was going headfirst into the car's backseat when I suddenly felt someone watching me. I grabbed Nan's two bottles of wine and stood up quickly, thinking, *Luc*.

But it was Richard who leaned against the next car, Richard who was watching me with those dark brown eyes. "Hello," he said. "Nice *bouvre*." He was wearing beat-up green fatigue pants and a white T-shirt with the sleeves ripped off.

"Do any of your shirts have sleeves?" I asked.

He gave me a little grin. "In the winter." He grabbed the hem of his shirt and pulled it over his head so he was naked from the waist up. I saw he had another thorny tribal tattoo on his smooth chest. Then he leaned through an open car window and pulled out his own *bouvre*, which was raw silk, streaky brown and gold, like his hair. He pulled it on, and it settled lovingly around him. Then, as if I wasn't even there, he reached under it, and I heard his pants unsnap. Immediately I turned and started walking away.

"Wait," he said.

I turned to him, glad I was wearing two-inch wedge espadrilles. He was only an inch or two taller than me now. I stood there stone-faced as he kicked out of his fatigues and picked them up off the ground.

"If you're trying to make me go mad with lust, you're failing," I said in a bored tone.

He gave me a slight grin and pushed his clothes into the car. Then out came the ever-present cigarette, which he lit.

"I have to go," I said impatiently.

He pulled on the cigarette, his head down, as if he was thinking. Then he looked up at me again and blew the smoke out of his nose, like a dragon.

"I wanted to say I'm sorry," he said, and I blinked in surprise.

"For what?"

"Kissing you. The other night."

I looked at him suspiciously, but there was no irony in his eyes, no second meaning behind his words. I shrugged and shook my head, not knowing what to say.

"I didn't mean to," he went on. "I won't do it again."

He gave me a little smile, almost sad, then turned and walked to the clearing. I heard Daedalus call his name. I stood there frozen, pulling in a shallow, silent breath. Swallowing hard, I realized I felt shaken, which was ridiculous. There was absolutely no reason why I would feel upset or even, goddess, hurt, just because Richard hadn't meant his kiss.

It didn't matter to me at all.

• • •

"Can I have some wine?" I asked Nan breathlessly when I got back.

She poured me half a glass. "That has to last you all night."

"Okay." She moved off, now talking to Axelle, Jules, and

Ouida. I took a sip, feeling its warmth as it went down, and realized wine was the last thing I wanted right now. I put it down.

"Do we have any lemonade?" I asked Thais. "Or water? Iced tea?"

"Tea. Here." She handed me a glass already poured. "So, the wine—it doesn't matter that you're underage?"

I thought about it. "Well, I'm not driving, and it's just half a glass. You know, it's just tradition. Family tradition. French families start giving their children a tiny bit of wine at dinner when they're just little kids. I mean, I'm not hanging out at the 7-Eleven, swilling beer."

Thais nodded, processing. "You know, these boo-thingies are really comfortable," she said. "And it even looks okay on the male people."

I drank almost half the tea right away. "That's better. Yeah, they're like kilts," I agreed. "On the right guy, they can even be really sexy." Then I winced. We both knew who we'd be seeing in a *bouvre* tonight.

Besides Richard, that is. I kept my back to the clearing, not wanting to see him again. I hadn't told Thais about his kissing me, hadn't even told Racey. Usually I told Racey everything, so I didn't know why I had kept it to myself.

I felt Thais stiffen by my side and turned. She was staring at me, her eyes wide and leaf green. Then I felt Luc's presence getting nearer. I reached out one hand and patted her arm, and she tried to smile.

We turned to look at him at the same time.

"Loser," I said coolly in greeting.

Luc's beautiful dark blue eyes looked into mine, as if he could see my soul. Goddess, what was it with me and guys? A guy had never knocked me off balance before in my life, yet Luc and now even Richard seemed to do it as easily as breathing.

Luc nodded. "Yes. I have lost," he said, and just hearing his voice sent shivers down my spine. Instantly my body woke up, every nerve ending coming to life, remembering his touch, his kisses, the way he felt when we were lying together.

Thais wasn't even looking at him, just staring at the ground, her body as stiff as a statue. I felt a second of irritation with her—I wanted her to have the Clio coolness, Clio strength. I didn't want her to seem this young, this vulnerable. It was almost like it made *me* look weak.

"How's your boyfriend?" Luc asked her, his voice chilly.

She looked up then, and I saw a spark in her eyes that surprised me. "He's fine," she said evenly, and I almost smiled. "Maybe I'll see him later tonight." She sounded distant, uninterested, and I was proud of her.

Luc's face flushed, and his eyes narrowed. He wasn't going to win any awards for his ability to conceal emotion. My jaw clenched. Emotion he felt for my *sister.* "We won't be done till late," he said, his voice tight.

Thais shrugged casually and took a sip of tea. "That's okay."

"It didn't take you long," he said, sounding angry.

Thais shrugged again. I saw a faint pink tinge on her neck—she was about to flush. She wasn't as unaffected by Luc as she was pretending. She put her glass down and walked away without another word, leaving me and Luc alone.

"Why don't you run after her?" I asked snidely. I shook my hair back over my shoulders, feeling anger erupting inside my chest. "She's the one you care about."

Luc turned to face me. I thought he would snap something and take off, but he didn't. "It isn't only Thais I care about," he said, sounding tired. He ran one hand through his dark hair and looked at me. He was almost six feet tall, much taller than Richard. "I absolutely care about you, Clio, sincerely."

I was so taken aback I couldn't come up with an acid-etched answer.

"I met you first, and it was your beauty that first captured me," he went on in a low voice. "I love your fire and your strength. You own your body, you know how to use it. You knew what you wanted from me. You know what you want in general. That all appeals to me greatly."

I took a quick sip of my tea so I wouldn't run screaming into the woods. The worst part was, I wanted to believe him—even almost did believe him. I wanted him so much, I needed his lies to be true.

"Then you met my sister and went for the two for one?" I asked, proud of myself for my voice not wavering.

Luc winced, and I wanted to hold him, press his head

against my chest and stroke his hair and comfort him. Can we say, "masochist"?

"I made a huge mistake. I treated you both unfairly and faithlessly. I'm very sorry, Clio—believe me. I never meant to hurt you. I was happy when I was with you, and I had hoped to make you happy too."

"Then you might want to try not two-timing me with my twin sister." My teeth were clenched tight, my hands curled at my sides. I was furious at him for lying, for manipulating me, and I was even more furious at myself for wanting him *anyway*.

I stalked away, trying to calm down. It was bad enough I felt this way without anyone knowing. Having it be public would be more than I could bear.

Nan and Thais were setting up the large circle, helped by Manon and Jules. Daedalus seemed to be reading from a large, old book. Sophie and Ouida were talking, their arms full of leafy branches. Axelle was at another table, putting a piece of cheese on a cracker. Everyone was busy—I could take a minute to get a grip. I ducked into the woods and almost immediately yelped when someone grabbed me.

"What do *you* want?" I sputtered, yanking my arm out of Richard's grasp.

"I don't know," he said, frowning. "I don't know."

Then, before I could say a word, his head came down and his mouth was on mine. He leaned against me with enough force to push me back a foot against the broad trunk of a live oak. My eyes opened wide in surprise, and then his arms were around me, protecting my bare back from the rough tree bark. He slanted his head a different way to kiss me more deeply, and still I hadn't reacted, hadn't pushed him away, wasn't even kissing him back.

All I could think was, *He just* said *he wouldn't do this again.*

And, *He said he hadn't meant it.*

And, *Luc was just yanking my chain. He loves Thais.*

Finally, *This . . . feels . . . good.*

I put my hands out and gripped Richard's upper arms, thinking, *I've got to get out of here.* Then every thought I had just evaporated. My eyes slowly shut and my whole body relaxed, pressed between him and the tree. His arms were smooth and hard under my hands, his skin warm. I opened my mouth and kissed him back, felt his surprise, his body tighten. My hands slid up his shoulders and held him more closely against me, one hand keeping his head in place.

I was so heartsore over Luc, over everything that had happened. It felt so wonderful to feel good again, just for a minute.

Suddenly Richard broke the kiss, leaving me gasping. "Say my name," he said, breathing hard while I blinked stupidly at him. "Say my name."

"Richard," I said breathlessly. "*Ree*-shard."

He kissed me again, harder, and I gave up completely, pressing myself against him, feeling his lithe hardness, his smooth, wiry muscles. The cloth of his robe was soft and thin, and our bodies felt so close. Richard was more my size, fit easily into my arms, against my body. He pushed one knee between mine, pressing my *bouvre* back against my legs.

I heard myself making little sounds, hungry sounds I'd heard before, and I thought, *I want him.*

"Clio? Clio!"

Someone was calling me. Nan. I pushed Richard away. We stared at each other, panting, my hands on his shoulders, his around my waist.

"Thais, go find Clio, will you?" I heard Nan ask.

"Oh, God!" I whispered. I whipped my hands away from him as if electrified. "God!"

Richard stepped back from me, his face flushed, hunger in his eyes. He looked as shocked as I felt.

"I—damn it," he said, breathing hard, sounding appalled. "I didn't—"

I just stared at him, unable to process what I had been doing.

I turned and walked quickly away, smoothing my hair with my hands. I tugged down on the skirt of my gown, feeling limp and overheated. When I was closer to the tables, I came back out of the woods.

"Nan?" I called, striving for normalcy. "Did you want me?"

She turned at the sound of my voice. I saw that the other members of the Treize were gathering in the circle. The sun was setting; it was time to begin. I took off my shoes and walked barefoot through the grass, not looking at Luc. On the opposite side of the woods, Richard came out into the clearing. He carefully didn't look at me, and I didn't look at him.

✦ Chapter Thirty-One

Thais

IT WAS HOT AND STICKY, AS USUAL. CLIO'S FACE
was flushed and pink from the heat, and I guessed that I looked
the same. The circle was forming, people were gathering. Luc
walked over from the tables, and Richard came out of the
woods across the clearing. I wanted to be next to Clio or Petra
or Ouida, but people started linking hands, and I ended up
between Jules and Richard. After Jules, there was Sophie,
Daedalus, Petra, Manon, then Clio. On Clio's other side was
Axelle, then Luc, and finally Ouida, Richard's other side. Richard's hand was warm and dry, his fingers firm and strong.

I glanced at Clio, and she gave me a little smile. She looked
upset or tense, and I figured seeing Luc again was throwing
her off. I actually felt weirdly calm and confident. I finally
knew what my element was, and this was the first time I would
make "big" magick with that knowledge. I hoped I would feel
magick coming alive inside me. It was a little scary, but Petra
and Ouida were here, and somehow they made me feel safe.

"Friends," Daedalus began. "Our journey to this point has

been unexpected and harder than we could have known. Yet how glad I am to share this Récolte celebration with you, the people I have known longest, the people I grew up with. And how glad I am to welcome Clio and Thais to our circle."

He smiled and nodded at both of us, and Ouida smiled at us encouragingly. As Daedalus went on, I remembered to calm my breathing and release any lingering tension inside me. Luc—I just had to let it go. I rolled my shoulders and breathed out, counting to four, and then breathed in, counting to four. I tried to clear my mind of everything around me and open it to everything I could receive from everyone else.

Slowly we started moving clockwise in our circle. The sun would set in another three or four minutes—it was deep twilight, and the woods behind me were black.

I closed my eyes and listened as Daedalus started the chant. I'd never heard it before, but Petra had told me that each sabbat had its own traditions, songs, and foods, just like with Christianity or any other religion. I liked how the *Bonne Magie* emphasized having a cycle, with no beginning and no end. Everything we did here tonight could be done next year at Récolte. Everyone around me had done almost exactly this at every other Récolte they'd celebrated throughout their lives. And after this, the next holiday was Monvoile, which came on Halloween, and then Soliver at the winter solstice. The sun rose and set, the seasons bloomed and died, everything was a circle, an unending rhythm. I'd never thought about life like that, and I really liked it. It gave a sort of structure and sense of permanence to my confusing, impermanent life.

All at once I realized that the Treize itself was unnatural, out of cycle. These people had been born and should have lived and then died, their natural cycle. Then they would have been born again, and their souls would have another lifetime to try to improve and advance farther on their paths, according to their beliefs, as Petra had explained them to me.

But the Treize hadn't died. They'd been born but become stuck in a static, linear life. How weird. Was it having some effect? Like, on their souls or even on the world around them? I didn't know—didn't even know if I believed all that.

Next to me, Jules's beautiful, deep voice started to weave in and out in the chant. Most people were singing now. I didn't have my own personal song, but I just closed my eyes and thought about water, my element, and everything it meant to me. Then I opened my mouth and let whatever came to me become a sound.

At first I sang very softly, not wanting to mess anyone else up if I was doing it wrong. But I felt like I was actually singing a song and not just making a bunch of unconnected sounds. It felt like there was a song already written inside me that I was letting out. It felt good and natural. I let my voice join the others lightly, following them without trying to be louder or alone, just blending. Slowly, as I concentrated, faint impressions came to me.

I focused on opening my senses, and gradually I was able to separate out emotions and people. I almost caught my breath—it was incredible. I could actually feel that Manon was unhappy and that she also felt guilty. About what? And Daedalus was already sending out waves of triumph, as though some goal had been achieved. That was creepy.

I tried deliberately reaching out to Sophie, just to see what would happen. To my surprise, I was hit with a wave of sadness that was so strong I opened my eyes. Her face looked impassive, the same as always, but her large brown eyes were haunted, and I felt a sense of desperation—almost steely resolve. To do what?

From Ouida, I felt calm, radiating peace and love—what a relief. She felt wary but was concentrating on sending out only good. Thank heavens. Then there was Luc. I couldn't help it—I opened my eyes and shot a quick glance at him. His eyes were closed; he was singing, joining in with the others. I felt a deep wave of remorse and longing coming from him. He was so beautiful, so haunted in the deepening twilight. Suddenly I was fiercely glad that he was there, that we were both part of making magick, no matter how far apart we were. With no warning, I felt a powerful rush of love and sad desire for him. I tried to squelch it immediately, but it was too late. He felt it. His eyes popped open and he stared at me. Quickly I looked away, swallowing my feelings, but my eyes caught Clio's. She'd been watching Luc. She'd seen us looking at each other. Miserably I wondered if she'd felt my emotions. I hoped not. Deliberately I closed my eyes and cleared my mind again. I held Jules's and Richard's hands firmly, our feet doing a grapevine to the left endlessly, over and over.

Okay, Axelle now. Mostly I got a sense of impatient irritation.

Richard, right next to me, felt more closed off, as if he were concentrating on not sending out anything. What little I picked up felt like confusion, anger, doubt.

I opened my eyes a slit and looked at Clio again. Her eyes were closed, her face flushed and damp. She looked—beautiful. Did that mean I did too?

Relax. Concentrate. In the middle of the circle a small fire burned. Near it, at the four points of the compass, were thick gold pillar candles inside tall hurricane-glass holders two feet high. The fire was ringed with stones, and between the candles were stone bowls of water. I let myself feel each element, concentrating on water—cool, flowing, powerful, endless, timeless.

I let my voice grow stronger. Our circle was moving more swiftly now. Petra had explained that the Récolte song had once had actual words, but that they'd been lost over the centuries. It seemed so odd that this had been going on for centuries and until now, I hadn't ever heard about it. But the song had once praised the earth for growing people's food, praised the sun for keeping everything alive, and praised rain for nourishing them as well as their crops. It was all about how the earth had given to them and they had taken. Next spring, they would give back to the earth when they planted things and enriched the soil. It was about the promise of returning life in return for the life they had received.

It was a haunting, beautiful, otherworldly-sounding song,

and I felt weirdly emotional and thankful for everything I had. I'd lost so much, and after losing my father, I hadn't been able to imagine ever feeling close to whole again. But now with Clio and Petra, I had a family again. And even more than that—I had a connection to this deep magick within me. It had terrified me at first, but now . . . now that I was finally feeling close to it, close to *myself,* it was like a door had opened to another entire part of my life.

Suddenly I began to feel a strong thread twisting through the woven song. I realized the energy of the circle felt off balance, discordant. There was anger in the thread, and it was coloring our magick dark. I opened my eyes and looked at Petra, who was facing straight ahead, her chin firm as she sang. She felt it too. Glancing at Clio, I saw that she looked puzzled, concerned. I kept singing, not knowing what else to do or what was going on.

I realized I was caught up in magick—it was overwhelming, stronger than me, stronger than anything I had felt before. I looked from face to face, but everything was a blur, a dizzying swirl of light and color and sound. I saw Clio staring at Luc, then turning away. I saw Ouida nod at Petra. Richard, next to me, was watching Daedalus, frowning, and when I looked at Daedalus, I recognized the Source of the dark magick.

Daedalus was using our energy to work some other spell. I wanted to break out of the circle but didn't know how, didn't think I could. I was hot, burning up, damp with heat, and my throat was dry and sore.

I closed my eyes for a second, starting to feel sick, and when I opened them, I saw Petra nod at Ouida and Luc. Suddenly she wrenched her hand out of mine. The three of them threw their hands up, shouting words I didn't recognize, and it was like the world had been pulled out from under us. Jules and I, still holding hands, stumbled and started to fall, and then with no warning the big glass flutes shielding the candles burst.

"Oh!" I cried, feeling my cheek and shoulder sting, and then I fell hard to the ground and felt the world sway beneath me.

Other people fell around me, crying out. Daedalus's voice was choked with rage, and then all was still and quiet. I felt terrible, nauseated. My head throbbed and my forehead stung, maybe from getting hit by flying glass. My eyes filled with tears.

"Thais." Painfully I turned my head to see that Clio had crawled over to me. Her face was unnaturally white, with greenish edges. Her shoulders were scratched and bleeding. "Are you okay?" she asked, and then she simply collapsed on the ground next to me. I reached out and felt her hand, her fingers closing around mine.

"I'm gonna barf," I croaked, starting to cry. "What happened? Did I do that?"

"No, no," she said weakly. "Nan and Ouida ended the circle unnaturally. You always have to bring a circle down slowly, the way it began, and finish it properly. If you don't, you feel like this."

"It feels horrible," I said, sounding like a baby. "Why did they do it?"

"I think Daedalus was doing something," she said.

I put my hand to my cheek. Blood trickled down the side of my face to the ground. My arms were cut in several places.

"I think he was working dark magick, using the circle," Clio went on, her voice breaking. "Nan and Ouida broke it to stop him."

My face crumpled and tears slid down my cheeks. "Was he trying to hurt us, you and me?"

She held my hand more tightly. "I don't know. But it's okay," she said. "We're fine. I'm here, and Nan is here."

"Girls?" Petra leaned over us, her face ashen. "Are you all right?"

"No," I said, starting to cry more. I remembered how excited I'd been to start the circle, how thrilling it had been, feeling the magick rise. Now I felt naive and stupid, duped. "I never want to do this again."

"I'm sorry, darling," said Petra, sitting by us. She reached out and put a hand on each of us. "I'm so sorry. It really isn't usually like this. Ouida, Luc, and I had to try to stop Daedalus."

"But you didn't, you know," said Daedalus, sounding wheezy but triumphant. Like I'd felt him before. "It succeeded."

"What were you *doing*?" Jules sounded furious.

With difficulty, I propped myself up enough to see that the others were in various stages of recovery. Manon was crying also, and Sophie was holding her, kissing her face. Axelle was leaning over into some bushes, being sick. Luc and Richard got up, and they both looked as furious as Jules sounded. Luc was pale and clammy, his deep green *bouvre* dark with sweat. Like the rest of us, Luc was cut all over from when the glass burst. Thin ribbons of blood trailed down his face and arms.

"A forceful summoning." Daedalus sounded so pleased with himself that I wanted to kick him. "For Marcel and Claire. There's no way they can resist coming now. I'll have my Treize."

"You fricking jerk!" Clio choked out, sitting up. "How dare you—"

He turned to her, his eyes like ice. "I dare much, little girl," he said. "And you'll thank me before this is through."

"Get up." Luc glared down at Daedalus.

"Oh, Luc, really," Daedalus said. He got to his feet a little shakily, and as soon as he was up, Luc swung back and punched him so hard it knocked Daedalus off his feet.

Daedalus lay still on his back, his mouth gasping like a fish.

"Get up," Luc said again, and spit blood onto the ground.

Ouida came over, moving stiffly. "Please, Luc, don't," she said, putting a hand on his arm. He ignored her for a moment, then turned to her. His chest was heaving, and his eyes gleamed with anger. "I'm asking you," she said more softly. "Please."

After several long moments, Luc swallowed and stepped back but glared down at Daedalus.

Richard came over, his upper lip cut, his robe sliced in several blood-rimmed places. He looked down at Daedalus.

"Try it again, old man," he said, his voice still and deadly. "Try using me again like that against my will, and I'll find a way to kill you. I promise."

Daedalus looked shocked. "Riche—" he began, but Richard had already turned and walked away, heading to the food tables.

I lay back down, feeling better as soon as I was touching the earth from head to foot. I looked up at Petra.

"Can we get out of here?"

"Yes," she said firmly. "As soon as you two can walk."

⚜ Chapter Thirty-Two

Hurricane Force

WHAT WAS THIS GUY'S NAME? PAK? PAKPAO? Whatever. Claire lifted her hair off her neck and fell over sideways on the bed.

The guy said something to her, but the only word Claire caught was *beautiful*.

She smiled and patted his arm sleepily. "Yeah, yeah."

In the next instant, the finely carved wooden screens on her windows blew inward with hurricane force. Empty bottles fell and smashed on the ground. The single lightbulb overhead burst, showering Claire with hot, fine pieces of glass.

The magick hit Claire in the chest like a fist, and she bolted upright, gasping.

Daedalus! That bastard! Claire sprang out of bed, swearing furiously. Pak was frightened, chattering in Thai, something about a storm. She ignored him, stomping around her room. Her feet were cut by the broken glass, but she ignored that too. Damn Daedalus! Picking up a heavy brass incense holder, Claire hurled it against the wall. It knocked a chip out of the plaster and fell to the floor with a crunching sound. She would kill him—somehow she would find a way. She would absolutely cut out his beating heart. Had anyone ever tried that?

Finally Claire sank back down on the bed. Pak put his hand on her shoulder, concerned. She shrugged him off, told him to leave now. At least she'd learned that much Thai. Very useful. While the guy, completely bewildered, got dressed, Claire hung her head, so angry she could hardly breathe. A liquor bottle had broken near her foot, and the sticky puddle touched her bare foot. The alcohol burned her cuts, but none of it mattered.

Pak tried to talk to her once again, but she waved him away. She wouldn't cry—Claire never cried, but she almost wished she could right now. In a few moments she had to get up, throw some things together, and grab a taxi to the airport. She was going to New Orleans. And once she was there, she was going to make sure that Daedalus understood he was never, ever to mess with her again.

Chapter Thirty-Three

A Spell of Forceful Summoning

MARCEL WAS DREAMING. IN HIS DREAM, HE WAS tending a garden by a river, back in Louisiana. There was water everywhere in Louisiana, rivers everywhere, like the canals in Amsterdam. When he was young, people had used the rivers much more than the rutted, muddy roads.

There were two kinds of rivers. One kind was opaque and green, with warm, slow-moving water. The other kind was clear and red-tinged, with cold water that moved fast. They were both good to swim in, drink from, catch fish in. Here in Ireland, despite the very different climate, Marcel had lots of seafood, like back home. Crabs and shrimp, all different kinds of fish. He loved that about Ireland, the greenness, the water. Like home.

In his dream, Marcel was tending a garden. Looking up, he saw a lone pirogue moving slowly down the river. It must have broken loose from somewhere. Marcel made his way down the slippery clay bank, avoiding the knobby cypress knees poking up through the water. He grabbed a long branch and hooked it on one end of the little flat-bottomed boat. He would pull it to shore and tie it up, find out whose it was.

The pirogue bumped against roots, its bottom scraping the shore. Marcel leaned down to grab its trailing rope, then stopped, frozen. Inside the boat was a body. His breath caught in his throat as he pulled the boat closer. It was a girl, not yet twenty. She lay peacefully on the boat's floor, eyes closed, arms crossed over her chest. She looked like she was sleeping except for the unnatural pallor of her skin, her blue-tinged lips and fingertips.

Now he saw that she was wet, her dress sodden and clinging to her, her black hair streaming back. Cerise's birthmark burned on her cheekbone, bright red.

Cerise? No—of course not. Cerise had been blonde. But this girl looked just like Cerise, if Cerise had had black hair. And this girl had drowned. Cerise had died in childbirth.

Who was she? Marcel reached out one shaking hand—and then the small, high window of his monk's cell burst inward, the shards of glass streaking across his face and hands, leaving fine red lines.

Marcel shot up, cold sweat breaking out instantly. His room was pitch dark; his window was shattered. Icy air rolled in through the small opening, pooling and settling all around him. His heart was pounding, and then it hit him—the knowledge of what this was, what Daedalus had done.

"Oh, God." Marcel moaned and pressed his hands against his face, feeling the warm stickiness of his blood. Bits of glass stung him, but it didn't matter. Daedalus had thrown a thick velvet rope around his neck, all the way from America. Now he was going to pull it in, and there was nothing Marcel could do about it. Everything in him was urging him to America. He felt like if he didn't get there as soon as possible, his skin would erupt and spiders would swarm all over his body. He had to get there fast, fast, fast.

That was what a spell of forceful summoning felt like. It made you panic, made every second's delay feel like torture. He would feel like he had the plague until he set foot in Louisiana again.

Marcel hung his head, biting back bitter tears. He wasn't strong enough to resist this spell. If he was truly worthy, he would be able to reject it, to pray his way out of it, work harder against it.

But he wasn't worthy. He'd always known that.

Stifling a sob in his throat, Marcel began to review what needed to be done. Not much. Just getting up, telling Father Jonah that he must leave, and making his way to the Shannon airport. Oh, God. He would see them all again. Daedalus, who had done this to him. Petra, whom he loved but also feared. Richard, his mortal enemy, who had killed Cerise. Manon, with whom he shared a terrible secret. And so on. All of them.

He didn't need to know why Daedalus had summoned him to New Orleans. He already knew what awaited him there: pain and destruction. And the absolute end of any hope he had of his salvation.

BALEFIRE

Cate Tiernan

BOOK THREE:
A FEATHER OF STONE

BALEFIRE

BOOK THREE:
A FEATHER OF STONE

✤ Chapter One

Clio

I HEARD A FAINT SOUND BEHIND ME AND FROZE, my hands inside my canvas bag. I waited, sending my senses out more strongly, but felt nothing out of the ordinary: only sleeping birds, neighborhood dogs and cats, mice. Insects.

Ick.

I let out a deep breath. It was a new moon, which meant this cemetery was even blacker than usual. I was tucked into a remote corner, kneeling on the grass between two tall crypts. I was invisible from all directions, unless someone was right in front of me.

It was almost midnight. I had school tomorrow and knew I would feel like crap in the morning. Too bad. This was my chance, and I wasn't going to waste it.

Quickly and silently I drew a five-foot circle on the ground with sand. Inside the circle, I set four red candles at the four compass points. Red for blood, lineage, passion, fire. I myself was in the very center, with a small stone bowl filled with chunks of coal in front of me. I lit the candles and the coal, blowing on the coal until it was glowing red.

Then I sat back, gently rested my hands palms-up on my knees and tried to calm my nerves. If Nan woke up and found me gone, I would be dead meat. Or if anyone else found out what I was doing, again, there would be much brouhaha.

But two nights ago, at a circle for Récolte, I'd been blown to the ground by a huge surge of power. My own power had been taken and used by someone else. I was still pissed at Daedalus for doing it. Yet here I was, trying to find out how he did it.

I'd practiced magick, the *métier*, pretty much my whole life. I hadn't had my rite of ascension yet, but I'd had great teachers and knew I was pretty powerful for my age. I'd seen any number of grown-ups work magick for years. But I'd never seen anything like what had happened at Récolte.

Where had Daedalus's power come from? Was it from being immortal? Tonight I was going to try to go to the Source—my memory. For some reason my sister Thais and I could tap into memories of our ancestors, the line of witches twelve generations long that led back to the rite, the first rite, the one where the Treize became immortal and Cerise Martin had died.

I'd *seen* what had happened that night. At the time I'd been too freaked to see the big picture. But now I knew what it was, what had happened. I would find out *how*.

I stilled my whirling thoughts and focused on the burning coal. Fire was my element, and I concentrated on the glowing red heat, feeling it warming the heavy air. On the ground I drew different runes: *ôte*, for birthright and inheritance, *rad*, for my journey, *lage*, for knowledge and psychic power. I slowed my breathing. The barriers between myself and the rest of the world slowly dissolved, our edges blurred. I took on an awareness of everything around me: the inhalation of a blade of grass, the microscopic release of old, weathered marble on a tomb. In my mind I chanted a spell, one that I'd spent the last two days crafting. It was in English, and I'd totally given up on trying to make it rhyme.

Chains of time, pull me back
Let me sink into memory
Follow the red thread of my blood
Back through the ages
Woman after woman, mother after mother
Giving birth, succumbing to death
Back to the first one, Cerise Martin
And the night of Melita's power.
Show me what I need to know.

I had never done anything like this before, never worked a spell this big. Also, I was deliberately invoking a memory of someone I knew to be evil—Melita Martin, my ancestor. In my earlier visions of that night, I'd been both terrified and horrified at what I'd seen. Now I was going there voluntarily. No one with any sense would think that was okay. But part of being a witch was an ever-present thirst for knowledge, a desperate need to have questions answered, an overwhelming desire to understand as much as possible.

Of course, part of being a witch was accepting the fact that there were many, many questions that could never be answered, and many things that would never be known.

I began singing my song, my unique call for power. I sang it very, very softly—this cemetery was in the middle of an uptown neighborhood, not far from my house, and was bordered by four narrow residential streets. Anyone walking by might hear. A thin shell of awareness was distracting me—I still felt the damp grass I sat on, heard the faint drone of distant grasshoppers.

Maybe this wouldn't work. Maybe I wasn't strong enough. Maybe I had crafted the spell wrong. *Maybe I should ask Melita for help.*

That last thought startled me, and I blinked.

It was sunny, and I was standing in the middle of a small garden patch. I held my long apron up with one hand, and with the other I picked tomatoes, letting them slide into the pouchy sling my apron made. I saw that fat green tomato worms were eating some of the vines. So my anti-tomato-worm spell hadn't worked. *Maybe I should ask Melita for help.*

But now I had enough tomatoes for Maman's gumbo. I hitched up my apron so they wouldn't spill and headed back to the kitchen. My bare feet felt the warm earth, the slightly cooler grass, the rough packed oyster shells of the path to the barn.

My back hurt. My big belly stuck out so I could hardly see my feet. Two more months and the baby would be born. Maman said my back wouldn't hurt anymore then.

I'd heard the English looked down hard on a girl unwed but with child. Our village was more accepting. Maman did want me to choose Marcel, make my own family with him. But I wanted to stay here in this house with Maman and my sister. Papa had left long ago, and since then we were only women here. I liked it that way.

I climbed up the wooden steps to the back room. We cooked outside—everyone did—but we kept our kitchen things in the workroom. Maman and my sister were inside.

"Here." I lifted the tomatoes onto the table, then sat down in a wooden chair, feeling the relief of not carrying the extra weight.

"The bébé grows big, no?" my sister said, going to the pail of drinking water on the bench. She dipped some up for me, filling a cup, and brought it over. "Poor Cerise."

"Thanks." The water was warm but good.

Melita knelt in front of me and put her hands on the hard mound of my stomach. She soothed the tight muscles, and her movements calmed the baby, who was active and kicking. One big kick made me gasp, and Melita laughed and tapped the plain outline of a tiny foot.

"You're full of life," she murmured and smiled up at me, her eyes as black as mine were green, her hair dark like Papa's.

I smiled at her, then caught a glimpse of Maman's face

as she snapped green beans. She was worried, watching us. Worried about me and the baby, about Melita and her magick. People said Melita worked dark magick, that she risked her soul pursuing evil. I didn't believe them and didn't want to think about it. She was my sister.

"Are you ready for the special circle tonight?" Melita asked, starting to chop tomatoes.

I made a face. "I'm tired—maybe I'll stay home and sleep."

"Oh, no, chère," she said, looking distressed. "I need you there. It's a special circle, one that will guarantee a time of plenty for the whole village. You must come. You're my good luck charm."

"Who else is going?" I bent down with difficulty and picked up some sewing from the basket. I'd begun making baby dresses, baby hats, baby socks. I carried a girl; I could feel her. Now I was working on a small blanket for the cradle.

"Well, Maman," said Melita.

I glanced at Maman to see her frowning. She too was unsure about this circle of Melita's.

"Ouida," Melita said cajolingly. "You like her. And cousin Sophie. Cousin Luc-André. Manon, the smith's daughter."

"That little girl?" Maman asked.

"She wants to take part in circles more," Melita answered. "Um . . ."

The way she hesitated made me look up. "Who else?"

"Marcel," she admitted.

I nodded and went back to sewing. Marcel was a dear. He

was so anxious about the baby. Had asked me to marry him a thousand times. I cared about him, truly, and knew he would make a good husband. I just didn't want a husband. He'd been so sure that I'd marry him when I knew I was going to have the baby. But why would I bother marrying when I had Maman and Melita to help me?

"Several others," Melita said, sweeping the chopped tomatoes into a bowl. "It will be perfect. I've been crafting this spell for a long time. I assure you it will bring long and healthy lives to everyone who participates."

"How can you know that?" Maman asked.

Melita laughed. "I've crafted it to be so. Trust me."

• • •

At sundown Maman and I walked from our little house to the place Melita had told us about, deep in the woods, not far from the river. I had rested and felt fine and healthy. I couldn't wait for two months to be past so I could meet my baby girl. Would she have light eyes or dark? Fair skin or warm tan? I looked forward to her fatness, her perfect baby skin. Maman had delivered many babies, and I knew it would be hard but not horrible. And Melita would help.

"Through here," Maman murmured, holding back some trailing honeysuckle. Their strong sweetness perfumed the air, filling my lungs with scent. It was hot and our clothes were humid, but everything felt fine.

We reached a small clearing in front of what Melita had described as the biggest oak tree in Louisiane.

"Holy Mother," Maman breathed, looking at the tree.

I laughed when I saw it—it reached the sky, taller than any tree I'd ever seen. It was so big around that five people holding hands could still not encircle it. It was awe-inspiring, such a monument to how the Mother nourished life. I touched the bark with my palm, almost able to feel the life pulsing under its skin.

"How could I have not known this was here?" Maman said, still gazing at it.

"Petra," said a voice in greeting. "Cerise."

It was remarkable, how I felt chills down my back when I heard his voice or knew that he was near.

Maman turned to him with a smile. "Richard, cher. How are you? Melita didn't tell us you were coming."

I turned slowly, in time to see him take off his hat and brush it against one leg. "Melita is very persuasive," he said, not looking at me.

"Petra." Ouida called her from across the clearing, and smiling, Maman went to hug her.

I looked into Richard's dark eyes. "Did Melita tell you what this was about?"

"No. You?"

I shook my head and looked for a place to sit. Finally I just sat on the grass, smoothing out my skirts and arching my back to stretch my stomach muscles. "She said it was about ensuring a time of plenty for the village," I said. "Long lives for everyone. I didn't want to come, but she said I was her good-luck charm."

Richard sat next to me. His knee accidentally brushed mine, and a ripple of pleasure shot up my spine. My mind filled with other memories of pleasure with Richard, and I wriggled a bit and smiled at him. He got that very still, intent expression that always meant I was about to feel good.

Then he turned away, his jaw set, and I sighed. He was continuing to be upset about Marcel. Just like Marcel was very upset about him. Sometimes the two of them made me tired— why should it matter if I wanted both of them? Why should I have to choose? I wouldn't care if they also wanted to spark some other girl in the village.

I fanned myself with my straw hat and saw that others were arriving. M. Daedalus, the head of our village, was there, and his friend Jules, who'd lived here for ten years now. M. Daedalus had just gotten back from visiting his brother in New Orleans, I remembered hearing. I wondered if he had brought back any fabric for the Chevets' shop. I'd go look tomorrow.

Melita's best friend, Axelle, arrived, slim like a snake even in her full skirts and sun hat. I smiled and waved at her, and she waved back.

"Greetings," said a voice, and I turned to see Claire Londine stepping through the honeysuckle. She saw me and came to sit down.

"You're as big as a house," she said, shaking her head. "How do you feel?"

"Fine, mostly," I said.

"I don't see why you would—" she began, then looked at Richard and stopped.

"I'm going to talk to Daedalus," Richard said abruptly, and left.

Claire laughed. "He sensed woman talk coming on. I wanted to say, why did you let this happen? It's so easy to prevent it. Or to stop it, if it comes to that."

I shrugged. "I decided I'd like to have a baby. I'm going to call her Hélène "

"But babies are so much work," Claire said. "They scream all the time. They never go away."

"Maman and Melita will help me. And I like babies."

"Well, I hope you do," Claire said, stretching her legs out in the sun. Her bare feet and almost six inches of bare leg were visible below her hem, but Claire had always been scandalous. She was nice to me, though, and she'd been in my class at our tiny village school.

"Everyone," my sister called. "It's time. Let's form a circle."

I stood ungracefully, holding my belly with one hand. It was almost sunset, but at that moment the light winked out like a snuffed candle. I looked up to see huge, plum-colored clouds sweeping in from the south.

"Storm coming in," I murmured to Maman. "Maybe we should do this another time."

Melita heard me. "No," she said. "Tonight is the only time I can work this spell—everything is perfect: moon, season, people. I'm sure the storm won't bother us."

She quickly drew a large circle that almost filled the clearing, then lit thirteen candles—one for each of us. The wind picked up a bit, an oddly cool, damp wind, but though their flames whipped right and left, the candles stayed lit.

Melita drew the rune *borche* in the air, for new beginnings, birth. I frowned slightly, holding my big stomach. Was that safe? I glanced at Maman. She was watching Melita very solemnly. Maman would stop this or send me away if it wasn't safe. I tried to relax as we all joined hands.

Marcel couldn't take his eyes off me, which irritated me. His gaze was like a weight. Unlike Richard, who was across the circle, talking in a low voice with Claire. He laughed, and Claire giggled and swung his hand in hers.

We started to move *dalmonde,* and Melita began chanting. Again I glanced at Maman, and again she had her eyes locked on my sister. I didn't recognize this song—I'd never heard it before, and it didn't match any of our usual forms. Melita's voice became stronger and stronger, seeming to fill my chest. It was very strange—not at all like other circles.

Rain began to fall, big, cool drops soaking my shoulders and the top of my stomach. I vaguely wanted to stop, wanted to let go, but as soon as I thought it, the idea was out of my mind. And Melita's song filled me again.

My hat flew off as we went faster. I felt awkward, unbalanced, and feared falling, but Jules's hand and Ouida's held me up. Then my throat seemed to close. Huge, heavy, powerful magick welled out of the ground as if it would swallow me up. Of course I'd felt magick before. But this was unlike anything I'd ever even dreamed of. This was overwhelming, an enormous wave made of earth and air and water and fire all at once. I was choking, truly afraid now, and still we circled the hissing candles, Melita's voice filling the air as if it came from somewhere else.

Rain poured down. People's faces blurred, smeared images flashing by. Every face except Melita's was afraid—some were angry, also. Thunder rolled through us, so deep that it rocked the earth. The sky was white with lightning, again and again turning us into sharp-edged indigo outlines. I was drowning in magick, caught in magick like a spiderweb, like pitch. I shook my hands to release them, but couldn't.

"Meli—" I cried, but at that moment the world seemed to end. A cannon boom of thunder and an unearthly blast of lightning struck at the same moment. The lightning hit Melita directly, and I screamed, seeing her dark hair flying out around her ecstatic face. The next second, the lightning imploded in me, shooting through Jules's hand, searing mine, and racing into Ouida's hand. We all cried out, and I heard my own screaming.

An agonizing, gripping pain seized my belly. Our hands flew apart, and I fell to the ground. My stomach felt as though someone had buried an ax in it, and I curled up, gasping.

"Maman!" I cried, sobbing. I held my stomach as though to keep my insides from spilling out, but the pain was too big for my hands, too horrendous to bear.

Then others were around me—Richard, Ouida, and finally Maman, who knelt quickly on the rain-soaked muddy ground. She smoothed my hair off my forehead, her lips already chanting spells. Her hand gripped mine tightly, and I clung to it.

"What's happening?" I cried. Maman's strong face filled my eyes, but she muttered spells and didn't answer.

Another searing wave of pain crested, and I closed my eyes and sobbed, trying to ride it out. I felt a gushing flood beneath my skirt, and then Maman's hands were pushing it out of the way and rain hit my bare legs. Richard grabbed my other hand. I pressed it against my cheek, ashamed to be crying and looking weak, but too panicked and in pain to stop. Maman and I had already rehearsed the calming and concentrating spells I would perform for the baby's birth, but every one of them had fled my mind. All I knew was a dark tide of pain crashing over me, submerging me in its depths.

My stomach was heaving, contracting, and after an eternity, I slowly realized that the pain was less. I felt far away, tired, hardly aware of what was happening.

"Oh, goddess, the blood," I dimly heard Ouida say.

I knew Richard was still holding my hand, but the pressure was faint. I was so glad that the pain had lessened, so glad that I was removed from the horror and fear and agony. I needed to rest. My eyes closed. Rain splashed my eyelids. The storm still rumbled overhead, but the ground beneath me felt safe and nurturing. I relaxed, feeling all the tension leaving my body. Thank the goddess the pain was gone. I felt perfectly well.

Then I was looking down on myself, on Maman and Richard and the others, looking down from a high distance. I saw the rain drenching everyone. Maman held up a tiny, writhing baby, its blood being washed away by the rain. I saw myself, looking peaceful and calm, as if asleep. *My baby, Hélène,* I thought.

I came out of it when I fell backward and hit my head on a rock.

Blinking, I looked up and saw dark, moonless sky and the tops of family crypts.

My head hurt, and I put up a hand to rub it, feeling a knot forming on the back of my skull. I sat up. A chunk of a name plate had fallen off a crypt, who knew how long ago, and I'd whacked my head against it. I didn't know why I had fallen—if I was dead, why did my head hurt? And my hands?

It took another minute for it to sink in that I wasn't dead, I wasn't Cerise. I was me, Clio, in the here and now. My four candles were guttered and almost out. The small bowl of coal was nothing but gray ashes. I looked around quickly, placing myself, then crawled over to my canvas bag and pulled out my watch. It was four a.m. I felt shaken and breathless. This time, instead of just seeing the rite happen, I'd been part of it. I'd heard the spell Melita had used, seen the glowing sigils and runes on the ground, the ones we hadn't seen her write because she'd put them there before the circle gathered.

I'd felt myself die.

I swallowed, sucking in a shallow, trembling breath, then

started to gather my things. I dumped the ashes onto the ground and rubbed them with my toe to make sure they were out. I snuffed the candles and cleaned up the wax that had dripped off.

"Petra would be very displeased if she knew about this."

The dry, slow voice made me jump about a foot in the air. I hadn't sensed anyone around me—still didn't, in fact. Looking around wildly, I finally saw a black shadow sitting on the stoop of a crypt, next to a cement vase holding faded plastic flowers. Daedalus stood and came over to me.

My heart was beating fast—I was afraid. I put my shoulders back, shook my hair out of my face, and began putting my supplies into my bag.

"You don't care what Petra thinks? She raised you." He knelt a few feet away from me, his black clothes blending into the night.

"Why don't you let me worry about that?" I said. I forced my breathing to slow, kept my face blank.

"Why are you stirring up the past?"

I looked at him. "You saw what I was doing?"

"A bit. Not a lot. It was an ambitious spell. Why were you working it?"

"Why should I tell you?" I stood up, my knees shaky, and shoved my feet into my slides. I began to head for the cemetery gate.

"I could help you."

I paused for just a second, then kept walking. Daedalus walked beside me.

"I could help you," he repeated. "I know more about Melita's spell than anyone. You obviously have a connection to her through your bloodline. We could combine our strengths. It could be . . . very interesting. Very rewarding."

I reached the rusty wrought-iron gate that led out of the cemetery and opened it. It squeaked loudly.

"I don't think so," I said. "Nan doesn't trust you, and neither do I." I turned and walked away from him, hoping he wouldn't follow me home, maybe wake Petra up to fink on me.

"Think about it." His quiet words floated through the night, but when I turned, he was gone.

✦ Chapter Two

Thais

"CHIP?" SYLVIE HELD OUT A BAG OF FRITOS AND shook it. Our school's cafeteria was always crowded and noisy, so my friend Sylvie, her boyfriend, Claude, Kevin LaTour, and I were sitting outside.

I took some. "Thanks. Trade you for my pickle?"

"Great." Sylvie leaned against Claude and bit the pickle. "At least it's Wednesday," she said. "Middle of the week. After this, it's all downhill toward the weekend."

I laughed. "I hope next weekend is better than last weekend," I said without thinking.

Next to me, Kevin groaned and covered his face. We'd had a date last Saturday, and we'd gotten hit by lightning. But that wasn't even what I was talking about.

"I promise," he said, putting his hand over his heart. "Our next date will be disaster-free."

I slapped his knee lightly. "It wasn't your fault."

Actually, I'd been referring to the nightmare of a Récolte circle I'd gone to on Sunday—but for a second I'd forgotten that I couldn't talk about it with my friends. They knew, in a vague way, that witches existed, but they didn't know that my family and I actually practiced the Craft.

I still found it hard to believe myself.

Kevin put his arm around me, and I smiled at him. He was a sweetheart—the more I knew him, the more things I liked about him. Plus, of course, the high adorableness quotient.

"Can you maybe grab some coffee with me after school today?"

My face lit up and then instantly fell. "'Fraid not. First I'm going to get my Louisiana driver's license, then I have to go home and wash, scrape, air out."

Kevin made a sympathetic face. Pretty much every day for the last week and a half, my sister Clio and I had spent most waking moments helping to repair, clean, and desmoke our little house. We'd set it on fire during a spell, and the whole back had been damaged.

"But this weekend?" I suggested. "I'm pretty sure if I whine enough I could possibly get out for one night."

Kevin grinned and kissed my hair. "Just tell me when."

I smiled and nodded, amazed at how normal I was being. Inside, I was still trapped on an emotional Tilt-a-Whirl. It was hard to know which end was up nowadays, with everything that was going on. The best thing about Sylvie, Claude, and Kevin was how unconnected they were to my other life, the life of my new family. With them I could be just Thais Allard, unassuming high school senior, northern transplant. At home I loved being a sister and a sort of granddaughter, but home was also where magick was made, where my troubling and surreal history seemed unavoidable. At home we talked about what had happened at Récolte, or the autumn solstice. We talked about the fact that some people we knew and were related to were immortal. Literally. And we worried about the rite that Daedalus was planning, the one that might kill me or Clio, or make us immortal too.

"I'm sorry, what?" I said, realizing that my friends were looking at me expectantly.

"Did you study for calc?" Sylvie asked again.

I let out a breath. Lovely normalcy. "Yep," I said. "But I still don't get most of it."

✦ Chapter Three

Clio

"FEEL THE LIFE IN EVERY HANDFUL OF DIRT."
My teacher, Melysa, paused to admire the black earth trickling
through her fingers.

I looked at her sourly. Gardening was one of my least
favorite things to do, and in our climate you can grow *something*
all year round. Plus, the firefighters had completely trampled
Nan's gorgeous front beds to get to the back of the house. So
here I was, gardening my little heart out in penance.

And as part of my lesson.

"Yeah, full of life," I muttered, wiping the sweat off my
brow. "Gotcha." I leaned over and pulled up a dead plant by
the roots. I threw it on the pile of compost and raked the
dirt smooth. On the sidewalk sat a tray of eight tiny cabbage
plants, waiting to be transplanted. *Great. Gardening* and *looking forward to eating cabbage this winter. Oh, joy.*

I stood up, stretching and groaning. "I feel like my back is
about to break." Not to mention my hands, which were red, as
if sunburned, and still stung from last night.

Melysa shot me an amused glance. "Number one, you've only been at it for fifteen minutes. Give me a break. Number two, you're seventeen years old. You don't get to complain about aches and pains until you're fifty. Now, do you remember green cabbage's true name?"

I looked at it. Not napa cabbage, nor red cabbage, but this particular kind of green cabbage. "Seste," I said.

"Very good." Melysa crouched on the ground and dug a small hole with a trowel. Expertly she flipped a cabbage plant out of its plastic cell and popped it in the ground, patting the dirt around it firmly. "Have you been working on a spell for your rite of ascension?"

I blinked at the change in subject. "Uh-huh." *If you only knew,* I thought uncomfortably. She couldn't know, I reassured myself. No one but Daedalus knew about the spell I had done last night in the cemetery. The one he had offered to help me with.

I raked and pulled, lost in thought. For my rite of ascension, I needed to craft a major spell, one utilizing several levels of power, several forms of spell crafting, several witch's tools. Last night I had done just that, and it had worked. It had been the first major magick I had done alone. It had been awful and scary. But I had learned more about what had happened with the Treize. And with Richard, I remembered, feeling my cheeks flush more. As Cerise, I had memories of him as a lover. It felt weird and uncomfortable, as if I had spied on him. Which I guess I had, in a way.

A totally bizarre, unbelievable, *X-files* kind of way.

But whatever. What was important was that I'd gotten a bird's-eye view of Melita's spell. I'd seen the sigils and runes that had glowed on the ground around the circle. Cerise hadn't been aware of them that night—I wondered if anyone had noticed them, with everything else going on. Cerise dying. But in my vision I had seen them. I had a more complete picture of what Melita had done, and I thought I understood how and why it had worked. But I needed to do more research. Especially with Daedalus still plowing forward with his plans to re-create the rite.

I'd been thinking a lot about it, about immortality. The idea had planted its roots in my mind and was taking firmer hold. Immortality. Going on and on. What would things be like two hundred years from now? What would it be like to never fear death? I didn't know exactly how it worked— like, could one of the Treize jump off a cliff and just get up afterward, like Wile E. Coyote? What would it be like to be frozen in time as I was now—young and strong and beautiful? I would never age, never get gray hair and wrinkles and have things droop on me. I would be able to learn magick my whole life. What would my powers be like a hundred years from now, with a hundred years of studying under my belt? Would I just keep getting stronger?

It was starting to sound pretty damn good.

Clearly I didn't want to die in the rite, which Daedalus was calling every member of the Treize to New Orleans for.

But—would Thais agree with me? Could I bear to become immortal while she went on to age and die? True, I'd had a sister for only a few months, but she was my mirror image. It would be like watching myself age and die. Now that we knew each other, we were joined. We were connected. It deepened with every day that passed. Could I bear for that connection to be broken someday?

Next to me, Melysa planted the other baby cabbages. I finished preparing my bed and knelt down to sprinkle weensy radish seeds in short rows. It was almost October, but we had plenty of time for another radish crop. And cabbages grew well in chillier temperatures—like if it got down in the fifties. I sighed and brushed my hair off my neck.

"Feel free to share," Melysa said.

I looked up. "Oh. Well—I've just been thinking about different things," I said. "Listen—do you understand the form of the Treize's original spell?"

Melysa looked surprised. She was the only non-Treize member who knew about Nan and her *famille*, knew their freakish history.

"Well, a bit," she said. "I don't know if anyone truly understands all its nuances or powers. Not even the people—who were there."

Daedalus says he does, I thought. He says he knows enough to re-create it.

And he wants to teach me.

I pushed that thought out of my mind.

"But what would the basic form be?" I persisted.

Melysa frowned slightly as she cut several small squashes off the vine growing on our fence. "Why do you want to know?"

"I'm just curious. It seems so amazing, so out of the realm of what we usually do."

Her eyes were serious when they met mine.

"It is," she said. "For good reason. That kind of magick isn't positive, doesn't add a positive presence to the world. It's harmful, it creates an unnatural situation, it affects other people without their will or knowledge. It's forbidden."

"Forbidden? Do people even know enough about it to outlaw it? Wasn't that spell with the Treize the only instance of it?"

Melysa, who I could usually ask almost anything, took on an uncharacteristically shuttered expression. She didn't answer, and a flash of excitement rushed through me. Did that mean there had ever been other spells like Melita's? Was there a whole school of magick that I—and most witches—knew nothing about? It would be incredibly interest—

Oh. Yes. Now I got it. Yes, there was a whole school of magick that probably dealt with spells similar to Melita's. It was called dark magick, and we did not practice it. It had never occurred to me that among all the awful, evil, totally wrong spells of dark magick, there would be some that could work a spell like Melita's. The kind of spell that would grant immortality to the witches present.

And that could kill a witch too, I remembered, trying not to shudder at the memory of feeling Cerise die.

I heard the familiar cheerful chugging of my little Camry and looked up. Thais found a parking space in the street right in front of our house—we didn't have a driveway or garage. She got out and walked through our gate, careful not to step on any plants.

"You get it?" I asked.

She smiled, looking exactly like me except for the clothes, and waved her new Louisiana driver's license.

"I'm legal now. To drive, anyway. You guys have gotten a lot done." She surveyed the front yard, which was being transformed from a trampled, sooty, demilitarized zone into a mere inkling of the glory of Nan's old garden. "Let me change and I'll come help for a while before dinner."

"Great, thanks," said Melysa, smiling at her.

Having an identical twin sister was starting to feel a teensy bit more normal, but waves of "This is unbelievable" still flitted through my head. I'd spent seventeen years as an only child— having my entire world turned inside out in the last couple of months had made me feel like I was tripping sometimes.

"What's that?" Thais asked, pointing to the baby cabbages. "Not more okra?"

I laughed. Thais was still getting her Southerner's taste buds jumpstarted.

"Cabbage!" I said brightly, and she made a face.

Melysa stood and brushed off her hands. "It's time I was

going. Now that you've got a helper. Tell Petra I'll talk to her later, all right?"

"Okay. Thanks—see you soon." I stood up and followed Thais inside. It was time I found out exactly what she thought about immortality.

❧ Chapter Four

Black Like My Soul

THIS HAD ALL CHANGED SO MUCH. EXCEPT the heat, the mosquitoes, the smell of the water. Those were the same. But the way the land looked, the contours of the canals and the rice fields and the rivers themselves—all that was different. The small trolling motor on this old wooden pirogue made an annoying buzzing sound, like a big, sleepy insect. Richard sat in the stern, one hand on the tiller, maneuvering his way through water paths that had changed ten times since he'd seen them. How long ago had he been here, to this very place? Maybe forty years? Thirty? Decades blended together.

The sun was hot on his skin, warming his blood. Richard brushed his damp bangs off his forehead and lit a cigarette. He remembered Clio snootily telling him not to smoke in Petra's house. He guessed Petra hadn't told Clio she herself had smoked for, like, eighty years. Clio. He snorted smoke out his nose, feeling the heat, the chemical aftertaste.

Up there. A quarter mile ahead, the flat, treeless rice fields gave way to a flat swamp. This canal was about to become choked with weeds, so Richard shut off the motor and pulled it in. He got out a long, broad paddle, its paint worn away, and began pushing through the weeds. Water hyacinths. Really pretty, shiny green leaves, pretty purple flowers. Clogging canals, ditches, and rivers throughout the Gulf states.

But pretty.

Like Clio.

She too was pretty and useless—in fact, destructive. Look what she had done to Petra's house. At least he was pretty sure it had been her, her and Thais's spell going wrong. Unless . . . Frowning, Richard flicked his cigarette into the water. There was a quick hiss, and then Richard remembered that littering was really verboten nowadays. Damn.

He took off his shirt and began to push the pirogue through the thick weeds. He saw a nutria, as big as a housecat, race across the canal where the hyacinths were so thick they could practically support its weight.

Twenty minutes later he was clear of the canal and started the motor again. There was an almost hidden entrance along here, leading to a narrow, snaking river barely twelve feet wide. Here it was. He angled the boat in and cut the motor again. Too many cypress knees and trailing underwater weeds. Easy to chew up your propeller. Most of the trees were new growth, but something about the general contours triggered his memory. This was the place.

Mosquitoes buzzed around him, but he'd done a little spell

that kept them off. He took out another cigarette and was about to light it when he remembered Clio's face, her wrinkled nose. Swearing with disgust, he tossed the pack onto the flat bottom of the boat. God, what was the matter with him? She was stuck-up, snide, selfish—and still hung up on Luc, which only showed how stupid she was.

And yet.

When Richard was around her, his heart started beating again, and he suddenly felt more alive than he had in a hundred years. He remembered her long, bare, tan legs, stretched across the kitchen floor as she cleaned inside a cabinet. He remembered her in scarlet linen, the fabric floating across her stomach, her hips, at the Récolte circle. Something about her made him want to crush her to him, to bend her head over his arm. . . . But it would never happen again. She was out of his system now—those searing kisses at Récolte had cured him of her. He would never touch her again.

Looking up quickly, Richard took his bearings. Had he passed it? He'd been so distracted, thinking about Clio. Swearing again under his breath, he peered ahead, trying to see around the next bend. No. This wasn't it. He'd gotten lost. Now he was totally pissed at himself.

It took a seven-point turn to get the pirogue facing the other direction. Richard glanced at the sun—he had a couple more hours before the boat's owner would return and notice it was missing. Richard began to paddle, putting his back into it. He was sweating, the air so still and damp that it couldn't evaporate. He remembered he had a bottle of water and took a long drink, wishing it was beer.

Now he was at the last fork. Looking at it again, he saw he needed to take the other arm. Grimly he put his oar in the water. That was what thinking about Clio would get him. Turned around. Lost. She wanted Luc? She could have him.

Fifteen more minutes of paddling brought him to another juncture. He knew where he was now and unerringly took the left fork. Five minutes later he saw it: a thick, bent, twisted cypress hanging arched over the water like a bow. Long ago a length of chain had been wrapped around its trunk; now it was almost buried beneath the bark. Ducking down low, Richard slid the pirogue under the arch. He stepped out into the shallow water, feeling the smooth clay squishing beneath his sandals, and tied the boat to a tree.

The bank was steep but not high, and he pulled himself up it by grabbing tree roots.

He reached the top and headed inland, pushing aside vines and thick underbrush. Again he checked the position of the sun, squinting up through the thick treetops. He had enough time, barely, if he didn't get lost again.

Clio was destroying his peace of mind. Why? She was nothing to him. Another tragedy in a long line of tragedies. Richard had thought he could solve that situation, but now he knew he was powerless. Something occurred to him, and he stood still for a moment, struck. If Clio didn't get over Luc, and Luc, that bastard, took advantage of that fact, then Clio could very well end up in the same situation as the twelve generations of women before her. Including Cerise. She could get pregnant. And then she would die.

A month ago Richard hadn't known Clio or Thais. He'd distanced himself from that whole line of doomed women, knowing that he would eventually hear that the latest version of the marked line had died. He would have felt bad for a moment and then shrugged it off.

But now he knew Clio. Clio and Thais. Clio was the only woman of that line that he'd wanted, besides Cerise.

What if Luc knocked her up? She would die. A sudden image of Clio's beautiful face flashed through his mind. He saw her green eyes wide with fear, her black hair streaked with sweat, her hands covered with blood. In a split second he pictured her face still and lifeless, her eyes open, her entire body wet, soaked through, as if rained on. Dead.

The ground spun beneath him, and he dropped to his knees. He closed his eyes, swallowing hard, and leaned forward, resting one hand on the warm ground. Clio dead. He blinked several times, trying to erase the image from his mind. It had been unusually clear and real, like a premonition. Slowly he sat back on his knees, wishing fervently that he hadn't left his smokes back in the frigging boat. He swallowed again and wiped the cold sweat from his forehead. He felt shaky, chilled.

He looked around and cast his senses, making sure he was alone. He felt nothing out of place—plants and animals and insects. And a very thin, very tremulous thread of ancient magick, vibrating slightly in the air.

He got to his feet and began walking toward it.

Clio. He hadn't had a vision like that in ages. It had happened to him only a couple of times in his whole life. The first time had been the afternoon before Melita's circle. He'd been hoeing his father's field, and then suddenly he'd seen Cerise dead. She'd been drenched with rain, and Melita had stood next to her, laughing. Blood was everywhere. In that moment he'd seen that Cerise would die at the circle that night.

And yet he had gone.

Now he saw one of his landmarks, a granite boulder almost as tall as he. It would never occur naturally in Louisiana. He looked around and found the second boulder, then the third, forming a rough triangle. The rocks looked as if they'd been here for millennia, and Richard wondered how many casual hikers had seen them and not realized that they were completely out of place.

Inside the triangle Richard started with the northernmost rock and counted off paces. He aligned his arms with the other two rocks, made a half turn, and counted six more paces. Then he dropped to his knees again, pulled out his folding shovel, and started to dig. With his first hard thrust, the shovel bounced off the dirt and flew up, almost hitting him in the face.

He blinked, surprised for a moment, and then he smiled

ruefully. Under his breath he said a disarming spell. This time the metal blade sank easily into the dark, rich soil. He dumped the shovelful of dirt to one side and pushed his shovel in again, digging further, further into the past.

✤ Chapter Five

All the More Believable

I CERTAINLY AM SPENDING A LOT OF TIME IN cemeteries these days, Daedalus thought as he walked between two rows of graves. Some of them were simply above-ground cement troughs, built to hold a coffin, then backfilled with dirt up to the level of the sides. Not as durable as covered crypts, which were little houses for the dead, but of course cheaper and easier to maintain.

Cemeteries were always so peaceful. And hot. The sunlight bounced off the white marble and soaked into the cement, radiating out for hours after twilight. He didn't feel anyone else's presence here, at least no one he knew, but all the same he detoured past the weathered facade of the Martins' crypt. Petra's husband, Armand. Armand's brother and his wife.

Daedalus had been surprised when Armand had left Petra. Not that they were the picture of wedded bliss, but then who was? Losing all those children had taken a toll on them both, but that had been so common back then, even among witches. It would have been worse without all the protection spells and healing powers. Daedalus had visited New Orleans during those years, and there he'd heard of families losing ten children out of fourteen, or every one of their infants, one a year until they gave up in despair.

In his *famille*, they'd known how to prevent or delay the birth of children, and their child mortality rate had been one-tenth of their region. Still, losing any child feels like too much, Daedalus knew.

He retraced his steps, walking across the cemetery to the side closest to the river. Here was a small wrought-iron bench, somewhat rusted, but still sturdy. He sat on it, his hands moving in an automatic gesture to flip his coattails out of way. He shook his head at his own foolishness. He was wearing a plain white shirt and gray-and-white seersucker pants. A jacket hadn't been required wear for decades. Old habits died hard.

He sat back, resting his cane against the side of the bench. There had been a time when most people carried canes as a fashion accessory, but Daedalus had gotten his first one when he was barely eighteen. His mule had kicked him hard in the thigh, shattering the bone. Petra had wrought her spells, saving his leg—on anyone else, it would have turned gangrenous and been amputated. But he'd limped. In the 1970s he'd finally gotten it surgically repaired, but it had taken another fifteen years to learn how not to limp. Now he walked perfectly but still carried a cane. Some habits were too hard to break. Plus, of course, canes lent that distinctive touch of elegance.

The sun was low enough so that Daedalus sat in shade. It had been very, very interesting to find Clio Martin working spells last night. Spells he was certain Petra wouldn't have allowed. Spells that sought the origin or at least an understanding of Melita's power.

Very interesting, indeed. How long it would take before her thirst for power, for knowledge, exceeded her loyalties to Petra? Perhaps not that long.

Closing his eyes, Daedalus muttered a spell. It was the same spell he cast in this place every time he came here. Every few days whenever he was in New Orleans. He opened his eyes, feeling foolish again for his faint air of expectancy.

There was nothing.

Carefully Daedalus looked at the tomb directly in front of him, the tomb of the *famille* Planchon. His family. His parents and most of his other ancestors were buried down in LaFourche Parish, near where their *ville* had been. But not everyone. Daedalus's brother Jean-Marie had been buried here twenty years after Daedalus became immortal. Immortal and yet unable to save his favorite brother. Now he came when he could to his brother's grave.

Not once in 250 years had he seen what he'd been looking for: some sign that his brother's wife had come to pay her respects. That didn't mean she hadn't been here, of course. Just that she'd left no sign. And why should she? She'd never wanted to see any of them again. That night she had left Jean-Marie as surely as she had left all of them, and Jean-Marie had never heard from her again. Or at least, not that he had ever admitted to Daedalus.

Then he had died.

The bottom of the inch-thick marble faceplate had broken off and lay in big pieces on the ground. He really should have it repaired or replaced. He read the words as he had read them thousands of times before, and they made no more sense now than they did when he'd first paid to have them engraved.

Jean-Marie Planchon. Born: 1731. Died: 1783. Beloved brother of Daedalus Planchon. Faithful husband to Melita Martin.

Chapter Six

Taught by Evil

TIME HAD STRETCHED OUT INTO AN UNENDING emotional and physical pain that might very well drive him mad, Marcel thought. It had been almost three days since he'd been summoned. It had taken this long to get his passport in order, acquire a plane ticket, and get to Shannon, the closest airport. Three days of torment, as if spiders were crawling under his skin. The magickal urging of the summoning spell. He would feel increasingly worse until he saw Daedalus.

Now his flight was leaving in half an hour—people were starting to board out on the tarmac. This small plane would take him to London, where he would connect with a flight to New York, and then another one to New Orleans.

He threw away his paper cup of tea and picked up his one small leather valise. He felt more out of place than he usually did, surrounded by bright lights, radio noise, children, and women as brightly colored as parrots. He longed again for the monastery, with its silence and hushed sounds, the soothing gray stone and worn wood, the deep voices, the ever-present brown robes.

He was reaching for the glass door that led outside when a querulous voice hailed him.

"Father. Bless me, will you, Father?"

Marcel turned to see an old woman, bent with age but still dignified, her silver hair neatly coiled on the back of her head. She approached him with firm steps, sensible brogues seeming like boats on her narrow feet. Her tweed skirt was worn but once of good quality.

She smiled and knelt with difficulty. A gnarled hand reached for the hem of his robe. Before he could stop her, she kissed it. "Bless me, Father," she murmured, her head bowed.

Marcel felt another pang of sorrow and loss so acute that tears started to his eyes. He had never felt worthy of this traditional demonstration of faith, but now somehow, tainted anew by his past, he felt even more fraudulent.

Kneeling himself, wincing from the exquisite pain of this reminder of everything he was giving up and leaving behind, he took the woman's hand and helped her rise.

"No," he murmured. "I am so unworthy, it's you who should be blessing me. I should kneel at your feet. I am nothing."

The woman's face was uncomprehending as he went on as though talking to himself. "I am worse than nothing, because I am made of evil."

The woman drew back, her faded blue eyes searching his.

He saw her fear and forced himself to smile gently at her. Then he turned and pushed through the glass doors, out into the misty rain. *I am made of evil*, he thought sadly, crossing the tarmac to the waiting commuter plane. *I was born in evil, grew into evil, and was taught by evil.*

He climbed the slick metal steps that had been rolled over to the side of the plane. Ducking into the damp-smelling cabin, he saw there were only two passengers besides himself.

He settled into a seat, gazing out his tiny window. He wanted to rush outside and fling himself to the ground, physically holding on to the land of his adopted home.

A flight attendant offered him a drink.

"No, thank you."

Evil. His darkness spoiled everything he touched. At least it seemed that way after all this time. He put his head back and closed his eyes, feeling more wretched than he thought possible. Almost as wretched as that night, so long ago, when he'd watched Cerise die. Everyone had felt the lightning shoot through them, filling them with light and power, but that same power had killed Cerise as she had birthed her daughter. He remembered Melita's triumphant face, flushed and beautiful. She had run off that night. She'd destroyed the huge oak tree and the Source.

Marcel had tracked her through the darkness like a panther. He'd caught up to her, and he'd struck her down. He'd stood there, panting, howling inside with anguish and grief, as Melita lay facedown in the mud. The rain had pelted her dress like bird shot. His heart, his life and love had been destroyed, so it was only fitting that he destroy the cause.

Then Melita had raised her head, had turned to look at

him. She'd wiped mud out of her eyes as he'd stared at her, speechless. She had laughed at him.

Enraged, he'd raised his mattock again—but she'd thrown out one arm, speaking dark words that whipped around him like strangle vine. And just like that, she'd taken hold of his soul.

And she'd kept it, for years and years.

❧ Chapter Seven

I PULLED OFF MY CUTE SCHOOL TOP AND searched for an old T-shirt suitable for drudgery. "How about strawberries?" I asked as Clio came and lounged on my bed. "Planting strawberries—I could get behind that."

"Too late in the season," Clio said.

I rummaged through a drawer. "When will Petra be home?"

Clio groaned. "Who knows? Once she was gone for almost thirty hours, and then one time she went out to a case and was home in an hour. She said the baby just popped out."

I made a face at the mental image, and Clio grinned wryly.

"Listen," she said. "We still have to figure out who was trying to harm us. I mean, it seems like the attacks have stopped, but it would strengthen our position to know who was actually behind them. Let's do another reveal spell, before Nan gets home."

"Oh, *that's* a good idea. What else needs burning down?" Last time we had tried working magick, we'd almost destroyed our home.

"Very funny," Clio said, then sat up. "Hey, maybe we should do it right outside Luc's apartment. I bet lightning would hit it or a meteor would drop on it or something."

I tried to smile. Luc was still a very sore subject, despite how hard I was working to put him out of my mind.

"What do you mean, strengthen our position?" I asked. "Our position on what?"

Not answering, Clio raised one arm and trailed it along an Indian-print bedspread that I had hung over my window. It was weird, seeing myself performing these natural but dramatic gestures—like a hyper-feminized me.

I pulled on an ancient tie-dyed T-shirt. "Waiting, here."

Clio looked at me. "The whole immortality thing."

"What about it?" I asked warily.

"Have you been thinking about it? I mean, this whole huge possibility has been dropped into our laps, and we haven't really talked about it."

I stared at her. "Yes, we have. We talked about how we didn't want any part of it, how Daedalus was awful or crazy, how we wanted the Treize to leave us alone."

"No, we didn't," Clio said seriously. "Maybe *you* said something like that, but we haven't really talked it all out. I've been thinking about it more and more."

"Again, I ask, what about it?" I wasn't liking the direction this conversation was taking, and I headed out of my room and went downstairs.

In the kitchen I took an apple from the bowl on the

table and bit into it. "Man, apples suck here," I muttered. Clio came in and poured us a couple of glasses of iced tea. She and Petra didn't drink sodas much—they called them soft drinks and never bought them at the store. Maybe they weren't natural enough or something. "You haven't tasted a real apple till you taste an apple in the north, where they're grown."

"Okay, someday I'll make a point of it. Thais, don't you want to be immortal?"

There. She'd said it. Now I couldn't ignore the white elephant in the room. "Well, no."

The expression on her face said she couldn't believe I had said that.

"Thais! Immortality! The more I think about it, the more I want it. I want to freeze right here. I don't ever want to die. And I don't ever want *you* to die."

"I don't want us to die, either," I said. "But the idea of the rite terrifies me, especially considering what happened at Récolte! There's no way I would go through the actual rite! We have no idea what could happen!" Wishing she would just drop it, I got up to put more curtains in the washer. Then I paused, suddenly seeing Petra's face in my mind, but unsure why.

"I feel—" I began, as I heard the front door open. I realized what it had been. "Petra? I sensed you!" I said, amazed. "I sensed you before you came in!"

"Hi, girls," Petra called, heading back to the kitchen.

Excited, I glanced at Clio, but she looked upset and even

angry. "We'll talk about this more later," she said, and started loading the dishwasher.

"Pretty cool, huh?" said Petra, entering the kitchen. "You sensed my aura. It's easier the more you know someone, but you can do it with strangers too, or even animals, if you concentrate."

"Huh," I said, impressed.

"And hello to you too," said Petra, kissing Clio on her cheek. "Your powers are awakening, my dear. As time goes on and you learn more, your powers will increase. Then having a heightened awareness of everything about you will be second nature."

She dropped her large macramé purse in a chair. "I noticed the front garden. You two have been working hard."

"It was Clio," I said. "Clio and Melysa. She said to tell you she'd talk to you later."

Petra poured herself a glass of iced tea and leaned against the counter, looking tired.

"Hard day?" I asked, gathering an armful of curtains off the table. I opened the back door—our washer and dryer were in a tiny attached room, stuck to one side of the back of the house. The outside had been scorched, but the appliances were fine. The outside had already been re-weatherboarded and was being painted. It would look brand-new when it was finished. Which basically made the rest of the house appear totally dingey and beat-up-looking.

Back in the kitchen, Petra put her empty glass down. "I'm

going to change. Then we can think about dinner." Giving us a smile, she went into her small alcove room under the stairs.

"Thais," Clio whispered. "Please, just think about it. This is really important to me. Say you'll think about it."

I sighed. "Okay. I'll think about it."

Clio nodded, then went back out to the front yard.

Leaving me feeling totally uneasy.

✦ Chapter Eight

Not to Be Trusted

AXELLE RANG THE DOORBELL. ON THE SECOND floor, a casement window cranked open, and Sophie leaned out.

"Oh—hi," she said. Axelle knew why she was surprised—she and Sophie and Manon didn't usually socialize. But then again, this wasn't exactly a social call.

"Can I come up?"

In answer, Sophie pressed the buzzer that unlocked the downstairs door.

Upstairs, Axelle looked around. "This is nice," she said. There was one large room, a small kitchen off of it, and then a hall that Axelle assumed led to bedrooms. "Do you get tired of moving?" she asked, surprising herself. She didn't usually give a rat's ass about what Sophie or Manon thought.

Manon came down the hall, wearing a short silk dress. Axelle had the fleeting thought of the huge sum Manon could make as a child prostitute, then felt a little abashed. Manon never would, of course. But she *could* make a fortune, and it wasn't like she was actually a child, anyway.

"What's up?" Manon asked, sitting in an armchair.

"Axelle just asked if we were tired of moving," Sophie said, seeming confused.

"That's not what I'm here for," Axelle said, sitting on the couch. She leaned back against the arm and put her feet up.

"Do you want something to drink?" Sophie asked politely.

"God, yes," said Axelle. "What do you have?"

"Um, tea—or, or we have some wine open, and I think we have some Cointreau. Manon was cooking with it."

"A little Cointreau would be nice," said Axelle. "Thanks."

"What's this about our moving?" Manon asked.

"No—I'm here to talk about Daedalus," Axelle said, taking the small glass from Sophie. "Thanks. It's just when I walked in, I thought about how many apartments I'd lived in over the years, and I had a one-second thought about whether anyone else got tired of moving." Now she felt exhausted, having this stupid conversation. This was why she didn't socialize with Sophie and Manon.

"I get tired of it," said Manon, leaning her head back. Her fair blonde hair spread across the chair like a shampoo commercial. She would have been a knockout as a grown woman. It was too bad.

"There was a place in Provence, before it became popular," Manon went on. "We loved it there." She looked at Sophie, and Sophie smiled and nodded. "We would have stayed forever, but after a couple years, people always start to wonder why I'm not getting older."

A dark bitterness lay beneath her words. For the first time it occurred to Axelle that Sophie and Manon might have different agendas. She glanced again at Sophie, saw her face was drawn and sad, though she was trying to hide it. Axelle took a slow sip of her drink, inhaling the intense orange scent, letting the liquid burn slowly down her throat. Frankly, she preferred vodka. Vodka you could just knock back.

Did it matter to her plan if they wanted different things? Should she approach this differently? She didn't know. She was tired of thinking about it. *Might as well throw it out here.*

"I know what you mean," Axelle said. "The longest I ever stayed in one place was eight years. It gets tiresome, moving all the time. But anyway—of course Daedalus and I have maintained our friendship through the years. And when he told me of his plan, of finding the twins, well, it all seemed to make sense to me. We all have something to gain from doing the rite, no? But lately I've been wondering if Daedalus perhaps has some other plan that no one, not Jules nor I, knows about. To tell you the truth, I've been wondering if he can be trusted."

Sophie and Manon just looked at her solemnly.

"And not only him—Petra, also. She's so concerned about the twins and their safety that she might not be seeing the big picture. She might not care what Daedalus is up to, as long as the girls are safe. I've been worried. I feel like I need a back-up plan. Like we all need a backup plan. What do you say?"

"What do we say to what?" Manon asked, eyebrows drawn together.

"Forming an alliance," Axelle said, impatient. "The three of us. If we know that we're guarding each other's backs, we might be able to relax a bit, not worry so much. I mean, we're dealing with the Treize here. Who among them can you trust?"

"Yes, I see," Sophie said slowly.

"I don't know what Daedalus is planning," said Axelle, putting her empty glass on the coffee table. Her stomach felt pleasantly warmed by the Cointreau. "I don't know what anyone is planning. I want to talk to everyone, away from Daedalus. I want us, at least some of us, to be standing together when his plan goes down."

"That makes sense," said Manon, looking at Sophie.

"Well, you think about it," said Axelle, standing up. She smoothed her Lycra skirt over her hips and slipped her feet back into her high-heeled sandals. She remembered the horrible, ugly shoes everyone wore during World War II and shuddered.

"Think about it, talk it over, and let me know, okay?"

"Okay," said Sophie, walking her to the door. "Thanks for coming to talk to us about it."

Axelle paused, one step down, and looked up at Sophie. "You and I are different and always will be," she said. "After this drama is over, we might not speak again for sixty years. For the most part, I don't care what your life is like or what you two do with it. But if this situation is dangerous, if Daedalus is planning to use us for something, the way Melita did, then we need to stand together, tightly together, you know?"

"Yes." Sophie nodded, seeming sad again.

"Okay. So, later." Axelle went down the stairs and out onto the quiet neighborhood street. She took a deep breath, then stopped to light a cigarette. Goddess, that had been hard. It was so much harder being sincere than to spin a web of half-truths that wouldn't hold up to the light. It was so unnatural. She shook her head, blew out a long stream of smoke, and headed to her car.

✦ Chapter Nine

Clio

THAIS WOULD TAKE SOME CONVINCING. THAT much was clear. I needed to come up with Thais-like reasons for her to do it. Like, if she were alive long enough, she could figure out how to cure cancer. Something like that. Or, if we were immortal, we'd never have to worry about anyone attacking us again. We could laugh at muggers and light posts. How could she not want that, and right *now?*

I would talk to her about it later and maybe do some more research. But right now I had my other quest, my other spell.

In my vision of Cerise dying at the rite, I'd seen runes and sigils glowing on the ground for a split second, right before the lightning hit. They had burned like fire. Some of them I'd recognized, some I hadn't. But they all had to do with Melita's spell—

"Clio?"

So much for my sensoriness. I jumped at Nan's voice, then turned to see her in the doorway of my room.

"Sorry—didn't mean to startle you." She looked a bit

bemused that she'd been able to.

"Working on my ROA," I said, gesturing to my book of shadows, the notes spread everywhere.

"Then I hate disturbing you," she said. "But could you do me a favor? I'm showing Thais some basic centering spells, and I've realized we're all out of blue candles. I really think they'd help."

"You want me to run to Botanika?" I said, loving the idea of getting out.

"Would you? If you get the candles, we can keep working till you get back."

"Yeah, okay," I said, sliding my feet into some kitten-heel mules. I did it slowly, hoping Nan wouldn't wait for me. She smiled and headed back downstairs, and I whipped over to my bed, shoved all my notes back into my BOS, then spelled it and put it on my desk, very casual looking. I took a page of unknown symbols and stuck it into my miniskirt pocket, then hurried downstairs.

"Back in a few," I said, passing through the workroom.

"Thanks, sweetie," said Nan. "Be extra careful."

"Gotcha." I grabbed my purse and car keys and headed out the front door into the night. It was warm but not awful, and I was thrilled to get out for a while. I'd been so housebound lately, what with all the Cinderellaing, coupled with the humiliating lack of boyfriend. I mean, I always had *someone* around. But not since I'd met Luc. No, since that whole train wreck, I'd been alone, pathetically advising my sister on date wear while *I* sat home *knitting*. Okay, well, metaphorically knitting.

I drove down Magazine Street to Botanika. Inside, I got myself an iced latte, then took it into the store section. They had the best selection and collection of occult books in New Orleans, which was saying something.

First I looked in the spell-craft section. I found a couple of books that were a bit over my head, but even they dealt with spell forms I'd heard of before: the basic "cast circle, call on elements, delineate spell and its limitations, call power, enact spell, disband." Familiar stuff, and then some variations, including an interesting one that relied on natural limitations, like phase of the moon, etc. It seemed somewhat risky to me, but nothing hit me as very dangerous or dark or superpowerful.

I glanced around, but no one was paying attention to me. There was another, restricted area of the book section: a short, dark passageway lined with bookshelves. At one end was a fire exit. A gold cord and a sign blocked entrance from the store. *Not open to minors due to the sensitive nature of the works within.*

I slipped under the cord. My eyes adjusted almost immediately to the dim light.

Small, faded paper labels identified some shelves. There were sections for Biography, Spell Craft, Grimoires, Books of Shadows, Witch's Tools, Tantric Power, and so on. *Biography of a Dark Witch* was one title, and my eyes widened with interest. But first I needed to see what else was here. *Don't Invoke Danger* seemed pretty forbidding. There were more: *Celestial*

Omens, Personal Power, The Thin Line Between Light and Dark, and one titled simply *Dark Magick.*

All of them looked incredible, and I couldn't believe I'd never been in here before. Actually, I wasn't sure they would sell me any of them, anyway. I could try. But I wasn't finding anything about immortality, channeling lightning, or something. I would know it when I saw it.

I didn't have much time. Nan would give me only so long, then call my cell phone, worried. I would have to come back another time. Quickly I stooped down and looked at dark-spined books on the lower shelves. Many of them were in different languages. Curious, I pulled out one called *Mastering Life,* which I thought might be about immortality. It kind of was, but it didn't seem to parallel Melita's spell in any way.

A book called *Forbidden Symbols* caught my eye, and I pulled it out. Flipping through it, I saw one and then two of the unknown sigils from my vision. I tucked the book under my arm. I would try to buy it, and if they wouldn't sell it to me, then I'd come back later and copy its information. I was about to leave when I saw a thin, falling-apart volume shoved toward the back of one shelf. I could see it only from above—at eye level the other book's spine covered it. I eased it out carefully, its binding practically crumbling in my hands. Once it had been dark red but now was so old and grimy that it was almost black. I opened the cover.

"*Being the Personal History of one Hermann Parfitte; and How He Learned to Subvert the Power of Others,*" I read silently.

Subvert the power of others? Bingo. That was more like what Melita had done. I tucked that book under my arm too and stood, and just as I did, a rush of heat and awareness made me think—*Richard.*

I whirled and saw—Luc. Watching me from the entrance of the restricted area. As usual, a flush rose in my cheeks, and my heart started beating fast. Keeping my face neutral, I walked right toward him and ducked under the cord, forcing him to step aside. I brushed past him and headed for the candle section.

He followed me.

"What do you have there, Clio?" he said. His voice was beautiful, slightly accented, and reminded me of afternoons we'd spent lying in each other's arms.

"Candles." I grabbed some off the shelf, making sure they were unscented and the right diameter.

"The books," he said, and reached for them, his fingers brushing my side.

A tingling shock went through me, as if I had touched a live wire. I tried to pull away, but the books slipped out from under my arm. Luc read the titles, his eyelashes thick and dark as he looked down.

"None of your business," I said coolly. "Just like every other aspect of my life."

He looked up at me, his handsome face thoughtful. "How are you?" he asked, not commenting on the books. "Have you recovered from Récolte?" He'd been furious at the Récolte circle—he'd punched Daedalus, knocking him to the ground.

I took my books back, practically snatching them out of his hands. Inside, I felt trembly, uncertain, hurt. All the usual Luc feelings. I wondered if he wished he'd run into Thais instead.

Not answering him, I headed to the checkout counter. I hated this. I loved him, but he loved my sister. He was still everything I wanted. Why was he playing games with me? What could he possibly get out of it now?

The clerk rang up my candles and started to ring up the books. She paused when she saw the red "Restricted" stamp on the inside, by the handwritten price. Looking up at me, she seemed to weigh her options. She'd been working here for several months, and I knew she was Wiccan. Not everyone who worked here was a witch, but she was. She said, "Are you over eighteen?" She looked barely over eighteen herself, with her turquoise hair, pierced nose, and tattooed arm.

"Yes," I said clearly, wanting to will her into believing it but figuring it probably wouldn't work.

"Can I see some ID?"

Crap. Damn it. How freaking embarrassing, right in front of Luc. I really needed these books, had to have them. I didn't want to come back—

"Those are mine." Luc stepped up to the counter and put down some money and a driver's license.

The clerk glanced from Luc to me while I held my breath. Luc looked only a little older than I did—he'd been frozen in time when he was nineteen. He would be carded in bars forever.

The clerk finished ringing up my candles and handed me my change. She rang up the books separately, looked at Luc's license, and put them in a plain paper bag. Handing it to Luc, she gave us both steady looks, as if to say, "I hope you know what you're doing."

Outside, in the night air, I took the books back from Luc. "Thanks," I said ungraciously, and held out a twenty.

He shook his head no, waving it away. "Those books are dangerous, little Clio. Why do you want them?"

I turned to head for my car, but his warm hand on my shoulder, heating my skin right through my shirt, made me stop. I loved the way his hands felt on me. A wave of longing and attraction washed over me, practically making me whimper.

Slowly he turned me to face him. "What are those books for? Or . . . who?"

I shrugged. Who else would they be for? He didn't think Petra would want these titles, did he?

"Tell me. I might be able to help you."

The thought of making magick with him made me want to cry. This was unbearable. I pulled my shoulder away. "You've already done enough," I said, my voice shaky, and headed back to my car.

But again, as I was reaching for the door, Luc turned me to face him. I stood as he traced my cheek with his fingers, burning trails of awareness wherever they touched. He put his head close to mine, and I thought I would scream.

"I miss you," he said softly, gently raising my chin to look into my eyes. He pushed his other hand through my hair, holding the back of my neck. "I'm so sorry I hurt you." Then he lowered his lips to my temple and pressed a feather-soft kiss there. My knees felt weak, and I hoped they wouldn't buckle.

"Please tell me how I can help you," he said. "You don't have to go through this alone."

Somehow that did it—that word woke me up, made me snap back to reality. I drew back a bit and finally looked him in the eye.

"I'm not alone," I said, making my voice strong. "I have my sister."

Pain flared in his gorgeous, dark blue eyes. His hands dropped away from me and he stepped back.

I drove home, refusing to cry.

Chapter Ten

Someone Who Could Help

OUTSIDE OF THE AIRPORT TERMINAL, MARCEL inhaled deeply, then coughed out a lungful of car exhaust. Another thing to long for: the clean, pure air of his home, scented by the sea, by peace. The air in New Orleans had taken a dive since the last time he'd been here.

Still, the moment he'd set foot on the pavement, he'd felt immeasurably better. No longer did he feel as though a thousand insects were crawling under his skin. He'd lost much of his tension, his anxiety—and would lose even more as soon as he saw Daedalus.

The rage, however, would remain.

Here, in the city where virtually every kind of vice was tolerated and condoned, his worn brown monk's robes attracted even more attention than they had in Shannon. He needed help. He had no money, no other clothes. He was completely drained, an emotional shell. It had been days since he'd been able to sleep or eat, thanks to Daedalus.

A taxi pulled up to the curb, and Marcel climbed in. He would go to Petra. She would help him. She always had.

Chapter Eleven

THE NEXT AFTERNOON I EASED THE CAMRY into a parking space in front of our house, then forgot to put the clutch in and popped the brake. The engine gagged, then died with a shudder. I winced and turned to Clio, who was wearing her saintly hope-you-learn-to-drive-soon expression.

"Sorry."

"It's okay." Clio gathered her stuff and opened her door. "I'm sure my kidneys will bounce right back."

I laughed. "It wasn't that bad. I was able to pass the driving test, after all."

"Uh huh," she said, opening the front gate.

"Isn't all this stuff going to die when it freezes?" I asked, pointing to the plants.

Clio shot me a superior look. "You're such a Yankee."

"It freezes here, right?"

"Every couple of years," Clio admitted. "Let's go see if they finished the back yet."

We'd done as much of the work repairing the back of the

house as we could, but Petra had hired professionals to do the rest. Rain had delayed the final paint job, but maybe they'd done it today.

We started down the narrow alley along the side of the house. Without warning, Clio stopped so suddenly that I walked right into her.

"What's—" I began, but her hand motioned me to be quiet. I peered over her shoulder.

"Down there," she barely breathed, and I went on tiptoe to see better.

A brown snake was coiled on the sidewalk right in front of us.

"Is that a good snake?" I whispered.

"It's a copperhead—a water moccasin," Clio whispered back.

"So that's not good?"

She didn't answer. The snake's head swayed as it rose into the air.

"It's going to strike," Clio said without moving her lips. "It's poisonous."

I closed my eyes for a moment, and just like that, words came to me. I breathed them out. "Sister snake, leave us now. Return home to your young. Our place is here. Return and be healthy. Va-zhee, va, let, monche." I didn't know what those last words were, but the snake paused as if it heard me.

It pulled back, as if it was going to leave, but suddenly swung around. Clio backed up quickly, pushing me behind her, but the snake twisted toward us. Suddenly I remembered my nightmare, the one where the snake was coiled around my neck, choking me. This wasn't a constrictor, but still, this was bad.

Clio repeated the spell I'd just said, with the same words at the end. At the last words, she drew two signs in the air, ones I didn't recognize.

Again the snake paused, and again it swiveled back toward us. "Our magick's affecting it, but it's fighting us," Clio said.

I couldn't take the tension anymore. I slid my purse strap off my shoulder and hummed it right over Clio's shoulder at the snake. Clio shrieked almost soundlessly and pulled back. My purse hit the snake, and I mentally said, *Sorry, sorry.*

But it did seem to break the snake's concentration. With a last look at us, it turned and slithered under our neighbor's fence so quickly that it was gone in a flash.

I hadn't realized I'd been holding my breath until I let it out with a whoosh.

Clio turned to me. "A snake in our alley."

"Does that ever happen, normally?"

She paused, considering. "Well, copperheads *are* all over the place, but not usually uptown. They stay closer to water."

"We're only three blocks from the river," I pointed out. I paused, shivering despite the heat. "Or do you think it was magick?"

"I don't know," Clio said. "I mean, was this an attack? Have they started again? I thought they were over. But we should tell Nan."

She headed toward the back again, and I picked up my

purse carefully, looking all around in case the snake came back. I'd lived in Welsford, Connecticut, for seventeen years, and the only dangerous thing that had happened to me had been stepping on a dead bee. Since I'd come to New Orleans, I'd been living in mortal peril, like, every day.

We were almost at the back of the house when we heard Petra's voice and someone else murmuring back to her. The side windows were open, over our heads, since the house was raised up on brick pilings.

"Are you still worried that she's a dark twin?"

It was Ouida. Once again Clio and I stopped dead. She turned to me, her finger to her lips. *Dark twin?* I thought. *What are they talking about?*

"I'm thinking—" Petra began, but then she stopped. "Are the girls home?"

My eyes widened, and Clio pushed me back down the alley, fast and silently.

"She felt us," she whispered.

"What the heck is a dark twin?" I whispered back.

Clio shrugged, looking clueless. "Your guess is as good as mine." Turning around again, she strode toward the backyard, making sure her feet made sounds on the pavement. I followed, still keeping a wary eye out for the snake.

"Yeah, and so I've got to reread that whole section in chemistry," Clio said, pitching her voice just a shade louder than normal. "And I'm so bummed, because I already answered all those questions."

I wasn't nearly as good at subterfuge as Clio was. "Yeah," I said, my mind spinning. "Um, I've got lots of homework too. So did they finish painting back here, or what?"

Now we were entering the backyard. We walked past the little laundry shed and then "saw" that the back door was open. Inside, Petra was looking out the screen door.

"Hey," I said, waving, hoping my face wasn't too transparent. We hadn't been deliberately eavesdropping, but clearly Petra didn't want us to hear about the dark twin thing. My life was one circle of secrets within another—I was losing count of who knew what and who thought what and who I could maybe trust.

"Hi, girls," said Petra. "Why didn't you come in the front?"

"We wanted to see if they'd finished painting," said Clio. "And it looks like they did."

"Yes, the workmen left a couple of hours ago," said Petra, opening the door. "How was your day? Did you feel safe?"

"Yeah," I said, mounting the steps to the back door. "Until the snake welcoming party when we got home."

"Snake?" Petra looked amused more than alarmed. I dumped my backpack and purse on the kitchen floor. Ouida sat at the table, and she smiled and waved a muffin in greeting.

"A copperhead in the alley." Clio motioned outside with her head, already taking a bite of muffin.

"They're everywhere," said Ouida. "You always hear about people finding them on their car engines or under the fridges."

"What?" I asked in alarm. I looked at our fridge, humming away in the corner.

Petra smiled again. "They like warm places. So they coil up on top of your car engine or under your refrigerator, where the motor is. To be warm."

"Well, can we put an anti-snake charm around the house?" Clio asked. "I hated running into that thing."

"Snakes can be useful," Petra said. "Keeping down the mice and rats."

I sank weakly into a chair. "We have mice and rats now?"

Ouida and Petra both laughed.

"Welcome to New Orleans," Clio said. She looked at me. "Come on, we might as well do our homework upstairs."

I realized she wanted to talk to me alone, so I nodded and grabbed my stuff. My mind was reeling. I had done a spell, without thinking, out in the alley. It had almost worked. Now I wanted to know what a dark twin was. Plus we had snakes and rats and mice, apparently. Ugh.

In Clio's room, she got out of her sundress and put on high-cut jean shorts and a tight red T-shirt with a silhouette of Bob Marley on it.

"Okay, so what the heck is a 'dark twin'?" I stretched out across her bed.

"I don't know. Ordinarily I'd ask Ouida or Melysa, but I think Nan doesn't want us to know about it." She pulled her hair back into a ponytail and suddenly looked more like me—simpler, less like glamorous Clio. "We should go to the library and check it out, or use a computer at Botanika or Café de la Rue."

"Why can't anything be simple?" I groaned. "It seems like I just get used to one thing, and then nine other weird things take its place."

Clio smiled. "Believe it or not, *my* life was much simpler before all this too." She looked up. "Someone's coming."

My first thought was Luc, but it would be crazy for him to come here. He was lying low lately—I hadn't seen or heard about him since Récolte.

The doorbell rang, and Clio went to stand at her open door, listening. We heard Petra walk to the front door and open it.

"Marcel!" she exclaimed, and Clio looked at me with raised eyebrows.

"That's one of the Treize," she whispered. "One that Daedalus got here with his spell of forceful summoning."

"Which one was Marcel?" I came to stand by her. Downstairs we heard murmuring and voices. Petra and Ouida both sounded glad.

Clio frowned, thinking. "Uh—which ones aren't accounted for? He wasn't another slave, was he?"

"I don't remember."

"Wait. No." Clio's face cleared as she remembered. "Oh—Marcel was Cerise's lover, the father of her baby. Cerise wouldn't marry him." She looked solemn.

"Hm. Well, let's go meet him."

We went downstairs—everyone was still in the front room.

A young, strawberry-blond guy was standing between Petra and Ouida. He was taller than Richard, but not as tall as Luc. He had fair skin and blue eyes and looked more Irish than French. He was wearing . . . uh, like, a brown monk's robe.

When we walked in, he glanced up, then drew in breath with an audible gasp. He actually stepped back and put his hand up, his eyes wide. I wheeled to see if something was behind us.

Oh. It was just us, the miracle twins.

Petra gave a sad smile and took his arm. "Marcel, this is Clio and Thais—Clémence's daughters. Girls, this is Marcel Theroux, one of the Treize."

I stepped forward and held out my hand. "Nice to meet you."

The seconds ticked by awkwardly until Marcel seemed to force himself to touch my hand briefly. "Hello," he murmured, looking down.

"Hi," said Clio, not offering to shake hands. Marcel looked relieved.

"Clio, could you please see if any mint survived in the backyard?" Petra asked her. "I'll make us something soothing to drink. Let's go back into the kitchen."

"We have to get you some new clothes," Ouida said, taking Marcel's arm, almost like he was an invalid, I thought. "Where are you staying?"

"Nowhere," Marcel said faintly. He had a bit of an English? Irish? accent, and I wondered where he'd been and what he'd been doing. *Something monkish,* I gathered. They were walking in front of me, and I happened to glance up as he blocked out the sunlight in the doorway.

This time *I* gasped, stopping in my tracks. His silhouette, the outline of his head and shoulders—he was the man who'd leaned over the dark-haired woman in the vision Clio and I had shared, the day we set fire to the house. He had killed someone in the swamp.

They turned to look at me, and I shook my head, looking down. My face flushed. "Saw a spider," I said awkwardly.

"Spiders, snakes—I guess you haven't seen snakes in a while, have you, mon cher?" Petra asked Marcel.

"No," he said.

"Can you come stay with me?" Ouida asked as they sat down at the kitchen table. Clio came in the back door, the strong scent of spearmint preceding her into the room.

"Yes," Marcel murmured, not looking at either me or Clio. "I would appreciate it."

"Have a drink, and then we'll get you settled," Ouida said. "You must be exhausted."

"It was a—long journey." His voice sounded tense and sad, as if he were physically in pain. He was very different from the other men in the Treize: pompous Daedalus, quiet but kind Jules, weirdly dark Richard, and then Luc. Marcel seemed even more otherworldly.

And he had killed someone. But Ouida and Petra both seemed to trust him and care about him. Maybe they didn't know. Maybe they knew and didn't care. No—Petra would care. So either they didn't know, or—maybe that woman hadn't died that night? I thought about what I had seen. The woman had been facedown in the mud of the swamp. We'd seen someone chasing her—she had dark hair and dark eyes. *Think, think.*

Oh my God. Melita, the dark one who had worked the spell—it had been *her.* Marcel had killed *her.* Or had *not* killed her. Everyone in the Trieze assumed Melita was gone, since she'd never surfaced after that crazy rite so long ago.

But . . . if Melita hadn't died, if she was in fact still alive, then Daedalus wouldn't need both me and Clio for the rite, to make a full Treize. I stood, frozen in thought, my mind whirling.

What if someone knew that Melita was alive, knew where she was now? They would know that they needed only *one* of us for the rite. Would they be trying to get rid of one of us, then? Which would explain the attacks.

Then again, if Melita was out there, why wouldn't the person who knew it have come forward a long time ago, back when our mom was born, or her mom, or her mom before her. . . . Why wait until twins came along and just get rid of one twin? It seemed pretty farfetched. Then again, we were talking about a rite that could make people immortal, so I guess the term *farfetched* was kind of relative.

All I knew was I had to tell Clio about all of this as soon as I could.

✤ Chapter Twelve

Would That Kill Him?

THE TAXI GLIDED TO A STOP. LYING ON THE backseat, her eyes closed, Claire groaned. She was too tired to get out and deal with this. How much would it cost to just sleep here in the taxi for a while?

"Yo, ma'am, we're here."

The door opened, and Claire felt warm air on her legs. With great difficulty she opened her eyes, wincing at the glare. Her driver stood impassively on the sidewalk, no doubt wondering if she would have to haul Claire out herself.

"Okay," Claire managed, struggling upright. She coughed and got out of the cab. Her driver, satisfied that Claire was conscious, popped the trunk and got Claire's lone, battered suitcase.

On the sidewalk, Claire stretched, breathing in. Noticing the driver looking at her, she rummaged in her purse for American money, which, amazingly, she'd remembered to get at the JFK airport.

She paid the driver, remembering to tip her much bigger than she'd had to tip anyone in Thailand.

"Thanks, ma'am." The driver got back in the cab and drove off.

Claire stretched again, her short wrinkled skirt riding up, then lit a cigarette, getting her bearings. She looked around. This block of the Quarter hadn't changed much. Some things would be different, she knew, but it had been only about five years since she'd been here. So not too shocking.

She inhaled deeply. At least she didn't feel like she was detoxing anymore, now that she was physically in New Orleans. She had to see Daedalus soon, though, to get rid of the last of the twitching. Bastard. Whatever he'd called her for better be damn important. Yeah, she would go see him. First, though, she needed a bath and a drink, and in the best possible world, both at the same time.

Daedalus. Had anyone ever tried cutting his heart out and throwing it into a fire or something? Would that do it? Would that kill him? Because maybe the time had come for someone to try.

Heaving a sigh, Claire put out her cigarette and picked up the handle of her suitcase. One wheel had broken off, and now the suitcase lurched unevenly behind her. She bypassed the big pink house, heading down the crushed-oyster-shell driveway on one side. In the back was a small, long row house, cut into three tiny apartments. Two hundred and fifty years ago, slaves had lived here. Claire shook her head and sighed. *You'd think Jules would get over it.*

The air was still, as if there was a storm coming. Claire still hated lightning but didn't mind rainstorms too much now. For years after Melita's rite, she'd cringed every time it thundered. But that had been a long time ago.

Pausing for a moment, Claire concentrated, knowing her nerves were jangled. She was desperate for a drink, she was exhausted, and her powers were frayed and shot. Yet she was still able to pick up his energy right here in the first apartment. She climbed the three small steps and rang the doorbell, then pounded on the wooden door. She felt sticky and couldn't wait to get into the bath.

The door opened, and Jules looked out at her without expression.

Claire gave him a big smile and pulled open the screen door. He didn't step aside, so she pushed past him into the dim, cool interior.

"Oh, God, that's better," she said, letting her suitcase drop noisily. "It's bright out there." Finally she turned to face him. He was still standing by the door, though he had closed it. She gave him a big smile. "Hi, honey. I'm home!"

Chapter Thirteen

Clio

MARCEL AND OUIDA STAYED FOR DINNER. HE seemed shy and nervous, not big with the smiling. Now Claire was the only member of the Treize we hadn't met. It was so weird, thinking about these people living in a tiny, old-world village together, knowing each other for hundreds of years. Really hard to wrap my mind around.

They stayed up late with Nan, talking, while Thais and I went upstairs.

"I've been dying to talk to you," Thais said when we were brushing our teeth. She waved her toothbrush at me, mouth foaming like a rabid dog. "Number one, I think Marcel is the guy we saw standing over that woman in the swamp, when it looked like he'd killed her. In our vision."

It took me a moment to catch up to her train of thought. But it all came together, and I nodded. "You're totally right. I knew he looked familiar, and I couldn't figure it out, but that's it."

"And," Thais continued, "I think that woman was Melita.

And no matter how crazy this Melita woman was, does Marcel really seem like a guy who'd murder someone? So what if Melita *wasn't* dead, the way she seemed in our vision and the way everyone else sort of assumes she is? What if she had only *looked* dead, but she's really still alive, and someone knows it, then maybe that someone is the someone who's been trying to get rid of just one of us." Thais looked at me expectantly, holding her toothbrush like a wand.

I thought about it. She was right. The woman who had led the rite was the same one we'd seen fall in the swamp. It was also true that all of the attacks had happened to *one* of us at a time, except for the wasps. But maybe that had been aimed at Thais, and I'd only happened to get caught up in it by accident. I nodded slowly.

"Maybe so. But you know, if Melita's out there, then really, wouldn't it make more sense if it's Melita *herself*?" Thais and I stared at each other over the bathroom sink. "Like, she's back for some reason," I went on. "She knows Daedalus is about to do the rite, and she wants to lead it herself. So she's trying to knock off one of us."

It seemed plausible for about a minute. Then, at the same time, we shook our heads.

"That seems too much, even for this completely screwed-up situation," I admitted. "First of all, we'd have to be right that Melita's even alive, and everyone seems to think she's the only person who managed to actually die after that rite—along with Cerise, obviously. So, she'd have to be alive and just somehow disappeared off the face of the planet for two hundred and fifty years."

"Then," Thais jumped in, "she'd also have to have come back right at the same time I got here, figuring out that Daedalus wants to do the rite again and thinking she has to get rid of one of us to guarantee her spot. I mean, if she wanted to be a part of the rite before, why wouldn't she have just shown up way earlier?"

"Yeah," I agreed. "I mean, it's possible . . . but it seems pretty out there. Way too many *ifs*."

Eyes narrowed, Thais said, "But we have to figure it out."

"We will soon," I promised.

In my room I lay awake, watching the shadows change on the walls. Thoughts careened around my brain like pinballs. By the time I heard Ouida and Marcel leave, felt Nan and Thais drift off into sleep, I was both so tired and so wired that I felt like jumping out of my skin.

Finally I couldn't wait any longer. Still lying in bed, I crafted a sleep spell, sending it out to waft through the house like the scent of a flower. It would coil around Thais and Nan like a comforting blanket, pressing them deeper into sleep, soothing their dreams, quieting any need to get up for a drink of water or anything. It was a lovely little spell that I'd found in one of Nan's old books.

Of course if Nan or Thais ever found out I'd done it, they'd kill me. Using magick on anyone without their permission was about the biggest no-no there was in our religion. If someone did it to me, I'd want to take them apart. Yet here I was.

I crept downstairs and past Nan's closed door. In the work-room I gathered a few supplies, then let myself out into the darkness of the backyard. It still smelled like ash out here. I wondered how long it would.

Out back, I went into the darkest area, by the brick wall that separated our yard from the empty lot behind us. Nan's compost heap hid me from the house, which felt better, even with the sleep spell.

Quickly and quietly I set up my circle, setting out power stones, filling our four cups, lighting incense. But there was so much on my mind, I kept doing things out of order, kept jumping at the slightest sound, knocked over the cup of wa-ter. I thought about seeing Luc yesterday at Botanika and wondered why I'd felt he was Richard just for a second. And Richard—why had I kissed him when Luc was the only one I wanted to kiss?

They were both part of the Treize, this new entity that seemed to be taking over my life. Now Marcel was here, and Claire probably was too. All of them were here in New Or-leans—this city was like a cauldron, and the Treize was going to come to a boil very soon.

I had to be ready for it—which was why I was out here.

I had two goals: to have a protective spell in place for me and Thais, and to control the power that the rite would create, to make us immortal. Thais and I wouldn't die. I was sure Thais would want it too, once I had convinced her. Immortal. Even the word sent shivers down my spine—the very thought of it. Going on forever. Learning more and more. A hundred years, two hundred. I smiled bitterly. Maybe in two hundred years, things would work out between me and Luc and Thais. Maybe I could have him for the first hundred, and she could have him for—no.

But I had the magick that would accomplish this.

Finally I had everything in place. I opened the old grimoire I'd found at Botanika last night. There was a spell in here that Hermann Parfitte had described as "basic."

Feeling nervous, I reread it and made sure I had set everything up correctly. This was a spell to draw the power of others to you—the first step in learning how to control or subvert that power. I was going to start with smaller creatures like bugs and work my way up to humans.

It was both terrifying and darkly thrilling, doing this. It went against everything I had been taught my whole life. It was among the most forbidden magick there was. And certainly, in the wrong hands it could be evil beyond comprehension.

But I wasn't doing it for evil purposes. I was doing it to protect myself and my family. I was going to learn to do it before Daedalus did it to me—again.

After a last look around at the darkened yard, the windows of the sleeping house, I closed my eyes, let my hands rest on my knees palms up, and concentrated. I let every muscle relax, from the top of my head to my smallest toe. I felt the tiny release of each one, my shoulders, my wrists, my neck. The boundaries between me and magick began to dissolve.

I became part of the world, and the world was part of me. I never got tired of that joyful feeling of oneness with everything, where it all made sense, where everything seemed whole and complete and perfect, just as it was. I didn't know why it didn't last, once I came out of my trance—I only knew that it didn't. In the regular world, colors were paler, sounds more discordant, emotions more jangled.

I began to sing very, very quietly, almost silently. The spell had been written in French so old I couldn't translate half of it. I was praying there wasn't an unsaid evil purpose beneath the words. I sang the spell and then sang my own song, that contained a whisper of my true name, that put me in context within the world. It called power to me, connected me to the power in all things: tree, rock, air. With my eyes closed, I drew sigils in the air, the ones described in the grimoire. This spell was strange in that it didn't specify exactly what creature's powers it would call to you. I assumed it would be insects or perhaps lizards or frogs.

So when I opened my eyes and found seven neighborhood cats and Q-tip waiting patiently for me, I was shocked. Cats were mammals—higher, very complex beings, compared to insects. They surrounded me, watching me even as they washed a paw or followed a wind-shaken leaf.

"Cats," I murmured, amazed. This was *powerful* magick. Q-tip looked at me, wondering what I wanted. Ordinarily he would chase strange cats out of the yard, so I knew without a doubt he was under my spell.

The next part of the spell was to access the creatures' power. I was scared—I had no idea what would happen and worried that doing this one spell, taking this one step, would somehow color me evil forever. Like it would take away any hope I had of general goodness. Not goody-two-shoes goodness, which, face it, I'd never had a lot of. But goodness in the sense of . . . lack of real badness.

But the stakes were so high. My life. My sister's life. Would it be better to be tainted dark forever, but keep my free will, or to be good but controlled by someone else?

I closed my eyes again and murmured the words that would let me access the cats' power. It wasn't gradual, a slow, gentle twining of our spirits. It was sudden, shocking. Within seconds I felt their feline life forces standing all around me, animal sentinels in the darkness. They were alien, totally *other*, not like anything I'd ever felt, even during the wildest circle. Each cat was an unmistakable individual. Their energies were sharp and pointed, little clumps of crackling force; small, wild, and primitive. Even Q-tip, my baby, who was about as domesticated as they come, felt like *animal*. It was freaky in the extreme.

Feeling shaken, I went on to step three: joining their energies to mine. I sang the third part of the spell, checking the words again in the grimoire, which was open in front of me. I sang the words that let my spirit glide out and encircle theirs, one by one, as if I were a stream and they were bits of debris that I was picking up and carrying downstream with me. I sat quietly, feeling the joining. I began to assimilate them—I began to feel catlike.

My eyes popped open. The seven cats were completely still, staring off at nothing. Totally under my power. I had taken their strength, their force, and they were diminished and hollowed because of it. I felt ashamed that I had done this to them. But I also felt an exhilaration: I was super-Clio, more than I had been, more than I had *ever* been. I felt bursting with life and power, and a dark and terrible joy rose up in me. Standing, I held my arms out, trying to encompass this hugeness, this surge of strength.

And then I jumped. The strong feline power within me insisted on showing itself, and without thinking, my muscles coiled. I crouched and jumped easily to the top of our seven-foot brick wall. Right to the top of it. I landed on my toes, arms out for balance, but felt solid and secure. I could do anything.

Laughing aloud, feeling glorious, I raised my face to the sky. I saw differently, heard differently, tasted the air more powerfully. Every scent the air carried was distinct, clear, strong. The last of the blooming jasmine, the sweet olive, the roses in our neighbor's garden. I smelled other animals, damp brick, green leaves, and decaying plants and dirt. Everything tasted exciting, and my senses seemed close to overload. I was giddy with sensation, thrilled with fierce anticipation about exploring the whole new world opened to me. Laughing, I spun in a sure-footed circle on the eight-inch-wide wall. My night vision was amazing, and I gazed at everything, seeing every dark leaf, every swaying plant, every cricket in the grass, one crisp, clear snapshot at a time.

And I saw seven cats, still as stones, on the ground in my backyard.

A sudden fear overtook me, an animal fear, unthinking, strong, violent. *Were they dead?* Had I killed them? If I'd killed them, I'd killed part of me—and worse, I'd become something that filled me with horror. Quickly I jumped down and touched Q-tip's fur, gleaming whitely in the very slight moonlight. He was alive. Alive, but not himself. And I understood with shame and crushing disappointment what I had done.

I sat down again in my circle, trying to still my frantically beating heart. I didn't *want* to lose this feeling, this incredible, exhilarating extraness. It would be so easy to just take it, take it and keep it, and not care about the consequences.

But seventeen years of Nan's teachings and examples were worn into me too deeply, and I was grateful. Her lessons gave me the strength to do what I might not be able to do on my own. Closing my eyes, I chanted the fourth, last part of the spell, the one that would undo what I had put together. Even before I had finished saying the strange, ancient words, I felt the feline spirits leave me, felt myself becoming less. Less dimensional, less powerful. Flatter, completely human. Our energies flew apart from each other, and each cat came back to life, blinking, sitting up, looking confused and startled and afraid.

In an instant all the cats scattered. They associated this

place with something ill, something they must escape from, and so they ran, slinking under fences, jumping over them, racing down our alley to the street. They were running away from *me* and what I had done.

Except Q-tip. He sat in front of me, his eyes on mine. He hadn't heard any of the spell, but it had affected him. He was only a cat, but there was an unblinking knowledge in his eyes. He knew what I had done to him. He knew I was the kind of person who would take his power and use it against his will. Slowly he turned away from me and walked to the house, the offended line of his small back seeming a bitter accusation.

"I'm sorry," I whispered. But of course he didn't hear me— none of them did. Guilt and shame crashed down on me. I had taken a lesser being's power and made it my own. And I had loved it so, so much. And I wanted to do it again.

My face crumpled. I tried to hold it in but couldn't—sobs broke out of my chest. I kicked over the candles, the cups of water and sand. Falling to my side, I curled up on the ground and sobbed and sobbed, my arms covering my face, making myself as small as possible. As if I could make myself so small and insignificant that the goddess wouldn't see what I had done, the terrible line I had crossed.

♦ Chapter Fourteen

Thais

MELYSA WAS IN OUR HOUSE WHEN I GOT HOME on Friday.

"Thank God this week has ended," I groaned, dropping my backpack. "Lately it seems like every week takes months and months to get through." I went to the fridge and got some iced tea and a yogurt, and sat down at the kitchen table.

"Where's Clio?" Petra said. She glanced out the window, and I realized she was checking the time. I'd become very aware of this lately—whenever Petra or any of the other witches wanted to know the time, they glanced up at the sky first, then sometimes double-checked it against a clock or watch. I couldn't believe figuring out where the sun or moon was could really narrow down the time that much—they were probably constantly late for appointments or TV shows.

"She said she had to run a quick errand. I took the streetcar home." Clio had seemed a little off all day—she'd looked tired and kind of drawn, like sad. I'd asked her if she was okay, and she'd said nothing was wrong. I wondered if she was still pining over Luc. I sighed. We'd both loved him so much. And Clio didn't have Kevin to help take her mind off of it.

"Did anything happen at school today?"

I felt Petra's blue-gray eyes on me and knew she meant anything weird. I shook my head. "Nope. No snakes, wasps, or streetcar accidents."

Petra shook her head. "I've questioned everybody," she said. "Of course all of them are terrific liars—we've all had to be over the years. But someone must also be using a spell of concealment."

"The snake might have been just a coincidence," Melysa said. "They're everywhere. I've seen copperheads in the lagoon at City Park. Maybe the attacks really are over."

Petra nodded, looking like she wanted to be convinced. "Maybe so." She smiled at me. "At any rate, I'm always glad when you two get home."

I smiled back and finished my yogurt. I was glad I had a home to come to, no matter how weird it was sometimes. The months I had spent at Axelle's in the Quarter had been totally unsettling. Even though Petra and Clio were witches, even though I was now even more caught up in the Treize's drama than before—still, I had a home and people who cared about me. I didn't know if I would ever get over my dad's death. But at least I wasn't floating, lost, in a world I couldn't relate to.

I did my homework at the table while Melysa tied herbs in little bundles to dry. There were racks in the outside laundry room, and now I knew what they were for. Many of Petra's herbs and medicinal plants had been destroyed in the fire, but she'd gathered the ones she could save. And now we had yarrow, skullcap, catnip, lemon verbena, herbs, and other plants I hadn't learned yet, all hanging upside down to dry.

Petra was steeping other plants in small copper pots on the stove. She had a whole system where she strained the infusions through cheesecloth into small glass bottles, then stuck preprinted labels on them. These she stored in a cabinet in the workroom. I would never learn everything they knew.

"This stuff I'm going to save till Sunday," I said, closing my chem book. "I got the worst out of the way."

Petra smiled at me. "Clio always leaves everything till the last minute."

"I know. But I hate having it hanging over my head."

Melysa looked up. "Would you like to learn more about a witch's tools?"

I knew about the four cups and the special gowns witches usually wore during circles. Clio had mentioned other tools, but I didn't know much about them. I nodded. "Like what?"

"Well, there's the wand," Melysa said. "You don't have one, do you?"

"No."

"Clio does—why don't you use hers?" Petra suggested. "I'm sure she wouldn't mind. You won't do enough magick to alter its vibrations very much. I think she keeps it in a box under her bed."

"Okay." I got up and hurried upstairs. A wand. Like Harry Potter! In Clio's room I got on my hands and knees and pushed her bedspread aside. She never made her bed, and the covers always looked like a wrestling match had taken place there. An instant image of Clio and Luc together on this bed flashed into my brain, and I literally winced and drew in a breath.

I sat back on my heels and let that breath out. I didn't know if they'd gone to bed or not. I didn't want to know. I thought they probably had—Clio was way ahead of me in that department. I'd never even gone to third base. But thinking about it, picturing them doing it, was intensely painful, and I'd tried to banish the idea from my mind.

Which I did now.

Another deep breath out, and then I looked under her bed for the box. It was made of inlaid wood and looked very old, but well-kept. An intricate rose made of several different kinds of wood decorated the top. I pulled it out, and as I did, I noticed the edges of some paper sticking out from between Clio's mattress and her box spring.

I bit my lip. There was no reason I had to know what those papers were. If they were love letters from Luc, I didn't want to see them or even know they existed. If they were Clio's diary, I didn't want to read it.

But I slid my fingers in and pulled it out as if I was watching someone else do it.

It was a tattered old book, with crumbling pages and a

threadbare spine. The cover had been red once, but you could hardly tell anymore. I opened it.

"Being the Personal History of one Hermann Parfitte; and How He Learned to Subvert the Power of Others." Oh my God. What was Clio doing with *this*?

I opened the first few pages and skimmed some lines. It was partly in English and partly in French. I saw what looked like spells, but they were in a language I didn't recognize, as if French had been put in a blender. Clio had made some notes in the margins, translated some words. Her handwriting was worse than mine, and I turned the book this way and that, trying to make out what she had written.

A minute later I sat there, quietly freaking. It felt like the pages themselves were sending out tingles of magick. The few words Clio had translated were *control, will, spirit, power, afterlife,* and *living beings.* Oh, jeez. What was this about? Daedalus had taken over our energies at the Récolte circle. Had Clio stolen this from him? Was she trying to learn how to do it herself? Was she trying to figure out how to make herself—and maybe me too—immortal? What was she *thinking?* This seemed so dangerous.

I closed the book and pushed it back under her mattress so that none of it was visible—I was betting Petra didn't know about any of this. Clio and I had to talk about it. If she didn't bring it up, I would.

Quickly I opened the box, hoping I wouldn't stumble on any other dark secrets. Thankfully, there were only recognizable tools inside. I took Clio's wand, closed the box, and hurried back downstairs.

Swishing it experimentally, I went back into the kitchen. "Okay, ready," I said.

Chapter Fifteen

Not by Ordinary Means

IT WAS STILL BEAUTIFUL. RICHARD TURNED THE knife over and over in his hands, feeling the cool, razor-sharp obsidian edge. The hilt was finely carved and polished to an infinitely black gloss. You could practically see each individual feather strand. He stroked his fingers slowly over the almost imperceptible ridges, thinking about the last time this knife was used. Ordinarily it would be impossible to hone an obsidian knife to such sharpness. But of course, this hadn't been made by ordinary means.

Richard uncrossed his legs and rolled his shoulders, stretching out the kinks he had from paddling and digging. The metal box rested on his mattress on the floor. He'd brushed off most of the dirt, enough to see that the metal was untouched by time or rust, the painted symbols still clear and precise. One symbol on the box's lid, black and spiky and flowing, matched exactly the tattoo on his chest, across his breastbone.

There were other things in the box, but just as Richard replaced the knife, the doorbell rang. He frowned, trying to feel who it was, but couldn't really tell. Someone knocked hard on the door. Shaking his head, Richard slipped the box under a loose floorboard beneath his bed and said a quick spell over it.

The doorbell rang again. The last thing Richard felt like doing was dealing with someone, but it sounded like they weren't going to go away.

He was almost to the door when the doorbell rang *again*.

Richard unlocked the door and pulled it open. "Okay, keep your pants—"

Clio looked back at him, her eyes the clear, deep green of a camellia leaf.

"—On," Richard finished. He hated the way his heart sped up when he saw her. What was she doing here in the middle of the day? Or at all? "Aren't you supposed to be in school?"

"It's four o'clock," she said in that superior way of hers, where the *you idiot* was implied at the end. "Is Luc here?"

His eyes narrowed. Just like that, his heart burned as if someone had tightened barbed wire around it. "Afraid not. Lover boy's out." His voice sounded even and disinterested. Good. He turned and walked down the hall, leaving her. The door shut behind him, but he refused to look back. Then he heard her footsteps, and his throat tightened. For some reason Clio tied him in knots. It was infuriating. No one got to him this way.

His jaw set, Richard went back into his room, saw his mattress on the floor, and cursed under his breath. *You stupid ass.*

Why didn't you go to the damn kitchen? He grabbed his cigarettes and lit one, knowing how much she hated it.

Clio stood in the doorway of his room, seeing it for the
first time—the dark blue walls, the painted silver symbols. The
room was practically empty except for a low nightstand, the
mattress, a small altar in one corner, and a broken dresser.

He turned to look at her, blowing smoke in a stream toward
the ceiling. The fan blades chopped it up and it disappeared.

"When will he be back?" Clio asked, her face closed,
eyes guarded. She didn't seem to be craving alone time with
Richard. Fine. As long as they were on the same page. She was
probably still pissed about his grabbing her at Récolte.

"Don't know," Richard said, sounding bored. "I'm not his
keeper. Sometimes he stays out all night." Pain and anger
flared in her eyes, and Richard felt maliciously pleased. Served
her right, mooning over Luc. He'd never had much problem
with Luc, but somehow this just rankled him. He blew more
smoke toward the ceiling, keeping his eyes on her.

"Do you have to do that?" she asked tartly. She was standing in the doorway, holding tight to the purse on her shoulder
as if he might mug her.

"It's my room," he told her. "Whatever I want in my room
goes."

Clio flicked him a glance, and just like that, the atmosphere
between them changed.

Which he wasn't going to mess with. "Go on, then," he
said. "Go home."

But she stood there, and for the first time Richard noticed that she didn't look model-stunning, like she usually did. There were circles under those green, almond-shaped eyes, and her face looked drawn and tight. She was upset about something. Well, he didn't give a damn. She could stew in her own juices.

"Quit," she said, her voice faltering. Richard just looked at her. "Quit kissing me." She raised her chin a fraction, trying to summon defiance, but instead looking only vulnerable.

Biting down his anger at both her and himself, Richard forced his voice to be neutral. "Fine. You got it. I wouldn't touch you with someone *else's* pole."

For ten seconds—Richard counted—Clio looked at him, emotions crossing her face like clouds across a sky. His cigarette had burned down, and he ground it out in his ashtray. Why wouldn't she go?

She launched herself at him just as he straightened up, and he grabbed her arms in surprise. It wouldn't be the first time an angry woman had come at him, but—

In the next second Clio was holding his head in her hands, kissing him. Richard heard her purse hit the floor.

This is stupid, this is not good, this is not what I should be . . . uhh . . .

His hands slid down her slim, strong arms and held her at the waist. She pressed her lips harder against his so his mouth would open. His brain shorted out and his senses went on overload. She was insistent, molding herself to his body, and then she slid her arms beneath his unbuttoned shirt, her fingers spreading across his back.

He groaned as he felt her heat and urgency, her anger and pain and uncertainty. It was more intoxicating than anything he'd come across so far, and his search had been wide and varied. *Now, now, now.* She pushed her tongue in his mouth, and he reciprocated, feeling like the top of his head would come off. He wanted her, wanted her raw heat, her wildness. Breaking the kiss for a second, he pulled her down to his bed on the floor, keeping his eyes open so he could see her fine black hair fan across the white sheet. Clio's gaze was locked on his, her face serious and flushed, mouth half open. He gathered her under him, wedging one knee between hers. She pushed at his shirt, and he helped her get it off. And then her hands were all over him, across his chest and holding him to her and smoothing over his tattoos, leaving heated trails of raw nerves.

He kissed her again, feeling her surge against him, kissing her so deeply it was like they had fused together, were drinking from each other. She tasted wild and sweet, not like whiskey, not like cigarettes. Beneath him she was strong and curvy, not tiny, almost as tall as he, and their legs tangled together. Her sandals came off, and he pushed them onto the floor.

He slid one hand up her thigh to her waist, pushing her dress up. She made little sounds against his mouth, sounds he'd heard before, and knew she wanted him. Suddenly she pushed against his chest, pushing him off her. He pulled back, breathing hard, wondering what the hell she was doing. Then she pressed his shoulders back against the bed and climbed on top.

"Oh, yeah," Richard breathed as she came down again, kissing him hard on his mouth, his face, his neck. Her teeth bit his neck gently, then she kissed the same place, touching it with her tongue. Silky hair brushed against his face, and he held it back, framing her cheekbones, one thumb touching her birthmark. Goddess, he wanted her, he wanted her more than anyone. . . .

Clio was wearing a thin white shirt over a pink camisole, and now that she was on top, he tugged her shirt off easily. Keeping his mouth glued on hers, he slid his hand under her camisole, feeling no bra strap in the back. Richard couldn't believe this was happening, knew he should stop it, knew it was Luc she wanted. But here they were, and she wanted him too. He stroked one hand inside her shirt in front, feeling her breast, the roundness of it, the softness, and Clio made an incoherent yearning sound against him, coming from deep in her throat.

"Oh, God."

His eyes flashed open to see Clio staring down at him. Her face was flushed, her lips red and swollen. Inside his mind was screaming, *Don't stop don't stop don't stop.*

She was breathing hard, her hand flat on his chest, stroking him, making him crazy. "I thought—I had the thought that I needed to do a nulling spell," she whispered, her voice sounding broken.

Richard blinked as his brain tried to translate her words. Nulling spell. Oh, so she wouldn't get pregnant.

"Good thinking," he got out, reaching for her, but she pulled back, her eyes huge and sober.

"Then I thought—what are we doing?"

What did she *think* they were doing? He stared up at her, breathing hard, and then it hit him: What the hell were they *doing?*

"We don't even like each other," Clio said, sounding horrified. She scrambled off him, one hand at her mouth.

It was like someone had thrown ice water on him. In one *second* the heat and the wanting and the fierce longing to join with her fled, leaving him cold and appalled.

"No, we don't," he said hoarsely. He swallowed. But he'd wanted her so bad. . . .

Sitting up, Richard pushed his hair off his face with both hands, not looking at her. His hair was damp with sweat, his skin felt on fire. Anyone else, he would spin a string of lies, say anything that would get him where he wanted to go. But they wouldn't come now—he couldn't do that to her. He got off the bed and leaned against the dresser, a thousand thoughts crashing into his brain. They'd been one zipper tug away from having sex.

"You've never slept with someone you didn't like?" he asked, feeling appalled at what had almost happened.

She looked down, her hands stroking the sheet. She realized her skirt was still up practically to her underwear, and looking embarrassed, she tugged it down, smoothing it over her thighs. The thighs he'd just had wrapped around his waist. *Déesse.*

She moved to sit on the edge of the bed and scooped up her white shirt from the floor. Pulling it on, she lifted her hair out of the collar. Her hair looked like she'd been caught in a tornado.

"No, I have," she said, so quietly he could hardly hear her. "It . . . wasn't anything. It was like . . . eating, or taking a bath. Neutral, not bad. But this—is way different."

"Yes." No argument there.

"I don't know why—it's too—" She shrugged, unable to explain.

"Yeah. But we—really don't like each other," he said, sanity returning like harsh sunlight. "We're just . . . on fire for each other." It was horrible to admit it out loud, but he dared her to deny it.

Frowning, looking unhappy and still flushed, she reached for her strappy sandals and put them on. He tried not to look at her legs, her face, her collarbone where he'd kissed her so hard she might have a bruise. She seemed completely unlike the arrogant, totally self-assured Clio he'd met, the one he knew could chew up guys and spit them out. Five minutes ago he'd thought he had to have her or die. Now it was like they were both already dead.

Clio stood up, pushing her hair off her shoulders. She reached down for her purse. Richard couldn't go near her.

She hadn't looked at him for several minutes. Now she left

without a word, walking down the hall, shutting the front door behind her. All without meeting his eyes.

Despair was nothing new to Richard—it was more of a constant companion. But this gut-turning misery, this twisted yearning, the desire and the horror all mixed up—that was new.

Now that she was gone, Richard lay down on his bed. In a minute he would get up and drink about a half a bottle of scotch. That would be good. Shut his mind down, shut his body down.

The front door opened again and closed. Richard's heart flared—had she come back? If she'd come back, he would take her. No matter what, he would hold her and kiss her and lose himself in her and not think about anything but the deep pleasure of not thinking for a while.

"Hey." Luc stood in his doorway. Richard felt like his life had become a surreal movie.

"Hey," he managed, his mind reeling.

"You okay?" Luc frowned at him.

"Yep."

Sighing, Luc leaned against the doorway. "Marcel's here. In town."

Richard's stomach clenched tighter if that were possible. Perfect. His day was now complete.

"And Claire. She's at Jules's."

"Good." Richard liked Claire.

"You wanna get something to eat?"

Richard thought about it. "Yeah. Give me a minute to grab a shower." A really cold one.

Chapter Sixteen

True Love

IT WAS GETTING DARKER EARLIER EVERY DAY, Sophie thought, hurrying down the street. She'd left her car several blocks away, seizing the first free parking space she'd been able to find. Now she walked quickly away from the river, away from the more touristy parts of the French Quarter, toward the quieter, residential blocks.

Even here in the city, surrounded by lights and noise, one could still notice the changing of the seasons. Sophie thought longingly of the several years she and Manon had spent in Northern Virginia. For an almost perfect balance of storybook seasons, Virginia was the place to go—even better than Paris. Three months of real winter, including actual snow. Three months of a glorious spring, the kind of spring that had first inspired the goddess's festivals; a giddy, heady rebirth of life in all forms, painting the earth in a wash of fresh, bright colors. Three months of an actual hot summer, hot enough to go swimming in rivers and lakes, hot enough to bask in the sun, feeling languid and soft. Then autumn. The first tingly breezes leaving one's cheeks chilled; the fiery, painted leaves as trees shut down for winter. Apples, leaves crunching underfoot, Récolte and Monvoile celebrations. Each season brought its own particular joys, own painful beauty. The rhythm and cycle of seasons and time, the yearly death and rebirth that was the basis for the *Bonne Magie*.

Now she was back in New Orleans, and though the days were growing shorter, week by week, still it was hardly a real autumn.

Sophie crossed a street, easily walking between two cars that were inching toward Canal Street.

New Orleans basically had nine months of summer, then three months of ugly weather. Very few trees lost their leaves, and the ones that did didn't turn gorgeous colors first. Just brown. Then an ugly, wet, usually chilly but sometimes depressingly warm and muggy winter. Then a spring that lasted about a week. Then summer again.

Some of it was beautiful. There was a certain attractive lassitude that came over you after months and months of unrelenting heat. As if keeping up emotional and behavioral standards was too much effort after so many hot months. It broke you through to another place, a place where you acted differently, thought differently, went further and dared more.

Sophie smiled slightly. She'd written a dissertation on this topic in 1983. It was still fascinating to her. She'd shown that to Ouida, hadn't she? Ouida had probably enjoyed it.

Looking up, Sophie saw the big pink house, the address that

she remembered. There was a crushed oyster-shell driveway on the right side, and she walked down it. Jules could afford any place he wanted—they all could. After two hundred years, even the most imprudent of investments paid off. All of them were well-off, never needed to work again. Experience had shown most of them that lack of purpose led to madness. They needed occupations, jobs, interests, responsibilities to keep sane.

She wished Richard would admit that, get his life together. And Luc.

Her lips pressed together for a moment, then she shook her head. This was it, the first apartment. She rang the bell, feeling Jules within. He answered the door and smiled when he saw her.

"Salut, Jules," she said, leaving the *s* off his name.

"Come in, petite," he said, holding the door open.

Inside, it was dim—the windows faced east, and the sun was setting. The furniture was mismatched, but everything was severely tidy and well-cared for.

"Something to drink? Sherry?"

"Oh, yes, please. Lovely." Sophie sat on one of the couches, feeling herself relax for the first time in days. Axelle probably hadn't talked to Jules—she seemed to think Jules's loyalty to Daedalus would overrule his judgment. Sophie wasn't sure of that.

Jules came back with two small, delicate glasses of sherry. Sophie inhaled its scent, warm, a bit woody, rich. She took a sip and let it trickle down her throat.

"I wanted to talk to you," she said, loving the honest warmth of his eyes. "Have you been thinking about what—"

The slamming of the back screen door interrupted her. Sophie's eyes widened as Claire came through the back bedroom and the kitchen to the front room. Daedalus's summoning spell had worked. Of course. And Claire was staying with Jules. This was awkward.

"Well, hello, Sophie," said Claire. She was wearing Hawaiian-print capris and a red spaghetti-strap top. Plastic flip-flops with big red flowers over the toes seemed to glow against the floor's dark, scarred wood.

"Hello, Claire," Sophie said politely. Her mission would have to wait till another time. Claire's green eyes were sharp, taking in Sophie from head to foot.

Sophie waited, wishing she had never come, though of course she'd have to see Claire sometime. Claire was one of them, just like Sophie. One of the Treize. She and Claire hadn't gotten along since Sophie was eight and Claire was nine. Even then they had been the antithesis of each other, and almost 250 years had done nothing to change that.

"Why, you haven't aged a day," Claire said, smirking. She sat down in a rocking chair across from the sofa.

Unfortunately, neither have you. Sophie thought, giving a tiny smile at Claire's tired joke.

"Whatcha got there? Sherry? How about a little *coup* for me, eh, Jules?"

Getting up, Jules went to the tiny galley kitchen.

Sophie took a sip, trying to finish her drink quickly so she could leave.

"I hear you're still with Manon."

Sophie looked up. "Yes," she said warily.

Claire leaned back in the rocking chair, looking at the ceiling. She gathered her wild magenta hair in both hands, twisting it into a ponytail. "Well, good for you," she said.

Sophie waited, but Claire didn't sound sarcastic.

"I guess it's true love," Claire went on. "If I ever found true love, I'd stay with it too." She glanced at Jules, but he wasn't looking at her. He poured some burgundy liquid into a small glass and brought it to her.

"Thanks, babe," said Claire. She turned back to Sophie. "Manon got a tough ride. Her and Richard—their situations suck. But it's good, you with Manon. You seem good together."

Sophie nodded, wondering how sincere Claire was being. This was the most personal they had ever gotten, except for an ugly fight back in 1931.

"I'm going to see Richard later, I think." Claire took a big sip, emptying almost half her glass. "Him and Luc. I guess they're batching it, more or less, over on Ursulines."

"Yes." Sophie finished her drink with relief and stood up. "Thank you, Jules—I'll call you later. Nice to see you again, Claire. I'm sure we'll all be getting together again soon—whether we want to or not."

Claire laughed, sounding bitter. "What do you think of Daedalus's scheme, Sophie?"

It was a direct question, one that many members of the Treize had skirted around but not voiced.

Shrugging, Sophie edged toward the door. "I need to think about it some more," she said. "I don't know how much he's worked out, and I need to know more about what's going to happen."

Jules nodded at her—they could talk about it later.

"Thanks." Sophie opened the door. The sun had just set, and there was a magickal sensation in the air, the everyday magick of day turning into night. She headed out into it, retracing her steps back to her car. That visit had been a complete bust.

Then she realized, if Claire was here, Marcel probably was too. Sophie grimaced at the thought of Marcel. She didn't want to see him. It would be lovely if she never had to see him again.

✦ Chapter Seventeen

No Room for Her

DIVINATION WAS ONE OF DAEDALUS'S LEAST favorite disciplines. It was imprecise at best, positively misleading at worst. And not a fun way to spend a Saturday morning, either, in his opinion. He'd wanted Jules to help him with this spell, but Jules hadn't answered his phone this morning. Of course, with Claire staying with him, they might have been out, or perhaps Claire had unplugged the phone.

Daedalus's lip curled with disdain. If he could possibly do without Claire, he would, in a heartbeat. He had no idea what Melita had seen in her, what purpose she had served. In the centuries since, she'd proved to be as useless and weak as she'd seemed in their village. Now he was shackled to her for all time and was even in the nauseating position of being dependent on her, needing her for his rite.

Yet another thing Melita had to answer for. Admittedly one of the smaller issues.

Now Daedalus made a circle on the wooden floor. Axelle was out—perhaps she had joined Claire and some of the other dissolutes Daedalus was saddled with. Richard, Luc. He was fond of Richard but had no illusions about him. Of all of the Treize, Richard probably had the least moral compass, was the least caring of the subtle differences between right and wrong. Luc cared but was compelled to choose wrongly, again and again. Then was tortured about it. Axelle was easily swayed, easily led, content to do whatever served her best, as long as it wasn't too inconvenient.

Working calmly and efficiently, Daedalus set up the rest of the spell. It was one he had performed countless times over the decades. Always without result. But now—now things might be different. He felt it. He felt that there were signs all around him, telling him that now was the time.

Daedalus's element was air. He set up five thin sticks of incense in a wooden holder and lit them. Their coiling streams of smoke twined together, weaving a rope of scent. Daedalus began chanting softly, letting himself drift into concentration. This was the hardest part: the releasing of self to merge with and access the world of magick. Daedalus hated the feeling of vulnerability, letting down his walls. True, it lasted only moments before that vulnerability was replaced by a surge of power—still, it had never gotten easier.

He forced himself to sit quietly, to release his mild irritation at Jules not being home, his disapproval that Axelle had stayed out all night, his disappointment that so few of the Treize had lived up to his hopes or expectations. One by one he set these thoughts free, like balloons floating away into the atmosphere.

His gaze became unfocused as he became aware of his connection to magick. It was there; it was always there for the taking. As usual, it caused an unstoppable flood of joy within him, almost embarrassing in its strength and the eagerness with which he embraced it.

Unseeing, tracing the symbols by memory in the air before him, Daedalus wrote the runes *ôte*, for birthright, inheritance; *deige*, for clarity, awakening; *is*, for obstacle, something frozen or delayed. Then he wrote the sigil for things revealed, veils dropped, and another sigil to enhance the sensitivity of his vision.

Then he waited. Inhale, exhale. The beating of his heart. *Don't search; let it be revealed.*

The smoke formed a thin, hazy curtain in front of him. He watched, trying to divorce himself from want, trying to just be, with no expectations. Which was almost impossible for him even after two centuries' practice.

But there—there. In the smoke, the haze, an image was forming. A face. Black eyes, straight nose, generous mouth. A woman, not a girl. She was laughing.

Is this what I need to see? The image seemed to realize he was there. Its expression froze, looking surprised. Then it was gone, as if a wind had swept it away.

Daedalus blinked and shook his head.

He'd done that spell, what—thirty times? Fifty? Seventy? He'd never gotten an image before. He wasn't great at scrying—he found it hard to believe stories people told about seeing this, that, and the other thing. Only a few times had he received useful or pertinent information. So this was hard to take at face value.

Melita's face, that was.

If he believed it, then she truly was nearby, after all this time. She wasn't dead. He'd been searching for her for so long—could this be real? *Was* she nearby? Was she aware of what he was doing?

Lost in thought, Daedalus automatically cleaned up evidence of his spell. He hadn't heard Axelle come home, but he cast his senses to make sure. No—no one was here but him. He put away the incense, the chalk, the stones.

Melita. If she were back, it could be either really incredible or really, really disastrous.

✦ Chapter Eighteen

She Can't Hide It

THE WOMAN BEHIND THE COUNTER LOOKED at Luc, then down at the collection of ingredients he was buying.

"Dove feathers, honey, dried foxglove," she murmured. Her squarish brown hand turned a small green glass bottle so she could read its label. "Dried snakeskin."

Luc kept his face impassive.

She met his gaze, as if weighing the light and the dark within him. He tried not to breathe a sigh of relief as she rang up the items and put them in a small paper bag. He paid and slipped the bag into his leather sack.

"Thanks," he said.

"Do you—" the clerk said, making him pause. "Are you sure you be wantin' these things, now?" Her voice was warm, her brown eyes knowing. She had a slight, singsongy Jamaican accent.

"Yes," Luc said briefly.

"Do you be careful, then, man," she said solemnly.

"Yes," he said again, and left.

• • •

It seemed like decades ago that Clio had taken him here. Luc leaned against the broad trunk of the live-oak tree, looking down into the cradle formed by its thick roots. He and Clio had lain together in this hollow, hidden from passersby.

Now he stepped over the roots and set his small leather sack on the ground. He wished he were in . . . Africa. Or somewhere far away. Where he wouldn't have to deal with Daedalus or any of the Treize.

Then Daedalus would just summon him by force. He grimaced. Claire was doing a burn, no doubt about it. She'd spent most of last night fantasizing about ways to kill Daedalus. It had been pretty funny. But goddess, she and Richard together—they were both so bitter and hard. It got to be too much after a while. Of course they all had cause to be. But after hours of eating and drinking with those two, Luc had felt like he'd been dipped in acid and rubbed with sandpaper. It had been a relief to leave them.

Luc heard voices. Probably students from Loyola or Tulane. He lay down, sinking onto the warm, dry earth. Someone would have to be practically on top of him to see him now. On his back, he looked up through the leaves at jigsaw pieces of cloudy sky.

Clio. Clio and Thais. As usual, the thought of Thais made his jaw clench and his gut ache. Her sweetness, her acceptance. He was dully surprised that she was still so angry, so hard against him. At Récolte, she'd been cold and unyielding—at least, until they were in the middle of that awful circle, their emotions being ripped out of them and used as fodder. He'd felt her then. Felt the deep and powerful love she had for him. He'd felt her anguish, her anger. And her love. She was much stronger than he would have thought possible.

Now she was seeing that boy, that stupid boy, kissing him, wrapping her arms around him. If Luc were dark, really truly dark, no holds barred—that boy would have had a car wreck by now.

Good thing he wasn't that dark.

Sitting up, Luc unpacked his supplies. With a stick he drew a circle in the dirt around him and set four stones at the four compass points. This was dark enough. This was sinking to new lows, even for him. Already he was going further than he'd thought he'd have to. Ten years ago—five—none of this would have bothered him. But there was something about the twins—a vulnerability coupled with an incredibly compelling strength. He hadn't felt so strongly about anyone in—ever? He frowned, trying to remember. He'd loved Ouida, in his way. He'd loved other women over the years, the centuries. But who had *gotten* to him this way? Who had ever caused this deep hunger in him? Had anyone? He couldn't recall.

It was almost sunset. Luc sat in the middle of his circle, closed his eyes, and let himself sink into a trance. *Leaf of tree, cloud of sky, come to me and know not why. I draw you here with blood and bone. I know you're near, Clio my own.*

There. He sent it out into the world, feeling it leave him,

aiming straight and true toward the one he called. Similar to what Daedalus had done, but on a much smaller scale: If Clio were even fifty miles away, she wouldn't feel it. Daedalus's spell had reached to the other side of the world. Also, Clio could resist this one if she wanted to, if she was strong enough. Not by just shrugging it off—she'd have to work a little. But she could do it. He wondered if she would.

The sun had almost completely set by the time he had his answer.

He felt her before he heard or saw her, felt her angry energy. But she had come.

When she was close, he opened his eyes. She was striding toward him, her face set in a grim expression.

"How dare you!" she practically spit at him, when she was close enough. He had the sudden thought that if he'd been standing up, she would have punched him. As it was, she swung her woven straw purse and smacked him in the head.

"Ow!" It hurt, but was so unexpected he almost laughed.

"You used a *spell* on me!" she snapped furiously. "A week ago you punched Daedalus out for doing the same thing to you! You hypocrite!" She actually kicked him, but she was wearing soft-soled beaded ballet slippers, so it probably hurt her more than him.

He stood quickly, holding up his hands. "Yes, yes," he said, speaking softly. "I'm sorry. You're right. It was a terrible thing to do—"

"*Another* terrible thing to do," she said, her green eyes

narrowed. "You just seem to keep coming out with them, don't you?"

"I'm sorry," Luc said again. "I was desperate—I had to see you, talk to you. I'm sorry I used a spell, but I didn't know what else to do. Clio, please, please, just sit and talk to me for a minute. Please."

She crossed her arms over her chest, pressing her breasts upward against her olive-green camisole top. A couple of circuits in Luc's brain threatened to short out, but he ruthlessly damped them down.

"You have one minute," Clio said, her voice like an arctic wind.

"Okay, all right." Luc ran one hand through his hair. He'd rehearsed this speech so many times, but as usual, seeing Clio in person made all his thoughts go haywire. "I—miss you."

Clio's perfect upper lip curled in a sneer.

"Clio—I screwed up. I'm sorry. I hurt you and Thais both, and I can't ask for forgiveness. It was inexcusable."

She didn't contradict him.

"But I miss you," he said, forcing the words out. Not that they weren't true—they were. But he hated feeling so exposed. "I'm not—a bad person. I'm just someone who's been around too long, seen too much, done too much." He shook his head, feeling bleak. "You made me feel new again. Like—everything was new. New and exciting, because I was sharing it with you. You brought life into my world. And I destroyed it."

Clio waited.

"For the last 250 years, I just wanted time to speed by, to hurry up in case I could finally have a chance to die. When Daedalus approached me, he said I could use the power of the rite any way I wanted. I could get more power, change the course of my magick—or die. I wanted to die, to end this pointless, endless existence." He looked up. Clio's face was calmer, watching him with alert interest. He felt the slightest stirring of hope.

"Then I met you. You changed my world, changed how I felt. Stupidly, I destroyed it. When I met Thais, it was like— she was the part of you that you were holding back. And you were the part of her that she doesn't let go. I wasn't thinking, wasn't using my head. It was just, my heart told me to try to have every aspect of you."

Those green eyes narrowed. Not good.

He shrugged, hopeless again. "I'm sorry. I've said it was stupid, and it was. I was overwhelmed, I was out of my league, and I made a huge, hurtful mistake. You've told me what you think of me, that you never want to see me again. And if it were anyone but you, Clio, I would take you at your word and leave. Not bother you anymore."

He wished she would sit down. He wished he could touch her.

"But you're too important," he went on. "In more than two hundred years, you're the one who stands out, who my heart yearns for. You've had too much of an impact on me. Anyone who's reached me the way you have—I have to pursue. Don't you see? *Letting* you go would be an even bigger mistake than making you want to go in the first place."

They were standing within a triangle of three enormous live oaks. It was almost completely dark; minutes had passed since Luc had been aware of anyone passing by. Clio was leaning against a tree trunk, arms still crossed over her chest. She didn't say anything, and her face was closed, not giving away her thoughts.

"I'm not asking you to love me again," he said with a bitter, self-deprecating laugh. "I'm not asking you to even *like* me. I'm asking you to let me love *you*, even if from a distance. Let me care about you. Let me try to make it up to you. I *can* be loyal. I *can* be true. I can make you happy. Please let me."

Now he saw indecision flicker in her eyes.

"And where does this leave Thais?" she said coolly, her tone not matching her expression. "Out in the rain? She was stupid enough to care about you—I think *she* actually loved you." The words were snide, meant to hurt, and they did. But he couldn't let himself think about Thais now. If he did, everything was lost.

Luc bit the inside of his lip and nodded, determined to take whatever she dished out.

"Thais has recovered, it seems," he said stiffly.

Clio scoffed. "Kevin? God, you're an idiot."

Luc met her eyes. "I care about Thais," he said honestly. "I'm appalled and horrified at how I hurt her—and you. I met you first, Clio."

Several emotions passed across her eyes as she looked at him. Then she pushed off from her tree. "I have to go," she said flatly.

In a split second, Luc reached out and took one of her hands, pulling her gently back. She would kill him if he tried to kiss her mouth, but instead he pressed his lips against her warm, soft palm. A flare of passion seared him, almost making him pull back in surprise. Clio wasn't as aloof as she seemed. There were still strong feelings between them.

He stood up, searching her face. She looked upset, still angry, but also torn with longing.

Pulling her hand away from him, she strode away over the dark grass, not looking back.

✦ Chapter Nineteen

Clio

THANK THE GODDESS I HADN'T DRIVEN, I thought as I slammed through our front gate. I would have wrecked the car, I was so furious. I'd thought I was losing my mind earlier—one minute I was standing in the kitchen, washing dishes, and the next I was practically shrieking with the need to see Luc immediately. Then I'd had the image of him waiting in the park just a few blocks away.

I'd almost gasped with shock. *He'd put a spell on me.*

And the truth was, I still loved him. Still longed for him. It had taken everything I had to resist him. Here's the sick part: I almost wished he had put a spell on me to make me give in, so I could just do it and not blame myself for being stupid and weak and betraying Thais. I was pathetic.

Opening the front door, I was greeted by air only slightly cooler than outside. Nan hated air conditioning, and even when she ran it to dry the house out so we wouldn't have mold and mildew everywhere, it still wasn't the frigid blast I wanted. I headed upstairs, deciding to stand under a cold shower for a long time. I heard Nan's radio playing in the kitchen and figured she and Thais were still cleaning up after dinner. Thais had a date with the Kevster.

I wished she were really in love with him. If she were, if she had really moved on from Luc, then maybe—

"Hey."

I started, not expecting to see Thais sitting on my bed. Had she felt Luc's summoning spell too?

"Hey," I said, putting down my purse and pushing off my shoes. I was glad I had kicked Luc. I should have done it harder. I released a tight breath, hoping I appeared somewhat normal. "Here for a pre-date fashion consultation?"

I scooped my hair up in both hands and secured it with a clip, trying to look bright and chipper, but Thais was watching me with a serious expression on my face. Our face. "What," I said.

"So, whose energy do you want to subvert?"

In books they always talk about how "the blood drained out of her face," or whatever. But this time I *actually felt* the blood draining out of my face, leaving me cold and clammy. This was so far from what I'd been expecting that I suddenly needed to sit down in my desk chair. *Oh, goddess, I could be in such huge trouble.*

"What do you mean?"

She gave me a *please* look. "I mean, why do you have Hermann Parfitte's book hidden under your mattress? What are you doing with it?"

For at least a minute, I just looked at her, trying to decide the best course of action. Denying everything seemed to be out. All the scary, dismayed feelings from the night I'd worked the spell on the cats came back to me, and I really didn't want to talk about it.

But.

This was my sister. Was it true, what Luc (the bastard) had said to me, that together Thais and I made up one whole? Was Thais everything about myself that I suppressed, and vice versa?

"Well," I began. Then it all crashed down on me at once: seeing Luc just now, practically having *sex* with Richard just *yesterday,* the spell with the cats. . . . I felt tears well up in my eyes and blinked them back.

"Clio," Thais said softly. "Just tell me what's going on."

"You can't tell Nan." I felt totally bleak.

"Yeah, okay, thanks."

Blinking back more tears, I looked at her. "It's . . . important. This is between you and me."

Thais smiled at me, and it was so weird—it was a really old, *wise* smile. For just a second she wasn't Thais at all, but someone different, someone much older. I blinked again and she looked just like herself. I must have imagined it.

"*Everything* is between you and me," she said.

I nodded and let out a couple breaths. "I bought that book," I said, so low I could hardly hear it myself. "From the restricted area at Botanika."

"Why?"

"I'm curious," I said. "Daedalus was able to take our power, at Récolte. I wanted to know how." I opened my mouth to tell Thais about trying that spell, and being so horrified at what I'd done to all the cats. What a relief to blurt out everything, to tell my twin everything. But it was like a train coming to a junction—I meant to take one path, but the tracks switched, and suddenly I was on a different path.

"I thought if I knew how he'd done it, I could figure out a way to stop him from doing it to us again." Perfectly true.

Thais frowned, looking out my window at the top of the mimosa tree in the front yard. Its leaves were just starting to turn yellow, and they shone under the reflection of the street light. Soon the leaves would fall off. It was one of the few trees that changed with the seasons.

"Is this about Récolte or the other rite?"

"Both."

"Are you learning how to become immortal? Is that it?"

"Well . . ." I hesitated. I had to convince her. But something told me if I blurted it all out now, she would be turned off and wouldn't go for it. "Not really. More about how to control power once you have it. So no matter what happens with this rite or any rite, no one can use us like that again. I want to make sure you and I are safe from whatever these freaks try to do next."

"So have you learned anything? Have you tried any of the spells?"

"No." I shook my head, feeling so tired. I grabbed a tissue

and blew my nose. "I mean, yes, I'm sort of learning stuff, but no, I haven't tried any of the spells."

"Are you learning how Daedalus got our power at Récolte?"

"I don't know," I said slowly. "Sometimes I just don't understand it—it doesn't make sense. I can't see how something would work. But I just got the book a few days ago, and I haven't been able to spend a lot of time on it. I just wanted to, you know, learn about it."

Thais nodded, then glanced at the watch on her wrist. "I want to talk about this more," she said. "But I have to get ready—going to a movie with Kevin. Listen, tomorrow, or some time when we're both free, let's go over everything together, okay? Maybe it'll seem clearer if we just hash it all out."

"Yeah, that would be good." What else could I say? Thais nodded, looking serious, as if she wanted to delve deeper into my motivations. "Are you going to wear that?" I asked, just as her mouth opened.

She glanced down. "No. I'm going to put on a sundress. With a sweater, in case the movie's cold."

"Do you have a cute sundress?" I asked, raising one eyebrow skeptically.

"Yes." Her chin lifted a fraction.

"No, I mean a *cute* sundress."

Sighing, Thais stood up and opened my closet doors.

• • •

There was nothing good on TV, as usual. It was unbelievable to me that popular Clio was home alone on a Saturday night, while wallflower Thais had a date with a really cute guy. The more I moped around the house, the more I felt myself weaken about Luc. I could call him. I could see him. Thais wouldn't have to find out.

It felt horrible.

Time to go to Racey's. Luckily, she didn't have a date either. How the mighty had fallen. But Della and Kris and a couple others would be there, and we were going to eat junk food and listen to music and do something girlie, like paint our toenails. It would be distracting, which was what I needed.

"Okay, later, Nan," I said, popping my head into the kitchen.

"You're going to Racey's?" she asked, marking her place in her book.

"Uh-huh."

"Be careful," she said. "Don't be too late, okay? You have your phone?"

"Okay, okay, and yes." I grabbed an apple from the bowl on the kitchen table and took a big bite. Nan smiled at me, and I wished I didn't know that she'd lied to me for seventeen years. I smiled back and grabbed my car keys.

The Camry was right outside. I cranked the windows open to get the heat out. When would it cool off? November? December? Ugh. I took another bite of apple and left it in my mouth as I pulled away from the curb. Good thing Luc couldn't see me now—no makeup, hair in a sloppy clip, and the crowning touch, an apple stuck in my mouth. Lovely.

What was Luc doing? Was he just yanking my chain? I thought so, but then, he seemed so serious, so sincere. *Right,* I thought sarcastically. *And his sincerity means so much.* And then Richard. What was I doing *there*? Why did he have that effect on me? I couldn't stand him—but every time I saw him I wanted to knock him down and rip off his shirt.

At St. Charles Avenue I took a right, and the steering wheel grabbed a little bit, almost locking up. Surprised, I yanked it hard and made the turn. Should I pull over? Was something wrong?

I glanced down at the dashboard and felt my breath sucked right out of me. The temperature gauge was as high as it could go, and I'd only gone about eight blocks!

I looked over the street, searching frantically for somewhere to pull over, but there were parked cars everywhere. Adrenaline flooded my veins as I scanned anxiously for a place to stop. Suddenly actual flames and smoke erupted from beneath the car's hood, and cars started blaring their horns at me. At the very next corner I wrenched the steering wheel as hard as I could, making a wide and clumsy turn off St. Charles. As soon as I was close to the curb, I jerked the keys out, grabbed my purse, and jumped out of the car.

I ran across the street, my hands shaking as I fumbled for my cell phone to call for help.

A loud *whoosh* erupted behind me and I turned and stared as flames completely engulfed my car. This was impossible. I'd had the Camry serviced three weeks ago, and they'd checked everything.

Numbly I started to dial 911, then heard sirens already screaming closer. I remembered that the car had a fricking *gas tank* and rushed away, running halfway down the block. The first fire engine wheeled around the corner as tears started streaking down my cheeks. My car. How had this happened? Had I fried the radiator?

Or.

Was this an attack? I still thought the snake might have been—it had seemed to resist our magick. Maybe this was a follow-up.

Thirty yards away the firefighters connected a hose to a hydrant and flooded my car. I started weeping in earnest like a total crybaby. Clouds of white steam and black smoke billowed into the night sky, obliterating stars. A small crowd had already gathered, and now a firefighter was striding toward me.

"Miss? Is that your car?"

I nodded, wiping my eyes and getting to my feet. "I don't know what happened," I said, trying to pull myself together. "I was driving, and then the steering wheel felt funny, and then I noticed that the temp gauge was way high, and then *boom,* the whole car was in flames." More tears rolled down my cheeks, and I wiped them off with my sleeve.

"Had you filled the radiator recently?"

I nodded. "Just three weeks ago. And I'd only gone eight blocks! How could it overheat so fast?"

The firefighter shook his head. "I don't know, miss. Your insurance company will check it out. A tow truck is on its way to take it to a car shop—but you know it's totaled."

"Uh-huh," I said brokenly, leaking more tears.

"Do you have someone to call?"

"My . . . grandmother." When Nan got here, maybe she would be able to tell if someone had tampered with the car.

It was now official: Every single aspect of my life was dark, negative. I didn't feel good or happy about *anything*, not like I used to. It was like I wasn't even me anymore.

⚜ Chapter Twenty

Two Black Sheep

THE NAPOLEON HOUSE WAS PACKED, SINCE IT was Saturday. Frowning, Luc pushed through the crowd and debated whether it was worth it to wait for a table or even a spot at the bar. The smell of warm muffalettas reached his nose. Maybe he should wait.

"Luc!"

Luc turned to see Richard and Claire sharing a table at the edge of the courtyard. Richard raised a glass of scotch at him, and Luc walked over.

"Hello, tall, dark, and immortal," Claire said, grinning. She took a gulp of a frozen piña colada and waved him to a seat. "Sit down. You hungry?"

"Yeah." Luc caught the eye of a waiter and ordered a scotch straight up and half a muffaletta. "So what are you two up to tonight?"

"Drinkin'. Eatin'," said Claire. "You?"

Luc shrugged. *Putting a spell on Clio* would probably make them laugh, but he didn't want it getting around.

"So give me your take on the old crackpot's scheme," Claire said. She finished her drink and ordered another when the waiter brought Luc's food.

Again Luc shrugged. "The problem is, he's not a total crackpot. He wants power and he knows how to get it. He's willing to run us all down doing it."

Claire nodded, mulling it over, and Luc saw the shrewd intelligence in her eyes. It was so easy to forget how smart she was, how sharp. "How many of us are onboard with the rite?"

"Axelle, Jules," said Richard. He lit a cigarette and blew the smoke upward. "Me, Manon. Possibly Ouida. Possibly Petra. Possibly Sophie."

Claire looked at Luc. "Et toi?"

"Onboard," he said, taking a bite of his enormous sandwich. Warm cheese, spicy salami, olive salad, Italian bread—it was damn near perfect.

"Interesting," said Claire.

"What about you?" Richard asked.

"Onboard, I believe," she said, sounding coy. "Trying to come up with a Christmas list."

Richard laughed dryly. "Aren't we all?"

"Tell me about these surprise twins of Petra's." Claire bummed one of Richard's cigarettes and lit it, the smoke obscuring her face for a second.

There was silence, and Luc felt Richard's dark eyes on him.

"They're the latest in Cerise's line," he said slowly,

pushing some olive salad back under the bread. "The thirteenth generation. Apparently Petra helped the mother have them, and when she saw it was twins, she took one and didn't tell the father. So one grew up with the father in Connecticut, and one of them grew up here with Petra."

"Petra wanted them apart," Claire said. "Did she already suspect Daedalus of wanting a complete Treize?"

"Don't know," Luc said. "She just thought the two together wouldn't be safe for some reason. Then the dad died this summer."

"We think Daedalus, and probably Jules and Axelle, killed him," Richard put in matter-of-factly.

"Jules wouldn't do that," Claire said, somewhat sharply.

Richard raised his eyebrows. "Jules has followed Daedalus for years. And he might very well have plans of his own too. But the dad died, and they wrangled it so Axelle got custody of the northern twin."

"Thais," Luc murmured, and felt Richard looking at him again.

Claire laughed. "Yeah, 'cause Axelle has always had maternal yearnings. That's hysterical."

Luc couldn't help smiling, and so did Richard.

"Yeah," Luc said. "So Axelle brought Thais here. Bizarrely, she and Clio ended up going to the same school, ran into each other, and figured everything out."

"That's the abbreviated version," Richard said, taking a drink of his own scotch.

"Really," Clare said, alert and interested. "What's the long version?"

"Yes, Luc," said Richard. "Tell Claire the long version."

Luc shot him a look. "Not much to tell."

Richard laughed, and Luc narrowed his eyes at him, aware that Claire was following this exchange.

"And then at Récolte, Daedalus seized our power and summoned you and Marcel," Luc went on, skipping several chapters. "And now we're all waiting to see how it plays out."

"Mmm," said Claire.

Luc could practically see the gears in her head turning.

"And while we're all waiting, Petra has the twins." Claire took the piece of pineapple out of her drink and bit into it. "Petra has the twins, and the rest of the Treize is fermenting in the cauldron of New Orleans, eh? No one's worried about the twins? No one's trying to keep them separate?"

"Worried? Well, Petra made everyone promise that they would leave the twins alone," Luc said.

"Too late." Richard smiled sardonically into his glass. He was really getting under Luc's skin. He hoped this wouldn't turn into a bar fight in the middle of the Napoleon House.

"Why would they keep them separate?" Luc asked, trying to keep his anger down. "I never understood why Petra separated them in the first place. I mean, the whole twin-power thing is just a myth, right?"

"Luc." Claire's eyes, green but nothing like the twins', were quietly amused. "Of course it's not a myth. I can't believe

Petra's being so reckless, having them together. Thank God the northern one doesn't know magick yet. The two of them doing magick together could blow you, me, and Daedalus right out of the water."

"But . . . they wouldn't," Luc said, surprised. "They're not—dark."

"They don't need to be," Claire said. She held the head of a crawfish up to her bright red mouth and sucked the juices out of it. "They don't need to be dark or light or know what the hell they're doing. They only have to be together. Did you sleep through this part of the histoire de famille?"

"They're dangerous?" Luc just couldn't take it in. "How? Why?"

"Because they're twins, they're the thirteenth generation, they're marked—I mean, hello. What part of disastrous prophecy do you not understand?" Claire drained her latest drink and shook her magenta hair off her shoulders.

"What's this prophecy say again?" Richard asked. He seemed weird, tightly wound, angry, worried—Luc couldn't put a finger on it.

Claire slowly ran a finger around the top of her glass, making an annoying, high-pitched hum. "The marked girl brings you death," she said. Then, laughing, she shrugged. "They will bring eternal life and also death. The Twin Angels. You know. The Twin Angels of Life and Death."

"Angels, yeah," Richard muttered. His eyes were glazed. *Drunk off his ass,* Luc thought. *And in a weird mood. Time to get out of here.* Richard drunk and in a bad mood meant that blood was going to be spilled. Luc wasn't up for it. Let him and his pal Claire get into a screaming fight here in front of the tourists.

The waiter brought him another scotch without being asked. *All right, one more drink.* They didn't have any at home, after all. "I can't believe you buy into all that crap, Claire. They're just twins. They're innocent. Neither one has much power. Don't worry about it."

"They have power," Richard said in a low voice. He looked up at Luc, his eyes unreadable. "They have power over you, over—all of us."

Luc shook his head impatiently. "Fairy tales. The famille probably made it all up to keep kids in line."

Both Richard and Claire looked at him solemnly, identical glassy-eyed gazes not hiding their sharp intelligence, their experience. All of it hard-won.

Luc shook his head again and took a gulp of his drink. "You worry too much."

✦ Chapter Twenty-One

Thais

"UH-*HUH*," I SAID, NOT CROSSING THE THRESHOLD.

Kevin looked at me innocently. "What?"

"No one else is home, and we're going to go in and watch a movie. I'm using air quotes around the 'watch a movie.'"

He laughed and took my hand, gently pulling me through the back door of his enormous house. Inside it was dark and cool. A clock chimed somewhere—it was eight thirty.

"Who checked on the movie times?" he asked.

"Me," I admitted. The Website had been wrong, and we'd missed the first twenty minutes of what we'd wanted to see. Kevin had said we could watch a movie at his house. But I had expected at least one of his parents to be home.

"Don't you want to see *Before the Day*?"

"Yes, but—" The house stretched out all around us, pristine and decorated and bigger than any private house I'd ever been in. I loved the fourteen-foot ceilings, the tall French windows, the gleaming wide floorboards.

Kevin quit tugging on my hands. "Hey, if you don't want

to stay—that's cool. We can go somewhere else, do something else. I wasn't trying to push you."

That was one reason why I liked Kevin so much. He was totally sincere about that. I mean, Luc might have said the same thing, but he wouldn't have meant it as much, would have really wanted me to change my mind. Kevin was willing to take me at face value.

Don't think about Luc.

I kind of wanted to go home. I felt worried and distracted—Clio wanted to be *immortal*. She was messing with what even I could tell was dark magick. Everything felt off-kilter, and smiling and being nice was taking a lot of effort. But I didn't want to be mean to Kevin.

"I'm assuming the TV is downstairs?"

Kevin grinned. "I was thinking the one up in my room."

Laughing, I pushed against his chest gently. "Think again."

He raised his hands in defeat and led me into a family room that was bigger than the front room and workroom at Petra's house put together. He opened an antique-looking entertainment center to reveal a gigantic TV.

"Oh my God," I said enviously, and he smiled.

"You'll have to come to our Super Bowl party. Or maybe not—it gets pretty ugly. You want something to drink? I can make popcorn."

I just gazed at him in appreciation. He would be so perfect—if I didn't have the memory of someone else.

• • •

"Is this okay?" Kevin's voice was muffled and kind of hoarse.

Feeling like I was about to jump off a cliff, I managed to nod before our mouths met again. The only light was a dim table lamp across the room. We were lying on the wide sectional sofa, making out, the movie a muted background noise that we hadn't paid any attention to.

Kevin was a great kisser, smooth and sure and gentle, with an underlying determination. It was—really nice. Great, even. But my brain never went haywire, I never lost myself, never felt like we were becoming one person. I really, really liked holding him, liked the way he felt and kissed, felt comfortable making out, but didn't feel desperate to go further. I didn't feel like being more assertive, or demanding as much as I was giving.

We were lying side by side with one of his legs over mine, and now he put his hand on my leg, right below where my dress ended. I felt flustery and kind of anxious about already going as far as we had, and now he was gently asking for more. His hand slid up my thigh slowly, giving me time to stop him.

"Um," I said, breaking away from our kiss. I felt sleepy and dopey and thoroughly kissed, and it was so nice, such a good feeling. Breathing hard, Kevin waited, then leaned in and kissed my neck, sending shivers down my spine. His hand went a little higher, and it was exciting—it felt risky and safe at the same time, and part of me wanted to see where it would lead.

Except I knew where it would lead, and I couldn't go there.

I put my hand over his, and he stopped, pulling back to look at me.

"I want to touch you," he whispered, kissing the side of my face. He felt warm and so, so nice, and it was incredibly tempting. If I could have said yes, I would have.

But I couldn't.

"I—can't," I whispered back. I remembered how angry Chad Woolcott had been, the ugly fight we'd had, how his nice facade had dropped away, leaving a hateful jackass. *Please don't let that happen now.*

Kevin hesitated, and I imagined the war inside his head— push now and see if she gives in, be a good guy now and see if it pays off later. . . .

He took his hand away. Holding me in an embrace, he kissed my face and then my mouth, snuggling closer.

I couldn't relax. "Are you . . . okay?"

He looked at me and gave a little smile. "I'm here with you. Everything's fine."

I relaxed, and right then became aware of a dull humming sound. "What's that? Is that—just the fridge or something?"

Kevin listened, then he sat up and tugged his shirt down. "Oops. That's the driveway gate opening. Someone's home." His smile was beautiful and teasing as I bolted into a sitting position and smoothed out my clothes.

Getting up with quick grace, Kevin flicked on several more lamps. I grabbed the remote and turned up the TV's volume. And there we were, watching a movie neither of us could name, when Kevin's stepmother came in.

"Kev?" a woman called.

"Hey," Kevin called back, Mr. Innocent. I gave him a look, and he smirked at me.

"Hi, sweetie," a woman called. I saw her dark form moving in the back hallway. After a moment she came into the family room, sorting through a thick stack of mail. "I saw your car," she said without looking up. "Didn't you have a date tonight?"

She was tall and elegant, with black hair swept up into a chignon. Even Clio would have approved of her tailored, probably designer pantsuit. Her skin and eyes were darker than Kevin's, but of course there was no reason they would look alike.

"Uh, yeah," Kevin said, muting the TV again. "This is Thais. Thais, this is my mom."

His stepmother looked up sharply and saw me. I projected an air of goody-two-shoes while her eyes narrowed at Kevin.

"Nice to meet you, Mrs. LaTour," I said politely.

"You too, sweetie," she said to me, then turned her attention to Kevin. "Home alone with a girl? Minus five points."

He looked a little embarrassed while she made a big show of examining the situation. My cheeks started to heat up.

"But you're downstairs. Plus two points. And everyone's clothes are on. Another two points."

Now I was mortified.

"So it could be worse," she said, putting the mail down on a bookshelf. "I'm not trying to embarrass you, sweetie." Her eyes were kind as she looked at me. "But Kevin's father and I know how easy it is to get carried away, make a mistake."

"Mom," Kevin groaned, putting his head in his hands.

"Especially in a house with a liquor cabinet and a swimming pool."

"The liquor cabinet's locked!" Kevin protested.

"I don't drink," I said quickly.

"We're almost eighteen," Kevin pointed out.

"Yes, and eighteen is a great age to get married and have babies," Mrs. LaTour said brightly. "Or better, have babies and *not* get married. I mean, college schmollage! Careers are for losers! Right?"

Kevin just groaned, shaking his head in his hands.

I wished I could melt into the couch and disappear. How would I ever be able to face his stepmom again?

"We were just watching a movie," I said faintly, my face burning. I could never come back to this house, never meet Kevin's dad—not after tonight. She'd tell him that Kevin was making out with some girl, and that would be me, and I would never—

Believe me.

The thought flew away from me as if it had its own destination.

Believe what you see, not what you fear.

Have trust in your child whose heart you hold dear.

I hadn't meant to send it out, wasn't even sure what it would do. But I was so embarrassed and mortified and just wanted this to end.

Mrs. LaTour blinked and put her head to one side, and then she leaned against the doorway into the kitchen. "Gosh, I'm . . . so tired," she said, sounding sapped. "I didn't realize it." She looked up at us. "What was I saying?"

"Um," Kevin said.

"Well, it's late—I really should get going," I said. "I have a curfew." I didn't really, but let her think of me as the nice girl with the curfew.

"All right, Thais, is it?"

I nodded.

"I'll take you," Kevin said, practically springing off the couch.

"It was nice to meet you, Mrs. LaTour," I said.

"Dr.," Kevin whispered. "Dr. Hendricks."

"Sorry. Dr. Hendricks," I said. I grabbed the sweater Clio hadn't wanted me to bring, and Kevin and I hightailed it out of there.

When he dropped me off at home, Clio's car was still gone. Kevin walked me up to the porch, and we stood out of the streetlight's glare for a while, kissing and murmuring good-byes.

"I'm sorry my mom walked in on us," he said.

"It's okay," I said. "But I was so embarrassed."

"She'll forget about it," he promised.

Yeah, I think she will. I found that unsettling.

Finally we tore ourselves away from each other, and I went inside. Dropping my purse on the little table by the front door,

I headed back to find Petra. Sure enough, the kitchen lights were on. I felt Clio in the house, which was weird—

—except, when I reached the kitchen, she was sitting there with Petra at the table. They both looked grim. *Uh-oh,* I thought. *What now?*

"I didn't see your car," I said. "I thought you were still out."

"There's a reason for that," Clio said bitterly.

"I've been trying to call you," Petra said.

Frowning, I pulled my cell out of my purse. I hadn't turned it on. "Oh."

Then they told me about how, while I'd been making out with my boyfriend, my twin sister had almost been killed. Again.

My first thought was: *Melita?*

✦ Chapter Twenty-Two

Get Over Her

THE FRENCH QUARTER HAD SUNK EVEN LOWER into its iniquity. It had been forty years since Marcel had been here. It had been shocking then, but now it was like he was at the entrance to hell.

Well, he'd seen enough. Here, surrounded by gaudy lights, gaudy people, horrid scents, and ear-deafening noise, he missed his home at the monastery with a raw pain. He would never be able to go back. Something would happen here to prevent it, he was sure of it. How could he return to Father Jonah with fresh blood on his hands?

He turned and headed back up to St. Charles Avenue. It was three in the morning—it might take a while for the streetcar to come. Not many locals would wait for it at this hour—crime here had spiraled so far out of control that most natives lived behind locked iron gates, burglar alarms, and private security firms.

However, Marcel didn't worry about getting mugged. He had nothing to lose, not even his life.

As he walked past a place Ouida had taken him to for

lunch back in the '50s, the door swung open, and three drunks stumbled out, laughing and holding on to each other for support. They almost ran right into him, and he stepped back, weary and revolted.

Oh.

He knew these drunks. They were three of his least favorite people in the whole world.

They were gasping with laughter and righted themselves clumsily.

"Oh, pardon me," said Claire, blinking hazily up at him. Then her face changed with recognition, and she stood up straighter. "Marcel."

Richard and Luc also straightened, as if they were willing themselves to sober up to deal with him. Maybe they were—frivolously doing system-cleaning spells to rid themselves of pollutants. It would be just like them to misuse magickal power. He himself hadn't used or made magick in a long, long time—not since he'd devoted his life to the Christian God, back in 1919. He tried to not even think about magick. It wasn't up to mere humans to bend the power of God to their will, and that was what magick was. Only the hand of God should alter things out of their natural paths.

Looking at these three, he knew that distinction was lost on them. He tried to keep his face impassive but felt his lip curl slightly in disgust. Of course Luc was still completely dissolute. Where were this week's women? Usually he had two or three hanging off him.

And Richard.

Richard was the embodiment of the hand of God, put on earth to humble Marcel and remind him of his all-too-human weaknesses. To hate someone as deeply as he hated Richard, to be stirred to violence at just the sight of him—these were tragic character flaws that Marcel had spent decades trying to improve.

Without success.

"Marcel," said Luc. He held out a hand. "Sorry you got brought back like that. Daedalus is having another lust-for-power banquet. You and Claire were the appetizer."

Marcel forced himself to shake Luc's hand.

"Luc."

"I got in Thursday," Claire said. She fished a crumpled pack of cigarettes out of her big, lumpy purse and lit one.

"Tobacco," Marcel said. "Satan's agent. Slavery, cancer, corporate lies, deliberate poison—it all stems from the tobacco industry."

"Glad you've lightened up," Luc muttered.

Claire looked at Marcel and blew smoke away from them, out the side of her mouth. "Marcel, honey, you must have missed the memo. There is no Satan. No Satan, no hell. We've got la *Déesse*, le Dieu, the life force that exists in everything. We've got ourselves and our free will. You can't pretend to believe different."

"I don't believe different," Marcel said. "I *know* different. There's the one true God, his Holy Son, the Holy Spirit.

And there is surely Satan and surely hell." He'd seen both, close-up.

Claire let out a deep breath. "Okay. Tomato, tomahto. Anyway, we've been talking about possible ways to kill Daedalus." Her face brightened, and Luc smiled again. "Got any ideas?"

"If I had, I would have used them long ago, before I committed my soul to God. But not necessarily on Daedalus."

From the corner of his eye, he saw Richard's muscles tense. Looking at him straight on, Marcel saw a mirror of his own hatred and resentment.

Luc sighed and rolled his eyes.

"Dammit!" Claire smacked him in the chest with her fist, surprising him. She looked back and forth between him and Richard furiously. "Damn both of you! That was 250 years ago! Get *over* it! Get over *her!* You stupid jackasses! Just let it *go!*" Some people walking by stopped to watch the spectacle unfolding.

Richard and Luc looked as surprised as Marcel felt. Claire had always been a drama queen, but she'd never spoken to them like this before. Pain and heartache bored her, she'd said. She'd rather just have fun.

She spoke again, her voice low and trembling with anger. "You're both so *stupid*, so *blind*. Centuries later, and she's still squeezing your hearts. Cerise was a sweet girl—she didn't deserve what happened to her. Goddess knows we've been playing out the tragedy ever since. But you two are the most single-minded idiots I've ever—you're *pathetic*, both of you. Poor Marcel. Poor Richard. Lost their true love."

Marcel stepped back, stung, feeling blood burn his cheeks.

"All this time, it's always been Cerise, Cerise, Cerise," Claire went on. She seemed stone-cold sober now, her green eyes fiery. "You can't even *see* anyone else. You can't even *recognize* love—" She stopped abruptly, shutting her mouth like a trap. White-faced with anger, she glared at them for a second more, then rubbed her hand over her eyes. "I'm tired," she said. "I'm going back to Jules's."

Without another word she turned and crossed the street, heading away from the lights on Chartres Street. She seemed to be weaving a bit, and after a pause, Luc said, "I'll go with her, make sure she gets back."

Then he was gone, leaving Marcel and Richard facing each other. Marcel's head was spinning. What had Claire meant?

Richard was watching him steadily, but Marcel knew he was just as shaken.

"She's talking rot," he heard himself say. "She's drunk. As usual. Doesn't know what she's talking about."

Richard, barely two feet away, close enough to strangle, gave him an odd smile. "Claire always knows what she's talking about. She knows more than you and me put together. Despite everything you learned, being Melita's bitch half your life."

Pain stabbed Marcel's heart so strongly he almost gasped.

He actually staggered, one hand on his chest, and leaned against the crumbling stucco of the Napoleon House. Several people glanced at him in alarm, but they faded away, out of his sight. All he could see was Richard's face, that hateful, beautiful angel's face that Cerise hadn't been able to resist.

"How did you—" he choked. "Who else knows? How could you—"

But Richard only gave him another small, tight smile, then turned and walked away.

✦ Chapter Twenty-Three

Clio

ANOTHER SLEEPLESS NIGHT. I WAS EXHAUSTED
to my bones—this day had been endless, and the evening horrible. Every time I closed my eyes, I saw my Camry billowing
black smoke toward the sky.

*Okay, okay, Clio, think. Think it all through. Someone is trying
to kill you or Thais—again.* The more I thought about Thais's
theory about Melita, the less ridiculous it seemed. Sure, it was
a stretch, but none of this made sense anyway. The only reason
I could think of for anyone wanting me or Thais out of the way
was if the *two* of us made more than a full Treize. Daedalus
needed a full Treize—but no more—for the rite. Someone
needed one of us gone before the rite. As much as I was drawn
to working with Hermann Parfitte's book, as much as I needed
to know how to control the rite's power, still, I needed to know
who was behind the attacks *more*.

If we knew that, then other things would fall into place.

At least, I hoped so.

Okay. Now I knew what I needed to do. I got out of bed

and walked quietly into Thais's room. She was deeply asleep, her layered black hair in an aura around her head. Kneeling next to the bed, I shook her shoulder.

"Thais," I said softly. "Thais, wake up."

She stirred, then blinked, then startled. Her eyes focused on me, and she instantly looked alarmed. "What is it? Are you okay?" Sitting up, she looked at me anxiously.

"Hi," I whispered. "Sorry to wake you. But I need you for something."

"What?" She rubbed her eyes, still looking worried. "What's wrong?"

"I'll explain on the way," I said. "First we have to steal Nan's car."

• • •

No one did stiff disapproval better than Thais. I had to hand it to her. She was much better than Nan, even.

Now she sat next to me in the front seat of Nan's Volvo. The only time she'd uncrossed her arms had been to eat a McBiscuit.

"Since I'm going to get hanged when we go back, can you fill me in on what my crime is going to be?"

"Yeah. Right now we're going to a safe place so we can do a spell," I explained. "Last night—was it only last night? God. Last night someone blew up my—our—car. It convinced me that the most important thing right now is to find out who's trying to kill us. When we know that, we can figure out how to protect ourselves from them *and* figure out how it relates to the rite. We can't even plan what to do in the rite until we know who's behind the attacks."

I glanced at her, jotting a mental note to avoid ever making that face.

Thais let out a heavy breath and looked out her window. "The rite."

"Yes."

"Where you want us to become immortal."

"Yes. Thais, I've thought and thought about it. We can't die. We have to go on living, like this, young and beautiful and healthy. Think of everything we could do with all that time to do it in."

"Yeah, and it's worked out so well for the Treize," she said sarcastically. "They're the poster children for mental health and stability."

"We're different. We're choosing this on purpose. We have goals for ourselves, our lives. They weren't prepared."

"I'm not prepared either."

I stayed quiet, letting her wrap her mind around the idea. Several miles later, she finally spoke.

"I've thought about it. I just don't know. I think the rite is going to kill someone, like it killed Cerise."

"Not if we know who to protect ourselves against," I pointed out. "Not if we're strong. Not if we're the ones controlling it."

She shook her head, looking out her window. Her face was troubled, reluctant. "We're just going to set something on fire again," she said.

"Not if we're in the middle of a river," I said.

• • •

"They don't make floating cups?" Thais asked unenthusiastically.

"No. But we can do this without the four element cups," I said. We were waist-deep in a small river close to the town of Abita Springs. The water was red and cold, mostly clear. Where we were, the river was about forty feet wide. I wished Racey were with us—remembering what had happened the other times that Thais and I had made magick together didn't reassure me. But Nan hadn't been able to figure out who was trying to hurt us, and now my fricking *car* had been blown up.

"Maybe we should talk about this some more," Thais said, eyeing my supplies.

"Look, we have to do this," I said. "Once we know who's trying to kill us, we'll be able to focus on the rite, and becoming immortal." I realized what I'd said—how bizarre my words were, and how they actually made sense in the craziness of our lives—and laughed.

"You must have been a fun child," said Thais.

I laughed again, glad we were together, that it was daylight, that we were far away from anyone.

"Okay, we're standing in water, which is your element," I said. "So this should be good." Glancing at the sky, I saw that it was still clouded over. It didn't look like rain was near, though. The only candle I'd been able to find that would float was a goofy one in the shape of a yellow duck. I lit it, and then I dropped four stones in the water around us: one for the past, one for the future, one for now, and one for the problem. Thais and I held hands over the water, and I began to recite:

We walk in sunlight
Shadows follow us.
We are facing fire
We are standing beneath stone
We are underwater
A storm is coming toward us.
With these words reveal the signature
Give the shadow a face, a name
Show us who kindles fire against us
Who holds a stone over us
Who pulls us underwater
Who conjures a storm to destroy us.

I began my song. The last time I'd done a spell, I'd taken Q-tip's soul from him. That had been a huge and powerful spell, and this was another one. Beneath my nervousness and determination, I felt deeply tired and tainted. Maybe Melita had begun like this. I don't know where the thought came from, but it chilled me. I pushed it down and kept singing, closing my eyes, trying to concentrate.

Thais didn't join in, but I felt her power rising with mine, joining mine through our clasped hands. I actually *felt* her power—it had become tangible, stronger, since the last time we'd done a spell together.

Ideally, a photographic image would have popped up in

our minds, with a big yellow arrow pointing to the guilty party. But noooo. Magick doesn't work like that. You have to meet it halfway.

I sang for a while—I don't know how long. I was getting nothing and decided this was a bust. I quit singing and opened my eyes to tell Thais. She opened her eyes at the exact same time, and we stood looking at each other for a moment. In the next second, I was pulled into her eyes, the green striations like veins on a leaf. It was like sinking into a vortex, like a wormhole in a sci-fi movie. In the depths of her eyes, I started getting images.

There was the hazy outline of my car, like a smudged Polaroid. I saw a dark figure off in the distance, and somehow I knew its lips were moving, its hands making motions, but I couldn't tell if it was a man or a woman.

I saw my car explode into flames again, and I winced. Like a fuzzy old movie, I saw myself, a blurred stick figure, jump out of the car and run away, and I felt someone's dark pangs of disappointment that I hadn't died.

It made my blood boil.

More images flowed. I saw Thais sitting on a streetcar, saw a red pickup fly soundlessly through the air, snapping a light pole in slow motion. Inside the streetcar, Thais got to her feet and moved out of the pole's way, seconds before it would have impaled her.

Was Thais seeing this? I blinked several times, trying to retreat to see her, but I couldn't—my spell had unlocked this knowledge, and it had to spool out until it was finished.

I was sleeping in bed—no, it was Thais, sleeping. Her sheet twisted thickly and coiled around her neck. She began choking, flailing, trying to pull it off. It must have been so terrifying. . . . Next Thais and I were standing in front of our house under the streetlight. A huge dark cloud engulfed us, and I grimaced, remembering the searing pain of the thousands of wasp stings that had almost killed us.

Next I got to relive that skuzzy guy pulling a knife on me in the alley in the Quarter. I felt the fear all over again, the cold pounding of my heart, my numb lips as I tried to summon a spell. Luc had run up, right afterward.

Had it been Luc, all along?

The images got smaller, farther away, and I thought, *no,* because I hadn't learned anything. Again I saw the same things happening, the streetcar, the wasps, the mugging—but now I saw another person on the edge of each scene, someone standing, watching, working the spells that called the danger to us. Who was it? *Reveal yourself!*

The figure sharpened, took on features, clothing . . . and I felt like I had been clubbed in the head with a brick. It was *Richard. Richard* watching the streetcar and feeling disappointed that Thais hadn't died. *Richard* summoning the wasps, watching them surround us, *Richard* working the spell to choke Thais with her sheet, *Richard* compelling that poor sap to attack me.

I couldn't breathe, couldn't get air. In my mind I saw

Richard and me tumbling on his bed, me pushing his shirt off, holding him tightly, holding his head and kissing him, wanting him, *burning* for him. He had tried to kill me and Thais, again and again.

Oh, God, I was going to be sick.

With a heaving gulp I fell backward, breaking the spell. I splashed down into the water. It closed over my head, but I forced my legs to straighten and righted myself, gagging and holding my stomach.

Thais grabbed my arm. "Are you okay?" She sounded near tears. "Did you see Richard?"

I was barely able to nod, trying to control the dry heaves that shook me.

"I can't believe it," Thais said. "I just can't believe it!"

"It's true," I choked. And then I felt a huge, dark presence well up behind me. A shadow fell on Thais's face, and she looked up. Her eyes widened and her mouth opened.

Turning, I saw today's version of our combined magick going ballistic: We'd created a waterspout, a tornado made of river water, and it was spinning at us with a hissing howl, faster than I'd ever seen something move.

In one second the twenty-foot cyclone of water swallowed us, gulping us greedily into its unnatural strength. I tried to hold on to Thais, to scream, to summon a spell to save us— but our hands were wrenched apart. The last thing I saw was Thais's pale, terrified face, whirling away from me in the side of the cyclone.

✦ Chapter Twenty-Four

The Bottom of It

SOMETHING WAS WRONG.

Petra awoke in an instant, as she always did. Unconsciously she cast her senses throughout the house and yard, taking a quick reading of her world.

The twins weren't here. She couldn't detect their vibrations anywhere in the house or yard.

A glance at her clock said six forty-five. On a Sunday, she could count on Clio sleeping in till ten. Leaping up, Petra began muttering reveal spells that would show if someone had lured them away magickally. Two minutes later she knew that they had left of their own accord not too long before, and that they had taken *her car*. And would be grounded until they were in their late twenties.

She grabbed the phone as she pulled on some baggy gardener's pants. "Ouida? I need your help."

• • •

"This way?" Melysa looked to the right.

Ouida nodded, her eyes vacant. She and Petra sat in the

backseat, holding hands. Together their concentration was revealing the twins' route, all the way to Abita Springs. Abita Springs! What were they up to? Petra's mouth set in a grim line. She knew it wasn't good. They weren't over here at a pick-your-own pumpkin patch.

Melysa turned to the right and headed down a narrow, barely paved road.

"A river," Petra murmured, seeing it in her mind. Then she and Ouida sat up straight at the same time.

"Oh, goddess," Ouida breathed.

• • •

She heard it before she saw it. As she, Ouida, and Melysa crashed through the woods toward the river, Petra heard a high wailing sound, like a train engine. The closer they got to the river, the more leaves and twigs whipped through the air. They tangled in Melysa's hair and scratched Petra's face.

"Is it a tornado?" Melysa called over the rising sound.

Then they saw it: a muddy waterspout spinning its way across the river toward the shore. Its sides were blotched with dark objects, pieces of driftwood, a snake, some fish. And the merest glimpse of a pale face, pale arms pinned to the wall of water.

Instantly the three witches flung their arms out and began shouting a dissipation spell. Each one used a version unique to herself, but the forms were the same, and they all had the same goal. Petra felt every muscle in her body quiver with magick as she called on a deeper power than she had used in decades.

"Water, lie down in your bed!" she commanded, holding out her wand. Electricity crackled around her, though she couldn't see it. Behind her Ouida and Melysa were chanting and drawing sigils in the air. "Water, lie down in your bed!" Petra shouted, feeling as if her magick was going to sweep her up into its arms and fling her into the air.

Then it stopped. The waterspout fell all at once, smashing down into the river. Two human figures lay crumpled in shallow water, twenty yards away. Petra raced toward them, already calling on healing powers.

She reached Thais first and dragged her up onto land. The girl was unconscious but breathing. Ouida raced up and took over while Petra splashed into the river to get Clio. Clio's eyes fluttered, and she raised her head weakly, but she collapsed again and would have gone under if Petra hadn't grabbed her arms. Melysa supported Clio's other side, and together they dragged her onto the small sandy shore. In addition to the spells they were muttering, they pounded the girls firmly on their backs. At last the twins started coughing and gagging up water.

"They look like drowned rats," Melysa muttered, wiping Thais's hair away from her face.

Clio's eyes opened blearily and she looked around, trying to orient herself.

Petra held Clio's head in her lap, stroking her hair. "Clio, are you all right?"

Clio blinked several times, finally placing where she was and what had happened. "Thais?" she said hoarsely.

"Will be fine," said Ouida, kneeling in the sand next to her. "*What* were you two *doing?*"

"I'm sorry, Nan," Clio croaked, struggling to sit up. Petra helped her, supporting her back. Her anger had been tempered by the girls' danger and her relief at their safety.

"I'm sorry we took your car without asking. But we had to know who was trying to hurt us. I had to know who blew up my *car.*" Clio's eyes were brighter and her voice stronger. Petra recognized Clio's sense of outrage and knew that it wasn't in her personality to take anything lying down.

"You almost got yourselves killed!" Petra said. "Did you cause this, or was this another attack?"

"Flip a coin," Thais said weakly, also sitting up. Her face was still pale, and she had an ugly bruise already developing on one shoulder.

"I'm not sure," said Clio, looking thoughtful. "I thought we had done it, putting our magick together. But I guess it's possible. . . ." Suddenly her eyes flared, and her face looked furious. "It was Richard, Nan!" She grabbed Petra's arm and shook it. "It was Richard! Richard who's been trying to kill us! We saw it!"

"*What?*" Petra was shocked. Of all the people she'd suspected, none of them had been Richard.

Thais nodded, getting stiffly to her feet. She had sand in her hair and dripping off her clothes. "It's true, if that spell worked. We saw him casting the spells, waiting to see what happened. *Richard.*" She sounded angry and sad, but Clio sounded truly incensed, as if she took the news more personally.

Petra met Ouida's eyes. Ouida looked as shocked as Petra felt.

"*Richard,*" Ouida repeated, amazed.

Grimly, Petra got to her feet and helped Clio stand. "Richard. I'm surprised, but I can't say it's completely unthinkable. But this ends *now*. Melysa, can you drive the girls back home? And stay with them till I get back? Do not let them out of your sight, okay?"

Melysa nodded solemnly. "Yes. Ouida, are you coming with me or going with Petra?"

"I need to see Richard alone, I think," Petra said, brushing sand off her wet canvas pants.

"I'm sure we'll be okay," Clio began. "We don't need a babysitter. We'll be fine—"

Petra gave her a piercing glare. "You will stay *home* with Melysa until I get back. You will not leave the house, not even to take the *garbage* out, which by the way you forgot to do yesterday. You will not be taking anyone's *car* without permission, you will not *leave* Melysa's side, or I will slap you with a homing spell so strong you'll live out the rest of your life in your *rooms*. Understand?"

"I can stay with them too," Ouida offered. "Until noon, anyway."

A mulish look crossed Clio's face as she weighed Petra's words. She must have realized that Petra was dead serious because she shrugged her shoulders ungraciously and said, "Whatever."

The five of them started to trudge back to their cars. Petra couldn't believe she almost lost the girls today. In their head-strong *stupidity*. She walked closer to Clio and put her arm around the girl's shoulders. "I don't want you hurt."

"I know."

"I can't believe it's Richard. But I'll get to the bottom of this, I promise."

Clio looked up at her and gave a tiny smile. "Okay."

"I just can't imagine—" Petra thought out loud. "I wonder . . . does it have something to do with you two looking like Cerise?"

Next to her, Clio stopped in her tracks. "We look like Cerise?"

"Yes, of course. Didn't you see her in your visions?"

"I told you that," Thais said. "We look just like Cerise, we saw it in our vision."

Clio shook her head slowly. "Not clearly enough to see her face. It was dark and rainy."

"I saw her," Thais said. "And we do look like her, except she was blonde."

Petra saw the two girls exchange a look.

"I'm sorry," she told Clio, continuing on to her car. "I thought you knew that." As always, her heart felt pained at the memory of the night she lost her last two remaining children.

"How much alike?" Clio asked.

"Exactly," Petra said sadly, opening her car door. "You two look exactly like Cerise, but with black hair. But other than that, spitting image."

Ouida nodded, looking sympathetic. "She was a beautiful girl, as you two are. Clio, you get in the front seat with Melysa. Thais and I will ride in the back."

Petra watched her girls get bundled into Melysa's car. Melysa had thought to bring large beach towels, and now she made sure the twins were wrapped up warmly. Petra followed Melysa's car all the way back to New Orleans until Melysa took the Carrollton exit off the highway, and Petra continued on to the French Quarter.

✦ Chapter Twenty-Five

When They Had Met

EACH DAY WAS A BLESSING. EACH DAY WHEN HE opened his eyes, whether it was sunny, rainy, clammy, or freezing, he was glad to be alive. It hadn't always been that way.

Jules got up out of his single bed and stretched. It was raining lightly—he heard it pattering against the roof. The floor beneath his feet was cool—could autumn really be showing her face? He moved quietly like a cat into the bathroom, glancing into the front room as he did. Claire was asleep on the couch, in her clothes. He'd heard her come in early this morning, heard Luc put her to bed. She hadn't changed her ways. She never would.

It was strange, really, how little any of them had changed over such a long period of time. Not only had they been frozen in age, but in their personalities too. You'd think that over almost 250 years, at least some of them would have undergone huge changes, but none of them ever really had. Certainly not him.

Back in the kitchen he put the kettle on to make coffee.

Claire would want some when she woke up. The small window over his kitchen sink had an uninspiring view of the brick fence next door, covered with fig ivy. In the front room, Claire stirred, shifting position, curling up almost like a child on the narrow futon couch. She'd teased him about his meager surroundings. Told him he still thought like a slave, after centuries of freedom. He admitted it was true. Slavery, like a broken love affair, was not something one ever really got over.

In the kettle, the water made a rough purring sound. It was about to boil. He got out the sugar cubes, knowing Claire usually took three.

In some ways, it seemed just a short while ago that he had met her.

He'd run away from the tobacco farmer who had owned him. He'd been beaten badly, and his hands were manacled, but he'd escaped. He'd wandered for days, moving as he could, though in the end it was hardly moving. Crawling. He reached a swamp and was only five feet into it when he fell, tripping on a hidden root, splashing down, hitting his head on another root. The world swirled, and he smiled, because now he was dying. They hadn't found him, and now they would find only a corpse. He almost laughed, thinking how mad they would be. The top of his head, his face, was barely out of the water. It was warm and pleasant. Surely it wouldn't take long now.

But—being dead couldn't hurt this much, could it? He was in so much pain it shocked him. The bumping, the jolting . . . he forced himself to open his eyes. *Please let me be dead. Please,*

please let me see nothing, see the white men's angels, see devils, see anything but—

Trees. Above him were trees. It was barely light out, but whether it was dawn or twilight he couldn't tell. He was being dragged somewhere. He was alive. Tears escaped his eyes and rolled down the drying mud on his face. A rolling boom of thunder made him tremble, and then warm rain was pelting him through the trees.

A face looked back at him. A white face, with orange hair and blue eyes. A boy. The boy was dragging him on a plank, over the ground. The boy would take him back to the farm, turn him in, collect his ten dollars.

Crying, he'd raised his hands to his face, but the manacles were heavy and he banged himself in the nose. The white boy looked back at him, then rested the plank on the ground and came to kneel by his head. He tried to stop crying, tried to look brave, like a man, but he wasn't a man—he had no name.

The white boy spoke in French. "Vous pourriez vous récupérer," he said in a soft voice. "Dans ma ville. Ce n'est pas loin. Calmez-vous."

Those words made no sense.

That had been Marcel, who'd found him in the swamp, dying, and fashioned a travois out of a plank and dragged him three miles to Ville Du Bois. Twelve-year-old Marcel turned him over to Petra, the healer. Jules burned with fever for a week, hallucinating, rigid with terror. Petra made him teas and soups, some bitter, some not. She washed the swamp mud off him, put salve on all his injuries. The smith came and broke the manacles off his hands.

"Vous vous appellez Jules," Petra murmured one night, late, just after his fever had broken. "Nous allons vous appeller Jules maintenant."

A dark-haired man came in. Armand. He explained things to Jules in English. And when Jules recovered, as Marcel had said he would, he stayed there in the Ville Du Bois, living as one of them, as a person, for the first time in his life. It was a hidden paradise. Jules never ventured far from the village—misery and pain waited outside. He never wanted to leave—everyone was so kind. M. Daedalus taught him to read and write. Everyone, even the children, helped teach him the natural religion, the *Bonne Magie*. It fell into place in his life like tumblers in a lock, being set into place with the right key.

One day, some ten years after he arrived, he talked to Claire for the first time. He knew what the village said about her—she had loose skirts—but it wasn't like back in the other world, where she would have gotten beaten or exiled.

Jules was walking home, a string of catfish over his shoulder. As he walked, he murmured a litany of thanks for everything he had, everything he saw around him, every scrap of happiness he felt. He gave thanks for all of it, as often as he could.

Not far from the village, he heard voices raised in anger. Several more steps showed him Claire and a young man—Etienne somebody—arguing.

Claire slapped Etienne with her free hand. Fury washed Etienne's face with an ugly red hue, and he raised his fist above her head. Just as he was sweeping it down, Jules grabbed it from behind.

"Now, now," Jules said, keeping his own anger firmly locked away, "you know we don't hit women."

"Mind your own business, old man!" Etienne snapped.

"This is my business," Jules said. His strong fingers pried Etienne's hand off of Claire's arm, and she fell to the ground, then scrambled to her feet. "I'm stopping you from making a mistake that will haunt your soul. You know the threefold law."

Etienne sneered. "That's only for magick, old fool!"

"No," Jules said, shaking his head. "It's for everything, all the time."

"You'd best let me go," Etienne snarled. "And continue on your way. This is between me and my girl."

"I'm not your girl!" Claire said.

"You're everybody's girl." The disdain on Etienne's face pained Jules. The younger man turned back to him. "Last warning. You let me go now, or—" He showed Jules his clenched fist.

"I'm not a girl you can threaten, boy," Jules said mildly. "And my fist is bigger than yours."

It was almost twice as big, in fact; Jules was a much bigger man than most of the villagers—the little French people, as he thought of them.

Etienne looked at Jules's huge fist, with its fingers that had been broken and not set properly. He looked at Jules's face, which was not mean but iron-hard. Jules saw the moment when the boy realized that Jules was maybe seven inches taller and had about fifty pounds on him.

The fight faded from the younger man. The fight, but not the fury.

"Have it your way," he spit, and wrenched his hand loose.

"I'll be upset if I hear you've bothered this young lady again," Jules said.

"She's no lady," Etienne tossed over his shoulder.

It deserved no response.

"Are you all right?"

Claire nodded. "Thank you." She seemed embarrassed and unsure of herself, very different from the brash, flirtatious girl Jules saw around the village.

They began walking together.

"It's a shame our paradise is marred by one like him," Jules said.

"Paradise!" Claire stared at him. "You mean prison! I would give anything to leave! In fact—Etienne had promised to take me to New Orleans if I lay with him. But he was lying."

"This village is the last Eden on earth," Jules said seriously. "The world out there is full of pain."

He saw her glancing at his scars from when he'd been whipped, back on the farm.

"I'm smothering here, day by day," Claire said. "I've got to get out." She stopped in the path and looked at him, her eyes clear and without guile. "If you ever leave here, take me with you."

He almost lost his breath. What was she saying?

Oh. That she wanted someone to protect her on the way or a mule or horse to ride if he had one.

"I won't be leaving, mamzelle," he said gruffly. "You take care now." He split off from the path and followed another way to his own little house, his sanctuary.

"Hey."

Jules jumped as Claire shuffled up and reached for a coffee cup. It was now, again, and the memories of then twisted away like leaves in a breeze.

"Time is it?" she mumbled, pouring coffee.

"Not quite noon."

Her magenta hair smelled like cigarette smoke. She had four small silver rings in her left ear. Jules was thankful she'd let her brow piercing heal over.

"How was it last night?" Jules asked.

Claire shrugged, leaning against the kitchen counter. "All right. Ran into Marcel."

"Then Daedalus will want to convene the Treize soon, now that you two are here."

Claire's face looked bleak as she sipped her coffee. "Yep."

Chapter Twenty-Six

Clio

I LAY ON MY BED, MY WET HAIR MAKING MY T-shirt soggy. Thais and I had both had hot showers, and Melysa and Ouida had made us valerian and catnip tea. Now I lay on my bed, feeling Melysa and Thais's presence downstairs.

Richard was the one who'd been trying to kill us. Richard, who I'd jumped just two days ago and practically slept with. *How could he?* He had actually tried to *kill* me. *And* sleep with me. He was a total *psychopath*. It was terrifying—especially since I hadn't seen it in him, hadn't felt it. Hadn't seen it in his eyes or felt it in his touch. What was wrong with me that I hadn't picked up on it? The same thing with Luc—they had been both pursuing me and simultaneously betraying me. The two of them.

What was wrong with me? Here's what was worse: Knowing Richard had tried to kill us made me feel pretty murderous myself. And goddess knew Luc was still on my forget-it list. *Yet*—I still wondered what was wrong with me that they didn't just love me. Which was so twisted and pathetic and unhealthy that I started bawling all over again, pressing my face into my pillow so no one would hear.

Luc had wanted me because I was the missing part of Thais. He'd *loved* Thais. Petra wondered if Richard trying to kill us had anything to do with our looking like Cerise, whom he had loved. Did he not see me as Clio, but only as a modern version of Cerise?

I almost cried myself sick, working through half a box of tissues, crying until my guts felt twisted and raw. How many times was I going to cry over guys? It had already been too many.

Another question: When could I escape to go confront Richard myself? Because I was going to rip his lungs out. Somehow I didn't feel afraid of him now or worry about what he might do next. It was like knowing who it was had granted me immunity from his attacks. I was burning with fury, itching to take it out on him. As soon as I got a chance.

✦ Chapter Twenty-Seven

Someone Unseen

DAEDALUS OPENED HIS EYES SLOWLY. THE SKY
had clouded over significantly in the hour since he'd started his
spell. The sounds of the swamp were intensifying as twilight
neared—animals were foraging, birds going on the hunt—he
was making magick. The palm of his right hand tingled, and
even before Daedalus looked, he knew what he would see there:
a small, glowing green orb that hovered right above his skin.

It had worked.

He'd never done this spell before—he'd found the form
in an ancient text at the Oxford Library in England. It had
been mistranslated from old Persian, and Daedalus had hired
a modern scholar to retranslate it. His hunch had paid off. As
far as he knew, no one had manifested a locator orb before, not
in centuries.

"Go," he whispered. "Find the Circle of Ashes."

Fifteen minutes later, it did.

Once again Daedalus stood inside the charred circle that
was such a visceral reminder of that night so long ago. The

night of creation and destruction. Now he had a full Treize, the circle, the rite. He was ready, at last, after centuries of waiting.

His goal had been achieved, but he knew that others had helped him get here. Jules, through the years, Axelle, others. And lately, someone unseen had helped him. Someone who would possibly rejoin the Treize, rendering one of the twins superfluous.

✦ Chapter Twenty-Eight

The Endless Cycle

BY THE TIME PETRA GOT TO RICHARD AND Luc's apartment, she was nursing a deep, smoldering rage.

Richard answered the door, wearing ragged jeans too big for him and an unbuttoned, faded denim shirt.

"Hi," he began, but Petra stepped forward and slapped him across the face as hard as she could. He staggered backward, taken completely off guard, and almost fell against the hallway wall.

"Are you *nuts?*" he exclaimed, one hand over his cheek. He straightened quickly, but not before Petra hauled off and smashed her fist into his ribs. "Ow! Stop it, you crazy old bat!"

Now totally alert, Richard danced away from her.

"I'm going to skin you!" Petra hissed, advancing on him. "And then I'll sew you back into it! You lying *bastard!* You son of a *bitch!* You murdering monster!" Belatedly, Petra had the fervent hope that Clio's vision hadn't been wrong.

"Uh, *what?*" He sounded incredulous, staring at her, still with his hand to his face.

"The twins' spell finally worked," Petra spit out, trying to corner him. "They *saw* you, you bastard! *Saw* you watching the streetcar, summoning the wasps, blowing up Clio's car! It was *you* all along, you bastard! You tried to kill *Clio!* Clio is my child! I raised her! And Thais, an innocent! They're *my* family! And you stood there and *lied* to me, said they were safe! Said you wouldn't hurt them! You're lucky I don't strike you down where you stand!" She raised one hand in the air, as if to call down a spell that would split him in half.

Richard backed away and held up both hands, ready to ward her off. "I didn't blow up Clio's car," he said quickly. "What are you talking about?"

"Oh, good, look concerned," Petra sneered. "Last night Clio's car exploded. Congrats. Your spell worked. But you must know that."

"Her car explo— Is she okay?"

"You do surprised concern very well." Petra's voice sounded like acid dripping. "You missed your calling—you should have gone onstage."

"Is she all right?" Richard's face was stony.

"I'm sure it's a disappointment for you."

Richard stepped forward and grabbed both of Petra's arms, his grip biting into her. "Is. She. All. Right?"

Petra looked at him. This was weird, even for a murderous, lying, son of a bitch. "She jumped out a split second before the whole thing went up in flames."

He released her and stepped back, rubbing his fingers

across his forehead. "So she's okay. And it wasn't an accident?"

"What are you playing at?" Petra exclaimed. "Of course it wasn't a bloody accident! You know it wasn't!"

"I didn't do it," he said strongly, looking at her.

"They *saw* you," Petra said. "The twins did a spell, and they saw you do those things."

"They didn't see me blow up the car, because it wasn't me."

"You're saying you didn't almost impale Thais on a light pole, didn't summon the wasps, didn't send a guy to mug Clio?" Going through the litany made her anger burn again.

"I'm saying I didn't blow up Clio's car yesterday."

Petra looked at him, the tight line of his body, his shuttered face, the tattoo she could see on his chest. She shook her head. "You've lost me. You didn't do the car, but you did the other things?"

He frowned and moved away from her, walking down the hallway to the kitchen. His tan feet were bare and made no sound on the wooden floor. She followed him.

"If I'd brought my athème, I would be cutting out your liver now."

He shot her a glance as he filled a dishtowel with ice. "You've become unexpectedly bloodthirsty in your old age, Petra." He held the towel to his cheek, wincing slightly. "Bloodthirsty and weirdly strong." He moved to a cupboard and got down a glass. There was a new bottle of scotch on top of the fridge and he filled the tumbler half full. "I'd offer you some, but—"

"I'd only spit it in your face." There was something off here, but Petra couldn't put her finger on it.

Richard took a swallow of the liquor, not even wincing when it went down. "I didn't do the car. But I did the other things."

In her deepest heart, Petra had hoped that somehow the girls were wrong, that Richard hadn't been behind the attacks. He'd always been in her heart, from the time he was a boy. She'd felt his pain over Cerise and knew what a bad deal he'd gotten out of the rite. For him to have done this—it broke her heart.

"You did the other things." Her knees felt weak, and she sat abruptly in an aluminum kitchen chair.

Richard pulled out another chair and sat down across from her. "I did those things before I knew the twins. I wanted them dead."

"In the name of the goddess, *why?*"

He stared into the bottom of his glass. "When Daedalus called me here, I didn't know what was going on. Then he told me about the twins. I knew you'd had Clio—I saw her when she was just a little kid. But twins—as soon as I knew there were two, I wanted to get rid of them."

"You didn't want a full Treize."

"Hell no, I didn't want a full Treize! Why would I? So some other horror could take place? What would it be this time?"

"You think the rite would be worse than your killing inno-cent children?" Petra didn't drink—maybe a sip or two of wine every once in a great while. But she would have welcomed a sherry right then. She let out a heavy sigh, feeling tired and discouraged. "Why didn't you come talk to me?"

Richard scoffed. "Yeah. 'Hey, Petra, is it okay if I off those kids?'"

"I could have helped you come up with another way. I thought you wanted to do the rite."

He made an impatient gesture. "I don't need more power—I don't use what I have. Maybe if the rite would make me age naturally, or die, then I might go for it. But it's just going to be Daedalus's power grab."

Petra sat and thought for several minutes. Something else was going on, something he wasn't telling her. "Or is it because the twins look so much like Cerise?"

His dark eyes flicked up to meet hers. "Oh, do they?" he said woodenly.

"Is seeing them painful for you? Are you still angry at Cerise for not choosing you?"

"Cerise did choose me," Richard said, and drained his glass. "Yes, Thais and Clio look like Cerise, eerily like her. But once I got to know them—they don't actually remind me of her very much at all. They're—really different."

"Yes, they are." Petra twined her hands together. "What do you mean, Cerise chose you? You said the same thing the other day, that she hadn't rejected you. What are you talking about? Everyone knew Marcel was sparking her, and she got pregnant, for God's sake! You couldn't court her, not really. You were too—young."

Pain flashed across his face but was gone in an instant. When he looked up again, he had that oddly knowing, adult expression that he'd had even at fifteen, more than two hundred years ago.

"I wasn't too young," he said. "I was too young to marry her, couldn't support her. But I wasn't too young to spark her, and I wasn't too young to get her pregnant. Cerise's baby was mine."

"No." Petra frowned, thinking back.

"Yes. It's true that she was with Marcel," he went on, his face twisting with bitterness. "But she'd been lying with me for six months before. She was already pregnant when she was first with him." He got up quickly and poured himself more scotch. Petra wanted to take it from him and give him something else but knew better than to try.

"It was your child?" Petra was awash with emotions, memories, old pain, healed wounds. "You're—quite sure?"

He laughed bitterly. "Oh, yeah."

"Then what was she doing with Marcel? He hoped to marry her!"

Shrugging, Richard sat down again, pulling his shirt closed around him, as if cold. "I don't know. I thought I'd die when I found out. She just scolded me for being jealous. Maybe she felt sorry for him. Maybe she wanted to thank him for everything he was doing for you all, your family. After Armand left. Maybe she really cared about him. I don't know."

"Both of you." Petra shook her head. How much she

hadn't known about her daughters. Had she been blind? Stupid? Or just too wrapped up in her own unhappiness and disappointment to see what was happening in front of her nose?

"Yeah. Both of us. Never at the same time, though."

Petra winced.

"Sorry," he said, shaking his head. "She was your daughter, and she was a good daughter. But goddess, it was hard, loving her. Knowing it was my child she carried, and her still dallying with that stiff, stuck-up fool—and then she died. And I couldn't even claim the baby."

"Why didn't Marcel?"

"He knew I would kill him if he tried." Richard gave a little smile and drank.

"So he thought the child was yours?"

"I think he hoped it wasn't. He knew I was in the picture, though. Cerise never kept either of us secret from the other."

Standing up, Petra went to get a glass and filled it with tap water. She leaned against the sink and looked at him. "And how does this tie in to the twins?"

Richard sighed and rested his head in his hands. It was several minutes before he spoke. "After the rite, we all split apart, right after. Melita disappeared that night, and Marcel within days. All of us split away from the ville, and my daughter went to live with the Dedouards. I planned to get back to the village when she was old enough to take with me. *But then I didn't age.* I didn't become a grown-up, on the outside, at least.

So I only kept tabs on her from a distance. I kept in touch with some people, and they let me know how Hélène was. I watched her grow up from a distance. Grow up and get married and get pregnant and die."

Petra nodded sadly.

"They always die," Richard said.

Petra could tell he was trying to sound cold and distant.

"Daughter after daughter of that line—they always die. I just—want it to stop."

She could barely hear his voice.

"If the twins died now, they wouldn't give birth, and that line would end," Petra said. "Is that what you mean? We'd never have to feel the pain of another daughter dying."

His nod was barely imperceptible, and he drained his second glass. An ordinary man would have no liver left by now.

"And you were willing to commit murder for that."

"I didn't know them. I freaked about Daedalus wanting to do the rite. I don't know—it was like I went crazy for a while. But—also. I couldn't follow through. I mean, I'm not Daedalus, but I know my way around a spell. If I'd really, truly had wanted them dead, they'd be dead. My spells always had an out."

Petra glared at him. "And that makes it okay?"

"Petra." He gave a bitter laugh and shook his head. "Of course not. It will never be okay. Nothing will ever be okay for any of us, ever again. But bottom line, I didn't kill the twins. And I quit trying after the wasps."

"What about my house catching on fire?"

"Wasn't me."

"Clio's car didn't just explode on its own."

"I didn't do it. Petra, I know them now. They're . . . nice kids. I truly regret trying to harm them, and I stopped as soon as it got through to me that they were . . . real. I'm sorry."

"I can't ever trust you again."

Richard looked sad. "I was never that trustworthy to begin with."

"No—you were unreliable, but I did trust you. I trusted you not to hurt me or the people I love."

He was silent for a minute. "If you feel they're still under attack, then you need to figure out who's behind it, and fast. Amazingly, there are people who are even more ruthless than I am."

She looked at him. "If I find out you're lying now, if I find out that you're still trying to hurt those girls . . ."

"You'll cut out my liver with your athème, skin me alive, and sew me back into it, and what . . . oh, spit scotch in my face. Got it."

"I will make you pay for the rest of your life," she said, getting up. "And as you're all too aware that will be a very, very long time."

She left without looking back. Oddly, she pretty much believed him. Which meant someone else was now trying to hurt the twins.

✦ Chapter Twenty-Nine

Thais

"ARE YOU SURE YOU DON'T WANT A RIDE?" KEVIN asked me on Monday afternoon. He pointed to his car and looked hopeful.

"I would love one," I said. "But I can't. Maybe tomorrow?"

"Tomorrow," Kevin said. He came closer and put his hand on my shoulder, and I felt a comfortable excitement at his touch. "Can I call you later?"

"Of course," I said, and we kissed for just a moment, breaking away before the inevitable catcalls and teasing started. Kevin got in his car, and I headed for the streetcar stop.

Petra had put yet more layers of protective spells over me and Clio this morning before school. Last night she'd told us that Richard had confessed to everything up until the wasps, but that he swore he wasn't responsible for the house fire or Clio's car. Petra had believed him. Which meant we still had an unknown enemy.

Clio had been hoping that Petra wouldn't even let us go to school today, but she had. Clio told me Petra had always worried that if Clio missed too much school, social services would try to take her away. So Petra had given us a ride here this morning. I'd half expected her to be waiting for us after school, but I hadn't seen her car.

Which was just as well because I had no intention of going home right away. Apparently neither did Clio because she'd left with Racey and said she'd see me later.

The streetcar heading downtown came within a few minutes, and a crowd of students got on. I sat on a wooden seat, remembering the light-pole incident. Richard. It was unbelievable—sure, he seemed mysterious and kind of hard, but trying to kill us? I remembered the first few times I'd met him, how cold and weird he was. But the more I saw him, the more okay he'd seemed, and I'd been starting to like him as a friend. Petra had said he'd been determined for the rite not to happen, and that he had lost his head. He'd tried to hurt us before he'd gotten to know us, and now that he did, there was no way he could try to hurt us.

It just went to show, you never really knew anyone. Everyone lied, or left stuff out, or distorted things—especially everyone in the Treize. Even in my own family. Petra had lied to Clio about our dad. Axelle had lied to get me to come live with her. Even Clio had probably lied to me at some point about something.

But it was time to get some straight answers.

Now I knew it was Richard who'd been trying to kill us. I knew the whole Treize was here in New Orleans. I knew that

Clio and I would play a vital part in the rite—if we agreed to it. Now I needed to know how I had gotten here in the first place.

I got off the streetcar at Canal Street, crossed it, and headed into the French Quarter. It felt like I'd lived in New Orleans a long time. Like every day had a year's worth of emotions packed into it, so it was a lifetime ago that I'd lived in Connecticut and years since I'd lived with Axelle.

I'd never given Axelle her key back, and now I let myself in through the side gate. At the apartment door, I put my hand out, flat against the door, and closed my eyes.

I got nothing.

Wait—I concentrated hard and felt myself sink surprisingly quickly into a focused state of awareness, where I almost melded with the door, with things around me. Inside the apartment I felt Axelle. But no one else. Good.

Unlocking the door, I opened it into the familiar dim, smoke-filled entryway that led directly into the main room. A moment later Axelle walked out of her bedroom.

"Who's—Thais? How did you get in?"

I dangled the key from my hand. "I want some answers. And you're going to give them to me."

Axelle paused, looking confused. "Clio?"

I stared at her. "No. You can't tell us apart? I used to live with you!"

"Sorry." Axelle curled up in the black leather armchair, crossing her legs over one overstuffed arm. "I knew it was you.

But you seemed different. Just for a second. What's up?" She picked up her old-fashioned silver cigarette case and took one out, lighting it.

I came into the main room and dropped my backpack on the newspaper-littered floor. Axelle was probably missing her personal maid and cleaning service.

"I told you—I want some answers. Let's start with: Did you kill my father?"

Axelle looked startled. "This is out of the blue, isn't it? What's going on?"

"I'm just starting at the beginning. Believe me, we're going to get to more recent stuff." I felt very sure of myself, in control. It was unusual, but it also felt natural, like it had been inside me all the time and now was finally coming out. "Now, about my dad?"

Axelle shook her head briskly, swinging her silky black pageboy like a bell. "No, I didn't kill him. Absolutely not."

"So Daedalus did, then?" I asked with surface calm.

"He told me he didn't."

"Do you think he did?"

Axelle seemed to choose her next words carefully. "I'm not sure. I didn't think so at the time—I believed it was all coincidence. But now I'm not sure. It's possible."

Having my dad die in a freak accident had been the worst thing imaginable. Now, believing that he'd been killed—and I did think that Daedalus had killed him—the pain came rushing back at me with a fresh, razor-edged presence. My dad had been killed so that Daedalus could get to me for his own purposes. My dad had died because of me. In that moment, a small, sharp burning ignited inside me, deep in my chest.

"Okay then." I took in a deep, steady breath, trying to stay calm, not to jump up shrieking and wailing. "Next. What's a dark twin?"

Across the room, Axelle's eyes were as black as her hair, as black as the leather chair. Bottomless. "I haven't heard that phrase in a long time," she said slowly. "I think it's an old wives' tale. Where did you hear it?"

"What is it?"

Shrugging, Axelle said, "Well, it's a myth, really. It's when you have identical twins, one egg that splits apart. Instead of each half getting a mix of light and dark, one twin gets mostly light, and one gets mostly dark."

"So one twin is evil?"

"Not necessarily." Axelle thought, tapping one finger against her chin. "It's more like, that twin is more *likely* to go dark. But, I mean, no one really thinks it happens. Not really."

Petra does, I thought. *But which one of us is she worried about?*

"What's Daedalus up to, really? With this rite and the full Treize? Is he planning for one of us to die?"

"No." Axelle frowned. "I don't think so. It's never sounded like he expects anyone to die. Certainly not you or Clio. He was so thrilled about you two. He needs you both to complete the rite. There's no way he would harm one of you, the way Petra worries."

I was about to ask my last question when someone pounded on the apartment door. My breath stilled in my chest as I recognized those vibrations. *Luc. Oh, no.*

Axelle rose with languid grace and sauntered to the door. She opened it, and I caught a glimpse of Luc's dark shadow, followed by a smaller one. I forced myself back to the cool calm I'd been channeling with Axelle and raised my eyes to meet his.

He wasn't expecting to see me, and something lit for just a moment in his dark blue eyes. I clamped down on any response and knew I'd gotten all the answers out of Axelle that I would get. At least for today.

Axelle and someone else came into the room, and the other person gasped. I looked at her—her magenta hair, multipierced ears, the wild clothes. This must be Claire, I realized. She stared back at me, her hand over her mouth.

"Yes, they do look alike," Axelle said with dry humor. "I assume you two want a drink?"

"God, yes," Claire said with feeling. "It's pretty freaky."

I grabbed my backpack and stood up.

"I've seen maybe eight of that line," Claire went on, still looking at me. Axelle handed her a martini glass, and she took a big sip. *What was it with the Treize all being lushes,* I wondered. Because they didn't need to worry about killing themselves with alcohol? "They've all had the mark, the fleur-de-lis. But none of them has ever looked so—exact. Axelle? Did you ever see one like this?" She gestured at me with her drink.

"I'm standing right here. But go ahead and talk about me. It's okay." I couldn't remember ever being so snippy. I moved past Claire toward the front door, not looking at Luc. I hadn't gone four feet when there was a huge crack of lightning that polarized the room for a moment, and then an enormous boom of thunder that actually made my chest flutter.

Then the lights went out.

"Damn it," Axelle muttered. "Let me find a candle."

"I can't believe this still happens all the time," Claire said. "Talk about a third-world country."

I made out the dim outline of the door and headed for it again just as Luc's hand brushed my arm—I was inches from him. That barest touch set off a chain reaction, melting my icy shell. I stiffened, pulled my arm away, and moved past him.

"Where are you going?" His low voice still thrilled me, and I so hated it.

"Home." I opened the door and was blasted with sheets of rain and a bolt of lightning so close that I quickly stepped backward. Shoot. This was going to be so awful, slogging up to Canal Street to catch the streetcar. Well, I could duck into a shop or café and wait till it blew over. Getting me home even later. Petra was going to have a fit.

"Thais, wait till it lessens," Axelle said.

"How can she even stand lightning?" I heard Claire mutter. "I hate it."

"You can't go out in this." I felt Luc's heat behind me. What if I closed my eyes and leaned back, felt his arms come around me? God, I was such a jerk. Very nice, very nice to be thinking this when I had Kevin. I was *awful*—not only stupid, but disloyal.

Ignoring all of them, I stepped right out into it, and rain instantly washed over me, pelting my face and hair, gluing my shirt to me.

"I'll give you a ride." Luc turned to Axelle and Claire. "I'm giving Thais a ride to Petra's. I'll be right back."

"No you're not," I said, crossing the courtyard as fast as I could and getting to a momentary shelter under the covered driveway to the street. Luc caught up to me and touched my arm, and that motion and the rain and my jumbled thoughts added up to a powerful déjà vu of when he had first kissed me in our private garden. It sent pain jolting through me, like lightning, and I whirled, ready to snap his head off.

"Please," he said gently. He dropped his hands to his sides and looked at me. "I won't touch you again. I won't even talk to you if you want. But let me give you a ride home. My car is right there." He pointed through the wrought-iron gate at the street. "It's pouring—I can get you home in ten minutes."

I was suddenly so tired of keeping up my guard and my hurt against him. It took so much effort. I pushed my wet bangs out of my eyes, unwilling to think this through. "Fine," I said. "Whatever."

Luc walked quickly to the gate, as if he wanted to get me in his car before I came to my senses. The sidewalk was covered by the balcony overhead. Luc went ahead of me to unlock the passenger door—what a gentleman—and I followed him.

Jump!

Some sixth sense shouted that at me, and I obeyed instantly, leaping sideways, pushing Luc ahead of me. A split second later a heavy metal planter plummeted down right next to me, scraping my arm, and crashed onto the curb, spewing plants and dirt everywhere.

I stared at the planter. It must have weighed sixty pounds at least and would have cracked my head open if it had hit me. Luc and I were semi-sprawled across the hood of the car in back of us. His arms were around me, his face shocked, and he looked up at the balcony where the broken, twisted metal supports dangled from the balcony railing.

"Holy Mother!" Luc exclaimed. "Are you all right?"

"Uh . . ." I didn't know. I was so shaken. A dim stinging feeling made me look at my arm.

"My arm is scratched."

Luc pulled me farther into the street, standing next to me in the pouring rain, and looked up at the balcony. "That whole section is rusted through," he said. "It's amazing it hasn't fallen before. Let me see your arm."

"It's just a scratch," I said, not wanting him to touch me.

Adrenaline made me even shakier. I felt unsure of myself and just wanted to get home. "Well, I guess it wasn't Richard this time, anyway."

Luc's eyes narrowed. His face went still and cold. "What do you mean, not Richard?"

✦ Chapter Thirty

Clio

RACEY GAVE ME A RIDE DOWNTOWN AFTER I promised that Nan wouldn't turn her into a toad for aiding and abetting me.

"If she gives me a hard time, I'm going to take it out on you," Racey promised.

"Fair enough."

I had her drop me a couple blocks from Richard's so I'd have a few minutes to get a grip. Ever since Thais and I had recovered from almost drowning, I'd been dying to get my hands on Richard, and not in a good way. I was still reeling from our discovery. Inside I felt charred, hollowed out by betrayal and disappointment. Out of the fifty guys I'd ever dated, I'd cared about only Luc. Since Luc, the only guy who'd gotten to me at all was Richard. Both were disasters. It made me feel like I wasn't even myself. Things like this didn't happen to fabulous Clio, the envy of most of the girls at my school.

At Richard's, I leaned on the doorbell. I didn't try to see if Luc was there—I didn't care if he was. I was going to tear into Richard no matter what. Overhead, a bank of dark purple clouds was rolling in fast. We were in for a storm in more ways than one.

No one answered. I forced my breathing to slow, forced my chaotic emotions to quiet. I leaned against the wooden door, resting my forehead against it. Richard was inside, but his presence felt subdued, not lively. Maybe he was sleeping.

In our religion, we have several really important rules. The threefold law, for example, where you acknowledge that anything you do, anything you send out into the world, comes back at you three times over. So heads-up, basically. And there were other rules about not controlling people, not manipulating events that affect other people, not subverting others' will—I had broken that rule and was walking a dangerous line with it.

Another rule is about not using magick to invade other people—themselves, their thoughts, their space, their things. Not without permission. I was about to do that.

Glancing around first, I traced several signs around the lock on Richard and Luc's front door. I focused, seeing the lock's mechanism inside my head, seeing the tumblers gently shift and fall, and then the lock opened with a gentle click. I turned the doorknob and burst in, slamming the door behind me as hard as I could.

I was halfway down the hall when Richard came out of his room, wary concern on his face. When he saw it was me, his shoulders fell with resignation.

"I know why you're he—" he began, as I swung my heavy messenger bag at him with all my might. It caught him squarely in his side, knocking him over into the wall of the hallway.

"God da—" he began again, holding up his arm, but I was swinging my other fist. He grabbed it, holding my wrist in a manacle grip, and yanked the messenger bag away. He grabbed my other wrist, and I was horrified by how strong he was, how quickly I'd been thwarted. I had pictured him taking my wrath, apologizing, groveling, letting me get my rage out—like most guys did.

I drew back one foot to kick him, but in a second he had hooked his ankle behind mine and pulled so that I fell heavily to the hard floor. He fell on top of me, since he was holding my hands, and my breath whooshed out, leaving me gasping. Quickly he rolled off me so we were side by side, and he got as far away from me as he could before I could knee him where it hurts.

I sucked in a deep breath and started yelling at him. Every bad name, every swear word in English and French that I knew, every hateful thought I'd had about him in the last thirty hours, every ounce of rage and hurt and venom I'd been bottling up since yesterday, I let it all out. My whole life, if anyone had crossed me, from kindergarten to this year, they'd known about it, and I'd made them wish they'd never been born. All of those times rolled together weren't a tenth of what I spewed at Richard now.

Toward the end of my tirade, there was a huge flash of

light, as if God had just taken a picture of the world, and then an explosion of thunder that vibrated the floorboards beneath me. The apartment went dark. I struggled as hard as I could, but he held my wrists like iron until I had angry red marks from his fingers.

Heavy rain pelted the windows in the other room, and more lightning flashed and thunder boomed. I paused to take a breath, and he quickly said, "I was going to come see you and Thais today. I know you're pissed, and I don't blame you. But I can explain."

"Save it!" I spit, trying to jerk my hands free. "You effing bastard! I *hate* you!"

"No you don't," he said. "You don't love me, but you don't hate me, either."

"Okay, then, I *despise* you! I *loathe* you! I spit on the ground you walk on!"

In the dim light, Richard's dark eyebrows raised, and then I saw him bite the inside of his cheek, like he was trying not to laugh.

I stared at him. "Don't you dare laugh, you fricking *jerk*!"

He went solemn immediately, shaking his head. "No, no, I'm sorry. I'm not laughing. You've got every right to be furious. It's all my fault. I just—was crazy. I can't explain it. But then I met you, and . . . " He looked down at me, and I caught my breath, remembering another time he had looked down at me. "And I knew I couldn't hurt you." He cleared his throat. "Couldn't bear to see you hurt." His voice was husky now, and because I'm completely *insane,* I became aware of his hard body pressed against me.

"Even though you're stuck-up," he went on, unbelievably.

My eyes snapped wide open.

"And have had your own way far too much," he went on, "and are spoiled and have Petra wrapped around your little finger and are way too beautiful for your own good and are used to stupid little boys hanging on your every word and—"

His words were drowned out by my outraged screech, and I bucked hard, trying to break his grip. Then he was smiling down at me, as if he thought I were fabulous, and, goddess help me, he was beautiful in a weird, young way, completely unlike Luc.

"Don't you look at me like that," I hissed. "You tried to *kill* me and my sister! And then you made out with me! When I think about it, I want to throw up!" Abruptly my throat closed, and I felt my nose twitch with impending tears.

Richard was solemn again. "I don't want to hurt you," he said quietly in the darkness. "I only kissed you after I had given up the whole plan. And last time, *you* grabbed *me.*"

"Don't remind me," I snapped. "I'm so ashamed, I don't know if I'll ever live it down!"

He drew back then, and I was amazed to see that he looked hurt. He seemed like the tough-as-nails type, who'd seen and done too much for anything or anyone to get to him.

"Well, it'll be our secret," he said evenly.

That deflated me. I slumped against the floor, away from him, trying to figure things out. Richard was very still and quiet, his face the same cool mask as when I'd met him. I hadn't realized how much emotion he'd been showing me, how much his guard had been down, until I saw him again like this.

I wriggled my hands tiredly. "Let me go."

He did, releasing my wrists. I looked at them, the dark red marks, and knew I'd have bruises tomorrow. I rubbed my wrists with my hands, easing the ache, and just lay on the hard wooden floor, my back to him. Clio the Magnificent, as some guy had called me in tenth grade. *Look at me now,* I thought dully. *I'm a freaking waste of space. Like a crumpled pile of dirty clothes, lying here on the floor.*

"Why did you do it?"

"Didn't Petra tell you?"

I shrugged. "Just wondering if you had anything to add."

"Only that I am so sorry, and I would *never* hurt you, now that I know you."

"Nan said we looked like Cerise. I hadn't realized that," I said dully. The next question was obvious—was that why you wanted me?—but I didn't want to know the answer.

"You're not anything like her," Richard said.

"What?" I closed my eyes, feeling like I couldn't get up. It was dark, and the rain and thunder and lightning were soothing, so much bigger than my pathetic life. I wanted to be in a cocoon of gray light and rain.

"Cerise. You're not anything like her. You don't remind me of her. You don't even look like her, really. Just a superficial resemblance."

"We look exactly like her," I said in a monotone. "People gasp when they see us." *And that was the only reason you ever came after me.* I remembered Marcel's reaction and realized why it had been so strong. Had Thais told me we looked like Cerise? I didn't remember.

"They're not seeing you. Cerise was—light, like honey. Like sunlight. Easy to hold but impossible to keep. Like a butterfly."

"Not like me." It seemed like one more damning thing against me.

"No." Richard gave a short laugh. "You're not a butterfly. You're not light or easy."

There was silence between us for some time.

"You're not honey," Richard finally went on. "You're wine. You're the deepest, darkest shadow under a tree on a blazing day. You're strong and hard, coursing like a current at the bottom of a river."

I started crying silently, my tears running across my face to drip to the floor.

"I don't love anybody." Richard's voice was bleak. "I don't love you. But I see the value of you, the incredible worth of you, more than anyone I've ever known."

We were there like that for a while, with me weeping silently and Richard not touching me. I wished someone could hold me. Eventually I stopped crying. Finally, feeling like I was a thousand years old, much older than *him,* I sat up. I had the thought that if I felt like this now, immortality was going to be harder than I imagined.

"I have to go." I got to my feet awkwardly. My wrists burned.

"Clio—believe that I'm so sorry about how I tried to hurt you and Thais. I can't really explain it, except I just went crazy. But you have to know that I would *never* hurt you now. I wouldn't let anyone else hurt you, if I knew about it. When Petra told me about your car catching on fire, I was—"

I picked up my purse and my messenger bag and brushed dust off my clothes. Not looking at him, I headed to the front door, knowing I must look like I was dragged through a hedge backward. Whatever.

His warm hand touched my upper arm, holding it lightly, keeping me there. "Clio."

"Don't touch me."

He let go at once, and I walked to the door. It was going to be a long, wet walk to Canal Street.

As I reached the front door, I realized that someone was talking loudly outside, and then the door flew open and Luc was there, right in my face.

"Where is he?" Luc said, his eyes cold and hard.

"Luc, come *on*," said Thais, and I saw her right behind him.

"What's going on?" I asked as Luc pushed past me.

"You bastard!" Luc shouted, lunging for Richard, who already looked beaten down and weary. Luc slammed his hands against Richard's shoulders, shoving him into the wall—I heard Richard's head crack against it, saw him wince.

But not fight back.

"What were you thinking?" Luc yelled. "What were you doing? Have you finally gone totally insane? Clio and Thais!" He pushed Richard hard again, and Richard staggered but stayed on his feet.

"Get in line, Thais," Richard said over Luc's shoulder. "First Petra, then Clio, then Luc, then you. And I guess Ouida and Sophie and whoever else gives a crap will show up soon."

"How could you do it?" Luc shouted again. "How could you try to *kill* them? Are you a *murderer?* How could you possibly stand to hurt them?"

Richard frowned, straightening up. "I don't know," he said. "You tell me."

Luc's face flushed, his hands curled into fists.

"I mean, how could I *possibly* do something stupid and boneheaded that would hurt the twins when I don't even know them?" Richard's voice was mocking and sardonic.

"Shut up! I didn't try to *kill* them."

"No. But I wonder who hurt them more?"

They stood there, glaring at each other, both tense, ready to spring.

I looked at Thais, the only person I was happy to see in this whole mess. I would worry about what she was doing with Luc later. Right now, she was my sister and the only person in the room I didn't want to shred.

"I'm sick of both of them," I told her. "Let's split."

"Oh, God, yes," Thais said, holding the door open.

Then we were out in the rain, walking toward Canal Street. The rain actually felt good, and I knew I couldn't possibly look worse.

"So," said Thais after a couple blocks. "You gave Richard a hard time?"

"Yeah. It was pretty ugly." I shifted my bag to my other shoulder. "What were you doing with Luc?"

"I went to Axelle's to wring some answers out of her." Thais sounded as fed up and tired as I felt. "Luc was there, and he followed me out of Axelle's when I left. And then we almost got plantered to death."

"What?"

She told me about how a huge, heavy planter had narrowly missed her. A long scratch on her arm looked red and painful.

"Was this another attack, or was it a coincidence?" I asked, knowing that there aren't any coincidences.

"I don't know," Thais said. "It looked all rusty, like it might have happened anytime. Anyway, I was freaked, and I said something like, 'I guess it wasn't Richard this time.' And then Luc ran with it from there."

"Well, maybe they'll kill each other," I said hopefully.

Thais looked at me, and a smile turned up the corners of her mouth. Suddenly it felt okay to smile myself, and we grinned at each other. Sisters.

✦ Chapter Thirty-One

Tonight

PETRA FINALLY SAW CLIO AND THAIS ON A streetcar, with rain running down the window next to them. They looked alive, if not well, and Petra couldn't see or feel any sense of dark intent around them.

The crystal icicle she was scrying in was still spinning in the window when she realized that someone was knocking on the front door.

Daedalus.

Wonderful. This would be the crowning touch to an already tense, frustrating day.

Petra opened the door, and as soon as she saw his exultant face, she realized that the time she'd been dreading was at hand.

"We have everything," he announced, stepping across her threshold as if walking onto a stage. "The final form of the rite is complete. We have a full Treize. And I have found the Circle of Ashes."

With long practice Petra kept the dismay off her face.

He'd found the Circle of Ashes? They should have cloaked it better.

"The time is now," Daedalus said grandly.

"Now? You mean, before Monvoile?"

"I mean now, tonight," Daedalus said.

"Tonight!"

"Yes. Everything is aligned, as if it was all decreed by the heavens." Daedalus smoothed his hair back with one hand.

What a load of—hot air, Petra thought.

"Please get Clio and Thais and meet us at the circle at midnight tonight." Daedalus handed her a printout of a map and directions. He didn't know that she, Ouida, and Sophie had found the circle weeks ago. "The rite will begin at precisely twelve twenty-seven, when the moon is at its utmost fullness."

"I don't think we're ready to do the rite," Petra tried.

"You will be." Daedalus looked down at her, and then his face softened. Unexpectedly, he took one of her hands in both of his. "Petra. We've had more than two hundred years to think about this, to dream about it. To prepare for it. On that terrible night, so long ago, Melita gave us all a gift and a curse. This is our chance to heal past injuries, enhance our gifts, correct our curse, and achieve that which is dearest to our hearts. You're ready for it. You've been ready for it for a long, long time."

She looked directly at him. "I don't trust you."

He laughed, putting his head back. Petra remembered that he had been handsome as a young man. But he hadn't aged well. Instead of achieving distinction, he had acquired only superciliousness.

"The beauty is you won't need to, my dear," he said. "Each of us brings to the rite his own strengths, her own powers. None of us is a Melita. Each of us may have a different goal. We might not agree with or support each other's goals—they're inherently personal, relating only to ourselves. Take care of yourself, and everything will be well."

He let go of her hand and walked to the front door. "At midnight, then." His eyes were sparkling, his face animated and alive. Still smiling, he let himself out, not seeming to mind that Petra hadn't promised to come.

• • •

The rain had stopped. Petra was in the newly replanted front garden when she felt the girls walking home from the streetcar stop. They had deliberately disobeyed her, completely flouted her authority, and what's more, hadn't been stopped by the knowledge that she would be out of her mind with worry.

What a surprise that teenagers would act this way.

They paused at the front gate, seeing her kneeling on the damp brick walk next to the small bed of herbs.

"Nan," Clio said.

Petra looked up. They both looked like drowned rats, almost as bad as when she'd pulled them out of the water spout—oh, goddess, had that been only *yesterday?* But looking more closely at Clio, Petra saw that she had been crying, and looked shaken and upset. She'd gone to see Richard, Petra assumed immediately. But surely he hadn't put those bruises on her wrists? Not unless he'd lost his mind for good this time.

"Um, hi, Nan," said Thais.

"You're both really wet. Go inside and change your clothes. I'll put the kettle on to make tea. Then we need to talk."

✦ Chapter Thirty-Two

Thais

HALF AN HOUR LATER THE THREE OF US SAT around the kitchen table, mugs of hot tea in front of us.

"If you believe that Richard didn't blow up Clio's car, then who's doing it?" I asked. "I mean, maybe the planter wasn't an attack, but maybe it was. It has to be one of the Treize."

"Yes, I think you're right," Nan said, frowning. "I truly don't know who, though. However, I think it will all probably come to a head tonight." Her clear blue-gray eyes met mine and then Clio's across the table. "Daedalus stopped by. He wants to do the rite tonight, at midnight."

My heart seemed to seize in my chest. We'd been dancing around this idea for weeks now, almost pretending it wasn't real, wasn't coming. Now Nan was saying that it was coming right at us right now.

"Tonight?" Clio said, looking alarmed. "But I'm not ready. I mean, we're not ready, none of us. Right?"

Nan sighed. "I'm about as ready as I'll ever be. I've put certain plans in place for the rite. I know you two will be safe. I don't know what else will happen."

"That's just it!" I exclaimed. "No one does. Everyone seems to think something different will happen. But I've got no idea what it will do to *me*. Plus, the last time we did a circle with Daedalus, he used our power without permission."

"I've thought about that," Nan said. "But Ouida, Sophie, and some others are all in agreement. I'm sure that neither of you will be harmed tonight. Nor can Daedalus take anyone's power, unless they give it to him."

I took a sip of tea, my mind whirling. "This is all happening much too fast." I thought about Clio and how she was studying Hermann Parfitte's book.

"Couldn't we wait a couple of weeks?" Clio asked, as if she had read my mind.

Nan looked at her. "Why? I don't think it will make any difference to you two."

Clio and I met eyes, and I knew she wanted more time to work on her spells. But she wouldn't tell Nan that.

"Tonight is when a lot of different elements come together," Nan explained. "The phase of the moon, the position of the stars, the time of the year—apparently it's all just right, perfect for the rite to happen tonight."

"But what's going to *happen?*" I asked pointedly. "What will happen to *us?*"

"I think you'll get a huge surge of power," Nan said. "After the rite, I believe your magick will be much stronger, though neither of you has gone through your rite of ascension."

"What else?" After Récolte I'd felt terrible.

"I don't think you're going to become immortal," said Nan. "Is that what you're worried about?"

"Among other things." I couldn't believe this conversation was part of my life. "I thought I would have a lot more time to think about this. Why don't you think we'd become immortal?"

"No one will be spelling you to be." Nan looked into her tea mug, as if the answers lay there. "I'll be spelling you to be protected, to be safe. But no one will be trying to make you immortal."

Clio looked disappointed, but then her face became determined, which gave me a bad feeling.

"Can we refuse to go?"

Nan looked thoughtful. "We could, of course, but actually, honey, I don't think it would make much difference. There are reasons to do the rite—to become more powerful, more in tune with magick. To help our friends if we can. To learn. Because I'm sure you won't be harmed, it seems pointless to refuse to go."

I didn't know what to think. I'd been hoping that if enough time went by, I could ride out Clio's plan to become immortal. Maybe with time I'd feel more prepared, more braced. Now it was happening much too fast. I was somewhat reassured by Nan's promise of safety and the knowledge that no one could spell us to be immortal. But I was worried about what Clio was thinking, what she might be planning to do.

I sighed. "Maybe I'll be able to think better with a full stomach," I said. "What are we doing for dinner?"

Nan looked regretful. "Have some more tea, sweetie, but you don't want to eat anything if we're doing the rite tonight."

"Why?"

"It's really big magick," she explained. "It's kind of like swimming. You don't want to eat a lot before you do it."

Oh, and that made me feel so much better.

Q-tip jumped up on the kitchen table, rubbing against Nan's arm.

"Hi, baby," Clio said gently, reaching out to pet him. He shied away from her, hurrying across the table and jumping off next to me. Clio gazed after him, looking upset.

I had too many thoughts and emotions to even begin to deal with them. The rite seemed much too huge and unbelievable and soon. And before this, I'd seen Axelle, almost been killed *again*, and saw that awful scene with Richard and Luc. I'd been flooded with adrenaline too many times today to count, and I felt almost ill. I really, really wanted to eat something.

I got up and put my mug in the sink. "I'm going to take a hot bath."

"Good idea," said Nan. "Put some rose petals and lavender in the water, and relax."

That didn't seem too likely.

Upstairs I got my robe and was heading into the bathroom when Clio appeared at the top of the stairs.

"Can you come in my room for a sec?" she whispered.

In her room I sat down on her bed, the only clear surface. She shut the door and sat next to me.

"I don't want to do the freaking rite," I said.

Clio nodded. "I need more time to get ready. But still—if we have to do it tonight, I feel like it will be okay. I do know how to protect myself—us—from Daedalus taking our power. And Nan's covering the other bases."

I shook my head, not convinced.

"I do," she insisted. "I won't be trying to get anyone else's power. All I'd be doing is protecting us."

I put my head on my hands. "You can't make us immortal?"

"I don't think so," she said regretfully. "Maybe in another month . . ."

"I'm just . . . afraid."

"So am I," Clio surprised me by saying. "I've never been part of anything like this. I mean, you know—things like this just don't happen. Not anymore. Not that anyone would hear about, anyway." She leaned back against the wall, her legs straight out. "This is some freaky stuff, Thais. But . . . I believe Nan. I believe that she'll make sure we're safe. She may have lied about a lot, but she's always protected me. I know since you've discovered magick, you've seen it get all wonky pretty easily. But remember, this is different—these are people who've spent all this time working on their powers. And I can protect us too, guard against our power being used. I mean, isn't it kind of exciting in a way? Tonight is the culmination of hundreds of years of history."

"Tonight is why they killed my dad. Our dad."

Clio's face went white. "What?"

"I talked to Axelle. I'm pretty sure Daedalus killed him to get me here," I explained. "So how can I do this? Just on principle, I hate everything about it, don't want any part of it. It would be like justifying what they did." My poor dad. From the time he'd met our mom, he'd stumbled from one lie to another. That she was a witch. That he'd had two children, not just one. That we could live a normal life if we weren't in Louisiana. And then he'd been killed. What a bad deal he'd gotten, just because he'd fallen in love with our mom. And no one ever talked about her. I had no idea what she'd been like.

"Yeah, I get what you mean," Clio said. "But . . . see, if we do this but play by our rules—it'll show them that they can't control us like they think they can. We're strong, Thais. We're weirdly strong together. The two of us can show them that they can't mess with us, that we're calling the shots for ourselves, now and for the rest of our lives."

I gazed up at the ceiling, seeing the fine cracks in the old plaster.

Clio was silent for a minute, regarding her sparkly purple toes. "It might not even work," she said finally. "Who knows if they've really re-created the rite the way they need to? But as long as we're there for each other, with Nan watching out for us, you and I will be okay. And if we don't go . . . we'll never know who's trying to kill us. They'll just keep trying, and what if it works next time?"

I shivered, already knowing there was no point saying anything else.

We were going to this rite.

Chapter Thirty-Three

Please Forgive Me

SOPHIE GRIPPED THE STEERING WHEEL TIGHTER, hoping Manon would assume she was tense because of the rite. Which she was, of course. She and Manon had talked everything out exhaustively, over and over. She felt like she'd been crying for years. But now she knew without a doubt what Manon planned to do.

Next to her, one small hand reassuringly on Sophie's leg, Manon was oddly calm.

Sophie swallowed and peered into the darkness, looking for a road sign. She only hoped that someday Manon would be able to forgive her for what she was about to do.

Chapter Thirty-Four

A Burst of Divine Power

"ARE YOU ALL RIGHT?" OUIDA'S CONCERNED voice was soothing in the car's darkness.

"Yes, quite. Thank you." Marcel felt more all right than he would have thought possible, thanks to Petra. Now he was quietly exultant, filled with hope and anticipation. At last, at last, his hope and dream, his longing would come true. It would serve Daedalus right.

✦ Chapter Thirty-Five

Had He Learned Nothing?

PETRA GLANCED AT THE TWINS IN THE backseat. Thais looked sad and afraid. Clio looked both calm and expectant. Which was worrisome. What was on her mind? *Please, goddess, don't let her be planning anything stupid,* Petra prayed silently. *Well,* she thought, *I'll just have to be alert, ready to circumvent it.*

Petra was sure Thais was regretting every aspect of her new life, new religion, new relatives. But after tonight, things would settle down some, at least for a while.

It wasn't hard to find the site. Daedalus had written very clear directions, and besides, Petra had been here recently. She turned into an unmarked, unpaved road; its crushed white shells practically glowed in the bright moonlight. She glanced up at the sky through the windshield. It was perfectly clear, the stars popping brightly.

That would change soon.

Two miles down the road, they were deep in a wooded area, the trees so close on either side of the car that leaves brushed the windows. Then it suddenly opened up into a rough-mown meadow where several other cars were parked. Petra stopped her Volvo next to Ouida's rental and killed the engine. Turning in her seat, she looked back into the solemn identical faces of her descendents, her adopted granddaughters, the people she had chosen to value above all else.

"From here we have to walk a bit," she said, her voice sounding loud in the still night. "Are you guys okay?"

They nodded, and Clio muttered, "Yeah."

Together the three of them walked down the narrow path that led into the blackest part of the swamp. The air was cool and damp here, and mosquitoes buzzed all around them.

Behind her, the girls were quiet, trying not to stumble on the uneven ground. They were unusually subdued, despite Petra's promise that they would be safe. It was almost as if they knew what Petra knew: Someone had to die tonight, for the rite to work.

And Petra knew who it would be.

✦ Chapter Thirty-Six

Clio

AFTER A TENSE, SILENT CAR RIDE, PETRA finally parked and told us to follow her through the dense woods. I walked with her and Thais toward the spot where we would meet the rest of the Trieze, and almost froze when I realized we had reached the Circle of Ashes, the place Thais and I had seen several times in our dreams and visions.

It was creepy and amazing to be standing here, and I was so wound up I could practically feel the earth's energy entering me through the soles of my feet.

I wished I'd had more time to work on my spells. I hadn't gotten far enough in Hermann Parfitte's book to really understand how to achieve immortality. I'd done only that one spell, with the cats, to subvert power. But we would be okay tonight. I could at least keep Daedalus from using my power if he tried. Nan would keep us safe from harm; I would keep us from being used.

That awful scene with Richard had replayed itself in my mind twenty times while I had gotten ready for tonight. Again it had struck me how unlike myself I felt lately—weaker, less brash, less bold. And Thais was seeming just the opposite—stronger, more sure of herself.

I blinked as something hit me. That spell we had done to join ourselves. What if it had gone farther than we intended? I frowned, thinking back to the limitations I had put on it. Had I forgotten some aspect of the limitations? Were Thais and I merging, or worse, becoming each other?

I didn't want to be Thais. It was hard enough being Clio.

Maybe it had been the spell. Or maybe I was just turning into a huge crybaby wuss. That was going to stop tonight.

I had taken extra care with my appearance, like old times. My hair was glossy and shiny, parted in the middle, hanging down to frame my face. My makeup was subtle but effective and counteracted the pale, drained, weepy look I'd come home with. I wore solid copper bracelets to cover the bruises on my wrists. For magick like this, no mixed-metal jewelry could be worn.

Finally, I wore the bouvre that I'd been saving for my rite of ascension. Tonight seemed important enough for it. It was made of heavy green silk several shades darker than my eyes. The sleeves were long and tight to the elbows, then flared out in bells around my hands. It fitted more closely than most bouvres and had embroidery around the waist, like a belt, and around the hem. We would be barefoot, but I wore solid copper anklets.

I looked fabulous. Very much like the old Clio.

"Petra."

A young woman stood next to Jules at the edge of the circle. Her hair was wild, spiky, and dyed magenta. Her ears gleamed with lots of silver earrings.

"Hello, Claire," Nan said kindly. They embraced, then Nan introduced us.

"Thais I met this afternoon," said Claire, coming to shake my hand. "So this is Clio." She gave me an open, slightly mocking smile, and I realized I liked her right away. She didn't seem as stuffed-shirty as some of the other Treize did.

"Hi," I said. She had green eyes like us, but a different shade.

"Welcome, all," I heard Daedalus say, and I turned to see him, arms outstretched, at the opposite edge of the circle. "Thank you so much for coming."

"Your guest speaker will be Father Daedalus," Thais murmured in my ear. "Refreshments will be served by the Ladies' Altar Guild."

I stifled a laugh.

"It's now almost midnight," Daedalus went on. "And we're all here."

I hadn't looked around, hadn't looked for Richard or Luc. Now I shook my hair back over my shoulders, chin up, looking calm, cool, and collected. I hoped. I kept my eyes on Daedalus, but it was torture, not examining everyone's expression.

"My friends and our two newest members, more than two hundred and forty years ago, we first began this journey together," Daedalus began. And basically he went on like that for ten minutes, droning on about their incredible voyage of discovery that made it all sound like a *National Geographic* special.

I eased myself behind Nan and surreptitiously looked around. Sophie looked white-faced and tense; Manon calm and unafraid. Ouida and Nan both looked alert and kind of stern somehow. Marcel stood next to Ouida, and he seemed okay, almost excited. Jules was impassive, head lowered, listening to Daedalus. Axelle was nervous, moving from foot to foot, like a racehorse. Claire's expression was outwardly calm, but the tight lines around her brightly painted mouth hinted at more under the surface.

Luc. The one time I glanced at him, he was looking at me. At me, not at Thais. He looked like he wanted to be anywhere but here. Across the circle, opposite Luc, Richard stood, his face hard, his jaw set. He was looking around at everyone, and I thought I saw a glance pass between him and Petra. For a moment his eyes met mine, and I got a jolt of emotion from him, which then immediately shut down. I glanced away, confused. During a circle, if people have a connection, you might pick up feelings from them, but we were just standing here.

"So let us join hands," Daedalus said, "around our ceremonial fire."

One by one we walked into the large circle he had drawn around the charred circle of earth. A small fire blazed in the middle, and four smallish, beat-up wooden cups held the four elements around it. Next to the fire was a slab of white marble, and on the marble was some kind of a stone knife with a carved handle. Daedalus closed the circle around us, and at that moment an unexpectedly cool breeze rustled my hair and brushed against my skin. Clouds had rolled in while Daedalus was speaking, and now every star had been wiped out. The sky was dark purple, and in the distance I saw clouds lit up by lightning.

Next to me Thais touched my hand. She'd just noticed the sky. She was trying to keep her fear down, but I could feel it. I was open to everything right now, receiving impressions from everyone and everything around me.

In the circle Ouida came and deliberately put herself between me and Nan, taking my hand in hers. So it was Nan, Ouida, me, Thais, Claire, Richard, Sophie, Jules, Manon, Luc, Daedalus, Axelle, and Marcel next to Nan on her other side. Thirteen of us. A Treize. Someone here was frustrated that Thais and I were alive and here. I couldn't see any sign on anyone's face that told me who it was.

"Let us begin," Daedalus said, and as if on cue, lightning flashed and thunder sounded threateningly. Thais let out a breath, and I squeezed her hand. The circle began moving dalmonde, clockwise, and Daedalus began to sing something that I couldn't understand. I assumed it was in old, old French, just as it had been in 1763 when this rite was first done. I had a quick thought: myself, two hundred years from now, doing the rite once again.

Jules began to sing, blending his deep voice smoothly with Daedalus's. Under my breath, I began my own spell, first outlining the limitations, hoping I wasn't leaving anything out, and then weaving the rest of the spell around Thais and me. Again I wished I'd had more time to practice, but the words spun out of my mouth smooth and light and easy. To me that felt like the magick was right. As the circle moved more quickly around the crackling fire, the air around us dropped in temperature, and the wind felt cool and damp.

Everyone was singing now. Daedalus's voice was like the main branch of a wisteria vine, with everyone else twining their voices around him. They wove in and out and around each other, each one distinct and yet blending into an almost seamless whole. I caught the words *collet, tâche, plume, cindres,* which I'd heard somewhere before. Holding tightly to Thais's hand, I finished the second section of my spell and began the third.

Nothing startling seemed to be happening, except the magickal energy was rising faster and fuller than I'd ever felt it. The wind kicked up, blowing our hair, our gowns, making leaves swirl in tiny cyclones here and there. The fire cast a pretty, rosy warmth on everyone's faces.

From time to time I closed my eyes so I could concentrate on my own spell. Thais was singing next to me, and I recognized her song. She didn't know Daedalus's spell, of course, so she was simply calling power to her. Our clasped hands felt hot. The ground itself pulsed with energy and power. Wind whipped my hair into my face for a moment, and I accidentally skipped a verse of my spell, only remembering it halfway through. Damn it. I had to begin the third section all over again.

Thais squeezed my hand. Opening my eyes, I saw her worried face.

"Is this a hurricane?" she managed to get out.

Around us, trees waved and bent. The wind was strong and cold and smelled like rain. The clouds above us were churning, lit from within by almost constant lightning.

I shook my head. My heart was pounding. I felt frighteningly full of energy. "Just big magick."

Her face fell, and I wasn't thrilled either. Nan's eyes were closed as she sang strongly, her feet sure on the packed-down grass. The fire's glow glided over her face, softening it, making her look younger.

Quickly I plowed on with my spell, needing to finish it as fast as possible. Everyone was singing loudly, though the wind snatched our voices away, twisting them up into the clouds, spiking them with lightning.

Luc's face was flushed, unbearably handsome, and my heart ached to see him. Ouida, on my right-hand side, was intent, her smooth brown skin glistening with mist. Manon was joyful, almost skipping to keep up with the circle's speed, her face alight with hope. And Richard—was looking at me, his eyes dark and intense. I saw his mouth moving but couldn't distinguish his voice. He had kissed me. I had kissed him. We didn't love each other, didn't even like each other, and he'd tried again and again to harm me. But I somehow believed that he would never try to hurt me now.

Drawing in a deep breath, I began the last part of my spell.

Lightning struck so close by that I jumped. My hair felt electrified, standing on end. A gray sheet of rain drew over us, soaking us with one sweep. My gown stuck to me uncomfortably as thunder rumbled through my stomach.

My chest felt full and tight, my body so strung with magick that I might burst. I blinked and for just a second was back in my vision, watching the circle do exactly this: the storm, the song, the rite, the rain. Only this time there was no Cerise.

Just her look-alikes.

Fear rushed over me then, huge and terrible and stunning. In one second I couldn't think, couldn't breathe, could hardly move: I was paralyzed with terror, an unnamed, animal-like terror that this was too big, dark, dangerous, deadly, and I shouldn't be here, I shouldn't be here, I shouldn't be here. . . .

Boom! The world whited out, like a blizzard. The blast of electricity knocked me backward several feet, wrenching my hands away from Ouida and Thais. Thunder shook the actual ground, like an earthquake, shaking people apart, wrecking the circle. My skin sizzled, and I felt the lightning even before it snaked down from the sky, crisp and thorny and whiter than the sun. It blasted down, blowing a hole in the world where our fire had been. Daedalus, Marcel, Richard, Ouida, Nan,

Sophie, and Manon—they each shouted, all different things, all at the same time.

The lightning splintered, whipping into each of us, throwing me to the ground. Daedalus raised his hands in exultation, laughing, feeling the power. In the next moment the lightning jumped, enormous and horrifying. Nan threw her arms out as if to embrace Marcel, and he held his arms open, his face to the sky. Instantly the lightning coalesced, leaving all of us, and speared Marcel in his chest, blowing him off his feet. In its glow I saw Marcel's shock, his face twisting in pain—and then he fell heavily to the ground, dead.

The aftermath was still and quiet. The storm lessened immediately, leaving a stunned vacuum in its wake. The drumming rain became a gentle shower. We all stared at Marcel, who lay faceup, glassy-eyed, on the ground.

"Oh my God," said Claire. "He's dead!" She looked at us all, dumbfounded. "Marcel is dead!"

Thais made a small sound of terror, and I looked at her. She was greenish around the edges and swayed on her feet. I staggered over and caught her as she was going down. Clumsily we both collapsed just a few feet from Marcel's body.

"What have you done!" Daedalus shouted, his face a mask of fury. "How *dare* you! How *dare* you circumvent the rite!" He shook his fist at Petra, who sank down next to me, looking ill.

"He wanted to die," Petra said weakly. "He wanted to die, and someone had to die for the rite to work. You know that."

She met Daedalus's glare. "I had to make sure it wasn't either of my girls. So Marcel and I made a pact."

"How *dare* you!" Daedalus shouted again. "Who helped you? Anyone who helped you will answer to me!" He looked around wildly from face to face.

Sophie was gaping, leaning against a tree. Her long, dark hair streaked down her back. Manon, on her hands and knees, stared at Sophie.

"No one helped me," Petra said, her voice hoarse. "It was just Marcel and me. I'm sorry, Daedalus. I know how much this meant to you. But I couldn't let you kill the one you wanted to."

He opened and closed his mouth several times as members of the Treize turned to look at him.

"And who would that be, Daedalus?" Richard asked quietly.

Daedalus shut his mouth with a snap. "You don't know what you're talking about," he ground out. "I wasn't going to kill anybody! I need everyone here! You've destroyed my life's work! You've destroyed our one chance to have everything we've ever dreamed of!"

"I've destroyed your chance to have everything *you* ever dreamed of," Petra said sadly. "But knowing you, I'm sure you'll create another chance for yourself."

I heard a gasp but couldn't see where it came from. Then a groan.

Claire drew in a breath. "Marcel!"

On the ground, Marcel coughed and groaned again. He blinked several times, then seemed to register that there were trees overhead and rain hitting his face.

"Am I not dead?" his voice was a rusty metal whisper.

Luc knelt next to him, his face bitter. "Marcel—you're immortal, man. Get used to it."

Standing, Luc looked at Daedalus, at Petra, at the rest of the Treize. Not at me, nor Thais. He shook his head, seeming disgusted, then walked off in the rain in the direction of the cars.

"There's no Source," said Jules. He pointed at the charred ground, the jagged hole blasted into the earth. "The Source didn't reappear. This was all for nothing."

"So this is it," Thais said so softly I could hardly hear her. "All of this, the lies, the manipulations, the secrets, the alliances, the research—it was all for nothing."

"Not for nothing, my dear," Petra said just as softly. "Maybe Daedalus's rite didn't work, but there were many spells being worked here tonight, many people calling on magick for their own uses."

I looked down at my hands, where the bright copper bracelets still rested against Richard's bruises. *Interesting*, I thought. How many other people were working spells, and for what? Had any of them taken?

Had mine?

BALEFIRE

Cate Tiernan

BOOK FOUR:
A NECKLACE OF WATER

BALEFIRE

BOOK FOUR:
A NECKLACE OF WATER

Chapter One

Thais

FIRE. IT WAS CREATION AND DESTRUCTION AT once. It made life possible, yet could so easily snatch it away. It was a beacon in the darkness, warmth in the coldest winter, an eternal symbol of hearth, home, and comfort.

And it could cook steaks.

I glanced beneath the half-moon kettle standing on rusted legs in our backyard. With one hand I felt around the back—

"Where's the switch?"

My sister looked at me pityingly, then struck a match and laid it on top of the small pile of coals. Nothing happened, and she pulled out another match. Then I saw the barest disturbance—a wavering around the edge of a briquette, as if air itself was bent.

"There," said Clio, pointing. Sure enough, a timid flame was licking a coal, sliding over it like liquid light, and in another minute the other coals wore tiny frills of dancing orange heat.

The sun was sinking rapidly—though it was still daylight saving time, night was coming sooner every day. Now it was twilight, and shadows and shapes in our yard were becoming less distinct, grayer.

"Huh," I said, lost in the way the flames were consuming, covering, eating into the coals. I looked up at Clio, who was as transfixed as I was. "On mine, we just pressed a switch."

"That's 'cause you're a Yankee," she said absently.

I kicked her shin with my bare foot, and she looked up with a faint grin. "The truth hurts," she said. "I understand." She sat down on our back steps and gathered up her long, straight black hair, using a big plastic clip to hold it off her neck. "Whew," she said. "Hot."

I sat next to her, my own straight black hair awkwardly growing out a hairstyle I hadn't kept up. Back home in Welsford, Connecticut, I'd had it cut in precise layers every seven weeks. Now I hadn't had a trim in over four months, ever since my father had been killed and I'd been shuttled down here to New Orleans to live with strangers.

Clio and I let out heavy sighs at the exact same time, then met each other's eyes in a wry acknowledgment of our "twin thing."

I focused on the grill, trying to find words that wouldn't set off yet another argument between me and Clio. In the end, all I could come up with was, "Don't do it."

Clio frowned, not looking at me, and my chest tightened.

Ever since we'd taken part in the horrible, failed rite of the Treize two days ago, Clio and I had been locked in a battle of wills, and we were both losing. It had been an incredibly powerful rite, a rite that could have—should have—been deadly, and Clio and I never should have witnessed it, much less participated.

But we had. And during it, at the climax of power and magick and energy, each person in the Treize had privately spoken their deepest wishes. Mine had been to know for sure what had happened with my father last summer. One minute he'd been standing in front of an ice-cream shop, and the next he'd been under the front wheels of a Crown Victoria.

I'd been in France on a class tour of Europe. I'd gotten a phone call from Mrs. Thompkins, our next-door neighbor and closest friend. My life had ended with that phone call, and the surreal existence I'd been living since then still seemed like it belonged to someone else, most of the time.

I'd needed to know: How could it be such a coincidence that Dad had died, and that I'd come to New Orleans, and found not only my identical twin sister but also a bizarre web of history and pain that had been going on for almost 250 years?

It wasn't a coincidence. In my vision I'd seen Daedalus performing the spell that made old Mrs. Beale have a stroke. I'd seen Daedalus magickally guiding her car onto the sidewalk. He'd smacked his hands together right as the car hit my dad. I'd seen him clench his fist as he ended my dad's life from hundreds of miles away.

Now I wanted to kill him.

Which was impossible, what with the fact that he was immortal and all. Maybe there was some unknown way I could *try* to kill him, but I'd never be able to carry it out, despite what he'd done. I wasn't a murderer, like he was.

But I was planning to destroy him. I still didn't know hardly anything about *Bonne Magie,* my family's traditional religion, but I'd learned that what you put out into the world, you got back threefold. If breaking Daedalus came back on me three-fold, it would be worth it, to avenge my father's death and my life being blown apart for Daedalus's dark purpose.

After the rite, when we were more coherent and less sick, I'd told Clio what I'd seen. Clio had never known Dad, but he was her father too. I was sure she'd feel the same way I did. And she *was* angry at Daedalus, but it was hard to grieve for something she'd never had.

I didn't know what spell she'd tossed into the tornado of magickal force that night. Each person there had been further-ing his or her own agenda. Clio told me she'd had a vision of herself drowned. Dead. Her skin pale and bloodless, her sight-less eyes staring up at a sky black with storm clouds. It was haunting her.

Clio got up and stirred the glowing coals, edges rimmed with fine white ash, and spread them on the bottom of the kettle. She gauged their temperature with her hand, then set the metal grill in place. We'd marinated a steak, and when she dropped it onto the grate it sizzled and sent up sharp hisses of steam.

Petra, who Clio had always thought was her grandmother, had been hit hard by the rite. Since then she'd hardly left her bed, and we were both worried about how frail she suddenly seemed. Maybe making her a steak would strengthen her, along with all the healing spells our friend Melysa was doing.

"I'm going to do it," Clio said, her back still to me. Anger bloomed fast inside my chest like a scarlet carnation.

I opened my mouth to speak, but Clio turned to face me.

"I don't want to die," she said for the hundredth time. "I saw myself *dead*. Dead *now*, at this age, not older, not as a grown-up."

"You aren't sure that's what it meant," I said carefully, keeping reins on my anger.

"Yes, I am!" she snapped, her green eyes flashing in the deepening night. The birthmark on her left cheek, identical to mine on my right, seemed to blaze brighter, like a splash of blood. "I saw myself *dead*, and it wasn't a dream, it was real. It's what is *about* to happen. And I won't *go*. Not *now*. Why are you so sure what you saw is real, but mine isn't? You're not even a witch!"

I jerked back as if slapped. Clio had grown up as a witch with Nan and her coven. I'd only found out about the craft a few months ago. Neither of us had passed the rite of ascension, which in *Bonne Magie* would make us full members of a coven. Compared to Clio, I was as stupid as a toddler, with all the stuff I didn't know. But it was all too clear that I was a witch, as much a witch as any woman in my family, going back hundreds of years. It was clear that I was going to follow that course till the end of my life.

Clio's lips made an angry, hard line, and I knew she regretted saying that.

"All I'm saying," she went on tightly, "is that you seem to think what you saw is more real than what I saw."

I did think that.

"No, I don't," I insisted. But *I'd* seen details of something that *had* really happened, and *she'd* had a premonition, at best. Who knew if it would ever come true? "I just don't see how you could bear to study with someone who killed our *father.*"

Which brought us to the crux of it: Clio had seen herself dead, and it had terrified her. Now she was willing to ally herself with my father's murderer in order to cheat death—death that wasn't even certain.

"Daedalus knows the rite, knows the magick behind it, better than any of them." Clio jabbed a long fork into the steak and turned it over. Blood dripped onto the blazing coals. "He can teach me what I need to know to make sure the rite works the next time."

"So you'll be immortal," I said tonelessly, and Clio shrugged.

And there you have it: Clio wanted immortality; I wanted to destroy the man who had so coldly ended my life, ended my dad's life. My dad had been forty-one! Daedalus was, like, 270. Who deserved to live more?

"I know you don't want to die," I said, coming to stand next to her. "I don't *want* you to die. And I don't want to die myself. But you *don't* have to study with Daedalus."

"He knows the most, he's the one who got this together," she said stubbornly.

How could she be so *stupid*? How could she be so disloyal to Dad and to me? "Don't you study with him!" I shouted in frustration, and Clio wheeled on me, looking furious. Her mouth opened to blast me, but in the next second she froze, as if hearing something.

"Luc," she said, frowning. She glanced at the freshly painted back of our house. "Luc—and Richard."

"Here?"

"Yes." Clio picked up my hand, but only to read my watch. Turning, she stabbed the steak with the fork again, sliding it onto the platter. She headed up the steps with it, telling me once again that this fruitless discussion was over.

I wanted to punch the kettle but knew I'd burn myself. Now I had to go inside and face Luc and Richard, neither of whom I had the energy for.

I couldn't believe Clio wouldn't change her mind.

Which was why I could never tell her about my plan to destroy Daedalus.

✦ Chapter Two

Clio

THAIS WAS REALLY PISSING ME OFF. OF COURSE I hated the fact that our dad was dead, that I would never know him, that he'd never known me. If Daedalus had done it, then I would have it out with him. Someday.

But in the meantime, I myself was going to be dead *any day!* In my vision, I'd looked exactly the same as I did now, not even a year older. I'd seen myself *dead*, drowned, gray, looking almost exactly like my ancestor Cerise had when she'd died.

Cerise. My jaw tightened as I set the steak platter down on the kitchen table. I heard Nan in the front room, talking to Luc and Richard. Great. Just who I needed to see now, together, with Thais. Luc, the man we had both loved, and, I was guessing, both still loved, and Richard, another member of the Treize, Luc's roommate. Someone who set me off like gasoline on a fire. Someone who had tried to kill me and Thais. And then made out with me.

I frowned, trying to get it together, as Thais came in from the backyard. Our small wooden table was set for dinner for three. Iced tea had been poured, baked potatoes were ready, and a dish of sautéed okra sat in the middle of the table.

"Come in," I heard Nan say, and felt footsteps vibrating the floorboards. It was interesting, how our house felt when a man entered it. We were three women, our footsteps light, our energy relatively smooth. Our house felt calm and strong around us. But when a man came into it, everything changed. The energy was charged and jagged, their footsteps so much heavier, voices louder, taking up more space than a woman.

"Oh, Clio," said Nan, her voice still weak. "We . . . have visitors."

The way she said it made me look up. She knew that I had felt them arrive. I wondered if she was still furious at Richard, or whether she'd forgiven him. And she knew that Luc, Richard, Thais, and I had tensions and resentments and weirdnesses between us—though she didn't know the complete picture of any of it. At least, I prayed she didn't.

"Well, dinner's ready," I said shortly, pulling out my chair and sitting down. Nan came into the kitchen, followed by two people I had rolled around with and now kind of hated. I took a big swig of iced tea, wishing it was Jack Daniels.

Then I saw Luc's face and almost spewed tea out my nose. I heard Thais's gasp behind me, and suddenly Nan's odd tone of voice made sense. I gulped, coughing, trying to get tea down before it blew all over the table.

Finally, holding my napkin to my mouth, I managed, "What happened to your face?"

I flicked a glance at Richard's dark eyes. The expression on his face told me he'd definitely wanted to be here when I saw Luc for the first time.

"Sit down, Luc," Nan murmured, pulling out her chair. Our kitchen was small, our table smaller, big enough for only three people at one time. I looked at Thais, where she was leaning against the stove, her eyes big and startled. She met my eyes and mouthed *holy crap* at me, and I nodded.

Luc sat down across from me, looking miserable. Or at least, I thought he seemed miserable—it was actually hard to tell from his expression. I mean, it was hard to tell that he was *human*. Luc—one of the hottest, most handsome guys I'd ever seen in my life, with beautiful bones, beautiful dark blue eyes, a beautiful sculpted mouth that I had been unable to resist— now looked like the Thing.

His face was grossly swollen, his features obscured. His eyes seemed small and piggy, almost closed with extra flesh. His skin itself, usually gorgeous, perfect, and tan, was now waxen and pasty, covered with thousands of tiny pustules. Clearly he'd had trouble shaving: several days' worth of dark stubble mottled his cheeks and chin, and not in a sexy way.

He looked like a monster.

"Yep," Richard said, walking to the fridge and helping himself to one of Nan's beers. "I'm guessing someone at the rite wanted everyone's outside to match their inside."

"Shut up," said Luc, his voice sounding like it had been put through a cheese grater. He sounded very subdued, very different from his usual world-weary irony.

Richard grinned and toasted him with the beer, then tilted his head back and drank. I tried to put all images of kissing and biting that neck out of my mind.

"But what happened?" said Thais, sounding appalled. "Did someone do this? Or is this, like, from something you ate or touched? Poison ivy?"

Luc laughed wryly. "No, this is magickal. I don't know why or how or who. Someone wanted to teach me a lesson, I guess."

His gaze flicked past Thais to me, and I frowned. He knew Thais and I had every reason to despise him, but neither of us would ever do anything like this.

Tempting though it would be.

"It wasn't me," I said.

"It wasn't me," Thais echoed.

"It wasn't me," Richard put in. "Though God knows I'm enjoying the hell out of it."

Luc shot him an angry glance, and Richard grinned. It burned Richard up how I felt about Luc—not that he wanted me himself. Or at least, for more than twenty minutes at a time.

Nan took Luc's chin in her hand, tilting his face in the red-tinged twilight to see it better. "It would help if we knew who had done this," she murmured, and she suddenly looked so old that I almost drew in my breath. Nan had looked exactly the same for my entire life—seventeen years. Now, two days after the rite, she looked five years older than she'd been on Monday.

"But I think we can do something, not knowing who it was, or what they used," she said. "Skin problems are usually caused by something acting on the liver—the seat of anger or hostility. I would guess some kind of anger recoiled on the liver, and it's pushing a psychoenergetic poison out through your skin, from the inside."

Yep, that would have been my first guess too.

Nan looked up at me, her pale, blue-gray eyes tired but still bright. "Honey, go into the workroom and get me some broad-leaf dock leaves and some red clover and vervain. Asabarraca. And there's a jar labeled *French Clay,* if you could bring that, and . . ." she paused, thinking. "I guess that's it—we'll start with that. And Thais, fetch the rosemary and sage out of the pantry. Oh, and the comfrey tea."

"Comfrey tea wrecks your kidneys," I threw over my shoulder as I headed to the workroom.

"You can't drink it for more than three days," Nan reminded me. "Or it will."

I was standing in front of Nan's work cupboard when I felt Richard come up behind me. For one second I felt afraid—I couldn't forget that he'd tried to hurt me and Thais. But I also believed, as Nan did, that he would never do it now.

"Go away," I said, my back to him.

"Come to help you carry," he said in that sardonic voice that always felt like a challenge. "'Cause I'm that kind of guy."

I gave him a narrow-eyed look. "Don't even get me started on what kind of guy you are." I saw his jaw tighten as he tried to keep his temper from flaring. Turning back to Nan's cupboard, I examined small brown glass bottles filled with essences and extracts, dried this and powdered that. I set the asabarraca on the worktable, then found the ceramic jar of French clay. Next I went through files of pressed, dried leaves and flowers, organized not alphabetically but according to what larger family they were from, and within that, subcategories of what effects they would cause.

I knew this stuff pretty well and usually could put my hand on what I needed pretty quickly. But having Richard breathing down my neck made me tense, and I forgot what I was looking for.

"Go away," I said again irritably.

"Look, we have to get this straight between us," he said in a low voice.

"Get what straight? The fact that you tried to kill me and my sister?" Wide-eyed, I cocked my head, looking confused. "Is that what you're talking about? The attempted murder stuff?"

"Yeah, yeah," he said tensely. "My bad. Can we move on from that?"

I gaped at him. "Move *on?* Move on from attem—" I was literally speechless.

He waved his hand impatiently. "I explained all that. That was before I even *knew* you. Just—get over it. We need to figure this out, what we have between us."

"We don't have *anything* between us!" I hissed, trying to keep my voice down.

"That's bull, and you know it!" he said just as angrily. He moved closer to me, and I felt his indescribable force, as if we were literally magnets, positive and negative, irresistibly drawn together whether we wanted to be or not.

I kept my arms at my sides, as stiff as poles. I hated this! Hated what he did to me. "We have *nothing*," I said again and turned back to the plant file. Red clover, Red clover . . . my fingers flipped through plastic sleeves, all neatly labeled and dated.

In the next moment he curved his arms around me, pressing his body against my back from shoulder to hip. His arms crossed, holding me tightly, his right hand pulling my hips against him, his left hand curling up to hold my right shoulder.

"Don't say that," he murmured into my hair while all my nerve endings started exploding. I felt his breath, warm on my neck, and then he bit me gently, right where my neck curved into my shoulder. I shuddered, and my brain shorted out for a moment.

But just for a moment. I brought my arms up hard, breaking his hold, and though he'd trapped me between himself and the cupboard, I wheeled, ready to rip into him.

I didn't have a chance. He lowered his head lightning fast and kissed me, pushing me against the open cupboard so it teetered on its legs. He pressed hard against me, trying to make as much of me touch as much of him as possible. *Not again.*

His mouth was warm and hard, and I instantly recognized it. My body recognized his, my mouth knew the touch and pressure and taste of his. I could smell the slight smokiness of his clothes and hair and the fresh detergent scent of his shirt. It felt like, *At last.* I started to weaken, like honey warmed by the sun, becoming softer, more fluid.

But because I still somehow had two synapses left to rub together, I broke out of his hold again, pushing his chest hard, shoving him. He was breathing fast, chest rising and falling, and his dark, dark eyes looked lit by flames.

"Get off me!" I said too loudly, and lowered my voice. "Get away from me," I whispered furiously. "There's nothing between us, there'll *never* be anything between us! Now get the hell out of my way!"

Staring at me angrily, he held up his hands—surrender. He picked up the jars of French clay and asabarraca and headed toward the kitchen. "Get the rest of the stuff."

Then I was alone in the workroom, feeling like I was losing my mind.

Unfortunately, I knew myself well enough to know that I was partly angry at him and partly angry at myself for physically wanting him despite everything. He'd tried to cause fatal accidents to happen to Thais and me. He didn't love me, didn't love anybody. . . .

But something about him caused my body to go into hyperdrive. Something inside me wanted him, wanted desperately to meld with him, no matter what he or I rationally wanted or thought. I took some slow, steady breaths, trying to calm myself. I pressed my palms against my cheeks, which felt like they were on fire.

I forced myself to remember what else Nan had said. Thais was getting rosemary and stuff—oh, broadleaf dock leaves. Red clover. All this stuff had purifying, cleansing properties. The vervain would give everything an extra boost.

I brought the vervain and dried leaves back into the kitchen, where the kettle was boiling.

"Thank you, sweetie," Nan said, getting out her mortar and pestle. "There's a small jar in the back of the cupboard marked *Cendres*. Get that too."

I nodded, refusing to look at Richard, who leaned against the fridge, drinking his beer. In moments I came back with the jar of ashes, collected from various sacred fires.

Our food was cold on the table. I had lost my appetite, anyway. My hands clenched and unclenched nervously. I had to get out of here. Just being around Richard, much less Richard and Luc together, was making me feel like I was coming out of my skin.

"Okay, Luc," said Nan, sounding a bit more brisk. "Four things. A tea to make and drink one cup of, three times a day. I'll write it out for you. It'll help cleanse and strengthen your liver. A wash to use on your skin also three times a day. A mask to use once a day. You put it on, let it dry, then gently wash it off. And finally, a spell to perform twice a day, at noon and midnight, that will help channel this anger and energy out of you."

"Thank you, Petra," said Luc, his voice muffled. "I really appreciate this." I'd never seen him like this—it was like his gorgeous outer shell had split to reveal this ugly, less cocky version of himself.

Someone had done this to him magickally. Someone pretty strong. One of the Treize.

I wish I'd thought of it.

No, not really—I still felt burned about what he had done to Thais and me. My heart still felt broken. And in weak moments that I hadn't admitted to anyone, I still wanted him to be mine and only mine. But I had to say—seeing him like this made it a little easier somehow.

"Has anyone else been affected like this?" Thais asked. I'd been avoiding her eyes, not wanting to know if she was watching Luc, but now I looked at her. She seemed stiff and uncomfortable, but whether it was because of Luc or Richard or our fight, I didn't know.

Luc and Richard glanced at each other, and Luc said, "No, not like this. But Manon has moved out. She's left Sophie. Right now she's staying with Axelle."

"Such a good idea," Richard murmured.

"Why did she move out?" Thais asked.

"It turns out she'd tried to use the rite to kill herself, like Marcel did," Luc explained. "But without anyone else's help."

Nan shrugged wryly.

"But Sophie worked against her, preventing her spell from taking effect, not that it even would have," Luc went on.

"Manon realized it and felt like Sophie betrayed her. They had a fight, and Manon broke up with her."

"Oh, my goodness," Nan murmured, her hand to her chest.

"Wow," said Thais. "How long have they been together?"

"Uh . . ." Richard thought. "About a hundred and twenty years, I think. Something like that. They have a big fight every forty years or so. This will probably blow over."

"I don't know," said Luc. "This seems different. Manon was—more than furious."

"Women!" Richard shook his head, and I gave him an angry glare. He grinned at me and I quickly looked away. When Richard smiled, he looked like an angel who had been kicked out of heaven. A bad angel. A dangerous angel.

"Daedalus seems to still feel weak from it," Luc said, his eyes on Nan. He must have noticed how she was looking, how she was acting.

Nan nodded gravely.

"But no one else has anything like this," Luc said, gesturing to his face in disgust. "This is all mine."

"I think it will improve," Nan said. "It's not permanent. Just follow this regimen and in three weeks you'll be recognizable."

"Three weeks?" Luc sounded horrified.

"You'll be okay," Richard said, patting Luc's shoulder. "It'll be good for you. Character-building. See how the other half lives. Man on the street and so on. Instead of that male-model babe-magnet thing you usually have going."

Thais made a strangled sound, and I had to forcibly swallow a shriek of rage. Luc's babe-magnet effect had broken my heart and Thais's as well. Trust Richard to rub our noses in it.

"I'm going to Racey's," I said abruptly.

"But you haven't eaten," said Nan.

"Not hungry anymore."

"Well, okay," Nan said, "but don't stay out late. It's a school night."

"Okay." I made sure Nan wasn't looking, and then I stuck my tongue out at Richard. His eyebrows shot up and he grinned again. I turned and hightailed it out of the kitchen, but not before I'd glimpsed Thais's startled face—she'd seen me. But she didn't know the whole story between me and Richard, and she never would.

My purse and the keys to our dinky little rental car were by the front door. Outside, it was completely dark, a pleasant, balmy evening, maybe in the sixties. It was October. In a little less than four weeks our most important festival, Monvoile, would take place. It was a time of supreme magick, when the mists between the worlds thinned and pulled back slightly. And I had a plan for it.

I got in the car and started the engine, picturing tired little squirrels pedaling, making the engine run. As I pulled away from the curb, I felt Richard's presence lingering behind me. To hell with him. Jerk. I pulled out my cell phone.

"Race? Listen, if anyone asks, I'm at your house, okay?"

✤ Chapter Three

A Hollow Shell Within a Year

DAEDALUS TILTED THE SHADE OF HIS DRESSER lamp to throw light more directly on his face. Peering into his mirror, he turned one cheek forward, then the other. Two days after the rite, his eyes were sunken, his forehead furrowed, his lips thinner.

His powers were weakening, and it showed on his face.

He had no idea how this had happened, only when—at the rite. The failed rite that he had planned for, dreamed of, researched for more than two hundred years. It hadn't been the perfect recreation—no one had been pregnant. Several people had been there by force. The actual Source had not been bubbling up from the ground at their feet. Plus, the twins, with their powers—that could have been enough to throw the whole thing off. Everything that had been under his control—the timing, tools, the spells themselves, the location—all that had been perfect. But he wasn't able to completely control the Treize—not the way Melita had.

And, of course, Petra had actively worked against him.

Petra, Marcel, Ouida, probably others that he wasn't aware of. They'd worked against him, betrayed him. And now look at him—getting weaker every day. He wasn't positive that someone had specifically spelled him to weaken him like this, or whether it was just an effect of the rite's energy going haywire, being misused. But he would find out.

He had to prevent anyone from realizing what had happened to him. He couldn't afford to look weaker. Now, in front of the mirror, he practiced standing up straighter, holding back his shoulders, trying to firm his jaw.

Depression settled on his shoulders, making them sag. His power was leaking slowly out of him day by day, as if it were sugar trickling from a tiny hole in a sack. At this rate, he would be a hollow shell, a grotesque, powerless, walking skeleton within a year.

He had no choice now. Melita *must* be found. Then the two of them would do whatever it took to reopen the Source and completely re-perform the rite again in its entirety. With any luck, someone would be pregnant by then. He would have to speak to Luc, find out what was going on with that. If Luc hadn't made such a monumental blunder in the first place—

Anyway. His own path now was clear. But with Melita back, they would no longer be a Treize. One person would be superfluous and need to be eliminated. One of the twins, to break up their joint power? Or someone whose loyalties were clearly not with him? Or the weakest person?

He would have to decide, and soon, before he lost any more strength.

His doorbell rang, startling him. This problem had so consumed him that he hadn't felt anyone approaching, even coming up the stairs.

He cast his senses and frowned when he realized who it was. What would she want?

Before he opened the apartment door, he squared his shoulders and stood up straight, putting a stern frown on his face to seem stronger.

"Hello, Daedalus." Clio was trying to look casual, but he read tension in her shifting feet, the way one hand held her purse strap so tightly.

Daedalus quickly glanced past her out onto the covered balcony. She was alone.

"Who sent you?" he asked brusquely. "What do you want? I'm very busy."

"I know," said Clio, sounding more sure of herself.

"Well?"

"I want—I want you to teach me." Cerise's beautiful leaf-green eyes looked at him out of Clio's face. In a moment, he was transported back 250 years.

"I want to be immortal," she said.

✦ Chapter Four

Clio

I WAITED ON DAEDALUS'S DOORSTEP, TRYING to look brave and calm. "You offered to teach me that night in the cemetery," I reminded him. "I want to take you up on it."

"Petra just worked against me during the most important rite of the last two centuries," Daedalus said coolly. "Does she know you're here?"

I hesitated. If I said no, would he take it as permission to kill me and chop me up into little pieces?

"No," I said just as coolly, raising my chin. After all, I was Clio Martin, and I'd been making guys—young and old—quake in the knees since I was fourteen. "But Thais does."

In a general way. Not a specific right-now way. And she would kill me if she did know.

Daedalus looked at me. Lamps cast a soft amber glow over the walls, making the fourteen-foot ceilings look even higher. He seemed to make a decision and stepped back from the door. He gestured me in, and I expected spooky symbolic music to start playing, like "crossing the threshold, oooh."

As he had the first time we'd all met in his apartment, Daedalus went to a small table with crystal decanters laid out as though part of a movie set. He poured some plum-colored liquid into two miniature wine glasses and handed me one. It smelled nutty and warm and sweet. I waited for him to drink his first, since I didn't just fall off the turnip truck. He took a small sip, seeming to savor it before swallowing.

I decided to wait on mine. Time to get to business.

"Look," I said, taking a deep breath. "Monday night—the rite. I don't know what happened with everyone else. But I had a vision. I saw myself dead. Drowned. I don't know why." I walked past him to the tall French windows that led to his balcony overlooking the narrow street. "I don't want to die. Not now, not ever. I want to be immortal, like you and the Treize. Teach me how to do the rite, whatever I need to do to make it work."

I looked at him, still standing by his drinks tray. What if he had changed his mind?

"I saw myself *dead*," I said, trying to keep desperation out of my voice. "It wasn't just a vision—it was real. It's going to happen. I don't know when, but soon. I have to stop it."

I forced myself to wait, looking as calm as I could. I didn't want to give him any more power over me than I had to.

Finally he spoke. "So you want to participate, to help raise the power and channel it, instead of merely watching?"

"Yes."

His eyes narrowed at me, and his glance flicked down to my untried glass of port.

"Who sent you?"

"No one. I want you to teach me. Are you up for it or not? Do you *have* anything you can teach me?" I injected just the faintest tinge of skepticism into my voice, figuring that his Y-chromosome bullheadedness would kick in.

It did.

"I've forgotten more about magick than you'll ever learn," he said, anger flushing his hollow cheeks.

I paused and took a sip of the wine. It left a trail of heat down my throat and into my stomach. I *so* hoped I hadn't just done something stupid. "How pithy," I said, watching him casually as if he were a science experiment. "Did you make that up?"

His jaw set, and the way the light hit him just then made me realize that he looked older today than he had before the rite. Like Nan. Crap. Were they *aging?* Were they no longer immortal? Then Daedalus seemed to get ahold of his anger, and he relaxed.

He smiled. "You're tough, aren't you, Clio?"

I stood there and tried to send out "tough" vibes.

"How tough, I wonder?" Daedalus said, almost to himself, and walked toward me.

I am immoveable, I thought. *I am a rock.*

When he was close enough, he reached out one hand and gently placed three fingers at my temple. Too late I realized what he might do and jerked away, but he grabbed my arm tightly with his other hand and held me in place.

I closed my eyes, panicking, trying to shut my brain down, shut everything—

But it was too late, and he was too strong. In moments he had gained access into my consciousness, and then things became blurred. Second by second, I received lightning-fast patchwork impressions of a thousand different memories, over and over—for how long I don't know. Memories of my childhood, my first kiss, my first spell, being afraid, nightmares, being sick, feeling triumphant, a thousand pictures and emotions flashed inside my head like a film sped up to incomprehensibility. I felt terrified, on a roller coaster of emotions from hell, and wished desperately that I hadn't come. I had to get out of here, had to escape, had to— And then Daedalus turned me loose. I staggered and almost fell.

I caught myself on the back of a wingback chair, seizing the tapestry, rough under my fingers, and held on. I was breathing hard and felt like he had poured Drano on my brain and then caught my rushing memories in a steel basin. My other hand was curled into a claw, and I realized with amazement that I hadn't dropped the port glass. Slowly, slowly I came back to myself, trying to contain my consciousness, to pin my fear beneath my heel. When I could, I raised my eyes and looked at Daedalus, unsure how much time had passed, what he had seen, how he had done it. I'd heard of people doing this, witches, and Thais and I together had done a mutual version of it to become closer. But I hadn't realized that someone could do it so easily, at a moment's notice. He really was much stronger than I'd realized. I was in over my head.

No I wasn't. I could do this. I *was stronger than I realized.*

I stood up straight, trying too late to look unaffected, to control my breathing, and took another little sip of port. It felt like drinking blood, warm, rich, heating my veins and filling me with life.

Suddenly I wondered if it was spelled. *Oops.* What the hell was I doing? If Thais was right about him, then I was being about as stupid as I could possibly be. But if she was wrong—

Daedalus was standing several feet away, watching me.

I tilted my chin a little as if issuing a dare, pretending I wasn't terrified that he might have just wiped my brain clean of all memories.

No. I knew I was Clio. I had a sister. We lived with our twelve-greats-in-a-row grandmother.

"You do want to learn," he said.

"Yes." My brain understood his words. Oh, thank God.

"You came on your own."

"Yes."

"Thais doesn't know. She thinks you're at Racey's."

Crap.

Would I survive if I threw myself out the window and over the balcony to the street below? How high was it? Eighteen feet?

Suddenly Daedalus turned away, all business. He put down his glass and smoothed his goatee in the empire mirror over the table. "Well, come here. Let's see what you make of this."

I followed him to his formal dining room, which had paneling below the chair rail and old-fashioned flowered wallpaper above. As in Axelle's apartment, a heavy molding had been used for the chair rail, and more edged the high ceiling. Daedalus paused by a section of the wall and lightly drew his fingers across the wallpaper, whispering things I couldn't hear.

I heard the faintest click, and then a small doorway, invisible before, opened inward. Thais had told me about something almost exactly the same that Axelle had in her apartment. Did every witch have something like this? Just the Treize? Did Nan have one somewhere that I'd never found?

The interior of the space was dark. Daedalus picked up a four-armed silver candelabra and brushed his fingers over the candlewicks. They ignited instantly, and I thought, *So effing cool.* He went inside, gesturing to me to follow him.

In a movie, this would be the part where the audience is screaming, "Don't go in!" And then of course the stupid heroine goes in, and then the axe murderer gets her. I stepped in, my heart beating in my throat, hoping there would be enough left of me to identify the body.

We were standing in a space about five feet wide and maybe seven feet long. The interior was painted black, making the space seem smaller. Everywhere were painted silver symbols, making borders along each edge, covering the walls. I saw a cornucopia spilling tears or blood that made me shudder, though I tried to hide it. There were words in Old French, most of which I knew. And of course there were runes—all the usual ones I recognized and then some I didn't. I tried to have no reaction when I saw the same symbols here that I'd seen on Richard's walls in his room at Luc's apartment.

Come to think of it, there were a lot of similarities. Both had used silver paint on a dark background, both had these unknown symbols. What did that mean?

Black candles in small silver holders were everywhere, some new, some guttered. I looked down to see if they had dripped onto the floor and saw that the floor was also painted black, and a large silver-painted pentacle almost touched all four walls. For a minute I just looked around, hoping I wouldn't see a shrunken head or a jar of newt eyes. And I'm a *witch*.

"How do you think immortality works, Clio?" Daedalus asked. On a narrow ledge, a large, leather-bound book lay open.

"The Source," I said, looking at him. "It was like the fountain of youth or something."

"I'm not sure what the Source is," he said, setting his candelabra on a very small, narrow table. He flipped through the yellowed, deckle-edged pages of his book. "I think it's a power enhancer, whether it's a life force, or magickal power, nature, growing things."

"But it by itself isn't a fountain of youth?"

"It might be," Daedalus said. "But I don't think so. I think it just lent us power to prolong our lives. And I think we need to find it again if we're going to lend immortality to anyone else. But we can still accomplish a great deal without it. I can teach you how to get power from other things, and then, when we find the Source, you'll be ready."

That sounded like what I wanted. "What other things?" I pictured small dead animals and knew I just couldn't do anything like that.

Daedalus looked at me, his black eyes glittering. "Almost anything," he said, his voice mild. "From fire, from water, from plants, from the ground itself. From animals. From people."

I had a split-second image of Cerise, dead on the ground, followed immediately by an image of myself, also dead on the ground. Drowned. Was that what was going to happen to me? Would someone kill me to use my power? It wouldn't make sense—there were so many people who were stronger than me and would be more useful for someone to seize their power.

But they were immortal.

Oh.

"I see," I said, nodding. I had wondered whether to tell him about the awful, wonderful spell I had done on the neighborhood cats and decided not to. I didn't want him to think I was more evil than I actually was. I mean, I'm totally not evil at all, but telling him about that spell might give him the wrong impression.

"I'm not sure you do see," Daedalus said, "but I can show you. Let me walk you through a simple spell, teach you how to take something's power."

"You mean subvert its power?" Which was what I had done to the cats. Borrowed their power.

"No. Actually take its power. To keep."

Please, Deésse, don't let him bring out a live animal, I prayed, feeling my stomach tighten.

Instead he opened a wooden box, painted black and inset with a silver D, which seemed kind of prosaic—like, it should be another pentacle or a rune or some other symbol instead of just his initial. He took out an egg-size chunk of smoky quartz, uncut, just an irregular, flawed hunk of crystal.

"Everything has energy, Clio," he said softly, holding it out in his hand. I didn't know if I was supposed to take it or what. "Everything is vibrating, according to its nature. If you attune your vibrations to its, you can assume them. Then it will become part of you, and its power is yours to use."

A tingle of excitement stirred among my nervousness and tension. I licked my lips, looking at the crystal.

"How do we do it?" I asked.

"Ce n'est pas facile," he said, unexpectedly switching to French.

"Oui, je comprends," I said, not knowing how I should respond.

He gave a quick nod, then gestured to my purse, which I was clutching like a lifeline. "Put that down, and any electronic things you might have, like a phone or digital watch, or a— what do you call it—a pager."

I set my purse outside the door of the little secret room, fully aware that my cell phone was in it and that without it I was completely alone and unreachable. Daedalus waved his hand in the air, and the small door silently swung shut. I could only just barely make out its outline in the black wall, and I thought, *Oh frick*. My heart started pounding so hard I wondered if Daedalus could hear it.

My whole life I'd lived with a witch, Nan, and around witches. Nan had always been much, much stronger than anyone else. I had been the second strongest. Now I knew it was because of our heritage, because of the Treize. Even so, I'd never seen Nan just wave her hand and close a door. *She'd probably think it was tacky,* I thought with rising hysteria.

I looked up at Daedalus, at his dark, unreadable eyes. He looked very intent, focused on me, and I hoped it was because he was glad to have someone who wanted to learn.

"Come," he said, holding out his hand, and I stepped closer to the exact center of the silver pentacle on the floor. A long, slim black wand was resting on a shelf, and he took it and traced the pentacle's circumference with it. Our circle was cast. Then he placed my right hand over the crystal in his hand, so we were holding it together.

"First we center ourselves, where we are, and get in touch with our own power," he said softly. I'd never been this close to him before, and I was uncomfortable and unbearably tense. Suddenly I was afraid that I wouldn't be able to concentrate, that I would choke and look weak in front of him. I had to show him that I was strong, that I could do this.

Clio, do not screw this up. It felt like my whole future was tied up into this moment, whether I would live or die, literally, depended on the outcome of this situation.

I shut my mouth and breathed out slowly through my nose. Consciously I released all fear and regrets, just let them go and agreed to accept whatever happened.

Which, of course, is always the first step to getting in touch with magick.

"The first part of this spell binds us to the earth," Daedalus said. "Even though we're on the second floor."

His eyes twinkled. I'd never seen any sense of humor about him before, and it made him seem a bit less scary. A tiny bit.

"The second part recognizes the crystal's vibrations," he went on in a soft, soothing voice. "And the third part aligns our vibrations with its. Can you tell me what the fourth part of the spell would be? The quatrième?"

Spells were divided up into parts, anywhere from just one to as many as twelve or thirteen, depending on what you were doing. I knew spells existed with even more parts or steps than that, but I'd never done any of them, never seen them done. Putting the prefix *fin* in front of it meant that it had only four parts; the fourth part was the last.

"The fin-quatrième would be taking its power," I said. I had no problem with taking a crystal's power. It didn't seem alive, couldn't feel pain or fear. This was fine.

Daedalus started teaching me the spell. I knew the basic form, the grounding and centering, and I copied it perfectly. He seemed pleased, and I started to feel better.

The second part was also familiar—anytime you use

anything whatsoever in a spell, you have to recognize it, learn it, identify it. The third part was a variation on what I had done that night with the cats, but it seemed less scary and dangerous. I concentrated hard, memorizing it, and almost gasped when I felt my vibrations subtly align with the crystal's. My eyes were closed, and I was breathing shallowly through my mouth. I felt the crystal practically burning between our hands. Then we joined the crystal, and it was like we were no longer two beings, Clio and Daedalus, but one new, alien life-form made up of our two vibrations, plus this additional, weird vibration of the crystal. You couldn't picture it in your mind, and I can't describe it. But that was what it felt like.

Then Daedalus started singing the *quatrième partie*. I paid intense attention, though since we were linked, the words weren't even words. They were images and emotions and meanings, and they went straight into my brain from his. I started singing them too, though I'd never heard them before. It was a beautiful spell, elegant and precise, sparely written with no extraneous showmanship or clumsy, unnecessary elements. It was actually a much better spell than I would have thought Daedalus would craft—but then again, maybe he hadn't crafted it.

Suddenly the tone changed. I was in the middle of admiring it, memorizing it even as I sang it for the first time, and then it was as if the world went dark. I didn't open my eyes, but a heavy gray veil suddenly seemed to drop down over everything, separating me and Daedalus and the crystal from the rest of the world. A tendril of fear uncoiled at the base of my spine, but I ignored it, concentrating on the spell.

The spell started to unravel the crystal, separating its vibrations and energy from its form. It wasn't a clean break; it wasn't as if you could simply assume its power and still be left with a whole crystal. With horror I realized that the only way to get power from something was to destroy it utterly. The vibrations were being dismantled, untwined from their hold on the crystal's perfect, beautiful structure of neatly aligned atoms. Like a storm pulling a rose bush off a trellis, the spell slowly ripped away the crystal's energy. It was devastating. Then I was almost thrown backward as a sharp, clear burst of energy jolted into me, spearing my chest and filling me with light and fire.

My eyes popped open to stare into the glittering black eyes of an ancient witch. His face was alight, younger, his cheeks flushed and not so sunken. An insane riptide of joy submerged me as I felt the huge, spiraling power within me, far more powerful than anything I'd felt before, either at a circle or with the cats. I felt like I was glowing in the dark, that I could walk down the street and bring trees back to life, heal children, wave my hand and solve any problem.

Daedalus smiled at the look on my face. I realized his hands held mine firmly, which was why I hadn't been knocked out of the circle when the crystal's energy entered me.

"Do you see, Clio?" Hip lips didn't move, but I heard the words clearly. "Do you see how something's power can become yours for the taking? Do you see what life can feel like?"

I nodded, speechless, my head buzzing with wonder, my knees shaking. If I opened my mouth to speak, white light would pour out, lighting this black room like sunlight at noon.

I was ecstatic, intensely happy, filled with light and love and power beyond all comprehension. It was the most incredible feeling I could possibly imagine—I'd had no idea such a thing was possible, and in one second I knew that I wanted it, needed it, had to have it all the time. *What now*, I thought eagerly—*do we do another spell to keep it with us? How long will this last? Can I add to this?*

With no warning I felt it start to drain away.

Alarmed, I looked into Daedalus's eyes and saw my knowledge confirmed there. He knew it was already fading.

"No, no," I whispered. "Don't let it go!"

He shook his head, and we continued to breathe slowly in and out in unison. The power leached out of me, like bones being bleached in the sun. I wanted to cry as I felt it leave me, felt my joy and passion and power and strength fade, leaving me diminished, heartbroken, a pale reflection of how glorious I had been only minutes earlier.

I felt utterly shattered, as if my bones were turning to lace. My right hand clenched around the crystal like a frozen claw, and with difficulty I unpeeled my fingers.

Where the chunk of smoky quartz had been, there was now only a pile of ashy white powder. As soon as I took my hand away, it began to sift through Daedalus's shaking hand.

Abruptly my legs gave way, and I fell to the ground.

✦ Chapter Five

Effortless, Like Melita

IT WAS AMAZING, AXELLE THOUGHT. HER BLACK eyes focused unwaveringly on the black candle, hovering an inch over her black marble countertop. Her thought was a nebulous ribbon fluttering at the edge of her brain while most of her consciousness spun magick.

Axelle had never been able to levitate a candle, even after Melita had increased their powers, after Axelle had been studying magick off and on for almost two hundred years.

Now look at her.

It felt effortless, a smooth extension of herself, as if her will extended beyond the boundaries of her person to affect the world around her without even touching it.

This was all new, since the failed rite. During the rite she had asked for more power. She had gotten it. And this newfound power was intoxicating. She knew that all of magic was a balance—that if she had gained power, someone had lost it. But truly, why should she care?

"Mrew?" Minou jumped up on the counter next to the

hovering candle. His pupils flared when he sensed the magickal field, and when he saw the candle, he batted at it.

Axelle blinked, the candle fell, and the spell was broken. Minou's tail puffed instantly, and he jumped off the counter to hide under the couch. The whole thing had taken two seconds.

Nearby, Manon managed half a smile, which was the most Axelle had seen since Manon had shown up on her doorstep, suitcase in hand. Yeah, Sophie had screwed up big this time. Not that Manon's plan would have worked anyway—it wouldn't. Look at what Marcel had gone through. Axelle sighed. Marcel. When was he going to get tired of being a little storm cloud, raining on everyone's parade? Goddess knew *she* was tired of it.

But Sophie had blocked Manon's plan, when if she had just sat tight and not done anything, it would have ended up how she wanted. Now Manon felt betrayed, like Sophie had stabbed her in the back. Which, as they all knew, wouldn't have helped her plan either.

"You couldn't do that before, could you?" Manon asked.

"No," said Axelle, picking up the candle. "I'm stronger since the rite. I don't know how, but I am." She looked up at Manon, used to her childish face and body, the blonde hair, the dark eyes so oddly old and jaded and bitter in that pretty, girlish face. "You know, this is what Melita feels like all the time. More than this. Stronger than this." Axelle looked down at her perfectly manicured hands, the slim fingers that now seemed able to command magick at will.

"I never really realized it before," Axelle went on. "We all knew she was wicked strong, but I never understood what that meant. It meant this." She twined her white hands in the air, not making magick, but moving slowly and gracefully through space. "It felt like part of her, easy and natural. I mean, I think things, and they come to me. It always seemed to take so much effort before. Studying books, memorizing things, practicing forms again and again. This is the difference between taking endless years of violin lessons and being born a virtuoso."

Manon looked at her. "Do you feel like a virtuoso now, with magick?"

Axelle thought. "Kind of. I don't know. It's just—so much easier. It makes more sense. It comes to me. Before, I had to hunt magick down, wrest it out of the world, force it to my will. Now it feels *there*, everywhere, accessible. I can pluck it out of the air like a kite string." She made a pinching motion with one hand. "It's easy. Smooth."

"That's amazing." Manon sounded bitter—clearly she hadn't gotten what she'd asked for from the rite. Her dark eyes looked bruised from crying, her small face pinched and pale. Axelle still had no idea what Manon saw in Sophie—Sophie seemed so staid, so boring and prissy and goody-goody. Not that Manon was that bent. But she could have done so much better. If Axelle had been Manon, been made immortal as a beautiful child, she would have found a way to turn it to her advantage instead of whining about it for a quarter of a millennium.

"The thing is," Axelle said, going to the fridge and taking the bottle of vodka out of the freezer, "this is what Melita felt back then. And who knows what she's got now, what kind of power. But back then, she had this, possibly more, and she kept it to herself."

"What do you mean? She showed us all the Source; she did the rite," said Manon.

Axelle poured herself three fingers of vodka in a glass she hoped was clean. Manon wasn't the little homemaker Thais had been, and the place was a wreck. "But she didn't truly share her power. Yeah, she did the rite, made us all immortal, yippee. But only because she wanted it for herself as well. Before then, she was this strong for, what, ten years? A long time. And she didn't share that, didn't tell anyone else how to get it."

Manon frowned, then picked up her glass and went into the big main room. She sank down on a black leather chair with her back against one arm and her legs dangling over the other. "Well, why would she? People who have power want to keep it for themselves."

"You don't understand." Axelle lay down on the couch, her clothes sliding against the leather. She punched a pillow into place so her head was still high enough for her to drink. "I was Melita's best friend since we were six. I was more her sister than Cerise was—*she* was always off in her own little fairyland, all fey and golden and otherworldly. Of course we now know she was apparently boinking half the village."

"Only Richard and Marcel," Manon said.

Axelle waved a hand. "Uh-huh. How many people were you boinking? Or me? None. Because nice girls didn't. Even naughty nice girls didn't. But anyway, I was practically Melita's sister, but she didn't share her power with me. She could have made me stronger, and she didn't. I was the person she loved best in the world, and she left me behind in the dust, just like she left all of you."

"Huh," Manon said thoughtfully.

Axelle wanted to backtrack; she hated Manon knowing how hurt she felt now, today, at what Melita had done more than two centuries ago. But she couldn't help herself—these last two days had been a revelation.

"I mean, I was proud of her all those years. Yes, maybe I was also envious, but mostly I was proud. And she told me how sorry she was that she couldn't just wave her wand and tell me how to do it, that she had no idea what had happened to her—maybe she had been born that way. Yeah, right!"

Now that Axelle had gotten started, she couldn't stop. "She *wasn't* born that way—she discovered it. Or someone showed her, someone none of us knew about. If she had shown me, we could have made incredible magick together. But she kept it all to herself and lied about it."

Manon was watching her now as the implications of this started to sink in.

"And you were best friends," she said.

"More than best friends. Blood sisters." Axelle felt her cheeks heating up with anger, or maybe it was the vodka. For so many years she had let these thoughts go. But now they were stuck in her craw, a constant irritant. "But she didn't want a blood sister—she wanted a *lackey*. She wanted me to stay *beneath* her. She *wanted* to leave me behind. I never would have done that to her." Axelle drank angrily. She'd already said too much.

She was pissed, really pissed, at Melita, for the first time. She'd hated Melita leaving her behind, but she hadn't really known what had happened. Maybe something bad had happened to her—maybe she couldn't come back, maybe she hadn't become immortal for some reason, maybe she was dead.

But now Axelle felt, deeply and certainly, that Melita wasn't dead, that she could have taken Axelle with her. She could have shared her power, helped Axelle be much stronger, and she had decided to keep Axelle down.

✦ Chapter Six

Clio

I WOKE UP FEELING LIKE I'D SPENT THE NIGHT in a cement mixer.

My alarm sounded like the world coming apart. Groaning, I leaned over and smacked it off. Then looked at the floor, spinning crazily, and realized I was going to hurl.

Our small bathroom was between my room and Thais's, and I stumbled toward it, whacking my shoulder hard on the doorframe. I drew in my breath with a hiss, kicked the door shut behind me, and *almost* made it to the john before I tossed. Operative word being *almost*.

After I was done heaving, I splashed water on my face and rinsed out my mouth. A quick look in the mirror told me I looked horrible—splotchy, greenish, hollow-eyed. My birthmark stuck out against my unnaturally pale skin as if someone had smashed a raspberry against my left cheek. I grabbed a towel and swiped up the floor and toilet as best I could, then pushed the towel behind the big, old-fashioned tub, figuring I'd get it later and slip it into the wash.

I felt like walking death. Or in my case, staggering death.

This was a hangover, but the worst effing hangover I'd ever had in my whole misspent youth. This was a hangover caused by doing risky magick. *Dark magick,* I admitted to myself with a searing sense of shame and remorse. Magick I was hiding from Nan and especially Thais.

But that burst of power I'd gotten from the crystal—

My throat tightened again. I grabbed my hair with one hand to keep it from getting hit and hunkered over the toilet.

"Clio? Time to get up!" Nan's voice came dimly to me from downstairs.

Oh, goddess, I had school today. *Frick.*

"Coming," I croaked, hoping she could hear me.

A couple of dry heaves later, I groped my way to the bathroom door and headed downstairs, hanging on to the handrail so I wouldn't fall and break my neck. Obviously, I had "an awful stomach bug," and Nan would definitely let me stay home from school.

The smell of coffee and toast almost made me hurl again, but I forced myself into the kitchen so I could evoke as much sympathy as possible.

"Clio?" Nan called again. "Thais, maybe you should—"

"Hey," I said weakly, entering the kitchen.

"Honey, what's the matter?"

Thais was pouring me a cup of coffee, but she turned around at Nan's tone.

"Whoa," she said. "What's wrong?"

"I don't know," I said miserably, and right then I truly did feel miserable and scared and deeply ill down to my bones. Tears welled up in my eyes, and I rested my head on the table. If they knew . . .

Nan put a cool hand on my forehead. I had the sudden fear that she would feel the dark vibrations left in my skin like a scent.

"Hmm—you don't feel feverish," she said, looking at me with concern. "Let me get you something to settle your stomach."

"Yes, please," I said with feeling. "I ate something at Racey's last night—maybe it was bad. Maybe I should call her and see if anyone over there is sick." Still able to think on my feet.

"What did you eat?" Thais asked, coming to sit next to me. "You want some plain toast?"

My stomach recoiled, and I grimaced. "Um, a taco. And no thanks."

Five minutes later I was carefully sipping tea made with fennel, ginger, honey, and ground aniseed, still feeling like death might be a good option at this point. I didn't know why I felt so wretched and wondered if Daedalus did too. Maybe one got used to the effects of dark magick. Right now I never wanted to find out.

"Sip that slowly, honey," said Nan and sat back down to read the newspaper.

"I don't think I can go to school today," I ventured.

"No, not if you're this sick. Thais can get your assignments. Another good thing about having a sister."

I looked at Thais, who gave me an overdone perky nod.

"Yep," she said brightly. "I know you don't want to fall behind."

Nan gave me a knowing smile, and I moaned and hung my head over my tea. My stomach felt a tiny bit better.

"Oh, goodness," said Nan, reading the newspaper. "Your school—they've done asbestos testing and have found that some of the old insulation contains asbestos."

"It's an old building," said Thais, finishing her coffee.

Nan kept reading, one hand absently breaking off pieces of cinnamon toast. It smelled really good, and I started to wonder if I could maybe handle a small piece. Then my head throbbed again, a wave of exhaustion came over me, and I decided against it.

"Listen to this," said Nan. "Because they've found evidence of old asbestos, they need to shut the school down for several days while they determine whether they need to rip it all out or if they can just seal it up."

Thais's face lit. "We don't have school?"

This was too good to be true.

"Not for the rest of the week," said Nan, frowning as she read. "They'll make an announcement on the school's Website on Sunday night about what will happen next week. If they actually need to rip the asbestos out, they'll try to divide up the classes and house you all in other buildings, like at Tulane or Loyola."

"Yes," I said gratefully and drank more tea.

"Wow," said Thais. "Back in Welsford, there was a grade

school and a courthouse that had asbestos. They just sealed it all up, though."

"Well, you two have gotten a reprieve," said Nan. She still sounded tired, not totally herself, and I wondered again what had happened to her and Daedalus during the rite.

"Excellent!" said Thais. "No school!"

I remembered to be Clio. "So I'm wasting a perfectly good illness. Way unfair."

Nan sent me a tolerant look, one I knew well. "The injustice. Go on back to bed, honey. I'll come check on you in a little while. Is that tea helping?"

"Yeah. I'll take it up with me. Thanks." I carried it upstairs, feeling like I was made of glass and might splinter apart at any moment. I'd never felt this bad from a regular hangover, not that I'd had many. One time of throwing up Cuba libres through my nose had pretty much taught me how to cut off my liquor before it got to that point.

This felt much worse, like my *soul* had a hangover. What had I done?

I set the tea on my bedside table and crawled back under the covers. Thank God there was no school—the universe was looking out for me. I wanted to sleep for a year, and then wake up to find life back to normal.

I felt Thais coming closer, then heard her footsteps on the stairs. I closed my eyes when she came in and gently sat down on my bed. If she suspected that I'd started studying with Daedalus, she would be so mad. And worse, so hurt.

"Where were you last night?" she asked.

I opened my eyes. "Racey's. I told you."

She nodded. I couldn't tell if she believed me or not.

"Too bad about Luc's face," she said.

I watched her expression, which looked guarded. As mine probably did.

"Yeah. Bastard."

"Yeah. Anyway, Petra seemed to think it was only temporary. So—" suddenly her eyes met mine, sharp and green. "Richard. I think he's hot for you."

"What?" I practically yelped, my heart starting to race. "What are you talking about? Richard and I can't stand each other."

Except for when we were locked together, our mouths fused, our hands all over each other, getting under each other's clothes . . . But Thais didn't know about that. No one did, except me and him.

"I don't know," she persisted. "I saw him yesterday, how he was looking at you. He looked—like he wanted to eat you up."

"I don't know what you're talking about," I bluffed. "He can't stand me. And I can't stand him. He's so . . . supercilious. Like he's always sneering."

"Yeah," Thais said thoughtfully. "Well, watch him the next time he's around. See if you notice anything." She stood up. "I can't believe there's no school! I'm going out. Petra still looks kind of under the weather—I'll see if she needs anything. What about you? You want some ginger ale or something?"

"No thanks. I've got this," I gestured to the tea. "What are you going to go do?"

"Go to the grocery store, other stuff," she said vaguely, heading out the door. "Hope you feel better—I'll see you later."

"Okay." Once she left I snuggled down under my covers again, trying not to cry, knowing I would only feel worse if I did.

So Thais thought Richard was hot for me. I had an image of myself lying on the cool wooden floor of his apartment after I had furiously and unsuccessfully tried to take him apart. After the hitting and screaming and crying, I had lain there like a sack of laundry, and he had said, "I don't love anybody. I don't love you. But I see the value of you, the incredible worth of you, more than anybody I know."

Now, lying here in my bed, knowing what I had done last night, how I had taken something beautiful and utterly destroyed it for my own purpose, I started weeping silently. Richard was wrong. Right now I felt like I had no value and no worth.

Chapter Seven

Thais

WE DIDN'T HAVE ANYTHING LIKE BOTANIKA back in Welsford. I'm sure occult bookstore-coffee shops existed in Connecticut, but I'd never been in one. I wasn't totally comfortable here, still felt like an imposter somehow, among the nose rings and dreadlocks and pink and blue hair. There were *some* normal-looking people too. But I was pretty much the most boring person there.

Botanika took up the whole front half, almost a block long, of a building that looked like it had been a department store back in the '30s. Huge glass windows overlooked the street, and the interior showed what it might have been like eighty years ago, with pressed-tin ceilings painted a dark copper color, ceiling fans on long poles, all connected to each other by pulleys, and tall columns supporting a roof that must have been eighteen or twenty feet high.

Inside, all the way to the right, was the coffee shop, with its small square black tables and old-fashioned library chairs. Each table had a green-shaded banker's lamp, and the whole place had Wi-Fi, which explained all the students with laptops and iPods.

In the middle section, right when you came in, was a small area with funky clothes, bookshelves lined with all kinds of alternative books, and other shelves with candles, incense, herbs, and oils.

To the far left was a smaller section, less well-lit, with more shelves of books. These were more serious, books about witchcraft and voodoo, with deep knowledge of herbs and stars and the tarot. These were for scholars, people who practiced the craft. The books out front were more for dabblers, people who were curious but not necessarily serious.

At the back of the darker section was an area that was actually restricted. Two rows of bookcases faced each other, with a gold cord across the opening, saying no one under eighteen was allowed in.

It was easy to duck under.

After the rite, I'd been so upset about Daedalus and what I should do. I couldn't believe Clio didn't feel the same way. But my huge emotions had boiled down into one cold, coherent thought: revenge. I was here to figure out what form that revenge could take. After seeing Luc, I'd thought about doing something like that, only permanent. But Daedalus didn't seem like he would care about his looks much. Daedalus was all about power.

So I wanted to take his away from him.

Of course I had no idea how to pull it off. As Clio had

pointed out just yesterday, I wasn't a trained witch. I did have some power, and Clio and I together had tons of power. But she'd made it clear I would be doing this alone. This was my first recon trip—I needed to do research, figure out what was involved. If there was anything that I could do now, I would. If it was something that would take years of training, well, I probably had the time.

The books on these shelves looked older, beat-up, as if their lives had been hard. Who knew how many generations of witches had used these books, and for what purposes? They were loosely organized, but nothing was labeled *Dark Magick (Revenge)*.

I started pulling things out. There were books all about garden spells, crop spells, spells that used the moon phases, ones based in herbs or crystals or other tools. A few of the books had spells that seemed kind of dark—like how to make your neighbor's crop fail while yours thrived. But nothing seemed big enough, specific and ruthless.

One by one I examined titles, and again and again I had to stop myself from getting lost in something fascinating that didn't relate to my mission. There was a whole book about how women could use spells in conjunction with their monthly cycles, drawing on their changing powers. Who knew if that was real or not, but it would be so awesome to read. I had to flip through as many books as possible before someone kicked me out. Next month I would be eighteen, but they probably didn't care about that today.

Finally I saw a book with *Beware* written on its spine in faded, flaking gold leaf. I pulled it out carefully and opened it, half expecting its pages to crumble into dust in front of me. In fact, inside, its ink was so faded that I could barely make out the words on the pages. Frustrated, aware of time ticking by, I rifled the pages with my thumb, wishing that suddenly one page would be totally clear and exactly what I need.

Which didn't happen. All that happened was a small piece of folded paper fluttered out from between the pages and see-sawed its way to the dark green linoleum floor. I picked it up and of course opened it. Maybe it was an ancient shopping list. Maybe a love note from someone.

It was an address. Scrawled in faded pencil, hard to make out. It said, *Mama Loup's*. I didn't recognize the address. Which meant nothing, because I was still finding my way around this city and constantly got lost on the meandering streets. I slid the book back onto its shelf, ducked under the gold rope again, and headed to the front door, where a stand held tourist stuff in case someone happened to wander in off the sidewalk.

I pulled out a map of New Orleans and looked up the street, just out of curiosity. I mean, I'd found it in a book called *Beware* in the restricted section of Botanika. The street turned out to be really short, maybe three blocks long, stuck between two longer streets that framed it like the letter *H*. It was on the edge of the Quarter, close to Rampart and Esplanade.

I decided to go.

It took me a while to find it, despite having looked at a

map. I drove down the block, looking for a parking space, and I noticed how run-down everything looked here. New Orleans in general seemed to have a laissez-faire attitude toward litter and keeping public spaces tidy, but I was always shocked when I went through the poorer neighborhoods and saw how incredibly third world they looked. And that no one seemed to think this was unusual or alarming.

This was one of those streets. Only four blocks from the bustling French Quarter, with its tour buses disgorging tourists by the thousands, this street seemed far removed from anyone's attention. It was distinctly run-down, with crumpled wire hurricane fences sagging on their posts, trash, and weedy brown grass clumps everywhere. It was mostly residential, and the houses here were small and unkept, with tiny, raggedy yards, peeling paint, shutters lurching on one hinge.

After circling the block, I took a parking spot on the street that had first seemed too far but now was a reasonable option. I sat in the car for a moment and said every protection spell I could remember of the ones Petra had taught me. I tried to protect this pathetic tin-can rental car, myself, the air around me, and so on. I was aware of people walking by, looking at me, a white anomaly in their neighborhood of color.

I read the numbers on the address again, then got out of my car, locked it, and headed down the street. The address led me to a regular house, and I stood in front of it, frowning. Then I noticed it wasn't a totally regular house. A strip of broken sidewalk led around the side, and there was a crude, handwritten sign that said *Mama Loup's* with an arrow point-ing toward the back. As I was wondering what to do, a woman came down the side alley and walked past me.

"You can go on if you want," she said in a friendly voice, gesturing toward the back, then passed me through the rusted iron gate.

"Okay," I said, still hesitating. Then I thought, *If I can't even walk down a slightly spooky alley in broad daylight, how did I ever expect to take revenge on one of the world's most powerful witches?* Did I want to do this or not? Had I thought it was going to be easy? That it would be clean and fun and light?

Feeling disgusted with my lameness, I strode down the alley. Ragged bamboo fencing made a six-foot screen to one side, hiding this house from its neighbor. At that moment the sun blinked out. I stopped and looked up to see that typical rolling thunder clouds had filled the sky. Great. Because this place didn't have enough atmosphere.

A man came out, letting a screen door slam behind him. He brushed past me fast in the alley, head down.

I stopped in front of the door. A single lightbulb in a rusted fixture hung crookedly over the doorway. The door needed painting, and the screen had several holes rusted out. I couldn't see anything behind the screen. I swallowed hard and pulled it open.

I stepped in, unable to focus on anything. Blinking rap-idly, I stayed right inside the screen, ready to leap backward if I heard something—a gun cocking, for example. Oh, God,

I was so scared. It suddenly occurred to me—everything bad that could happen to me here, how stupid I'd been, how I was going to end up floating down the river, Jane Doe—

"You need help, sugar?" someone asked, and I almost screamed and leaped into the air. The Southern accent was so strong I could hardly understand it.

"Uh," I said, looking around wildly. Now I could see things, I realized. Shelves and posters on the walls and another bare lightbulb casting a weak light over in the corner.

"You looking for something? You lost?" The voice seemed bemused by my presence, but not unkind.

"I was looking for Mama Loup's," I said, my voice wavering.

"You done found it, honey. Whatcha want with Mama Loup?"

The shelves held candles of all colors. Some of them were shaped like people. Or body parts. Including a—

"Need a spell," I mumbled, my eyes taking in the old posters thumbtacked to the bead-board walls. I saw a faded, ripped one for a concert, a band called the Radiators.

"What kind of spell?"

Now I focused on the person talking to me. It was a woman somewhere between the ages of thirty and sixty. A brightly colored kerchief covered her hair. She wore African-style robes of intricately patterned material, and plastic flip-flops on her feet. One hand held a feather duster, which she had been flicking over the shelves.

"Honey, you want, like, a love spell for your boyfriend?"

She was amused now, starting to head toward a cracked glass counter case. "He foolin' around on you? You want him back? Want to make him sorry? I got what you need."

"No," I said, barely audibly. I cleared my throat. *Get it done, Thais.* "No," I said more clearly. "I need a spell to strip a witch's power away from him."

The woman paused halfway behind the counter and looked at me. Adrenaline had flooded my veins, and my heart felt like it would pump right out of my chest. I stepped closer, trying to look strong and unafraid.

"I'm a witch," I said firmly, hoping it wasn't a lie. "Another witch has wronged me. I want to strip his power away, leave him like an empty shell."

The woman blinked, then looked me up and down as if a stuffed animal had suddenly started talking to her.

I don't know what made me do this, but I stepped closer still and touched my fingers to the back of her hand. I had to convince her, make her help me. I looked deeply into her eyes, concentrating on the power flowing from my fingertips.

Her brown eyes widened. She stared down at my hand, then looked up at my face. I saw her gaze rest on my birthmark for several seconds. She was solemn now, not joking, not patronizing.

I saw her thinking, felt her indecision. I waited, trying to calm my breathing.

She drew her hand away, looking uncertain, then murmured, "Wait a minute." Turning, she went through a hanging bamboo curtain that almost concealed a doorway behind the counter.

I waited. No one else came into the shop. The air was full of incense that tickled my nose and throat. My eyes had adjusted, but everything still seemed unusually dim, as if light was actually being sucked out of the room. I'd gone from terror to a milder, barely controlled panic.

"Hello."

The voice came from behind me—I hadn't heard or sensed anyone nearby. Whirling, I came face-to-face with another dark woman. I couldn't make out her features—it was as if she wore a thin, invisible veil over her face.

"Mama Loup says you need a spell."

My voice was gone. So this was not Mama Loup, then.

"My name is Carmela," she went on. I couldn't make out her accent or whether she was black or white or Hispanic.

"I'm—" I began automatically, then stopped. Give a fake name?

"What are you looking for?"

"Someone killed my father," I got out, the words sounding harsh and bald in that quiet room. "I want revenge. He's a witch. I want to strip his powers away."

Suddenly this all seemed so impossible, so unbelievable. What was I doing? Who was I? This wasn't even *me*.

"You believe in witches, then?"

"I have to. I am one." Oh, God, what if this was a cop or something? Was I doing something illegal? Was this a trap? Get me out of here!

"And this witch wronged you?"

"He killed my father. I want to destroy him."

"Destroy but not kill?"

Going into the Treize's immortality would be too much. "Losing his powers would be worse than death for him."

"Yes," the woman murmured, moving away from me. "It would be for a witch."

She walked slowly through the shop, as though thinking things over. Every once in a while, I felt her dark eyes on me. I prayed a SWAT team wasn't about to bust in here. All I wanted was to run screaming down that alleyway, out to the open street and my car. *Let me make it out of here alive,* I prayed, holding my breath.

"A spell that would strip his powers away is dark magick."

No, duh, I thought with rising hysteria.

"It's very dark magick. You'll bear a mark on your soul forever."

"He killed my father." I felt like tears were not far away.

"I will teach you a spell," the woman said. "If you are truly determined to do this. It won't be easy. Are you prepared for pain? For fear? For darkness?"

His or mine? "Yes," I said, quaking.

"You will need these supplies. Come back when you have them."

A slip of thick gray paper seemed to materialize out of the air.

I took it, my hand shaking. "Okay," I barely whispered.

"Go home, little girl," she said. "Do not come back until you're ready."

"Okay." I nodded. Then, without waiting for her to say anything else, I wove my way through the dimness to the screen door and its patch of gray light leading to the outside. I crashed my way out, flinging aside the door and then breaking into a run down the alleyway. The air felt heavy and still, but so much fresher and real than the air inside Mama Loup's.

What had I done?

⚜ Chapter Eight

Damned All Over Again

MARCEL WISHED SERVICES WERE STILL IN
Latin. How much more majestic they had been, more mysterious,
seeming truly more divine than human. Now everything was in
everyday English, boring, pedestrian. Impossible to communicate
the glory and terrifying omnipotence of the Christian God.

Marcel winced. He meant, God. His God. The One God.
Deep in his soul he still had doubts.

This church was pretty, St. Louis Cathedral, right on Jackson Square. He remembered when this one, the third church
to stand on this spot, was built in the 1850s. It still held daily
masses and three services on Sundays.

The sparse congregation, consisting of a handful of ancient
women in black veils, some tourists, and a couple of nuns in
modern habits, stood. Marcel stood with them. People opened
hymnals, but Marcel had no need to. Everything in the hym-
nal and the Book of Common Prayer had been memorized
decades ago. Sometimes the wording was updated, modernized,
but Marcel always found his footing again.

The priest and altar servers made their way down the wide middle aisle, singing the final closing. Marcel filed out behind them, heading out into an afternoon that had clouded over and dropped about eight degrees. Which meant it was about seventy-eight. Welcome to October.

Marcel kept walking, through Jackson Square and across the street to Café du Monde. Having done today's penance, he could indulge in coffee and beignets, a silly, childish treat. And completely inconsequential compared to a lifetime of burning in a Christian hell.

He was standing inside the outdoor railing, looking for a free table, when he heard his name called.

"Marcel!" Looking over, he felt his stomach knot. Claire and Jules. He'd always liked Jules, liked his quiet dignity.

But what Jules saw in Claire, Marcel would never know.

There was no avoiding them; they'd seen him and were waving him over.

"Hello," he said stiffly, pulling out a chair and sitting down. A tiny Vietnamese waitress hurried over, and he gave his order.

Claire took a bite of beignet, sending powdered sugar raining down. The server brought Marcel's coffee and his own three beignets, and he took a deep breath, inhaling the rich coffee scent, tempered by chicory and made with boiled milk. The best coffee anywhere.

"So, Marcel," Claire said, still chewing. "Looks like heaven spit you back out again, eh?"

Jules paused in mid bite, his dark eyes turning to look at her.

Marcel also froze. Trust Claire to be the bull in a china shop. He didn't answer her, but cooled his coffee and took a sip.

"I'm just saying," said Claire. "I mean, what were you thinking? Jesus, if a measly knife in the heart would do it, you think I wouldn't have checked out long ago?"

"Claire." Jules frowned.

She looked at him impatiently. "Come on, you know it's true. And I'm not the only one." She turned back to Marcel. "What made you think it would possibly work?"

Again a black, bleak depression settled on Marcel. His chest actually still hurt where the knife had gone in. He'd been so hopeful, so ready to die. And then to find out he was cursed to continue walking the earth for who knew how long . . .

"I thought, the power from the rite," he got out with difficulty, then prevented himself from saying more by biting into his hot doughnut. It was, as usual, as close to heaven as he would probably ever get.

"Well, it's not gonna be that easy," Claire said. "That bastard pulled us all here for his big magic show—like we're effing puppets—and then he's all surprised when, lo and behold, not everyone's being their most cooperative. Idiot."

Marcel glanced at Jules over the rim of his heavy china coffee cup. Jules was pretty much Daedalus's oldest confidant. It was a somewhat unlikely alliance, but Marcel knew they'd been traveling together, studying together, off and on for about a hundred years.

"Daedalus is very ambitious," Jules said now. "He feels that he—that all of us—were wronged during Melita's rite, and he wants to repair what he can, enhance what he can . . . in essence restore some kind of balance to our lives."

Claire looked at Jules for a minute. She leaned over and put her hand gently against his cheek. "Dear, sweet, naive Jules," she said in a honeyed voice. "Yes, I'm *sure* that's it. I'm sure Daedalus is trying to *restore balance to our lives.*" She dropped her hand and rolled her eyes while Jules looked uncomfortable. "You guys—Daedalus has *never,* in his long, controlling, avaricious life, *ever* done *any*thing for someone else—unless it benefited him somehow."

Marcel watched Jules, watched the emotions cross his face. Jules looked like he wanted to refute it, but seemed to realize that example after example proved Claire right.

Claire ate another doughnut, like she had all the time in the world for Jules's illusions to be stripped away one by one.

"Then what do you think he's doing?" Marcel asked.

"He wants to re-create the rite. Why, I don't know. I think we need to find out." She looked at Jules meaningfully, but he stared straight ahead and drank his coffee. "Maybe he just wants more power. Maybe he's trying to pull Melita back. Maybe it'll reverse our immortality, but strengthen his. I don't know. I just know I'm getting more pissed by the day, being here. I tried to go over to the coast yesterday to visit some friends, and I got as far as Ocean Springs before his spell kicked in and I had to turn around." She sounded very bitter.

"I just want this to end," Marcel said quietly.

"Your life should be celebrated." Jules looked serious, despite the tiny bit of powdered sugar dotting his lip. "All life should be celebrated. You've been given a gift—the chance to rejoice every day, to do whatever you want to give your life meaning."

"Here it comes," Claire muttered.

"Both of you—so caught up in yourselves," Jules went on. "Instead of sitting around being unhappy, why don't you do something to give your life purpose?"

"Orphans in Africa," Claire said under her breath.

"There are people all over the world who need help," Jules said earnestly.

"I know," Marcel said, feeling defensive. "I've been taking care of the poor in Ireland for the last hundred and forty years."

"And that didn't give your life meaning?" Jules asked. "Didn't it give you some measure of joy, to know you were making a difference in those desolate lives?"

"It was all right."

Jules let out a deep breath. "You have been granted the opportunity to live extraordinary lives. Quit wasting them." He stood abruptly and dropped some money on the table for a tip. With a last, unreadable look at Claire, he made his way through the crowded tables and disappeared toward the levee.

"That's Jules for you," Claire said, sounding not bothered

at all by his lecture. "Sincere as shit. Still—" Her eyes followed his broad back. "He's a good person." Her voice sounded uncharacteristically soft, affectionate, and Marcel looked at her curiously.

"What is it with you and Jules?" he surprised himself by asking.

Claire looked surprised too, that Marcel would address it so openly.

"Oh, you know." She waved her hand vaguely, watching the crowd where Jules could no longer be seen. "I love him. He won't have me. And so on."

"But the question is," she said, looking at Marcel shrewdly, "what are we going to do about Daedalus?"

"What *can* we do?"

"You know who we should talk to?" Claire asked. "Axelle. Our Axelle has become quite the powerhouse."

Chapter Nine

Thais

"YOU'RE GONNA LOVE THIS PLACE," KEVIN SAID, patting my knee between shifting gears.

"Good—I'm hungry." I looked over at him and smiled, trying to seem normal. This had been such a bizarre week. Kevin had been asking to get together every day. I'd missed him, but he seemed so removed from the rest of my life—there was so much I couldn't share with him. Or with Clio, or Petra. Meeting Carmela, starting on that path, was weighing on me like a heavy, dark cloak that I couldn't take off. What would they say if they knew?

I looked out the Miata's window, seeing the shadows slanting steeply from the tall oak trees. It was as hot as summer, but the sunlight looked autumny: its quality, its angle. Every day I stepped outside, expecting a crispness in the air—and every day I was disappointed. Back home I'd be wearing sweaters by now and a jacket at night.

"And no school next week!" Kevin smacked his hands against the steering wheel. "How cool is that? Let's get Sylvie and Claude and go do something tomorrow, maybe get a little sailboat, have a picnic out on the lake."

"That sounds great," I said, loving the idea of doing something so aboveboard and normal. With Kevin, I got a glimpse of my old life, when I was a regular teenager in a regular town. More and more I felt like I was leaving him behind—and last night, at Mama Loup's . . .

"You cold?" Kevin's face was concerned, and he adjusted the AC. "You're shivering."

"No, I'm fine," I said. "Thanks."

"Hey—are you okay?" He steered with one hand, lacing the other through mine on my lap. Every so often he released it to shift, then he'd take it back. "You seem kind of—distracted."

"I'm sorry," I said. "It's been a crazy week. I haven't been getting much sleep, and my grandmother seems to be getting sick or something. I'm having a hard time focusing. Sorry."

"That's okay—I know how those crazy weeks go."

I bet you don't, I thought.

"Is there anything I can do to help?"

He was literally the sweetest guy I'd ever met. I gave him a bigger smile.

"No, this is good, right here. Getting po-boys with you, and then a movie. It's just what I need. A perfect Friday night." Nope, no witches here.

"Okay. But anything you want, you tell me."

"Thanks—you're a sweetie."

Kevin smiled at my endearment, then turned off of

Magazine Street toward the river. The houses here were small, but mostly nicely kept. Kids were playing and dogs were running around barking.

I got lost in my thoughts for a moment; these small houses such a contrast to the ones I had seen just yesterday. Yesterday. That whole experience had shaken me to the core. I'd made the decision to start down a dark path, one that would mark my soul forever, according to Carmela. And when witches said dark, they meant really *dark*, good-versus-evil kind of stuff. Stuff that could, well, mark your soul forever.

Was I ready to do it? This morning I'd bought some of the supplies from Carmela's list at Botanika. The clerk had looked at the assembled pile and then examined my face, as if to judge whether I should be buying this stuff. Some things I'd been able to get from Nan's cabinet in the workroom, very quietly when I was supposed to be in there studying.

I'd felt weird and kind of off all day. Now I seized a chance to feel normal and innocent.

"Where are we going?" I asked, seeing nothing but houses, no businesses anywhere.

"Around the corner," Kevin said. "It's a little hole-in-the-wall, but they make the best roast-beef po-boys anywhere."

"Sounds great," I began, but at that moment, a little girl chased a puppy into the street right in front of us. I gasped, and time seemed to slow down, each second taking thirty seconds to get through. Everything happened simultaneously, and it was only later, replaying it all in my mind, that I was able to follow the big picture of what had happened.

"Whoa!" Kevin said and jerked the steering wheel to one side, but not enough. The little girl, maybe four years old, froze with fear, staring at us. Someone yelled from the sidewalk, and I think someone leaped up toward the street. Words came into my mind, and I repeated them unquestioningly. Not knowing why, I put my hands together like an arrow, then split them apart fast, as if sending a burst of air between our car and the little girl.

The next moment, she was blown backward, right out of the street and against the curb, where she landed with a small skid. The puppy was flung to the opposite side with a startled, high-pitched yelp. An adult dropped next to the child, gathering her up into strong arms. She started wailing.

"Oh my God," I exclaimed, watching all this happen. "That was close!" Then I realized that our car was still moving, listing to one side of the street. "Kevin?"

Next to me, Kevin's head hung limply toward one shoulder. His hands had fallen off the steering wheel, and his eyes were closed. The car jumped the curb with a jolt, and I grabbed the wheel just in time for us to hit a fire hydrant on the corner.

Wham! I was jerked forward. My seat belt caught hard and slammed me back into my seat. I felt shaken like a rag doll. When I looked at Kevin, he looked dead.

"Kevin! Kevin!" I grabbed one shoulder and shook it, and he blinked groggily.

Then, just like in the movies, I heard a loud rushing sound, and a geyser of water shot out of the broken fire hydrant, shooting twenty feet in the air, then dropping heavily onto the hood and roof of our car.

"Wha?" Kevin mumbled. He blinked again, looking around in a daze, and slowly took in my anxious face, the car lurched up onto the sidewalk at an angle, the crashing water.

"What happened?" His voice sounded thick, and his face looked gray.

"What's wrong? Are you okay?" Starting to freak out, I saw that his lips looked faintly blue. I grabbed one of his hands. It was ice cold.

People had gathered around our car, and now the doors opened on both sides.

"Miss, you okay?" A gentle brown hand extended to help me out. On Kevin's side, people were helping him out too, but he sagged against a man, who quickly set him down on the grass by the curb.

"Kevin! My boyfriend!" I said, hurrying over to him, then remembered I had a cell phone. I dialed 911 as fast as I could and started babbling at the calm person on the other end.

"Sit down, honey," said a woman, tugging on my arm, and I sank down moments before my knees gave way.

Someone took the phone out of my hand. While I stroked Kevin's clammy forehead and patted his hand, I heard a heavy Southern accent say, "I don't know what happened. This girl and her boyfriend just knocked over a hydrant. Uh-huh." I heard him give an address.

"Get an ambulance!" I said urgently, because Kevin wasn't snapping out of it.

"This girl wants an ambulance," the man repeated. "And her boyfriend don't look so hot, I gotta tell ya."

After that, different choppy scenes intruded into my consciousness. The little girl we'd almost hit was okay, though scraped on one elbow. The puppy was okay. Most of the front end of Kevin's car was crumpled. I got my purse out of the car, getting soaked, then sat down next to Kevin again, holding his hand. I put my other hand on his heart and felt it racing uncontrollably.

Jeez, slow down, I thought fearfully. *Slow down, calme-toi.* Within seconds his heart did seem to slow down, but I didn't know if I had done it or if it had just happened.

"What happened to you?" I asked him.

"Don't know." He shook his head, still looking sick and gray.

An ambulance came. Police came. The fire department came and pushed Kevin's car out of the way and sealed the broken hydrant. The police questioned everybody, and I was pretty incoherent. They gave both me and Kevin alcohol tests, which were negative of course.

One paramedic said, "It's like he got hit by lightning or something. He's seriously out of whack."

The sky was cloudy but not thundering or lightning. They picked Kevin up and strapped him onto a gurney.

I remembered to call Kevin's house and explained it all to

his stepmother, who promised to meet him immediately at the hospital. She urged me to go home and lie down if I felt I didn't need to be seen by a doctor.

"We barely hit the hydrant," I said. "But Kevin was out before we hit it."

Finally they took Kevin to the hospital. I held his hand and kissed his cheek, but he seemed oblivious. A policewoman helped me into a cruiser and drove me home.

And that's when I had the thought—what if this had happened to us, to me, because of what I had set in motion last night?

✦ Chapter Ten

Thais

"THANK YOU." I WAS SO GLAD TO BE HOME.

"Let me walk you to your door," said the policewoman as I climbed out of the cruiser.

"No, that's okay, thanks." I was embarrassed that she was seeing me all upset and weak-kneed and just wanted her to go.

As soon as I opened the front door, Petra called, "Thais?"

"Yes." I headed toward the kitchen, practicing sending out my Spidey senses to see if Clio was home. I didn't feel her, but maybe she was upstairs and I couldn't get that far yet.

I stopped in the workroom and concentrated, but my nerves were so jangled, and all I wanted to do was sit down, so I blew it off.

In the kitchen, Petra looked the same as when I'd left less than two hours ago: a bit pale, tired. She glanced out the window, seeing what time it was.

"That was quick," she said. "I thought you were going to a movie."

"I was." I headed to the fridge and poured myself a glass of the ever-present iced tea.

"What's wrong, honey? You feel upset."

Startled, I thought, *Like, you're informing me?* Then I realized I felt upset *to her*. My aura felt upset; she could pick up on it. I sighed.

"Well," I began reluctantly, sinking into a kitchen chair. "Something happened to Kevin, and he wrecked his car. And we almost hit a little kid." It all came rushing back, and I almost collapsed onto the table, my head on my arms.

"What? Goddess, Thais, what happened? Are you okay? Where's Kevin?" Petra immediately got up and came to me, stroking my hair, her long, sensitive fingers tracing my forehead as though to get the information out of me by osmosis.

"I'm okay. Kevin's at the hospital. His stepmom said I should come home."

"But what happened?"

I tried to put it all together in my mind. "We were just driving, not too fast, down a little street. On our way to Del-Rays for po-boys. And suddenly a little girl ran in front of our car."

I sat up, trying to remember what had happened in what order. "There was a puppy. She ran after the puppy. She saw us, but was too scared to move. I gasped, and Kevin said something and jerked the steering wheel, but there was no way we wouldn't hit her."

"Oh my God," Petra said, rubbing my shoulders.

"Then—I don't know what happened, but I remember thinking I had to stop it somehow. Words just popped into my head, and I said them. And I did like this with my hands." I showed Petra the splitting-arrow thing. "And then, boom, the little girl flew over by the sidewalk, and the puppy went in the opposite direction. So we didn't hit them."

I looked up to see a bizarre expression on Petra's face. She focused on me solemnly, as if I'd just given her some terrible news.

"What?" I asked.

"Words came into your mind, and you said them, and you did that with your hands, and the little girl flew out of the way?" She looked deadly serious.

"Yeah, pretty much."

"Have you been studying displacement spells?"

"No. What's a—oh, when you move something out of the way? No, you know I haven't. I'm still learning the bazillion words for herbs." I tried not to sound bitter, but the amount of sheer memorization required for the craft was overwhelming.

"You haven't studied anything like that? Has Clio shown you something similar? Or anyone else?"

I thought. "No. I don't know how I knew it. It was just there, and I said it, and it saved the little girl. She just had a scrape. What?" I was starting to feel alarmed at Petra's expression.

"Okay," she said, sitting down across from me. "Then what happened?"

"Well, I did the thing, and the little girl was out of the way.

But we headed toward the left curb, and I said, 'Kevin,' and then I saw that he was unconscious, passed out."

"Unconscious?" Petra looked awful.

"Yeah—I don't know what happened. It's like he's—diabetic or something and just passes out. The paramedics said it was like he'd been hit by lightning. This happened once before," I said, the word *lightning* triggering a memory. "That night we did get hit by lightning. Remember? Kevin almost passed out, and that guy had to help us. I mean, I wonder what's wrong with him. Maybe I should talk to his dad or stepmom about it."

Petra gazed at me with her clear, blue-gray eyes. "He's not diabetic," she said.

"How do you know?" Could she really tell without even examining him?

"It's you. It's what happens when you make magick around him."

I stared at her. "What do you mean?"

"I don't know why you're able to perform such powerful spells without studying," Petra said slowly. "That's something we should look at. But with Kevin—what you're doing is, essentially, sucking his energy out of him. His life force."

Horrified, I gaped at her. "What?"

"Magick doesn't come out of thin air," Petra explained. "Though it might look like it does. Magick is everywhere, and when you make magick, it's mostly *gathering* magick. Though you can increase what you have to work with."

I wasn't following her.

"Trained witches create boundaries around their spells, so it doesn't affect any living thing around them, except of course whatever they want to affect. But you're not trained, and when you do powerful magick, it grabs force from wherever it can. In this case, from Kevin."

I could hardly take it in. "*I* did that to him? But he was—he was gray. His heart was beating way too fast. He's at the *hospital*."

Petra nodded. "It happened before, at the fountain. At the time, I thought maybe the lightning itself had affected him. But now it seems like it was probably you."

"Oh my God." I was appalled and felt my throat close and tears spring to my eyes. *I* had done that to Kevin. My making magick had sent him to the hospital. And now all sorts of memories came to me—of Kevin suddenly seeming dizzy a couple of times. Even his stepmother swaying against a doorframe. Every time I had called up the tiniest little spell, it had affected him badly. Today the spell had been pretty strong, and it had practically killed him.

"Oh my God," I said. "What am I going to do?"

"You have to learn how to put up boundaries, as fast as you can," said Petra. "But that can take a long time. Or you have to stop making magick of any kind, for any reason, around Kevin—or any other non-witch, for that matter. Witches have an inbuilt defense mechanism—you'd have to try really hard to take our power."

I swallowed, not looking at her, steering my mind away from what I wanted to do to Daedalus.

"The third option is, you have to stop seeing Kevin."

Today, last night, this whole week, had been too much. I couldn't stand it. "I'm going to take a shower," I said, my voice breaking. Standing up, I hadn't made it through the doorway before I started crying.

"Thais," Petra called.

I turned back and saw her looking very serious.

"You need to make some hard choices," she said, her voice gentle. "But you must make them. Let me know if you need help."

I nodded and headed upstairs. In the bathroom I pulled the shower curtain around the big, old-fashioned tub and turned on the water. I lay in the tub, eyes closed, with the water raining down on me as if it could wash away all my darkness.

✦ Chapter Eleven

Another Hundred Years

"I'M NOT SURE SHE WANTS TO TALK TO YOU."
Axelle sounded apologetic, but Sophie knew better.

She had come prepared. "I need to speak to Manon now,
Axelle."

When Axelle continued to block her apartment door,
Sophie brushed past her and entered the cool, dark interior. It
was amazing, Sophie thought, how they each managed to find
their own environments in whatever city they happened to be
living in. Axelle's apartments always looked like this. Daedalus's was unmistakably his. Where she and Manon settled, it
had always seemed homey and warm, welcoming and safe.

Except now. Now Manon was gone, most of her clothes
out of their closet. It felt unbearably bleak and empty, awful to
come home to. And she'd been gone only four days.

Axelle's short, dark foyer opened up into the large main
room on the right and a small galley kitchen on the left, separated from the hallway by a half counter. A black cat sat on
the counter, drinking water from a bowl. Sophie wanted a

cat. Maybe she would get Manon a kitten. Though actually, Manon had said she didn't want to be tied down to taking care of an animal.

It took a moment for Sophie's eyes to adjust—the kitchen light was on, but the main room was lit by only two inadequate lamps. The first thing she saw was Marcel's bright, copper-penny hair, starkly visible against the black and white of the kitchen. What was he doing here? His unexpected presence unnerved her.

"Sophie," he said, nodding at her.

"Hi," she said, flustered, and then turned toward the main room. To her relief she saw Manon, draped over both arms of a big leather chair, reading a *Marie Claire* magazine.

"Hi," Sophie said, hurrying over to her. She sank down beside Manon's chair, gazing up at the face she'd loved for more than a hundred years. Manon looked tired, unhappy, and Sophie wanted to pull her into her arms, hold her tightly, tell her everything was going to be all right. Reaching out, she touched Manon's jean-covered knee, but Manon pulled away. Sophie's heart sank lower.

"Can we talk, please?" she asked in a low voice, all too aware of Marcel and Axelle.

Manon's expression was ungiving. "We've talked."

Sophie glanced behind her to see Axelle making no effort to disguise that she was listening in. She was making a gin and tonic at the kitchen counter while Marcel watched her, frowning slightly. Why was he here, anyway? He couldn't stand Axelle.

"Please, honey," Sophie said. "Please let's just talk it out. You know I wouldn't hurt you for the world."

"No, but you would hurt me for *you*," Manon replied quietly.

The words stung. Sophie wanted to deny them, but deep down she knew they were true. She'd been willing to sentence Manon to an endless lifetime of unhappiness and frustration just so that she, Sophie, wouldn't lose her. The really bitter thing was that she hadn't had to do anything at all—they'd seen that even a much more powerful suicide spell wouldn't work. If she had done nothing, if she had even pretended to support Manon's wishes, she would still have had the outcome she wanted.

And Manon wouldn't have left her.

"I'm so sorry," Sophie said, looking down at her hands, clenched in her lap. "I know it was wrong. You're right—it was inexcusably selfish of me. But I did it out of love—because I love you so much I can't bear the thought of living without you."

"That's the thing," Manon said slowly, standing up. Sophie scrambled to her feet, watching the sweet, perfect face that had frozen in time when Manon was thirteen years old. "I believe that you did it because you couldn't bear the thought of living alone. But I don't know if that was about me, really *me*, or just about you being afraid to live alone."

"What are you talking about?" Sophie cried, following Manon to the kitchen. Glancing uncomfortably at Axelle and

Marcel, she saw they were watching with undisguised interest. "Manon—can we talk about it in private? Please?"

"I don't want to talk about it at all." Manon's voice was bleak. She got a glass out of a cupboard and helped herself to some gin and tonic. There was a lime already sliced, and Manon squeezed a piece into her drink, then dropped it in.

"You have to forgive me." Sophie was growing ever more alarmed. She and Manon had had fights before—had even broken up for a few days at a time, but that had felt different than this. Manon seemed so cold, so unyielding.

Manon sipped her drink, watching Sophie over the rim. "No, I don't." The words sounded sad rather than angry.

Sophie's heart froze. "Manon—can't you see that I need you? That I love you more than anything?"

"I believe that you need me."

"You think I don't *love* you?" This was beyond humiliation, having to beg like this. But Sophie was past caring. All that mattered was that Manon relented and came back.

"I don't know," said Manon quietly, touching an ice cube with one fingertip, not looking at Sophie. "Maybe you just can't be alone."

"*What?* Manon, how can you say that?" Sophie exclaimed, feeling close to tears. "I love you! You're the only person I've ever loved!" As soon as the words were out of her mouth, she had a cold, sinking feeling. But maybe Manon wouldn't remember. . . .

But she did. "That's not entirely true," Manon said evenly.

"I've had a lot of time to think." She gave a short, bitter laugh. "I mean, a *lot* of time. And now I wonder if I wasn't always second best."

Sophie gaped at her, horrified. *Oh no, oh no, oh no—don't say it, don't go there—*

"Compared to how much you loved Marcel."

There was dead silence in the small kitchen. Outside, someone shrieked with laughter, a car horn blared. Sophie felt far removed from this bright, untidy kitchen, with plates piled in the sink, Minou leaning down from a counter, pawing through the trash. She stared at Manon's small, heart-shaped face, aware only of a desperate, desperate wish that she had misheard, that Manon hadn't just said that in front of these two, that Manon would never betray her—

—the way she had betrayed Manon the night of the rite.

Oh, goddess.

Sophie pressed her hand to her mouth, feeling like she was going to be sick.

"Whaaat?" Axelle asked with fascination, her black eyes darting from Manon to Marcel to Sophie.

Sophie couldn't move, couldn't believe this was happening. She took rapid, shallow breaths, aware of Axelle and Marcel on either side of her in her periphery. Her eyes were locked on Manon's sad, angry, ashamed, triumphant face.

"Uh . . ." said Marcel, sounding shocked.

What was he doing? Thinking back over the last 250 years, looking for clues? Sophie thought hysterically.

"My God," said Axelle softly. "None of us knew. Except Manon."

"I have to go," Sophie breathed through a clenched jaw. Blindly she turned and stumbled toward the front door. Her car keys jingled in one pocket; she had no idea where her purse was. It didn't matter. Nothing mattered anymore. She clawed frantically at the locks, yanked the door open, and ran out into the courtyard. A motion sensor light came on, flashing white light into her face. Sophie shaded her eyes and ran down the flagstone alley to the street. She tried to remember where she had parked, but her mind was a complete blank. Instead she hurried down one block and then another, not knowing where she was going, not caring.

She couldn't believe Manon had done that to her. What a payback. Now Marcel knew. Manon might be giving them all the details even now, details Sophie had confided to her more than a hundred years ago, in the early stages of their affair.

Sophie had never wanted Marcel to know. She could have gone another hundred years without Marcel knowing. Finally she collapsed against an old brick wall overhung with long canes of Lady Banks roses, trailing to the sidewalk. Pressing her face against the soft orange brick, Sophie sobbed.

This, more than anything, meant that she and Manon were over for good.

✦ Chapter Twelve

Clio

THIS TIME LAST YEAR, I'D BEEN FIELDING THREE
different guys, including a twenty-two-year-old paralegal I'd
met at Amadeo's. Every Friday and Saturday night had been
taken; I was so busy I could hardly catch my breath.

Look at me this year: My only romance in the last three
months had ended in humiliating disaster. Other than that, I
had the occasional, incendiary smashmouth kiss with Richard,
who I didn't like and who didn't like me.

Now here I was on a Saturday morning in a cemetery with
a man old enough to be my grandfather, like, a million times
over. And yet this seemed more important than social butter-
flying, not that anyone would believe I ever thought that.

"Okay, now, is the whole earth going to crumble into lifeless powder when I do this?" I sounded grumpy, probably to
hide my fear and distaste. The last time I'd done this, a beautiful crystal had turned to horrible, dead-feeling powder in my
hand because I'd taken its life force, for want of a better word.
Its energy. Its chi. You might think a crystal is already pretty

dead, and, yeah, it isn't alive in the same way that a squirrel is, or a freshman, or an amoeba. But magickally, there's a huge, striking, palpable difference between a regular crystal, solid and integral, and what had been left after I'd taken its chi. The powder had felt repulsive to me—dead. I'd thought about it since then and decided it felt like antilife, anti-magick. Not just *nothing*, but a horrible absence of something. It had been like holding death and made my skin crawl.

Which made my sitting here, getting ready to do it on a bigger scale, seem astoundingly stupid, even for me.

"No," said Daedalus. "We can set the limitations to exclude actual vertebrates and invertebrates, so the energy would come solely from plants and the earth itself. Nothing will turn to white powder, I assure you."

I nodded, thinking about Thais and Nan. They would hate my being here. Since I'd started studying with Daedalus, I'd been hiding it every moment I was home. Usually when I felt bad, I'd go to Nan for help. I could even go to Thais. But not about this. Not about how sick this made me or how it felt emotionally. This I just had to handle on my own. It separated me from them like nothing else.

"The last time I did this," I told Daedalus as he continued to set up the spell, "I had the mother of all hangovers. Including barfing my guts up, which doesn't do much for a girl's looks. What caused that?"

"Everything has a price, Clio," Daedalus said, trickling salt in a circle around us. This was an unused corner of the cemetery with fine, short grass and the occasional weed popping up next to the crypts. Daedalus had set up a couple of spells to gently turn people aside if they came close to us and to make us hard to see if they somehow got through anyway.

"It will grow less with time," he went on. "I can also give you some herbs and a spell to help counter the aftereffects. But if you want to sail through with your beauty rituals and your make-him-love-me tisanes, then you've come to the wrong place."

His voice was suddenly harsh, his face forbidding. Now I felt like a wuss for even mentioning it.

"Whatever," I said, sounding ticked off. We worked in silence for ten minutes, Daedalus doing his parts, and me doing mine. When everything was set up, we sat cross-legged in the circle, facing each other. A heavy black pillar candle sat in its holder between us.

"You'll be drawing energy up out of the earth," Daedalus explained. "The earth is humming with the vibrations of the living things within it, of the life and growth and change happening on a huge scale and a minuscule scale at every second. Even deep, deep beneath the surface, where not even bacteria can live, you still have the energy of the earth itself, its inner core of burning iron."

I looked at him. "You couldn't tap into that. It'd be like tapping into a nuclear bomb."

"Yes," said Daedalus, sounding regretful. "It would take the strongest magick imaginable and probably end up killing you.

I'm just pointing it out. Now, are you ready? Do you remember the first part of the spell?"

Nodding, I let my hands rest palms up on my knees. This position is used a lot in mediation because it connects all the parts of your body to all the other parts, creating a circle of energy. Meditation and magick have a lot to do with each other.

It was a lot like it was before. The first part of the spell set the limitations and defined the scope of the spell. The second part put me in touch with my own personal power. The third part sought out and identified other magickal power, in this case from within the earth, the actual dirt beneath us. And the *quatrième* aligned the two powers, joining me to the earth's energy.

At first nothing seemed to happen, and I was disappointed. Then, just like when the charcoal briquettes caught on fire, I became aware of power licking at the edges of my consciousness.

"Open yourself to it," Daedalus murmured, his eyes closed. "Let it in."

I was afraid. It was a beautiful thing, a glorious thing to feel myself become one with the earth; yet compared to the crystal, this had the potential to be a tsunami, a terrifying tidal wave of energy that could fry my brain and leave me making pot holders at the state mental hospital.

"Don't worry," said Daedalus. "You will tap into only a microscopic section of the earth. You'll feel power, but will be in no danger."

I hope you're right, old man, I thought, then hoped he couldn't feel my thoughts. *Damn it. Had to be more careful.*

"Concentrate," came Daedalus's voice, and I yanked my focus back to the spell. There was a wall of energy pressing against me. It was very different—I'd held the crystal, and its energy had been right there, blooming in my hand like a flower. This was something pressing against me from the outside.

"Let it in," Daedalus said again.

I tried to relax, to take down my natural walls. *Come on, Clio, think! Do it. You can do this. You have to do this.* I relaxed every muscle, controlling my breathing, trying to release every bit of fear or alarm I felt.

And suddenly I was flooded with light and power.

The crystal's power had been a burst within me. This was a wave washing over me, bigger, unstoppable.

"Oh," I breathed, inhaling it in, feeling it fill every cell in my body. It was indescribable, an ecstatic feeling of omnipotence and joy. I felt like I could move cars with a wave of my finger or cure cancer by laying my hands on someone. I could topple bridges with my thoughts. Like the crystal, it was more than intoxicating. This was why I was willing to risk feeling like death afterward, willing to destroy a crystal, willing to rip power away from the earth itself. To feel like this. I wanted to laugh.

The crystal's burst of power had lasted less than a minute. This seemed to go on and on as I took in the world around me. I glanced at a sparrow, tucked inside a shrub nearby. Instantly

I became the sparrow, felt myself small and light-boned, bursting with quick-tempoed life. The world simplified in an instant, my entire existence made up of my feathers, the air moving in and out of me, the rustle of the leaves on the shrub.

Tearing myself away from the sparrow, I saw a dandelion growing in a crack in the cement. I felt its intense surge of life, growing upward, felt our roots digging deeply into the thin soil for nourishment. I started crying. I felt like the goddess. I *was* the goddess.

"Yes, and now . . . " Daedalus murmured, singing softly.

"No, no, no!" I cried, snatching out at the air, at the invisible, seductive life force that I felt draining away from me, escaping into the wind, into everything around me. Within a minute it was gone. The colors of my world had drained away, leaving everything in black and white. I came to, finding myself staring at Daedalus's flushed, ecstatic face, his eyes glittering. He looked younger, healthier. How long would that last?

Then I fell sideways, hitting the short grass before I'd even realized I was losing my balance. I lay sprawled awkwardly, unable to process how empty I felt, how desolate everything was, without that power.

That feeling was what Melita had gone to such extreme lengths to get, including even killing her sister.

I understood why she had done it.

❧ Chapter Thirteen

Thais

"HE'S ASLEEP?" I STOOD ON KEVIN'S FRONT porch. It was shaded by huge oaks, freshly painted, and dotted with white wicker furniture. These people knew how to live.

Mr. LaTour nodded. "Yes. I'm sorry, honey. We've only just gotten home from the hospital. The doctors said he's going to need several days of total peace and quiet."

"Did they figure out what was wrong with him?" My voice was small, and I hoped that extreme guilt wasn't written all over my face.

"No." Kevin's dad sounded worried, and I felt terrible. "It might have been some electrical aberration that won't ever happen again, but we're keeping him on a portable monitor for at least four more days. Good thing you guys don't have school this week."

"Yeah." I swallowed. "But he'll be okay?"

"He should be fine." Mr. LaTour sounded almost too hearty, and I knew he was worried—I could feel it. I was so much more in tune with people's feelings these days. Since I'd gotten in touch with my magick. The magick that had almost killed my boyfriend.

"Thais—I wanted to thank you for what you did that day."

I looked up, eyes wide.

"I know you steered the car away from the little girl and that you called 911 right away and stayed with Kevin until the EMTs came."

I couldn't say anything.

"The police report showed that neither of you had been drinking. I just want you to know that I was glad Kevin was with you when it happened."

Oh, God. I was going to fall apart. If Kevin hadn't been with me, he would be totally fine and not on bed rest with a heart monitor.

I nodded, trying not to cry, and pushed my small bouquet of Petra's flowers at Mr. LaTour. "If you could give him this," I said. "And this card."

He took them from me and nodded. "He'll be fine, honey," he said kindly. "And as soon as he's up to it, I know he'll want to see you."

I nodded again, turning to go. The only time I was going to see Kevin again was to tell him I was breaking up with him.

• • •

Fifteen minutes later I was walking down Daedalus's street. I'd been here only once, and hoped I would recognize his door. I couldn't exactly ask anyone for his address.

I had a totally lame excuse ready—wanting to ask him

Cate Tiernan

about the history of the Treize, as if it were a school report. All I needed was to get into his apartment for a minute, get close to him somehow. I just prayed that he wouldn't immediately be suspicious and kick me out.

I slowed down, looking at tall, white-painted doorways. He lived close to a corner in one of the fancy apartment buildings that bordered Jackson Square. I thought it was this one, on the north side. . . .

Tourists streamed past me, most of them watching the sidewalk artists that had set up their stands around Jackson Square. Each one had a subject perched on a stool, holding very still. I'd watched them work before, when I lived in the Quarter with Axelle. Interestingly, every one of them started a portrait by doing the person's eyes first.

Anyway. Where was it—it wasn't the one on the very corner. The second one in? An iron-gated doorway led down a short, very narrow alley to the back courtyard, where the stairs were. This had to be it.

I rang his doorbell, wiping my sweaty hands on my peasant skirt. I had rehearsed what to say a hundred times on the way down here. Minutes passed. No one leaned out over his balcony, no one buzzed me in. Just then, a woman came down the alleyway. Not even looking at me, she opened the iron gate, then held it a minute for me to go in.

"Thanks," I murmured casually, pretending to put a key back in my purse. My heart in my throat, I headed down the alleyway. Could I do this? I had come this far.

Now that I was in the courtyard, I was relieved to definitely recognize it as Daedalus's. His apartment was on the second floor—all of them were, since the first floor was for stores and restaurants. I cast my senses, sending my thoughts up the stairs I was climbing, seeing if I could possibly feel Daedalus or anyone else in his apartment.

Impressions came to me from other apartments, which was really interesting. I could tell if they were male or female and what kind of energy they were putting out. It was amazing, and if I hadn't had a mission, I would have been happy to sit on the top step, close my eyes, and just see what else I could pick up.

At Daedalus's apartment I leaned against the front door, hearing nothing and feeling no presence inside. Which didn't mean anything—he could very easily cloak himself from me. Except none of them seemed to do that at home. We could always tell who was where if we were close enough. I didn't know how to cloak myself very well.

I knocked several times. No one answered. Maybe he wasn't home. Damn. I needed to do this now, so I could meet with Carmela later. Just thinking about her and the ingredients she'd demanded filled me with tension and a deep sense of foreboding. Making the decision to strip Daedalus's powers from him had been my first step on this path, meeting Carmela had been the second step, and what I was doing here was the third step.

Still, this was all reversible—if I changed my mind, no

harm had been done. But eventually I would be past the point of no return. What would that feel like?

I took a deep breath and let it out, looking at this thick front door. Okay, what to do?

It came to me in an instant: the memory of the secret room at Axelle's apartment, which had been locked. One day I'd thought about the lock opening, and I think I had actually opened it. This was before I knew I was a witch—it must have been my latent, personal magick.

This time felt different, clearer; my power seemed to flow in a clear stream from me to the lock. Within a minute I felt the tumblers fall into place, heard the faintest click of the bolt pulling back.

A door opened at the other end of the balcony, and an older couple carrying several shopping bags headed toward the stairs. Quickly I opened Daedalus's door and slipped inside, locking it behind me. I heard the couple pass, heard them bickering quietly the way old married people do.

Now, quick, quick, quick. I scanned the room and saw the door to his bedroom. This was going to be horrible, but I had the grim knowledge that this was far from the worst thing I would end up doing. I took a baggie out of my purse and walked through his bedroom, seeing the fastidious neatness, the beauty of the antiques, the old mirror losing its silvering, reflecting my scared face across the room.

The bathroom was through a set of narrow double doors like shutters. My heart was pounding so hard I could hear it throbbing in my ears. I tried to listen, tried to feel if anyone was coming, and got nothing. Quickly I opened drawers, looking for—

His hair brush. This was so gross. Putting my hand inside the baggie, I plucked several gray hairs off the brush, then turned the baggie inside out and sealed it. I stuck it in my purse, tried to set the brush in exactly the same position it had been in, and carefully closed the drawers.

I was almost to the front door when I felt Daedalus coming. Was someone with him?

I froze. Then instinct kicked in, and I bolted into the dining room, on the other side of the living room. My first thought had been to hide under the bed, but I couldn't cross to the bedroom without being in clear sight of the front door.

Instead I crouched under the dining-room table, climbing on its cross beam and holding my skirt up tightly. I squeezed my eyes shut, realizing that Daedalus would pick up on my vibrations any second. I said all the *hide me* words that popped into my mind, but clearly this was going to end in complete disaster.

I started formulating an excuse and, better yet, an attack. *The best defense is a strong offense,* my dad used to say. About football.

Damn, damn, damn. *Hide me, hide me, hide me.*

I heard his voice in the living room, and I realized who was with him. Clio! So she had already started on her plan to increase her power. I bit my lip, feeling angry all over again.

How could she do this after what he had done to me, to our father? After I'd asked her not to?

I heard books being moved on the living room shelves.

"Here, take this," said Daedalus. "This will help paint a broader picture."

"Okay, thanks," said Clio. She sounded tired, or maybe sick, and I remembered how sick she had seemed just two days ago. What had she been doing then?

"Are you all right to get home?" Daedalus asked. "Did you come down on the trolley?"

"Yeah, I'm fine," Clio said shortly. "Thanks for the stuff."

There was a pause, then Daedalus said, "I'll drive you. I didn't realize you were so affected."

"I said I'm fine," said Clio, but her voice was muffled, as if her hand was over her mouth.

"No arguments," said Daedalus, and I heard the jingle of keys. "You're ill. I'll drive you home. What you tell Petra is your business."

I heard a muffled assent, and then, unbelievably, they left! They left, and I felt them going down the stairs. Oh, I couldn't be this lucky—it seemed like even thinking about what I wanted to do would be enough bad karma to ensure that I got caught immediately.

I waited several minutes in case one of them forgot something. Finally, feeling shaky from adrenaline, I scuttled out from under the table, made sure my baggie was still in my purse, and slipped out the front door. My breath felt stuck in my throat, and I had literally broken out in a cold sweat like they do in books.

I hid in the shadows of the courtyard for at least a minute, making sure the coast was clear, and then I zipped out the iron gate and lost myself in the crowds in Jackson Square. Inside the square I sat on a bench in the sun and tried to calm my shaking. It was almost half an hour before I felt like I could drive and made my way back to the rental car.

Clio, I thought, starting the car. She was studying with Daedalus anyway. How could she do that?

Probably the same way I could do what I was doing.

Chapter Fourteen

Her Face

LUC LOCKED HIS CAR AND HEADED UP THE block to Petra's house. You couldn't tell from looking that it had been in a fire, but there was still a faint scent of charred wood, burned plants, wet ash that would linger for years. It was Saturday afternoon. Would the twins be home?

Luc paused for a moment before he rang the bell. He felt Petra inside, but neither twin. Both a good and a bad thing. Probably mostly good, considering his appearance. After three days of Petra's wash and mask spell, Luc thought he noticed a slight difference. He was still a complete monster, though.

Petra opened the door in moments.

"I'm not sure which of us looks worse," Luc said bluntly, shocked by Petra's change.

She smiled wryly and stood back to let him in. "You do, I assure you."

Luc sighed and followed her back to the kitchen. "Yeah, I know."

"Sit down," Petra said. "Iced tea?"

"Do you have any wine?" He glanced outside—it was about two o'clock. He'd grown up drinking wine with every meal except breakfast, and it still seemed civilized.

Petra got out a bottle of red wine and poured two glasses. She didn't usually drink during the day, and Luc watched her, wondering what was up.

She sat across from him, and they toasted each other silently. Petra cocked her head and examined his face, illuminated harshly by the slanting sunlight coming through the window.

"It's a little better," she said.

"A little."

"We're on the right track," Petra said. "I'll work another healing spell with you, and that will speed things up."

"Are you sure you should?"

Petra met his gaze. "The rite seems to have sapped my strength," she admitted quietly. "But magick is a muscle—if I don't use it, it will atrophy."

"What happened to you during the rite?"

"I don't know. A lot of things happened that I wasn't aware of. I was so focused on Marcel. . . ."

Luc nodded. "The lost boy."

Petra's clear blue-gray eyes looked at him. "Did you ever have sex with either of the twins?"

Luc almost spit wine all over the table. He coughed several times and wiped his mouth on his sleeve. "*What?* No! You know I didn't."

Petra just looked at him.

"Petra. You asked before, and I told you. No, things didn't get that far with either one." The memory of Thais in his arms, making little sounds as he kissed her deeply, touched her everywhere, rose in his mind. He shut it down, feeling the familiar sharp pain in his heart, a pain that hadn't lessened. He tried not to obviously catch his breath, to keep his face blank.

"Which one do you love?"

He frowned. "What *is* this? Look, if you don't want to work on this"—he gestured to his face—"that's fine. No problem. I appreciate what you've done so far. But what's going on?"

Letting out a breath, Petra sat back in her kitchen chair. "I don't know." She shook her head and put one hand to her cheek. "I don't know. I'm getting weird stuff—"

Luc waited, concerned. Petra was usually very calm, very centered. Right now she felt kind of ragged around the edges, unbalanced.

Finally she met his eyes again. "I don't know," she repeated. "There seem to be—plots in the air around me." She waved her hand gracefully. "I feel like things are developing, plans and schemes, like they're becoming thicker all around me. But I can't see them, can't tell exactly what they are or who they're from."

Tread carefully, Luc. "Plans and schemes? Like what?" He felt the pressure of tension in his chest and tried to release it.

"I don't know."

"What's this have to do with me and the twins?" *Just put it out there.*

Petra didn't say anything, looking at her hands resting on the scrubbed wooden table. She took another sip of her wine. Luc waited, wondering if everything was about to be blown apart.

"Cerise was pregnant at the first rite," Petra said slowly. "If someone was trying to re-create the rite more exactly, if they really needed it to work for reasons of their own, then someone might think that a member of the Treize has to be pregnant. Only the twins are capable of getting pregnant."

"Oh come on!" Luc scoffed. "That's crazy. Who would think that?"

Petra looked at him steadily.

Luc shook his head. "I don't know what you're feeling, Petra. I can tell you that I myself am not involved in any plan or scheme about the twins or the Treize or whatever. My only goal right now is to fix this face."

She wouldn't try to get into his mind. Surely. They never did that to each other, or almost never. A minute slowly ticked by, measured by the almost imperceptible creeping of the pepper-shaker shadow on the table between them.

"I don't know what I'm thinking," Petra said finally. "The twins both feel odd to me, off. I don't know what's going on." After another moment she shook her head, as if to shake off bad feelings. "Don't listen to an old woman, Luc. It's probably nothing. I'm still trying to figure out what happened at the rite."

"Are *you* all right?"

"Yes, I'm sure I'm fine. Anyway. Let's see what we can do to speed up the healing."

Luc nodded and sat forward, waiting for whatever Petra told him to do. Then an impression of Thais seemed to press against him, filling his arms and his heart. He caught his breath, putting a hand to his stomach to hold the feeling of her tighter.

The front door opened. Petra looked up.

"Thais," she said, and Luc's stomach tightened more. He saw her so rarely—actually, when he thought about it, he'd probably seen her less than fifteen times, ever. Could that be possible? She was part of him, in his blood, under his skin. Every memory he had, Thais was part of. Every thought of the future contained Thais. She was still the first thing he thought of when he awoke and the last image in his mind before sleep. Luc would look at the moon's shadows moving across the walls in gray trapezoids and relive all the moments he'd had with Thais.

Of course, she hated him. Or did she? The night of the rite, he'd suddenly felt a burst of emotion from her. He'd looked up in surprise, found her eyes already shying away from him.

Now he looked like someone had thrown lye in his face.

"Hi, sweetie," said Petra. "Did you get everything you needed?"

"Yes," Thais said, moving to the counter. "I did."

Luc watched Thais set down her grocery bags. Her face was closed to him, her back stiff. He'd held her like that, her back to him, his hands curving around her stomach, pulling her to him. How had he made such a tragic mistake? How had he miscalculated so disastrously?

He knew how. He was used to getting away with everything. He'd left a thousand broken hearts behind him without losing a moment's rest over any of them. Things went his way—everything went his way. No problem had ever been so big that he couldn't just leave town over it. Ten, twenty, thirty years, things died down, people forgot. He'd gotten too sure of himself. He'd seen himself as untouchable.

And it had cost him the only person he'd ever loved, besides his sister.

And look how well that had gone.

There, she was turning around—was she going to ignore him? He felt heat rising to his scarred, ruined cheeks, felt his swollen eyelids widen as he watched her.

She put milk in the fridge, then emptied a plastic bag of apples into a basket.

"Thais—will you come join us? This healing spell would be useful to know."

Luc felt his face stiffen into an expressionless mask.

"Um, I'm supposed to go to a movie with Sylvie," Thais said, looking only at Petra.

"All right," said Petra, nodding.

Again Luc felt heat wash his face. He'd broken her heart and broken his own at the same time. Now, with the way he looked, he'd never have a chance to make it up to her, ever.

She'd moved on already. He'd seen her wrapped in some kid's arms.

"How's your boyfriend?" He was as surprised as she, hearing the words.

For the first time she met his eyes. He searched her face, waiting for her to flinch at his appearance, the way everyone did on the street. But she showed no reaction.

"He's fine," she said shortly. "We're breaking up." Immediately she frowned: She hadn't meant to say that.

His brilliant flare of hope was instantly extinguished by the knowledge of what he looked like. He had no hope of this pain being eased, and he looked down at the table.

"I won't be late," Thais told Petra, then she turned and left the kitchen.

"All right, honey," said Petra. "Be careful."

"Okay."

He heard her run lightly upstairs, imagined the way her full, colorful skirt would swirl around her legs. She was down again in a minute. Then all that was left was the fresh lavender scent of her hair and the echo of the front door closing.

Slowly he let out a deep breath, as if that would ease the pain. He met Petra's eyes. "Can we do the spell?"

✦ Chapter Fifteen

Perhaps Thais

CLIO WAS AN APT PUPIL, DAEDALUS THOUGHT again, entering his apartment. True, she was affected badly by the magick they'd made—but that would lessen in time. It was like anything else; one became inured to it. One developed calluses.

But really, she was gifted. He had to show her something only once, and she remembered it with certainty the next time. It was very gratifying.

And she seemed grateful for his lessons—she had a goal and, like himself, was single-minded in her pursuit of it. It was a quality he admired. The twins, more than anyone of Cerise's line, seemed to embody the old spirit of the time they sprang from, in their looks as well as strength.

He couldn't kill Clio to make room for Melita. It would have to be someone else. Someone had to go, and Daedalus was biding his time, waiting patiently to make the best decision. Should he kill the weakest? That would be Sophie. The one most likely to betray him? That was harder to discern.

Petra? Jules? Not Jules, not after all these years. But he could do the most damage if he did betray Daedalus. Jules was above reproach, though, Daedalus was sure of it.

Daedalus moved to the kitchen and poured himself a glass of *eau gazeuse* with a twist of lime. Clio was very strong—she'd been in his apartment only a few minutes, and yet he imagined he could still pick up her vibrations, barely perceptible but there.

Perhaps Thais should be the one to die. She wasn't on his side, he could feel it. She could become quite a liability with her unusual strength and lack of respect for his position. He would have to ponder this.

He paused halfway through the living room. Axelle. What did she want? He sighed, moving to turn on the ceiling fan. Axelle could be extremely tiresome sometimes. But useful, too, he admitted. Better to be gracious and keep on her good side.

He opened the door just as she reached up to knock.

"My dear," he said, ushering her inside. "I've been thinking about you. No ill effects from the rite, then?"

"No," she said. "But you look like hell."

Trust Axelle to acknowledge the elephant in the room.

"Do I?" Daedalus said smoothly, moving to open the tall French windows that led to the streetside balcony. He held his shoulders back and moved with firm strides.

"Yes, you do," she said, reclining on one of his Empire settees. "Rough night?"

And just then a thought crept into his head, the dim recognition of something he'd been missing. Since the rite, he'd been weaker. And so had Petra, he'd heard. The two of them, the most powerful witches in the Treize—aside of course from Melita—suddenly struggled for energy. It only followed that someone had taken their power at that rite. Someone had used the rite to draw in more magick, and that magick had to come from somewhere.

It had come from himself and Petra, and it had been taken by . . .

Axelle.

Daedalus smiled at Axelle patronizingly, carefully blocking his thoughts from her. "Is there something I can help you with?" He sat across from her and set his water on a silver coaster. Now wasn't the time to share what he knew. He would wait, and he would find the right way to repay her.

"Yes," she said, crossing her long legs and putting her red-painted toes up on the settee's arm, which was obviously calculated to annoy him back. "Let's get Melita home."

❧ Chapter Sixteen

Thais

IT WASN'T ANY EASIER GOING BACK TO MAMA Loup's now that I knew the way. The neighborhood seemed even more threatening, and though it was daytime, the light around Mama Loup's house seemed dimmer and the air heavier. I parked the rental as close as I could, said spells of protection around it, and tried to look brave and untouchable as I passed people sitting on their stoops, dogs barking at their chain-link fences, kids racing by on too-small bikes.

I went through the rusty iron gate and headed around the side, an old pro. The alley was barely two feet wide, and wild vines covered the thin bamboo fence. This house, like ours, like most houses in New Orleans, was raised up several feet on brick pillars. I could smell the damp soil from beneath the house and had no desire to see what else might be under there.

The same bare-bulb fixture was lit above the same broken screen door. Again, the wooden inside door was open. I pulled open the screen and stepped into the dark interior. After the daylight, blinking made things look polarized and orange. I stood still, wishing my eyes would adjust faster.

There were other people in the shop—the same woman who had waited on me before, who I thought was Mama Loup. She was talking seriously with another woman who looked thin and strung out. A plump baby sat on her hip, clinging to her T-shirt with small, wet fists.

I wandered over by the counter, not wanting to interrupt them, hoping Carmela would see me and come out. Old metal shelves made short aisles in the room, and I started looking at dusty glass bottles with handwritten labels and baggies sealed with twist-ties, instructions tied to them with black string. One baggie had what looked like several dried green lizards in it, and I tried not to grimace.

"That'll make him come back to you for true," I heard Mama Loup murmur. "You rub that *Perlainpain* on anything he wears, he can't help but come back to you, no."

A love spell. I'd gotten the impression from Clio and Petra that to stoop to such a thing was embarrassing, humiliating. I remembered Luc in my room at Axelle's, angry, saying, "I could make you love me." Luc.

I didn't hate him. I was still angry, furious, at what he had done. But I couldn't seem to muster up hatred. Now, looking at him, so different—his natural confidence, almost arrogance, had been obliterated along with his handsome face. That was what was different. He seemed humbled. *That could only be a good thing.* I thought meanly, then turned as I heard someone come through the hanging bamboo beads that curtained a dark doorway.

It was Carmela, I knew, but once again she seemed to carry her own personal storm cloud around with her, making herself harder to see, to distinguish.

"You're back, child," she said. "I said not to come back until—"

"I have everything on the list," I interrupted her. Her dark eyes blinked once, which I took as surprise.

"Everything?"

"Yes." I patted the canvas carryall I had on my shoulder.

For several moments she gazed at me, and looking back at her, I saw only her eyes, as black as Axelle's.

"Then come this way." She held the beaded curtain aside with one hand. My heart in my throat, I stepped around the back of the counter, passed her, and entered the black room beyond.

It was a hallway, short and unlit, like a cave, and I could see only the barest outline of a doorway on the left. Feeling slightly hysterical, it occurred to me that this warren of rooms was like the magick tent in *Harry Potter*—small and normal on the outside but going on and on impossibly long on the inside. Already it seemed like there was no way all these rooms could be contained in the small house I had entered.

"In here." In this room there was more than just an absence of light—the walls seemed to actually deaden light. The idea of warmth and sunlight outside seemed like distant memories.

My throat was dry—I couldn't swallow. I felt hyperalert,

as if going through a carnival funhouse, on guard against anything that might spring out at me. But the truth was, I had put myself in a dangerous situation, and if things went south, I probably wouldn't be able to save myself.

And I was so glad I'd just had that thought. *Put it out of your mind.*

"Show me what you have."

I blinked at Carmela's voice, my eyes widening to let in as much light as possible. A faint scratch, then a match flared into a swaying dance, and I saw Carmela's tan hand lighting black candles, three of them, held in a twisted silver candelabra.

The flickering candlelight showed me that we were in a room maybe nine feet square. The walls weren't painted black, as I'd thought—they were a dark, oxblood red. Out of nowhere I flashed on the fact that on wooden warships, in the olden days, the doctor's little room for surgery was painted red everywhere so the men couldn't see all the blood and get scared.

Great. Thank you for that.

I tried again to swallow, unsuccessfully, then started pulling things out of my bag. Three forked twigs from a weeping willow. Red clay dust made from rubbing an old brick on the sidewalk. Little pieces of unworked silver that I'd bought at Botanika. A hard cone of pressed brown sugar I'd gotten from a bodega on Magazine Street. The baggie with Daedalus's hair. Some powdered sassafras leaves from Botanika.

I laid everything out. Carmela examined it all.

"What's this stuff for?" I asked.

She looked up at me, eyes glowing like a cat's. "The silver is because I'm making a necklace and thought it would look pretty. The brown sugar is good in coffee—you scrape it with your spoon. The sassafras is called filé, and you sprinkle it on gumbo to thicken it right before you eat it. The brick dust is useful for different spells, and the willow twigs were just for fun, to see if you would bother finding them."

I stared at her.

"But this, this is very interesting," she said, picking up the baggie containing a few silver hairs. "I didn't think you would get this, child." She looked at me appraisingly, as if this one ingredient made her take me seriously.

"Tell me more about what you want to do." Her English was fine grammatically, but she had an accent that didn't seem quite French or quite anything else.

"I want to—strip someone's power from him. A witch," I managed to get out. I'd told her all this already. "He killed my father with magick. I can't kill him, but I could take his powers away, which would be worse. If you help me."

"Why can't you kill him?" Oddly, in this bare room, her words had no echo but fell from her lips like stones falling silently into still water, leaving no ripple.

Because he's immortal?

"He's a murderer," I said. "I'm not. And stripping his magickal powers would be worse for him."

"For any witch," Carmela said thoughtfully.

"Yes." *Even for me?* I wondered.

"Do you have any idea what stripping a witch's powers is like?"

No. "I think it would be really bad, but not kill him."

"I'll show you on something smaller," she said, pushing back the full sleeves of her caftan. Like Mama Loup, she wore a long, African-print robe and a matching turban. "And then you will decide."

"Okay." This didn't sound so bad. Unless—"You don't mean, like an animal, do you?"

Carmela paused and turned toward me. "Would that bother you, Thais? Surely an animal is less than a human being?"

"Animals are—innocent," I said, tension winding around my spine like wire. "People aren't."

She looked at me consideringly. "Surely some people are?" It sounded rhetorical.

I thought of Clio, who was studying with my mortal enemy behind my back. I thought of Luc, who had betrayed me. Petra, who had lied to Clio for seventeen years. It was inextricably part of being human, I thought sadly. People lied, cheated, hurt the ones they loved. "No," I said. "No one."

She laughed, showing small white teeth. "So young to be such a cynic. So very young."

"I'm more of a realist," I said.

"Not an animal, then," said Carmela, in a tone that made me think she'd never planned to use an animal anyway. She reached beneath the table and took out a potted plant, a perfect long-stemmed orchid. Totally anticlimactic.

I blinked. It was a potted plant, not even having its roots in the ground. What power could it have?

"Come." Carmela walked past a small table to where a silver circle was painted on the floor. All around the circle were painted small runes and other symbols I didn't recognize. It was weird—as soon as I stepped into it, it was like stepping into a . . . well, *a windstorm* is too dramatic. Not a tornado. But like a faint vortex of some kind, held solely within this dinky painted circle in this little back room of a house in New Orleans. I definitely felt it, like a fan beneath the floor, pulling at my skirt. It was so weird.

"Sit," said Carmela, gesturing to the floor. She sat down across from me and put the plant between us. "Everything has power, magickal power," she went on. "And a life force. Those two things overlap, and in some cases they overlap completely, inseparable. The thing is, if you take something's life force, you also take its magickal power. But sometimes you can take something's power, but not its life force. You can do that with people. And most animals. And some plants."

"Okay," I said, feeling my palms get sweaty on my knees. "Now . . .

The beginning of her spell was familiar in that we centered ourselves, like for meditation. Then Carmela began singing in a chanting, singsong kind of way, like I'd heard others do. Then, with no warning, I was sucked into the spell, pinned motionless by what was happening, and could only sit and watch.

Carmela's spell was like turning a black light onto a black-light poster, where unseen colors suddenly popped and the whole thing looked different. One minute I was looking at Joe Orchid in a pot, and the next it became an alien vibrating thing, practically glowing with a faint green light, visibly radiating energy or power or whatever it was.

"This is its life," Carmela said softly, stroking her tan fingers along one glowing-edged leaf. "And this is its magick." She gestured to the plant's vibrations, how it seemed to be spiky with movement, vibrating like a plucked string. "We leave its life but strip its magick. We're not going to take its magick for ourselves. This time."

She began to sing again, and I recognized about every tenth word as sounding French.

She moved her hands over the plant, and I swore I could see a dim outline of the plant slowly untwine itself from the actual plant. It was like a thin, shimmering blue-green line, orchid-shaped, and Carmela's hands seemed to coax it away. I was frozen in place, eyes wide, wondering if I was hallucinating. Clearly this was magick on a different scale and with a far different intent than anything I'd been exposed to.

I felt the outline's small, fluttery vibrations, like a butterfly's wings brushing against me. Carmela seemed to gather it in her palm, then opened her fingers in a starburst shape. The outline coiled and then broke apart, a silent firecracker shattering into thousands of tiny shards. They arched and fell, but dissipated almost instantly, and I felt nothing fall around me.

"Oh my God," I whispered, awed. "That was amazing. That was its power, its magick?"

Carmela nodded seriously, then gestured down at the orchid.

I sucked in my breath, recoiling instinctively.

The orchid was . . . not dead. Still alive, it drooped in its pot, but I had the shocking feeling that it was obscene somehow, something grotesque and perverse. I blinked a couple times, trying to figure out what I was seeing.

I was seeing . . . an orchid in a pot. Visibly, its colors were definitely duller, faded. But besides that, there was something about it that filled me with revulsion, that felt awful and horrifying, like I'd stumbled on a rotting corpse in a wood.

"What's . . . wrong with it?" I managed to get out.

"We stripped it of its magick. Like you want to do to your witch."

"It's not dead?"

"No. It won't live long, but it's not dead."

"Why does it feel so awful?" I could barely speak; my eyes were riveted to the plant.

"Because it has no magick."

I met her dark eyes, confused.

"Magick is what makes life worth living," she said matter-of-factly. "This has no magick."

I stared again at the plant, how it seemed so repugnant to me, worse than dead.

"And this will happen to Daedalus? The witch?"

Carmela's eyes flashed. She seemed to look right through my pupils to my soul itself. "Yes."

I swallowed, feeling like I might be sick. "Good," I whispered.

✦ Chapter Seventeen

Clio

"WHAT?" NAN LOOKED SHOCKED, AND TWO spots of heat appeared on her cheeks.

I scraped my plate into the garbage and picked up Thais's. Neither of us had eaten much dinner, but I didn't think I would be sick. The herbs and spell that Daedalus had given me earlier had helped a lot, and I was acting pretty normal. As opposed to Thais, who had slept all afternoon after some strenuous shoe-shopping.

"Here." Thais put our three glasses on the counter, then took a dishcloth to wipe down the table. She'd been acting weird since yesterday—cold, not looking at me or talking to me. But she couldn't possibly know about me and Daedalus, so I had no idea what was going on. I hadn't had a chance to ask her.

"I said, *what?*" Nan was looking at me in horror.

I knew this conversation was going to be really hard, but it had been on my mind, and I wanted to get it over with. Since Nan had just told me to call Melysa to set up a time to study for my ROA, this seemed like a good moment.

"I don't want to do my rite of ascension," I repeated. "At least not right now."

"Clio—you're going to be eighteen next month." Nan left the trash where it was and folded her arms, looking at me.

"I know. But with everything that's been going on—the Treize, the rite, everything—it's impossible for me to focus on it," I explained. "Maybe next year when things have settled down."

"No, not next year!" Nan exclaimed. "*This* year, next month, like we planned."

"Plus, I think it would be great if Thais and I did it together."

Thais snorted over by the table.

"Thais won't be ready for her ROA for maybe five or six years," Nan said. "And you know it."

"Well—" There was something else that I wasn't telling her. Usually in our religion a witch made her rite of ascension as both a test and a tool to help her solidify her strengths and knowledge. I didn't need to do that. Right now I couldn't see how it would help me feel more centered in my power. I was studying with Daedalus, learning a lot, and I already knew I was more powerful than any other witch in Nan's *cercle* besides her. The witches of the Treize were all so much more powerful than ordinary witches, and it looked like that power had been handed down to me and Thais.

I just couldn't see the point.

"Clio, you've been working toward this for a long time," said Nan, leaning over and tying the top of the trash bag.

"I know. I don't want to disappoint anyone," I said. I scrubbed a plate with soapy water and rinsed it. "But I've got too much going on. You have to admit, the last month has been a roller coaster. There's no way I can focus on the ROA."

"The party has been planned."

I looked at her. "No it hasn't," I said, smiling. "There's a huge difference between *thinking*, 'Oh, we should have a party when Clio makes her ROA,' and actually having it all planned, invitations sent, and stuff. You know you haven't gotten that far with it."

Nan pressed her lips together, clearly thinking, *Smart ass*.

"Look, I'll do it later," I said, thinking that I wasn't really lying. "But goddess, Nan—I've had so many huge things explode in my life lately. I can't take one more huge pressure."

"No, I can't allow you to throw this away so easily," Nan said crossly. "You've been working and studying for a long time, and I won't have you waste it."

"Knowledge is never wasted," I said, keeping a lid on my temper. "*You* said that."

"Look, you're going to make your rite of ascension next month, and that's final."

I didn't say anything but dried my hands on a dishtowel. There wasn't any point to arguing more. Later I would probably have to dig my heels in again, but for now I was going to drop it. I looked up to see Thais watching us, and I was sure she was happy to be out of it.

"What are you doing tonight?" I asked her. "How's the Kevster?"

After a quick, startled glance at the change in topic, she looked away from me, her face guarded. "Fine."

I wasn't positive she needed to break up with him, myself. Maybe this was why she was acting weird. No—it seemed to be about me in particular.

"I'm going to meet Racey downtown," I said. "Want to come with?"

For a moment she paused, as if considering, then gave me a cool look and shook her head. "I've got a killer headache," she said. "Maybe it's allergies. I'm going to stay in and go to bed early."

"Okaaay." We couldn't have it out in front of Nan, but if she wanted to be that way, fine. I draped the dish towel over the sink to dry, and when I glanced up, Nan was giving me an eagle-eyed look.

"What?" I said.

"This discussion is not over," she said.

I sighed. "Please just think about where I'm coming from. But right now I'm going to meet Racey." I prayed that she wouldn't suddenly put her foot down and say I couldn't go. I wasn't up for a big battle.

I saw the thought processes going on in her head. Finally she nodded shortly. "We'll talk about this later. Don't be out too late."

I nodded. "Okay. Hope you feel better, Thais."

"Yeah, thanks."

Then I grabbed my purse and car keys, and I was gone.

• • •

In the car I pulled out my phone and dialed Racey's number. At the last second, I didn't hit *send*. I steered with one hand, holding my phone in the other, and thought about where my head was. What did I feel like doing? Who did I feel like being with?

No one. Someone new and fabulous.

With irritation I remembered how Richard had grabbed me the other day, when Nan was working on Luc. No one had ever pissed me off as regularly as Richard did. If only I could wipe that smirk off his face once and for all.

And Luc. Goddess, what had happened to him? I really did think it was a shame, but it also seemed to be a living example of the threefold law. He'd put some bad energy out into the world, some real pain, and lo and behold, he'd gotten the same back.

I was amazed at how resigned he was to how incredibly horrible he looked, after so long of looking like a god on earth. He seemed to accept it as his fate—he wasn't raging against it or saying it was unfair. To me that meant he got the fact that what he'd done had been wrong and bad and that he should pay for it.

My thoughts exactly.

But I did feel sorry for him. Nan had said that he felt like a leper walking around town. That people actually gasped and turned away. That had to suck. If this had happened to me, I'd be hiding under my bedcovers for the rest of my life, or until it got fixed somehow. At least Nan had mentioned that his face was improving a bit.

Looking up, I saw I was already at Jackson Avenue, half-way downtown. Maybe . . . maybe I would go see Luc. See how he was. He didn't deserve my help, and I wouldn't offer it. Still, if everyone was freaking out when they saw him, it would be nice for him to see someone who could deal with his face the way it was.

• • •

Richard answered the door, unfortunately. He was in his standard uniform of unbuttoned plaid flannel shirt, ratty jeans, and bare feet. His sunstreaked hair looked like he'd just gotten out of bed. I'd been taking extra care with my appearance to cheer myself up, and I looked hot in a gauzy peasant shirt you could see my bra through and a pair of tight red capris that stopped just below my knees.

It was nighttime, but the Quarter was well-lit, and I was standing practically under a streetlamp. I frowned up at him, and something hit me as different—he looked different somehow, but how? I couldn't put my finger on it.

"I was hoping you were out," I said bluntly.

"You're out of luck," he said. "What's up? Selling something door-to-door?" His mocking gaze looked me up and down, making it clear what he thought I should be selling. Bastard.

"Here to see Luc," I said, crossing my arms over my chest.

"Should I frisk you for weapons?"

I tried not to shiver at the thought of his hands patting me down. Instead I smiled sarcastically and didn't answer. He stepped back from the door and made a sweeping motion with one hand, waving me inside.

I walked through the doorway, careful not to touch him, but as I passed I smelled his detergent, the scent of cigarette smoke, and . . . some kind of spice? Unmistakably Richard. I knew it very well.

He inhaled as I passed, and from the corner of my eye I saw the smooth tan skin over his collarbones, saw the beginnings of his tribal tattoos. Keeping my eyes fixed straight ahead, I went down the hall to Luc's room, which I'd never been in. Ironically enough.

Their apartment was a typical half of a double: The front door opened into a long hall that had a row of rooms on the right-hand side. First was a living room, which I'd never seen. I didn't even know if it had furniture. Then Richard's room, with its single mattress on the floor. Then Luc's room. At the end of the hall was the bathroom, and the last room was on the left in a stuck-on addition, making a T: the kitchen. The ceilings were at least twelve feet high, the floor moldings maybe fourteen inches. Two small brass chandeliers, one at each end of the hallway, cast inadequate light. It would be beautiful if someone with money bought it and redid it.

"I'll leave you to it, then," Richard said behind me, and I heard the door to his room shut. I knew it had to be burning him that I was here to see Luc and not him.

Tough.

I knocked on Luc's door. He must have known I was here from my voice, if not my vibes.

"Let me in," I said. It was then that I realized he wasn't alone—I felt a female presence. My jaw dropped, and without thinking I turned the doorknob and pushed.

Luc sat on the side of an antique sleigh bed. His arms were around a girl who was covering her face, clearly sobbing. I stood there, dumbstruck, thinking, *My God, even with that face he's getting girls.* Then she looked up, and I was struck again: It was *Sophie,* and she looked like hell. I knew she and Manon had broken up, that Manon had moved to Axelle's—but here she was on Luc's *bed*, with his arms around her. Was he taking advantage of her wrecked emotional state to get somewhere with her?

I gave him an icy glare.

"Clio!" he said, clearly surprised.

"Never mind," I said, stepping back and pulling the door shut hard. My face burned, and I was furious at him all over again.

"Clio, wait!" he called through the door.

Sophie sobbed again, and Luc said something to her. But I was already striding down the hallway, incensed, reaching for my phone to call Racey to meet me at Amadeo's.

Predictably, Richard's door opened, spilling a rectangle of warm light into the hallway, and I whirled around on him.

"Get a good laugh out of that?" I hissed. "You knew he wasn't alone!"

He pretended not to know what I meant, looking confused. "No, Sophie's in there."

"No fricking duh!" I said. "Thanks, jerk!" I spun away and headed for the front door. Richard caught up to me, and since he never had a problem putting his hands all over me, he grabbed my arm. I stopped with a jolt.

"What did *I* do?" he demanded. "I didn't make her go in there. And it's just Sophie."

"Just Sophie," I mimicked. "And they're on his bed, and his arms are around her!"

Richard looked at me oddly. "Well, we *are* in the South."

I stared at him, no idea what he was talking about. Did being in the South make people act crazy from the heat? Make them hornier? I shook my head and tried to yank free, but instead he dragged me into the living room.

It was dark and unfurnished because Luc and Richard were perhaps the two least domestic guys I'd ever met. The long French windows overlooking the street were shuttered, but their transoms let in the streetlamp's light, so I could see Richard's face.

He pushed the door shut with one foot, keeping hold of me. "Let go of me!" I hissed.

"Why are you so mad at *me?*" he said, his eyes watching my mouth.

My eyes widened. "Where should I *start?*" I pulled my arm one last time, and he let me go but stood between me and the door, looking like he wasn't going to move.

"How long are you going to be mad about that? Ballpark figure?" he said irritably, and I assumed he was talking about the whole "attempted murder" wrinkle.

"Um, *forever?*" I'd never had a crush on Richard, never needed to win him over, so I'd never tempered my anger or watched my words or tried to pretty things up. I always let him have it with both barrels. And he always took it. And came back for more. Come to think of it, he was the only guy I spoke totally straight with, all the time. Basically, it probably confirmed his opinion of me as a total bitch.

In the next second, just like that, it was like he'd flicked a switch and went from regular annoying Richard to deadly seductive Richard. Eyes staying focused on my mouth, he stepped a bit closer and visibly let go of his irritation and impatience.

Oh, no, I thought, backing up. *No.*

"No, not forever," he murmured, his voice silky.

"Leave me alone," I said.

He never listened to me. His hand reached out and curled around the back of my neck. I stiffened, narrowing my eyes at him in a way that had once made someone cry.

"Clio," he said, so close that I could feel the heat of his skin. "We don't like each other. But we have this between us. If we gave into it, maybe it would go away."

Yes, said my stupid, easily convinced body.

"No. Don't be an ass," I said.

I braced myself as he leaned closer, tilting his head to kiss my neck. I pulled back, but he pursued me, pressing his lips against my skin. Again, I had an odd, vague sense that something was different. He was just slightly . . . different. It made me crazy not being able to put my finger on it. His mouth was warm and firm and familiar, and shivers ran down my spine. I instantly felt my knees start to melt, which pissed me off. He left another kiss on my neck by my collarbone, and my heart sped up and my breath got shallow. He always did this—the Richard effect.

"No, go *away*," I said crossly and pushed against his hard shoulders. Then my hands slid over his shirt, feeling his heat through the cloth, and my brain went dead. He pulled me to him, one hand against the small of my back, one hand sliding up my side. His bare stomach seemed to burn me through my thin shirt, and all I could think was, *Uhhhhh . . .* Slowly, slowly, he kissed his way up my neck and across my cheek while my eyelids fluttered closed.

Somehow, when he kissed me, everything else went away—my pain over Luc, my fear and dread about working with Daedalus, Nan, Thais being upset with me—it all faded. All I was aware of was Richard's scent, how he felt, how his hands felt moving over me.

Just as his mouth covered mine, I heard Luc's door open and footsteps come down the hall. My eyes flew open, and I quickly stepped back.

"Damn it!" Richard said, reaching for me, but I had my sanity again and dodged around him, lunging for the living room door, opening it.

Sophie, still looking upset but not crying, nodded at me. "Clio," she said, as if it was no big deal I'd found her in Luc's bedroom. After all, they'd known each other for two hundred years. Who knew if they'd been lovers before she'd gotten together with Manon? She opened the front door and left, with one last look at Luc.

I almost choked when I saw how he looked back at her—I actually saw the love in his eyes, which were the only things on his ruined face capable of expressing emotion.

The front door closed, and Luc looked at me. Then he looked at Richard, standing close behind me, and saw that we had just come out of the living room. He frowned, looking back and forth. I could hear Richard breathing hard.

"What's going on?" Luc said.

"Nothing," I said shortly, heading for the front door. Once again, I was disgusted with both of them and guys in general.

"You two—what's going *on*?" Luc said, but this time in his voice I heard comprehension.

"Nothing. You're the one with the girl in your room." I reached the front door and pulled it open.

"What?" Luc asked, sounding incredulous. Little Mr. Innocent. "That was *Sophie!*"

"Uh-huh." I stormed outside and slammed their door behind me. Damn both of them! And damn *me* for giving in to Richard *again*.

The door opened, and Richard came out as I stomped down the steps.

"We have to sort this out," he said in a low voice, gesturing between himself and me.

"No, we don't," I said and began to head to my car.

"Clio!" Luc's voice. Disbelieving, I turned around.

"What are you doing with Richard?" He sounded almost outraged, which was a big laugh and pushed me over the edge. I was so mad at both of them and even more mad at myself that I just lashed out stupidly.

"I'm *sleeping* with him!" I snapped, and then felt worse than mortified when a passerby turned because she'd heard me. My cheeks flamed, and I wanted to scream.

Luc's jaw dropped open, and Richard started in surprise, then got a lopsided grin.

I pressed my lips together so I wouldn't start shrieking swear words at the top of my lungs. Shaking my head, keeping my mouth shut tight, I whirled and practically ran down the sidewalk.

"Oh, Clio!" Richard called after me. I ignored him. "Sophie is Luc's *sister!*"

✦ Chapter Eighteen

Stupid Idiot

LUC CAME BACK INSIDE AND SHUT THE DOOR hard, glaring at Richard.

Richard just grinned and headed for the kitchen.

"She's lying," Luc said, following him.

"Yep, uh-huh," Richard replied in a tone calculated to make Luc insane. He flicked on the kitchen light and got a glass out of a cupboard.

"She's totally lying," Luc said. "You didn't get in her pants."

Richard poured himself half a tumbler of whiskey and took a sip, looking innocent. This was too good. He would have to thank Clio later for giving him the most fun he'd had in weeks.

"Admit it," Luc demanded, his hands on his hips.

"Why do you care? I thought you were hot for Thais."

Luc started to look angry. "Tell me she's lying."

"I'm not going to tell you anything," said Richard, brushing past him.

"Listen, you stay away from her."

He really sounded mad, which was *verry* interesting. Richard knew Clio still had warped feelings for Luc, but he'd thought Luc was resigned to his disgraced status. The two of them pissed him off—Clio, still thinking she loved Luc when clearly she was all wrapped up over Richard, and Luc, for being the greedy bastard that he was, being dog in the manger. He couldn't have either twin, but he didn't want Richard to have Clio either.

Which was too bad.

Because Richard was coming to terms with the fact that he did want her.

Really, really wanted her.

"What's it to you?" Richard asked, leaning in his doorway, drinking his whiskey. He needed to get something to eat—the alcohol reminded him of how empty his stomach was. What time was it? He couldn't tell.

"You stay away from her," Luc repeated, actually pointing his finger at Richard. "She loves me, and I love her."

Richard laughed. "No you don't."

"Yes, I do," Luc insisted.

Richard shook his head in disgust. "Whatever. May the best man win."

"You're not even in the running!" Luc almost shouted. "You're her frigging grandfather!"

Richard stared at him. "What the hell are you talking about?"

"Clio and Thais are the thirteenth generation of Cerise's

line," Luc said deliberately. "Where did Cerise's line come from?"

Right. Richard had fathered Cerise's baby, and he felt the familiar barbed-wire feeling in his heart at the memory of it. Thirteen generations later, the baby he had made had descendants, Clio and Thais. Yes, he *was* related to them. But incredibly, incredibly distantly. The connection certainly wasn't close to significant by now.

"I'm not their grandfather," Richard said. "The percentage I'm related to them is so small I can't even figure it out."

"You're still related! I'm telling you, Richard, don't touch her!"

"Why not, Luc?" Richard made his voice mild, knowing that Luc would recognize this as a sign for caution, if not outright alarm.

"She's mine."

Richard's eyes narrowed. "Really. Does she know that? Is that why she can't keep her hands off me?"

Luc looked stunned, then quickly recovered. He stalked back to his own room, shaking his head. "You're lying."

"Yeah," said Richard, raising his voice so Luc couldn't help hearing him. "She and I are *both* lying."

Luc slammed his door.

Richard swirled his drink in his glass, then looked around his room for some socks and his motorcycle boots. He had to go get something to eat.

✤ Chapter Nineteen

If He Had Loved Her

"SMELLS AND BELLS," THEY CALLED IT, THE "high church" style of service. A typical Sunday in a town still very Catholic. The priests swung the heavy brass censer, and they carried the Bible around the church, doing the stations of the cross. It was beautiful, ultimately civilized and yet very primitive at the same time.

Everyone stood, and Marcel stood also. He had this rear pew almost to himself—only an old woman shared the very far end. A strand of jet beads, her rosary, dangled from one hand. Automatically Marcel tapped his pockets, but the plain wooden beads he'd once carried everywhere were no longer tucked into his monk's robe.

It was time for the sermon, and the priest ascended into the pulpit and turned on the microphone. Marcel sighed, wishing for the churches of a hundred years or more ago. As the priest began to talk about how they, as ordinary people, could embody the reflection of Christ in everyday living, Marcel let his mind wander.

Axelle, Claire, and Sophie.

Three women he now unexpectedly found himself in relationships with. Three women he doubted he'd spoken to more than a dozen times in two hundred years. Axelle was still self-serving and duplicitous, but also unexpectedly shrewd and unexpectedly generous. Claire he'd written off when she was fifteen and already had a reputation as a loose skirt. God knew she'd only gone downhill from there—with each new age of civilization, it seemed she found new opportunities for depravity. Now she seemed—fun loving and lovelorn. She was in love with Jules. Now that he finally recognized it, Marcel, looking back, couldn't remember a time when Claire had not apparently been in love with Jules.

And Jules wouldn't give in to her for some reason. Why? Marcel saw love in his eyes as well. What was holding Jules back? Now, at last, Marcel could see that, if you loved someone for hundreds of years and they didn't love you back, you might very well want to try every diversion you could to take your mind off of it. When he looked at it that way, it was much easier to empathize with Claire and even admire her courage.

And then . . . Sophie. That whole concept stunned him, still. Long, long ago, Sophie had loved him, had pined for him. And he'd never seen it. He'd focused his sights on one person—Cerise—and never looked to either side.

People around him stood again, and Marcel mindlessly began singing the closing hymn.

The priest in his white robe and embroidered alb passed,

palms locked together in prayer as he sang. Everyone filed out after him: deacon, altar boys, choir.

Sophie had loved him. She'd been a lovely girl. Marcel grimaced—clearly, she was lovely still. How long had she pined for him before giving up? How many shy signals, glances, slight overtures had she made toward him that he hadn't noticed?

Almost groaning, Marcel rubbed his temples and waited to exit his pew.

Sophie. He had missed out.

Marcel went out into a humid, too-warm Sunday afternoon. It was thickly overcast, and the breeze carried the scent of rain. He wandered aimlessly onto the wide slate flagstones that bordered Jackson Square.

Sophie. Sophie was beautiful in a quiet, deeply feminine way. She was one of the few truly nice people he'd ever known, someone truly without avarice or meanness or anger.

What would his life have been like if he'd loved Sophie instead of Cerise? He could have been loved instead of given a number and fit in whenever Richard wasn't in her bed.

Acid burned his stomach, and he forced himself to control his anger. It had all been so long ago. Richard had been just a kid. Only recently had Marcel actually realized that. Richard had been only fifteen. Cerise was four years older—she should have known better. In a way, she'd taken advantage of Richard. And Marcel, both of them. Gotten what she wanted without giving either of them what they'd wanted.

Marcel found himself on the corner of St. Ann and Chartres.

Sophie.

Sophie and Manon had broken up—possibly for good.

Marcel turned and headed deeper into the Quarter. Maybe Axelle would want to get some lunch somewhere. Or Claire and Jules.

Marcel's mouth quirked in a slightly surprised smile. He had friends.

Chapter Twenty

WWCD?

"MARCEL, HUH? I HAVE TO ADMIT, I MISSED that one." Claire handed Sophie a Snickers bar, then lay down on Jules's pink futon sofa. She ripped open the end of her own Snickers and took a bite.

Sophie nodded miserably and looked at the candy bar as if needing instructions.

"Just eat it, honey," said Claire, chewing.

Looking like she had nothing to lose, Sophie carefully undid the wrapper and took a tentative bite. Claire tried hard not to roll her eyes. It was a frigging Snickers bar, for God's sake. What rock had Sophie been living under?

Jules hadn't had any Kleenex, so a roll of toilet paper sat next to Sophie's chair along with a paper grocery bag of used tissue.

"I never wanted anyone to know," Sophie said. Her voice was thick with chocolate and crying. "I only told Manon because—" She sniffled again and took another bite of peanutty goodness. "I told her after we became . . . friends, years after the rite. When she was closer in age, not just a little girl."

"Hmm." Claire carefully scratched her nose next to her silver nose ring. "Well, Marcel knows now. The question—well, one of the questions—is, are you and Manon going to patch things up?"

Sophie looked stricken, her face gaunt and pale. "I don't know," she whispered. She shook her head and bit off more Snickers. "I thought for sure we would—we always do. But now I don't know. Manon says she'll never forgive me."

"Yeah," Claire said quickly, wanting to steer the conversation to a less weepy topic. "But if you don't get back with Manon, how about hooking up with Marcel? God knows he's still single."

Sophie looked struck by the thought. Had it not occurred to her? Maybe Claire should hand over the "dense" award.

"I don't know," Sophie said, seeming lost. "But he doesn't care about me—he doesn't know I'm alive."

"He does now," Claire assured her.

"And—he took a vow of celibacy when he became a monk," Sophie went on. "I remember hearing that."

Claire rolled her eyes. "He's a guy."

"And I still love Manon," Sophie said, her voice wavering.

Sitting up, Claire balled her candy-bar wrapper and threw it across the small room into Sophie's tissue bag. "Okay, so you still love her. She'd be a hard habit to break. But if she's ready to move on, then you have no choice but to move on too. And if you don't want a regular guy, one with a short life span, then Marcel might be the way to go."

"I can't even think about it now," said Sophie, brushing her long dark hair off her face.

"Well, plenty of time," Claire said in a massive understatement. "The thing about unrequited love is that it doesn't tend to go away."

She felt Sophie looking at her and hoped her voice hadn't sounded really bitter.

"Where's Jules?" Sophie asked, following Claire's train of thought.

"He got a job," Claire said. "Inexplicably."

For several minutes the two women were quiet. Every once in a while, Sophie sniffled or blew her nose.

Who would have thought, Claire mused, looking at her bright red toenails, that she and Sophie the Ice Maiden would ever have anything in common? "Have you ever been with a guy?" she asked, out of the blue.

Sophie blushed. "No. When I was younger—well, it wasn't done." Then she seemed to remember that Claire had in fact done it quite a bit with boys and men in their village. She hurried on. "I just couldn't—with my parents watching me all the time. Then I was in love with Marcel for a long, long time. When he disappeared after the rite, I wondered if he was with Melita—if he'd run away with her, if they were lovers. Maybe he'd loved them both."

"I doubt it," said Claire.

"But he was gone. So even though Cerise was—dead, Marcel wasn't there, anyway. I mean, I wasn't happy about Cerise—what happened to her. It was horrible. But if she was gone, then maybe Marcel would—" Sophie let out a sigh. "But no one knew where he was. And then I became friends with Manon. With the way she looks, she needs someone to be with her—help her get stuff done. She's had it really hard." Her voice broke again.

"I bet." Claire didn't think about Manon and Richard much, how much harder their lives had been. Especially Manon. Richard could almost pass for his late teens if you didn't look at him too closely.

"I guess that'll get easier now," Claire said.

Sophie looked at her, sniffling. "What do you mean?"

Claire shrugged. "They're aging."

For a minute Sophie just looked at her uncomprehendingly. She blinked a couple times and then frowned. "What are you talking about?"

Now Claire was surprised. She would've thought this news would spread like wildfire. "Richard and Manon are aging since the rite. I saw Richard last night, or this morning, around three or so, coming out of Lafitte's. It took me a second to figure out what was different. But then I realized he looked older. When's the last time you saw Manon?"

"Friday, at Axelle's. She hasn't let me come over since then."

"Today's Monday—a week since the rite. When you see her, you'll notice it."

"But that's impossible! Why didn't you say this earlier?"

"I thought you knew—I thought everyone knows. It seems to be just those two who are actually aging. But apparently Daedalus looks like crap, and Petra definitely seems weaker, according to Luc. He's worried about her."

"But I can't believe it," said Sophie, standing up and starting to pace. "It isn't possible."

Claire shrugged. "Ooh, must be magick."

"Richard's *aging*?"

"Either that, or all the alcohol's really taking an effect on him."

"Manon?"

"Yeah. She's taller, older. She looks like she's around fifteen now."

"How long will this last?" Sophie's brown eyes were wide. "When will it stop? What caused it?"

Claire made checkmarks in the air. "Don't know, don't know, don't know."

"I've got to go see Manon!" Sophie grabbed her lavender sweater and her purse. "She wouldn't be dependent, she would feel more equal. She might not even want to die. This changes everything!" She hurried to the door.

"It doesn't change the fact that you betrayed her." Claire didn't pull punches.

Sophie stopped dead at the door and looked around, stricken.

"Her age wasn't the main problem," Claire went on more

gently. "The problem was that you put yourself first. You deliberately screwed up her plan, blew off something she really wanted bad, because it wasn't what you wanted. Her looking like slightly less dangerous jailbait doesn't change that."

Slumping against the old wooden door, Sophie rubbed a pale hand across her eyes.

"Then what now?" She sounded defeated.

Claire shook her head. "I'm a witch, not a psychic. It's anyone's guess."

❧ Chapter Twenty-One

Clio

"OKAY, CHALICE OF WIND, GOT IT." I HELD THE smooth wooden cup in my hand, rubbing my thumb on the fine grain. "Circle of ashes, check." I gestured at the burned circle on the ground, where we'd done the rite a week ago.

"Yes." Daedalus leaned on his walking stick and looked around.

He definitely seemed weaker to me today, and so had Petra, this morning. Had it happened to all of them? There was no way to tell with Luc, with his face being so messed up. What about Richard? I frowned, thinking back. I'd seen him just two days ago. Something about him had felt different. Had he been weaker? No. But something was different.

"Anytime you're ready, Clio," said Daedalus, and I snapped my attention back to him.

"Um, where's the feather of stone?" That was how the rhyme had gone, the spell. A chalice of wind, a circle of ashes, a feather of stone, and a necklace of water.

"Richard has it. It's a knife carved of obsidian. In the shape of a feather."

I nodded. "I saw it at the rite."

"Yes. It's been in our famille for hundreds of years. I'm not sure how he ended up with it. It was always used in our important circles, our days of observance. That night Petra used it to cut Cerise's baby's umbilical cord."

"And the necklace of water? I don't remember anything about that."

"The old rhyme never specified what the necklace of water was, and that night Melita didn't clarify it. I thought that it was something real, maybe something she had found or created and imbued with deep, strong magick. I remember her wearing a necklace—a string of moonstones. It disappeared when she did. Since then, I've often wondered if that was the necklace of water. You know what moonstones look like."

I nodded.

"But Petra thought it meant something different," Daedalus continued. "Like, tears or blood or something. It was foolish to try to re-create the rite without knowing for certain what that was—or without Melita, for that matter."

He sounded resigned, sad.

"You worked really hard for a long time to create that rite," I said.

"Yes. And who knows if I'll ever have another chance?" He glanced over at me. "Perhaps with your help."

An idea came to me then, and I put it out into the world without thinking it through. How many times in my life had I done that—sending an idea, an action, a thought out into the world like a butterfly? And like a butterfly altering the world's climate, what effect had I had on the world so far?

"Maybe," I said slowly. "Or maybe you've been going about this all wrong."

Daedalus's eyes flashed, and he looked offended in the way that only an old-fashioned, proper gentleman can look offended. "Pardon?" he said coldly in French.

"I mean, you've been trying to *re-create* Melita's rite because it was the most amazing, most powerful thing you could think of. But now, two hundred and forty years later, don't you think you and Jules and Petra and Ouida could write a new spell from scratch? It wouldn't be exactly the same, and it might not have the exact same effect. But I bet you guys could do something awesome. Come at it from a different angle." I paced around the charred circle, where nothing would ever grow again. "If Melita's rite set up the form one way, that isn't the only way to do it, is it? Like, a spell to make your vegetables grow better." I drew on what I knew, having helped Nan a million times. "You can achieve the same results lots of different ways. You can strengthen the life force of your tomato plant. Or do a spell to increase its attraction to bees, so more bees come and pollinate the flowers. Or do a spell to ward off bad insects. The effect is the same, but there are lots of ways to get there."

Daedalus was quiet, watching me, and I tried not to sound like an idiot. "You know the form of Melita's rite and the elements she used. Maybe there's still something missing, something you don't know about, which is why the rite didn't work, or at least didn't work the way you thought it would. But what if you, and maybe some others, put your strengths together and wrote a new rite, using what you know, what you've studied for two centuries?"

There were only the two of us in the middle of these woods. It was barely mid-afternoon, but already the autumn light made deep, slanting shadows. Things felt quiet here, hushed, as if birds and animals were giving this place wide berth.

"I've tried," Daedalus said, his voice thoughtful.

"When? With who? The whole Treize?"

"No. It must have been back in the thirties. And with barely half of us."

"So what do you want this rite to do exactly?" I persisted. "Melita wanted power and immortality. But you already have power. You've got immortality. You have plenty of money. You can basically do anything you want. What do you need from this rite?"

Funny how I had never thought to ask that before.

"More power."

I stared at him. "You're already incredibly strong. What would you do with more power?"

"I would just—have it. I would be able to work beautiful, incredible, powerful magick. I would be able to achieve whatever goal I wished. I would be independent, not needing others for anything."

I digested this for a minute. "Is this like a megalomaniac kind of thing?"

Daedalus was startled into laughter. "Does it matter?"

I considered this carefully. "No, not to me. Unless you were to harm or control me or anyone I loved." Thais believed he already had, that he'd killed our father. She was certain of it, but I wasn't. Visions could always lie, if someone manipulated them the right way. But if he did anything in the future . . .

"What would happen then?" He seemed amused, indulgent.

I looked up at him, met his dark eyes that now seemed faded. "Then we would become enemies." I expected him to laugh, to dismiss me with a wave of his hand.

Instead he looked at me and stroked his short gray goatee. "I see."

We waited, watching each other, as if a challenge had been thrown down.

"So, write a completely different spell myself," he said. "It's interesting. I would have the whole Treize. And I have you, my dear. Your help, your power."

Was this a test? What was I committing to? "Yes, you would."

✣ Chapter Twenty-Two

Thais

I LOOKED AT KEVIN, SITTING ACROSS FROM ME at our small table in Botanika and thought once again about how much I cared for him, how happy I was with him. Being with him felt clean and light, and I longed for it, after working with Carmela. I still felt tainted by what she'd done to the orchid and the knowledge of what was ahead of me weighed heavily on my conscience.

"I'm so glad you're feeling better," I said.

"Me too. They still don't know what was wrong with me. I'm supposed to take it easy, no football or track or anything. But no school this week! That rocks."

"I know," I said, smiling. "And your car will be okay?"

Kevin made a face. "The front end needs to be replaced. But insurance will cover it."

"Yeah—it wasn't your fault."

It was mine.

But I'd been learning limitations, how to keep magick focused so it didn't affect others. . . .

My latte was too hot. Nervously, I placed my fingers against the tall mug and mentally crafted a limitation around it. Then I cooled it, drawing the heat into my fingers. I watched Kevin carefully—he seemed okay. Yes!

If I learned enough limitations, if I really studied hard, or if I never worked magick around him . . .

Smiling, Kevin put his arm around my shoulders and kissed me. "I've missed you."

"I've missed you too. I was so worried about you."

"It was weird, but I'm fine now. Listen—Halloween's coming up. And the Halloween dance at school. And the haunted house at the fire station on St. Charles, by Nashville. Would you want to do any of that?"

"Oh, yeah," I said feelingly. It would be so great to be a normal teenager with a boyfriend, doing "spooky" things that didn't involve actual, sometimes terrifying magick. "I have to check with my grandmother." Halloween was the most important sabbat of the year in the *Bonne Magie*. I was sure a big circle or celebration was planned, and I had no idea if I would be able to make the school dance. Or if I would still be with Kevin by then.

"Great. We'll need costumes. But nothing stupid, like salt and pepper. More like, I'll dress up like rice."

"Rice? What do you mean?"

He grinned. "You go as 'white,' and I'll go as rice, and you just be all over me all night."

I laughed—he looked so pleased with himself. "Very funny!"

And this was my ongoing dilemma: If I wanted, I could choose. I could turn my back on magick, be just a girl again with a sweet, normal boyfriend who would live a regular life span. My life would uncomplicate itself, my future would simplify. All I had to do was choose.

Kevin stroked his fingers up my arm. "What are you thinking about?"

About how I'm lying to myself. I smiled at him. "Just enjoying being here."

"Me too."

And so it went. I was on a seesaw, teetering between safety and desire, selflessness and selfishness. Right now, selfish desire was winning. I felt good with Kevin: calm, comfortable. Everything I hadn't been with Luc. Kevin was a cozy hearth; Luc had been a wildfire.

Wildfires destroyed everything in their path.

Kevin and I were talking about going to see a movie when I suddenly felt: Axelle.

Turning, I saw her and Manon coming out of the book section. Axelle's eyes caught me, and she smiled and waved in a patently artificial way. I smiled and waved back just as artificially and then smiled at Manon.

Good Lord. Was that Manon? It had to be—it was her, definitely—but she was *older*. Not instantly recognizable as a child. She was—a teenager. She raised her eyebrows at me and smiled in a friendly way, and I pretended to let my jaw drop open. She grinned and nodded, and they went toward the exit.

"Do you know them?" Kevin asked.

"Remember my crazy guardian, when I first got here? The dark-haired one was her."

"Oh. Yeah, not very motherly. Or parently of any kind."

"Nope." Just then, I felt Axelle in my mind and almost jumped. I could literally feel her, as if she were trying to eavesdrop, know what I was thinking. I was shocked and in the next instant wondered if she had done that when I lived with her, but I hadn't recognized it. Maybe the reason I could recognize it now was because I'd become more sensitive to magick.

Which was amazing. But I didn't want Axelle in my head and tried to remember what I'd been taught about that. I could put up walls around myself. Clio had told me that the Treize pretty much blocked their minds all the time without thinking about it.

But now I quickly put up barriers around my mind—a small spell that wouldn't stop anything big or powerful but would prevent casual eavesdroppers. At once I felt Axelle's presence disappear. As she left Botanika, she cast me a thoughtful glance, as if surprised by this show of strength.

That's right, be surprised, I thought smugly.

"Uh . . ." Kevin said.

I looked over at him and realized with horror he looked gray. Oh, no! I had done it again! I had done magick without protecting him, and now he was paying for it!

"Oh, God, Kevin, I'm sorry!" I blurted, putting my arm around his shoulder. Instantly I dropped my magickal barrier.

He blinked several times as I rubbed his back and felt overwhelmed with guilt.

"Do you want some ice water?" I asked. He nodded and reached out with a shaky hand. After he drank some water he took a deep breath and shook his head, already looking better.

"I'm okay," he said, but he sounded concerned and upset.

It was all my fault. I was literally damaging him, hurting him by being around him. Kevin was the nicest guy in the whole world, and I was hurting him carelessly again and again. Seriously hurting him.

I had to break up with him.

• • •

We drove to his house in his dad's car. I said I would walk up to St. Charles and catch the streetcar home—I didn't want him driving by himself. The whole way to his house, I tried to get the nerve to go ahead and break up, but I just couldn't. He was upset and worried about his "relapse," and breaking up felt like kicking him when he was down. I couldn't even think of a good excuse. Not one good reason.

Overwhelmed and miserable, I kissed him good-bye and walked down the driveway to the sidewalk, trying not to cry.

I was an idiot. A dangerous idiot. This was what Clio and Petra had been talking about, how unschooled I was, how dangerous it was to know just a little bit of magick. I was a bullet, careening around, hurting people right and left without meaning to.

I started crying, trying to hide it. Getting on a streetcar

with a bunch of strangers was totally unappealing. Instead I kept walking uptown on Prytania Street, trying to distract myself with the incredibly beautiful houses along this section.

A car honked behind me, but I ignored it. Sometimes frat guys from Tulane or Loyola drove around, honking at girls, yelling stuff. If they pushed me, I was going to rip into them.

"Thais!"

I turned to see Clio waving at me through the open window of our rental car. She immediately pulled up to the curb next to me. My first thought was, *Thank God, my sister,* and then I remembered I was still mad at her and turned away.

"Thais! Get over here!"

Sighing, I went and leaned in the open window. "What?"

"What is the matter with you?" she asked. "You're walking along crying, and you won't even come over to the car? What's going on?"

I just shook my head.

"Get in the car," she said briskly, sitting back and checking her rearview mirror.

Unable to fight anymore, I got in.

Clio pulled quickly out into traffic, making people honk. She flipped a general bird out the window and took a left, heading toward Magazine Street. It was a relief to be sitting down, even a relief to be with my sister. Glancing at her, I saw she looked pale beneath the summer tan that hadn't faded much.

"What did you do today?" I asked, sniffling. *Study much?*

"This and that," she said offhandedly. "I was going home,

but why don't we go to PJ's, get some coffee? I feel like I haven't seen you in ages."

I'd been avoiding her for days, since I'd heard her at Daedalus's. "Whatever." But I felt glad that maybe we could clear the air now. I sniffled again, wiping my eyes with my hand.

PJ's had a back courtyard with rickety metal tables and overgrown plants that made it feel junglelike. I got an iced tea, and we took our drinks out back.

"Okay, now tell me what's going on," Clio said once we sat down.

"I don't know where to start." With, I'm killing my boyfriend because I'm stupid and out of control? Or, I'm studying dark magick with a creepy stranger so I can get revenge on a murderer that my own sister studies with? Or even the old standby, I lost my dad and moved two thousand miles away, and sometimes I'm still not on my feet?

Pick one.

"I tried to break up with Kevin," I said. "But I couldn't get the words out. I feel like I don't have any reason to give him."

Clio stirred her coffee, thinking. "How about, I met someone last summer, before you, and we broke up, but I really loved him, and now he wants to get back together. So, bye?"

I frowned at her. "What are you talking about?" Did she mean Luc?

Clio shrugged. "It would be an excuse."

"It would be awful! It would make me look like—" I shook my head. "That's the thing. Any reason I give him is going to make me look bad. I care about him so much. I don't want him to hate me."

"You're kind of between a rock and a hard place," Clio said. "Tell him you need to take a little break because you're under so much pressure with school and your new family and stuff. Then later, when you have all your limitations and barriers down cold, you can look him up again."

She was actually trying to help me. I thought about it. "That's not bad. How long do you think it'll take me, with the limitations?"

"Well—like, two years?" Clio made a "sorry" face. "That's to be really good, able to have them up most the time without thinking about it."

"Great." Mentioning barriers made me think of what had set all this off. "Oh my God—just now, Kevin and I were at Botanika, and we saw Axelle and Manon. And get this— Manon looks like she's about fifteen. She's older!"

Clio's eyes widened and her brows rose. "Really? It was obvious?"

"Yeah. I mean, she's taller, she's getting boobs—she's a teenager! Isn't that weird? Do you think it's happening with all of them?"

"Well, Nan *seems* older for sure," Clio said, looking thoughtful. "Richard—I don't know about because I haven't seen him. Who else have we seen recently? Luc you can't tell because of his face."

What about Daedalus? How did he look? I wanted to say. It

was hard sitting here, knowing she had this huge secret from me. But I had a huge secret too, I admitted. True, I wasn't studying with someone she hated, someone who had killed our father, but I also knew that Clio wasn't convinced Daedalus really had. It was hard to blame her for not believing my vision. Reluctantly I remembered that I hadn't really believed *her* vision. So we were kind of even in a way. I sighed, not knowing what to do with all my conflicting feelings.

"Yeah," I said, trying to remember if I'd seen anyone else. "God, if she and Richard age, it would make their lives so much easier. But—do you think they're aging, like, until death?"

"I don't know. All kinds of stuff happened at that stupid rite that we don't know about—like everyone did something different, caused different things to happen."

"Yeah. It's all so complicated."

For a couple of minutes we sat there, lost in our own thoughts.

Clio looked up at me, her eyes green and clear. When I'd first met her, we'd seemed so identical I'd practically fainted. Now when I looked at her, I found her very familiar, but it wasn't as if I were looking at myself. We're such different personalities that she didn't seem like another me.

"The thing is," she said slowly, "I'm not sure who to trust anymore. I always thought I could trust Nan, but she lied to me my whole life. I thought I could trust Luc. Ha ha. I sort of thought I could trust Richard. I thought I could trust our circles. Now I don't trust anything—except myself. And you."

"You trust me?"

"I do." She made a wry face. "I'm not even sure why—I hardly know you. But we're twins, identical twins. Two halves of one whole. I feel like I have to trust you. Listen—I think we should make a magickal pact, where we swear to not betray the other no matter what."

"Are you serious?"

"I'm telling you—you can trust me no matter what. Trust that I would never do anything to hurt you."

What about studying with Daedalus? I wanted to shout. But following her logic, if she believed that I was wrong about Daedalus, then studying with him wasn't really hurting me because he hadn't really killed our father. This was all making my head hurt.

"I want to know for sure that there's one person in the world *I* can trust, and that's you," she went on. "Will you swear with me? We could do a spell."

"Yeah, because we haven't gotten thrown across a room lately," I said.

She frowned. "Thais, this is important."

I thought it through carefully. Six months ago, in my old life, I'd have thought I could trust anyone in my family, anyone I was related to. I would have trusted most people. Now—it was true: There wasn't anyone I felt 100 percent certain about. Could I really trust Clio? Could she really trust me? Yes. I wasn't doing anything to hurt her. Only myself.

I nodded. "Yeah, okay. We'll do a spell. And we'll swear to

each other, on our mother's grave, that we'll never betray the other no matter what. That whatever happens, we'll have each other's back. Right?"

Clio stood up, looking relieved. I was touched that this meant so much to her. "Right. Let's go do it. By the way— where *is* our mother's grave?"

"No idea."

✦ Chapter Twenty-Three

Maman

GODDESS, BUT SHE WAS EXHAUSTED. PETRA PUT down her bag and smoothed a hand over her silver hair. The house was empty—she'd felt that as soon as she'd come through the front gate. Thais was with Kevin, breaking up with him. It was sad, unfortunate. Kevin was a nice kid. It wasn't Thais's fault that she hadn't grown up with the Craft and didn't know how to control her power.

It was Petra's fault.

But if she hadn't split the twins up, they might very well be dead now. It was only chance that they hadn't been killed in the last two months, first by Richard, and then by—who? It was still unclear. Oddly, Petra had been unable to discern any culprit among the Treize, and it seemed like the attacks had stopped.

Well, it was all twigs down the river at this point. She was doing the best she could.

In the kitchen, Petra put the kettle on. What did she feel like having? Her joints ached, she felt scattered and unfocused, she was bone-tired. . . . She laughed wryly. She could drink her whole pharmacopoeia and it wouldn't help.

She was weakening and perhaps on the downhill slide toward death. Actual death after so long. It was a bizarre thought. What would happen to the twins if she died? Once again, Petra damned Daedalus for setting all this in motion.

Glancing at the light outside, Petra saw that she had maybe an hour before something had to be done about dinner. Where were the girls now? She wasn't exactly worried; things had been more or less quiet since the rite. But—everything that had once seemed solid now felt tenuous, rickety, as if it could fall apart at any moment. She'd spent centuries getting to this place, where she could create a good life. She'd brought up Clio here. After such a disastrous experience of motherhood the first time, it had taken more than two hundred years for her to want to do it again. But somehow, when she'd seen Clémence die, seen the two tiny babies take their first breaths, she'd known that these were the ones she would save. She would somehow try to break the curse of Cerise's line.

Clio had been six months old when her birthmark had appeared on her left cheek. Cerise's birthmark. Petra's mother had had it, and her grandmother. Their line was marked.

The kettle whistled, making Petra snap back to the present. She took a bag of plain Earl Grey tea and dropped it in her cup, then poured steaming water over it. The scent rose through the air on a ribbon of steam: the magick of tea.

Petra had invested almost eighteen years into Clio, and

now she had Thais as well. These were two children she would not see die or turn to the dark side or disappear.

Petra poured some tea into the plain white saucer on the table. She concentrated, closing her eyes, building the scrying spell one elegant layer at a time. Like anything else, magick was a skill. It could be done badly or done well. It was the difference between a rough-hewn, three-legged milking stool cobbled together by a farmer and the highly polished burl maple of a Boston highboy with its perfect proportions, joints like the tail of a dove, and wood as smooth as silk.

Opening her eyes, Petra gazed down into the pale, shallow liquid. Faint tendrils of steam rose from it, and when they cleared, Petra saw Clio and Thais sitting, their heads together, talking seriously. Thais picked up a glass and drank. There were plants in the background. Clio said something, and they both laughed.

They were fine. Petra exhaled deeply, feeling tension slowly uncoil from her bones. She lifted the saucer to pour the tea back into her cup, but another image, unsought, was forming.

Petra watched in astonishment as a beautiful face, framed by waves of hair as black as her eyes, formed within the shallow saucer.

Her heart slowed to three beats per minute. Petra couldn't breathe as she absorbed the details of that face, the face she hadn't seen in 242 years.

The face smiled, showing even white teeth. "Maman," Melita said. "Comment ça va?"

✦ Chapter Twenty-Four

Could This Be Happening?

DAEDALUS STOPPED AND TOOK HIS BEARINGS. As often as he'd been in this cemetery, still, the way the sunset was dappling the tombs made things look different. A large angel had fallen off a mausoleum dedicated to firefighters, and that had made him miss a turn.

Could this really be happening now, when he was nearing his own personal sunset? Or at least felt possible for the first time? Everything was coming together, happening all at once, and it was incredibly exciting and gratifying. Having the whole Treize, having Clio studying with him, so eager to learn . . . this was the least discontent he'd been in decades.

Ah. Daedalus stopped in front of his family tomb. Clio had teased him about his name—how he didn't use "Planchon." Everyone knew him as Daedalus. "Like Cher," Clio had said with an impertinent smile. No one had teased him in a very long time. It both irritated and amused him. As usual, he lowered himself to the small cast-iron bench directly across from the nameplate. It was a different lifetime, the lifetime when he'd had a brother, and his brother had been secretly married to the strongest, darkest witch anyone had ever seen.

Now 242 years of history were coming together right here. Daedalus had front-row seats. In fact, he was the ringmaster.

He felt her before he heard the almost silent footsteps on autumn-dry grass. A deep thrill went through him—this was almost unimaginable, what was happening. Every tiny hair on his arms rose. He felt so tightly strung with tension that if he stood up suddenly, his bones would snap.

There she was.

He didn't turn as she seemed to glide across the grass toward him. In the deep shadows of new sunset, he saw her place a white rose on his brother's tomb.

Finally he spoke. "I'm here, as you directed."

She turned, and if possible, was even more beautiful than he remembered. Unusually tall for a woman from their time, slim, dark-haired and black-eyed, she favored her father much more than she did Petra, and Armand had been an incredibly handsome man.

He remained seated as she bent down to brush kisses against each cheek. When she sat next to him, he picked up the scent of spices he couldn't name.

"Of course you are." Her voice was at once foreign and also frighteningly familiar, the voice whose words had commanded more dark magick than he'd seen before or since. "Now, tell me everything."

✦ Chapter Twenty-Five

Thais

"YOU'VE COME VERY FAR, VERY FAST," CARMELA said, as I sat, dazed, my eyes on the black candle that only moments before I had actually levitated. By myself. I felt drained and queasy, as usual.

"I've been practicing," I said, wondering if taking Dramamine would interfere with magick. I also wondered if my eyes had changed to see in the dark. I was in the same dark red, windowless room that Carmela had first led me to. Then I'd felt like I was moving through fog, unable to see more than a foot in front of me, unable to see Carmela clearly.

Now, after working with her for only five days—what was today? It was hard to keep track without the regular school rhythm. I felt like a cat, able to see in complete darkness. I'd worked with Carmela every day this week, sometimes for five or six hours at a time, sometimes for only an hour or two, depending on how long I could sneak away. I'd learned more in this past week with her than the last two months with Petra and Clio.

"You come from a long line of witches?" Carmela asked, picking up the black candle and setting it back in its stand.

"Yes."

"Light the candle."

I loved doing this. I'd done it for the first time yesterday, after Carmela had explained how it worked. Basically, everything exists all the time all around you, wherever you are. Every element, every substance can be called out of "nowhere" because it already exists and is there for the taking. Magick was simply a way to call something to you, so that it took on a form or substance.

I focused on the wick, already burned black. Closing my eyes, I pictured tiny molecules of the element fire all around me, infinitely small, dispersed so widely that they had no form, no cohesion. I began a spell to gather them to me, then direct them to the wick, then coalesce into something strong enough to take form and ignite.

The best part? This took about twenty seconds. Carmela had made me do this over and over yesterday until it became second nature, like plucking a feather out of the air.

I opened my eyes in time to see a teardrop of fire swirl around the wick, lighting it. This one candle seemed to light the room like a stage because I was so used to the darkness.

Carmela's bright black eyes were on me.

"What?" I said.

She gave me an odd half smile and shook her head, still wrapped in its African-print turban. "I enjoy our lessons, Thais." She sounded bemused.

"Oh. Does it—bother you, what I want to do?"

"Strip an old man of his powers? No." Carmela laughed, the sound echoing off the painted walls. "I've done far, far worse." Immediately her face was solemn, and a chill made me shiver.

Yes, of course you have, I thought, remembering I was afraid of her.

"No. It's just—you're very strong, unusually strong in a way I haven't seen in a long time," she went on. "I enjoy it. It seems familiar. You remind me of someone I used to know."

I didn't know what to say to that. "When do you think I'll be able to do it? Strip him of his powers?"

"Sooner than I had imagined, when you first asked me to teach you," she said.

"When?"

"Perhaps even—on Monvoile?" she said. "I can't be exact."

I nodded. Monvoile—Halloween—was about two and a half weeks away. "That would be perfect."

"Today you're ready to practice on something more complicated than a plant," said Carmela. Standing, she went to the small black table by the door and picked up a basket that I hadn't noticed. She set it in front of me. Timidly I peeked inside, expecting a snake or something to leap out. But it was empty. I looked harder, and then in the basket's black interior, two amber eyes blinked. Instinctively I jumped, then my brain processed that they were cat eyes.

Smiling, Carmela reached into the basket and pulled out a

sleepy black kitten. "Cats and humans are similar enough that if you can strip it of its power, you'll be seven eighths of the way to being able to do it to a person."

I stared at her and at the chunky, fuzzy kitten that was now wandering within our drawn circle, unable to cross its barrier. "You want me to strip this cat of its powers?" I asked. After the orchid I'd felt repulsed and tainted and had gone to sleep crying. Two days ago we had done an earthworm. After *that*, I'd felt almost crazy. You'd think an earthworm—slimy, faceless, not cute—wouldn't even cause a ripple across your conscience if you stripped it of its powers. I mean, it wasn't like I'd killed it.

It had still been alive when I finished.

I had thrown up outside in the alley. And again in the gutter after I'd pulled the car over. About a stupid *earthworm*. How would I feel after I took magickal power from this kitten?

"Use the same form as before," Carmela said in her rich, slightly accented voice. "When you get to where you identify your subject, I'll fill in the words to cause the spell to surround this cat." Absently she stroked the kitten's black fur, and it arched slightly and purred.

I looked up at Carmela's dark eyes. She was watching me intently. This was a test, of course. How far was I willing to go? How far into the darkness? What I wanted to do to Daedalus would take me very far down the road of dark magick. So far that I might not ever be able to return. I knew that. I wanted to do it anyway.

By stripping this cat of its magick, I would be closer to my goal.

The cat was a mammal, a vertebrate. If I could do it to a cat, then I could do it to Daedalus. The cat sniffed closer to the lit candle. I felt its consciousness, its simple feline instincts. It was alert but not afraid.

I sat back. "No."

Carmela frowned. "No? No what?"

"I'm not going to do the cat. The orchid and the earthworm were bad enough."

A look of surprise transformed Carmela's face. It looked almost—clear for a second. Not so, well, blurry. She frowned, and her eyes narrowed. "Thais," she began, a dangerous, impatient note in her voice.

I raised my chin. "This cat is an innocent creature. I won't do it."

Carmela opened her mouth, but I interrupted her.

Leaning forward, practically over the candle's flame, I said, "Look, don't question if I can do this to that witch. He killed my father and ripped my life in half. Believe me, when it comes time, I'll be able to strip his powers without a second's hesitation." My voice was tense, taut—I felt unlike myself. Stronger, more ruthless. "He's guilty and deserves what he gets. Every person, every human, is guilty. No animal is."

All I could see were her black eyes, which were focused narrowly on me.

"You believe every person is guilty of something?"

I thought for a moment. "Maybe not kids under the age of four," I conceded. "But even they have the capacity to be evil, to do wrong. Animals don't. The earthworm was bad enough. The cat is out of the question."

"You believe that you'll be able to put your squeamishness aside and take the magick of another person because of how guilty you think he is?"

"Yes." I had no doubt about that. It was hard and even devastating to realize that about myself—that I was in fact willing to perform this heinous, horrific act on another person for revenge. But I was grimly coming to terms with it.

I stood up and broke our circle, not caring if my lesson was over for today. I put on my jean jacket, then picked up the kitten and tucked it inside. I still had that hollow, sick feeling that seemed almost incessant these days, but managed to stay on my feet without swaying. I turned to look at Carmela, barely able to see her sitting deep in the shadows of the room.

"I'll be back," I said. "Tomorrow."

✦ Chapter Twenty-Six

Clio

I WENT DOWN THE OLD CURVING STEPS THAT led from Daedalus's apartment to the courtyard below, holding on to the rail for balance on my shaky legs. I felt like crap. Again. Though it was getting less, as Daedalus had promised.

I'd parked the rental car three blocks away on another street and at the time had congratulated myself on my clever stealthiness. Now, of course, realizing I had to walk three blocks (even short Quarter blocks) made me curse myself. It was barely five o'clock, but clouds covered the whole sky and made it seem later. When I passed a tiny corner store, I bought an orange soda and chugged it. The jolt of sugar immediately made me feel less shaky. By the time I got to my car, the bottle was empty, and I felt vaguely human.

A tall weeping willow hung over a brick wall, shading the sidewalk where I'd parked my car. I unlocked the door and practically fell into the front seat, so thankful to be sitting down. Goddess, I needed to get my act together before I drove home. This wasn't like being drunk, where I could do a spell to clear my blood out. This I just had to get through. I needed to go home and get under a hot shower. The idea of home was very appealing. Though Nan was still weak and preoccupied sometimes, Thais had quit freezing me out since our pact. I still felt bad about studying with Daedalus, knowing how much she didn't want me to, but it was getting easier to not feel as guilty about it.

"What the hell are you doing with Daedalus?"

The tense, quiet voice from the backseat made me jump about a foot and stifle a shriek. Even before I hit the seat again, my brain had registered that it was Richard, that he had somehow gotten into my locked car, that he'd waited for me.

"What the hell are you doing in my car?" I shot back, my hand to my chest as if it would slow down my electrified heartbeat. Then I really looked at him and almost gasped again.

He *was* older, like Thais had said about Manon. Richard was *older*. I mean, of course, he was ancient. But he'd always looked like a kid, about fifteen. Now he was bigger—his baggy clothes seemed almost too small. His face, once smooth and almost pretty, had harder planes. He still looked young, under twenty, but so, so different.

And he was *stunning*. I was so taken aback I just gawked at him while my brain went, *Damn, he's hot*. Then I shook my head to clear those thoughts and remembered to frown at him.

"Yeah, I know," he said. "I look older. What the hell are you doing with Daedalus? And why do I think it's something incredibly stupid and dangerous?"

"You do look older," I said snidely. "I can't wait to see what you look like when you're two hundred forty-two. And what makes you think I'm doing anything with Daedalus?"

"If I keep going, I'll be two hundred fifty-seven," he corrected me. "Maybe because I saw you go into his place six hours ago and just saw you come out. And you look like *that*." He pointed a finger at me.

Irrationally, I thought about what I usually looked like when I left Daedalus—pale and sick—and wished I looked better. I hated Richard seeing me vulnerable, not at my best. Then his words sank in.

"Are you *stalking* me now?" I put total outrage into my voice.

"Yes." Richard actually climbed over the seat and dropped down next to me. He was at least three inches taller and maybe fifteen pounds heavier—it was hard to tell.

My cheeks heated. I wanted to kick him out and race home but felt if I did anything too vigorous, I would hurl.

We faced each other with angry faces and narrowed eyes.

"What do you want?" I said impatiently.

He looked at me so intensely that I leaned back an inch, and then his beautiful, hard mouth smiled. My breath caught. Slowly he looked me up and down, like he'd done before, and I crossed my arms over my chest when his gaze lingered.

"Stop it and get out," I said, trying to sound bored.

He leaned against the car door, calmer, not as angry. I had no idea why I couldn't control him—I'd always been able to control guys. Not like with manhandling but just the force of my personality. No one had ever defied me as much as Richard did every time I saw him. It was infuriating.

"Okay, if you won't get out, I will." I wrenched open the car door and got out, then realized of course I had nowhere to go. Richard came and stood face-to-face with me on the sidewalk.

"What are you doing with Daedalus?" he demanded.

"Nothing."

He changed tactic. "Why'd you tell ole Luc that we'd had sex?"

Oh my God—I had managed to forget about that. It all came back in a rush, what I had shouted angrily when I left their apartment. *Crap.* My face flushed with embarrassment. Good—at least I wasn't pale and pasty anymore.

"To shut him up. Now it's your turn. Go away." I looked for an escape route—and saw a small wooden door set into the brick wall I was parked beside. Someone's private garden. I leaped for it, pushed it hard, and tried to slam it in back of me.

Effortlessly, Richard held the door open. "I don't scare off that easy," he said, pushing his way in, shutting the door behind him.

I looked for another way out, trying not to show how mad and sick I felt. This was me, *Clio,* actually on the run from someone. This had never happened before—I was a different, weaker person, and it was freaking me out.

A marble bench gleamed faintly in the twilight, and I sank down on it before I fell down.

"Please go away." I rubbed my eyes, keeping my hands over my face.

Slowly he pulled my hands away, waiting until I looked at him. I wasn't used to older Richard, his appearance.

"Daedalus can't be trusted." His words were quiet, and in the shadowed garden, it felt like we were the only two people alive.

I swallowed. "I know." But, of course, I *was* trusting him.

"He has his own agenda that you don't know anything about." With big-cat grace Richard sat next to me, and I felt his warmth from inches away.

"What do you mean?"

"Daedalus is playing out a couple of centuries of history right here, right now, in this city. You and Thais are caught in the middle of it. I don't know what he's doing or what his plan is, but I do know that when the hellfire shows up, the only person he'll save is himself."

I didn't understand. There was so much that wasn't clear. I swallowed. Why did Richard seem so incredibly caring sometimes and so angry and bitter other times? Why should I trust him when I knew he'd tried to hurt me and Thais? I looked at him, his dark brown eyes, hair still tortoiseshell colored, summer-streaked, his skin still tan.

"What hellfire?" I asked.

"I don't know. I just know he's got something going. And it

won't be good for anyone but him. I mean, I can't help caring about the old bastard. He's helped me out of some hard places. But in the end, he would gladly throw me into the furnace if it would save his ass."

"Why are you telling me this?" The bench was hard and cold. I was exhausted and prayed that I wouldn't end up crying.

"I don't want you to get hurt."

"You mean, by anyone else but you?"

His face didn't change; he wasn't going to rise to my bait.

"Clio," he said very seriously, "I don't want you to get hurt."

"Why? Why do you care?" Impatiently I met his eyes, took in his new face again. "Why are you even *here?*"

I saw his indecision.

"Because you want to use me against Luc? Because you care about Petra and she'd be upset if something happened to me? Because you'd rather hurt me *yourself?*" I was fed up—fed up with him, with everyone, with feeling this way.

"No!" He was frowning again, taking on his look of perpetual irritation. "You know that's not true."

I stood up. I was done. I was leaving, and if he still hassled me, I would—

Typically, he moved fast, standing and yanking my car keys away. He stuffed them into his pants pocket as I gaped at him.

"What the—"

"Shut up," he said, holding me hard by the shoulders. "You know I—" He looked like this was really costing him, and I thought, *Good.* "I—want you."

My mouth almost dropped open. "That's it? That's the big drama? Give me my damn keys back! Of course you want me, you idiot! Everyone wants me! What are you—"

"I'm not *everyone*," he interrupted me furiously. "You stuck-up, full-of-yourself bi—witch! This is *me!* I don't want *anyone*. I don't *love* anyone. I don't need *anything*." He took a deep breath. "I'm telling you that—I . . . want *you*. I—" He looked awful, as if saying this was ruining his life. I felt stunned—he couldn't be serious.

I didn't know what to think. Richard had loved Cerise a long, long time ago. As far as I knew, he hadn't loved anyone since, though I was sure he'd been with a million people.

What did this mean? Was he setting me up? If he was serious, how did I feel about it?

"I know you think you still love that joker," he said, his voice bitter.

I did still love Luc. I would always love him.

"But he doesn't even see you."

"What does *that* mean?"

Richard's face was hard and set. "He looks at you and sees—Thais's sister."

My eyes flew wide. "Shut up, you bastard!" I spit. "You don't know anything about it! You don't know me or him or anything!" On top of the intense magick I had made today, this was pushing me over the edge. I rushed toward the exit, not caring that he still had my keys.

"Clio!" Richard's hand held the garden door shut, and he

expertly dodged my kick aimed at his shin. "I'm not trying to hurt you or make you upset." His voice was oddly quiet and gentle.

"Well, you've goofed then," I snapped, trying to kick him again.

"Why does it have to be like this?" Richard's voice was loud, exasperated. "I'm trying to talk to you! There's something between us—there always has been. Why can't you just calm down and see it?"

"Because you're a jerk?" I guessed.

"Clio." The one word was warm, inviting, and alarms went off. "We're two of a kind, you and I. You don't want Luc—he's cold. You want me. You and me—we're fire together."

Oh, no, I had enough time to think, and then of course, Richard was reaching for me, and of course I wasn't going anywhere, only half pretending to push away from him. He gathered me to him easily, slowly, giving me time to protest.

"No—stop," I whispered as his head came lower. Already excitement was igniting in my chest, my body recognizing him. It was *so stupid,* how I gave in so easily, but he was the only thing in my life that felt good right now.

Richard stopped and looked at me, how I was waiting for him to kiss me. "You always say that," he said softly. "You never mean it. You want me."

There was no way I could admit it.

One hand curved around my lower back, pulling me closer to him. I felt his height, his new muscled weight—he was so familiar, but different.

"Ask me to kiss you," he whispered, his soft hair brushing against my skin.

I couldn't.

"Ask me, and I'll kiss you," he coaxed so softly I could barely hear him. "You can have anything you ask for." He waited, and I still couldn't say anything, but inside I was trembling, aching for him. Like I always was, despite everything.

"Whatever you want," Richard said, his words setting off tendrils of anticipation along my nerves. "All you have to do is ask."

Oh, goddess, I hated myself. And I wanted him so much.

"Kiss me." My words had hardly any sound, but it was enough. His mouth came down on mine, firm and warm, and his arms tightened, as if keeping me from falling off a cliff. Suddenly I felt warm and safe, which was ludicrous. I felt happy and loved. I wrapped my arms around him and held him hard against me. Our mouths opened, and I kissed him as deeply as I could, feeling his heart speed up, his breathing quicken.

It wasn't enough. I pushed my hands under his shirt, feeling his new body with its same silken skin, same hard muscles. He groaned against my mouth, sliding his fingers through my hair, holding my head so he could kiss me however he wanted.

There, in the dark garden, I asked him for more and more, and whatever I asked for, he gave me.

✦ Chapter Twenty-Seven

One Daughter Is Alive

"YOU LOOK MUCH BETTER." PETRA SAT BACK and surveyed her work. Next to her, Ouida nodded, her face serene and powerful, emanating magick. The two of them had spent the afternoon working on Luc, and Petra knew it had taken longer than usual because she'd found it almost impossible to concentrate.

She'd seen Melita for the first time in 242 years.

Her one child, out of five, who had lived.

"Really?" Luc tried to look unconcerned, but Petra saw the hope in his eyes. She knew he was forcing himself not to jump up and look in the mirror.

She was so tired, and now her nerves were stretched to the breaking point. Ouida, as if reading her mind, got up and brought her a cup of hot black tea.

"Thank you," Petra said, taking a sip, feeling the warmth go down. She glanced at the window—it was dark out. They'd started at four in the afternoon. "What time is it?" Answering her own question, she checked the kitchen clock. Almost eight. "Where are the girls?"

On cue, Petra felt Thais on the front porch, then heard her unlock the door.

"Thais?"

Luc tensed across from her, and Ouida started clearing away their supplies.

"Hi, Nan," Thais called, sounding tired herself. She came into the kitchen. "Sorry I'm late—did you get my message?"

Petra looked at the lit-up answering machine. "No, I'm sorry—I'd turned the ringer off. Is everything okay?" It was more than just a casual question.

"Yeah. Hi, Ouida." Ignoring Luc, Thais reached into her jacket and pulled out a small black kitten, who blinked in the kitchen's light. "I found him in a gutter by Kevin's house," she said. "He didn't seem to belong to anyone."

"Poor thing," said Ouida. She held the kitten up and looked into its small face.

"Mew," it said.

Thais leaned against the kitchen doorway, looking wiped. "Well, I'm going to go take a shower," she said.

"Okay," said Petra. "Come down if you're hungry."

"Okay, thanks," Thais said, turning to go.

Luc was trying not to watch Thais's every move, but clearly her presence had affected him. He stood up quickly and grabbed his jacket. "I better go," he muttered. "Thanks, Petra. Thanks, Ouida. I really appreciate it." He gestured at his face. It hadn't yet recaptured its perfection, but he definitely looked normal. People wouldn't stop and point at him at least.

Petra watched him hurry after Thais, heard him murmur something to her. She replied, but Petra couldn't hear it. She and Ouida exchanged glances. Then Thais went upstairs, and Luc let himself out.

He still loved her, Petra mused. Luc, whom she'd known for so long, loved Thais. He'd always been a rake—charming, ruthless, conscienceless. She'd thought he'd given up on trying to seduce either twin, but he seemed to sincerely love Thais; Petra felt it. It made her uneasy. She needed to think about this. She had a lot to think about.

After he left, the two women sat at the kitchen table, watching Q-tip examine the new kitten. After sniffing him cautiously, Q-tip put one big white paw on the kitten's back, pinning him in place for a vigorous, unasked-for washing.

"Thais looked exhausted," said Ouida. "Not herself, in a way."

"Yes. She and Clio have both looked like that this past week."

"What are they doing?"

Petra was thankful for Ouida, a friend who always spoke straight. "I don't know. They won't tell me, or they lie."

"What are you going to do?"

"Wait."

Ouida nodded thoughtfully. "Are we thinking boys, drugs, sex, worse?"

"Worse." Petra had thought it over again and again. She'd had time to come to terms with the fact that the twins were possibly getting involved in something big, magickal, and probably dark. And now Melita was back. She hadn't mentioned the twins, but Petra assumed she knew about them.

Thais and Clio didn't know it, but Petra had put sigils on the doorways, so she could see who came and went, and when. Her next step was to make a gris-gris and sew it into their jackets or purses. It would help her know where they had been.

"Have you tried scrying?" Ouida asked.

"Yes. There are times when they're blocked, when I can't see them."

"That's not good." Ouida took a sip of tea.

"No. But actually—that isn't all." Petra looked over at the woman who had been her friend for almost 250 years. "Melita's back."

"*Sppfftt!*" Ouida sprayed the kitchen table with tea, making Petra jump. She started coughing and trying to suck in air, and Petra patted her back firmly, trying not to smile.

"Jesus, Mary, and Joseph!" Ouida wheezed when she could speak. "What are you talking about?"

Despite everything, Petra couldn't help laughing. Blotting up the table with a napkin, she said, "Melita contacted me a few days ago. She's alive—well, we were all pretty sure about that. Now she's coming to New Orleans. She wants to see me."

"Oh, goddess," Ouida breathed. "How do you feel about that? I can't believe it. You must be about to climb the walls."

"Yes." Petra smiled wryly. "*Astonishment* is a small, ineffectual word to describe my feelings. I don't know." She spread her hands across her lap, trying to find the right words. "Melita is dark," she said, meeting Ouida's eyes, seeing agreement there. "I know that. I never wanted to know it back then. Never wanted to believe it. But of course I do now. I'm assuming she's very dark indeed."

Ouida looked sympathetic, but didn't deny it. "What . . . did she want?"

"She wants to see me, says there's no real reason. Like a whim, really."

Ouida looked like she didn't believe that for a minute. "What are you going to do? Petra—if Melita's back, and Daedalus finds out . . . if she wants to be part of the Treize for some reason—" Her brown eyes were large with worry.

"Yes," Petra agreed calmly. "Then we're fourteen, with the twins. Too many. I know. And there were the unexplained attacks on the twins, though I have no way of knowing if it was Melita. It seems—kind of beneath her, if you know what I mean."

Ouida nodded slowly. "She makes lightning and earthquakes—making a planter fall on a teenager would be scut work for her."

"Yes." Petra was quiet, thinking. "She's my daughter," she said, "the only one who survived. I love her, and I'll always love her, but . . .

"I know," Ouida said.

Chapter Twenty-Eight

They're Very, Very Strong

RICHARD WAS BUZZING, LIT UP, AS HE WALKED down the street.

Him and Clio. It was unbelievable.

Of course, he hadn't made it to 257 years old without wising up. He knew this probably didn't mean anything. Unfortunately. Or maybe fortunately. He didn't even know what he wanted it to mean. But right now, he felt great, better than great.

Looking up, he saw that he was passing Axelle's house and decided to drop in for a drink and some distraction.

Axelle buzzed him in, but as he approached her front door and felt who was inside, he paused. But the door was opening, and Axelle was waving him in.

"Holy crap, look at you!" she greeted him.

"Hey." Richard suddenly felt self-conscious. He heard Manon's voice and wondered how much she'd changed since yesterday.

"Richard, ah," said Daedalus warmly. He raised a glass of sherry at Richard.

Richard smiled and eased onto a black and chrome barstool, aware that everyone was examining him closely. Jules held up a bottle of whiskey, and Richard nodded. "Thanks." He took a sip, thinking that he should have just gone home, savored his feelings by himself. This was a mistake; he didn't want to be here. One quick drink and he'd go.

Manon looked like a striking, cheerleadery teenager. "Riche, I'm legal to drive. For the first time." She showed him her official license.

"Clearly there was no street test."

Manon made a face. "That was a long time ago. I'm taller; I can reach the pedals and steer at the same time now."

"That's a blessing. But good for you, Non-non."

Manon grinned at the use of her pet name. Richard wondered for a moment if Manon questioned at all how it had happened—the two of them, the only members of the Treize to begin aging. If she'd realized that the development was coming from the spell Richard has used the rite to cast, giving himself and Manon the bodies and faces of adults after all these years.

It didn't matter, really, if Manon ever knew how. He was just glad for the happiness it gave her.

And it was certainly worth it for him, seeing how Clio looked at him now. That he could finally be a man for her. With her.

"Ahem. We were just talking about the Source," Daedalus said.

Richard was so sick of the frigging Source he wanted to break his glass. "Really? What about it?"

"I think I can open it," Daedalus said. "Not with the rite, but with a simpler spell that I'll write myself. I think it will work if it's powerful enough. But we'll need the most powerful members of the Treize."

"Like me," said Axelle with a self-satisfied air.

"Yes," Daedalus agreed, looking like he was still getting used to the idea. "All of us here, obviously," he went on diplomatically. "And Petra's twins."

Richard's chest constricted. "Oh, come on," he said, sounding bored. "Why involve the twins? They're kids. They'll just muck everything up as usual."

"The twins are very, very strong," Daedalus said. "Together, the two of them are probably as strong as the rest of us put together. We need them. All we have to do is convince them, and that won't be hard."

"Would this be dangerous?" Jules's voice was quiet and measured.

"No." Daedalus sounded more sure than he looked.

"I'm in," said Manon.

"Why?" Richard asked. "What's the point? Isn't it kind of moot now?"

"No." Daedalus's eyes flashed. "I need the Source. I need its power to recreate the rite."

Because you're getting weaker all the time, and you don't want to die, Richard thought. *Why can't you let it all rest?*

"Well, whatever," he said casually, setting down his glass. "Let me know when it is, and I'll help. That is, if I'm strong enough for you." He made a sardonic face at Daedalus, and Daedalus rolled his eyes.

"Of course," the older man said.

"I'll let myself out," said Richard.

• • •

His bed had no Clio in it. Richard dropped to his single mattress on the floor, pushing aside the bunched covers. He lay on his back, one arm under his head, and started thinking things through.

When Luc came home half an hour later, Richard feigned sleep and wished he'd shut his bedroom door earlier.

"I know you're not asleep," Luc said from his doorway. He was holding a po-boy, taking bites off one end while trying to keep the drippy parts contained in its wrapper.

"Pretend I am," said Richard.

"I guess if you're asleep, you're not hungry," said Luc, shaking a paper bag.

Richard propped himself on his elbows.

"Roast beef," Luc clarified. "Dressed, tiny bit of gravy. Don't say I never gave you nothing." Luc headed into the kitchen.

"Damn," said Richard, getting up and following him. He sat across from Luc at their small metal table and unwrapped the wax paper. The French bread was already getting soggy from gravy. He took a big bite and savored it. "This is perfect. I wish your face had gotten messed up a century ago. It's made you so thoughtful."

"Screw you," said Luc, eating his own sandwich.

Richard thought of Clio, pulling him to her in the dark garden, kissing him, her skin hot under his hands, and very carefully didn't meet Luc's eyes.

"You missed the powwow at Axelle's," he said. "Daedalus, Jules, Axelle, Manon. They have a harebrained scheme to open the Source to boost everyone's power. And then, I guess, to redo the rite *again*. And they want to use the twins' power."

"Hmm."

Richard glanced at Luc out of the corner of his eye and saw that in fact his face really did look much better. Clearly Petra had been working her usual miracles.

"He should leave the girls alone," Richard said, watching for Luc's reaction. "They're young and don't know anything."

"Hmm."

Was Luc still pissed about what Clio had said, about sleeping with Richard? No—he hadn't even believed her. Probably. And no one knew about tonight, except him and Clio.

"As annoying as the girls are, we don't want them in Daedalus's clutches," Richard pressed on.

"No," Luc agreed, chewing.

This was weird. Something was going on with Luc, and Richard didn't know what.

Which was not good.

✦ Chapter Twenty-Nine

Clio

BY THE WEEKEND THINGS SEEMED ODDLY normal. Nan looked better, and when she got a call to go to a case, she felt up to it. She kissed us both good-bye, warned us to be careful and to take our jackets, like we were little kids.

"What are you doing today?" Thais asked me, pouring herself a cup of coffee. She'd been asleep when I'd gotten home last night. I was glad because I didn't want to blurt anything out—not until I knew how I felt. Did I love Richard? Were we a couple? Had it been just a one-time fluke? Did he actually care about me? Now that he'd gotten what he wanted, was he going to drop me like a hot coal?

He wasn't the only one who'd wanted it. I admitted that to myself. I'd wanted him too, so bad. Then having him, actually having sex with him, had blown my mind. I turned away so Thais wouldn't see my secret smile. My emotions were wrecked; I was confused and worried and anxious not only about Daedalus, but about everything else in my life—Nan, Thais, Luc, me. I shouldn't even be capable of smiling at this point.

But when I thought about Richard, being joined with him, kissing him, the way we felt together, how intense and incredible and even—yeah, sweet—it had been, I couldn't help smiling.

"I don't know," I answered her. "I'm feeling kind of freaked." That was honest enough. I sat down next to her at the kitchen table. "I don't know what to do with myself. Everything feels like too much, you know?"

Thais nodded soberly. "I know." She sighed heavily, and I saw the dark circles under her eyes. "I broke up with Kevin last night. On the phone."

"On the *phone?*" I mean, yeah, *I* had dumped guys by phone, but that was me.

She nodded, looking miserable. "I'm such a waste. But I just couldn't do it in person. I tried a couple times. Anyway. I did it last night. It was awful."

"I'm sorry. Maybe eventually you can work it out with him."

"Maybe."

The phone ringing made us both jump—it was so normal and prosaic compared to everything else going on.

I went out into the hall and answered it.

"Clio?"

Daedalus's voice made me shiver. He'd never called me before, and I was glad Thais hadn't answered the phone.

"Yes?" I wandered into the workroom.

"Meet me at the cemetery tonight at nine o'clock," he said. "We'll do some last-minute practice before tomorrow."

"Tomorrow?" He couldn't mean . . .

"Yes, tomorrow. I've arranged for the others to meet us at the Source at six. You and I will get there first and set everything up. I'll come pick you up at four thirty."

"Four thirty?" *Please let him mean afternoon.*

"Yes, before the sun comes up. We have to be ready by daybreak. Understood? I'll see you at nine."

"Yeah, okay."

•   •   •

That night Daedalus and I went over things I already had down cold. He was excited and even nervous, snipping at me to do everything just so. Finally we were just snapping at each other.

Daedalus rubbed his hand over his eyes. "This is pointless. Go home, get some sleep. You know it well enough."

Damn right I do, I thought.

"Fine." I gathered my tools, slipping them into the heavy silk bag I carried them in.

"Remember, be ready at four thirty," he said.

"Right."

It was a relief to leave him. I got to my car, half hoping to find Richard lurking in it again. Part of me was dying to see him and part of me never wanted to see him again.

Halfway home I realized that what I really needed was a margarita. Yes, alcohol screwed with magick a bit, but I would have just one and then do a spell to clear it out of my system. There were no downsides.

Amazingly I found a parking spot only two short blocks from Amadeo's. It felt like I hadn't been there in ages, and it was hopping. Flashing my fake ID, I got to the bar and ordered a margarita, then took out my cell phone to call Racey to come meet me.

"Fancy meeting you here."

I turned to see Claire leaning against the bar, waving a ten-dollar bill at the bartender. "Two scotch on the rocks!" She faced me and asked, "Would it be '*scotches* on the rocks'? I never know these things. How's tricks? You look like someone put you in a blender on 'whip.'"

Since I thought I'd been looking more like myself, this made me frown. I tried to see myself in the mirror over the bar, but there were too many people.

"Come on, honey," said Claire, picking up her drinks. "It's quieter in the back."

I followed her through the crowd, unable to see anything except her torn black *Ramones* T-shirt. In the back room I almost bumped into her when she stopped abruptly.

"Push over," she said to someone. "Make room. Look what I found."

She suddenly sat down, and I saw with horror that she had been speaking to *Luc and Richard*. Both of them. Together, at this table. With Claire and now me. In a moment I zipped through possible consequences of just turning tail and running away.

Claire smiled at me, and it almost looked like a challenge,

though not a hostile one. Richard's dark eyes were full of alert watchfulness, and I felt a flutter in my chest when I saw him. Remembering what we had done last night—how good it had been . . .

And Luc—Luc was looking better. Much better. Nan's stuff had been working. But the weird thing was . . . even though his face was closer to normal again, he just didn't seem to have the same effect on me now.

I sat down.

Claire pushed one scotch over to Richard, and he took it and drank. He seemed to be trying not to look at me, but I could feel his tension from where I sat. Luc also seemed hyperalert, and I felt like a pinned beetle.

"Hello, Clio," said Luc.

"Hey," I said shortly, trying not to gulp down my margarita.

"No date?" Richard said, looking innocent. As usual, being the one comfortable with throwing gasoline on a fire.

I gave him a look that had once made Nan ground me for two weeks. He put on a cheerful smile, so obnoxious and audacious that I had to bite back a laugh.

"So!" said Claire, rubbing her hands together. "This is cozy! Anyone got any hot gossip?"

Let's see, where to begin . . . I was working gray magick with Daedalus. Thais broke up with Kevin. And, oh yeah, Richard and I did the wild thing last night.

Yep, that pretty much covered it.

"I'll start," said Claire, since no one had spoken. "*A guy asked Manon out on a date.*"

"You're kidding!" I said. "What'd she say?"

Claire's eyes widened. "I believe she said yes."

Richard groaned and covered his eyes with one hand. "Does Sophie know?"

"Not yet. But I'd give big money to be there when she finds out," said Claire.

"Claire," said Luc.

"Come on," said Claire. "This is serious stuff." Frowning slightly, she blinked, and then looked at me. Moments later Luc's eyebrows rose, and he also looked at me. I checked Richard: His eyes were locked on me.

"What?" I asked. "Did I spill something?" I checked my tight cotton sweater.

Glances passed between the three of them like lightning.

"Magick's coming off you in waves," Luc said quietly. "I just realized it was you. What have you been doing?"

Was Richard going to rat me out here?

"Just practicing," I said offhandedly. "Got my ROA coming up."

"Petra says you aren't doing it," Luc said.

Damn it.

He and I looked at each other for several seconds, and without realizing it, I compared his deep blue eyes, so beautiful and expressive, with dark brown ones that made me catch on fire.

"*This* is interesting," Claire almost purred, looking from me to Luc and back again.

I felt Richard's tension coiling tighter and wondered if they could feel it too.

"Good for you, Luc," Richard said. "Save her from herself." He sounded snide and on the wrong side of angry.

Luc turned to Richard and his face hardened. "Maybe I should save her from *you*."

Richard scoffed. "Screw you." He knocked back the rest of his drink in one big gulp, and his jealousy seemed so clear and obvious that I was sure the whole bar could see it.

"No, Richard," said Luc coldly. "You're quite the lady-killer. In more ways than one."

Richard's face tightened and flushed. "You better shut up."

"Have you told her yet?" Luc pressed him.

"Told who what?" Claire asked, leaning forward.

Luc turned to me. "You said you were doing Richard." Claire practically gasped.

"Oh, please," I said, mortified.

"Luc, you don't want to go there." Richard's voice was like a knife, like stone.

"Has Richard told you why that wouldn't be a good idea?"

"You mean, besides all the obvious ones?" I said, trying to save myself with sarcasm.

"Luc—" Richard said warningly.

"You're the thirteenth generation of Cerise's line," Luc went on.

Richard stood up fast, knocking over his chair. "Luc, I swear to God, if you—"

Luc's body tensed as if he knew battle was coming.

"So?" This was all over my head, so far.

"Richard's family," Luc said quickly as Richard lunged. Luc leaped out of the way, but kept talking. People around us turned to stare. "Richard was Cerise's baby's father. He sired your line. You're *related* to him."

My mouth dropped open. I was horribly aware of strangers watching us with interest. In the next second, Richard crashed over the table, furious, his hands going for Luc's neck. Glasses and drinks went everywhere—my margarita spilled into my lap, making me jump up. Richard managed to snag Luc's shirt, popping a couple of buttons off. One hit me in the cheek, hard. Richard had Luc on his back on our table. I could hardly take it all in.

Richard had fathered the baby Thais and I had seen in our visions, Cerise's baby. The one she had died giving birth to. That baby had been my great-a-bunch-of-times-over grandmothers. Richard was *related* to me, like a super-great-grandfather or something. And last night he and I had . . .

Oh, God. Oh, oh, oh, God.

Claire had jumped up too. "Boys, boys," she said warningly, but they continued to struggle. Muttering under her breath, she stroked her fingers down Richard's arm and onto Luc. Instantly they both sagged, as if their breath had been knocked out of them. They moved in slow motion, turning to glare at

Claire, whose lips were still moving, her eyes focused on them. Richard, I was sure, was trying to curse her out, but couldn't form words.

I stared at them in disbelief. Richard had *known* he was my ancestor and still had come after me. He'd known I'd probably be grossed out, but he hadn't told me. We'd actually *had sex* last night, and he hadn't *told* me.

"You bastard," I said with quiet fury, my words cutting through the noise and commotion. I leaned closer to make sure Richard heard me. "How many times are you—going to do me wrong?" That was all I could come up with—I was freaking out and close to tears.

His eyes took on a look of ravaged pain. "No, no," he said, his words slow and slurred.

"Oops! These boys have had too much to drink," Claire said brightly to our audience. She clapped her hands as if to dispel the onlookers. "Guess I better get them home!" She grabbed Richard's T-shirt in her fist and hauled him off of Luc. He came with her like a rag doll. I was already turning and pushing my way through the crowd.

I raced out of Amadeo's, suddenly feeling like the magick and the drink and being horrified were all making me ill. Somehow I made it back to my car, mumbling the words to de-alcoholify myself. By the time I cranked the key in the ignition, I was more desperate to get home than I'd ever been. I backed up to get out of this tight space, and suddenly the right-side passenger door opened, and Luc threw himself in.

Because I wasn't going to learn to *lock my freaking doors* in a million *years.*

"Get the hell out of my car!" I snapped, backing up again and easing forward. I was shoehorned into a space only inches bigger than the rental car, and there was no way to peel out and leave Luc in a satisfying cloud of exhaust.

"Clio, please listen to me." He sounded pretty normal, as if Claire's spell had already worn off.

"Shut up and get out of my car!" I shouted, backing up too quickly and tapping the car behind me. Its alarm started going off, and I swore loudly.

Lurching forward, I cleared the car in front of me by a hair and finally pulled out into Quarter traffic, which was dense but pretty slow. Someone honked angrily, and someone else swerved. I headed toward Rampart Street to go back uptown, wondering how I could kick Luc out of my car like they did in movies. A satisfying image of Luc rolling in the street, all scraped up, came to mind.

"I know you're upset," Luc said, using a calm-the-hysterical woman voice.

"You think?" I snarled, taking a turn too fast, making my tires squeal.

"Slow down before you kill yourself!"

"I guess it wouldn't kill you, though, would it?" But I slowed down. Nan would be devastated if anything happened to me. I was the closest thing to a daughter she had.

I screeched to a halt at a red light and took the opportunity to reach across and pound Luc with my fist. "I don't know which one of you is the biggest jerk! I hate both of you!"

Luc winced when I hit him, then gestured at the light. "Green."

I slammed the gas pedal down and roared forward as fast as the little chipmunk engine could take me.

"Clio, listen," Luc began, sounding so reasonable I wanted to scream.

"I'm done listening to you, you jackass!" Ignoring him, I wheeled around Lee Circle and raced up St. Charles Avenue. Luc's eyes were on me, but I stared straight ahead. After several minutes I tried to calm down enough to drive less like a maniac.

"Are you sleeping with Richard?" Luc's voice was quiet inside the car.

"None of your damn business." My knuckles were white on the steering wheel.

He'd been expecting me to vehemently deny it and was shocked when I didn't.

Tough.

Finally I turned down Broadway, heading toward the river. I had no idea how Luc would get home, and I didn't care. After turning onto our street, I went two more blocks, then jolted to a halt at the curb. I leaped out of the car and slammed the door behind me.

As I rushed toward Nan's house, the streetlight overhead winked out, casting almost the whole block in darkness. In the split second I paused to look at it, Luc caught up with me. I whirled to face him, knowing if he grabbed my arms like Richard always did, I would deck him.

"Go away," I hissed.

He put his hands up to show he wasn't dangerous. "Clio—please—just stop. I'm worried about you. I don't want Richard to hurt you or lead you on. You don't know him like I do—he might look like a kid, but he's one of the coldest, most ruthless guys I know. He makes *me* look like an innocent babe. I promise I just want to be your friend now after all the hurt I caused."

Luc seemed incredibly sincere—just like he had all the times he'd lied to me.

I turned and walked away. I had to get up at four fifteen. After tomorrow and doing the spell with Daedalus, I would be able to rest for a while. I wouldn't have to work hard magick and feel sick afterward. I wouldn't have to lie to Nan and neglect Thais and Racey and everyone else. Life could be a teeny bit more normal after tomorrow. And I wouldn't worry anymore about Richard, about Luc, about these people I loved but could never trust.

"Clio," he began, but I shut out his voice as if he were a siren, calling me to smash my boat on the rocks.

✦ Chapter Thirty

Thais

IT WAS STILL DARK OUTSIDE. HALF AWAKE, I couldn't see the moon out my window, which meant it was after three a.m. Then I realized that I even knew that, and marveled sleepily to myself.

So after three but before dawn. I snuggled down into my pillow, already slipping back into my dream. I didn't know why I'd woken up. I was so tired, and this was so delicious, this almost asleep feeling. It felt incredibly good, and—

Clio was awake.

We hadn't shared a dream, had we? I wondered, barely conscious. I lay still, my eyes closed, vaguely wondering what had woken her up. My body felt like lead, my arms and legs boneless and weighted down. My bed felt perfect—the sheets were perfect, I was the perfect temperature, and I didn't have school tomorrow.

After a minute of dozing, some niggling feeling at the edge of my consciousness told me again that Clio was awake. For no reason I forced my eyes open and focused. She wasn't sick, was she? Didn't sound it. And everything in me was dragging me back down to sleep, as if—

As if I'd been spelled, actually.

This thought opened my eyes again, and I ran a systems check, wondering if I would recognize a sleep spell. I thought I could—this felt like I was being cradled in a golden web of sleep, and it was drawing me down into perfect, unworried slumber.

But Clio was wide awake. Why was she awake if I'd been spelled? Had I even been spelled? Thoughts flitted out of my mind like tissue in the wind, sliding away before I could even focus on them. All I wanted to do was drift off again.

Deliberately I lay still, keeping my breathing deep and even, but trying hard not to slip into unconsciousness no matter how inviting it was. I closed my eyes and concentrated. It came to me that Clio felt nervous or excited or scared. What should I do? Could I even get up? I was afraid to try: If I was bound to my bed magickally, I would freak out and panic.

Almost silently, Clio left her room and crossed the small landing at the top of the stairs. She passed by my half-open door and padded downstairs barefoot. Something told me everything was fine, everything was all right, I should just go back to sleep and not worry about it.

Which made me freak out even more—those feelings were the classic signs of sleep spells, as Petra had described them to me. I fought against exhaustion, blinking again and again, and propped myself up on my elbows, even though being in a coma sounded good right now. Casting my senses, I felt that Petra, downstairs, was asleep herself.

Which meant that Clio had done this; she'd spelled the house so we would all sleep deeply. But why?

I need to wake up.

My sister had spelled me to sleep through something. I forced myself to sit up, even though my arms and legs felt like they weighed hundreds of pounds. Again came that reassuring thought: *Everything's fine, it's nothing, go back to sleep.*

Clio left the house. I felt her presence leave, and then I heard the faintest of clicks as the front door closed behind her. I finally thought to look at my clock. It was four twenty-five.

What in the world was she doing?

I got clumsily to my feet, feeling dopey and wiped out. I tried to think of a spell to counteract this—I was sure there was one, I just couldn't think of it. Instead I groped my way to the bathroom and hunched over the sink, splashing cold water onto my face.

That woke me up enough to remember to draw some runes in the air—*Deige*, for dawn, awakening, clarity. *Uche*, for strength. *Seige*, for life and energy. Then I muttered:

Repel the fog that clouds my brain

Bring me to myself again.

Whatever spell thus binds me so

I now compel to let me *go*.

Within moments I felt myself waking up, feeling more normal. I splashed more water on my face, then remembered that Clio had already *left*. I raced into my room and pulled on yesterday's jeans and a sweatshirt, then sped downstairs as quietly as I could. I ran into the front room and looked out the window by the front door, knowing that Clio must have left minutes ago when I was trying to clear my head in the bathroom, and I had no hope of knowing where she had gone.

But to my amazement, she was standing in the front yard by herself. She was dressed in dark clothes, and of course her hair was dark. But I had eyes like a cat and could see her outline against Petra's plants by the fence. What the heck was she doing?

In the next instant, I raced back upstairs, taking the steps three at a time. Behind a poster in my room was a niche I'd made in the wall. My supplies were in there—my usual magick tools, plus the things I used with Carmela. I threw them into a canvas bag and rushed downstairs.

At the front window, I was just in time to see a dark blue car pull up in front of our house. Clio went out to meet it. I stared, even as I shoved my bare feet into my sneakers by the front door. When Clio opened the passenger side door, the interior light went on.

It was Daedalus. What a big surprise. They'd been working together; now they were going to do something, put some plan in action. *Oh, Clio,* I thought in anguish. *How could you?*

I accepted the fact that I would follow them even before I decided to. I grabbed the keys to the rental and hovered by the front door. As soon as they were down the block, I slipped out the front door and hurried to our car. The streets were virtually empty: They were easy to follow. But I had to stay far back, since I would be obvious.

Clio, he killed our father. What are you doing?

⚜ Chapter Thirty-One

She Will Be Pleased

BESIDE HIM IN THE FRONT SEAT, CLIO LOOKED tired but alert. She'd asked about stopping for coffee, but he'd reminded her that they should perform this spell on an empty stomach. For the last forty minutes, she'd been uncharacteristically quiet, none of her usual bravado on display. He felt the tension coming off her and felt also how she was working to control it.

He was proud of her. He congratulated himself on finding her, discovering her talent, taking her under his wing. Melita would be very pleased, he was sure.

"And this will open the Source?" Clio's voice was quiet but startling in the dark car.

Daedalus shot her a glance. "Yes."

"And we'll increase our power with those spells?"

"Yes. We'll take power from the nature around us, as we've practiced. Then we'll be able to take greater power from the Source itself."

Clio nodded, not looking at him.

On the farthest horizon, the sky was lightening almost imperceptibly. It would be dawn in half an hour. He would be ready. And so would Melita.

✤ Chapter Thirty-Two

Clio

I'M NOT A MORNING PERSON. THERE'S A REASON I started drinking coffee when I was five—I'd needed that jolt of joe to gear me up for kindergarten. Right now I felt like my eyeballs had been fused open. I was hyperalert, every nerve ending tingling, but I also felt a bone-deep weariness from a combination of working hard magick again and again and getting barely any sleep last night.

Each road Daedalus turned down was narrower than the last, and by the time it was almost dawn, we were bumping down what felt like a dirt cattle path. I recognized where we were; he'd told me we were going back to the Circle of Ashes.

"What about everyone else?" I asked, as Daedalus rocked to a halt beneath a huge live oak. I looked around—no other cars were visible.

"They're joining us at daybreak," Daedalus said, getting out of the car. As usual, he was dressed in dark, somewhat old-fashioned looking clothes and had his walking cane hung over one arm. "We'll start with the purity of just we two, and then add others as needed."

I looked at him, and once again kicked myself for putting myself into what had the potential to be an incredibly stupid, if not deadly, situation. I seemed to have a death wish of some kind, or maybe I was just dumb as an effing rock.

Daedalus popped the trunk, then leaned around to call me. "Come, my dear. It isn't far now."

This whole area felt deeply familiar after being here less than two weeks ago, not to mention all the visions of the place that Thais and I'd had.

Well, here goes.

We cast our circle literally within the Circle of Ashes, just before dawn lit the clouds with scalloped edges of pink and orange. It was almost cool right now but would be warm again later. Around us, some trees had lost their leaves, but mostly there were pines and live oaks. Though the woods looked scraggly, they weren't bare.

No measly candles for us—instead Daedalus kindled a small fire on the patch of bare earth in the center. We stood, facing each other but not touching. Closing my eyes, I sang the spell to reveal my power, perfect and whole and strong, the inner essence of who I was. Then I felt Daedalus's power, and together we sang the bridge that twined them together. We weren't an even match—when Thais and I did this, it felt smooth and almost indistinguishable. But Daedalus and I were two very different beings, and I was glad we wouldn't have to do this much.

Just yesterday he had taught me the next section, where

I joined my power to the nature around me. Here, surrounded by huge trees and leaves and rocks, I would feel like the Incredible Hulk when it was over. I'd memorized this phonetically and recognized only about half of the words. It felt very ancient, and as I sang, I realized for the first time that a dark thread ran through it. I hadn't noticed it yesterday, hadn't felt it. But now that I was here, setting it loose, its dark undercurrent set off an alarm in my head.

But the alarm vanished in the next moment as a rush of power so beautiful and pure and intense swept me from head to foot, making me sway and gasp. Light and strength filled my chest and spread throughout my body as if I'd been empty before and was being filled with life and oxygen for the first time. I was awestruck—this was a hundred times more powerful and intense than anything I'd done before. I felt unbearably ecstatic and at the same time overwhelmed.

I opened my eyes. Opposite me, Daedalus looked flushed, healthy, younger. He smiled faintly, dark eyes glittering, and the rising dawn had painted a golden outline around his head.

I smiled, every breath I took feeling like pure sunlight. If I raised my arms, I would float right off the ground—possibly. If I touched a flower bud, it would bloom. If I brushed my hand over the ground, sleeping insects would waken, seeds would burst with life, new plants would push through the surface. I felt like I would live forever.

I laughed, and Daedalus smiled at me, his face lit by the fire.

"It's so beautiful," I whispered. My voice was otherworldly, musical, so perfectly in tune with nature that it was barely human.

"Yes," he agreed softly. "Power is beautiful."

Colorful leaves fluttered to the ground behind him—I saw them, despite the weakness of the daybreak's light. Joy rose up in me at the very idea of autumn, seasons changing, the endless cycle of death, rebirth, and growth. All around me life pulsed in time to my heartbeat; I was connected to everything, one with everything, surging with power, bursting with magick.

"Now, let's open the Source." Daedalus's words came to me as a thought, a feeling, and I felt a new rush of exhilaration at the idea of creating more magick in this exalted state.

"Yes," I breathed, and the leaves falling from the trees looked like nature's jewelry. I wanted to hold out my hands and have a leaf land on me as lightly as a dragonfly.

Daedalus started his spell, first casting the limitations. The song went on for a while, and our surroundings grew more light with each passing minute. I was paying attention to Daedalus, but the gentle sound of leaves falling distracted me, and enchanted, I focused on one wavering in the air.

And in the next moment was chilled with a horror so complete it was like someone had thrown a bucket of icy water on me.

My mouth opened in an *O*. Quickly I looked around, here, there, all around, and had my horror confirmed. It wasn't *leaves* falling to the ground—it was *birds*. Everywhere around us, one by one, small songbirds were falling from their perches, their nests, and dropping to the ground. Appalled, I realized that the magick pulsing with each heartbeat was in fact the power, the life, that these birds were losing to me. Each new pearl of light that swelled inside me meant another bird had just died, and I had absorbed its power.

"Daedalus!" I choked. "Daedalus! Something's wrong!"

It took almost twenty seconds for my words to register. Slowly he opened his eyes, stilling the spell. He looked angry.

"Clio! You realize I'll have to begin again."

"Look! Look!" I pointed all around us. "The birds—birds are dying everywhere! Something's wrong! Stop the spell! Break it! We did something wrong!"

Daedalus didn't even flick a glance over my shoulder. In that second I realized he wasn't shocked, wasn't horrified. Wasn't even surprised, in fact. This was the spell he'd had me memorize yesterday: a spell to take power from birds by taking their lives and adding them to ours.

"Oh, goddess!" I cried.

"Clio, don't overreact," Daedalus said more calmly. "This is what we talked about; this is what you wanted. Everything has a price, and you are willing to pay that price."

"Not *this* price!" Littering the floor like crumpled tissue were ten, twenty, thirty, *more* songbirds, too many to count. I knew their names; I had memorized these and so many more as part of my working magickal knowledge. Carolina wrens, brown-headed nuthatches, thrushes, sparrows of various kinds, and even some tiny, delicate, jewel-like painted buntings that are so rare to see. All dead everywhere I looked, and others were falling.

Tears flooded my eyes. Choking on sobs, I got out the words that would break any spell I was working. Daedalus lunged around the fire and grabbed my shoulders, looking furious.

"Stop it!" he shouted. "How dare you! Now you've made their deaths in vain! We need their power to open the Source! This is what you wanted! You don't understand! Stupid girl!" He shook me so hard my teeth rattled, but I still managed to draw the end sigils in the air, managed to get out the last words, and then it was over. Beauty, life, and power left me, and I dropped to the ground like a sack of dirt.

"You don't understand!" Daedalus cried again, sounding close to tears of rage and frustration. "You don't understand!" He sank to his knees by the fire, then dropped to all fours, gasping and trying not to cry.

"No," I said. I lay on the ground, feeling as if I would never be able to move. Without the magick, the whole world was in shades of washed-out gray. I was diminished to a point where I wasn't sure I was human or alive or anything. But something had occurred to me, the answer to a puzzle. "You're the one who doesn't understand. Now I know why Cerise died that night."

"What?" he rasped, raising his head with effort. "What are you talking about? She died in childbirth! Many women did back then."

"No." I managed to shake my head, though it felt leaden. "You didn't see it—you didn't want to see it. Cerise died because Melita took her life to get her power—the power of Cerise's life is what's kept all of you alive all these years. You stupid *idiot*."

Daedalus gaped at me, his eyes now bloodshot, face deathly pale.

"No—you're wrong," he insisted. "You don't know anything about it."

"I'm right," I said with certainty, feeling like death. "Cerise died to give you immortality. Like these poor birds died to give us power." I started to cry hard, sobs racking my chest, threatening to break my throat.

Out of the corner of my eye, I saw Daedalus freeze and then look up. I focused on him in time to see confusion cross his face.

"Wha—" he said faintly.

With huge effort, I turned my head. And saw Thais, my sister, walking toward us with a wand in her hand.

✤ Chapter Thirty-Three

THE FIRST TIME A DEAD SPARROW PELTED MY shoulder, I gasped and jumped. The second time, the little bird bounced off my shoulder, and I caught it in my hands.

It was a small brown bird, nondescript, the kind you see thousands of throughout your life. Nothing special. Its eyes were closed, feet curled, feathers soft and light and warm—a thing of beauty. In my hands it felt as grotesque and repulsive as the earthworm had after I'd stripped its powers. I smothered a shriek and dropped it, and then I saw that more were falling like rain, like slow, feathery raindrops splashing onto the wet leaves on the ground.

What in God's name was happening here?

I rushed forward, no longer trying to be stealthy. I'd followed Daedalus's car pretty easily, then parked out of sight and taken a roundabout way to the Circle of Ashes.

This was it. Clio would never forgive me, but this was the perfect opportunity. Carmela didn't think I was ready, but I was. I'd learned the basic form—and I'd crafted a short section that I would insert into the spell where the earthworm part had been.

Death was everywhere, morning light showing the stark corpses. I lost count of how many birds dropped around me, and I tried not to step on them. It was a nightmare, so desolate and horrible that I thought these woods would feel tainted forever.

Especially after what I was about to do.

At the edge of the woods, I stopped. I heard Clio crying, saying something about the birds, and I saw Daedalus grab her and shake her hard. Trying to tamp down my anger, I quickly began the spell. It was long and took minutes to set in place, with the limitations, and having to exclude Clio. I sang very softly, even after Clio dropped to the ground sobbing and I wanted to run to her. Then Daedalus fell to his hands and knees. Clio's words about Cerise came dimly to my mind, but I couldn't process them: I was ready. I aimed my wand at Daedalus and held out my left hand, which had a black silk cord wrapped around it.

I walked out of the woods toward him, and he felt it, looking up in surprise. With four words I hit him with the binding spell and pulled the cord tighter around my fingers. He froze, and part of me couldn't believe it was working.

Steadily I kept on, weaving the spell line by line, phrase by phrase. I drew runes in the air for victory in battle, and the one that meant frozen, obstacle, delay. I drew sigils in the air, big, with my whole corded hand, the one that tied the spell to this place right now, the one that solidified my strength right here.

"Thais?" Clio asked brokenly, trying to get up. "What are you doing?"

I couldn't answer, but now Daedalus was wide-eyed: He'd realized what I was doing. I felt him trying to move, to break free like a bug from a spider's web, but I held him there. I thought about him chanting the spell that made the car jump up onto the sidewalk. I thought about how scared my dad must have been, to see it crashing toward him. It must have taken Daddy minutes to die, minutes where he thought about me, about my mom who had died giving birth to me.

I hadn't been with him. He'd been gone by the time they got to the hospital and called me. I didn't have a chance to say good-bye.

Daedalus's mouth opened, and his lips formed a terrified "No!" But no sound came out. Still, I kept going, thinking of my dad dying, thinking of the life I'd lost. Daedalus's magick began to leave him. I caught it with my spell and began to pull. He screamed and collapsed on the ground, curling up in agony.

Clio shouted, "No, no!" and tried to get up. I held out one hand, and she was trapped on her hands and knees. I'd had this all planned out for days, waiting for the right opportunity, and I had to execute it. Daedalus writhed on the ground, a tortured old man, and still I kept going, pulling his magick from him as if I were uncoiling wool from a skein. He lay among the ashes of the circle, their dust streaking his face, his hands. Clio watched the scene with astonished horror, but she was helpless to stop me.

Still, I pulled it from him, and it was infinitely harder than it had been with the orchid or the earthworm. Sweat broke out on my forehead. I gritted my teeth, feeling an indescribable pain at working magick too advanced. Daedalus's power felt ancient and dark and unknown, and I knew it was so much more than what an ordinary witch would have. It flowed through my wand, and I dissipated it out into the world because I didn't know what else to do with it. My studies hadn't gotten that far.

I don't know how long it took—I had estimated it would take about ten minutes, but of course I had no idea. Once I started, there was no telling how much time had passed. But finally I felt Daedalus's magick lessen, his thread become thinner and weaker, and I saw his body lying like a shriveled husk on the ground. The last of it came away from him gently, dandelion fuzz releasing itself from him as lightly as air.

I had done it. I had taken my revenge on the man who had killed my father.

The spell collapsed on itself ungracefully, leaving me standing there as if I'd been hit by lightning. I met Clio's horrified eyes, saw her blur, and then I too fell to my knees onto the damp, leafy ground. The world was spinning crazily, and I dry heaved, my stomach empty. I felt horribly ill, like I was having a bad-drug reaction. But I didn't care what happened now.

"Very good, child," I heard a voice say. Amazed, I looked

up to see Carmela stepping out of the woods, her own wand raised.

"Who—?" Clio muttered, just as I said, "Carmela!"

"I thought you weren't ready, but you decided different, I guess," she said in her seductive voice. "It takes a lot to surprise me, but you've done it. Unfortunately, I really didn't want you to strip Daedalus of his powers—at least, not yet. I needed him. Now I'm in a bit of a pickle."

"What are you doing here?" My voice was thin and broken, and speaking made my head feel like it was going to explode. Carmela smiled pleasantly in a chilling way that awoke fear I hadn't thought I could still feel. Now that I saw her in weak daylight, her features were clear in a way they hadn't been before in the darkness.

"Melita." The word was barely sounded. I whipped my gaze to Daedalus, who was staring at Carmela with hope and, I thought, humiliation.

"Melita? That's not Melita," I said, trying to swallow. "Her name is Carmela."

Carmela smiled at me, and an icy hand seemed to seize my throat. I coughed as she shook her head fondly. "Thais, Thais," she said affectionately. "So smart, so strong, so unexpected. But not smart or strong *enough*." She raised her wand again, pointing it right at me. "You've thrown quite a wrench in my plans."

"What plans?" I tried to say, but could barely make a sound.

She started speaking, and I felt rooted to the spot, on my knees on the wet leaves in this cursed place. Her eyes narrowed, she lifted her wand. I had time to think, *Oh, God.*

"Wait!"

The voice came from the woods. Carmela and I both turned, dumbfounded. Petra rushed forward and threw herself in front of me just as Carmela snapped her wrist down. Petra's own wand was pointed at Carmela, and she was hissing words I didn't recognize.

Petra's body jolted, and Carmela snapped her wrist up, looking astonished.

"Maman!" she said, which made no sense to me.

"Carmela?" I said, feeling brain-fogged.

"Carmelita," Petra said weakly in front of me.

✦ Chapter Thirty-Four

Darkness Reigns

MELITA LOWERED HER WAND, THEN SHOOK her head. Her face tight with irritation, she went and knelt in front of Petra, touching her shoulder. "Maman, tu es bête comme un chou."

Petra couldn't argue with her.

Then Melita looked over at Daedalus, who was still curled on the ground, and at Thais, who was trying to get up, her face white, eyes huge with shock.

"Carmela is Melita?" Thais got out, and Petra wondered with dread how on earth Thais knew her and why by that name.

Slowly Petra got up, and her daughter Carmelita helped her. She hugged Petra briefly, and Petra closed her eyes, feeling deeply how long it had been since their last hug, and how she might not ever feel it again. Then, stepping back, Melita pulled off her turban. Long hair as black as Armand's had been spilled past her shoulders.

Again Petra looked at Thais. She was staring at Melita in

shock and—what else? Shame. Mortification. *Oh, Thais,* Petra thought. *What have you done?*

"Thais—Clio," she said. "Are you all right?"

Clio nodded, getting up with effort.

Thais struggled to her feet, swaying slightly, looking green.

"Quite the pair you have here, Maman," Melita told Petra. "They're very smart, very talented. And, of course, very, very powerful. I felt their power all the way in Europe."

"Is that where you've been?" Petra asked.

Melita laughed, and Petra saw Thais shudder at the sound. "I've been all over, Maman. Everywhere." She looked pityingly at Daedalus, who seemed to be barely breathing, then focused on Thais. "I wish you had been not so smart, not so talented, and not so powerful." She switched her gaze to Clio. "And you—you saw in a moment what the rest of them haven't seen in two hundred and forty-two years."

"What?" Petra couldn't help asking.

"The truth," Melita said simply. "The fact is, we're not immortal, we Treize. Your lives have only been extended for thirteen generations. Our time is running out. It's time to renew our contract for another thirteen generations." She smiled again. "That's where your twins come in, Maman."

"What do you mean, *extended?*" Petra asked. "I don't understand."

"Melita killed Cerise that night," Clio said, more solemn than Petra had ever seen her. "As part of the rite. She took the power of Cerise's life and gave it to all of you who were there. Now it sounds like she needs to do it again."

Petra's mouth dropped open, and she stared at Melita in shock. "No."

Melita made a regretful face. "I loved Cerise, you know I did, Maman. But I chose her carefully—*she* would die, but her line wouldn't. See? I let you have her baby at least."

Petra couldn't speak.

"Not . . . immortal?" Daedalus's voice was so faint Petra could barely hear it.

"No," said Melita. "Just extended for thirteen generations." She pointed at Thais and Clio. "They're the thirteenth generation. I'm here to do it again, give us another thirteen generations of life. But I need the Treize, the twins, and—the chalice of air, the circle of ashes, and the feather of stone."

And the fourth thing, Petra thought with dread.

"Unfortunately, Daedalus is of no use to me now." Melita shook her head at Thais. "I should have been more wary about someone whose darkness rivals even mine."

Petra heard Thais gasp and saw Clio look at her twin in shock.

"Don't look so surprised, Clio," Melita said. "I'm very proud of you too."

"*What?*" Petra said.

Thais hung her head, and Petra was dumbfounded. This was impossible.

"What are you talking about?" Clio asked in a choked voice.

"Of course, dear Cerise wasn't," Melita went on. "We all saw that. *I'm* clearly dark, but they're not my descendents. No, they got their darkness from Cerise's baby's father."

"Richard," said Clio. Petra had no idea how Clio knew that. Thais was surprised, though, judging by her face.

"Not Richard," said Melita.

"Marcel?" Petra felt like she needed to sit down, soon, before she fell.

"Not Marcel."

"But there were only those two," said Petra. "I didn't even know about Richard until recently."

"There was a third. Just once," said Melita. "Our little Cerise, all fey and light, *un papillon*. But she got around, apparently. And no one knew. Except me."

Daedalus made a choking sound.

"Yes," said Melita, her eyes gleaming. "It was none other than our village elder. Just the one time—he lost his head, she didn't resist, and now here we all are."

This didn't make sense. Petra didn't understand. "Daedalus was the father of Cerise's baby?"

"Yes," Melita said. "And anyone looking at him can tell that he's quite, quite dark. And his darkness has been carried down in that line, generation to generation. Right into our twins."

"They're not dark," Petra said more strongly.

"Of course they are, Maman," said Melita. "Look around you. A forest full of dead birds, Daedalus stripped of his powers, your never knowing what they're doing or who they're with . . . don't blame yourself. It's in their blood."

"They're not dark," Petra insisted, but she saw the look of guilt and shame on Thais's face. How could it be possible that she had stripped Daedalus of his powers? Oh. Because she had been studying with *Carmela*, and Petra hadn't known. Goddess, how she had failed.

"Not as dark as they're going to be," Melita said. Fast, before Petra understood what she was doing, Melita hissed a spell and twisted her hand in the air. She seemed to grab something and hold it in her hand, and then she threw it to the ground right in front of the charred and broken tree stump where the Source had been.

Nothing left her hand, there was nothing to see—but the tree stump split with a huge *crack!* as if cleaved by a giant maul, and the ground groaned under their feet like an earthquake, almost shaking everyone off their feet. Then water erupted from the ground.

It bubbled up through the split tree and welled over, spilling onto the leaves. The earth continued to split beneath it, an actual crack in the ground, growing bigger and bigger, and the water filled it. Within a minute, right in front of their eyes, Melita had reopened the Source.

✤ Chapter Thirty-Five

Clio

I FELT LIKE I'D BEEN HIT WITH A BASEBALL BAT, and it had permanently reduced my brain to mush. So much had just happened right in front of me, and I couldn't understand any of it. But somehow I knew that Melita had thrown magick at the ground and made the Source appear after all this time, after all Daedalus's effort.

"That was Daedalus's power," Melita said, then turned to Thais, who looked just as pole-struck as I felt. "You never let power that big or that dark loose into the world, ma chérie. Someone dark might find it, might use it to reopen a magickal well that would only make her stronger. Poor Daedalus. But it saved me from performing a difficult and time-consuming spell."

On the ground, Daedalus wasn't moving. I hoped he wasn't dead. I couldn't believe Thais had really done it, stripped his powers from him. It would have been better if she could have killed him. She must have been planning this, this whole time, and she'd never told me.

And now I had the horrible knowledge that *he* was my ancestor. I hadn't minded learning from him, but to know I was related to him, however distantly long ago, was sickening.

I saw Nan start to edge her way closer to me. The earth had literally split open, and the crack was widening and filling rapidly with water. It was maybe eight feet across now, twelve feet long, and who knew how deep. Melita had split the actual earth, and I knew that I would never see magick that big or strong or dark again.

Melita said that Thais and I were dark, as evil as she was. I prayed that wasn't true for either of us. But I'd just seen my sister strip a powerful witch of his powers, practically killing him. He'd been writhing in pain, clearly tortured and anguished, and she had kept on. I don't think I could have done it. But she was my identical twin. If she had darkness in her, maybe even more darkness than light, then so must I.

But she was still my sister, and she looked as awful as I did, horrified and sick and ashamed. I went to her, putting my arm around her shoulders just as Nan came up to us.

"Are you both all right?" she asked.

I just laughed, a brittle, choking sound.

"No, they're not all right." A new voice coming from the woods made us all start.

I saw Manon—the new, older Manon walking toward us, her fists clenched—and remembered that Daedalus had asked some of the Treize to meet us here at dawn. Dawn had come and gone, and I'd barely noticed.

"Manon—you look . . . different," said Melita.

"You don't," Manon said shortly. "I wish you'd never come back. The twins aren't all right," she repeated. "They'll never be all right. I don't want a full Treize, I don't want the Source, I don't want there to ever be another rite. I want to stay just like this." She gestured to herself, no longer a child, almost a woman.

"But Daedalus—" Nan began as Manon raised her hand.

"Manon, don't be stu—" Melita began, but Manon cried out words that sent a chill down my spine and threw something at us. A rock? It glinted in the sun—a crystal? Melita shouted over her, but the crystal hit me and Thais where our shoulders were pressed together. And before I blinked again, I realized I was frozen, completely bound in a way I'd never been.

✦ Chapter Thirty-Six

Thais

MY EYES SLANTED AT CLIO, AND SHE WORE THE same wide-eyed look of fear I was sure I had. I tried to move but felt like I was encased in ice. *This must be how Daedalus had felt.* Panicking, I realized the Source had widened until it was practically under our feet. I looked for Petra and saw that she was reaching out for us, but everything was moving in slow motion. Her mouth opened, but her words were incomprehensible. Her hands grabbed at us but never reached us.

The ground beneath my feet gave way, and I felt the rushing coldness of the Source lapping at my ankles. Then it was under our feet. I screamed, but no words came out.

Then we were falling, stuck together, eyes wide, the earth beneath us splitting to take us in. The cold water was shocking, and I was stunned that we were sinking into the Source, the water sucking us under.

This is how my darkness ends. As the water closed over our heads, an unexpected calmness came over me. It was over, it was all over. Somehow it suddenly made sense. Starting with my dad's death, everything in my life had been building up to this moment. Something bad had happened to me and brought my own darkness to the surface, as Melita had said. And now it was ending with my death. It seemed appropriate after what I had done to Daedalus, after the revelation of what I could do in the future.

These thoughts passed through my brain in an instant as I stared into my sister's eyes. We were in the Source, and instead of giving us life, it was going to bring us death. Melita had just opened this split, but we'd already sunk out of sight of the surface, into water colder and darker with each passing second.

We couldn't move. Our eyes opened wide, we could only stare at each other, unable to speak or struggle in any way. Manon had killed us to prevent another rite from ever taking place. With me and Clio dead, they wouldn't have a full Treize ever again—not only would we not be there, but we'd never have children to continue Cerise's line. And Manon would—what? Keep aging? Grow old and die?

Clio's hand tightened on mine—we could do that at least. I was a good swimmer. Daddy had taught me. But I was frozen like a block of ice and couldn't kick my way to the surface. All I could do was hold my twin's hand and watch her drown.

How much time had passed? We were both still holding our breath.

I was going to die today, right now.

It was incomprehensible. I understood it but couldn't wrap my mind around the idea.

The water was dark but clear. I could barely make out Clio's face. I'd gone seventeen years without knowing she existed, my other half, my identical twin. I'd known her barely more than two months, but I was about to lose her forever. And she would lose me.

I thought about Luc, and my heart twisted. Clio was the other half of *me* but Luc was the other half of my soul. I knew my death would hurt him. And it would hurt Petra too, but not nearly as much as Clio's death would. Petra would be devastated by Clio's death. I would miss her. But I would be seeing my dad soon. I hoped. Frowning, I wondered what the *Bonne Magie* had to say about the afterlife. I didn't know! There was so much I didn't know.

A look of pain crossed Clio's face, and then a stream of air bubbles escaped her lips. My eyes opened wider, and I saw she looked panicked. I clutched her hand tighter, though the water was so cold my fingers were getting numb.

No, Clio, don't give up, not yet. I tried to send her thoughts, but I couldn't tell if she could feel them.

She coughed soundlessly, and I dimly saw her mouth open and inhale water. *No, Clio, stop, stop! Hold your breath!* This was it. She was drowning! *God, Clio, please don't leave me!* My chest felt like a mule had kicked it, and my ears were about to burst, but I hadn't given up.

Inches away, Clio met my eyes one last time, and she smiled

slightly. *I love you,*, her mouth formed, and no air bubbles came out. Her fingers tightened a tiny bit on mine, then her eyes, identical to mine, drifted closed. I felt her body go limp.

I held on to her hand as hard as I could.

My twin was dead. Now it was just me again.

And it was my turn to die.

Should I repent for everything? Dad and I hadn't gone to church much—I didn't know what I was supposed to do. Ask for forgiveness? Part of me could never be sorry for what I'd done to Daedalus.

I'd spent my whole life obeying rules, following directions, trying to do what was right, but I didn't know the rules about dying. I didn't know how to do it.

I'm scared. I guess I should close my eyes. . . .

Chapter Thirty-Seven

Not Part of the Plan at All

PETRA LUNGED TOWARD MANON, WHO WAS leaning over the Source, a satisfied look on her face. She pushed Manon's shoulders as hard as she could, which in her weakened state meant she barely budged her.

"Stop! Stop! Are you crazy?" Petra said hoarsely. Bracing her feet on the ground, she knelt by the water, trying to grab the twins. They were out of reach already, sinking like two flawed, beautiful stones to the earth's core. "Help me, someone!" she cried. Daedalus was useless, barely alive, but the others were supposed to be here! Daedalus had asked Ouida to come this morning with a few others, and Ouida had told Petra and the rest of the uninvited.

Manon was snatching at her shirt, trying to pull her away from the Source. "They're gone! I'm sorry, but they're gone!" she cried.

Vaguely Petra heard voices, but she was trying to hold off Manon and couldn't look.

"Melita! Melita, no!" Jules's voice overlaid Melita's, and

Petra realized her daughter's voice was shouting a death spell. Aghast, she turned in time to see Melita fling a hand at— Manon. Manon stiffened, her head pulled back, eyes open in surprise, and then she crumpled. Petra caught her as she fell, and she was dead. Actually dead after all this time. Days after she'd finally wanted to live. Her face was more beautiful than it had been when she'd looked like a child. Her eyes were open, the color of the sky on a clear night.

"Manon!" Sophie shrieked, running forward.

A death spell? Manon could die from a death spell? But others of them had tried it before—it had never worked. Nothing had worked. But now Manon was dead. Petra was beyond grief, beyond tears. Manon had killed the twins, and her own daughter had proved herself a murderer—again.

The cloudy skies opened up then as if to cry for her, and a chilled rain began to fall. Then Sophie was dropping onto the wet leaves next to Manon, Luc was shouting something, and Ouida was crouched over Daedalus.

"How could she die?" Sophie said wonderingly.

"Where are the twins?" Richard said, grabbing Petra's shoulder. "Where are they?"

"Thais!" Luc shouted. "Thais! Where are you?" He wheeled to face Melita. "If you've done them harm, I swear by the goddess I will hunt you down."

"Luc! They're in the Source!" Petra pointed at the deep fissure in the ground and barely registered the horror and anger on his face.

"Sophie, Sophie—I'm sorry." Marcel's voice was quiet as he knelt next to where she was sobbing over Manon's body. He put his arm around her shaking shoulders.

"Move, move!" Melita said, pushing him out of the way. Petra watched, numb, as Melita closed her eyes and began an incantation that Petra immediately recognized as dark and ancient. The surface of the Source began to roil. Petra stared at it uncomprehendingly as Claire and Jules came and helped her up.

"Pauvre petite," Jules said, looking down at Manon, but Petra was transfixed by the clear water, bubbling over the edges of the hole. She stood unsteadily, holding Claire's hand, and felt like she was a thousand years old.

Melita kept speaking, words Petra had never heard, and then, shimmering in the water, getting closer to the surface, she saw the white skin of the twins' faces.

"Clio! Thais!" Dropping again, she lunged for the water and felt the silken swirl of soft black hair. The girls' faces bobbed above the surface, but their eyes were shut, their faces still. "Help me!" Petra cried.

Together she, Ouida, Richard, Luc, and Jules pulled the twins' bodies from the Source. As soon as Petra touched them, she knew: One was dead; one was alive.

"Clio!" Richard said, his face ashen. Roughly pushing Petra aside, he scooped up Clio's dripping body and cradled her on his lap, wiping wet, black hair off her beautiful, tranquil face. He rocked slightly back and forth, smoothing her hair, her face, her skin under his fingers. His face was a mask of pain. "Clio, Clio, Clio," he whispered.

Petra thought dimly, *Richard?*

A few feet away, Luc had turned Thais on her side and was slamming his palm against her back again and again. Waiting through a lifetime of slow seconds, Petra thought she was imagining things when Thais coughed, water running out her mouth.

"Thais, Thais," Luc murmured, holding her, rubbing her back. Thais gagged and choked, coughing, and then sucking in breath. She was alive. Petra had lost one and kept one.

"Actually, I need them both," Melita said quietly. Furious, Richard tried to block her, but Melita dropped like a bird of prey and struck her fist hard against Clio's chest. The few words she spit out sounded as if they had come straight from hell. Except that Petra knew none of them believed in hell.

Richard stared, and before Petra's eyes Clio's white face seemed to color again like Snow White's did in the kids' movie. Melita could give life as well as take it away.

✦ Chapter Thirty-Eight

Thais

I WAS SLEEPING, AND THE NEXT THING I KNEW, I was coughing up water and gagging while someone pounded my back too hard.

Blinking groggily, I realized I was on wet leaves on the ground, and it was raining. The only part of me that was warm was the hand on my back. I looked around. Petra sat a few feet away, her face tragic, almost skeletal. Luc hovered over me. It was his hand on my back. I'd thought I'd never see him again. Now, realizing I was still alive and he was here, I started crying but tried to sit up.

"Where's Clio? Where's my sister?" She'd died in front of me—I'd seen it, felt it.

"Shh, shh," Luc said, smoothing my sodden hair.

"*Where's Clio?*" I said, my voice sounding like a croak.

"Here."

I turned to see Richard looking down at Clio, transfixed, and I thought, *I was right. He loves her.*

And she was dead.

Except she was blinking.
Blinking? I sat up.
My sister was alive.

✦ Chapter Thirty-Nine

Clio

IS THERE A WHITE LIGHT, A TUNNEL, PEOPLE who have passed before, holding out their hands?

Maybe. I'm not going to spoil the surprise.

Richard was holding me, stroking my hair. Thais was alive. Petra was alive.

Every member of the Treize was there: Claire and Jules, holding hands. Sophie, weeping over Manon's body. Ouida, kneeling next to Daedalus. Marcel, sitting next to Sophie. Axelle, who had arrived and was sitting on Daedalus's other side, looking amazingly broken up at his broken condition.

And Luc, who had chosen Thais, not me.

Richard held me tensely, seeing me look at Thais and Luc. I looked back at him, into his dark eyes that showed every emotion I never thought he had: fear, hope, love—you name it, I saw it there, in his tears.

"I'm glad to see you," I whispered and reached up to touch his face.

✦ Chapter Forty

Beginning Again

RICHARD PAUSED AT THE FRONT DOOR OF Petra's house. Inside he felt Petra, Ouida, and Luc, and he grimaced. Well, might as well get it over with. He rang the doorbell.

This morning felt like a hundred years ago. He'd seen Clio dead, wearing her necklace of water, just like Cerise had 242 years ago. There was still a lingering pain over Cerise, there always would be. He was both sad and relieved to know that he hadn't fathered her baby. The idea that she'd been with Daedalus even once disgusted him—he really hadn't known Cerise, had he?

What he felt for Clio was a thousand times deeper, stronger. Scarier.

Ouida answered the door. Examining his face, she hugged him silently. He hugged her back, relaxing into her embrace for the first time.

"How's Petra?"

"Surprisingly good, considering everything," she said.

In the kitchen, the kettle was whistling. Luc and Petra sat there, and Ouida was right—Petra didn't look nearly as bad as he'd feared.

"Richard." Petra looked at him, and he saw acceptance in her eyes. "I'm so glad you're all right. What a day. Poor Manon. And Melita—"

"Is gone again," said Ouida.

"Girls okay?" Richard said.

"Thais is upstairs," Luc said, sounding pompous and possessive.

"They're fine, thanks to everyone," said Petra, sipping a steaming cup of something herby and medicinal.

"How the hell could Melita kill Manon?" Richard asked bluntly.

Petra's face twisted in pain. "I think—I just think Melita is still the strongest of us all. As strong as she made us, she kept the most power for herself."

"Was she the one who was trying to kill the twins?" Richard's face flushed. "I mean, after me," he mumbled.

"If she was, they'd have been dead," Ouida said. "No— actually, we still don't know who it was. Maybe Daedalus? He's not coherent enough to ask. We just don't know."

Richard stayed standing, casting a curt glance at Luc. "I want to see Clio." He looked at Petra as if daring her to try to stop him.

"She's upstairs," Petra said. "I don't know if she's awake or not."

Richard nodded, then turned and started up the stairs. He had no idea what he'd find. He braced himself for the cool, disdainful Clio to be firmly back in place, death-experience notwithstanding. Well, he would just start over. He had time.

At the top of the stairs, one door was shut and one was slightly open. Thais was behind the closed door, Richard sensed, and crossed the landing. He tapped gently on the other door, mostly as a formality, then pushed it open and immediately shut it behind him.

Clio was propped up in her bed, not reading or doing anything, just looking at the ceiling. She seemed startled to see him, especially here, in her bedroom, and he was surprised she hadn't felt him come up the stairs.

He stopped a few feet from her bed, taking in her scrapes and bruises, her still-pale face. She was wearing some unsexy kind of flannel something with pictures of sushi all over it. He had no idea what to say, so instead looked at her challengingly, hoping to start an argument at least, because it would be some kind of interaction.

Her slanted, leaf-green eyes looked at him, and then—she held out her hand.

Taken aback, Richard didn't move for a moment, then stepped forward and took it. Amazingly, she shifted on her narrow bed, making room for him. After a tiny hesitation, he sat down next to her, his heart pounding. She leaned against him, putting one arm over his chest, and his throat closed up.

He held her to him, stroking her hair, thinking about how he'd almost lost her forever.

"I guess it's all over," she said, her voice still raspy and weak.

He sighed and kissed her forehead. "It's never over, baby."

Clio seemed to accept this. She looked up at him with her beautiful, cat-shaped eyes, the rose-colored birthmark of a fleur-de-lis on her left cheek.

"Just hold me, okay?"

He nodded, and they snuggled closer together. It began to rain outside, the drops hitting the windowpanes. But in here they were warm and dry and safe. At least for now.

✦ Epilogue

Thais

WHAT WAS LEFT OF THE TREIZE HAD GATHERED
and built the magickal equivalent of Fort Knox around us
in protection spells. I knew Petra was still worried that they
didn't know who'd tried to hurt us, but with Melita gone and
no chance of a rite happening, I felt safe enough to venture out
of Petra's house. My house. My family's house.

It was a beautiful fall day, which everyone had told me was
very rare for New Orleans. It was chilly and clear, and the air
was almost crisp. I'd decided to take a walk up on the levee,
by the river, which was only three blocks from our street. A
shell road topped the levee all the way up to Baton Rouge, and
people rode bikes and horses along here all the time.

Now I walked along, watching the endless river with its
traffic of barges and steamboats.

Clio seemed happy with Richard, and the two of them
suited each other better than I would have guessed. I was
happy for her, seeing glimpses of the old, fun Clio peeking out
in the last couple days.

As for me, I was alive, and I had a family and a home. I was fine.

Sighing, I left the shell road and went down the levee a bit to sit on the fine, soft grass there and watch the water. I'd sat on the levee another time, a lifetime ago, where the river ran next to the Quarter. Now I put my face back, closing my eyes, enjoying the sun on my skin.

I sat like that for minutes, not thinking, just letting myself be, aware of all the ways I was connected to the world, all the things I felt now, life and magick and beauty.

"Thais."

I jumped—I'd come to rely on being able to sense people around me. Hearing a voice at my back without sensing someone coming was really startling.

Especially considering who it was.

Luc sat down next to me, a Greek god once again, the sunlight glinting off his perfect, chiseled profile.

"You look better," he said, appraising me.

"So do you," I replied.

He laughed dryly and touched his cheek with one hand, as if to make sure he hadn't uglified again. He was wearing worn jeans and a soft button-down shirt under a leather jacket, and he looked—beautiful.

"Thais," he said, taking a breath. "When you and Clio realized that I'd betrayed you, I thought I'd lost you forever."

My face stiffened, and I looked away. He was only inches from me, and I felt the heat of his knee reaching mine.

"Then, when I did this to myself at the rite, I was really sure that I'd lost you forever." He gestured at his face, and I glanced up, startled. He nodded. "At the rite I asked for the chance to make you love me again. That face was what the spell produced. It was meant to knock the wind out of my sails and make me figure out who I was inside. To help me understand what was important, what I really cared about, about myself and my life."

I didn't know what to say.

He let out a deep breath. "Then when we hauled you and Clio out of the Source, and I saw you . . ." He looked away, plucking at the grass with nervous fingers. When he spoke again, it was barely a whisper. "Then I knew what losing you would really feel like." His dark blue eyes met mine, and somehow I understood that he was different—he wasn't trying to win me, he wasn't asking anything of me.

"And I wanted to say—everything seems all right, since you're alive." He cleared his throat and looked out at the river. "I don't care how I look or where I live. I don't care if you learn magick or not or stay with Petra and Clio. It doesn't matter if you don't love me, it doesn't matter if you love someone else—whatever makes you happy. As long as you're alive in this world, then everything is all right. And I want to be alive too. As long as you are. That's the only thing of real value to me."

I couldn't speak for a moment. "Melita said—I'm as dark as she is. It's in my line, inescapable. I stripped Daedalus of his powers. Only someone . . . awful could do something like that." I looked down at my scuffed clogs, picked at a hole in my cords.

Luc didn't say anything, and finally I looked up at him.

"Darkness is in everyone, Thais," he said gently. He reached across and took one of my chilled hands in his. "In me, in you, in Petra and Ouida and everyone. And so is light. Darkness is a choice, a path. Every day we all have to make the choice, to choose good, choose light. We make the choice against darkness, against evil, every day, a thousand times a day, our whole lives."

"I'm afraid I don't have choices," I said, my words barely a whisper. This was my deepest fear, and it was devastating to say it out loud.

Luc leaned over and kissed my hair. I didn't flinch away from him.

"I promise you, you do," he said firmly. "Even Melita has choices. Everyone always does. I believe that from now on, you'll make the best choices you can." He laced his fingers with mine, and it felt so incredibly comforting, incredibly perfect.

"Thais," he said, sounding very unsure. "I would . . . be grateful . . . if you would choose . . . somehow . . ." He cleared his throat again. "To be my friend."

I could hardly hear the last words. I looked down at our fingers, his long tan ones, my smaller, paler ones, and I knew that I wanted to hold his hand forever, despite everything.

"Yes," I said, and in that moment, the burden of my dark inheritance seemed to lighten a hundredfold. "Yes, Luc. I'll be your . . . friend."